Barbara Erskine is the auth
well over a million copies
and *Child of the Phoenix*,
one of her own ancestors. *Midnight is a Lonely Place* and *House of Echoes* were shortlisted for the W H Smith Thumping Good Read awards of 1995 and 1997 respectively and were followed by *Distant Voices* and *On the Edge of Darkness*. Her most recent novel was the bestselling *Hiding from the Light*. Barbara Erskine's novels have been translated into twenty-three languages.

Barbara Erskine has a degree in mediaeval Scottish history from Edinburgh University. She and her family divide their time between the Welsh borders and their ancient manor house near the unspoilt coast of North Essex.

BY THE SAME AUTHOR

Lady of Hay
Kingdom of Shadows
Child of the Phoenix
Midnight is a Lonely Place
House of Echoes
On the Edge of Darkness
Whispers in the Sand
Hiding from the Light
Sands of Time
Kingdom of Shadows

BARBARA ERSKINE

ENCOUNTERS

DISTANT VOICES

Grafton

HarperCollins*Publishers*
77-85 Fulham Palace Road
Hammersmith, London W6 8JB

This omnibus edition published in 2004
by HarperCollins*Publishers*

ISBN 0 00 771204 9

Phototypeset by Input Typesetting Ltd, London

Printed and bound in Great Britain by
Mackays of Chatham plc, Chatham, Kent

ENCOUNTERS

Contents

Preface

I have always loved reading short stories and, like many authors, tested my literary wings experimenting with them. At first glance anyway, the short story seems an easy route for the beginner, largely because it is, axiomatically, short; one is not aiming for some distant horizon two or three hundred thousand words away. Short stories are self contained, feisty, fun; they are tricky, challenging – compact crystallizations, each of which must have as much substance in its own way as its big brother, the novel.

Having started to write them, hooked by the lure of so many plots, so many characters, so many scenes and the technical challenge of construction, I have found that I cannot resist the form, and this selection is taken from the hundreds I have written over the past fifteen years.

I did not plan to be a short story writer. I wanted to be a novelist – specifically a historical novelist – and it was years ago while a student at university in Scotland that I decided to write my first novel, the story of Robert the Bruce and the woman who set the crown of Scotland on his head. Consumed with excitement as I worked on the outline, spending much more time on it than I did on my studies, I visited the sites of the story and, absorbing the atmosphere, walked alone along mist-shrouded rivers and around the remains of countless castles. I wrote several thousand words, then I stopped. I realized I couldn't go on. I hadn't the experience of writing or of life to cope with the huge task I had set myself. Quietly and sadly I put my manuscript away. I knew I would write it one day – but not yet. (That book eventually became *Kingdom of Shadows* and, secretly, I incorporated those few thousand words unchanged into it – a debt to that student writer who had felt Robert and Isobel's suffering but had not then been able to put it down on paper.)

My confidence was shaken. I had wanted to be a writer since I was three years old and yet I had fallen at the first major fence. It was a case of wanting to run before I could walk. Obviously I had an apprenticeship to serve and so came the idea of trying to write short stories. I studied the markets and began to write articles and stories to fit those markets. Miraculously the first story I wrote was accepted and published by the *London Evening News*. I was much encouraged!

It was when we went to live in the Welsh Borders that again the longing to write historical fiction grew too strong to resist and I recognized consciously for the first time that I was one of those writers for whom the spirit of place is all important. The land around me, the hills, the forests, the seas, evoke echoes I cannot ignore. I have to write about them. I have to try and make my readers see and hear and even smell the landscape and its history as I see and hear and feel it.

Once more I began to plan a novel and this time I felt I had the experience and the confidence to do it. Not the story of Robert and Isobel – I still wasn't ready for that – but a novel of history and passion and mystery which was born of the mysterious, ancient landscape around me.

While I read and researched and visited the sites which were to become the background for *Lady of Hay* I went on writing short stories and, eventually, half a dozen short historical romances as well, perhaps to complete my apprenticeship before at last I could start writing the big novel.

But by now I enjoyed writing short stories too much to stop. Heavily involved in a book full of passion and hatred and fear it is nice to come up for air from time to time to write a humorous story, or an unashamedly sentimental one; a modern thriller or a plain old-fashioned love story, and I have chosen some of each of these for this collection. There are also, of course, ghost stories and a couple of stories where the past and the present slide together and the curtain which separates us from the past is temporarily drawn aside. Most of the stories are about places as much as about the people who find themselves within them, and most of them are, in one way or another, about encounters. I hope you enjoy them.

Barbara Erskine
Great Tey, 1989

A Step Out of Time

The house at the end of the long, winding drive was elegant Georgian. The windows, all perfectly proportioned, looked out across sweeping lawns – not quite as smooth as they might have been, but nevertheless beautiful – towards the Black Mountains, brooding in the heat haze of the August afternoon.

Looking through the windscreen Victoria tried to suppress the quick catch of excitement which she felt in her throat. They had already seen so many houses which looked idyllic. Before there had always been a snag. This house, she felt suddenly, would be right; it was as if, in some secret part of herself, she knew it already. She glanced at Robert and saw that he felt it too: the hope, the anticipation, the agitation. When they found the right house it was going to be very special. Their home. The first since he had come out of the army. The place where they could start their new life.

The young man from the house agent was waiting for them, standing beneath the porticoed entrance proprietorially jangling the keys as they drew to a halt. Robert glanced at Victoria and winked as he set about climbing stiffly out of the car. She fumbled with the door handle, not wanting to watch, knowing better than to help. Each time it was easier. Each time it hurt him less. Each time the excitement that this might be The House helped.

They shook hands and the agent, introducing himself as William Turner, inserted the key in the lock and pushed open the heavy door. Beyond it a cavernous hall opened up, elegantly if sparsely furnished, with at the far end of it a graceful staircase winding up to a galleried landing. There was a faint smell of dogs.

'Lady Penelope is away this weekend.' William's voice was reverently hushed. 'So we can go all over the house as we like.'

They followed him soberly from drawing room to dining room to sitting room to morning room – a room for every hour of the day – and on through to the large north-facing kitchen.

'Not modernized, I'm afraid.' William looked round in barely disguised disgust at the unmatched cupboards, the painted deal table and the small electric cooker. The water, Victoria noted with amusement, ran from an old wall-mounted water heater into a deep stone sink.

William was watching her. He gave a broad smile. 'Grim, isn't it?'

'It is rather.' Victoria liked the young man. He had not mentioned exotic fitted kitchens; he did not pretend it had been left like this for the convenience of the buyer. Besides, after the initial shock, she loved it. The kitchen had a quaint, old-fashioned charm.

'What's through there?' Robert nodded towards one of the internal doors. Beneath the grubby roller towel he had seen a key and three bolts. Three bolts seemed excessive for a door into a larder.

'Ah.' William gave his most charming professional smile, followed by a deprecatory shrug of the shoulders. 'Well, every house has a few drawbacks.'

'Oh?' Robert glanced at Victoria. His heart, like hers, had sunk. He flipped through the glossy brochure in his hand. 'No mention of any drawbacks here.'

'Perhaps you'd like to see the upstairs first? The principal bedrooms have glorious views across into Wales,' William said hopefully. He had seen how they felt about the house; he had seen her growing secretly more and more excited. He should have told them from the first. He glanced at them sympathetically. Robert Holland was tall, distinguished, in his late forties perhaps, his upright military bearing marred by an awkward limp. His wife was much younger, attractive, dark haired; slightly reserved, he guessed. The kind he thought of as deep and therefore probably interesting. He prided himself on his character analyses of potential clients. These people were understated, but that did not mean they weren't wealthy. He had learned that one very early in his career. Money, particularly old money, did not always show. It was new money that liked to flaunt it. They could afford the house; he knew already that they would not buy it.

'I think we should see the drawbacks first, don't you?' Victoria put in firmly.

'You're sure?' His humorous smile was putting them all on the same side – allies against whatever eccentricity was the other side of the door. It also helped to hide his fear.

The key was stiff and the bolts unyielding. He had opened the door some half a dozen times now, but it never grew any easier and he could never overcome his reluctance to go through it. When at last he managed to push it open they peered into a long dark passage. 'This,' he said dramatically, 'is the west wing. Lady Penelope seals it off more or less completely. I think she prefers to forget it's there. To be honest, the best plan would be to demolish it.'

They could all feel the cold striking up from the dirty stone floor. The rest of the house was hot and airless in the humid summer heat but here it was abnormally cold.

Victoria felt her mouth go dry. Suddenly her optimism

and her excitement had gone. 'I don't suppose there is any reason to see it if it's that bad . . .' she said uncertainly. A tangible feeling of dread seemed to surround her, pressing in on her from the cold walls.

'Nonsense.' Robert stepped into the passage. 'What's wrong with it? Dry rot? Again?' The again was for William's benefit. It might help to knock a thousand or so off the asking price.

'No, not dry rot.' William glanced at Victoria. He gave a tight protective smile as he saw that she had grown pale. About half of his clients seemed to feel it. The other half walked through without any comment, but even they hurried. He motioned her through ahead of him and reluctantly followed her.

With a quick, doubtful look at him she stepped into the passage after Robert. He had pushed open the first door on the left. Sunlight flooded across the empty room and into the corridor showing up the dust and scattered newspapers on the floor. 'It's a good sized room.' Robert walked across to the window, his shoes sounding strangely loud on the bare boards. He peered out. 'That must have been a formal garden once.'

'It still could be.' William was standing near the door. 'It only needs tidying up. There are seven acres here. The grounds are one of the best features of the house.'

'Why is there no mention of this room here?' Robert had turned back to his brochure. The inconsistency irritated him. He wanted room dimensions and particulars at his finger tips.

'There is.' Almost reluctantly William went over to him. He riffled through the pages and stabbed at one with an index finger. 'There. "Behind the kitchen quarters there is an unconverted wing with the potential for fourteen extra rooms".'

'Fourteen!' Victoria exclaimed in dismay. 'But that would make the house enormous. Much too big.'

'It does seem a lot, doesn't it?' Once more the disarming charm. 'The wing was added about a hundred years ago. As I said, I don't believe anyone ever uses it.' He glanced over his shoulder uncomfortably. The feeling was worse today; it was beating against his head like the threat of a migraine – fear and pain and nausea, gripping him out of nowhere. He swallowed hard, trying to stop himself retching. 'Look, Mr and Mrs Holland, would you mind if I left you to wander round for a few minutes. I have to make a phone call from the car . . .' He didn't wait for their reply. Already he was edging out of the room and back along the passage towards the kitchen.

Robert ignored him, but Victoria watched him disappear, fighting the urge to follow him. 'He doesn't like it through here, does he?' she said softly.

'It does have a bit of an atmosphere.' Robert squared his shoulders. 'You want to see it, though, don't you? I suggest we hurry round this bit, see the upstairs, then we can drive off somewhere and have tea. I'm frozen.'

'So am I.' Victoria shivered. 'And it's about 80° out there.'

'It must be damp in this bit of the house.' Robert walked back into the passage and peered through the next doorway. 'Another good sized room. And another. Good God, look!'

Victoria stared over his shoulder nervously. In the corner of the room was an enormous heap of old tin hats. Opposite them, near the window, a dozen long poles were stacked in the corner.

'Those hats must have been here since the war.' Robert picked one up.

'Don't touch them!' Victoria was suddenly frightened. 'Please don't touch them. Let's go. I don't like it here either.' She could feel the unhappiness, the desperation. It seemed to pervade the room.

'Don't be silly. We must see it all now we're here. Look, the stairs are along here.'

'No, Robert. Please.' She felt panic clutching at her throat. 'Don't go upstairs. Don't . . .'

'Victoria!' He stared at her in astonishment. 'OK. You go back. Go and look at the garden with young Mr Turner. I'll have a quick shufty up here and then I'll come and find you, OK?'

'Robert . . .' She raised her hand as if to stop him but already he had set off up the steep stairs, awkwardly pulling himself up by the handrail.

She took a deep breath. At the foot of the stairs a door led out onto the old terrace. She rattled the handle, not expecting it to open, but to her surprise it turned easily. It had not been locked.

The heat in the garden hit her like a physical blow. After the unnatural cold in the house it was wonderful. She threw her head back and raised her arms towards the sun with relief, then abruptly she dropped them to her sides. There was a young man standing on the terrace. Dressed in shabby corduroy trousers and an open-necked shirt, he had his arm in a sling. He turned and grinned at her.

'Hello.'

Victoria smiled back. 'I'm sorry. I didn't know there was anyone else here.' She was embarrassed, and at the same time relieved to see him. After the silence and the oppressive atmosphere of the west wing it was wonderful to see another human being. 'Are you looking round too?' she asked. She paused and found herself staring at him again. She knew him. Confused, she fumbled for a name, but none came. She couldn't place him.

'Looking round?' He looked puzzled. 'No. I live here. For the moment.'

'Oh, I'm sorry.' She was still desperately trying to think where she had met him before. 'We understood the place was empty.'

'Empty!' He seemed to find the word ironic. 'Well, I suppose it is in a way. I hate it in there. It's so cold, did you notice? However hot it is out here. As cold as the tomb.' He shuddered. 'Why were you staring at me?'

She hastily looked away. 'I'm sorry, but we've met before somewhere, haven't we?'

He was the most attractive man she had ever seen. Shocked at her own reaction, she was trying to cope with the sheer physical impact he had on her. It confused and frightened her.

He didn't seem to have heard her question. He was concentrating on the flower bed near them. And he obviously hadn't seen the admiration in her eyes, for when he glanced back at her he scowled. 'Not a pretty sight, am I?' He half raised his injured arm. 'Don't look at me. Wouldn't you like to see the garden?'

'Yes. Please.' Desperately she tried to get a grip on herself. Middle aged – well, nearly – women did not go round the country ogling handsome young men and feeling their breath snatched away by waves of physical longing for complete strangers. She concentrated hard on the flowers, as he seemed to be doing, hoping he had not noticed her confusion. 'The garden is very beautiful.' She hoped that her voice sounded normal. 'Mr Turner told us it had gone wild, but it seems very neat to me.' A crescent of rose beds curved around the neatly mown lawn, brilliant with flowers; beyond them a herbaceous border stretched towards the cedar tree, a riot of lupins and gladioli and hollyhocks.

The young man glanced at her and smiled. 'A few of the chaps work on it when they've got the strength. I'm not much good. I can't keep my balance without this damn thing.' As he turned to step off the terrace onto the soft mossy lawn she saw he was using a stick.

'You look as though you've really been in the wars,' she said gently.

He frowned. 'Who hasn't? But I'm lucky, I suppose. I made it back. Look. Look at the roses. God, they're lovely.' He stopped and stared at them with a strange intensity.

There was a long silence. Victoria felt uncomfortable, as though she were in the way. He had withdrawn from her into some unfathomable pain. Glancing nervously back at the house, she remembered Robert suddenly and wondered where he was. She wished he would come. He had been there: through the fear and resentment; he knew how to cope with pain.

The house on this side was smartly painted. She frowned. Several windows stood open and from somewhere she could hear the sound of music – a band playing on a scratchy record. Staring up at the windows, hoping to see Robert, she glimpsed a shimmer of white at a window. Her exclamation of surprise brought the young man's attention back to her.

'What's wrong?'

'I thought I saw someone up there. Someone in white.'

He gave a strained smile. 'Probably one of the nurses.'

'One of the nurses?' She stared at him. 'Do you have nurses to look after you?' Her eyes were wide with sympathy.

'Of course.' His eyes were clear grey, his face handsome, tanned. He glanced down at his arm ruefully. 'They're threatening to take this off.' Just for a moment she could hear the fear in his voice.

She didn't know what to say.

Visibly pulling himself together he stared at her. 'You were right. We do know each other, don't we?'

'I thought so.' She forced herself to smile.

'Yes.' He paused. 'Yes,' he repeated with conviction.

She frowned. Her emotions were sending her conflicting signals. There was something achingly familiar about his eyes, his mouth, his hands; something so familiar that, she realised suddenly, she knew what it was like to have been held in his arms and yet he was a stranger. She turned away abruptly. 'Perhaps we met when we were children or something.'

'Perhaps.' He smiled enigmatically. 'Who did you come to visit? It obviously wasn't me.' There was a trace of wistfulness in his tone.

'We came to look at the house.'

'Oh?' He stopped, gazing down at the grass. 'Interested in history, are you? It must have been lovely here, before they moved us in.'

Victoria smiled. 'Your family have lived here for a long time, have they?'

'My family?' He looked at her in amusement. 'No, my family don't come from here.' He stepped down onto the soft soil of the flower bed and picked a scarlet rose bud. 'Here. For you. It goes with your dress.' He held it out to her. As she took it their fingers touched and the electricity which passed between them left them both for a moment confused. She slipped it behind the pin of the brooch she was wearing.

'Thank you.'

He was frowning. 'You're wearing a wedding ring.'

She looked down at her hand, startled. 'Yes.' She bit her lip. 'My husband is here. He was looking round upstairs. I ought to go and join him, really.' She hesitated. She couldn't bear the anguish in his eyes. 'He was injured too – in the Falklands. He's out of the army now.' There was another long silence. 'I can't remember your name,' she said at last.

'It's Stephen.' He said it almost absent-mindedly, 'Stephen Cheney.'

The name meant nothing to her. Nothing.

'May I go and bring Robert to meet you?' she asked after a moment.

He was staring at her again, leaning heavily on his stick, his eyes intense. The silence between them was tangible. It stretched out agonizingly. Then at last he spoke. 'You and I were lovers once,' he whispered, 'in a land, long ago.'

She went cold.

For a moment they were both silent, stunned by what he had said, then he laughed. 'I'm sorry. I don't know why I said that. It's a quotation. At least, I think it is. If not it ought to be. Perhaps I'll write it myself. Yes, go and fetch your husband. I'd like to meet him.'

Victoria turned and walked slowly back across the grass towards the door into the house. She stopped as she put her hand on the handle and turned to look back over her shoulder. He was standing watching her. Jauntily he raised his stick in salute.

She let herself into the cold corridor with a shiver and ran to the stairs. 'Robert? Are you up there?'

'Here. Come and see this.' His voice was distant. 'This place is really weird,' he went on as she found him in the end room. 'Look at these – ' He broke off. 'Victoria, darling, what is it?'

For a fraction of a second she hesitated, then she threw herself into his arms. 'Oh, Robert!' She buried her face in his shirt, clinging to him. 'Robert. Where have you been?'

'Only up here.' He steadied himself with difficulty and pushed her gently away from him. 'Victoria, what's the matter?'

'Nothing.' She took a deep breath. 'I'm sorry. I don't know what's the matter with me. I was suddenly so afraid

I was going to lose you.' She could feel it again; the terror; the pain; the dread. It spun around them in the air.

He laughed. 'No such luck, Mrs Holland. You're stuck with me. How was the garden?'

'It's beautiful.' She had to be outside again. She couldn't bear to be inside another minute. 'You must come down and see it. I met one of Lady Penelope's guests. He said he'd like to meet you.' She knew she was gabbling.

'I thought what's-his-name said the house was empty.'

'He obviously didn't realize. It doesn't matter.' She glanced round again, at the long empty corridor and the silent rooms leading off it and she closed her eyes, trying to stave off the overpowering feeling of unhappiness which swept around her. 'I saw Stephen's nurse up here from the garden. Did you meet her?' The air was stuffy; no windows were open. There was no music. The upper floor echoed with emptiness.

'A nurse?' He looked puzzled. 'No, there's been no one up here. No one at all.'

They both glanced over their shoulders.

'That's strange.' She bit her lip, trying to keep her voice steady. 'When I was out there, I could hear music. The windows were open . . .'

'No.' He shook his head. 'You must have been looking at another part of the house. Come on, I've seen enough.'

'We're not going to buy it, are we?' Suddenly she minded terribly. Irrationally, she wanted the house. She wanted it as she had never wanted anything before.

He shook his head. 'It needs too much money spending on it, I'm afraid and it is far too large for us, you must see that. Sad, though. It's a lovely place.'

She bit her lip. 'I want to live here, Robert. I must live here.'

He stared at her and something in her eyes alarmed him. He was swamped by a sudden sense of foreboding;

he could feel the cold coming at him from the walls, threatening to overpower him. Somehow he forced himself to smile; somehow he kept his voice calm. 'Well, let's see the rest of the place, then we can talk about it some more.'

At the foot of the stairs she put her hand on the door handle. 'Come and see the gardens. They're so lovely.' Her fear had subsided as quickly as it had come. It had been an irrational, silly moment. She pushed at the door and frowned, rattling the handle. It seemed to have locked itself.

'Here. Let me.' Robert shook it hard. 'You are sure it was unlocked?'

'Of course I'm sure. It must have latched.' He could hear the rising panic in her voice again.

'Never mind, Victoria darling, it doesn't matter.' He put his arm round her, pulling her to him. 'We can walk round the outside before we go.'

Victoria moved away sharply from his strangely alien embrace and with a little sob she turned and ran down the passage.

Robert stared after her in astonishment and fear, then slowly he followed her.

William was waiting for them in the main entrance hall. 'Ready to go upstairs?' He glanced at them surreptitiously. They both looked agitated; uneasy.

'Why not?' Robert followed him towards the staircase.

'What did you think of the west wing?'

'Not a lot,' Robert smiled tightly. 'What on earth happened to it?'

'The house was used as a nursing home during the first war and they used that wing for the operating theatre and wards for the worst injured men.' William glanced at Victoria who had gone white. 'When the family moved back in about 1920 they left it as it was. Just closed the door and pretended it wasn't there until they forgot about it. And I think each successive generation has done the same since. Did you see the stretcher poles? They always give me the creeps.'

'So that's what they were.' Robert shuddered. 'Something I know a bit about.'

'It's an unhappy place,' Victoria put in quietly.

William nodded. 'I suspect a lot of young men died here. Luckily the rest of the house seems unaffected. I wouldn't let it worry you.' He didn't give them time to react. Turning, he led the way up the broad unlit sweep of stairs. Halfway up he stopped. 'Mrs Holland?'

Victoria was standing where they had left her. Her face was drained of colour.

'The nurse. Stephen's nurse. She was wearing some sort of big white head dress . . .'

'No, Victoria.' Robert limped back down the stairs towards her. 'I know what you're thinking. Just stop it. What you saw was a real nurse. A modern nurse. She probably saw me in the distance and decided to go back downstairs.'

William was frowning at them from the staircase. He felt a shiver touch his spine. What had she seen? One of his colleagues from the firm had seen something when she had stayed to lock up after showing some people around a few days before. That was why she had refused to come this morning. 'You can deal with that place,' she had said. 'I'm not going there again!'

He glanced at Victoria. 'What happened?' he asked cautiously.

'I met someone in the garden, that's all.' Victoria said. 'A house guest of Lady Penelope's. He's been in some sort of accident and he has a nurse to look after him. I thought I saw her in the window upstairs, that's all.'

'Lady Penelope said the house would be empty.' William swallowed hard.

'Well obviously it isn't.' Suddenly Robert was impatient. 'Let's look round upstairs, quickly, then I think we should go.'

Hastily they trailed through the main bedrooms of the house, through the bathrooms and the guest rooms. The only one showing any sign of occupation was Lady Penelope's own. There there were piles of books by the bed, a bottle of aspirins and some spare reading glasses. The other rooms were all neat and impersonal and unused. There was no room obviously allocated to Stephen. Or his nurse. Victoria felt a pang of disappointment. His face, his voice were still with her. It was as if for a few short moments he had been a part of her.

'So. That just leaves the gardens.' William had escorted them finally back to the kitchen via the second staircase. Checking the door into the west wing, he noted that the bolts were all firmly closed. 'As you probably noticed when you came in they were once very beautiful. With some care and attention they could bloom again.'

He led them back to the front door and down the steps. The sun was high, beating on the gravel with the white reflective heat more commonly associated with a Mediterranean afternoon than with an English countryside, even in August.

They walked slowly round the south side of the house and wandered across rough uncut lawns, through untrimmed hedges, an overgrown vegetable garden and between rampant woody herbs. The garden was very silent. It was too hot for birds. The only sound came from the bees.

Beneath the cedar tree on the western side of the house they stopped. Victoria looked round expectantly. Then she frowned. 'I don't understand. I thought it was here I saw Stephen. It was near this tree. There were rose beds full of flowers and the house was painted on that side, and the windows were open. There must be another tree like this . . .'

'No.' William shook his head firmly. 'There is only one cedar.'

'But we were standing there, by the door . . .'

They all stared at the door into the west wing. It was boarded up.

'No.' She shook her head. 'I've got confused. It must have been another door. There were rose beds, and a bank of hollyhocks and a garden seat, and the grass was short. There were daisies everywhere. And music. Music coming from the open windows. He picked a rose for me.' She hadn't realized that her voice was rising.

William swallowed. He shivered again.

She had the rose in her hand. It was a deep damask red. Several small thorns still adhered to the stem and as she held it out to Robert one pricked her. A fleck of blood appeared on her thumb. 'It didn't mean anything. He just gave it to me. It was a silly gesture.' She could feel her eyes filling with tears. 'I . . . I'll go and look. There must be another part of the garden we didn't see. The other side perhaps. Somewhere . . .'

Before either of the men could say anything she began to run, ducking through the thick laurel bushes which edged the grass onto the gravel of the drive.

William looked at Robert, embarrassed. 'We have been all the way round the house, Mr Holland. There are no other gardens. There are no rose beds. Not now.'

Robert laughed uncomfortably. 'Perhaps she fell asleep and dreamed it all. In this heat anything is possible.'

Slowly they walked after her. Both men were thinking of the rose.

'There isn't anyone else staying here, Mr Holland,' William said after a moment. 'Lady Penelope rang us this morning to say she'll be away another week. She wanted to check we were locking up properly. She said the house was empty.'

'Victoria, this is crazy. You can't go back there. I've told the agents we're not interested. And that's that.' Robert threw down the paper. Pushing his hands into his pockets he went to stand in front of the open window, trying to hide his despair.

Since the previous weekend she had not let him touch her. She had been tense, edgy and tearful and obsessed by the house.

'I can and I'm going to. I've already rung Lady Penelope. And I'm going on my own, Robert.'

He stared at her. 'You're mad.'

'It will only take me a couple of hours to drive over there and back. She's asked me to have a cup of tea with her.'

'But why? Why go? I've told you. We can't afford it. That house is going to go for more than we could pay. Be reasonable, Victoria.' He turned to face her desperately. 'I don't understand you, darling. What's happened to you?' She was a stranger.

She shrugged unhappily. 'I don't know. It was meeting Stephen. I have to find out who he is; where I knew him before. I can't get him out of my mind . . .'

You and I were lovers once, in a land, long ago.

She closed her eyes and shook her head, trying to rid herself of the echo of his voice, the image of his clear, grey eyes.

'OK. Go then.' Robert threw himself down onto a chair. 'Who was he? A boyfriend? You fancied him, did you? He was younger than me, I suppose; not crippled? Are you in love with him?'

'How could I be? I only saw him for a few minutes.'

She realized suddenly what he had said and for the first time she saw what she was doing to him. 'Robert!' She ran to him and put her arms around his neck. 'It's not like that. Perhaps he didn't even exist! Perhaps he was a dream! I don't know. That's why I've got to find out, don't you see? And he was crippled, as you call it, too. I told you. Look,' she hesitated. 'Come back with me. Come and meet him yourself. Please.'

He shook his head and tried to smile. 'No. You go. Whatever it is you have to prove, Victoria, you have to do it alone.'

Lady Penelope opened the door herself. She was a slim, elegant woman in her early eighties, with bright intelligent eyes. Once she had poured the tea she sat quite still behind the tea tray listening with complete attention as Victoria told her story.

When Victoria finished there was a long silence. 'Stephen Cheney,' she repeated at last.

'He and I knew each other once,' Victoria said softly. She looked down at her hands, covertly twisting her wedding ring around her finger.

You and I were lovers once, in a land, long ago.

'You do know him?'

'Oh yes, I know him.' Lady Penelope frowned. 'After tea, I'll take you to him.'

'He looked so ill.'

'Yes, poor boy, I expect he did.' Lady Penelope glanced up at Victoria. 'What made you and your husband come to look around this house?'

'The agents sent it. My husband has just been invalided out of the army and it seemed the sort of place we would like to live. We inherited Robert's father's house in London and neither of us wanted to live in town, so we sold it. But

I'm afraid this is going to be too expensive.' She smiled anxiously. 'Mr Turner from the agents said you'd already had offers above the asking price.'

'Even if I hadn't I wouldn't sell it to you, Mrs Holland.' Lady Penelope's smile belied the harshness of the words. 'This is not the house for you, my dear. You'll see why presently.' She stood up. 'Now. If you've finished your tea, I'll take you to see Stephen.'

The heat wave had broken at last and the air was cool and damp after a night of rain as they walked slowly round the side of the house, through the laurels and across the lawn beneath the cedar tree. The west wing was still tightly closed up. No music rang across the grass. Victoria stopped and stared at it. The whole place gave off a sense of deep sadness. Lady Penelope watched her, but she said nothing and after a moment she moved on. Victoria stayed where she was. He had been here. On the grass. Near the flowers. She closed her eyes. She knew already where they were going.

Her hostess moved with deceptive rapidity in spite of her eighty years and Victoria found herself almost running to keep up with her as they cut through the shrubbery and found themselves on another unkempt lawn. Beyond it a high yew hedge separated them from the church.

Opening a gate in the hedge Lady Penelope glanced at Victoria. 'I hope you're strong, I think you are.'

She set off up a path between huddled gravestones, overgrown with nettles, some of them lost beneath moss and lichen. One of them had been recently cleared. They stopped in front of it.

Stephen John Cheney
Born 20 June 1894. Died 24 August 1918
in God I trust

'I remembered the name when you mentioned it on the phone.' Lady Penelope poked at the grave with her walking stick. 'I came up yesterday to see if I was right, and cleared the stone. Then I went back to the records. We still have the nursing home ledgers in the house. My son found them years ago. I suppose they got overlooked with all the other stuff at the end of the war. Stephen died two days after they amputated his arm.'

'No.' Victoria stared down at the grave. 'No. You don't understand. I saw him. I spoke to him.'

'There is no Stephen Cheney now, my dear.' The old lady's voice was gentle.

You and I were lovers once, in a land, long ago.

'It's not possible.' It was a whisper. 'He gave me a rose.'

'Everything is possible.'

'Perhaps it was his son – or his grandson,' Victoria said uncertainly.

The old lady shrugged. They both stood, staring down at the mossy tombstone. Both knew somehow that Stephen had had no son.

'I learned the names on all these stones, walking to church every Sunday over the years,' Lady Penelope said slowly. 'My family have lived in this house for more than a century. We had to move out during the last war, just as we did during the first one. But they didn't use the place as a hospital again. The last time round it was the home guard. I brought my husband here in 1940, but we never lived here. He was killed in 1941, before our son was born.' She paused for a moment. 'The house is too much for me now. And my son doesn't want it. So, sadly, it must go.' She smiled. 'Are you all right? Do you want to sit down?'

Victoria was fighting back her tears.

'I'm sorry. It's such a shock.'

'There was no gentle way to tell you.'

'You must think I'm mad.'

'Oh no, my dear. I don't think you're mad. Far from it. On the contrary. I've heard their music from the old gramophone. I've smelt the Lysol in those wards. But I've never seen any of the boys. You are lucky.'

'Am I?' Victoria tried to smile through her tears.'Why did I know him? Why did he know me?'

He had touched her; given her a rose. She could hear his voice . . . see his eyes. She stared down at the grey stone, seeing it swimming through her tears. 'How?' she whispered. 'How?'

There was a long silence. Lady Penelope was staring across the churchyard into the distance where, through the trees, they could see the hazy mountains bathed in the afternoon sun. 'Maybe you knew one another in a previous life,' she said at last. 'Maybe you should have known each other in that life – his life – but he died too soon and you missed one another on the great wheel of destiny. Who knows? If it is still meant to be, you'll have another chance. You both stepped out of time for a few short minutes and one day you'll find each other again.' She put her arm around Victoria's shoulder. 'When you reach my age you know these things. Life goes round and round like the records those boys used to play endlessly on those hot summer afternoons. Once in a while the needle slips; it jumps a groove. That's what happened when you walked out through that door onto the terrace. You and Stephen heard the same tune for a while – then the needle jumped back. If it is meant to be, you will see him again one day.'

'You really believe that?'

'Oh yes.'

'But it won't be in this life, will it?'

'You have a lover in this life, Victoria,' Lady Penelope pointed out gently.

'You mean Robert?'

'If he is your lover as well as your husband.'

'Yes, he is my lover as well as my husband.' How could anyone doubt it? How could Robert have doubted it? She had left him alone, his face a tight mask of misery. But he had made no further attempt to stop her coming.

'Then don't hurt him.' It was as if the old lady knew what had happened. 'Stephen has had his life; now you must live yours.'

'How does it work? How could I see him? Was he a ghost?'

Her companion shrugged. 'It doesn't matter what he was. He was real. For you. And for me.'

They were both looking down at the grave.

'He told me he was afraid they would take off his arm,' Victoria said sadly.'He was so frightened. I wish I'd said something to reassure him.'

'Your being there reassured him.'

'Did it?' Victoria bit her lip. 'Do you mind living in a haunted house?' she asked after another long silence.

Lady Penelope smiled. 'Every old house has its ghosts, my dear. You grow used to them. I'm fond of mine. But that poor boy from the agents hates it here. He doesn't understand.'

'Why did you say we couldn't buy the house?'

Lady Penelope smiled. 'If you hadn't seen Stephen, it wouldn't have mattered. But you have and you recognized him. You cannot live in a house with two lovers, Victoria. It wouldn't be fair to your Robert, or yourself. Or to Stephen for that matter.'

'But fate must have brought me here.'

Lady Penelope smiled. 'There are times, my dear, when we have to turn our backs on fate. For the sake of our sanity. Always remember that.' She glanced towards the house. 'I'll go on back, my dear. You catch me up when you're ready.'

Victoria stood looking down at the grave for several

minutes after the old lady had gone. She made no attempt to reach him. Her mind was a blank. The churchyard around her was empty. There were no ghosts there now. Wandering on down the path she passed a wild climbing rose, scrambling over some dead elder bushes. Picking one perfect bud she took it back and laid it on his grave. Then she turned away.

As she walked back across the lawn she glanced up at the windows of the west wing as they reflected the late afternoon sunlight in a glow of gold. One or two of them were open now, she saw, without surprise. And, faintly, she could hear the sound of music. But the gardens were empty.

Visitors

'You know, I'm not sure that I do want to see you again after all, Joe.' I leaned back, beginning to enjoy myself, and shifted the receiver to the other hand. 'How long did you say it was?'

'Oh, come on, Pen. Don't be like that.' His voice was starting to sound the tiniest bit tetchy.

I hoped the smile on my face didn't come over in my voice. 'OK, then. As it's Christmas. You can come for the night. Spare room.'

'Spare room?'

'Spare room.'

I put down the receiver and stood up. Twenty minutes, he had said. Twenty minutes to tidy up, fix my hair and nails, slip into something infinitely casual and arrange to be very, very busy when he arrived. I glanced out of the window. The village street glistened beneath the dusting, melting snow. Rather as it had been when he walked out on me three years before. I had sworn I would never see the swine again.

Well, three years and a couple of morale-boosting affairs can do a lot for resolutions like that one. Anyway, I was curious. What had happened to my Joe in the last three years? I put a couple of logs on the fire and poured myself a drink.

*

I stayed where I was at my writing desk when I heard the car drive up outside. I counted to ten when the bell rang and then, slowly, walked to the door.

Damn. The sight of him could still make my pulses race. I stretched out a hand. 'It's good to see you again, Joe.' There were tiny unmelted snowflakes caught in the crisp curl of his hair. But his eyes were the same. Mocking; insolent; irresistible . . . 'Come and have a drink.' I put my hand on the door behind him to push it closed, but his foot was in the way.

'Pen, I'm not alone . . .'

As his voice tailed away I felt my nerves begin to throb warningly. 'Don't tell me you've brought a woman, Joe.' My voice was melodious, but I could see it made him uneasy.

'Of course not, I told you. It's all over. There's no one. But . . .'

Never in all the time I've known him have I seen Joe look shifty before. His eyes skidded away from mine and fixed, concentrating, on the battered coal scuttle on the hearth. I was taut with suspicion.

'I'm all alone, Pen,' he had said, on the phone. The liar. 'All alone, and it is Christmas Eve. Couldn't I come?'

I had been trying to forget it was Christmas Eve, in spite of the cards around the room, in spite of the coloured lights around the church and the village pub. Christmas is for families, not for the orphaned unmarried like me, however sociable we might be the rest of the year. But the crackle of sentiment in his voice had got to me.

'Come on in, Joe,' I said now, wearily. 'The house is getting cold. You'd better ask her in. One drink and you can go to the pub. Both.'

I turned my back on the door and stood, folding my arms defensively around me, in front of the fire. What did I care how many women he brought. No doubt he'd come for my approval before popping the question to someone who had finally been fool enough to say yes. It was the sort of crazy tactless thing Joe might do. I kicked a log and watched the shower of sparks. Whoever she was, she was a bitch.

There was a click as Joe quietly pushed the front door shut behind him with his foot. One. Two. Three. Four. Five. Six. Seven. Eight. Nine. Ten . . .

Slowly I turned.

Nobody. He was standing there with a basket in each hand, and he was looking sheepish again. What the hell was he up to?

'OK, Joe. Have a drink.' I sighed and went for the bottle as he set down the two baskets and came forward.

He took the glass from my hand. 'You're a real brick, Pen. Did I ever tell you that?'

Of course, I could have stepped back in time to avoid that kiss; as it was I stepped back just a little too late. As an experiment it was a success.

'I like your hair long. You look fabulous; really good.' He took a deep drink from his glass. I waited smugly for his eyes to water as he swallowed, but they didn't. I was impressed. It was neat and he had taken a big gulp. Perhaps he had been practising.

'Happy Christmas, fella,' I whispered. 'Now, stop flannelling and show me this friend.'

'His name is Paul.' He set down the glass.

'Paul?'

I watched as he went to the shopping. One of the baskets was stuffed with blankets and – I felt my eyes growing enormous – a small baby.

I stood there, for the first time in my life speechless, as Joe tenderly scooped it up and brought it to the fire. It had delicate, tiny features and warm pink cheeks. It was asleep.

'Isn't he beautiful?' Joe's voice was very gentle.

'Whose is it?' I don't think my voice was as harsh as it should have been. It really was, now he came to mention it, rather beautiful.

'This is my son.' There was no mistaking this time the pride in his voice.

And there was no mistaking the jealousy and disappointment that swept through me as he said it; silly fool that I was, still caring for a man like him.

'Do you want to hold him?' He spoke with the voice of one about to bestow a rare and lovely treat. I stepped back and firmly picked up my glass again.

'I'm not used to babies,' I said. 'I'd drop him.'

'I expect you want to know where he came from?' The shifty look had gone and the old mischievous grin was back, teasing me.

I raised an eyebrow. 'I've no doubt you have as many gooseberry bushes in town as we do here.'

'His mother doesn't like children. We had a conference when we split up and she said I could take him. So I did.' He was grinning all over his face.

'So you did.' I was stunned. 'Do you *know* anything about babies, Joe?'

He shook his head. 'She gave me a manual. It's quite straightforward, really. I've got all the gear. It's in the car, actually.'

'But, Joe, what'll you do when term starts? Who will look after it then?'

Joe, like me, teaches.

He shrugged. 'I'll find someone to keep an eye on him.'

Gently he laid the child down on the sofa and unwrapped a layer of shawl. I was torn between indignation and curiosity.

'Hadn't you better tell me who his mother was? Is?'

'Was. It has all been made legal. A lovely lady, Pen. You would like her . . .'

Like hell, I thought.

'. . . She's tall and dark and quiet, but absolutely set on being a top dancer. And she'll do it. She's good. And she's definitely not the maternal type. She nearly killed me when she got pregnant. Lovely girl.'

He positively licked his lips.

'You are a swine, Joe.' I thought it was time I said it out loud.

He laughed. 'You know, none of them have ever been like you, Pen. None of them.'

It was my turn to look modest. 'And how many of them have there been, if I might enquire?'

He shrugged. 'Trade secret, love. Who's counting? It's you I've come back to.'

'You and who else,' I said.

When he went to unpack the car I had a look at the baby. It was very like him, I had to admit.

I pulled back the shawl to have a better look and the infant Nureyev opened its eyes – and then its mouth. I leaped back as though it had bitten me. The squalling was deafening.

Joe was beside me in an instant. 'Did Penny frighten you, den?'

I put my hands over my face. 'Joe! I don't believe it. Not you. Not baby talk. Surely your son is an intellectual?'

'Of course he is.' Joe drew himself up.'Who is an intellectual, den? Daddy's boy.' He laughed. 'You should see your face, Pen.' He put his arm around me and gave me a squeeze. 'Come on. Are you going to feed him? It's time he was asleep.'

'Me?' I hit an unseemly falsetto. 'I couldn't feed him.'

'Why not? Women do these things by instinct.'

'Evidently his mother doesn't. And neither do I,' I said firmly. 'It's all up to you, Joe.'

I watched fascinated as he bent and, rummaging in a paper bag, produced a feeding bottle.

'It's only got to be warmed up.'

'Can't we give it brandy, or something, just this once?' I quavered. Babies, it seemed, unnerved me completely.

He remembered where the kitchen was; and the kettle; and the mixing bowl. Damn him, he was completely at home!

I hovered ineffectually, listening with increasing unease to the baby's screams from next door.

'Pick him up, will you. Tell him it's coming.'

I had been afraid he would say that. Nervously I edged an arm under the convulsed little bundle and heaved it up. It was surprisingly heavy. To my amazement it stopped crying at once, and after a moment, beamed at me. I found myself beaming back. I felt ridiculously pleased.

'See, he likes you.' Joe appeared with a towel wrapped around his waist, the bottle in his hand.

I watched goggle-eyed as he stuffed the teat into the baby's mouth and tipped the stuff down and I almost asked if I could have a go myself.

'I knew you'd turn up trumps, Pen.' Joe took his refilled glass from me and raised it in salute. We had made the baby a bed in a drawer upstairs after he had changed its nappy – blessedly out of sight, to save my sensibilities – and it had gone off to sleep at once. Its mountain of belongings tidied away, my cottage began to look familiar again.

'You can't keep it, Joe. It's got to go back to its mother.' I looked at him earnestly.

'Rubbish. It's mother doesn't want it.' Joe grinned affably. 'When are we eating?'

Men!

He had to make do with an omelette; hardly Christmas fare, but he produced a bottle of wine from one of his paper bags, so I made the effort to go into the garden where the snow was beginning to settle a little and I cut some frosty thyme. One *fine herbe* at least. He sniffed over my shoulder as the eggs sizzled in the pan.

'None of my other women have been able to cook like you. You know, I sometimes used to lie and dream about the nosh I got in this cottage.' He licked his lips and I had to laugh.

'I should kick you for talking about all these other women all the time. Why on earth did you leave if I'm such a paragon?'

'You were a bitch as well.' He was warming the wine, like the feeding bottle, in a basin of hot water. 'And I wasn't mature enough to cope with you. Besides, you were becoming too set in your ways. I could see you getting bossy. My God! You've moved the glasses.' He straightened from the cupboard in the corner. 'Do you know, Pen, that is the first thing that's been different in this cottage. Three years and not a bloody thing has changed. That's what I mean about being set in your ways.'

'A lot has changed.' I could feel myself getting defensive. He had caught me on a sensitive spot. I knew I was in a rut without him spelling it out. 'The walls have changed colour for a start. There are new curtains in the sitting room. I've got new chairs and . . .'

'Stop!' he raised his hands in surrender. 'Stop. I didn't mean it. Forgive the old campaigner the gaps in his memory.' He grinned again. 'So, where are the glasses these days?'

'On a tray next door.' I flipped the omelettes onto two

warmed plates and piled some French bread and salad round them. At least he wouldn't starve.

We were half-way through supper when the carol singers came. It was the moment I had been dreading most before Joe arrived. The year before, I had put out all the lights as I heard them down the street, put my head under my pillow and wallowed in self pity as they missed my darkened porch, as I had intended they should.

This time we listened. Happy. The joyous sounds were slightly off key, but who cared.

I hadn't any change.

'My God, woman, you're still after my money!' Joe groped in his pocket and produced a pound coin.

'Joe, that's too much!' I murmured, but it was too late. And it was worth it.

Oh, it would be so easy to have Joe back. So very easy.

We whispered so as not to wake the baby as we made up a bed for Joe in the spare room. 'You're right about things not being the same round here,' he muttered ruefully as I pulled the blankets over.

'Dead right, they're not,' I hissed back. 'You promiscuous so-and-so. You keep your child company.'

I didn't lock my door, though, and I was quite disappointed when the dulcet tones of Joe's snores began gently to vibrate across the landing.

'Happy Christmas, darling.'

I was struggling up through layers of exhausted sleep, clutching at daylight. It was dark.

I could feel Joe's arms around me. 'What time is it?' I managed to ask before his mouth closed onto mine. After a moment – a lovely moment – he replied, 'About three, I should think. I've just fed Paul.'

I sat up abruptly, pushing him away. It wasn't going to be that easy for him. 'Three in the morning? You're mad. Go away!'

'But Penny . . .' his voice in the dark was hurt and pathetic.

'Get out, Joe. I told you.'

I was indignant. Three in the morning is not on, by anybody's standards. Not after three years. Not after all those other women who didn't know how to cook.

He went.

At breakfast he was looking innocent again. Dangerously so.

'Happy Christmas, darling.'

'You've said that once today already, if I remember.'

'Have I?' He smiled. 'I've got a present for you.'

In spite of myself I was excited. 'Really?' I should have been suspicious.

'Really.' He looked suddenly serious. He felt in his pocket and produced an envelope which he pushed across at me. Hesitating I took it. It had something small and hard in it. Without looking I knew what it was. The ring I had thrown at his head so long before. I pushed the envelope back.

'No, Joe, it wouldn't work.'

'It would. I'm more mature now.' He smiled wickedly and left the envelope on the table.

'It wouldn't.' I got up to make the toast. 'So, when are you leaving?' I bent down to light the grill pan. It meant my face was hidden and he couldn't read my expression.

'Ten years, or so?' He sounded hopeful.

I laughed. And in spite of myself my heart leaped. 'We'll try it until lunch,' I said.

Cabbage à la Carte

Kate pulled the mini thankfully into the parking space and switched off. For a moment she rested her forehead against the cool rim of the steering wheel, breathing deeply. Her hands were shaking. The first, the lesser, part of the ordeal was over – driving the borrowed car through the overcrowded streets on market day and finding a meter. She leaned over to glance in the mirror and check her hair. Her face was pink and shiny again, her lipstick had turned too red.

She grabbed for her tapestry bag and applied a new layer. It looked artificial and hard. She wasn't used to bothering with make-up. She never usually dressed up. She had never owned her own car. But today she was endeavouring to be someone quite different. Kate Millrow, painter, recently – very recently – of St Agnes's School of Art, would never dare to try and sell her paintings to a smart town gallery.

Miss Rowmill (she was especially pleased with the name), artists' agent and talent spotter would be able to do it every day. 'Think yourself into the part, Kate, think yourself into the part,' she muttered desperately as she climbed out of the car and groped for the money. The coin, so carefully hoarded for this occasion, slipped from her fingers and rolled away towards a gutter. Frantically she leapt after it and caught it up before it disappeared down the grille. Even putting the money in the parking meter once she had recaptured it was something of an ordeal. She studied the thing intently, reading the instructions. The slot seemed to be the wrong way round. She couldn't get the money in. Then at last the needle buzzed across and she found herself with two whole hours in which to carry out her mission. She pulled out the portfolio, locked the car and made her way slowly towards the gallery. She knew it didn't open until ten so she made her way slowly towards a coffee shop, clutching the cardboard folder awkwardly. Its sharp edges at the top cut into her armpit, at the bottom they sliced into her fingers.

Sitting down thankfully with an espresso she set down her burden. By rights she ought to be at college now, settling into her final year. What had possessed her to think she could make it on her own? The offer of the cottage in the country? Somewhere where she could really paint? 'There's nothing much else to do there, Kate. It'll keep you at it. Then we'll see what you're really made of,' John had said as he handed her the key before setting off on his trek to Katmandu. For a year at least she had the place, rent free, to herself. It was a dream come true. Only John hadn't mentioned the fact that the rain came through the roof, there was no electricity and the nearest neighbour was half a mile away.

She had been shocked, afraid and then angry in that order when she first saw the cottage. Was it for this that she had thrown up college and antagonized her family? Then eventually she had begun to see the funny side. Perhaps fate had presented her with a challenge. Anyway it was too late to go back. There was nothing to do but weed cabbages ('You won't starve, love, help yourself from the kitchen garden'), eat cabbages and set up her easel.

And surprisingly she had painted. She had painted non-stop day after day, as long as there was light. But the moment had come when she realized that she could not live on cabbages for ever, and even if she could she had to pay for the calor gas to cook them, and oil for the lamps.

Nervously she had painted a board, 'Millrow Studios', and hammered it to the gate, thinking someone might come and buy at the cottage. She had waited heart-thumping for half an hour for a car to come down the lane and then she had run out and torn down the notice before anyone could see it.

Her only visitors had been her nearest neighbours from the farm up the lane. They had been kind and helpful and once brought her a chicken and often eggs, and now today she had borrowed their mini. They had looked at her pictures, made noises of polite incomprehension and suggested the gallery in town. They knew it opened at ten ('Lazy devils; don't know the meaning of the word work') and directed her to the coffee house. ('The pubs aren't open then, but if you need a stiffener, that'll be the next best thing.')

It was ten past ten. Her knees wobbling, she paid her bill and crossed the road.

The girl in the gallery had round moon glasses and an expression of disdain. Kate forgot she was Miss Rowmill, agent and became shy and diffident Kate Millrow, beneath the girl's supercilious gaze.

'Are you the owner of the gallery?' she asked in a strained falsetto, totally unlike her own voice.

To her surprise the girl gave her a friendly smile. 'No, but he'll be back any minute. Take a seat.'

Kate sat numbly, the portfolio balanced against her knees. The paintings on the walls of the gallery were to her eyes mannered and uncomfortable. But they were good and very professional. And, dear God, they were framed! Perhaps she should have tried to frame hers before she brought them in? She started to shake again, wishing she hadn't come.

Then the door opened and the owner appeared. He was a young man, tall and arrogant-looking. His lips, she decided instantly, were mean beneath the thin moustache.

Her only concern now was to get out as soon as possible, with the least embarrassment for everybody, especially herself.

The other girl had her coat on as soon as the man appeared. 'Here's Mr Chambers now,' she announced and she was gone without a word to him.

'Ask her to watch the place for five minutes and she acts as if I'd told her to swim the channel, the silly bitch,' he muttered angrily at her retreating back. 'Now, what do you want, young lady?' He sounded irritated.

He didn't seem to realize that she was Miss Rowmill, artists' agent. Nettled, she told him.

He was not impressed. 'We're fully booked well into next year,' he said coolly. 'But let's see what you've got.'

He leafed through the paintings and sketches casually, taking hardly any time to study them. Occasionally he muttered 'humph, not bad,' or 'weak, weak,' or 'very derivative'. Kate was mortified.

'They're all by the same girl?' he asked, not raising his eyes.

'Yes.'

'Where did you find her, art school?'

She was furious. 'No. She's a local girl. I think she has great talent, a great . . .' She hesitated, trying to think of a word.

'Potential?' He glanced up at her, smiling suddenly.

'Exactly.' She felt she wasn't playing her part sufficiently convincingly. 'I like to watch out for up and coming new names, and so,' she added pointedly, 'do *most* of my clients.'

'Indeed.' She did not like the way he raised one eyebrow.

He reached the end of the pictures and began to shuffle through them again. 'Did she have any oils, this Kate Millrow?' he asked casually.

'Oh yes.' Did she sound too eager? 'I didn't bring any today, but I could arrange to collect some.'

'No, no.' He held up his hand. 'I've seen enough. I'm afraid, Miss . . .' he hesitated over the name. '*Rowmill* was it? I'm afraid these are not really suitable for this gallery. However,' he glared at her as he saw her about to speak, 'however, I do believe like yourself in giving an encouraging help to the young occasionally, so,' he pulled out a watercolour and looked at it closely, 'I will take a couple of these if you agree. I'll have them framed and hang them in my next show. I'll take framing expenses plus ten per cent, agreed?'

Kate was speechless with joy. It wasn't the praise, the one man exhibition she had dreamed of, but it was something. Excitedly she gave him the address of the cottage.

'And now *your* address, Miss Rowmill. I generally prefer to deal through an agent direct if there is one.' He looked at her closely and waited, his pen poised. It nearly stumped her. She thought fast and then gave him her sister's address in London. It seemed to impress him.

It was not until she was nearly home that she realized that in real terms she had achieved very little. The condescending acceptance of two pictures by a stuck up opinionated gallery owner, out of charity rather than anything else, and a lot of quite unjustified rude remarks. 'Horrible prig!' she muttered to herself as she turned up the lane. And what was worse she realized, she still hadn't actually earned any cash, and her desire for some rather more exotic food than eggs and cabbage was increasingly daily, if not hourly.

Reluctantly, nervously, she rehung the notice on the

gate before she changed and took the car back to the farm. If Miss Rowmill could hang the notice up, she hoped desperately that she could persuade Miss Millrow to leave it there.

Once more dressed in jeans and barefoot, she selected the paintings Mr Chambers had made the least derogatory noises over and put them prominently round the room.

Then she sat back to wait. No one came. She left the notice on the gate, refused to be discouraged, went to dig some potatoes and then at last settled down to paint again.

'Derivative indeed,' she snorted. 'The man was an ignorant fool.'

It was on the Saturday afternoon that a car drove by, slowed and backed to the gate. Two people got out and wandered up the path, exclaiming at the honeysuckle and roses, pointing up at the fields behind the cottage.

Kate felt sick.

They knocked and she let them in, wishing she wasn't quite so shabbily dressed and that her toes weren't quite so grubby from the garden.

But they obviously liked to see her like that. She saw suddenly through their eyes a glimmer of the so-called glamour of the artist in the garret, and glad that for once she had got rid of the smell of cabbage from the house, she was content to let them wander around the room she used for a studio.

She crossed her fingers, praying they would buy some thing, but they completed a round of the paintings without seeming to see anything in particular.

Then the man turned to her hesitantly. 'Is anything for sale, Miss Millrow?' he asked.

Anything! He must be joking.

She smiled politely. 'Well, some of my best work is away on exhibition,' – was that Miss Rowmill talking? – 'but most things here are for sale, yes.'

She desperately tried to think of prices. Too high and they would be scared off; too low and they would think her valueless.

'I'll give you ten pounds for this, I love it.'

She could not believe her ears. Ten pounds for a tiny painting of a posy of spring flowers. It wasn't even modern in style.

'That seems very fair.' She smiled as graciously as she could.

She sat for a long time after they had gone, gazing at the two fivers on the table. Could it be true that at last she was earning her living by painting?

Two hours later she was chopping vegetables in the kitchen when there was a knock at the door. She opened it to find Mr Chambers standing on the doorstep. Her heart sank with embarrassment but he held out his hand blandly with absolutely no sign of recognition on his face.

'You must be Miss Millrow. How do you do.'

Had her make up been so good then? She stammered a greeting in return and showed him at his request into the studio.

Reaching into his pocket he produced an envelope. 'I'm glad to say I've managed to sell one of your paintings, Miss Millrow.'

'Already?' her voice came out in a squeak.

'Already.' He grinned at her amicably. 'It was lying on my table after you, that is your agent,' he corrected himself quickly, 'had left it with me and I had a buyer almost at once. It seems my initial judgement may have been a little harsh.'

'I'll say it was,' she muttered under her breath, and then out loud she asked. 'How much did you get?' She took the envelope with shaking fingers.

'There's thirty-five pounds there. I've already taken my commission.' He grinned again. 'I imagined that under the circumstances you would rather pay your agent her commission yourself.'

Kate felt herself blushing crimson. 'You must think I'm an awful fool.'

'Not at all. You'd be surprised how many people come in with pictures they say a "friend" has painted. Mind you,' he looked her up and down pointedly. 'Not many of them go to the lengths you did for a disguise.'

She blushed again. 'I'm afraid I'm rather a mess at the moment. I was cooking.'

He nodded. 'Cabbage. I had guessed.'

She smiled ruefully. 'I'm afraid I live on it.'

'Why don't you go and continue while I poke around here for a bit and investigate your,' he paused and winked, 'your potential.'

She fled.

It took only a few minutes to throw the vegetables into a pan and scrub her hands and then she ran upstairs to comb her hair and change her skirt. When she came down he had piled several canvases on the table.

'I'll take these next,' he said without preamble. 'Sale or return of course, and I'll buy this one myself . . .'

Again it was flowers, she noticed amazed.

'. . . if it's not exorbitantly priced. Now,' he looked at her again. 'Could that concoction you were making wait do you think? If you were to transform yourself, not into that hard hitting woman Miss Rowmill, but perhaps into a slightly tidier version of yourself I could take you out to dinner to celebrate your sales.'

She looked at him amazed. She had got the firm impression he despised her and her kind, and she certainly disliked him. So why ask her out? And anyway he was insufferably rude. A slightly tidier version of herself indeed. She curbed the desire to stick out her tongue at him.

Instead she lowered her eyes meekly to the floor. 'That would be nice,' she said. 'Much better than cabbage.'

She had a Laura Ashley dress upstairs and pretty Venetian sandals. Her hair beneath its gay scarf was at least clean. Oh yes, Mr Chambers. She could be tidier when she tried.

She debated over lipstick for several minutes in her bedroom and then decided against it. Miss Rowmill might wear lipstick, but she did not. She clipped on the silver bangle her parents had given her for her eighteenth birthday and gazed at herself in the stained old mirror. The image, she had to admit, was rather attractive.

Mr Chambers evidently thought so too, for he stopped being rude, told her his name was Derek and ushered her out to his car with exaggerated care. He even helped her with the seat belt.

'I have a ten per cent interest in you, my dear Miss Millrow,' was his only comment when she protested.

They drove back into town and he took her to the most delightful French restaurant she had ever been to. He almost talked her into having something called *Dolmas Maigre*, but the suppressed glee in his expression led her to guess it might have something to do with cabbage and to his chagrin she checked with the waiter before she ordered. Once that hurdle was over the evening continued fairly well. She found herself telling him about art school and John's offer of the cottage and her parents' anger when she had 'dropped out', as they of course put it. To her surprise he threw his head back and laughed.

'Dropped out, a prim little miss like you? Nonsense. Besides, they ought to be proud of you. You have a great deal of talent. And not only for painting. If you ever get bored with that, you could go on the stage.'

She looked at him to see if he was taking the micky, but his expression was all innocence. He quickly topped up her wine glass. 'Yes, Miss Millrow, you have a great deal of talent.'

To her annoyance she found herself blushing although she was quite sure he was teasing. His fingers had strayed towards her own on the blue table-cloth and as they so very casually, almost by accident, made contact, she snatched her hand away. She was not going to be that easy to placate. She took a gulp of wine.

When they parted that evening, however, it was on the understanding that they would meet again the following Saturday and that, if she could face the bus ride into town, she would go to see him at the gallery even before then.

'Now,' he said, looking up at her mischievously from the driving seat as he started up the engine. 'About what you wear when you come. Shoes, yes. Lipstick, no. Jeans, yes if decent. Right?'

She grinned. 'And next weekend?'

'Next weekend, if you're cooking for me, a large plastic apron, which I will personally provide.'

'Nothing else?' Her eyes widened.

He laughed. 'That, my sweet Kate, is up to you. But I'll live in hope.'

She stood waving as he drove off down the lane and then slowly she made her way back into the shadowy cottage where he had lit the oil lamp for her and left it, flickering slightly on the table. She was unbelievably happy.

'Damn cheek,' she muttered to herself. 'Who does he think he is?'

Metamorphosis

She couldn't remember how she came to be on the train. She knew the station had been huge and echoing and she had walked through it as through the rib cage of a dinosaur, to find the tiny womb of the compartment where she was to sleep. It was safe there; warm and dark and alone. When the man knocked and called out the different sittings of meals she hid her head beneath the blanket and he went away and then she still lay listening, as the wheels beat the rhythm of a foetal heart.

She who had been afraid to walk the streets of London, afraid of unknown lurking terrors, afraid of men and dogs and children and women like herself, somehow she had managed to change trains and between them she had bought herself a tea from an anonymous uncaring man who slopped the liquid across ranks of cups and watched it gurgle, stewed and wasteful through a grating. She dared not ask for a spoon, but she was well pleased with herself for the tea. It was hot and good to drink. The station had been alive with people and pigeons. Brisk sunshine streamed through dirt-encrusted glass. She realized that she was already no longer so afraid as she climbed aboard the second train and waited for it to travel north.

There was a taxi to find at the other end. She stood on the esplanade looking across at the fishing boats and sniffed the glorious sea. It gave her strength. She felt in her pocket for the key; a large cold key; the key to sanity.

Her driver had the soft-spoken gentle ways of the west. He made her welcome and gentled her as he would a doe come down from the hills in the snow. She had the great dark eyes of a doe, he thought. And the unnamed terror. Was it life she feared, or herself? She sat beside him, her fingers clutching the purse she needed to pay him and he knew she dreaded the moment she must pay, for the human contact it involved. He told her the names of the mountains and the lochs and he soothed her with softly-aspirated vowels.

Skies as wide as for ever opened now above her head and she felt light and free again. There were no more buildings. The taxi was bumping and swerving away from yesterday and carrying her inexorably with it. There would be no more hospitals now, no more drugs, no more fears. But memories; there were still memories.

'What you need now is a holiday, Miss Tansley,' the psychiatrist had said, briskly misunderstanding. 'Is there somewhere you could go, by the sea perhaps; someone you could go with?' and he had looked at his watch. She wanted to cling; to stay; to come again. But he had finished with her. Her case was closed.

The sun reflected on a silver loch dazzling her eyes with its beauty. 'There is Appin,' she had said. 'I can go to the cottage in Appin.'

'Fine, fine. Do that.' His mind had withdrawn from hers. He was already thinking of the next patient.

So she had done it. Slowly and methodically she had arranged it all. The cottage would be hers for a month with the seas and the lochs and the islands beyond the west where men go when they die and stay for ever young. All of it was hers.

But it had all been almost too difficult. The world was

still a menacing place; a place of greys and blacks and angry red. She had had to fight to keep the panic away. And she had thought silently in her bed, her eyes fixed on the cracked crazed ceiling which was no ceiling in the dark, but an infinite chasm, of the silver and the blues of the western shore where she had spent her long happy childhood holidays and she grasped towards the healing and the reality which the salt air must bring to her soul.

'Will you be all right, miss?' The taxi driver's face, beaten red by the wind and sun was crumpled with concern. He waved away the shaking hand which held a painfully calculated ten per cent and picked up her case to carry it to the door.

She proffered the key and he took it and opened it for her. The great stone hearth was unchanged. The rocking chair was still there. But the people were all gone.

She stretched her lips to smile at him and stood when he had gone, a shiver holding her in the centre of the floor. She could hear echoes. Echoes of her voice as a girl, pretty, carefree, happy as only the ignorant can be and of her brother, more raucous his and loud, but with the same intonation. And the Fairburn cousins, their two shouts indistinguishable twin from twin, and the gentle remonstrations of her mother; and her father putting his hands to his ears as he sorted out the lines for the sea trout. And the barks of Romany and Diddakoi, the two Battersea waifs, so long ago buried in the garden beneath the apple tree. She shivered again and felt the tears pricking her eyelids.

'Cry, my child. The day you can cry you will be on the way to being cured,' the psychiatrist's level voice echoed in her head. The tears were there all right, but still they would not fall. As they had not fallen since the car had spun out of reality and into nightmare taking mother, father, brother, lover all from her in one clap of thunder.

Slowly she walked into the bedroom which had once

been hers. It was the smallest and it overlooked the island, shimmering in the evening waters. She opened the window and looked out, breathing sweet thyme and lavender from the flower below. The stone was cold and hard to her elbows but she leaned there a long time watching for the luminous highland night which almost never came. Then at last she lay down on the bed, her coat still on, her shoes kicked wearily aside and she slept, not hearing the owls, the jumping fish and the hill noises of the night.

Instinct told her she had to walk each day. Exhaustion brought forgetfulness. It brought sleep and slowly appetite and a suspicion of colour to her sallow cheeks. She would take crumbs to the squirrels and sit for hours beyond the great rock gazing at the sky. She took a sketch book and slowly captured the growing beauty as it fought its way into her consciousness.

Once she saw a small boy looking at her from behind the rocks. When she looked again he had gone and she found herself half-smiling, sensing his peeking eyes. To her he was just another squirrel.

She watched the men with their boats, the tourists with their cameras, the children, shadows of her own past, as they crossed her path, but she stayed silent and withdrawn. In the village store they decided she was some kind of a natural, harmless, lonely, to be watched over with gentle unobtrusive care.

Then came the old man from over the hill. He knocked at the door and greeted her with a grin. 'How are you, lass? I heard you were here. Would you be the same little Josie Tansley who came in my boat with her dad?'

She looked at him frowning, remembering. Strangers' faces had gone; only the dead were with her. She grasped for a name: 'Ruaraidh . . . Macdonald?'

And he shook her hand the harder. 'You remember an

old man, lass. Tell me. How are your family? Is your father well?'

He alone in all the world did not know, had not heard the thunder clap. 'They're all dead, Mr Macdonald.' She felt her lips speak, as her mind receded from the truth. 'Killed.'

She turned away blindly, but the old man came on. His arm was round her, his faded blue eyes near hers. She saw his spontaneous tears and suddenly her own came flooding. At last the dam in her heart which had held back all things broke and she knelt, her head on the knee of an old highland man and wept.

He knew about broken hearts. He knew about the loss which is too great to bear. He sat all night, her head in his lap, his eyes fixed on the embers of the fire as they died one by one to white ash. The night came through the open windows almost as bright as day, scented, warm, moonlit. Only owls were abroad. His dog lay on the mat, its ear pricked to the night noises, its eye occasionally opening, watching its master and the girl in her grief.

Then the dawn came; rosy, gentle, feeling with hesitant fingers round the undrawn curtains and she slept at last. He picked her up, laid her on the bed and sat beside her, his lined face sad with the knowledge of generations of death and grief, pondering on the words of comfort he alone must give.

When she opened her eyes at last she lay purged and dreamlike, and she listened to his quiet voice telling the stories of the centuries which console and heal and she smiled at him at last and reached for his hand. The pain had dulled; the scar inside her mind had begun to heal of its own. Sadness there would always be, but he gave her resignation and a little hope that day.

When the squirrels came again she looked round for the little boy and seeing him called out. He came, nervous, chubby, a wicked cheerful child and she ran with him down to the water and watched him throw stones that skidded and bumped on the glittering surface and after a while she tried to do it too. And when her pebbles sank with a plop into the water she laughed.

In the store they noticed the change and were glad for her. People stopped to look at her sketches now and she found she could talk again. The world was no longer hostile, no longer viewed behind a wall of thick black glass, against which she beat with bloodied fists. It was sweet and young and she could breathe again.

Slowly she found she believed once more in the future. She went to the phone box and dialled a friend. Once he had been more. He understood; he bore no grudges; he came to be with her and gently took her hand. He would be the first bastion against loneliness. The first positive step. She accepted too a puppy from Ruaraidh Macdonald and together the four of them, the boy, the girl, her friend and the dog ran on the sands amongst the ribbons of emerald weed.

Each night she cried a little less, each day she laughed a little more. The agony was numbed. Her eyes were learning how to shine again; she was beginning to know hope.

The friend saw that she had fallen to the bottom of a muddy pool wide-eyed and gasping, flailing with arms towards the depths of darkness. Then slowly she had risen, inexorably and involuntarily, the will to survive triumphing over the will to die.

He slept in the bedroom that had been her brother's. Each day he saw her opening a little, like a flower. But he kept his distance, watchful, afraid lest he overstep some faint invisible line which would drive her once more from the sun. For him she was a sacred virgin, inviolable and goddesslike in her bereavement, with her delicate blue-veined pallor of the skin.

By the great rock he would sit, the width of the rock between them, idly throwing pebbles at the setting sun, while she dipped her brush in the carmine-stained waters of a rock pool and traced the scene on her page.

'Shall we take a boat to the Island?' he asked at last after many days, screwing his eyes to watch a cormorant flop from its perch on a weed-draped rock into clumsy flight.

She nodded absently. 'It could be fun.' Once her eyes might have sparkled. Now they looked at him with quiet detached amusement. She saw him as an overgrown school-boy, as playful and as harmless as the puppy.

They hired a boat and he rowed her, pulling quietly with the tide towards the dusky island. Trails of light still crossed the rippled water. The cormorant was back on its perch, its wings outspread to dry.

'The evening is like golden velvet,' she whispered, her fingers trailing in the cool. She faced him across the oars, watching his corded muscles contracting and expanding beneath the dark plaid shirt. Beads of perspiration stood on his brow. His eyes were over her shoulder fixed on the distance, the pupils small with the glowing sunset.

'Are you watching where we're going?' He had felt her gaze and smiled without looking.

'You're doing fine.' Her voice still cracked when she spoke from a long silence; cracked and hesitated before it sounded true. 'Don't hurry; it's so beautiful.' Her toes were bare in the warm greasy water which slopped on the bottom boards of the boat. A strand from the fringe of her shawl trailed in the wet, floated and unravelled, scarlet, unnoticed in the oily black of it.

When the boat grounded on the shingle he let the oars go, dead wings in the heavy rowlocks.

'Shall we walk or sit and watch the sunset?' he asked, his voice slightly raised above the rustle of the water on the stones and she stood up for answer, her arms out to balance as the boat rocked and she jumped clumsily to the shore.

They watched the clouds of midges dancing on the dusky water and whirling in columns above the beach. He slapped his neck and arms but her cool skin stayed untouched and she watched him, faintly amused again. There was a broch to see. They looked for it in the gloaming, amongst long dew wet grasses and listened to the lonely wail of a night bird echoing across the water. She held his hand over the uneven ground and to climb a fence and together they untangled the damp fringe of her shawl from the rusty wire. Their fingers touched by accident and she glanced up at his face.

He smiled and she felt the night wind cold about her shoulders. 'One day I must go back to London,' she whispered. 'To the flat.'

'I'll be with you, Josie. You needn't go alone.'

They gazed at the stones which had once formed a great tower.

'Was this it?' she whispered. 'Is this all that's left?'

'Josie, please.' His hand tightened over hers.

She was gazing at the black stones, thinking of the ancient hands which had built it strong and resilient. They were dead too, those men. 'What's it all for?' She sighed and turned away, not seeking an answer and he followed her, his eyes on the ground.

Near the boat she spread her shawl on the short turf and patted it as she sat down. 'Come. Make love to me now. That's all there is left to do.' She smiled enigmatically, the evening star in both her eyes. He knelt and held her shoulders, puzzled. Seeking to understand.

'You mean it, Josie? That's what you want?'

Slowly she unbuttoned her blouse and his fingers, gently seeking her breast felt a prickle of gooseflesh as the cool night wind stroked the warm skin. Somewhere an oystercatcher whistled down the strand as the man bent his lips to the small hard nipples.

She cradled his head in her arms and watched the distant loom of a lighthouse in the limpid night. She could still see the outlines of the trees on the opposite shore, even without the help of the silver crescent moon, lying on its back above the hills.

Quietly she slipped down till her head was resting on the ground and the night was eclipsed by the eyes of the man. She was not afraid any more. She was one with the past and the future, the day and the night. The living and the dead both were within her embrace.

They rowed home at last in the cool of the dawn, watching the spreading ripples as fish rose to break the surface and seeing the trails of weed colouring the turning tide's edge. Already she looked on the world with calm maternal eyes, sure of the seed she had desired. Her cool grey eyes met those of the man at the oars and lingered and at last she smiled, knowing that for her now there was a future.

She did not let him travel on the train. She carried within her a new self sufficiency such as she had not known before and she treasured it with the memories of the silver Appin seas. He stood to wave on the platform, half-guessing what she already knew, that she carried his child and that for now she needed no more of him.

She sat in her sleeping compartment once more quiet and alone listening to the beat of the wheels on the rails, her hands folded on her lap.

In her head she still carried the image of the velvet night in the north and she used it as an amulet against the towns the trains passed through, dense black jungles glowing with lights in the dark. Then came the outskirts of London in the early hours of the morning.

Josie slipped the key into the lock and stepped into her dusty flat, looking round with quiet resolution. The photograph of her broken family still lay face down beside the phone, where she had dropped it, splinters of glass scattered on the carpet. She stooped without stopping to take off her coat and picked it up, piling the glass carefully on to the frame. Beside it was a vase of dead roses. She swept them out, their stems long and dry and threw them in the bin. Then she went to open the windows.

'Come on, junior,' she said out loud. 'Let's choose which room you're going to have and then we'll go out and buy some paint. We're going to begin again, just you and me, as soon as we've unpacked.'

She caught sight of herself in a mirror and smiled gently, staring into her own dark grey eyes. 'It's all right, Josie my love, you're not talking to yourself. That's not been one of your troubles. You're talking to a real person; or at least he soon will be.' She unbuttoned her coat bit by bit and slipped it off, letting it trail from her fingers to the floor. 'And after you my little one, I have a feeling there may be another little brother to keep you company. I'll discuss it with your father when he gets in touch.' She thought of the quiet face on the platform, the wistful hand waving goodbye, and smiled again. Next week would be soon enough to ring him. She didn't want to hurry things. She couldn't go any further. Not yet.

Feline Express

It was one of those smouldering London nights when the air smells strangely bitter-sweet and exciting; a night for dancing on lawns or lying back in a punt and drifting beneath shadowy drooping willows. Those things were just dreams for me though. I was, as usual, at home; and in bed.

I sat up and groped for my clock. It was just after two. I must have been asleep, for the last time I had looked it had been midnight exactly. Cinderella's hour. I sighed uncomfortably, trying to find a cooler corner on the hot pillow for my aching head. Then suddenly I sat bolt upright, my heart thumping with fear. There was someone moving round in the kitchen next to my room. That must have been what woke me. I strained my ears. Silence. Then, quite distinctly I heard a scraping noise as though something were being pushed along the table.

I looked round desperately for a weapon of some kind to defend myself with. I didn't have a poker of course; the best I could do was a high heeled shoe. I crept out of bed and reached for my dressing gown, then, with the heel of the shoe held out menacingly before me in a shaking hand, I crept to my door and listened again. The whole flat was silent. Beyond my door lay the tiny hall off which led the kitchen door, next to mine, and opposite them the bathroom and the other room. Sally my flat mate had been sent to Brussels by her firm for six weeks, so I was alone. The telephone was in the kitchen. I quietly turned the handle of the door and opened it a crack. I looked out. The kitchen door was ajar.

Suddenly there was the most tremendous crash, followed by a terrified mewing and a scrabble of paws. I laughed out loud with relief.

Pushing open the door I clicked on the light. The kitchen, like my room, was at the front of the house. It had a small dormer window leading onto a broad parapet which ran along the house tops the entire length of the street. I had left the window wide open because of the heat. My visitor must have crept along from another flat and, seeing the open window, come in. My beautiful flowering geranium lay in the midst of its shattered pot on the floor beneath the window. There was no sign of the cat. It must have heard me and fled the way it had come, knocking over the plant as it leaped for the window. I got a dustpan and brush and swept up the mess, then checking everything else was in order I stopped to get myself a cold drink from the fridge.

'Mee-ow.'

I jumped. The frightened squeal came from very near me. Then I saw it. Hiding in the dark crack between the fridge and the cupboard was a tiny kitten, with enormous frightened eyes.

'Hello, puss,' I said quietly. 'Was it really you making all that noise?' I held out my hand and twitched my fingers at it enticingly. The eyes immediately stopped looking frightened and looked instead very intelligent indeed. It put its head on one side and scampered out to me.

I picked it up. It was a stripy kitten, with a ridiculous stump of a tail and enormous green eyes; clearly not old enough to be walking lonely parapets under the sky by itself at two in the morning.

I gave it some milk and took it back to my room. After exploring thoroughly for a while it scrambled up onto my low divan bed, curled up and went to sleep. It appeared that for the time being at least I had acquired a cat.

I slept beside it, not waking till the sun crept in at the attic-window and fell full on my face. I grabbed the clock. It was after eight and I was going to be very late for work. The kitten had gone. I called it vainly as I made breakfast and dressed, but it must have climbed from my bed to the bookshelf and jumped to my windowsill. I prayed it had not slipped on the parapet and that it could find its way back to its real home.

In the busy office during the day I didn't give the little cat another thought but at night, at home in the flat alone, I wondered where it had come from. It would have been fun to have a kitten for company in lonely London. Sally's friends were kind and often asked me out with them, but since she had been away the phone had stayed depressingly silent. I had only been working in London for a couple of months after all. I could not expect to know many people yet and I was bound to meet people soon, but that didn't stop me wondering and wishing as beautiful moonlit night succeeded moonlit night.

That night she, I decided she must be a she, came to see me again, about eleven this time, her tiny enquiring face all eyes, peering in through the open casement as I lay on my bed reading.

'Hello, Tiger, have you come to keep me company again tonight?' Pleased, I laid down my book to watch her. She jumped to the bookcase and stalked along it, her stumpy tail erect, mewing at me. She came and licked my hand with a tongue like sandpaper and then, politely, showed me where the door was. She licked her lips.

For four nights running Tiger came and had her evening milk drink with me and afterwards curled up with me to sleep. Each morning when I awoke she had disappeared.

The fifth night it poured with rain; heavy thundery rain which cascaded and bounced on the parapet and splashed into the room. Reluctantly I shut the window. Surely she would not come on a night like this. Entirely self-centred and demanding and affectionate only when it pleased her, my five square inches of visitor had a big enough personality to make up in many ways for my lack of human company in the evenings and I found I was missing her very much.

I left my windows open the next night and the next, but she didn't come and sadly I told myself she probably wouldn't come again.

Then one Saturday as I was cleaning the flat, my hair tied in a scarlet cotton handkerchief, she suddenly appeared at the kitchen window. Even in the short time she had not been to see me, she had grown.

I gave her some milk and let her play boxing games with my duster for a while, watching as she danced in the sunbeams on the rug. Suddenly she stopped jumping about, cocked her little head to one side and listened. Then in a minute she had leaped to the bookcase and out onto the parapet and was gone.

I went to the window and leaned out, edging forward beyond the angle of the dormer onto my elbows. To the left and right the long sunlit parapet stretched away the length of the street. I watched her trotting purposefully along, much too near the edge for my liking, till she came to another open window where she disappeared. I looked down nervously at the road, three storeys below and then began to wriggle back. As I edged back I glanced again at the window where Tiger had vanished. There was a young man leaning out, as I was, watching me. I smiled and raised a hand in greeting.

I pottered around with the duster for a while longer, but without Tiger to play with housework had lost all its appeal. So I collected my basket and my purse and ran down to go to the shops.

A few doors down from me a young man was tinkering about with an old car, his head under the bonnet. He stood up as I passed and I had a glimpse of brilliant blue eyes in a tanned face before I went on. I had the feeling he was watching me, but I didn't turn back. It was the young man at Tiger's window.

That night she came to me earlier than usual. I played with her and cuddled her for a long time before at last we fell asleep. Somehow I could not get the image of those blue eyes – her master's blue eyes – out of my mind.

I saw him again next morning climbing into his car as I set off for the post office. I almost hoped he would stop and offer me a lift, but he didn't. He glanced in his mirror though, to see me again after he had driven slowly by. The street seemed a hundred times more lonely when I got back later. The battered car was still missing and glancing up at our windows in the eaves of the high roof tops I saw that although mine were open, his were shut. Tiger would not be coming to visit me today.

His car did not return until after ten that evening, and although my windows stayed open all night Tiger never appeared. I stayed awake a long time hoping to hear her imperious voice from the windowsill, but it never came.

As I sat in the office next day leaning disconsolately on my desk I saw with sad resignation that the skies were clouding over. The heat wave, the weather forecast had said, was over. By lunch the first cold drops of rain were beginning to fall and I thought sadly of the long lonely evenings till Sally came back, my windows shut against wind and rain, my little visitor probably snug in her own basket beside someone else's bed. His bed.

It was coming down in big heavy drops when eventually I reached home that evening after volunteering to stay at work to do some overtime. I threw open the window and leaned my elbows on the sill. The streets were smelling of wet soot and sweet earth from the garden square round the corner. It was lovely to feel the cool freshness on my face.

Tiger arrived while I was still eating my supper, her fur wet and spiky. Around her neck was a little leather collar and attached to it by a little piece of string was some paper. I couldn't believe my eyes. My hands shook as I tried to untie it to take the paper. It was a note: 'How about dinner on Wednesday?' it said. That was all.

I stared at the writing, unbelieving. Was it meant for me? Putting the puzzled little cat firmly down on the carpet I went to the window and wriggled out a little way. His window was closed. He had put her out into the rain knowing she would have to come to me if she didn't want to get wet. To me, or someone else? I didn't know how many windows Tiger visited on her nightly rambles, how many lonely ladies she played with to earn a saucer of milk. There were many windows opening out onto her private cat walk.

I puzzled what to do; I wanted so very much to say yes. For a long time I sat in front of my writing pad, pen in hand while Tiger slept on my bed. At last all I could think of to say was: 'But I don't even know your name . . .' I tied it to her collar and crept at last into bed beside her.

In the morning she was still there and there was a huge puddle on the carpet from the rain which had poured in all night. I was furious. Picking her up I put her outside by force and shut the window behind her in spite of her pitiful mewing. I was angry as much with myself for leaving the window open as with her for not going out in the rain. Probably she wouldn't come back at all now after such an outrage, but my carpet was ruined and in the cold light of day I hadn't much faith in a silly scribbled message which was probably a joke. For a moment I regretted not removing my note and tearing it up. Then I shrugged. It would probably have dissolved by the time the poor little cat got home. I glanced out of the window. The rain was still sheeting down and the clouds were black and threatening.

I was like a bear with a sore head at work that day, as I sat gazing out at the rain. I so much wanted the note to be real, and for me. And I knew that it just couldn't be. Things like that don't happen in real life.

By about four o'clock the sky had cleared a little and as I walked home from the bus the sun broke through the clouds and glistened dazzlingly on the wet pavements. My heart lifted a little as I set the key in the lock. I had bought myself a new paperback and a pizza on my home to cheer myself up a bit. I was sure Tiger wouldn't come again after the way I had treated her that morning and I did not let myself even think about the message on her collar. I knew I wanted too much for her to come again with another.

She arrived about half past eleven, standing as if uncertain of her welcome at the window. I could see at once, with thumping heart, that she had a new message tied to her collar. I was terrified she would turn and run before I could scoop her off the windowsill and carry her to the kitchen. While she drank her milk I read the letter:

9 Westport Terrace (top bell)

To whom it may concern . . .
May I, Mowgli, being of sound cat-mind, introduce Jonathon Lazenby, bachelor of this parish. He is a respectable gentleman and most desirous of escorting a certain young lady, she being in the habit of tying her hair in a provocative red scarf, to the Bistro

Italiano at 7.30 tomorrow evening. Should she be willing to accept perhaps she would intimate the same to Mowgli who will pass on her message.

by Feline Express, Tuesday

I read the letter again and again, half laughing, unable to believe it to be true. Then at last I wrote my reply.

15 Westport Terrace (top bell)

Miss Anna Winton being the lady with the red scarf, thanks Mowgli very much for her impeccable introduction and has much pleasure in accepting Mr Jonathon Lazenby's kind invitation. She looks forward to meeting him tomorrow night.

by Feline Express

'I'll buy you a tin of salmon tomorrow, Mowgli,' I whispered in her ear as I tied the note to her collar. But I didn't have to. I found Jonathon had already done it and as he said, one tin at a time was quite enough for such a small messenger.

The Consolation Prize

'Would you like some more wine?'

Under the low ceiling with its criss-cross of darkened beams a curl of smoke levelled and drifted up from the log fire, from the cigarettes of the loudly talking guests, and from his pipe.

Annette stood watching, eyes half shut, her contact lenses not liking the atmosphere, as she clutched the empty wine glass in her hand. She was thinking about the church.

The baby had cried – a high wail, echoing up under the roof of the nave, the sound curling like the smoke around the rose window. A lonely sound which had made her drag her eyes back down to the font, which someone had decorated with threads of white daisies, as she blinked back sudden stupid tears.

Celia's child. Duncan's child. The child which might have been hers . . .

'Some more wine?'

She was beautiful; exquisite. Tiny hands waving indignantly over the pale lace. Natasha Anne. Her hair as golden as her father's; her eyes already the same blue. Or were all babies' eyes that colour?

'Wine?'

The pleasant face was smiling at her; the green eyes quirky and humorous as they watched her. 'If I could deliver it to your planet, I would.'

'Planet?' She turned her full attention to him at last, bewildered.

'You *are* on another planet?'

'Oh, I see!' Embarrassed, Annette looked back at Celia, still standing near the door, the child in the crook of her arm. Then she laughed. 'I'm sorry. I was thinking about the baby.'

'Very appropriate at a christening.' He smiled again. 'I'm Rick Jefferson; your colleague in the godparent stakes.' He captured her empty wine glass and filled it from the bottle in his hand, expertly fielding the slopping liquid as someone jostled him from behind.

Suddenly she felt more cheerful; she smiled. 'Of course. I'm sorry. I'm being very rude, I'm Annette.'

He grinned again. 'Can I fetch you something to eat? Say yes. Then I can put down this bottle and pick up a glass of my own when I go to the table.'

He wasn't very tall; not much taller than she. But his shoulders were broad and his frame solid. She found herself giggling at his pantomime of self starvation. 'I'd love something to eat. Thank you.'

'And you won't fly back to Mars or Venus or wherever?'

'Promise.'

She watched him thread his way across the room towards the long table. He paused near Celia and she saw him smile and touch the baby's hand – then he moved on. He collected a glass and two plates of food, and she saw him turning back in her direction.

'All alone?'

Suddenly Duncan was standing in front of her. She felt her throat contract a little as she looked up at his face. Could she have so soon forgotten how tall he was?

'Rick is fetching me something to eat. She's a lovely baby, Duncan.'

He was looking down at her intently. 'Annette. You

really didn't mind us asking you to be godmother? It was Celia's idea–'

'Of course not.' She forced herself to smile. 'I'm honoured.' And she turned to Rick, reaching with relief for the plate he offered her. For a moment the three of them stood there in silence. Then Duncan smiled and shrugged and walked away . . .

Later, as she and Rick let themselves out of the French window, there was a breath of summer in the garden and a soft evening shimmer in the air.

Annette shivered, her coat around her shoulders as they slipped out of the hot noisy room.

Rick grinned at her. 'Are you sure you want to go out?'

Nodding she sipped her wine and stepped onto the grass. 'I get claustrophobia at parties.'

'Me too.' He followed her, leaving his glass balanced carefully on the head of a lichen-covered statue at the edge of the steps. 'Are you going to tell me about it?'

'What?'

'You and Duncan. There was a "you and Duncan" wasn't there?'

She nodded, suddenly not minding his knowing. 'Oh yes. There was a me and Duncan.'

The scent of flowers was almost overwhelming. It had been summer then too. The first time she had come to this house . . .

Her office door was permanently open, so people walked through it. That was the idea, Annette's boss said with a laugh and Duncan was the third person to walk through it that morning. By mistake.

He was tall, lean and untidy, wearing a cotton sweatshirt and jeans and quite obviously not in the right place.

He leaned on her desk, towering over her, his hair tousled. He was grinning broadly.

'I'm on the wrong floor, right?'

She found herself smiling back, drawn irresistibly by the smile.

'Right. Wrong floor. You'll be wanting . . .' She hesitated, looking him up and down, her head on one side. 'The architect upstairs?'

He grinned. 'Try again.'

'The accountant?'

'No.'

'Then it must be the Inland Revenue.'

'As a humble supplicant and blood donor? No.'

'But that only leaves the dress designer.' She collapsed in sudden irreverent giggles.

'At last, you guessed my secret.' His solemn expression was belied by the laughing eyes. 'Don't I look like a potential customer for a dress designer?'

She shook her head, intrigued and disbelieving. But he did not explain. Not then. He did that over lunch.

'Black sheep?' She put down her knife and fork, her voice sliding up into a squeak.

'Five hundred of them.'

'And Kevin Spiggs uses your wool?'

'That's right. His dusky dream range!'

She was very late back to the office.

'Can you believe it, Meg? He breeds black sheep. And Kevin upstairs is going to take all his wool for a season to make sweaters and dresses and sell them for *hundreds* of pounds each!'

Meg raised her eyes to the concealed lighting of the low ceiling above the desk. 'Only you, Annette, could meet a sheep breeder here in St James's! And I suppose you are going to see him again?'

She was.

*

Two weeks later he took her to the farm. It was a long drive and she was tired but the countryside enchanted her. Soft rolling hills, stands of oak and birch, green and silver in the sunlight and then the sheep – not black so much as chocolate and mocha in the soft meadows.

'I can't get involved, Annette. I'm sorry.' The boyish grin, the rumpled hair as he strode at her side through the mud beneath the trees cushioned the words and made them light and easy to ignore. They laughed together so much, finished sentences for each other without even realizing it, liked the same music in the evening as they sat together on the sofa hearing the distant fluting of an owl above the soft notes of the woodwind.

His arm was around her shoulders, drawing her to him; he was solid and warm and reassuring and she was already half-way to being in love. Later, upstairs on the landing, he kissed her goodnight outside her bedroom door, then placed his finger against her lips as she tried to speak. 'No, Annette. I told you. Sleep well, my love.' And he was gone, leaving her lonely and disappointed as she let herself into the dark room and groped for the unaccustomed light switch.

They began to make it a pattern. Duncan would come up to Kevin's office on a Friday, fill in time until five o'clock then together they would climb into his car and wend the long agonizing route through the heavy traffic towards the west. Sometimes they bought chips on the way; sometimes she made sandwiches. Once in a while they listened to the car radio but more often they talked. They talked about everything. Life. Work. Holidays; and sheep. But never about love.

Yet she knew he loved her. It showed in his eyes; in his hesitant glances when he thought she wasn't looking. In the deep, lasting kisses when they lay together on the sofa, listening to the records they had brought with them from town, and finally and ecstatically in his tender love-making when at last he followed her into the now familiar bedroom and took her in his arms . . .

Next morning when she woke he had gone from the bed. She stretched happily and lay gazing at the faint light behind the curtains, listening to the plaintive whistling of a blackbird.

Duncan had gone out to the sheep; later he would come back with the papers and some coffee and perhaps climb into bed, his hair damp from the shower as he laid his head on her breast. Lying in his arms then, clinging to him, her heart full of love, she knew something was still very wrong. But she no longer cared what it was. It was enough that he was there and that she was with him.

Then he went away. 'Only for a couple of weeks, Annette. On business to Switzerland. I wish you could come too, my love.'

She'd known instantly, by the way he lowered his eyes and mumbled, unable to look at her, that he had lied. But which was the lie? That he was going on business, or that he wanted her to come too?

She swallowed her misery and worked extra hours at the office, trying not to think of what he might be doing in Switzerland, of what business a sheep farmer could possibly have in Geneva or the high mountains beyond.

When he returned she knew she had lost him again. Oh, he was pleased to see her; and his warmth when he drew her to him was real, but something had changed. His reserve had returned and she knew that, if she asked, he would say again, 'We must not get involved, Annette,' and that for him it would be true.

She cried a lot that summer, unhappy in her love, seeking comfort in the arms which were the source of her unhappiness, but unable to tear herself away.

It was his mother who told her. His parents lived not

far away, watching their son's farming efforts with tolerant amusement – but they were less amused by Annette.

She was a little in awe of his mother. Janet was so capable and hearty, so unruffled by anything. So it was a shock one morning to come down into the kitchen wearing Duncan's bathrobe to find Janet standing there, her coat still on, staring out of the window at the garden. The woman turned and looked at Annette, her face full of compassion. The expression hit Annette like a hammer. Her veins iced over as she guessed instinctively something of what was to come.

'Annette dear, Duncan tells me that you and he are not involved. That yours is an open relationship, whatever that means.' Janet's face had become unusually pink and shiny. 'I don't believe him altogether. I think you are more involved than he realizes and I don't want you to get hurt.'

It was suddenly so cold in the room.

'I won't get hurt,' Annette said cheerfully. 'Duncan's quite right. It is an open relationship.'

'And so you know about Celia?'

There was a lump of something in her throat, pressing down on her windpipe, stopping her breathing properly.

'Celia?' She had to pretend. She had to say she didn't care.

'His fiancée, Annette.' Janet's voice was unusually gentle. 'She will be coming back you know.'

'Where is she?' Her voice sounded strange in her own ears, thin and high, like a bird screaming in a storm.

'She's still in Switzerland, at the clinic. But she will be completely cured. And Duncan swore he'd wait for her, my dear. He swore.'

'Of course he did.' She sounded light and carefree now as she pulled the belt of the robe more tightly round her slim waist. 'You don't have to worry, Janet. Really.'

Oh God, why hadn't he told her? How could he have

let her go on imagining that it would all have been all right in the end.

The words echoed round her brain as she dressed and pulled on her light jacket. Duncan was out with a sick ewe. His mother had left the house, spinning the wheels of the car in her agitation. The house was silent and deserted; the house she had secretly, in her heart, thought of already as home.

She walked across the bare garden, hands in pockets and looked out across the fields. There were no sheep there now; they were desolate, like her.

Then he was there beside her, his face glowing, his eyes laughing, his warmth and humour reaching out to her. 'What about breakfast? I'm starving.'

'How's the ewe?' The steady cheerfulness of her voice amazed her.

'She'll be OK. Crisis is over. Was that ma's car I saw?'

Annette nodded. 'She couldn't wait. Just looked in to say hello.'

And goodbye. Because, of course, Annette could never come to the farm again. She didn't say anything in the end. What was the point of screaming and ranting at him? He had made no promises, held out no hope of the future. He had assumed they were still working from the first blueprint. 'No involvement, Annette my love. Just a good time while we're both at a loose end, OK?'

In the house, as she made the coffee with absolute concentration, Duncan said, 'Paula and Tony have asked us to dinner next weekend to see how their extension is progressing.' He did not look up. His face was buried in the newspaper.

'Oh what a shame. I'd love to have gone.' She was pouring the coffee, not looking at him, but she heard the rustle of the paper as he put it down.

'Why can't you?' Amazed. Even slightly hurt.

'I can't come down next weekend, Duncan, I'm sorry. In fact not for several weeks. I'm tied up.' She put the cup on the table without raising her eyes to his. 'It's nearly Christmas after all. I've so much to do. I'm ashamed I've allowed myself to come down here so much!' That was it. Bright and brittle. Don't ever show how much you are hurting inside.

She could feel him looking at her; imagine the thoughtful puzzlement with which he was watching. And she knew she would not be fooling him for an instant. She looked up at last and met his gaze, smiling. 'You'll have to do without me, Duncan. I think it's best.' She could not fight a sick enemy, one she had never seen. Another flesh and blood woman, yes, with nails bared and teeth set, but not this pale consumptive image, with her overtones of tragedy.

Duncan stood up and came round the table. 'Annette . . .'

'No, please. Don't say anything. Make my apologies to Paula. Perhaps I'll come back after . . .'

After what? Christmas? His marriage? His birthday? After it stopped hurting?

In the afternoon she packed slowly not waiting to read the Sunday papers with him by the fire, taking from the kitchen a couple of carrier bags to put all the extras in. The things which she had grown used to leaving behind week after week. Her records, her boots, a couple of books, the heavy Aran sweater she never wore in town. She piled them by the front door and took the old duffle coat off the hook. That, too, must go back. When she looked round he was standing in the doorway watching her.

'My mother did this.'

'No, Duncan. I always knew it wouldn't last. I just didn't know how long I'd got.'

He put his hands on her shoulders and drew her to him. 'Supposing I told you I'd change. I've grown so fond of you, Annette. I don't know that I can live without you. Not now.'

She felt her throat constrict. 'You must,' she whispered.

He took her to the train at last and found her a corner seat with her bags, then he jumped off as the train was already moving – no time for any goodbyes. But there was no one sitting opposite her to shame her into holding back her tears and she felt them run scalding down her cheeks as she turned her face to the window and saw the countryside gathering speed until it blurred and faded behind the dirty glass.

On Friday, in case he came, she rang the office and told them she had a migraine. The following week she went in as usual, thinking she felt more able to cope, but she did not have to. He did not appear.

She did not know whether he came up to see Kevin Spiggs again. She suspected he had never really needed to anyway, after that first time. He had come only to see her.

It was three months before she heard from him again. He phoned her at the office. 'How are you, Annette?'

Her heart, cured, distracted, no longer his, turned upside down at the sound of his voice.

'I'm fine. How are you?'

She thought she managed to sound casual. She fixed her mind determinedly on Robert, the new man in her life, who would be taking her out later that evening; Robert who had three times asked her to marry him.

'Can I take you out to lunch tomorrow?' Duncan sounded uncomfortable and quite suddenly she forgot her own unhappiness in a wave of sympathy for him.

'That would be nice. But it will have to be fairly brief I'm afraid. We're very busy at the office at the moment.'

'Fine. I'll pick you up around 12.30.'

She got up an hour early the next day to dress with special care and put on some make up, and one look at his face told her that there had been no point. His love for her, if that was what it had been, had gone. Rising from her desk she picked up her bag and followed him out into the street.

'I wanted to tell you myself that I'm getting married.' He said it at once, before they had even ordered.

'I'm glad for you.'

She realized as she said it that she meant it. For herself she was desolate, but the shining happiness she had seen on his face was so special she could not grudge him. Not that. That was what love did to a man, or a woman. 'To Celia, I take it?'

He nodded and grinned. 'So you did know. Afterwards I was so angry with myself. I thought perhaps I'd misled you. I couldn't have borne it if I'd hurt you, Annette.' His hand was on hers on the table. 'You're very special to me, you know. You always will be.'

'And you to me, Duncan.' She drew her hand away gently. Had he really never guessed how much she loved him? Had he really believed they were both just passing the time? She looked up at his face and then sadly she looked away.

They saw each other twice more after that. Once by accident in the foyer of the office building and once for coffee in the lunch hour two weeks before his wedding. He had a brown paper parcel under his arm.

'This is for you. From Celia and me. A wedding present for you.'

It was an exquisite sweater in soft chocolate-coloured wool.

She did not tell him she had given Robert back his ring. If you did not love someone with the all-consuming joy with which Duncan loved his Celia, there could be no future. She was sure of that.

She had not heard from Duncan again for two years.

Then had come the letter asking her to be godmother to his first child.

At first she was angry; then she cried. Then she laughed, and after writing two indignant letters of refusal tore them up and rang the farm. Duncan answered.

'Are you serious?' she asked.

'Perfectly. I want my daughter to grow up with humour and understanding. Who better to teach it to her than you?'

Was that really the way she had reacted?

'What happened to Robert?' he asked after a pause.

'No sense of humour and no understanding!'

'I'm sorry.'

'So am I.'

Behind the half drawn curtains the christening party was in full swing. But in the garden it was very quiet. Rick was watching her.

'You're telling the story against yourself,' he said gently. 'I think Duncan was a bastard.'

She shook her head. 'When you think about it, he displayed all the virtues. It just happens they were not directed at me.' She shivered suddenly. 'Shall we go back inside. I expect they're going to cut the cake or whatever they do at christenings. Did you go to their wedding?'

He shook his head, 'Did you?'

'I wasn't asked.'

Suddenly Rick laughed. 'Do you know who I am?'

'No. Should I?'

'I'm the man who asked Celia to marry him in Switzerland. And she nearly said yes. The only reason she didn't was this mysterious man she'd left in England who, she said, would wait for her no matter what. I told her she was mad.' He took Annette's hand and she found herself enjoying his warm grasp. 'So we're in the same boat, you and I. Rejected lovers.'

He grinned, looking anything but sad about it and suddenly she found herself laughing with him. 'You mean if I'd stayed with Duncan and fought, you'd have married Celia? She wouldn't have been left alone to fade away after all?'

'That's right.'

Annette was speechless for a moment. 'But she does love Duncan?' she asked hesitantly, after a long pause.

'Oh yes, she loves him again now.'

'And are you still sorry you lost her?' She looked at him squarely. He was staring up the steps towards the house, his expression enigmatic, his eyes narrowed in the dusk.

Slowly he shook his head. 'Not in the least. They deserve each other. After all, theirs is the classic love story. The happy ending against all odds.' He was still holding her hand as he led the way back into the house.

'And we were the odds?'

'I'd say so, wouldn't you?' He turned and winked at her as they slipped into the crowded room. Surreptitiously she looked at Duncan. He had grown stouter in the last two years and his hair was already thinning slightly. Perhaps, after all, she had not been as much in love with him as she had thought. She glanced up at Rick and found he was watching her.

'Do you think being godparents was the consolation prize?' she asked solemnly.

'It is often the custom, I believe.' He took two glasses of champagne from a tray and handed her one. 'Let's drink to Natasha Anne who introduced us!'

The Valentine's Day Plot

Of course it had to be a bouquet of flowers for St Valentine's Day. I chose them carefully, one by one, in the florist. Not less than 50p a bloom. She had always liked pink so those were the ones I selected. 'Would you like them gift-wrapped, Sir?' the girl in the shop asked, simpering, but I shook my head. That aspect of things I would deal with myself.

When I had finished with them I must admit they looked good. I tied an enormous bow of red satin ribbon round the bottom and stood back to admire the finished article. There was no way of seeing the little glass bottle deep amongst the glossy leaves until the bouquet was unwrapped. The bottle said Dior. I tied it in with thread to make sure it was secure; I didn't want it breaking and spoiling my surprise.

I knew she wouldn't be able to resist opening it and smelling it to make sure. And that, I confidently expected, would be the last inquisitive thing the lady ever did. It had after all been her nosiness which led to her finding out about me and to her lucrative career, at my expense, in blackmail. It's strange how some women take to that particular hobby.

I knew delivering the flowers would be a problem and I still hadn't decided at breakfast exactly how to do it.

Obviously I couldn't do it myself. One sight of me and she would suspect something.

Carefully I loaded the flowers into my car, propping them on the seat beside me and drove to The Avenue, which was just two streets away from her place. Then, pulling in to the side of the road, I sat and thought.

It was so easy of course, in the end. Two little boys came down the road, neat in identical grey shorts and blazer.

'Hey fellas!' I wound down the window. They stopped and looked at me suspiciously. I winked. 'Want to earn yourselves a pound on the way to school?' They looked at each other and hesitated. 'Each,' I added; that's inflation for you! 'Listen; it's not difficult.' I beckoned them close and lowered my voice conspiratorially. 'It's St Valentine's Day, right?' One of them smirked, and the other raised an eyebrow with horribly adult cynicism. I ignored it. 'I want you to take these flowers round the corner and give them to a lady. That's all. No problem?'

No problem. They took the flowers, listened politely to my instructions and to my threats of what would happen if they dumped the flowers and ran, and exchanged giggling glances when I gave them the address. Then they pocketed their money.

I sat back and watched them round the corner. They were just about young enough, I reckoned, to do as I asked with no lip. When they were out of sight I drove as fast as I could go to the office.

It was a pretty ordinary sort of day really, considering. I wondered when I would hear what had happened. I doubted if it would be on the evening news. It depended when that stuffy husband of hers came home and found her. I caught myself smiling quietly. After what she had done to me, the blackmailing interfering beautiful bitch, she deserved everything she was going to get. I glanced at my watch. Perhaps it was already over.

There was a lot of work to get through that day, so I ordered a sandwich lunch. When the phone rang I had just reached for my can of beer.

The strange thing was I didn't recognize her voice at first. Then she said, 'Thank you for the flowers, David.' Then I knew. She went on, sarcastically I thought, 'It was such a touching thought. Really the last thing I expected from you. You obviously chose them with such care.'

'What flowers?' The sweat stood out on my forehead suddenly. I had nearly been caught out and said, 'I'm glad you like them', or something equally fatuous.

'Oh come now,' her voice purred slightly. 'You don't have to pretend with me, David. Only you would send such a perfect bouquet. Your taste was always impeccable.

I stuttered slightly before regaining my cool. 'I'm glad someone still sends you flowers, love. Not me though, I'm afraid. Didn't they send a note with them or something?'

'No; no note.' She paused. 'It was so sweet, too, to put a bottle of scent in, David. You shouldn't have. Really. And Dior as well. You know, that's been my favourite perfume since we first met all those years ago.'

My hand was shaking a little as it held the receiver. 'Have you sniffed it to make sure?' I tried to laugh. 'You can't always believe the label, you know.'

'Oh indeed you can't, David.' She chuckled, and I could feel the small hairs on the back of my neck standing up at the sound. 'I'm afraid I didn't get the chance to smell your little gift, my dear. You see I'm afraid I dropped it. By mistake of course; out of the kitchen window actually. You'd never believe how concentrated they make perfume nowadays, David. It must have cost you a fortune. Do you know, it burned a hole right through the concrete. Imagine what it might have done to my poor nose.'

'Imagine!' I agreed sourly. The cunning female had seen through everything.

'What made you think it was from me, my love?' I asked casually. 'You know I can't afford to spend that kind of money on you. Not any more. You've milked me dry.'

She laughed, a beautiful tinkling sound, as though she were really happy. 'You had a spot of bad luck there, David. You see one of the little boys you bribed was my son. He'd been spending the night with a friend in The Avenue. You never met him before, did you? It just happens that they're both very keen on cars. You see you're the only person we know, dear, with a Bentley Continental with your initials on the number plate. Really, you should have come by taxi!'

I reached for my beer and swallowed the lot down fast.

'I don't think I will admit to anything,' I muttered. 'It might spoil the whole romantic illusion.'

'It would rather, dear.' I could actually hear her smiling. 'The trouble is, David,' she went on. 'I felt I had to tell my husband that you've started sending me flowers and I'm afraid he's immensely angry. You see he's a very jealous man. And he thinks you're in love with me.'

'More fool him,' I couldn't resist saying, but she went on as if I hadn't spoken.

'He really took it very badly, David. In fact he's on his way over now. I thought, for old times' sake I'd warn you,' and she hung up on me without so much as saying goodbye.

I sat gazing at the empty beer can for a few minutes, wondering. She couldn't be serious. Could she?

I don't quite know how he got past my secretary, but he arrived quite unannounced. He stood in front of my desk for a long minute, then he smiled.

'No other man woos my wife with flowers,' he said very solemnly.

'Dead right,' I was about to say, 'they don't,' but he

forestalled me. He took a revolver out of his pocket and hooked his finger over the trigger. He never gave me any time to explain.

But I won in the end: now I haunt them both.

'There was a time when I was almost happy . . .'

There was a brittle splintering as her foot slipped on the ridges of the cart track and the ice shivered delicately across the ruts in a labyrinth of crystal slivers. She hadn't been concentrating; she had been gazing into the distance where on either side of her the fields stretched like dull brown hessian towards the hedges. In the summer, when she had been here before, they had been a ripe, rich gold; somehow she had not expected them to have changed so much.

With a little shiver Jacie dug her hands deeper into her pockets and walked doggedly on. She had to get there before the mist-shrouded sun disappeared behind the hills and left her in the cold darkness. She almost wished now that she hadn't come at all. Perhaps it was a mistake to come back – to try and recapture those memories which haunted her. She hesitated for the first time, but already in front of her she could see the dark outline of the ruined arches rising starkly from the earth amongst the bare winter trees and irresistibly she was drawn on.

She stood for a while in the shadows, feeling the wind teasing her hair from the scarf around her head, gazing down at the patch of rimed grass where her feet and Brian's had stood, so close together. It had been like another lifetime then, in the summer, that time when she was almost happy.

She shrugged suddenly, shaking the loosened hair out of her eyes and pulled her collar up closer. The cool sun had gone now and night was coming faster than she had expected, moaning softly in the wind amongst the crumbling stones, darkening the fields. Suddenly, irrationally, she was afraid. She glanced over her shoulder, pressing back against the green damp of the stones, smelling their dankness, listening as she had that last time to the story they seemed to cry out of sorrow and pain. Her heart was beating fast somewhere high in the back of her throat and she pressed herself into the corner of the walls which had once formed the nuns' chapter house. It was then, glancing sideways, forcing herself to be calm, that she saw the web.

The spider had thrown its net across the corner between the rough stones, a hexagonal of perfect diamanté, glittering with frost even in the near dark. Jacie raised her hand in wonder and then swallowing a sob of relief held back, remembering the summer. Was it the same determined little creature which had returned and made good the wreck of its web which her clumsy fingers had torn into ashy fragments that last day? The sticky silken threads had been caught up and retied. She gazed at it until the dusk faded into darkness and she could no longer see even the frosty outlines of the shape. Would it be the same for her? Could the wreck of her own happiness be made good too? Would he come back to her and rescue her from herself again? Pressing her hands deep in her pockets she gave the dark corner where the web hung one last look, then she turned and slipping and stumbling in the dark she began to run back down the track towards the farm.

*

Ever since her childhood Jacie had felt different from other people. Partly, she now accepted, it was the way she was; partly it had been her mother's fault for not understanding.

'Jacie Stacey

Her silly vest is lacy!'

the children at school had sung, dancing around her as they changed for gym and the teacher had sent a note home to her mother: 'If Jane could wear something a little less elaborate . . . broderie anglaise is not really suitable for school wear . . .'

Jacie had looked up fearfully as her mother tore open the envelope, waiting for the explosion she was sure would come; somehow feeling herself to blame for the unacceptability of the trimming on her liberty bodice. There was an explosion, but not of anger; it was of laughter. Her pretty unpredictable mother had hugged her. 'Oh darling, I must buy you woolly vests and make you a conformist,' she had gurgled delightedly and Jacie had breathed a sigh of relief. She wanted nothing more than to conform in a woolly vest. It embarrassed her when her mother tried to make her different; it embarrassed her when her mother laughed and talked with the other mothers at collecting time and pulled her pigtails, saying, 'this one is mine'. All she wanted was to disappear and be wholly invisible. The more her mother drew attention to her and made her pretty – and she was pretty, there was no getting away from that – the more she hated it. If a teacher looked at her she trembled.

Later it had been the same. As she grew up she had hidden away from the other girls her own age, taking refuge in drawing which she found was the only way to express her feelings. She would hide in her bedroom, ignoring her mother's pleas to come out, endlessly sketching the roof tops and the trees which she could see from her window and putting into the strokes of her pencil all the pent-up emotion which she felt but did not understand.

'You'll grow out of it, darling. It's a phase. I was shy at your age,' her mother reassured her time and again, but Jacie could see the puzzled hurt in her mother's eyes and knew in her heart that her mother had never felt the way she did. She had never known the agony of not belonging and, worse, of not wanting to belong in spite of the ache of rejection, as first schoolgirls and then college contemporaries formed close circles which seemed to exclude her.

'What's wrong with me?' she asked in anguish, talking in the end in desperation to the same apple tree in the garden which she had addressed so often as a child. She received no reply.

Once she began working it was perhaps a little better. She gained confidence because she was good at her job. She was a designer; sometimes freelance, sometimes working for long periods for one firm and always, when she moved on, they were sorry to lose her. She was deft, competent and quietly efficient and managed to blend mutely with the grey carpet and beige wall, only occasionally being subjected to agonizing blush-making notice. Once or twice she went out with the men she met in these offices, but her terror and the rigid formality of her shoulders held them at bay. They never asked her a second time although long ago she had realized, catching sight of herself unexpectedly in a mirror, that she had inherited her mother's beauty..

There was one man she had liked a little; the partner in charge of her department at the last job but one. He was a rugged solidly built man with strangely flecked Irish eyes and enough shy charm to lull her into allowing a lunch hour break to drift on into the early afternoon, and they had gone for a walk in the park. They had stood side by side at the edge of the lake, watching the grey froth which lapped at the tarmac path beneath their feet.

'I like it here; it's so quiet.' She glanced up at him shyly with the half smile he found so intriguing glimpsed over the rim of her drawing board. Then avoiding his eyes she looked back towards the ducks, glossy in the plumage of early spring.

'I like quiet places too.' His voice took on a deeper note than usual as he moved little by little until, almost imperceptibly their elbows brushed. He had sensed her isolation; he did not want to hurry her.

'You can still hear the roar of traffic though,' he went on almost in a whisper. 'I'd like to show you somewhere really quiet. Why don't we take a drive down to the country at the weekend? Perhaps have lunch at a pub somewhere?' He too had been staring hard at the ducks as he spoke but now he turned to look at her. He found she was looking straight at him, her eyes wide, the pupils pin points in the light of the sun. Her face had drained of colour.

'It's awfully nice of you, but I couldn't. I couldn't possibly.'

'Why not?'

She shook her head emphatically. 'You hardly know me. You'd be bored. I'm not . . .' She was floundering unhappily. 'I couldn't. I'm sorry. I'm going to see my mother.'

She had drawn away, every muscle tense suddenly, resenting and fearing the brush of his elbow, the intimacy of his glance.

'Hey, I didn't mean – ' he found to his embarrassment that he was blushing too, disconcerted by her reaction. But already she was walking back across the grass, her shoulders squared beneath her coat.

'We're late for work,' she called behind her with a tight

apologetic smile and she almost ran in the direction of the park gates.

Later in the week she half hoped, half feared that he might ask again, but although his smile was just as friendly and his good morning relaxed and warm, he saw to it that they never found themselves alone together again.

And so the years passed. Time brought in the end a kind of serenity. Her shyness crossed the invisible road which turns it to reserve and she ceased to mind when her rejection of people led inevitably to their rejection of her. Or if she minded, she buried the hurt so deep that even she no longer noticed. Only her mother reminded her, and so now she seldom saw her mother.

Sketching, still her only passion, gave her the excuse for long lonely holidays in lonely places. There was one farmhouse in particular on a moor among the hills where she found solace and quiet dour friendship from the farmer and his wife. Once or twice a year, sometimes for long periods when she had saved enough, she made her way there, laden with sketchbooks and easel, to sit in the wiry heather with the wind teasing her hair and no companions save the sudden bulge-eyed hare and the distant wheeling, wheedling buzzards. It was a contented, restful time, for while she was there she forgot her inadequacies and her loneliness and found refuge and total confidence in her art and with the quiet couple with whom she stayed.

She had been going there for three years before she found the abbey. So often her footsteps retraced automatically the same paths through the heather and close-cropped tangled bilberries, taking her to landmarks of her own invention, that she rarely explored more distant valleys and dips in the rolling moors. There the fields, bright with ripening corn, encroached on the wildness of the landscape, reaching out to tame it with the richness of the fertile farms and thick growing woodlands. The ruins were hidden in a wooded valley of ancient trees, guarded by nettles and fierce sprays of thorn and bramble at the end of a cart track through the fields, and there she first met Brian.

She stumbled on him, almost literally, not seeing him until it was too late to turn and flee as he lay sprawled behind a low wall, field glasses pressed to his eyes, focused on a high fir growing out of the very stones themselves, or so it seemed. He turned furiously on her, mouthing silent curses and pulled her unceremoniously down beside him before turning once more to his watching. He never looked at her.

She lay trembling, her face pressed into the sweet grass, not daring to move although a nettle brushed her bare leg. Only when the great golden and russet bird which he had been watching lazily raised its wings and flew unperturbed away through the wood did he sit up and smile at her, obviously suddenly conscious of the formalities.

'Sorry about that,' he said, his deep voice softened slightly by the gentle lilt of the hills. 'She's nearly hatching her eggs you see and it would be a terrible crime if she were to desert the nest now. I've been watching her since she first laid.' He had a gentle quiet about him that reassured the scaredness within Jacie and allowed her to pull herself up to her knees, straightening her jacket and pushing the hair and grass and bracken tips from her eyes. The movement angered the nettle and she flinched as it rasped her skin.

'Hey, you've been stung – and it's my fault, I'm sorry.' His gaze had missed nothing and she sat wondering as hardly seeming to search for it his hand reached instinctively for some dock and soothed it against her skin.

'Do you know about birds?' he went on, as gently he replaced his salve with a fresh leaf. 'That was a kite. They're pretty rare round here and very timid.'

Jacie found herself smiling at him, reassured. 'I don't

really know very much, but I sketch birds sometimes.' Her glance went to the sketchbook lying in the grass where it had fallen with tumbled pages. He reached for it and slowly turned them, pausing here and there to look longer and nod. He came to sketches of birds – buzzards cleaving the sky on their arched golden wings; curlews, a pheasant – and she saw his face soften into something which was almost a smile.

'You've a good eye,' he said quietly and she found herself smiling, ridiculously pleased by his admission.

She was almost disappointed when he said suddenly, 'You'd best go now, before the other bird comes to sit his turn on the eggs,' but obediently she had taken back her sketchbook and half wriggled, half crept away from the ruins. Preoccupied again with his glasses he had not even raised his hand to say goodbye.

But he had found her two days later on the moor. And he smiled for the first time properly, his eyes matching the wash of ultramarine sky she was laying on the heavy-grained paper and for the first time in her life she was completely unembarrassed and at her ease with a man. The faint golden blush which he detected on her skin was put there by the wind and the green moorland sun, not by her realization that he was looking no longer at her picture but at her face. He had seen at once the beautiful eyes she had inherited from her mother.

It was then that he calmly asked her her name and told her that his was Brian. He stopped and picked up a discarded sketchbook from the heather and flipped through the pages. Then he set it down without comment, sitting easily beside her on an outcrop of slaty rock, one knee updrawn, clasped by his strong sun-burned hands. He watched as she bent once more to her paints, unselfconsciously continuing to work on the landscape. Their silence was companionable, uncommitted and she took his attention and lack of comment as a quiet compliment on the competence of her work.

She saw him several times after that; sometimes in the distance when he would lift a hand and stride on, making no effort to come over to talk and sometimes they would meet and would smile and walk together, falling naturally in step and talking of plants and birds and painting and sometimes of farming, but never of themselves. She thought he must be a farmer of some kind, but she never asked and he never told her what he did.

Nor did she see at first the quiet contentment in his face when he glanced in her direction as they walked together down the mossy tracks. When, almost imperceptibly, their hands touched she didn't draw away.

Then, once, turning to him, her face full of laughter as they talked she glimpsed suddenly the warmth in his eyes and the smile that was especially for her. Her laughter died for a moment on her lips and then she found herself smiling again, at him.

'It's good to have someone to walk with, Jacie,' he said quietly. That was all. But she understood.

It puzzled Jacie that she was at ease with him. One night she sat down in the dim light of her bedroom and tilted the flower-painted plastic shade on her dressing table lamp to throw a clear unflattering light on her face and gazed earnestly at herself in the mirror. It was an old glass, black-speckled with the image distorted slightly on one side, making her temple and hair ripple and move oddly. She smiled involuntarily and was amazed at the vivacity which suddenly lit her face.

Why, she was asking herself, was she not shy and embarrassed with Brian? Why should this man be the only man with whom she had never felt afraid – save her father, who had gone away so long ago and left an aching void in her life? She leaned forward to look more closely in the mirror, remembering suddenly how he would swing her up in his arms so she could wind her legs into the small of his back and bury her face in the strength and security of his chest. Always he had been there and she had known that he always would, until the day she came home from school and found her mother crying bitterly, face down on the bed. She knew now that her father had no strength, no security to offer and that he had made her mother miserable till the day he left, but rational adult explanations could not dispel that secure safe feeling which he had engendered and which lingered in her longing.

Brian seemed to have that feeling about him too. She knew instinctively that his were the kind of hands in which a wild creature would lie without fear and so – if ever he should ask it – would she.

She shook her head wearily and picked up her hair brush. It wasn't as though he were that much older than she either. Ten years? Probably less; automatically she ran her fingers over the tiny web of lines beneath her eyes, gently easing them flat. Then slowly she began to brush her hair.

'I hear you were talking to Brian Dexter up on the moors yesterday,' Mrs Finch commented as she fed Jacie scrambled eggs next morning. Who had told? The rocks? The lonely gossiping buzzards? 'He's a nice man, he is; but that wife of his . . . no better than she ought to be that one – Ann, she's called – having an affair with young Jim Lloyd like that! Serve her right that he's divorcing her. Divorce is too good I reckon. And he still loves her, you know; they say he still loves her. Some say he nearly went out of his mind when he found out and now he spends all his time alone on that moor, brooding. It's a wicked, wicked shame. And he's worth a hundred Jim Lloyds any day of the week.'

'I didn't know.' Jacie was gazing fixedly at her eggs.

There was a pause and then she went on quietly, 'He never talks about himself.' Nor of course did she.

She stared at the coffee pot as Mrs Finch picked it up, conscious of a sudden weight of sadness. It threatened her, this new intimate detail of Brian's life. She wished she didn't know, although it explained perhaps the nature of the bond between them now. For he too must mistrust the world, he too find himself apart . . .

That day, consciously, Jacie looked for him on the moors, but she didn't find him there and she didn't dare go back to the abbey. It belonged to Brian and his pair of kites. He would take her there in his own time to see his birds if he wanted and she must wait. For the first time since she had begun sketching the moors she found them lonely and a little melancholy as the warm summer wind rippled the heather and the green bracken and stirred the thorn bushes clinging to the scattered outcrops of rock.

He found her when he chose, which became more and more often as the weeks wore on. She never mentioned what she knew. She put the knowledge behind her as being part of his life which must never come between them, never spoil their careful impersonality. They talked though, all the time, and went for long walks across the countryside, climbing the hills and sitting on the edge of the river watching for kingfishers and laughing at the antics of the dipper as it plunged from its rock to walk beneath the water on the bed of the stream. And stealthily they went to visit the eyrie in its tall tree within the ruined walls of the abbey and Jacie saw the three ridiculous bald-fluffy heads of the young craning for their food as the parents swept down out of the sky.

They would picnic together, she and Brian, sharing her packed lunches which, though nothing was said at the farm, had mysteriously doubled in size and it seemed to Jacie that for the first time in her life she was almost happy.

'You must sketch the birds for me when they're flying,' he murmured as they crouched side by side behind the abbey wall watching the nest.

She nodded, her fingers gripping the cold crumbling stones which sheltered them. 'How long will it be now?' To her, the gaping beaks and the long necks visible in the nest seemed enormous already.

'Not long. Look! The hen bird.' His whisper made her look automatically up, but all she noticed was the firmness of the hand he had laid upon hers on the stones of the wall.

For a moment they forgot the birds and looked at one another and she saw the unspoken emotion in his eyes. Then he had turned away and abruptly releasing her fingers he raised his field glasses once more to the tree.

It was Brian who taught her, after he had teased her for huddling habitually under a scarf, to walk fearlessly in the rain, throwing back her head to feel the cold freshness of it on her skin as he made her shake out her hair to the damp and the fresh soft-scenting drizzle. And it was in the rain that he first kissed her gently, holding her against him and kissing her again as the cool drops ran down her upturned face, before he turned sadly away.

Summer grew heavy and languid and fearfully she began to count the days which remained of her holiday, willing time to slow down. In the abbey the young tested their wings and jumped up and down on the edge of their untidy nest high in the tree. They were ready to fly – and Jacie knew she was in love. But it was a humble, sad, compassionate, half fearful love that could not declare itself and dared not hint at its existence before the pain of the man at her side who still loved his Ann with such despair.

When at last the nest was empty they went more often to the abbey, walking up the cart track through the waist high ripening corn; they explored the woody valley in which it lay and the dark stone walls which so easily evoked an echo of pure voices sadly intoning the plainsong down the centuries. Jacie loved it there in spite of – perhaps because of – its sadness. It was Brian's place more than any other.

And there it was that she broke the spell of the summer. 'I have to go home soon, Brian. I hate to leave, but I must. I have to go back to work.' They were standing in the long seeding grasses in the chapter house of the nuns.

Silently he took her hand and squeezed it. 'I'll miss you, Jacie.'

Her eyes filled with tears. 'Brian, I shall come back. Next year.' And then it had happened. Her love and anguish had betrayed her and she had rushed on: 'By then the divorce will be over and you'll be free . . . I know you'll be free. You'll forget her one day.'

He didn't question how she knew. He said nothing, but his face tautened with pain and she saw misery and memories where only a moment before had been clear happy laughter.

In silent despair she walked away from him then, and there in the corner of the lichen-powdered wall she saw the neat intricacies of the spider's web looped across from stone to stone. She gazed at it for a moment and then bitterly swept her hand up through the threads, watching them snap and coalesce and cling fragmentarily to her fingers. That easy it was to break something fragile and beautiful. She could feel the childish tears welling under her eyelids. Then Brian was beside her. He said nothing, but she saw him looking at the ruin of the web and she felt desperately guilty and ashamed. She wanted to help him, to stand by him, to give him strength. But she did not know how. She wanted to be with him, but she didn't dare remain. Instead she walked away.

That was the last time she saw him. Two days later she

packed and went home, her shell once more tightly and protectively around her.

Mrs Finch sent her the notice of the divorce from the local paper. There was no editorial comment, just the bland headlines '*Well-known local farmer divorces wife*' and a few lines giving the names and addresses of the three people involved. So few words to cover so much that had happened.

She started to write to him then. But what do you say to a man in his position, when you ache with love and dare not say it? She tore up the half-written letter slowly and regretfully and let it fall, piece by piece, into the waste paper basket.

It was Brian who wrote in the end. A short note: 'Any chance of you getting up here in the New Year? You'd enjoy sketching the hills in the snow. The kites are still here.' That was all.

And so she went, and walked in the early dusk down the cart track to the abbey and found the frosted web which meant so much to her. She didn't find Brian that evening, but she didn't worry. She knew he would be there somewhere, and perhaps tomorrow, perhaps the next day, as she sketched in the snow on the moors he would come and find her, as he always had before.

Summer Treachery

The bedroom was high ceilinged and cool, lavishly furnished with a wealth of eau-de-nil silk.

'Well?' My sister was watching me closely as I threw my bag down on the double bed and looked round.

'Davina, it's lovely. Quite the most beautiful room I've ever seen.'

She looked pleased and for the first time since she and I had been alone together we exchanged a real smile.

I wasn't exaggerating. It was all quite fabulous: the room, the villa, the gardens which I had glimpsed as Tim and I left the car and walked up the broad flight of shallow stone steps to the porticoed front door. Everything.

I crossed to the windows and pushed back the shutters. Outside the Florentine sky was a blinding blue over the hazy valley. The shimmering afternoon heat hit into the room and I realized why every shutter on that side of the house had been closed. The view was breathtaking. If Tim and I could cement our love and happiness again anywhere it would be here.

Our marriage had not been happy. Perhaps I had been too young. Perhaps I had not realized what living with a brilliant but temperamental man would mean, especially when he was a man whose career as a sculptor brought him into intimate contact with so many beautiful women – and this while I had to keep on teaching to provide us with a steady income. Whatever the reasons, life had been hard for us. But now Tim was beginning to find recognition; I had given up my job and we had begun again.

Davina joined me on the balcony and we stood for a moment in silence. She was looking down the valley and I studied her surreptitiously. It was a year since we had met. That had been at her wedding to Simon Delacourt when I, her junior by five years, had already been married for eighteen months. Simon was rich, charming, clever; exactly what Davina had wanted. And who could blame her, with his country house in Sussex, his yacht, his executive jet and this fabulous villa in Tuscany?

We had always been close, but in her relationship with Simon she had been secretive; I had felt excluded, and wrapped up by then in my own unhappiness I had not paid my sister much attention, assuming that she had everything she wanted.

So why did she look so strained now? I studied her profile. There were lines at the corners of her eyes and between nose and mouth I did not remember.

She turned suddenly, groping in the pocket of her loose jacket and produced a pack of cigarettes and a small elegant lighter. 'Want one?'

'You know I don't. And you never used to, Davina.'

Her eyes met mine and she smiled again. This time it was brittle and automatic. 'You have to do something to occupy yourself.' She inhaled deeply on the cigarette and turned abruptly back into the room. 'How are things between you and Tim? Are you still supporting him while he lays every female in sight?'

I caught my breath. She hadn't used to be a bitch either.

I followed her back into the shadowy room, carefully pulling the shutters closed behind me. 'Actually he's becoming quite well known, so I don't have to support him any more,' I said. My voice was shaking slightly and I steadied it grimly. 'And we're happy now. Very happy.' We were also very hard up and praying that Simon might commission some work.

'Good.' She was studying her face in the lovely Florentine mirror over the dressing table and for an instant our eyes met in the glass. 'Let's go down and get a drink shall we?' she said tautly. 'I want to meet our other guests and we'll see where Simon and Tim have got to.'

Almost as soon as we had arrived Simon had whisked my husband away leaving us girls, as he put it, to get to know each other again. I could see why he thought we needed the time alone. Davina was a different woman.

The drawing room was rich and elegant, furnished in pale green and gold and it looked out across the formal gardens at the back of the villa. The line of tall windows shaded by ivory silk stood open. On the terrace outside I could see three figures reclining in the shade while beyond them in the sunlight the spray from an ornamental fountain hung like a rainbow in the still air. The two men stood up as we stepped out to join them. Both were casually dressed and wore dark glasses.

'Jocelyn and Maggie Farquer,' Davina introduced us offhandedly, 'and Nigel Godson – my sister Celia Armitage.'

Nigel Godson reached out a hand. 'Ah at last. The wife of the famous sculptor. I've heard so much about you both from Davina.' His grin robbed the words of some of their irony but nevertheless I felt a small flicker of warning. I had to be nice to these attractive rich strangers who came from a different world, for Tim's future success depended on the patronage of people like them.

Maggie Farquer patted the seat beneath the fringed

awning near her. 'Come over here, darling and have a drink. You must be parched.' She was a woman of about fifty, tanned, coiffured, jewelled, in Dior slacks and a crimson silk shirt. I smiled at her uncertainly as I accepted the tall frosted glass from Davina and felt myself grow suddenly shy.

My sister did not join us. She began instead to pace slowly up and down the terrace and I watched her as I answered Maggie's lazy questions about our trip through France in the car. I saw her stub out her half smoked cigarette in an urn full of tumbling pink geraniums and reach for another, then as I watched I saw her stiffen and return the cigarette to the pack. She was staring down the garden. I followed the direction of her gaze and saw Tim and Simon approaching slowly across the parched grass.

When the introductions had been made and Tim given his glass he sat down beside me on the seat. 'There's a cottage in the grounds I can use as a studio, Celia,' he murmured. 'I'll show you later.' He reached across and touched the back of my hand gently with his finger tip. It was a very private sign and I leant back against his shoulder sipping from my glass, happy and relaxed for the first time since I had sat down.

Davina was standing about three yards from us and I noticed suddenly that she had crushed the cigarette carton in her fist. Her eyes were fixed on the seat between Tim and myself where our hands touched on the cushion.

Tim was smiling later when he came back into our bedroom from the shower naked but for the towel knotted around his waist.

'What do you think of this set up?' he said softly. He put his arms around me and pulled me close. His hair was damp and he smelled of cologne.

'I love the villa.' I looked up at him.

'Not the people?'

'Not the people. Even Davina has changed.'

'We have to be nice to them, Celia.' He frowned. 'I hate to say it, but we need them.'

'Even men like Nigel Godson? I thought you said dealers were parasites and we could do without them.'

He laughed softly. His lips were in my hair. 'We can do without them only if we get the commissions direct.'

'And you think Simon will commission something?'

'Could be.' He sounded excited. 'He's had this cottage cleared of furniture so I can use it as a studio and work in peace while you're sunning yourself by the pool.' He grinned. 'He took me to see that too. You wait till you see it. Do you think I should suggest I do a head of Davina?'

'Do you want to?' My arms were around his neck and I could feel the towel slipping.

'Could do worse. She's very beautiful. I could tell the truth without offending.' He grinned again, reaching up for the zip at the back of my dress, beginning to slide it down. Reluctantly I wriggled away from him and went to sit out of his reach at the dressing table. I picked up my hairbrush.

'She is different, have you noticed?'

'A year older and wiser. So are we.'

'No, it's more than that. She's grown hard and neurotic.' I put down the brush and turned to face him. 'I think she's unhappy.'

He laughed. 'With all this?'

It did seem hard to believe, but as I watched her at dinner I became more and more certain I was right.

We sat at a long elegant table lit with candles in silver candelabra, waited on by the villa servants. Beside me Nigel Godson was attentive. Without his glasses he was also very attractive for his eyes were a warm hazel and they were without doubt fixed exclusively on me.

At the other end of the table my sister was dressed in white which against her tan looked quite stunning and she in her turn had eyes for no one but my husband.

He was studying her. I knew that look; I had seen it often and in the beginning I had resented it bitterly as beauty after beauty disappeared into his studio; I still found it hard to believe he was studying his subjects dispassionately and that he treated men to the same intense scrutiny. Davina had sensed his interest at once and was responding with an arch awareness which bordered on flirtation, looking up at him under her eyelashes as her fingers toyed with her wine glass. I felt a quick surge of hurt anger at her as I watched.

I dragged my attention away from the cameo at the end of the table to find that Nigel Godson was speaking to me again. 'Perhaps if your husband is going to work while he's here you would allow me to drive you down to the city to explore a little?' He smiled and I saw Maggie Farquer watching us through the candlelight from across bowls of stracciatella. On my left, sitting at the head of the table was Simon, a large florid man in his early forties. He was busy eating and did not appear to be listening. Nor had he noticed his wife flirting with my husband.

Maggie caught my eye and smiled. 'That's a splendid idea,' she murmured. 'I shall beg a lift down with you, Nigel. No – ' she made a deprecatory gesture with her hands. 'Don't worry, I'm not going to play gooseberry. I want you to drop me off somewhere on your way. A dear friend of mine has rented a house there for the summer and I've been dying for the opportunity to look her up. More than a friend actually, my erstwhile partner in crime.' Her smile had not faltered but I sensed she was no longer speaking to Nigel and myself any more; she was watching Simon. I glanced at him as well. He had laid down his soup spoon and was sipping from his glass. 'I believe you know her, Simon sweetie.' She was speaking to him directly now. 'It's Sarah. Sarah Cummins.'

Later we took our coffee and liqueurs out onto the terrace. An enormous orange moon hung above the cypress trees and the darkness had the quality of rich stifling velvet. I felt lost and a little miserable. Tim was still talking to Davina. They were sitting on the rim of the fountain together and she was stroking the still water at its edge into gentle ripples with the tip of her finger. Jocelyn and Simon were talking together as they wandered up and down the garden smoking cigars, tiny points of burning light in the night. Whatever reaction Maggie had expected from her host at her announcement at dinner, Simon had obviously disappointed her. His bland face had remained unruffled and he had merely smiled, rather bored, at her disclosure. She was talking now to Nigel, discussing people I did not know, laughing, touching his arm. I was sitting with them but I was an outsider, an observer who did not even speak their language and before long I rose with murmured excuses and tiptoed up to bed. I must have been asleep when Tim came up, for I never heard him.

When I awoke the room was cool and silvery with early morning light. Tim was already up and dressed in jeans and an open-necked shirt. He grinned when he saw me awake and came to sit on the bed beside me.

'Hi. Did you sleep well?'

I stretched in the soft silky sheets, my forebodings of the previous night forgotten, and nodded, holding out my arms as he bent to kiss me. But a moment later he was sitting up again. 'I'm going down to the cottage, Celia. I want to begin work at once. You don't mind, do you? Make the most of the sun and get a lovely tan beside their pool.' He ran his finger slowly down my breast.

I felt my nerves tighten. 'You're going to do a head of Davina?'

It wasn't really a question. I already knew the answer.

He nodded. 'She says Simon will pay for it for their anniversary and she can spare me a bit of time later this morning for a preliminary sitting so I thought I'd get straight to it.'

'Tim . . .' I reached out again and he caught my hands gently. Last night had been the first time we had not made love since our reconciliation, but what was the use of saying anything? It had all been said so often in the past. I just smiled at him, reached up to give him a kiss and lay back to watch him as he slung his denim jacket over his shoulder, winked at me and was gone.

Nigel Godson drove a British registration Lancia. I sat beside him in the front with Maggie Farquer, resplendent in a magenta jumpsuit, behind us, leaning forward with her forearms across the back of the seats as she directed us. She smelled faintly of gardenias.

We found it at last, a fourteenth-century farmhouse converted into a luxury holiday home. Sarah Cummins was the most beautiful woman I had ever seen. Elegant, ash blonde and charming she ushered us into the main room of the house and produced coffee and ricciarelli – delicious little almond biscuits – and it was only two minutes before I discovered that she knew Nigel as well as Maggie. It was an hour before Nigel and I could extricate ourselves from her hospitality and leave. I had not liked her; she was hard and I suspected clever, but with a hint of ice in her which touched us all. Even Maggie, who was effusive and voluble as she sat back on the Louis XVI sofa seemed a little uncomfortable.

Florence was hot and dusty and by mutual consent

Nigel and I agreed to forgo a trip to the Uffizi which we had planned and wander instead around San Lorenzo and down the Via Calzaioli towards the Ponte Vecchio. I had begun to like Nigel. He owned a smart gallery in Chelsea dabbling in art and antiques and was exactly the sort of man Tim resented, but he was also kind – a quality conspicuously lacking at the villa – strong and quiet and nobody's fool. And I sensed that his interest in me was real.

'How well do you know your brother-in-law?' Nigel asked suddenly as we examined some of the gilded leatherwork on a stall. I glanced at him, but he had retreated once more behind those dark glasses.

'I don't,' I said shortly. 'I've only met him twice in my life before and one of those times was the wedding.'

He said nothing for a moment, distracted as we wandered on through piles of intricately woven straw baskets, passed silver shops, silks and linens, antiques . . . Then he returned to his probing. 'Have you had a chance to speak to your sister at all?'

'What about?'

He looked uncomfortable. 'Nothing special. I just wondered how she seemed to you.'

I looked at him. 'I think she seems very tense,' I said cautiously. I was thinking of the last I had seen of her, wandering barefoot across the lawns after breakfast in the direction of the cottage, dressed in a simple Saint Laurent floating dress with a chiffon scarf draped over her hair like a 1920s film star.

He had taken off his glasses and I could see his face now in the blinding sunlight of the hot street. 'She's not happy, Celia. I don't think it's women – you gathered I suppose that Sarah used to live with him – I think it has something to do with his business activities.'

'You mean they're questionable?' I had a quick vision

of Simon in close conversation with Jocelyn Farquer, the man who had not, since I had arrived in the villa, addressed as much as one word to me directly.

Nigel shrugged. 'It's not my field of course, but I used to know old Simon pretty well and I get the impression he's up to something. Jocelyn and he are brokers of some sort in the City. Davina hates the Farquers, you know.'

I stared at him. 'I got the impression that Maggie was something of a bitch,' I said – I had also got the impression that Nigel disliked her intensely, 'but I haven't spoken to her husband. Not once.'

He laughed grimly. 'You wouldn't. He has no time for social niceties. He is one of those people who doesn't want to know you unless you are useful to him.'

'Touché!' I laughed. 'Why did they ask Tim and me to come do you think?'

Nigel looked down at me. 'Haven't you guessed?'

'I had hoped it was because of Tim's work.'

He grimaced. 'Perhaps a little. But something else as well.'

'To distract Davina?'

'Of course.'

'And you?' I was watching him intently.

'I am afraid my uses are very basic.' He smiled, suddenly humorous. 'I think I am the spare male to be used as distraction for any of the ladies who became too much of a nuisance. I thought when I arrived he had asked me to take Davina off his back – yes, I know it sounds pretty awful, but it gets worse. Now I think I've been asked to take care of you – so Davina can have your husband. I gather she's always rated her chances with him fairly high and Simon has never been a great performer in the sack so I'm told.'

I heard myself gasp. We were standing on the kerb, watching the noonday traffic roaring past in a haze of fumes and dirt. My head was spinning. 'I don't believe you! That's a wicked thing to say!' It was my own voice I could hear protesting but I knew what he said was true.

When we returned to pick Maggie up she dropped her little piece of news. 'I've asked Sarah to come back with us for dinner, Nigel. You don't mind waiting while she changes, then we can give her a lift.' It didn't cross my mind, then, to wonder how she would get back home again.

There was no one around when we drove up to the villa. The hall was cool and dim, the shutters closed as we trooped in and Nigel and I excused ourselves to go to our respective rooms to shower and change before meeting again on the terrace for drinks at six. Of the others in the party there was no sign and I vowed wearily as I climbed the broad sweep of stairs that I would not go to look for Tim in the cottage. Perhaps I was afraid of what I might find.

I showered and wrapped myself in a towel before lying down on the bed to rest. The walk around Florence had exhausted me and I was feeling very depressed at what I now realized was my sister's betrayal; I loved her, but I loved my husband too.

I must have dozed off for it was Tim who woke me some time later. He was stripping off his shirt by the window, staring out into the garden as he did so. The sun had gone round to the side of the villa and the shutters were open now onto the balcony. I could hear a pigeon cooing from somewhere in the trees.

'How was work today?' I murmured. I didn't sit up.

He turned. 'I'm sorry, darling. I was trying not to wake you. It was fine. How was Florence?'

'Hot and dusty and very beautiful. But I missed you.'

He came to me then and sat on the edge of the bed. 'I

missed you. Let's work out a way of taking a day off and making a trip together shall we – just us.' He leaned over me and I felt the warm touch of his lips on mine, then slowly he pulled open the towel which was wrapped around me and ran his hands over my body. It was only the sound of the ormulu clock on the landing outside our room chiming six which brought me back from the warm sated dream in which I was lying, and reluctantly I pushed him away. 'Remember our aperitifs on the terrace,' I whispered as his hand began once more to stray between my thighs.

He gave a grimace. 'I don't give a damn about the terrace. I want my wife!'

And oh how I wanted him. But I slipped out of his reach and went to the mirror to do something about my hair while he showered and found a clean shirt.

It was only when I went to pick up his discarded shirt, lying on the thick Chinese carpet by the window that I saw the lipstick on the collar and remembered that when he had cheated on me his first reaction always had been to come and try to make it up.

Davina was wearing a red and gold sarong, her hair piled up on her head to show a pair of exquisite emerald earrings which I had no doubt at all were worth a fortune. She came straight up to us when we appeared and slipped her arm through Tim's. 'Where have you both been? We thought you'd got lost,' she said. She glanced at me, and I saw the suppressed triumph in her eyes. So Nigel had been right.

I glanced round for him, but he had not appeared. Simon was standing on the lawn talking to Maggie and Sarah and Jocelyn was sitting on the wall of the terrace looking out across the gardens. Feeling sick and lonely I went to stand beside him, my drink in my hand, content to be silent. But to my surprise he spoke to me.

'My wife is unbelievably stupid. Have you any idea at all what she's done?' He was staring down at the group on the lawn, his voice icy with contempt and I took a step away from him in surprise.

'What?'

He turned and stared at me and I wondered for a moment if he had realized that it was me he was talking to. His face was hard and bitter, his lips thin as he looked me up and down.

'Sarah was Simon's mistress before he met your sister,' he said quietly, 'and the only reason she has come to Tuscany is to make trouble for him. For Maggie to invite her here is the most crass behaviour, even for her.' His look of loathing encompassed his wife and Sarah as they stood on the lawn and I wondered briefly what they could be talking to Simon about so intensely. For a moment I had forgotten my own grief in the shock of his statement, but as I turned to look at Davina I saw her still clinging to Tim's arm and I wondered suddenly whether she would care at all what her husband did, or to whom. I looked back at Jocelyn.

'And Davina has no clue about this?' I asked softly.

'No. Maggie and Sarah used to run a boutique together and Sarah even met Simon at our place in Midhurst. They were together for about three years but Sarah was too interfering; she poked her nose in where it wasn't wanted just once too often and Simon got shot of her.'

'Jocelyn,' I looked up at him searchingly. 'Exactly why did he marry Davina? She's hardly his type.'

He gave a small hard smile at that. 'Why, my dear young lady, does any man marry at all?' He looked rather pointedly at my husband.

I swallowed, hoping the wave of bleakness which swept over me did not show in my face as I turned away from him and walked back to the drinks table. I was not going to let Davina see that I cared. I refilled my drink with an unsteady hand and then I saw Nigel appearing from the house at last; he came over to me at once and gave a small smile.

'So, the cast is assembled,' he commented quietly.

I sipped my drink. 'To play tragedy or comedy, I wonder,' I said bitterly.

On the lawn the sets of couples had changed. Sarah had wandered across to join Tim and Davina, and Maggie and Simon were walking back to join Jocelyn on the terrace. Maggie was smiling as she looked up in our direction.

'Nigel, come and tell my husband about that painting you mentioned to me, my dear. I would so love him to buy it for me.' She came up and slipped her arm through his, edging him away from me.

I didn't mind. I knew her for what she was now, a bored rich manipulator who made up for her own lack of love by playing with other people. I just hoped that Sarah's presence would deflect Davina's attention from Tim when and if Davina found out who she was.

Time passed; drinks were replenished. Nigel made one rueful face at me behind Maggie's back and then settled into conversation. On the horizon behind the pointed cypress trees the rim of the moon floated suddenly into view, pale lemon in an aquamarine sky. I felt myself shiver.

'Celia, are you all right?' I hadn't seen Sarah approaching.

I smiled. 'A footstep on my grave, that's all.'

'You must be careful not to chill. I've just been talking to your husband and I hear he is to sculpt your sister's bust. Do you think I dare ask him to do mine?' Her laugh was a silver bell in the thin evening air as she ran the fingers of her left hand over the line of her breast. It was somehow an obscene gesture. She had been drinking heavily since six, and her thick make up could not quite conceal the blurring of her features.

'I'm sure he'd love to . . .' I hesitated. 'He is very booked at the moment though . . .'

'I can believe it.' She was watching me with an intensity which made me uncomfortable. 'Your sister is very beautiful.'

'Yes, she is, isn't she?' I took a sip at my glass with stiff lips.

'I can see how easily she must have captured Simon; he wouldn't have stood a chance.'

'No.' I didn't know what else to say.

'And now she's captured your husband,' she went on quietly. 'Do you mind? Or does he always sleep with his models? Perhaps an artist's wife gets used to it?'

'No, you don't get used to it,' I had replied with more feeling than I intended and I hastened to cover up. 'There's no need. His interest is purely professional.'

'Although there are exceptions.' She was still watching me as she drained her glass. She refilled it from the table and I saw she was drinking neat vodka.

I gave what I hoped was a worldly smile. 'There are always exceptions to everything,' I said, but I was aching with unhappiness as we both turned and saw Tim slowly leading Davina back towards the terrace. Their footsteps left a dark track on the grass where the dew was lying and she was leaning on him slightly, her arm through his.

They walked slowly up the steps towards us and I saw that she was talking quietly so that he had to lean towards her slightly to hear what she was saying. I felt a sudden surge of anger. I turned and, putting my glass down on the table, I walked towards them, conscious as I did so of Sarah's eyes watching me. They stopped, still engrossed in one another and for a moment I don't think either of them realized I was there. Then they were both looking at me and I was sure that I saw guilt on their faces. I forced myself to smile.

'You look so cosy there is speculation on the terrace about when you're moving in together,' I said with a laugh which came out far too brittle. Davina released his arm abruptly, but I saw the quick anger on Tim's face and I cursed myself for having said anything at all. But I couldn't stop myself. 'You're in demand, darling,' I said to him lightly. 'Sarah is wondering if you will have time to sculpt her bust too.' I knew she could hear every word I said. 'I told her you come expensive.'

Davina had opened her mouth, but her retort was lost in the sound of the phone relayed out onto the terrace by an outside bell. There was dead silence, then Simon began slowly to walk towards the french windows. Behind him Jocelyn put down his glass and followed.

'Well!' Davina laughed abruptly. She walked across to the drinks table and began rather obviously to tidy the tray and screw the caps onto various bottles. 'I suppose this means we'll be late for dinner and Stephano will hand in his notice again. It happens about once a week I'm afraid.'

'Business calls?' It was Nigel's voice from the shadows. Davina tensed. 'I expect so. Business can't be left at home even here.'

I recognized the strained note in her voice and instantly my hostility lessened. I thought I recognized her play for Tim as a plea; a cry for help. I wanted to reach out my hand, to hug her as I used to do when we were children and would comfort one another when things became too bad to be borne alone. But the eyes she turned on me were hard and rejecting and I took a step back as if she had slapped me.

Tim came forward. He smiled at me, his usual warm special smile as though nothing were wrong. 'We can't ask Davina to risk losing so great a treasure as Stephano; I suggest we go in and start to eat without Simon. I'll take the blame if he gets violent.' His smile took in everyone as he gestured to Davina to lead us into the candlelit dining room. There was no sign of Simon and Jocelyn. The double doors to Simon's study were closed; when we had come down earlier they had stood open.

We had finished the Parma ham garnished with figs and had already begun on the veal escalopes before the doors opened and Simon and Jocelyn reappeared. They both looked angry as they took their places and I found myself unwillingly catching Nigel's eye. He winked at me.

'Bad news?' he asked innocently.

Sarah laughed. She had already finished a second glass of Chianti. 'It must be bad,' she said, slurring her words slightly. 'It takes more than a bear market to make our Simon flinch.' She leaned forward across the table to put her hand on his. Her gold bracelet clanked heavily against the cut glass. 'That's right, isn't it, honey bunch?'

I was watching Davina's face. She had refused to look up as her husband came in, toying with her food with her fork, but now I saw her staring at Sarah in disbelief. She opened her mouth to say something but before she had the chance her husband spoke.

'I'm afraid it looks as if I'll have to nip back to London for a couple of days.' He cleared his throat. 'Awful bore. Sorry. But Davina will entertain you all.'

'And you, Joss?' Maggie was watching her husband across the table.

'Not Jocelyn.' Simon answered for him. 'Jocelyn has done enough damage.'

There was a moment of complete silence. Then Sarah started to laugh.

I cornered Davina in her bathroom. It was an amazing place of ornate marble and gold illuminated now by cruel hidden lights. She looked haggard as she bathed her eyes.

'What the hell is going on here?' I perched on the edge of the bath. 'What has happened to you, Davina?'

She looked up at me, her face wet. 'Did you know that Sarah woman used to be Simon's fancy piece?'

I nodded.

'Maggie's a cow. You know it was she who asked her here. I detest her.' She had drunk more than usual and her face beneath the heavy streaked layer of make up was flushed.

Privately I agreed with her. 'You haven't answered me, Davina. What is going on here?'

She shrugged. 'What do I care? Simon never tells me anything. I just have to sign things; and entertain his guests.' She was peering into the mirror now, her shadowed eyes expressionless. 'And you'd better mind your own business. Don't tangle with Simon.'

'How long has it been like this?' My sympathy for her had returned and I wanted to touch her, to comfort her. But I was not prepared to risk another rejection. She stared down at the mosaic floor.

'Ever since we married. I've wanted to see you often but I didn't dare ask you. I didn't want you to see what I had become. I could bear the thought of you and Tim as long as you were unhappy. It meant you were no better off than me. You see what a horrible person I am?'

There was a long pause. I closed my eyes wearily. 'And when you saw we were happy, you thought you'd take him for yourself, is that it?' I asked at last.

'You're my sister. I thought . . .' She stopped in mid sentence. Then she turned to face me. 'Oh Celia, you shouldn't have come.' And she began to cry.

*

Tim went into our room ahead of me. He didn't turn on the light. As I closed the door he came up to me and put his arms around me in the dark.

'Celia. What is it? What's wrong?'

'I talked to Davina. She thinks we ought to go. Can we, Tim? Please. Tomorrow. I know it's a disappointment but you'll get work from other people. You're good. We don't need to rely on Simon for any commissions.'

I felt him tense. He was stroking my hair gently. 'Celia, you can go if you want to, darling. But I can't. Don't you see?'

The room was very dark. The maid had pulled the curtains across the windows when she came in to turn down the bed and it was stifling. I pulled away from him wordlessly and went to open them. Outside the balcony was black. The brilliant moonlight flooded past the villa and focused on the lawn. The fountain was still playing.

'Do you love her?' I asked softly. I leaned on the stone balustrade and looked down.

'Who?' I felt the anger in him, the resentment which always came when I questioned him and I knew I could not fight it this time. What was the point? Tim came out onto the balcony beside me. 'Don't run away, Celia. I'm beginning to think you must be paranoid or something. Who do you think I'm having an affair with this time?'

'Davina.' I could hardly bring myself to say the name.

'Oh for God's sake. It's always the same, isn't it? The moment I show interest in a woman you imagine I've fallen into bed with her. What's the matter with you?'

What indeed? How could I explain to him how much I loved him; how much I feared to lose him; how much I had looked forward to these summer months in Italy as a second honeymoon? And now I saw the whole frail structure of my dream collapsing.

'You really mean it, Tim? You would stay here and let

me go home alone?' I didn't look at him. Below in the garden I saw a small glow in the darkness and I thought it must be a firefly. Then I realized it was a cigarette. There was someone walking slowly in the shadows of the trees.

'I've come here to work, Celia. And it's important that I do. More important than you know. Simon told me today that he is prepared to recommend me for a commission to do heads of all the members of a board he's on. It means security and freedom to work without worrying for a while; without you having to go back to that job. I'm not going to blow it, Celia, even if it means we can't be together. I don't want you to go. It's up to you.'

He turned and vanished back into the bedroom. A moment later I heard the door slam.

I could feel the hot tears burning my cheeks and I let them fall unchecked. The french doors below the balcony opened and someone stepped out onto the terrace. I knew it must be Tim. He would go to his improvised studio and work through the night, returning to fall into bed beside me at dawn. It had happened too often before after we had quarrelled. I did not call out to him. What was the point? He stepped out of the shadows of the terrace onto the grass and I saw him clearly walking towards the fountain. A figure detached itself from the shadows and joined him. A woman. The moonlight had washed the colour from her dress but I knew it was my sister. I watched as they stood talking then slowly they began to move, not towards the cottage but around the side of the house out of sight. Two minutes later I heard the sound of a car engine and the crunch of its tyres on the gravel of the long poplar-lined drive. Then there was silence.

I undressed and lay down on the bed, but my mind would not rest. I could not sleep and after a while I gave up trying. I rose and slipped on a thin sweater and some jeans.

The villa was in darkness save where moonlight slid through the windows on the staircase. I peered out. Our car had vanished from its place beneath the mulberry tree beside the wall. Behind me on the landing the clock chimed three. Tim had left the french windows open and I slipped out onto the terrace. I avoided the bright moonlight, following the dark shadows beneath the trees.

The cottage was in darkness, but the door was unlocked and I slipped in and at last allowed myself to turn on a light. The room was empty but for a large table and a couple of chairs. I recognized all the paraphernalia we had brought with us in the car. The plastic sacks of clay and plaster, the wire for armatures, the scalpels, the spatulas, the callipers and sketch books. Tim's overalls hung on the back of the door and the room already had the cold oily smell of the clay. On the table I could see the outline of the head beneath its cloth and I moved over to uncover it.

He had made a lot of progress. Davina stared out at me, her lips enigmatically smiling, her eyes still a blind sightless sketch in the glistening clay. I stared at it for a long time, then I covered it again and moved across to the stairs. The cottage had only one bedroom and it was fully furnished. The bed had been slept in. Beside it the bathroom was also fully equipped with toiletries and cosmetics. I unscrewed a bottle of cologne and sniffed it. It was spicy and rather strong. I did not recognize it.

A bell pealed in the silence and I froze. Then I realized it was the telephone beside the bed next door. I tiptoed across and hesitated as it rang. Then cautiously I lifted the receiver. A voice was talking in fast Italian on the other end and I realized suddenly that it was an extension from the main house. I was about to replace it when a second voice cut in. It was Simon and he sounded once more very angry. Holding my breath I sat gingerly on the bed and listened.

They were speaking in English now. 'I told you not to ring me!' Simon's voice hissed down the line.

'The deal is taking too long!' the Italian cut in. 'You have only twenty-four hours. Then I pull out.'

'You can't pull out, remember? Your currency is being held in my wife's name,' Simon snarled. 'I fly to London tomorrow. The transaction will be completed on schedule.'

'And if she asks any questions?'

'She won't. She never does.' Simon's mirthless laugh floated from the receiver in my hand. I could feel myself beginning to shake as I listened in disbelief, and for a long time after he had hung up and the line was empty I sat there, the phone still in my hand.

I could see the light on in his study as I tiptoed back across the lawn towards the french windows. I had no wish to meet Simon and I held my breath as I crept in. Then I realized he was not alone. Davina was with him and they were having a furious row. There was no question of them hearing me; they were making enough noise to wake the whole villa. The doors to his study were half open and I could see them both clearly. Simon was fully dressed still, but Davina was in a négligé and I could see from the stark paleness of her face that she had removed her make up. She looked as though she had just got out of bed and I wondered suddenly whether like me she had been listening on the extension.

I crept upstairs without them seeing me and peered out of the window on the landing. The car was still missing, and I realized bitterly that my husband's midnight rendezvous had been not with my sister but with Sarah Cummins.

Simon was missing from the dining room when I plucked up courage to descend at about nine, but the others were there, all except Tim. Maggie smiled at me. 'Is your divine husband at work already, Celia?' she asked.

'He's been at it all night,' I heard myself reply. I was watching Davina as she got up and went to the urn on the sideboard to pour herself a cup of black coffee.

She raised her eyebrows. 'How dedicated,' she said tartly.

'But I don't know where. He drove off with someone at about midnight,' I went on quietly, 'and the car's not back yet.'

Maggie and Nigel were listening intently; Jocelyn was engrossed in the *Financial Times* and did not look up. I saw the coffee overflow into Davina's saucer. Her face suddenly turned white.

'The bitch!' she said. 'The bloody bitch!' She put the cup down and flung her napkin on the floor.

There was a telephone in the hall – an ornate affair of gold and white – and she picked it up angrily. 'Maggie, what is the number of that woman you brought here last night?' she yelled through the door.

Maggie was smiling quietly. 'I wrote it on the pad by the phone,' she answered softly. 'I figured someone from this house might want to call her.'

Davina was connected almost at once and I listened in disbelief. This was my husband they were fighting over. Sarah Cummins had arrived at the house, bent on revenge on Davina for stealing her man, as she saw it, and in order to do it she had decided to steal Tim from her. Wordlessly I stood up and went to stand in the hall behind her, listening. There was no question that Tim was there, but he was refusing to come to the phone. After five minutes' vicious tirade Davina slammed down the phone and whirled round. She found herself face to face with me and for one second she had the grace to look taken aback. Then she smiled. 'Don't look like that, Celia. If you were any good at all with men you'd be able to keep him, wouldn't you! You deserve to lose him!' She ran to the staircase and vanished up it.

I was stunned. For a while I could not move, then I was conscious of the dining room door closing softly behind me, shielding me from the staring eyes within. An arm went round my shoulders. It was Nigel.

'Come on up to my room. I've some brandy up there,' he said quietly. I went without a murmur and sat on his bed sipping it until I had stopped shaking. His arms were round me, comforting, holding me close. I hardly noticed when he took the glass from my hand and set it down on the bedside table, then his lips were against mine and I felt myself lying back on the pillows. 'I'll take care of you, Celia. Forget him. He's not worth it,' he whispered, tickling my neck with a curl of my hair, wound round his finger. He looked down into my eyes with such concern and kindness that for a long time I lay still. I felt secure and safe. I was wanted. 'Oh Nigel!' My arms went round his neck and I was sobbing at last.

We lay like that for a long time and it was only the sunlight crawling across the carpet towards us until it threw a brilliant hot beam across the pillow which brought me to my senses. I pushed him away and sat up.

'Nigel. What shall I do?' I looked miserably down at the floor. I should have told him then what I had overheard on the phone, but I was afraid. Afraid for Davina but afraid of her too and I hated her at that moment almost as much as I hated Sarah Cummins. And myself.

Nigel did not try to touch me again. Getting up he poured another tot of brandy and put it into my hands. Then he walked across to the window and stared out. 'Let me take care of you,' he said. 'There is no point in staying with a man who makes you so unhappy, Celia. You can fight for years, but he's not going to change. Do you want to waste your whole life on him? He's not worth it.' He walked back and stood looking down at me. 'You're a hundred times more beautiful than your sister, Celia. You're natural; you're unspoilt. Don't let them corrupt you. Let me take you back to London.'

On my way back to my bedroom I listened at Davina's door. I could hear her sobbing and I raised my hand to knock. Then I lowered it again. There was nothing I could say to Davina. I had to think. I had to make up my mind what to do.

For a long time I lay on the bed in our bedroom staring at the ceiling. The house was completely silent around me. Nigel was going to drive down into Florence after lunch, he said, but I had declined his invitation to go with him. I wanted to be alone. His words were ringing in my ears. 'Do you want to waste your whole life?' Was that was I was doing?

The phone number was still on the pad by the phone in the hall. I sat down on the carved chair by the table and stared down at the scribbled figures for a long time before, hesitatingly, I picked up the receiver and dialled.

'*Pronto*.' The voice which answered was that of a stranger.

'Can I speak to Tim?' I said slowly, and groped for the Italian words.

There was a long silence, but he came in the end.

'Tim!' I tried to keep my voice calm. 'Tim, I must speak to you.'

'Can't it wait till tonight? I'm working, Celia.' He sounded exaggeratedly patient, like an adult humouring a fractious child. Something inside me seemed to break and I knew I was fighting; fighting for my marriage and my self respect.

'No, it bloody well can't wait,' I hissed down the phone. 'You get back here, Tim, and meet me at the cottage. I've got to see you now. I've found out something you've got to know about. Simon is involved in some shady currency deal and he's using Davina. You've got to tell me what to do. She's the one who is going to get into trouble. Now, get here.' I hung up before he had time to reply.

There was a sound behind me and I turned to see Simon himself standing in the dining room doorway. His arms were folded and he was watching me. 'I wonder what sort of trouble that could possibly be?' he said quietly, with a small smile. 'Perhaps you would come into my study a moment, Celia. It's time you and I had a short talk I think.'

He ushered me into a carved rococo chair by the fireplace. Then, half leaning on his desk he turned to face me. 'What exactly have you found out?' he asked. His face was quite bland and unthreatening, and yet suddenly I was afraid.

'That you treat Davina like dirt,' I replied. I had no intention of telling about my eavesdropping.

'I see.' He waited a moment, then he went to a cabinet beside the fireplace and produced a bottle. 'Campari and soda?' He put the glass in my hand. 'What do you intend doing about it?' A smile played across his lips for moment.

'Do you know what happened this morning?' I asked him suddenly, looking down at the glass in my hand without seeing it. 'Your ex-girlfriend has gone off with my husband because she wanted to hurt Davina. Don't you think that is rather funny?' I heard myself laughing, a high nervous sound which bordered on hysteria. 'Is that why you asked us here? So you could procure Tim for your wife and distract her from your illegal activities?'

I could have bitten my tongue out. His face had not altered but I saw the knuckles whiten on his glass. Slowly he raised it and drank.

'So. I ask you again, what have you found out, sweet sister-in-law?'

'Enough.' I stared at him defiantly.

There was a long silence. He set down the glass and looked at me thoughtfully. 'Do you love this husband of yours, Celia?' he asked.

'Of course I do.' It was true. It was agonizingly true.

'Then I suggest you keep very quiet about whatever it is that you think you have discovered, *cognata mia*, or I will break Timothy's career. Do you understand me? I can do it, you know. I'll see to it that he never gets another commission as long as he lives.' There seemed to be no animosity in his voice, no violence, just calm certainty. And I believed him. I stared at him, my heart hammering uncertainly in my chest as I set my glass down without tasting the drink.

'You bastard.'

He bowed in acknowledgement as though I had paid him a compliment.

When Tim returned Sarah was with him. The car crunched to a halt on the gravel outside the villa as I was descending the stairs from my room in search of a cup of coffee. I had had no lunch and my head was aching violently. I stopped dead as the ornate doors swung open and they appeared on the threshold. Sarah was laughing as the soft jacket thrown across her shoulders caught on the elaborate arrangement of flowers in the hall and a spray of stephanotis fell to the floor. Tim looked at me intently for a moment. The anger which had shadowed his face as he caught sight of me was replaced by concern. 'Sweetheart, are you all right?'

I glanced at the dining room door which stood open.

Beyond it Simon was still in his study. 'Come to the cottage,' I whispered. 'I must see you alone.'

Sarah was watching me. I saw a slight sneer flicker across her lips. 'Go on, Tim. I shall speak to Simon. I know exactly what this is all about. He tried it once with me.' She kissed her fingertips and laid them quickly on his lips. Then she went through the door and closed it behind her.

In the cool of the cottage Tim held me for a long time before he would let me speak. Then slowly he pushed me away, holding me at arm's length. 'I was only sketching her, you know. It never crossed my mind she was trying to make Davina jealous.'

His eyes held mine steadily and I knew that I believed him.

'And Davina? Did she have any reason to be jealous?' I asked softly.

'What do you think?' He was holding me tightly again and his lips on mine were urgent and demanding. It was a long time before I remembered my excuse for bringing him back to the villa.

'He said if I told anyone he'd see you never got another commission, Tim,' I whispered when I had finished telling him what had happened.

Tim laughed softly and the sound sent a shiver up my spine. 'I think I'm prepared to risk that,' he said.

Half an hour later I was packing when the door of our room burst open. It was Simon and his face was puce. 'Get up,' he said roughly and he bent to pull me from the bed where I was sitting. 'You silly bitch. You thought I didn't mean it? You thought you could double cross me, is that it?' He yelled at me. I heard a door open in the distance and I guessed it was Davina's.

'What do you mean?' I pulled away from him angrily. 'Take your filthy hands off me!'

'Simon, let her go!' It was Davina in the doorway. Her voice had risen to a scream.

'You told Sarah. She's just confronted me with my plans downstairs. She thinks I'm going to cut her in.' He gave an unpleasant laugh. 'I told her to go and screw herself.'

I wrenched my hand free. 'You're mad. I haven't told Sarah anything. I haven't spoken to her. She must have guessed.'

'I don't care how she knew,' his face was ugly. 'But there's nothing she can do. No one can, because it's too late and my plans are always foolproof.' He turned to look at his wife, then swung back to me. 'If you want to stop your sister going to jail you are going to do as I say for the next few hours. That is all I ask.'

Davina and I stared at each other. Her face was white and pleading.

I subsided onto the bed. 'What do you want me to do?'

He lifted my bag off the side table and wrenched it open to look inside. Then he threw it in my lap. 'Get downstairs and wait for me in the car,' he said.

In the hall the spray of fragrant white flowers still lay on the Bokhara rug where Sarah's jacket had flicked it. I bent and picked it up then I went out and climbed into the blue Alfa Romeo which stood outside.

He took the hairpin bends of the mountain road with screaming tyres as we swooped down towards Florence. The glare off the white road reflected through the windscreen and I closed my eyes.

'Where are we going?' I asked wearily.

'England.' He did not look at me.

My eyes had flown open. 'England!'

He chuckled suddenly. 'I told Davina that if anyone wanted to see you alive again they had better keep very quiet about what they know.' He glanced up at the driving mirror and smiled at himself. 'You could say, *cognata mia*, that I am using you as a kind of hostage.'

A wave of nausea swept over me and I felt myself clinging to the sides of the seat. The palms of my hands were clammy with fear.

'You're going to kill me?' I whispered in disbelief.

'Of course not. I don't want a murder charge hanging over me, Celia. I'm not that much of a fool. But they don't know that do they!' He laughed out loud. 'And I know you will behave because of what will happen to your sister – and your beloved husband – if you don't. You are merely an insurance policy, my dear. I have a plane waiting at San Giusto and like any good tourist you carry your passport in your handbag. So we should have no more problems.'

'I don't believe you. You're kidnapping me!'

'You are hardly a kid,' the scorn in his voice flicked at me and I flinched. He was right. I was no kid, and I understood perfectly that I had no choice but to do everything he said.

The Learjet was waiting on the tarmac near the terminal buildings, a beautiful glittering bird, poised for take off. Within twenty minutes we were cleared and in the sky.

I remember little of that flight. Europe lay beneath a haze of thin cloud which flattened the countries below into a tableau of white. I did not know when we crossed the Alps; I did not know when we crossed the Channel, but suddenly we were losing altitude and Simon himself took the controls from his pilot as we began to circle southern England. Gatwick was wet and glistening beneath a summer shower and very crowded, but Simon took my arm and guided me through the formalities with the minimum of fuss. Then we were in the chauffeur-driven maroon BMW swooping down the lush green lanes of Sussex.

Two cars were parked outside his Queen Anne mansion, an XJ6 and a sleek Rolls and he chuckled when he saw them. 'You see, I don't even have to go to London. They are here to meet me. You will excuse me, Celia, for half an hour or so, I know,' he said as he handed me out into the soft mist of the rain. 'This business won't take long.' He showed me into a pretty drawing room, furnished in pale greens and greys – Davina's favourite colours. 'Sit down. Help yourself to a drink,' and he was gone. This time I poured myself half a tumbler of Scotch.

There was nothing I could do. Outside the window the rain lent the countryside the smell of sweet grass and bruised velvet roses; somewhere a blackbird was singing undaunted. The house itself was very quiet.

Later I heard the cars leave. I did not move. I was too weary. When Simon appeared he was smiling. 'Celia. What about some food? Forbes has left steaks and champagne in the fridge.'

I followed him into the gleaming kitchen.

'How long do you intend keeping me here?' I asked. The house was quite empty, I discovered; his staff lived in cottages on the estate.

'Not long. You'll find a spare room that's comfortable – and I assure you I shan't bother you.' He eased the cork expertly out of the bottle and caught the bubbles. 'I find sex greatly overrated as a field sport.' He handed me a glass. 'Unlike so many of your contemporaries.'

I ate the steak and sipped a little of the champagne and then excused myself. Climbing the stairs slowly to the pretty chintzy bedroom which had been allotted to me, I kicked off my sandals and fell, fully dressed, onto the bed. It was barely half past nine.

Below me in his study Simon sat alone in the dusk with his telephones and his Telex and a new bottle of Scotch.

I was awakened by the sound of shouting. Somewhere

a door banged and there was a rush of feet. I sat up disorientated for a moment, then I ran to the door and looked out. It was pitch dark in the body of the house but I could hear the sound of shouting, muffled now, from downstairs and barefoot I ran down towards Simon's study.

Tim and Nigel were in the study with Simon and all three men were shouting.

'Tim? Oh Tim!' I ran to him and fell into his arms.

'Are you all right, Celia? Don't worry, the police are on their way.' I heard him reassuring me as his hug closed over me.

Nigel was grinning. 'I bought some air tickets when I went down to Florence yesterday,' he said good humouredly. 'I was hoping I could talk you into eloping with me, Celia. But I found myself eloping with this reprobate instead!' He punched Tim on the arm and both men laughed.

I stared from one to the other bewildered. 'Davina told you where I'd gone?'

'She told us everything,' said Tim grimly, 'including Simon's nasty little threat and Nigel here persuaded Jocelyn to fill in the rest. There was quite a show-down after you left.'

Simon broke in. 'You're too late, Armitage. If you've called the police it's too late to stop the deal. And it is Davina who will suffer if anyone does. And you. I'll break you for this. Ask your wife. I'll see you never sell so much as a flying duck to go on somebody's wall!'

Nigel turned to him slowly. 'Shut up, Simon, old boy,' he said tolerantly. 'You don't know what you're talking about. I'll see to it that Tim does all right. I do have a certain influence, you know. If you remember, that is the reason why you bother to know me at all.' His tone dropped in heavy sarcasm. Then he turned back to us. 'Now you two, I want you to get going. Take yourselves off to a motel or somewhere for the rest of the night. Borrow his car, he won't mind, and Uncle Nigel will take care of things here.'

Only when we had been driving for about half an hour did Tim tell me what had really happened. Jocelyn had convinced them that there was nothing they could do about Simon's activities. Davina was implicated too far and Simon too clever, so they had not called the police. Simon's only punishment would be a few hours' sweating until he realized that he had got away with it. Men like Simon always win.

'Davina's leaving him and I've told her she can come to us, Celia, do you mind?' Tim's hand groped for mine on the seat beside me. There was a long pause as we both peered through the windscreen wipers at the road ahead. I could feel the tears pricking at my eyes. 'I didn't sleep with her you know,' he said at last. 'You do believe that, don't you? It's you I love, and always will.'

I believed him.

The motel we found was small and shabby and the most beautiful place on earth. We were soaked from running from the BMW into the chalet and we had no luggage save my handbag with my passport, and we were both deliriously happy.

Trade Reunions

Jackie looked at her watch and then at the phone. Another half hour and Sue would be home from the cinema to relieve her, unless Bob and Phil were back by then. She glanced at the message pad. Two addresses so far this evening. Not bad, considering how hard it was raining!

The twenty-four-hour plumbing service had been her brother Phil's idea when she had joined the firm. The only rule was that she didn't go out on night jobs alone, which was fair enough by her. Instead she took it in turns to mind the phone with Sue.

She drained the dregs of her coffee and looked regretfully at the paperback on the table, finished twenty minutes before. If only it had lasted the evening because there was nothing worth watching on the box and if she made any more coffee she would begin to look like a Beautifully Blended Bean . . .

She took the phone call with her usual slight sinking feeling. Nightcallers were always dodgy: on the defensive for ringing late; or desperate; sometimes hysterical; sometimes downright abusive as if it were her fault; almost never what you would call routine. She picked up her pencil and waited.

And for the first time in her short career as a plumber it happened. The customer the other end of the line was someone she knew. She kept her voice carefully impersonal as she repeated his name and address.

'Someone will be there within half an hour, Mr Peters,' she said reassuringly.

She was smiling as she hung up and tore the page off the pad, folding it into her jeans pocket and when Sue appeared she was ready to leave.

'Only the two calls tonight, Sue,' she said happily. 'And the boys should be back soon, so I'll be on my way. I'm exhausted.' And she was out of the house and into her mini van before Sue could delay her another minute.

Stamford Avenue was much as she remembered it, quiet, respectable, really rather pleasant houses, not all that far from the school where John Peters and she had been sixth formers together. Number 35 was different though. Shabbier, not quite so imposing – or had it seemed so marvellous then because she had always seen it through rose-coloured spectacles?

Stupid, to feel her heart thumping again after all this time, just at the sight of his house. It wasn't after all as if she had even given him a thought in ages.

She pushed the gate and heard it squeak slightly on its hinges. Then she rang the door bell.

He was obviously waiting for the ring for the door opened almost at once. 'Thank God,' he said, 'come in quick!' Then his mouth dropped open. 'I'm sorry,' he said. 'I was expecting the plumber . . .'

She was used to it. Her bag of tools and the flat tweed cap she wore over her long chestnut hair usually convinced people in the end though. She walked on. 'That's right,' she said. 'I'm the plumber. Now, where did it happen?'

She kept her face straight with difficulty. He was wearing jeans rolled up to the knees and his feet were bare – and obviously wet. He looked distraught.

'Upstairs in the bedroom. I was nailing down the carpet and one went through this pipe under the board.'

'Have you turned off the water?'

He had not recognized her yet. And why should he? After all it was what, five years, and the light in the hall wasn't too good. She realized suddenly that there was no furniture. Just a ladder and some paint cans.

He was staring at her, but not with recognition or adoration. Just plain horror. 'I didn't think,' he said. 'I was trying to seal it off with towels . . .'

They found the main stop cock reasonably fast – not fast enough, she noticed sadly, to prevent a nasty brown stain appearing on the immaculately decorated ceiling of one of the rooms, but if a man didn't know where his own stop cock was then really she could not wonder if his house came to rack and ruin.

She followed him up the stairs.

The bedroom was a shambles. He had at least rolled the carpet back and torn up the boards. But the cavity beneath was full of soggy towels. Shaking her head she began to pull them out and pile them in a dirty revolting heap beside her on the floor.

'Nice new installation,' she commented critically. 'Been doing the house up I see.' She opened her bag and brought out the blow lamp and some spare lengths of copper pipe. Then she glanced up at him under her cap. Some stray wisps of hair had escaped and hung around her ears. He was staring at her.

'Jackie?' he said at last. 'I don't believe it!'

She grinned. 'You'd better. For the first time in your life you need me, John Peters.'

'But you went to university. You were going to teach . . .'

She made a face. 'Didn't anyone tell you that teaching jobs are hard to find?' she said, rummaging in her bag.

'You'll probably find lots of plumbers with English degrees these days. I did an apprenticeship and went into partnership with my brother.' She laid out her tools in a neat line. 'Do you live here with your parents?' she went on.

He seated himself on the end of the bed, still staring at her. 'No. They've retired down to Bournemouth. I'm buying the house off them. I teach at the old school now . . .' He looked down, suddenly abashed. 'Pure luck I got the job I expect . . .'

He had asked her out for the first time in the spring term of that last year at school. 'There's an exhibition I'd like to see at the Hayward Gallery. I thought we might go up by train and have a meal afterwards,' he had said. He was quite the best looking boy in the school then; tall, broad-shouldered, with a shock of fair hair and was considered by the girls of the top forms the supreme catch of the season.

Jackie was stunned by the invitation. Quiet and shy by nature she would never have dared so much as hope. She did not realize then the impact her coppery hair and green eyes could have on the opposite sex. Her eyes were nearly always fixed on her thumbed copies of Keats and Chaucer, so to raise them and find the smiling figure of John Peters standing before her was a considerable shock.

The day in London was a success. She had adored the exhibition and forgetting her shyness had blossomed under his attention. By the time they were ordering the hors-d'oeuvres she was madly in love.

Her work suffered of course, but not a lot. Being in love can help with the art of unravelling Keats or the sonnets of Shakespeare. Only John didn't see it that way. She was fun and a good doubles partner at tennis. That much he did not dispute. She was the right person to take to the cricket club dance at the end of term and fitted well with his old red MG but she did not particularly inspire his work; he was studying pure maths and physics.

He never asked her to his home. She knew where it was because once or twice she had quite by chance, of course, walked the dog down Stamford Avenue. That was how she knew the immaculate front garden with the row of standard roses and the shiny blue front gate.

To celebrate the end of A levels they had gone together on a picnic in the MG. He had prepared the food, in a real hamper; chicken, salad, wine, and they had stopped by the edge of the river and spread their rug on the bank. The water was cool and gentle against her toes.

'Where will you go if you don't get into Cambridge?' she asked him, lying back lazily, her arm across her eyes to keep out the sunlight.

'Cambridge,' he replied.

'You're pretty confident,' she retorted. Her own first choice was Bristol, a million miles away from Cambridge.

'There's always the vacations,' he said softly, for the first time since she had known him, reading her mind.

But vacations had come and gone and she had not seen him again. The anguish was lessened by the new faces, new places, by lectures and by the theatre, but always somewhere in the back of her mind she had kept alive the memory of John Peters and his old red MG.

'I never thought I'd see inside this house,' she said cheerfully as she wielded her hack-saw.

'I didn't bring people home.' He was watching her, fascinated. 'It was too distracting.'

'You were a real pig, you know,' she went on, neatly lifting out the damaged piece of pipe. 'I broke my heart over you that summer we left school.'

He gave a sheepish grin. 'Me too. But I was afraid you'd come between my work and me. I was always terrified I'd run into you in the vacations. One look at you and I'd have been a gonner again.'

She sat back on her heels. 'Should I be flattered?' She had never even guessed he felt as strongly as that.

'You should. I saw you as a *femme fatale. Fatale* to my career that is.'

'As a teacher? Here!' She was incredulous.

He pulled a face. 'No. I had something a bit more exciting in mind then. Research. The States. That sort of thing.'

For a moment they stared at each other. Then she burst out laughing. 'Looks as though we both came down to earth with a bump!' she gurgled. 'Poor John. Always so impractical!'

'You're married now, I suppose,' he said after a minute.

She shook her head. 'A career girl me. And you?'

'No. No one would have me.' He was surveying the shambles around them despondently.

'Not even for your good looks and your cooking?' She was teasing him now, remembering how he had grudgingly admitted that it was he and not his mother who had put together the food for their picnics. He was, she had heard later, a notable chef. But he never washed up.

She carefully measured out the new length of pipe.

'You,' he said, retaliating at last, 'couldn't boil an egg in those days.'

'Still can't,' she said cheerfully unabashed.

She was looking for her matches. They weren't in her pockets, or her bag or her jacket. He was watching speculatively.

'Lost something?' he asked at last.

She could feel herself blushing slightly. 'Matches,' she said. 'For the blow lamp.'

'Oh. I see.' He didn't move. 'I'd have thought a really efficient plumber would have had several boxes.'

She glanced up at him under her eyelashes.

'I've a confession to make. I shouldn't really be here,' she said.

'I thought not. What are you? A secretary or something?'

For a moment she was speechless with indignation.

'No, John, I am a plumber. A real plumber with a piece of paper to prove it. The reason I shouldn't be here is because Phil and Bob don't let me go out on night jobs alone.'

'I'm glad to hear it.' He was watching her closely. 'So, how come you're here?'

'I didn't log it in the book.' She bit her lip, trying not to laugh as she saw the knowing look on his face. 'I'm willing to trade, Mr Peters,' she said softly. 'You cook me a meal and I'll fix your central heating for free. How does that sound to you.'

'Pretty good,' he said. 'I don't think I can fault that bargain.' He stood up. 'Providing that you take off that appalling cap when you're eating!'

It was five minutes later that she found him in the kitchen. He was whistling.

'John,' she said. 'You've forgotten something.'

'Oh?' He turned and looked at her enquiringly.

'Matches.'

'Oh yes, matches.' He reached a box down from the dresser. Then he put his hands behind him. 'Not included in the bargain, of course. Matches are extra.'

She stuck her tongue out at him. 'It's your central heating. I can always go away and leave you to freeze.'

He grinned. 'I'd complain to your boss. Come on. They're not too expensive. One small kiss. For old times' sake.'

She thought for a moment. 'Payment deferred till after supper?'

Nodding he held them out to her. 'Payment deferred. Though there might be a bit of interest accruing by then of course.'

She laughed. 'I'll risk it,' she said.

All You Need To Do Is Smile

Once when Celia was about eight years old, her mother had said: 'You'll never keep your boyfriends, darling, if you look as grouchy as that when they speak to you,' and she had laughed and fondly punched the boy in question on the shoulder to comfort him for her daughter's disdain. Her cousin Michael it had been, Celia thought, frowning as she probed the memory.

Strange that she should think of that now, so many years later, as she walked slowly from the post office up the village street. Her mother's voice was vivid in her ears as was the memory of her own anguished embarrassment and her burning hatred of the unfortunate Michael.

But she had been right, her tall distinguished mother; Celia hadn't been able to keep her boyfriends and now, true to form she had lost her husband as well.

'It's not your fault, Cee,' he had said ruefully as slowly he packed his cases. 'I blame myself. Something went wrong somewhere. Perhaps it would have been OK if I hadn't met Louise. We might have struggled through and made it work but now there's no point. I'm sorry.'

And he had gone.

Bruised and alone she had refused to cry, to question fate. She continued to exist; to light the autumn-bitter driftwood fires in the cottage grate, to feed the cats, to collect the mail and the groceries every week at the village post office and walk the two miles back along the saltings home. But now there were seldom any letters; the post had always been for Don. For a week or two after he had gone they had continued to come, the letters and the packets and then abruptly they had stopped almost overnight. So presumably now they all went to his new address, his and Louise's, and all his colleagues and his friends knew that he had left Celia and no longer lived in the cottage at the edge of the ocean. The post which had accumulated she put into a drawer unopened. He had left no forwarding address.

She stooped beneath the heavy rucksack full of tins and packets and eased the shopping bag from one hand to the other. Soon now the winds would come, lashing the tides higher and higher up the beach, tearing the surface sand in spindrifts from the path, hurling rain and spume against the windows. That was when in any other year they would have put up the shutters and ruefully left their home for the worst three months or so of the year and gone to stay with Celia's mother in the town. But not this year. Celia was not going to tell her mother that Don had left her. She deliberately stopped her weekly phone call from the post office and wrote instead, a stilted, hearty little note which she knew would fool no one, and she posted it in the little box in the pebble wall beneath the shop window before turning for home.

Already it was growing dark and grey clouds were scudding in across the sea, trailing icy showers in their wake. Behind her the young man who had been buying stamps in the post office came out and banged the door, pulling the collar of his jacket round his ears before setting off after her up the street. His boots rang on the stone echoing beneath the blank walls of the cottages. The holiday-makers had gone now and most of them were empty. The fishermen lived further back in the lanes and alleys out of reach of the corroding air of the sea.

Celia hesitated, conscious suddenly of the hurrying steps behind her.

'Excuse me?'

She stopped and looked back. He had pleasant wavy hair and a shy grin which reminded her of someone: Michael. Of course, he was like cousin Michael who had complimented her on her pink dress all those years ago and been so rudely rebuffed. That's why the memory had returned unbidden. She smiled uncertainly. 'Can I help you?'

He grinned, pushing the fair hair out of his eyes as the first cold shower swept over them.

'I hope I can help you actually. Can I carry something? It is Celia Scott isn't it? I'm Brian Fraser, a friend of Don's. Did he tell you?' He was too busy lifting the pack from her shoulders to notice the smile freezing on her lips.

'Did he send you?' She stayed turned away from him, gazing out across the salt grass towards the sea.

'Send me? No, I haven't seen him in years actually. I thought I'd surprise him. How is he?'

She began walking again. Her shoulders straight now, not flinching as the rain misted across her face. The terns were wheeling and crying over the tide beside them. Brian walked beside her, the heavy bag swinging easily from one shoulder. Glancing at her he grinned.

'It's some place you've chosen to live! Trust Don to find a hide-out like this.'

She forced herself to smile. 'We love it here.' She had to tell him, make him turn back, send him away.

She walked on. 'It's a long way from the station. Did you take a cab?'

He grinned. 'I hitched. Not affluent enough for anything else I'm afraid. Actually,' he stopped and faced her, his face suddenly troubled. 'Actually I'm on the scrounge. I wondered if you and Don might be able to put me up for a few days and . . .' He looked down at his scuffed canvas shoes. 'It's a long story,' he added quietly.

A squall of wind grabbed the rain and flung it at them threateningly, moaning across the shore line. Celia shivered. The stove would have gone out and the cats would be huddling disconsolately by it, waiting for her to come and light it, waiting for her to talk to them. She talked to them a lot now; there was no one else to talk to.

She grinned at Brian, wiping the streaming rain from her eyes. "Course you can stay. Come on. Let's hurry.'

He lit the stove and stacked away her tins and took Linnaeus on his knee and drank hot soup as the shutters rattled and the lamp smoked. Then he looked at her and smiled. 'Where's Don?'

'Not here.'

'I can see that. Where is he?'

She shrugged. 'He left me for another woman. It's the oldest story in the book.'

'Do you care?'

She opened her mouth to protest, to assure him, to emphasize her love and then she stopped, watching the black paws stretch and flex on the rough denim on his knees. 'He likes you,' she said irrelevantly. 'He won't go to many people.'

Brian went on staring at her and she knew she had to answer. 'I'm numb without him,' she said at last.

His long gentle fingers were playing with the fur behind the cat's ears. 'You can't stay here on your own surely.'

'I have Linnaeus and Kizzy.' She smiled wistfully. 'I talk to them. And then I have my painting.'

He did not turn to look at the half-finished seascape on the easel. 'You're quite famous, I believe.' He did not make the statement sound sarcastic. He was stating a fact.

'I've had a few exhibitions,' she replied, guarded.

'And Don was still studying the seaweeds and the crabs?'

She smiled for the first time since they had seated themselves beside the stove. 'As usual. So this place suited us both.'

'Where has he gone, do you know?'

She shook her head. 'Her name is Louise.'

He stood up then, putting the cat down in his place on the chair, went over to the easel and stood looking at the painting on it. For a long time he said nothing then he turned, his eyes narrowed. 'Have you touched a brush since Don left?'

She could feel herself colouring. She bent and fed some sticks into the stove. 'I've done some sketching,' she said at last, defensively.

She watched as he walked around the room, turning canvases to face him, flipping over the sketches in the portfolio under a chair.

'You said you'd explain what you were doing here,' she said at last into the silence. Her voice was brusquer than she intended.

He straightened up abruptly. 'You're entitled to that.' He fumbled in the front pocket of his jeans and brought out a flattened pack of cigarettes. He did not offer her one. 'I would rather have told Don,' he said after a pause, his back to the shuttered window.

'Well, you'll have to make do with me.'

'I knew Don at college.' He struck a match and held it out for a moment, staring, waiting for the flame to steady. 'We were good friends once. I liked him.'

'And since?' She was watching him closely.

'Since, he went his way and I went mine. He went on to do a doctorate and became an expert on seaweed, I became a drifter.'

'You must have kept in touch, to have known about this place.'

He shook his head, absently putting the spent match back in the box. 'Someone gave me the address a year or so back; I never followed it up.'

'Till now.'

'Till now.' There was a long silence. 'I'm in trouble, Celia.'

'I thought perhaps you were,' she said softly. 'What sort?'

For a moment she didn't think he was going to answer. He threw the cigarette unsmoked into the stove and went back to perch on the edge of his chair. Behind him Linnaeus began to purr.

'Shall we say I borrowed some money? I need to pay it back.'

Celia stared at him, her stomach tightening. 'How much?'

'A hundred quid.'

She closed her eyes, feeling the heat from the stove beating against the lids. Don would have given it to him, would have shrugged and cursed him and given it to him without any questions. But Don was not here and she had no money.

When she opened her eyes he was looking at her. He smiled. 'No, Celia, I couldn't take it from you anyway. Don't worry. I'll think of something. I usually do.'

He was still like Michael. The hair, the smile, that disarming, gentle smile. 'Are the police after you?'

'I don't know. I shouldn't think so. It wasn't quite that bad. I didn't rob a bank or anything. If I had I hope I would have done a bit better than a hundred lousy quid.'

She stood up jerkily and picked up the coffee pot which stood on the stove. 'They would never find you here. No one would.' She swung round to face him. 'Don't tell me any more, Brian. I don't want to know about it.'

He reached down at his feet for his mug and held it out to her to refill. 'I'll go. If you want me to.'

She straightened up and stared stiffly past him at the shuttered window, listening to the scream of the wind, the crash of the waves against the sea wall beyond the saltings. There wasn't another human being for two or three miles.

'No. I'd like you to stay.'

Kizzy liked him, purring and flirting her tail as she wove intricate patterns around his ankles.

'I like coquettish females,' he said laughing as he bent to stroke her and Celia, watching, felt a sharp pang of jealousy.

'Most men do,' she said, unconscious of the longing in her voice.

He glanced up. 'You don't find it easy, talking to men, do you?' It wasn't a question.

She shrugged. 'Is that how it seems to you?'

'That's how it seems.' He grinned. 'We're only people, you know.'

She knew. Only too well. 'You'll never keep your boy-friends, darling,' the phrase came back again echoing in her head, the words pounding against her skull. Her mother had kept her boyfriends all right, after her father had died, flirting, giggling, simpering at them, hiding her brain, her talent, her ability. Anything to keep her escorts attentive, producing even now a new one every winter for her and Don's inspection. Celia at the age of seven had vowed never to be like that. She would giggle and flirt for no man. Ever. And she glared at Kizzy who had closed her eyes in ecstasy as she was tickled under her chin.

'I expect I drove Don away,' she said suddenly, her eyes meeting his in defiance.

And it was then, amazingly, that he had kissed her lightly on the mouth, his hand on the point of her chin, his eyes open and laughing. 'I doubt if you did,' he said softly. 'All you need to do is smile occasionally. I've seen you do it. I know.'

Perhaps it was the fact that he was not perfect which gave her the confidence she needed. She saw him not as a male, to be challenged and defied, but as someone who needed her help. As he himself had said he was, after all, only people.

She relaxed and unchallenging and unchallenged she did, almost without realizing it, begin to smile. The wind did not seem so cold now with someone else to share the blaze from the wood stove and she ceased brooding about Don, concentrating instead at last upon the beauty of the present, not the disasters of the past. Brian taught her that.

'Treasure what was good, forget what was bad,' he said, as together they watched an aquamarine sunset. 'That way, when he comes back you'll have a future together; something to build on. Otherwise you'll only destroy and tear down what is left.'

'When he comes back?' she turned and looked at him, her face illuminated by the pale light from the sky.

'When. If.' He was still trying to sound impersonal. 'Take what comes as it comes, Celia, and draw on it. Use it to make you strong.' He reached for her hand and held it and suddenly he could not pretend indifference any more. 'You know what I want. I'm hoping he never comes back.'

And he kissed her again.

*

Was it months or was it only weeks he stayed with her? She lost count in her new strange happiness, pouring out her confidence on canvas after canvas, not thinking at all of the decision she might have to make if Don returned. For the time being there was no word from him and that was enough. She no longer thought of him as her husband. Perhaps she never had, properly. Only now, for the first time in her life, was her whole being centred around a man. And it was not humiliating or servile. It was fulfilling. She felt complete at last.

Brian would stand and watch her at her easel, studying the fluent lines of her body as she wielded her brush or the palette knife, smiling slightly at her unconscious beauty, realizing that against all the rules – his rules – he had begun to love her, and as she sensed his eyes on her and looked up he would exchange with her a quiet smile before turning away to the stove or the cats, not wanting to distract her.

But he knew it could not last. He had watched the emergence from her shell, felt her relax and bloom beneath his hands; he realized her new dependence on him and he knew he could not allow it to continue. His own conscience was too stern. He had no right in her house, no brief to give her advice when his own life was such a mess.

'How long will it take you to finish that painting, Celia?' He was leaning against the door, feeling the buffet of the wind against his shoulder through the wood. He aimed the ash from his cigarette at the stove, frowning.

'A week perhaps. I don't know.' She did not look up as she spoke, squinting at the canvas, her thin face framed by its tangle of ash-blonde hair. Brian forced himself to look away.

'As quick as that?' Bleakness swept over him for he knew this painting would be the last he watched. He bent to pick Kizzy up from her nest in the chair and buried his face in her fur.

'You're going, aren't you?' Her quiet voice behind him made him swing round. He looked into her eyes, the cat still in his arms.

'Sometime. Yes.'

She held his gaze for a moment. Almost, but not quite, she heard her mother's voice but the pain in his face was too plain. This time she understood. She smiled and held out her hand. Her fingers met silky black fur and secure against his chest Kizzy began to purr.

Three days later he was gone.

She awoke to find the pillow next to her cold, the kitchen door swinging gently in the icy sunshine. The glare from the crystalline sea hid the path across the saltings, but somehow she knew he was already long out of sight.

For a long time she stood there clutching her towelling robe around her in the cold wind, then, slowly she turned back inside and closed the door. But the house wasn't empty as it had been when Don had left. It was still warm and welcoming and full of happy memories, and bereft as she was she knew she could continue with her painting and her life, for this time she had not driven anyone away.

She found his note pinned to her easel:

I wanted to stay for ever. You know why I couldn't. When I've settled my debts I'll come back to see you. Then if you're still alone and you want me, all you need to do is smile.

The Bath – A Summer Ghost Story

In the long, narrow back garden behind the house the grass they had so carefully tended through the spring was rapidly turning, beneath the children's feet, back to the dust from which it came. Cathy's anxious watering, walking up and down with a long-spouted can, refilled eight solemn times from the tap in the kitchen, did nothing but turn the dust momentarily into little swirling eddies which promptly vanished. If only they could use a hose pipe, but they had been banned until further notice. It hadn't rained for five weeks.

She turned from the kitchen window with a sigh. Ben and Sarah were occupied at least. Perhaps she could snatch a cup of coffee and five minutes with the paper before the children's onslaught resumed.

The crash outside in the street made her leap to her feet. A huge lorry had backed up the cul-de-sac of Edwardian terraced houses and deposited an enormous yellow skip almost outside their front door. She stared at it, watching mesmerized as the man uncoupled the heavy chains. Behind her two small heads pushed against the front window beside her, noses flattened against the glass.

'We heard the noise from the garden, Mum.' Ben's eyes were shining. 'Is it ours?'

Cathy was indignant. 'No. It's not ours.'

It was the new neighbours'. Liz knocked on the door half an hour later and introduced herself.

'I am sorry about the skip.' She seemed genuinely embarrassed. 'When I ordered it, I had no idea it would be bigger than the house!' She ran her fingers through a shock of short brown hair. 'It's only for a couple of days – while we gut the place.'

Cathy shooed away the children and offered her a cold drink. 'Is the house in a bad state? Ours was already more or less modernized when we moved in. We were lucky.'

Liz drained the glass of orange with apparent enjoyment. 'The place is a tip. I doubt if it has been touched since it was built. I only hope we haven't taken on too much!' She gazed reflectively into the empty glass. 'Come and see what we're doing if you like.'

One look at her children's faces told Cathy such an invitation could not be missed.

They told Tony about it later. 'There were still gas lamps on the walls, Dad. No electricity. Not anywhere. I didn't know there were houses without electricity!' Ben, a true child of the twentieth century, had been shocked speechless by the thought of there being nowhere to plug in the TV.

'You should have seen it, Tony.' Cathy had loved it. 'It was like walking into the past. Oh, it was dirty and everything, but the detail – the stained glass, the carved wood, the ornate shades on the gas lamps. It's a crime it's all going to be thrown away. There was the most wonderful old bath with wrought iron scrolling on it and beautiful ornate legs.'

'Sounds like you, my love.' Tony smiled at her fondly. 'Shall I take a turn with the watering can, while you put the kids to bed?'

Cathy cringed. A part-time feminist – part-time

between taking the children back and forth to playschool and cooking and cleaning – she had taught herself like so many of her friends to loathe what she considered sexist remarks. 'No, my love. You take a turn putting the kids to bed. Then you can roll up your trousers and show me your legs.'

'OK, sorry. Point taken. It was a joke.' No longer upset when his attempted compliments were rejected, Tony raised his hands in rueful surrender.

Two days later, when the bath appeared in the skip, Cathy could bear it no more. She went next door.

'You want it?' Liz looked at her amazed. 'You want that old bath?'

'I'll buy it from you.'

'No, no. We've thrown it out. You can have it and welcome. Where would you like it?' Jim, Liz's man, was vastly amused. 'I'll get our builders to put it round in your garden, shall I?'

Solemnly the huge iron bath was marched in through the front door, across the living room, through the kitchen and out of the back door into the hot dusty garden. They left it, standing forlornly on what passed for a terrace outside the kitchen window. Then Cathy rang Tony at work. 'I know you'll think I am quite mad, but . . .'

When he had stopped laughing, he told her she was, quite mad. 'You don't seriously want it installed?'

'I do, Tony. Please. After all there is room. The bathroom is big enough.'

'Cathy, you are out of your mind. We have a beautiful modern bath! And it matches the basin. It matches the loo for that matter.'

'The loo is next door,' Cathy retorted, 'so it hardly matters what colour that is. Anyway, I intend to paint the bath. It will match as well as the old one, I promise. Please, Tony. You wait till you see it. It will be magnificent.'

As she hung up she knew she had slipped disastrously down the scale in their relationship. To want the old bath was an illogical 'feminine' act. She had to convince Tony of its interior design possibilities or her personal five year battle for female equality would be lost on a momentary impulse.

The plumber they called to install it thought she was mad as well. As did the children. 'Mum, it's horrible! It's dirty and all black and grey at the bottom, and YUKKY!' Sarah was in no doubt at all how she felt about it. 'I will not sit down in it. I will NOT!'

Cathy was beginning to feel rather desperate. Family revulsion and ridicule were all very well in small quantities, but in such unanimity they were beginning to worry her. Doggedly she worked at the bathroom, throwing open the windows to the hot July night as she painted the outside of the bath a beautiful olive green to blend with what was left of the modern suite and resurfaced the pitted, stained inside. The result was dramatic and very effective. Pleased with herself, she called Tony and the children for an inspection. They were all watching TV and were not too keen on leaving their programme. With much protesting they solemnly trooped upstairs and crowded into the bathroom.

'Not bad,' Ben was grudging. 'At least it's bigger than the old bath.' The little boy had to stand on tiptoe to see over the edge.

'It's twice as big, you dope.' Cathy ruffled his hair affectionately. 'You'll be able to swim in that! But not yet. We've got to let the enamel dry.'

'I must say, they built man-size baths in those days!' Tony said with reluctant admiration. 'Even I will be able to stretch out full length in that! No more excuses about dirty knees because they never get under the water.' He grinned. 'We're not getting a Victorian loo next, by any chance?'

She shook her head. 'Pretty curtains, and perhaps a mirror from the junk shop on the corner – they've got one there which would be just right. He's had it standing out on the pavement for days; it's not expensive.' She glanced sheepishly at her husband. 'Old pine would be perfect, wouldn't it?'

'I dare say.' Tony frowned. 'But we're not made of money, love . . .'

She bought it, guiltily, after knocking the price down by a fiver, comforting herself with the thought that she would soon be working again. The mirror was perfect. Staring into it, she could see the whole bathroom behind her. The room had once been a bedroom so it was large; there was room for a chair and the old chest she had stripped the year before down to the warm soft honey-coloured wood. The new curtains blew gently in the hot breeze from the garden. From the trees at the bottom of the road she could hear the gentle moaning of a wood pigeon. It was very, very hot. The house was quiet. The children had gone out to play and Tony was at work.

Cautiously she touched the new enamel of the bath with her finger. It felt hard and cold. Impulsively she put in the enormous brass plug and turned on the taps. Dragging off her T-shirt and jeans she pitched them into the straw clothes basket, followed by her bra and pants. The draught from the window was cool on her skin as she pinned her hair up on top of her head. A mist of steam shaded the mirror and she rubbed it absentmindedly with her fingers as she reached for the bath crystals Liz and Jim next door had given her. 'As a sort of launching present,' Jim had said with a grin. They still thought her mad, although they had been in to admire the bath.

Behind her there was a shadowy disturbance somewhere in the mirror. She stared into the glass, puzzled. Some of the silvering had gone and parts of the image were indistinct and blurred, but there it was again – a light movement behind her in the room. She turned. There was nothing there. Only the gentle whirl of steam and the glittering patterns of water. Guiltily she turned off the taps. It would be wrong to try and fill such a big bath with the water shortage so bad.

She lay there a long time, luxuriating in the these days unaccustomed luxury of a daytime bath, then slowly she climbed out and dried herself and, dropping the towel on the carpet, began to rub some lotion lazily over her body.

As she balanced one toe on the chair, stroking the lotion up her legs she suddenly had the strangest feeling that she was being watched. She spun round, grabbing the towel, holding it tightly over her breasts, but there was no one there – only the cheerfully gurgling water spiralling out of the plug hole and, outside the window, the pigeon still crooning in the heat of the afternoon. She told herself she was a fool and, wrapping the towel round her, ran through into the bedroom to dress.

In the end the children loved the bath. There was room for both of them at once, together with Ben's fleet and they could still re-enact the Battle of Trafalgar with sound effects. Tony grinned at his wife as they stood for a moment listening in the kitchen. 'You sit down and have a cold drink. I'll sort them out.'

He disappeared upstairs and was still missing half an hour later. The sound effects had if anything worsened. Cathy smiled. The bath was obviously a success.

At half past ten that night Tony went upstairs yawning, while Cathy sat watching the end of the film. After it had finished she sat for a while on her own, relishing the silence and the cool. Upstairs the house was unbearably hot. When at last she followed him up, the light in the bedroom was already off and she could hear the gentle sound of snoring.

She smiled sadly. They were often too tired to make love these days.

She ran a cool, shallow bath while she undressed and stood naked while she brushed her teeth. Outside the closed curtains the night was very still.

The appreciative chuckle was almost drowned by the sound of running water. Spitting out the last of the toothpaste she rinsed out her mouth. 'I thought you were asleep,' she said over her shoulder. 'I'm glad you're not.' She turned, expecting to see Tony. The room was empty. She peered into the bedroom. He was exactly as she had left him, snoring.

Puzzled and disappointed she went back into the bathroom. She was obviously hearing things.

She was vacuuming in the bedroom next day when she smelt the pomade. The rich, spicy scent was drifting into the room from the bathroom next door. She sniffed appreciatively, then, puzzled by its source, she switched off the cleaner and looked into the bathroom. As always in the heat the window was flung wide. The room felt steamy as if someone had just had a bath and the exotic smell was very strong. She stared round, feeling the little hairs on the back of her neck stirring slightly. Then a shriek from one of the children downstairs distracted her and she turned away. When she came back, crisis over, half an hour later, the smell had gone.

That night she and Tony were going out. The children had refused to go to bed; the baby sitter was late and long after they were supposed to have left she was still desperately putting on some make up. She was leaning towards the mirror in the bathroom, squinting slightly as she stroked the mascara onto her lashes, when she caught sight of a movement out of the corner of her eye. The room seemed steamy and hot and faintly she could smell it again. The sweet spicy smell. She peered harder and her eyes widened in astonishment. Someone was in the bath. In the mirror she could see the water swirling around his middle, thick with suds. He was lying back watching her, an expression of quizzical amusement on his face. For a split second she saw him, saw the handsome, heavy-set face, the mutton chop whiskers, the wavy chestnut hair, the broad shoulders, the slightly plump hairy chest, then he was gone. She spun round with a gasp, staring into the bath. It was empty. She swallowed hard, trying to calm herself, but her heart was hammering furiously somewhere under her ribs. Cautiously she stepped towards it. She reached out and ran her fingers over the enamel. It was cold.

'Come on, Cathy, we're going to be late.' Tony appeared in the doorway. 'For God's sake, you're not even dressed!'

She stared at him blankly then without a word she turned back to the mirror. As she hastily finished her make up, the bath behind her remained bleakly cold.

She didn't say a word to anyone. In retrospect she wasn't afraid. She was really quite amused. Half of her – the rational half – knew she must have imagined him and yet – the smell of his hair oil, the steam, the gentle sound of water dripping into the deep, warm suds. They were so real! Real enough to stop her wandering round the upstairs with no clothes on! She would grab her bath robe and knot it firmly round her waist before going into the bathroom. When she actually had a bath it was different. She put in the plug and filled the bath, almost daring him to appear. But she knew he wouldn't. As she climbed into the two inches of water they were now allowed in the tenth week of the drought she knew she was alone. It was when she had her back to it, thinking about something else, glancing absent-mindedly into the mirror that she saw him.

But he only came when she was naked.

Testing him, half daring, half afraid she left her towelling robe on the bedroom floor and walked nude into the bathroom. She could feel herself self-consciously holding in her stomach and pushing back her shoulders, walking with a studied grace she had no time for in her real downstairs life. She did not even glance at the bath. Holding her breath she went and stood at the window, looking out across the parched gardens, feeling the clammy, thundery heat touching her skin.

It took a moment to pluck up the courage to look at last into the mirror.

He was there. She could see the clouds of steam, smell the soap, the spice, hear the splashing of water as he lifted a sponge and thoughtfully squeezed it over his broad chest.

Forcing herself to stand still she stared into the mirror until she caught his eye. He smiled and raised an eyebrow appreciatively and then, slowly, he winked. When she turned he had gone.

'I wish we knew something about the history of these old houses,' she said to Liz a few days later.

Liz nodded. They were side by side in her house stripping wallpaper on the landing. 'I do know something about ours, actually,' she said. 'It belonged to Ned Basset. He was a famous music-hall artist. "A notorious rake and a ladies' man", as that idiot at the house agents described him. I'm glad I never knew him. He sounds exactly the type of man I should detest.'

'A male chauvinist pig of the worst kind, no doubt.' Cathy found herself smiling as she agreed. 'Ned Basset,' she echoed after a moment. 'So that was his name.'

'Why, do you know something about him?' Liz ripped a strip of torn wallpaper off, screwing up her face at the dust.

'No.' Cathy threw down her scraper. 'Nothing at all.'

She didn't tell Liz about the bath. She didn't tell anyone. She knew Tony hadn't seen him; nor, she was certain, had the children. He was her secret. Her admirer. Perhaps he was her fantasy.

Was that it? Was he just a product of her imagination? The creation of a woman who had been conditioned by the age she lived in to reject compliments from men as sexist and unwelcome when deep down inside she craved them? Without realizing it she looked at Tony and smiled. That night they made love for the first time in weeks.

The next day after she had taken the children to play-school she came back and walked upstairs to the bathroom. She stood looking down at the bath. It was cold and empty. The enamel was dry. The room was just as usual, the children's toothbrushes lying on the basin, a streak of gaudy striped toothpaste decorating the soap, a wad of hairs in the plug hole, flecks of shaving soap on the mirror behind it, a pile of discarded clothes on the carpet. A towel lay near them, still damp, tangled and already a little smelly. Cathy felt a wave of depression sweep over her. Oh yes, she needed a fantasy. What woman didn't?

But she didn't want him to be a fantasy. That would be a weakness on her part; an admission of defeat. She wanted him to be real.

There was only one way to find out the truth.

Liz laughed. 'It's crazy, isn't it? We throw out that bath, and you make it so nice that you can invite people to come along and try it!'

'Only while your new bathroom is still disconnected,' Cathy said, all innocence. 'I thought it would be a change from the plastic bowl you were telling me about!' She had tidied the bathroom, laid out fresh towels, put a small bowl of roses on the windowsill.

Of course, it might not work. He never appeared when she was actually taking a bath, but sometimes afterwards, when she was drying herself . . .

And Liz did have, when one came to think about it, a

rather buxom figure beneath her habitual overalls. The kind of figure a rake and a ladies' man might appreciate. If he were real . . .

Liz took her time. Cathy could hear her singing cheerfully. There was a lot of splashing and afterwards the sound of water running away. Then there was a long, long silence.

When she reappeared Cathy looked at her hard. 'Was everything all right?' she asked as casually as she could.

'Fine.' Liz smiled. 'But what on earth was that fantastic exotic smell up there as I was getting dry?'

'Ah,' said Cathy with a smile. 'I've been wondering that myself . . .'

A Private Ceremony

She had slept in the room for nearly three weeks before she noticed that one strip of wallpaper was upside down. A spider showed it to her.

Lying gazing at the wall she saw the sunlight in the fine lace web. Behind it a rose hung stem upwards, its petals drooping. Lazily her eye followed to see leaves and buds and further blooms suspended as though by invisible wire over the creamy void. It hurt her to see the flowers thus. It seemed incongruous and cruel; a stroke of fate which left them for ever vertiginous, outcasts among their fellows on the wall.

Now she could no longer come into the room without her eyes immediately straying to this corner by the window. When someone moved the spider's web she was really very angry. It seemed the flowers' only redemption that they had been selected by the spider as the nearest thing to nature in the room. Now nothing distinguished them any more, save their own oddity.

Sitting at her mirror, brushing out her long hair, she heard again in her head the voice which haunted.

'The trouble with Samantha is of course that she is a teeny bit different from the rest of us, haven't you noticed?'

Her eyes as she gazed at them were a pure expressionless blue. They saw much. The silver-backed hairbrush made her arm ache. It was too heavy. But she kept up the endless strokes, listening to the crackle, watching the fine floating strands as her hair took on a life of its own around her head.

'Never, but *never*, brush your hair a hundred times, darling. It's death, positively death, and *so* Victorian.' She heard in her head the voice of the posturing little man who tended her hair and she brushed on harder than ever. This hairbrush had been made to brush hair a hundred strokes. It would be mortified if used to do less. When she had finished her hair then she would polish the brush. It seemed only fair.

In the mirror, in the corner where the silvering had gone in tiny freckles, she could see the angle of the room behind her. The casement window stood wide and she could see a fine mist of rain drifting over the garden below. The window still shone with wet and the pale green carpet beneath it darkened slowly as it grew damp. She could smell the grateful earth as its fragrance rose up in response to the rain.

Her roses, the upside down roses, could never smell like roses. But then they would never rot and grow black and die either.

She slammed her silver brush down on the dressing table glass and reached to clasp a bracelet around her slim wrist. Flinging off her dressing gown she stood naked on the carpet, throwing back her head and feeling the silky weight of her hair on her shoulders. It was strange that one was not allowed to appear naked before the world, even when one knew that one was beautiful.

She stood before the open window and felt the icy mist of rain on her warm skin.

A man stood outside in the garden, in the rain, his hair plastered blackly to his head, his tweed jacket heavy with moisture. He was standing looking up at her, not noticing the rain any more.

She smiled down at him and raised her hand. Then she moved away from the window and zipped herself dreamily into gold and embroidered chiffon. The spider was spinning again, she noticed suddenly, slightly further down the corner but still carefully, precisely, on the misplaced wallpaper. She watched fascinated.

She knew the man in the rain. In less than three weeks he would be her husband. His ring was on her finger; his kisses in her hair. Was it those she had been trying so hard to brush away?

The moth, its delicate finely traced velvet wings whirring ecstatically, stood no chance. Samantha put out her hand to ward it off, but she stayed the gesture in mid air, arrested by the sight of the diamond ring on her finger. It mesmerized her with its rainbow prisms and when she looked again the moth was caught. The spider's paralysing jaws were ready, and the straitjacket of fine spun silk. The spider embraced its victim tenderly, lost in caressing the silky fur on the tiny quivering body. How quickly beauty and freedom and life itself were lost.

She turned away, revolted and suddenly afraid.

The days passed. Showers of rain swept the gardens and terraces. From time to time she saw the man again standing beneath her window. In the corner the web was deserted, the moth no more than a frail dust caught in the still-sticky threads. The spider had gone.

Now when she stood at the window she kept her dressing gown on, clutching it to her, shivering.

Then she left the house in a haze of goodbyes. When she returned she would be its daughter. The web would have closed around her and the time for dreams would have gone.

In the taxi she looked into the mirror in her powder compact and saw that the haunted blue still shadowed her eyes. Where was their expression and their life? Her soul was shut down, secret, protected. It must be kept separate now or he would possess it as he must possess her.

She could not understand, suddenly, why she was afraid now. She recognized him as her friend. He was kind and gentle. He had not tried to rush her, had carefully controlled his own swelling waves of emotion. He recognized her fragility. He would treasure and protect her as a piece of fine porcelain. Again the voice spoke in her head:

'Samantha is a teeny bit different from the rest of us . . .'

'I'm not, I'm not,' she screamed silently. 'I am the same. I feel, I need, I fear. But I am trapped within myself. I am Rapunzel within the tower. He stands in the garden, at the foot of the wall, but he will not climb. He does not know that I have let the ladder fall. He strokes my golden hair, but he does not grip it, does not climb.'

The train carried her back to London where the rain smelt of soot and the plane trees wept in their concrete prisons, here and there their roots breaking free of tarmac and flagstone only to shrivel and waste in the dead air.

Her flat was dark and empty, a refuge she had always thought, for her soul. But her soul would not be comforted. It sought a mystic union now and would be satisfied with nothing less. Here where the wallpaper was immaculate, where no spiders dared to defile, where no mists of rain could spatter through the window glass, she had built for herself a temple of virginity. And she knew now what must be done. She picked up the telephone and dialled his number.

'Meet me at the station,' she said. Her voice was smiling. This time she needed no luggage; no gold bangles; no chiffon. No hairbrush save the wind.

He did not understand. He thought she had forgotten something. Never before had he seen her smile like this. His heart grew warm as he met her eyes. Now, she saw, he understood at last.

They drove up onto the moor. Still the rain surrounded them, misting the windows of the car, soaking the bracken and heather, filling the upturned bells of tiny flowers till they hung their heads beneath the weight of the water, and spilt it, nectar-like upon the ground.

Once more she felt the weight of her hair on her shoulders, the cold rain upon her warm body. She saw in his face delight and hope as she turned to him, her arms outstretched, at one with the soft wet earth, the grass and the heather. She felt his hand gently, hesitatingly on her golden hair.

Her eyes as she scanned them anxiously in her mirror in the train going home had a new depth of violet in the iris. She tore open the windows of the flat, bought armfuls of roses and trimmed her pure white wedding dress with blue.

She took her hair, tangled from the wind and heather, to be restyled and giggled as the voice said, 'But darling, the wind is death, positively death.' The posturing little man wanted her to wear her veil, but now she insisted on a garland of rose buds, entwined with the white moorland heather.

In the church the carol of gladness soared up into the vaulting and her heart with it. With him at her side and their own vows already made this formal binding no longer held any terror. It blessed the bond they had pledged in the rain with public ceremony. Her eyes and his held one another and knew their own secrets.

As she changed in the room with the rose wallpaper she drew apart from her attendants. While they fussed and gossiped over tulle and silver she looked for a new web. There was none on the wall, but outside, where a watery sun shone on marquee and grass, she saw in the angle of the window, a new, more delicate web, hung with diamond raindrops. It had ensnared nothing but a wisp of thistledown.

Satisfied, she returned to the voices. Let them say what they will, she and he were one; he did not find her different. He understood the way she thought. He had not laughed when she told him about the spider and the roses, but caressed her hair with his lips, wondering and gentle. Sympathetic to her needs he had made her glad by cancelling secretly the tickets for the south of France, people and society, and planning instead for a continuation of their private ceremony.

Soon, entertaining done and friendship appeased, they would leave for the far, empty north. Among the mountains the deep, reflective lochs and the purple heather they would find one another again. There they would nurture too the first foetal moments of the child she knew would be conceived. This room, she vowed, would be its nursery.

The Green Leaves of Summer

Grass the colour of young beech leaves stood high in the valley when the young man came to Cae Coch. Megan, her eyes blue with the freshness of forget-me-nots, would go quietly through the wood, down the way the brook went and peer through the hazel brakes to see him. He was tall and his skin was pale. She had never seen a man with pale skin before and her eyes rounded at the whiteness of it. The men of the hills had their faces reddened by the wind and tanned, young, into coarse leather. This man was smooth and she imagined his skin silky and cool like the keys of Dai Morgan's new piano.

Each morning Jeff would come out of his grandmother Lewis's cottage and sniff the sweet air with disbelief. After a city childhood and youth he had not dreamed such air could exist. He sometimes sensed the eyes watching from the wood beyond the brook and would peer into the undergrowth, wondering what small animal was hidden there. Never did he see a movement, save where the wind stroked the leaves and made them dance.

'Jeff, his name is,' Megan whispered to herself as she watched him. Raymond the Post had told her mother that, winking, as he put the parcel from Swansea on the scrubbed wooden table.

Today, as she watched, Jeff was wearing a dark green jersey, warm and soft. He must be cold inside himself she thought, to need the warmth of lambswool in the summer sun. She crouched lower and took a step forward.

It was shy she was or she could have taken eggs to Cae Coch, or warm bread from her mother's oven. She did gather roses once from the mossy ramblers on the back wall and tried to dare to take them down to the old lady, but then she gave them instead to her mother.

Often she sat with her books in the warmed stones of the ruined farm over the valley. It was quiet there. She felt secure, the crumbling wall with its curtain of ivy at her back. She did not look up as the shadows of the clouds chased one another over the hillside and a buzzard soared, mewing, out across the empty air.

The pony's hoofbeats must have been muffled by the grass for when he spoke she dropped her book with the fright of it.

'Hello,' he said. 'What a lovely place to read.'

The ride in the wind and sun had whipped a delicate shade of rose into his ivory cheeks.

Megan felt her hands begin to shake. Stupid it was when she had dreamed so often he would speak to her.

'May I sit with you for a moment to rest the pony?' His eyes were dark and secret like the eyes of the romany folk over by the town. Without waiting for her answer he lifted a long leg easily over the pommel of the saddle and slid to the ground. The pony dropped its nose to the sweet grass and blew gustily. 'Are you Megan?' he asked, sitting next to her.

She nodded shyly. 'How did you know my name?'

'Raymond the Post told me.' He smiled. 'I'm staying here for a few months' convalescence. I've been ill.'

'Are you better?' Her enormous blue eyes were turned to gaze at him, full of sympathy and concern.

'Much, thank you. The air is so good I'm eating like a horse now.' They both turned as the pony tore up a mouthful of weeds and stood champing them on her bit. Then they laughed.

'Is it buttercups you eat then?' she asked quietly.

'Even buttercups.' Unnoticing he had put his hand on hers. It was warm and dry and friendly. Without speaking they both gazed out across the valley towards the distant mountains to the west.

'My parents are coming over next weekend. You and your mother must come down and see them.' He looked down at the glossy curls of the girl beside him. 'I dare say your mother knew my mother when they were children.'

'Mam never said.' She screwed up her nose to think. 'She goes to Cae Coch sometimes, for a chat like, but she never said.'

There was silence again. Then he rose and went to take the pony's rein. 'Will you walk with me a little way, back to the stables?'

She shook her head, suddenly shy again and took up her book. 'I'll stay here a while if you don't mind, to read a bit.'

He shrugged and smiled and mounted the pony which laid back its ears and took a last defiant mouthful of buttercups. The small hooves made no sound on the grass as he went.

'Oh yes, I knew Sarah Ann,' her mother said thumping the dough with a floury hand. 'A fine madam she was. Got into trouble she did with one of the Jones boys from Llangoed, then she went to Birmingham. I never heard from her after that. Granny Lewis never talks about her and I never asked.'

'Will you go down there Saturday and see her?' Megan ran her finger round the edge of the jam pot on the table and licked it delicately.

'Take your hands away, girl.' Her mother slapped at her, scattering flour. 'Indeed I will not. I doubt if I've anything to say to Sarah Ann Lewis after all these years. And you'll not talk to that boy again, Megan. Like mother, like son, no doubt.' She snorted and turned the dough again, punching it.

For three days Megan took her books to the ruin, sitting, the pages blowing on her knees, her eyes fixed on the track at the edge of the wood. But Jeff never came. The fourth day she crept down the wood to the back of Cae Coch and waited to see him come out and breathe the fresh air.

A car was parked in the yard. When he came out there was a girl with him. She was tall and slim and had stylishly cut red hair. Megan could hear the sound of her laughter from across the brook. It was English laughter: strident, confident, and as she laughed the girl slipped her arm through Jeff's and clung to him possessively. Megan, in spite of herself, looked down at her own thin brown hands. She could almost feel the warm touch of Jeff's fingers again.

That girl would wear nail varnish and have smooth oval nails without a crack. Megan knew that. Her jeans were elegantly cut and her shirt immaculate.

Jess glanced up at the trees as though he felt the eyes watching him again, but already Megan had slipped back into the dark of the wood, her sandals making no sound on the leaf mould beneath thc trees.

She went back to her books, and back after two days of rain to the ruins of the farm. She sat on the stone wall to be out of the damp and wrapped herself tightly in her jacket against the wind.

Although she did not watch for him any more she knew when he came out of the trees. It was a different pony.

Behind on his sorrel came the girl, her head tied in a headscarf, her stirrup leathers too long.

Megan hunched her shoulders. He should not have brought the girl here. This was *her* place.

'Hello, Megan.'

She did not look up.

'Megan, I want you to meet my fiancée, Rose.' She heard him slide from the saddle. 'Aren't you cold up here in this wind, Megan?'

'I'm used to the wind, Jeff, thank you.' She looked up at last.

The girl, Rose, had not moved from her saddle. Her face was wary. Megan could see she had light blue eyes and gingery eyebrows. So the colour of her hair was real then. The slim fingers holding the rein were manicured. The nails were coloured; she had been right. They glowed a delicate shade of plum. Megan noted the sapphire with bleak satisfaction. So she hadn't got a diamond then.

There was no talking today; no need to rest the ponies. The sorrel pawed the ground, impatient to be gone. When they were out of sight, Megan closed her book. Quietly she slipped down into the wood to make her way home.

She didn't see Jeff again for many days but she thought of him in spite of all she could do to stop herself. Nor did she go to peer through the hazels at Cae Coch. The farm too was spoiled for her now. She took to rambling on the mountain, watching the sheep as they wandered through the bracken and gorse.

It would soon be time for her to go away to college. She put the date away from her. The rest of the summer came between her and that day. Her last freedom. She climbed higher towards the rocks and took deep breaths of the air, storing them up against a time when she would see the great open mountain sky no more.

She saw the galloping pony a great way off and stood to watch as he rode recklessly up the pony path, great clods of peat flying up from the thundering hooves. This time he was alone.

'Megan,' he called as he reached her. 'I've not seen you for ages.' He slid from the saddle and grinned at her. Now his skin was almost as brown as hers.

'You still have the book under your arm, I see.' He smiled, his dark eyes lighting with silver.

'How is your fiancée, Jeff?' she asked, not wanting to say it, not wanting to know. She saw his face fall, his smile go.

'She's well, thank you.' He sat down on a lump of rock and then he smiled at her again in spite of it. 'She's gone back to Birmingham now.'

'Has she indeed?' Megan felt her own heart lighten a little. She sat down beside him. The warm wind stroked her hair back from her face. He looked at her for a moment, then his fingers went gently to her forehead.

'You have lovely hair, Megan. Soft and shiny like nut-brown silk.' His eyes were serious as they looked into hers. She felt the message of them pierce right through her and she knew what he wanted so badly.

'Is it loving me on the mountain you're after?' she asked him direct, and she saw his eyelids droop in assent. His hands slowly strayed to the top button of her shirt, undid it, and the next. Gently, with his warm hands, he stroked her breast.

Towards the end of summer when the evenings were drawing imperceptibly in there was a wind; a storm from the west which brought with it the message from autumn that the leaves were doomed to fall from the trees as they turned colour and sent late harvesters scurrying to collect in the last of their store.

Then it was that Jeff told Megan he was leaving Cae Coch. She had borrowed his comb and was kneeling in the soft-brown leaves within the walls of the ruin, combing pieces of grass out of her hair.

'Back to your Rose?' She smiled up at him wistfully, still combing. He nodded, his eyes pained. He had expected her to cry. He buttoned his shirt and went to tighten the girths of the grazing pony.

'Will I see you again, Megan?' He asked it over his shoulder half afraid to turn, to see her face.

'I'll be here till I go.' She smiled enigmatically, slipping his comb into her own pocket. Without a word she began to walk back down towards the trees.

He stood and watched her go, gently stroking the pony's muzzle. In his heart there was already an ache of emptiness he had never felt before.

When he went two months later to her cottage Megan had left for college. In vain Jeff pleaded with her mother for her address.

'No son of Sarah Ann Lewis is going to follow my daughter,' she cried adamantly, hand on hip.

He walked back slowly through the wood to Cae Coch, his heart heavy with longing. The track he followed came out in the trees at the back by the brook, the place he had always thought he felt eyes watching him in the mornings. He smiled gently. So it had been Megan, that shy fawn of the woods whom so often he had tried to glimpse through the trees.

He groped in his pocket for the little box. Inside lay a ring, a tiny diamond on a band of white gold. The large sapphire, returned with such venom, had more than paid for it. He kissed the cold stone and put it back in his pocket.

Megan wilted beneath the dark city skies, but she worked hard and tried not to think of the mountain and the brook. Above all she tried to forget the image of the grazing pony and the buttercups.

Her first vacation she spent in Swansea with her Aunt Bethan. The next she went to London and met her mother for a three-week stay in a small hotel in Bayswater while they visited the shops and museums and had tea with Great Aunty Elen who lived in Richmond.

It was not until the sweet summer winds were blowing again over the mountains that she returned home. Granny Lewis had died at Easter and Cae Coch lay empty, the windows already broken by boys from the village.

Megan laid aside her new town clothes and climbed at long last back up to the ruined farmhouse. The stones of the mossy wall were familiar against her back as she sat reading in the sun. The gable wall had fallen some time during the winter and already the nettles were poking up thickly amongst the scattered stones, but she felt happy here; relaxed and safe again. No one else would come to sit beside her on the warmed stones.

She read through the long warm afternoons, watching only sometimes as the shadows of the trees lengthened across the path out of the wood the way he used to come with the pony.

The first storm of the autumn tore some slates off the roof at Cae Coch, leaving a gaping hole. The gate was hanging off its hinges.

Sadly Megan walked down out of the trees and stood in the yard for the first time, looking round. Raymond the Post had told her that it belonged to Jeff now. But he had never been back to see it. Never come back to the mountains.

She heard a soft whinny and shivered in spite of herself. It sounded like a ghost from the past. The sorrel pony was tethered to the fence behind the lean-to, out the back of the cottage.

She stood for a moment, uncertain, overcome with shyness. Then she turned and ran back towards the shelter of the wood. For a brief second she turned back to peer through the branches not letting the hope come. The yard was deserted and silent, the past a whole year away now. Sadly she made her way up the hillside, away from the brook towards the ruins of the farm.

Whistling, Jeff came round the corner of the cottage, his shirt sleeves rolled up, a hammer in his hand. He looked at the sorrel pony, munching sleepily at the net of hay he had hung for it and then he stiffened. Was he being watched? He turned towards the wood, his eyes scanning the pale-green hazel brake hopefully.

'Megan?' he whispered softly. 'Megan, are you there?'

The leaves rustled to the wind, but there was no answer.

Slowly he turned to the rucksack lying inside the door of the cottage. At the bottom was wedged the small ring box. He hadn't looked at it for many months. The diamond winked and gleamed in the silent sun and he gazed at it for a while, his head a little to one side. Then, his mind suddenly made up he stuffed it deep into the pocket of his jeans. Hitching his jacket over his shoulder he vaulted the fallen gate and set off into the wood and up the hillside towards the ruined farmhouse she had loved so much.

Encounters

I knew it was a mistake as soon as I held out my hand. His eyes behind their polite disinterest were mocking. He raised my fingers ostentatiously to his lips, then delicately, almost fastidiously, turned aside to sip his champagne; to rinse away the taste.

'Of course I know Jessica. Why it can't be more than five years since the trial.' Smiling, his teeth were immaculate as ever. I had a vision of the dentist's bill when he had them straightened. 'You knew she tried to murder me, surely?' He still held my hand and as I tried to pull away his grip tightened fractionally.

Our hostess's eyes became like marbles. A greenish tinge had appeared around her mouth and I felt a wave of sympathy. I tried to smile a reassurance.

'I expect he'll show you his scar if you ask him nicely. No, Sara, you guessed aright. You don't have to introduce us.'

My fingers, draining of blood in his grasp, were beginning to tingle uncomfortably. If I had had a glass in my free hand I could have dashed it into his face. As it was I reached forward for the centre button on his shirt. The scar was so small now. The incision appeared to have been made with such precision. A professional, considered thrust aimed, so the prosecution had maintained, with callous and cold-blooded premeditation. I felt a ridiculous giggle well up inside me and, unable to control it, let it burst forth like a hiccough. Abruptly he released my hand and groped for the button, concealing his wound.

Sara recovered some mastery of the situation. 'Well, dears,' she said with commendable sang-froid. 'Shall I leave you to talk over old times, or would you rather be parted at all cost?' She smiled, but not with her eyes.

His, on the other hand, were sparkling. Their appeal was irresistible. 'Let's talk, Jess,' he said. He took two fresh glasses from a passing tray and handed me one. 'There are things I want to know.'

'And I. My record of Verdi's *Requiem* for one. My begonia rex and the spaghetti jar from Habitat.' I sipped and he smiled. I let the bubbles effervesce for a moment against the roof of my mouth.

'Hostages to fortune,' he said. 'But you can come and get them whenever you like. I've taken cuttings from the begonia and I have the *Requiem* on tape.' He put his head on one side. 'Was it premeditated, Jess? I've often wondered. You must have hated me so passionately.' Shaking his head he took a gulp from his glass. He always closes his eyes when he swallows. It's an irritating habit when you're talking to him.

'Did you never look up in your *Anatomy*? X marked the spot I was aiming for. Only I could have missed so many vital organs so completely.' I lowered my lashes modestly and he nodded, understanding.

'You should have tried poison. It's the woman's method.'

'You can't have forgotten already that I do not like feminine compromise?'

Silently I applauded as he intercepted a tray of canapés.

'You take the plate and I'll help myself to enough for both of us.' He eyed my hand. 'You don't have a Borgia ring, I suppose?'

I raised an eyebrow. 'I was not expecting to meet you, and anyway, second attempts are so boring.'

'I agree.' He said it so heartily that I laughed.

It seemed natural then to head conspiratorially for the tables at the side of the marquee and sit down together with our plate and our drinks. Catching my eye he raised his glass and grinned. 'To the past before it went wrong,' he said and I drank to it with him.

We had, once upon a time, lived together for five years, he and I. We shared a love of Italian food and music. I suppose we shared a love of begonias. We certainly both enjoyed the making of our life and love together as we had enjoyed painting the flat the glorious plums and russets of autumn – 'So very sombre, my dear,' my mother had said once, but I could tell she was impressed.

We had stripped article after article to the basic weather-beaten pine and scoured our Cretan holiday haven for local wares, till our home was sophisticated and cool and I was secure in my liberated mutually-free relationship.

Then he had gone away to a medical conference. The day he was due back the doorbell rang and a woman stood there, tall and dark, her skin tanned and oiled.

'You must be Leo's sister,' she said, walking confidently in and throwing down her bag.

It was as much of a shock to her. She had known him only three months, but this holiday, for her the culmination of their relationship, had involved no conference that she could recall other than with one another.

We circled each other like cats. Then, our anger turning in despair on Leo, we kicked off our shoes and drank a bottle of gin, sitting together on the sheepskin rug, gazing through blurring eyes at the sunburst of corn in the fireplace.

It was her bitter suggestion that he deserved to die. And she admitted it at the trial, I never could decide whether from motives of self-sacrifice or malice.

Leo had not come back that night – perhaps some secret qualm had warned him of the passions that were smouldering beneath those plum and aubergine ceilings as I staggered round the flat after she had gone, tearful at last, to find a taxi.

When he came back the next evening and sat down to read the *BMJ* I gave him, silently, three minutes to explain. Then, as he closed the magazine to turn the page – he never laid a book or paper flat on the table as he read – I stood up and leaned across the table. It was laid, although I had prepared no food. I remember my sleeve catching at the carefully folded napkin as I stuck the stainless steel delicately through his sweater.

He had looked so surprised. Then the customary mocking glance had returned and he had said, 'Darling, Jess, was I late for supper?'

He had phoned for the ambulance himself before he collapsed and I in a fit of masochistic rage rang the police. I wanted reaction, drama; I wanted I suppose to be vindicated. I gave myself up and was half disappointed when they did not appear with handcuffs.

Then the game ended. They let me see Leo in hospital. We had a row, the first we had ever had, and I could remember even now, gazing at him across the canapés, how he had called out in despair, 'All right, Jess, if that's the way you want it, I'll press charges. I'll bloody well press charges.'

That was the last time I had spoken to him, till now.

'Did you qualify in the end, Leo?' The 'incident', as the police psychiatrist called it, had occurred four months before he sat his finals in medicine. He certainly looked respectable now. I eyed his immaculate morning suit.

'Indeed I did.' He grinned. 'Our little brush with the gossip columns does not appear to have harmed either of our reputations, I'm glad to say.'

I blushed. I was recognized now as a photographer and my name, the part of it I used these days, was occasionally to be found in glossy magazines beneath portraits of society personalities.

'You know what I do now?' I had been convinced that I no longer existed for Leo in any respect. The certainty helped me to bear my shame.

'My dear, I do have a certain proprietary interest in your career. Perhaps you have forgotten who lent you the money for your first decent camera.' He smiled encouragingly.

I couldn't help laughing. 'It was less than £5!'

'But you never paid me back.'

'I thought it was a present.'

'Oh.' He considered for a moment. 'Yes, perhaps it was.'

Behind his shoulder the creamy canvas of the marquee billowed slightly and a shadow was silhouetted by the sun.

'They make a very nice couple, don't you think?' I bit into some flaky pastry. 'Are you a friend of the bride or groom?'

'The groom's father. We're with the same hospital. How about you? Have you known them long?'

We were talking as strangers again. I shook my head. 'I was here to photograph the house. I know Sara, the bride's mother, through work.'

He laughed. Again those beautiful teeth. 'And she didn't know about your murky past?'

'I don't usually tell people.' I hesitated and then catching his eye and holding it, I found myself grinning ruefully. 'I'm not very proud of that effort.'

'Of course you're not. You botched it. You were never

one to crow over a failure.' His face was suddenly inscrutable but I thought, I hoped, he was still smiling inside.

Our glasses were charged and we rose to listen to the speeches. I stood bemused by champagne and the heady fragrance of trodden grass, surrounded by best dresses and hats in the cream twilight. Leo was beside me, tall, strong – alive. And then there was a surge of clapping and laughter, the formation changed and Leo was gone. I gazed round, trying to see him, but nowhere was there a sign.

I drank the next toast without enthusiasm and, bored with speeches, edged discreetly towards the entrance.

The garden was gaudy with roses and deserted now that everyone was crowding into the marquee. I could see a fountain playing at the end of a grassy walk. At the centre the slim bronze figure of a girl stood gazing down into the water, water trickling from her fingertips and her tresses and from the fronds that curled around her ankles.

I walked slowly towards her, my heels sinking into the velvet grass. I knew Leo wouldn't follow even if he'd seen me leave.

I sat on the surround of the fountain and lazily trailed my hand in the water. The afternoon was very still. In the distance there was a burst of shouting and laughter from the marquee. I ignored it.

I sat there until the light began to fade. After a time I realized that people were wandering around again. The speeches must be over. Then they began to disappear and, remotely, I heard the revving of engines as one by one the guests began to depart. One of those cars would contain Leo.

I hadn't told him that I was to fly to the States. Why should I? The next morning I boarded the jet at Heathrow and left England behind, leaving a cool hazy morning for the shimmering hothouse of New York and my own wedding.

I had a premonition that my marriage was doomed. Perhaps it was the thunder and lightning that raged round the slender spire of the wooden New England church as we exchanged our vows. Perhaps it was the helpless adoration I felt for George. A love like that could not be allowed. The gods are not sentimentalists. So when the end came I was almost prepared. The small plane he was flying from New York to Montreal dropped out of the sky and buried itself in the flaming glory of the Vermont fall exactly three months and four days after we were married.

When I came home the tawny of the English autumn wrapped itself gently around me like a familiar comforting arm. I walked in the mist and rain until the ache was dulled, then hesitantly I resumed work.

I had been staring at his back for some time. Perhaps it was the set of the shoulders. Perhaps it was the angle at which he held the *BMJ* over his head to ward off the streaming rain that held my attention. I was fascinated to see the water dripping from the page almost with deliberation into the perfectly angled upturned collar of his coat.

There were three people between us in the queue. I stood painfully hoping he would turn; dreading that he might turn. I wanted to run away, but I wanted my ticket for *Trovatore*.

Agonized, cold, wet, I shuffled on in the queue through the doors of the Opera House and across the foyer, regimented, obedient, hypnotized. Then I was gazing through the glass at the man in the ticket office. His gold-rimmed spectacles were slightly askew. A tiny puff of cotton wool supported one side of the frame over a red and swollen ear. He looked harassed.

'Ah yes, the lady in blue. Miss Ferindale. One ticket in the stalls. It has been paid for. Thank you. Next.' He pushed an envelope towards me and I took it.

I stood and looked at it. Then I looked for Leo. He had gone.

I arrived a little early and slipped into my seat while the Opera House was still half empty. The cool, clean sawdust smell from the stage hung in the air, then as the rows filled it was replaced by the scents of wet coats and expensive perfumes and people hurrying straight from work. An elderly couple side-stepped past me and settled in the seats to my right. The left-hand seat remained empty until the orchestra began to tune up. Then he came as the lights were dimming, wrapped in a heavy gaberdine raincoat. Not Leo.

The half glance I gave him told me I could sit back and relax. Obviously Leo's nerve had failed. The stranger had not even looked in my direction. But in the first interval he smiled.

'Leo had to go to the hospital,' he said. 'He said I could take you out to dinner and then I must deliver you to the flat later. I understand there is some plant you have to collect.'

The begonia.

It was a pleasant meal. The young man, a colleague of Leo's but specializing in paediatrics, played his part as escort well. I enjoyed myself. Until the coffee came.

'I wouldn't have put you down as being particularly homicidal,' he said, his hazel eyes serious. 'Of course, psychiatry is not really my line at all, but you seem quite rational to me. Have you ever felt the urge to repeat your violence?'

'Not very often.' I sat forward in my chair and began

to toy with the fruit knife. 'Do I gather that Leo's feeling nervous?'

He smiled enigmatically. 'Cautious perhaps.'

He called the waiter and then escorted me firmly to a taxi. He did not leave my side until we were standing outside Leo's door that had once been my door too. Then with a handshake and a stiff little bow he turned and left me.

The ceilings had been painted white. As Leo opened the door and I composed my face to greet him, I noticed the fact automatically. And I was pleased.

Nothing of my personality remained in that flat. Even my begonia, which stood ostentatiously on the table by the door, had changed. It had grown gnarled and whiskery and one of the umbrella leaves had blighted and curled up at the edges.

'It was kind of you to water it for me.' I might have been away for a week's holiday.

Leo acknowledged my thanks with composure and showed me to a chair by the fire. The hearth had been opened out and the glowing coals were sending out a radiant smokeless heat. I noticed that some of my carefully stripped furniture had been repainted. Some antiques and bric-à-brac had been introduced and the Greek island look had vanished completely. It was, I had to admit, very attractive in its own way, but not, I thought, entirely Leo's taste.

'Are you married now?' I asked as he handed me a coffee cup. He unscrewed the cap from a quarter bottle of brandy. I did not expect him to nod and when he did I did not expect the sharp wave of jealousy which flowed over me.

'Do I know her?'

I was relieved to see that it wasn't the tanned beauty who had incited me to murder. I gazed at the photograph he put in my hand. She was delicate and fair and had the gentle eyes of a dreamer very much in love.

'Can I meet her?' I gazed round, half expecting her to appear, but the door to the bedroom was closed. I knew suddenly that the flat was empty. Taking the glass from Leo I looked up at his face. His gaze was fixed on the photograph in my hand, and his eyes reflected exactly those of the girl.

Suppressing with difficulty the lump that persisted in rising to my throat I took a sip of brandy and set the frame down on the low table.

'I want to make love to you, Jessica.' He took my glass and cup away and sat down next to me, holding my hands. His eyes were sad, not searching, not demanding; just holding mine.

The bedroom was too tidy. I followed him to the bed and then stood looking down at the coverlet. There were no signs in the room of her presence. No make up, no slippers, no photographs, no lingering whisper of perfume.

And there were no signs there either of the time I had shared Leo's bed. It was a different place now. The rugs were changed, the pictures were different except for one. Glancing at Leo I felt myself smile just once. He had kept the hand-coloured print I had bought him of two goldfinches clinging to a head of thistledown.

'Why didn't you move?' I asked at last.

'I liked it here,' he replied.

His fingers fumbled as he unbuttoned my dress and as he slipped the material back across my shoulders I saw him stare and hesitate and frown.

'God, Jess. I must have had too much to drink.' His hands dropped to his sides and with a defeated little shrug he sat abruptly on the bed.

I stood before him for a moment and then, wriggling back into my dress I began to rebutton it. Perhaps he, like me, had had a vision of another, more recent love. I had been Leo's for so long, but my months with someone else had effaced the memory of Leo's hands and Leo's kisses. It was as though a stranger sat before me.

I brought his glass of brandy and my own from the drawing room and sat beside him on the bed.

'I've been married too, Leo. My husband is dead.'

His eyes filled with tears and I knew then for certain that he had lost her. I did not ask any questions and after a while we rose and went back to the fire. The bedroom door was closed behind us.

We talked of many things. Of our lives and careers, of old friends and memories, even of the trial and the horrors that surrounded it. On my third brandy I found myself giggling over the solemnity of the judge. He had turned out to be the grandfather of the dental student who had helped us with the beautiful ceramic tiles we found for the bathroom.

As the fire grew cold and the red, glowing coals faded to clinker I found the silences between us growing longer. I was too tired to move. My head began to roll on my shoulder and when Leo gently took away my glass and covered me with a rug I made no protest. I was content to be there.

The kitchen I found was almost unchanged from five years before. Leo had always been a keen cook. Evidently his wife had not challenged him on that ground. I found the coffee beans in the same place; the grinder was an updated model. I cooked his eggs and put the rolls in the oven while he shaved and in the fragrance of the cooking breakfast felt myself five years younger.

Looking for the butter I found two bottles of her nail enamel in the bottom of the fridge. When Leo wasn't looking I slipped them down behind a dresser drawer. It was better that he try to forget.

He drove me home on his way to the hospital, with my begonia, my spaghetti jar and my *Requiem* neatly stacked in a cardboard box on my knee. I would rather have left them.

'Will you come again, Jess, one day?' His smile was sad but genuine.

'I'd like to Leo. I'd like to very much.' He drew up outside my flat and sat for a moment gazing wordlessly through the windscreen. Then he got out and came to my side of the car.

Helping me out he pinched my cheek suddenly. 'I forgot all about the need to hide my knives. You must have lulled me into a sense of security.'

As I carried the box of treasures up to my flat I was feeling happier than I had for many months. And I had left another hostage to fortune behind me. In an envelope on the mantelpiece in Leo's flat I had put a five pound note and a message, 'Thanks for the loan', and my phone number.

The Touch of Gold

Pushing open the door the boy peered cautiously round it. The room was empty. On the bed, his uncle's suitcase lay with its lid thrown back, some clothes spilling over onto the patchwork counterpane. The curtains had been drawn against the brilliant afternoon sun and the room was a twilit cavern, scented with spice and pomade. He could hear the desperate rustling as a butterfly beat its wings, trapped somewhere between the curtains and the broiling glass.

Glancing back over his shoulder to make sure the passage was empty the boy tiptoed into the room. Lifting aside the heavy material he pushed open the casement. The frail wings beat against his cupped palms for a moment then the creature was gone out into the sun, leaving a dusting of gold on his fingers. He pulled the window to and slipped back through the curtains, holding his breath.

Full of curiosity, he looked round in the gloom. On the chest of drawers lay silver-backed hairbrushes, keys, pencils and a jar of some sort of cream. He unscrewed the lid and sniffed, wrinkling up his nose.

He hesitated before touching the suitcase. Then quietly and efficiently he went through it, searching the pockets, looking beneath every folded garment. He didn't know what he hoped to find. Some sweets perhaps or interesting photographs.

His eyes rounded in amazement when he found the sovereign. He held it for a moment, hesitated, then slipped it into the pocket of his shorts.

It was hard to remember to walk quietly, to shut his uncle's door, to stroll off casually towards the stairs. His gym shoes squeaked on the linoleum. He could hear his mother clanging saucepans in the kitchen and his uncle's drawling tones coming from the front of the house somewhere. Perhaps he had cornered one of the choirboys on their way to practice and was boring him with one of his interminable stories. His father would be in the study writing his sermon.

Stealthily he made his way out into the garden, his hand cupped protectively over his shorts' pocket. Sitting in the long grass behind the beech hedge he at last looked properly at the gold coin. He had never seen one before, never held one. He gazed at it and turned it over in his palm.

Then suddenly the awful realization came upon him that he had stolen it. He was a thief. In spite of the sultry heat he grew cold. His hand began to shake and unthinkingly he hurled the thing from him. It fell somewhere in the grass.

Hiding his head in his hands he sat for a long time, thinking. He knew what he must do. He must return the coin to its place in his uncle's suitcase. No one would know it had been taken. Only God.

The boy looked heavenwards and fearfully, fervently, hoped that God was busy somewhere else this afternoon. There had certainly been occasions when He had missed other misdemeanours, after all.

On hands and knees in the long feathery grass he began to search for the sovereign.

Peering between the cool green stems he covered every inch of the ground near him. Then methodically he crawled in circles further and further away from the small patch of flattened turf which showed where he had been sitting. His anxious eyes flitted over stones and a piece of amber glass, a ladybird and finally, miraculously, a glint of gold. It turned out to be a butterfly; perhaps it was the same butterfly. His head ached. His shoulders ached. Trickles of perspiration ran down his back and his shirt clung to him. His nose itched from the grass seed and his eyes watered as he forced them ever closer in the green twilight between his hands. The shadow of the hedge lengthened over him. It formed a darkness so black he doubted that he would ever see again.

Blindly, exhausted, he climbed to his feet. It was no good, he would never find it. Tears trickled down his cheeks leaving clean trails in the dust beneath his eyes. Then he spotted the gold piece shining in a patch of dappled sunlight ten feet from him.

He clutched it to him and ran as fast as he could for the house. The shadows of the tall yew trees in the churchyard had already engulfed the small vicarage: it was as dark as night in the hall and he almost collided with his father who was emerging from his study.

Up the stairs two at a time he ran and listened for a moment, his heart thumping, at his uncle's door. All was silent. Turning the handle he pushed his way into the room and looked round.

The suitcase, closed, stood on the floor by the dressing table. The hairbrushes and things had disappeared. Everything seemed to have been packed away. Hesitating, he wondered what to do. He could hide the coin in the room and hope people would think it had got lost. But his conscience told him otherwise. He must put it back. Silently he pulled the heavy case flat on the floor and tried the catches. They were unlocked. Relieved, he threw back the lid and slipped the sovereign back into the pocket where he found it. It was hard to reshut the case. He struggled to push the clothes down and to strain the lid back into position. The more he tried, the more untidy the contents seemed to become.

He sat on it, but his slight weight was not enough. He was so intent on his efforts that he almost missed the sound of heavy footsteps in the hall. Heart in mouth he left the case and fled to the heavy curtains, slipping through them as the door opened and his father and his uncle came in.

'I have something for the boy.' His uncle's voice had an affable confident boom which had always endeared him to the nephew. 'I'm sorry not to have seen him at all. Explain why I couldn't stay, there's a good chap.'

The boy heard the puzzled exclamation as his uncle saw the open case and unhappily he pictured his angry face. But no further comment was made. He heard a faint scrabbling and then his uncle spoke again, slightly breathless. 'Here we are. A sovereign for him. I know he'd like it.'

The boy, red-faced and unhappy pressed himself further back behind the curtain. With a slight click the window swung gently open as it had for the captive butterfly. He clutched wildly for a moment at the heavy material as he felt his balance go, then he fell, with a frightened shout, towards the scented flowerbeds in the garden below.

The Helpless Heart

Mark was standing in the warm evening sunlight gazing up at the front of the house. Watching him a little anxiously from behind her billowing curtains Susannah saw him hesitate for a moment before raising his hand to push the door then, walking slowly like a man in a dream, he disappeared out of her sight into the shadows below her window.

She was waiting for him at the top of the stairs when he reappeared in the hall and she stood quite silent until, glancing up, he saw her framed against the landing window. At once the preoccupied expression on his face vanished and she breathed a quiet sigh of relief; the magic was still there. He ran up two at a time and kissed her on the forehead and then held her at arm's length to see her better. On tiptoe she came only to his shoulder.

He followed her into her room. It was pretty and pastel-shaded, he saw looking round, feminine like her; the walls were hung with prints of flowers, festoons of blossom filled the vases on the table and bookcase and the shaggy rug was littered with her sewing. The flat was cool in the breeze from the open window.

Quietly she took his hand. 'I am glad you came, Mark,' she said softly.

Had she met him only two days before? It had been at a party which had been held in the big conference room at the offices where he worked. Long tables laid out with food and drink had been dragged across the length of the room and she scrutinized them anxiously from her corner. She had been feeling nervous about the party all day because she had supervised the catering and seen that all was ready; now it was up to the contract waitresses to cope for the rest of the evening. She eyed them critically; they looked smart and competent. She took a deep breath and pushed her fair hair back from her forehead. She knew she looked all right; she knew the food was good; so why was she worrying?

They began to arrive: the businessmen, the reps, the cool supercilious secretaries and at last, surreptitiously still rubbing little bits of wallpaper paste from beneath his finger nails, Mark. She didn't know why she noticed that one man amongst so many others. Perhaps because he too looked a little ill at ease. She watched him walk to the bar and collect a drink. Then he carried it into a corner and, sipping repeatedly, began to observe.

Susannah had known no one there at all except the managing director who had given her the job. He smiled at her distantly and bowed. She smiled back a little wryly, tempted to thumb her nose at so much pompous authority but not daring. It was then she caught Mark's eye and knew that he had read her mind. Glancing down she smiled, a little embarrassed.

He came over. 'Are you thinking what I'm thinking?' he asked easily.

'I'm afraid so,' she said.

'Are you with the company? I haven't seen you before.' Mark could not take his eyes from her face and a flutter of excited unease arose somewhere below her ribs. She took another sip from her glass. 'Actually I'm the cook. Free-lance. I arranged the food for the party.'

He didn't seem to be listening.

'I expect you work here?' she tried again, wanting to see him smile. They were jostled suddenly by a surge of loud-talking men and Mark slopped his drink a little on the skirt of her dress.

'I'm sorry.' He was jerked from his reverie abruptly. 'Here, let me.' He produced a handkerchief and dabbed her skirt. 'I'm Mark by the way,' he said glancing up at her, obliquely, almost on his knees at her feet.

'I'm Susannah,' she said, and he smiled.

For the rest of the evening they talked and laughed, inseparable; companionable; feeling as if they had known one another for years and he, realizing at last who she was, complimented her on her cooking, doing more than justice to his share as they talked.

Then the crowds began to thin. 'Do you have to stay behind to clear up?' he asked.

She shook her head. 'Not this time, no. I'm coming back in the morning to see to things.'

'But it's Sunday tomorrow,' he objected.

'I know. I don't mind.'

'In that case, can I give you a lift home?'

She would have liked so much to say yes, but she had a car. She felt panicky suddenly. She hadn't even known his surname, then.

But later, as the party finished he had offered to walk her to her car, opening the door for her as she stepped out of the hot stuffy building.

'I can never understand how people can lock themselves up in smoky rooms like that when it's so lovely outside,' she commented over her shoulder to him as he followed her, talking wildly to hide her nervousness and stretching her arms above her head, shaking her hair to rid it of the smell of smoke.

He smiled. 'It can't be the company tonight. It must have been your food.'

'Flatterer.' She walked ahead of him across the asphalt. Her car was parked with its nose almost in the dark sootiness of a privet hedge.

She paused and turned to look at him and hesitated for a moment. He was looking down at her, a frown on his face. Wasn't he going to say anything? The silence lengthened. Desperately she spoke up again, her voice sounding too loud in her own ears. 'Perhaps I'll see you around?' she hazarded, with an attempt at a casualness she didn't really feel. She wanted so much to see him again.

'Oh I hope so.' He took her hands in his and held them tightly, his eyes seeking hers in the dark.

He was going to kiss her. Susannah took a small step towards him, raising her face imperceptibly to his, but he released her quickly, as if afraid, and stepped back. 'Drive carefully, Susie,' he called as he turned away.

She stood still for a moment, unbelieving, disappointed, then she began to grope in her purse for her car keys.

The next day Susannah let herself into the office with a pass key she had been given and went into the room where the party had been. She wrinkled her nose in distaste. Dirty glasses and plates, overflowing ashtrays, crumbs trodden into the carpet, everywhere the stale smell of exhaled smoke and musty conversation. She threw open the windows and began to clean up, plodding methodically through the job, stacking, scraping, emptying. Resolutely she did not allow herself to think of the tall handsome man who had talked to her so caringly the evening before and who had left her so abruptly.

It was a long time before she realized that he was there. He was watching her through the glass door of the office. She took a deep breath to steady herself and raised a hand in greeting.

He opened the door. 'I had to come to collect some papers. Do you want some help?'

She smiled. 'I'd love some, but it's a dreadful mess in here.'

He shrugged. 'For you, ma'am, I'd brave the Augean stables if you asked.'

They had both laughed so easily together and it had taken her half the time with his helping her.

'Susie, I want to see you again.' At last he had said it. 'Soon. Tomorrow, if you can.'

And now he had come. Susannah watched him looking round her room, hungry for details of her life. She smiled again, understanding. She longed to know about him, too. But not yet. She liked him still to be a little mysterious; a stranger whom destiny had brought to her door. He told her that he had booked a table, she picked up her coat and they went out together.

They drove through the bright evening to a restaurant she had never been to before, she talking, a little puzzled by his long silences, and intrigued; he wanting to touch her, his hand straying every now and then to hers, not really listening at all, just happy to be close to her. He was already certain in his own mind, although she didn't know it, that what he wanted was a future linked indissolubly with that of this exquisite, fragile girl.

It was a dark, intimate restaurant, the tables barely lit by smoking night lights, hidden from one another by high-backed settles. Susannah sat opposite him and every now and then, as they talked, his hand would stretch out and gently, with a finger only, touch hers across the deep-crimson cloth.

'Would you like to come in?' She looked up and smiled at him at the door of her flat when he brought her home later.

For a moment his gaze met hers. Imperceptibly he nodded, but he said. 'I shouldn't.'

'Why not?' Her voice was gentle. She reached out to him and he came.

He watched as she filled the kettle at the sink and plugged it in. 'There's a drink if you'd like,' she smiled at him, but he shook his head.

'Coffee's fine.'

She knew he wanted her.

In the sitting room he smiled and put down his coffee cup and looked at her so long she began to feel strange – almost dizzy – there was such an intensity of feeling in his eyes. Then he put his arms around her and she let him kiss her.

She heard the little clock beside her bed next door chime midnight. He heard it too. Gently he pushed her away. 'Your coffee's getting cold,' he whispered, inexplicably sad.

She slipped to her knees on the soft carpet and sipped her coffee, leaning against his legs. His head was lying against the sofa back, his eyes closed in the lamplight. She couldn't know that suddenly and unwillingly he was thinking of Annabel.

Two days before, on the day of the party where he met Susannah, he and Annabel had at last bought the new wallpaper for their flat. She had chosen it and he was content to watch, knowing her eye for colour and her quiet taste. He had smiled at her fondly as she pulled out first this roll and then that until at last she had decided and turned to him for confirmation.

'Are you going to help me do it?' he asked as they paid for it, scrupulously half each.

She nodded. 'I'll do the painting round it; you do the

papering, Mark. Remember? You said you could do a better job than the men who did our bathroom and I seem to remember a small bet?' Her dark hair was curling into her eyes and he had longed to push it back for her, but his arms, like hers, were loaded.

They had worked hard and by mid-day she had painted a door and one strip of the paper was up.

'It'll dry flat,' he murmured hopefully as she came to inspect his handiwork and she hadn't criticized it.

'It'll be lovely,' she had said. 'I'll go on painting while you're at this party tonight. They shouldn't allow office parties on Saturdays. Do you really have to go?'

He hadn't wanted to go. If he could have thought up an excuse he would have used it. But this time, this once it was important that he be there. 'It has to be on a Saturday because the German delegates will be flying back to Frankfurt tomorrow. It's boring, I know, but there might be some good contacts there.'

'I know your kind of good contacts! Curvaceous, sexy Fräuleins!' She smiled at him.

That was the joke between them, just as when he said to her every so often, 'One of these days you'll marry one of the fat directors of that firm you work for, Miss Conway,' and she would solemnly nod and compute their salaries on her fingers. She wouldn't, of course. Mark and she might not be married, but he was the man in her life and had been for nearly five years.

That afternoon when he was wrestling with the second strip of paper she had slipped out for a while.

She walked slowly to the surgery, feeling the warm June sun on her hair, acutely aware of the colours and shapes of things in the road, as if her faint anxiety made her more alive. The waiting-room was nearly empty and it was barely fifteen minutes later before she was once more in the road. The test had been, against all probability, positive.

This time she was thoughtful as she walked and she saw nothing of the summer trees. It was strange that she did not wonder at once what Mark would say. Perhaps because she knew instinctively that what had happened would in a way make no difference; her future, as it always had been, was in her own hands – her future and now that of the baby. Decisions, if they had to be made, were her job and she was not afraid of them. Not usually. Unnoticing she broke a twig off a lime tree as she passed and twirled the stem in her fingers.

Mark and she were a partnership. They shared their lives and their home, but at the same time they respected each other's rights as individuals. Whatever she decided – and she knew that ultimately he would say that the choice must be hers – he would respect her for it when she told him. If she told him. She snapped the twig abruptly and threw the pieces into the gutter.

The future did not seem to be clear. There were so many aspects to face: to tell him, or not to tell him; to have it or not to have it; to have the child and then let it go perhaps, to someone else.

She and Mark had never seriously considered marriage. Their relationship suited them both as it was and she knew he valued it for its freedom. But now?

Her tongue suddenly tasted blood in her mouth, sharp and salty and she realized she had been chewing the inside of her cheek as she walked. She hadn't done that since she was quite a little girl.

She walked a long time before turning at last, as she began to feel tired, for home. Her only decision was that she would do nothing – not yet.

Strangely she began to notice things again now; her heightened sense of perception had returned with that one meagre resolution – to do nothing. The trees were again brilliant in their cloak of summer green, the last of their blossom white and creamy, with bees clustering to suck, their buzz droning above the cars. As she turned back into the main road she saw a couple walking towards her. The girl, obviously pregnant, turned to the man and laughed up at him with such trusting joy in her face as they walked that Annabel found that she too was smiling. She hugged herself a little and against all reason felt ridiculously happy.

Mark had left for the party at about six, not guessing anything, and Annabel, strangely contented, reached for her brush. 'I'll only look in at the party for an hour or two, and be back in time for supper,' he said as he left.

She stroked the paint onto the skirting board in long even strokes, concentrating on making the creamy ridges merge and glisten into a smooth flat strip. She almost decided to tell him when he came home. Something kept telling her that he would be pleased with her news. She pushed her dark hair out of her eyes with the back of her wrist and easing her cramped position a little, painted on. Behind her the clock struck nine.

Annabel stopped at last, finished cleaning her brushes and pressed the lid back onto the paint tin. She was exhausted but the painting was finished, all but the door. She could do that tomorrow. She glanced at the clock; it was after eleven. She frowned. Surely Mark should have been home long since?

Shrugging she went to turn on the bath. They didn't worry about each other as a rule. It was part of the way they lived. After all, office parties and office colleagues were a hazard they both lived with and on the whole ignored. It made for a free, happy relationship, and today's news should – would – make no difference. She flung open the bathroom window and leaned out, taking a deep breath of the fragrant summer night and wondering idly if Mark were still there, and she felt a wave of pity at the thought of him, bored but dutiful, still making polite conversation to the delegation from Frankfurt.

She was asleep when Mark got home. He let himself into the flat quietly and stood in the hall smelling the cloying tangy wet paint. Then, creeping into the kitchen he poured himself a glass of milk. He was restless, and he didn't feel in the least bit sleepy. The bathroom was a little steamy still and rich with the scent of bath essence and talcum when at last he began to undress and he let it relax him deliberately, standing a long time looking down into the clear water as it ran into the bath, allowing the reflections and the swirling transparent bubbles to mesmerize and soothe him, making his mind go mercifully blank.

Annabel was lying naked beneath the sheet, her dark hair tossed in a shadowy web on the pillow in the moonlight, an arm half across his side of the bed. He stood and gazed at her for a long while and then gently, so as not to wake her, he eased himself into bed.

Leaving the coffee perking quietly on the stove the next morning Annabel pulled on her jacket and slipped round the corner to the shop. Hot rolls and the Sunday papers were their special treat each weekend and they took it in turns to go out and buy them.

Mark was still asleep when she carried in the tray. She smiled at the sight of him so vulnerable with his face relaxed, half smiling in his dream. She set down the tray and dropped a kiss on the end of his nose. Lazily he opened his eyes and grinned up at her.

'Hi.'

'Hi. It was your turn, you know, but I went as you were so very asleep. What on earth time did you get in?'

Remembering the events of the night before he pushed himself up in bed. 'Midnight, I think.' He hesitated guiltily.

'It must have been a good party after all.' She was breaking open a crusty bread roll, buttering it, unscrewing the jar of honey. There wasn't any need to look at his face; she trusted him absolutely.

'It was quite fun.' He reached for the paper.

'Did you have a look at my painting when you came in?' She handed him the roll. This time, glancing up, she saw the look of guilt.

'I came in so late, Annabel. I'll go and see in daylight.'

'It doesn't matter. Not much to see, really; it's just a bit fresher, that's all.' She felt absurdly hurt.

They read and ate in silence for some time and then at last Annabel got up. She glanced at him again. 'Are you going to get on with the papering? We could finish that room today, between us.' She was collecting their plates.

Mark glanced at his watch. 'Annie, I'm sorry and I know it's Sunday but I've got to slip back to the office this morning. I was supposed to bring some papers home yesterday and I forgot. I won't be long.'

He did not look at her as he spoke.

She wandered into the kitchen when he had gone. She didn't as a rule spend much time cooking, but today she wanted to do something special. She began to search through the cupboards and the fridge and then when she started to lay the table and set wine glasses she realized why. It was today, after a special meal, that she would tell him.

The quiet happy assurance of the evening before had gone. That morning she had awoken early and lain in bed, gazing at the cool sunlight through the thin curtain, thinking. She had wanted to wake Mark then, tell him everything, ask what he wanted her to do, feel his comforting arms around her, but she had stopped herself in time. It wasn't like her to want reassurance and she lay puzzled and a little frightened, watching the hands of the clock tick round until it was time to get up.

He was late for lunch. She drew the cork from the wine bottle on her own and sipped a glass as she stirred the gravy, hypnotized by the circling creamy brown vortex beneath her spoon, thinking about Mark. When he came at last she could sense at once that something had happened and she knew she could not tell him now. He was elated and yet, as he refused to meet her eyes, in a strange way he was almost surly. She poured his wine, disappointed and watched him eat. Her own appetite had gone.

'You've remembered Bernard and Joy's dinner party tomorrow night?' she said at last, to break the silence.

He looked up and frowned. 'Oh Annie, I can't make it. I forgot to tell you. Something's come up at the office. We shall be having a meeting till all hours, I'm afraid.' He looked so ashamed as he spoke, tapping his knife on the plate until the gravy splashed across the cloth, that she shrugged her disappointment aside.

'It can't be helped. I know you're very busy there at the moment. I think I'll go though; I enjoy their evenings.'

'Yes, you go. Enjoy yourself, Annie. Please.' He was almost over eager. He put his hands on hers for a second. His skin was ice cold.

Annabel didn't enjoy the dinner party as much as she had hoped. She was too blatantly the odd one out; the single woman suddenly cast by the wives there in the role of predator. She might have laughed at the situation and flirted with the husbands deliberately if Mark had been there to egg her on; if Mark had known. But of course if Mark had been there she would not have been alone.

She smiled to herself climbing into her car. He would laugh when she told him; and next time he would see to it that he was at her side, mocking and teasing, there to enjoy the jokes with her.

She drove home fast, glancing at her watch. It was nearly midnight. He would be back by now. The flat would be warm and cosy, with Mark probably watching the late show on TV; perhaps a hot drink warming on the stove. She would tell him; now.

She parked the car and ran upstairs to their door.

'Mark?' Her key turned impatiently in the lock. 'Mark, I'm home.' The flat was in darkness. Puzzled, she clicked on the light and glanced round. He wasn't there. She went through to the bedroom to see if he was already asleep but the room was cold and empty. 'Mark?' she called again. 'Mark?'

For the first time she felt a tremor of unease.

Susannah was sitting with her head resting sleepily against Mark's knees. She was unbelievably happy. Still she could not bring herself to believe that this man could have fallen so deeply and so painfully in love with her so quickly. She was frightened too; vulnerable in her own sudden defencelessness. She felt his hand on her hair and she looked up at his face, strongly shaded in the lamp light as they smiled at each other. He set down his coffee cup and slowly pushing her head away he stood up and reached down for her hands. She let herself be led, trembling a little, into the bedroom. Deliberately he pulled back the counterpane and sat down on the blanket, still holding her hands, drawing her close so that she had to stand near him, her knees touching his. Gently he reached up to touch a curling tendril of her hair, which had fallen between her breasts.

He felt overwhelmingly protective towards this girl. She was so fragile, so defenceless; she brought out in him a strange almost fatherly feeling; the need to look after her, a feeling which he had never experienced before with Annabel and which he found exciting and stimulating. It was undeniable. He stroked her breast, feeling her shiver a little at his touch and then slowly he pulled her down beside him on the bed.

Annabel was sitting on the floor of the sitting room, her chin resting on her knees, her arms wrapped around her legs. She had turned on the television for company but she wasn't watching the screen. She had been deciding what to say to Mark. She could not carry the burden of her knowledge alone any more. He had to know. Now. She was uncertain and vulnerable and she needed him. She knew it was out of character and it was frightening to feel herself so undecided and exposed, but whatever his problems at the office, and ever since yesterday she had known that he had them, she knew he would help her. Her hot chocolate grew cold beside her and a skin formed on the surface as the minutes ticked by and she waited for him to come home.

She didn't turn round when at last she heard Mark's key. He crept in, not wanting to wake her and stopped abruptly as he saw her sitting on the floor, her narrow shoulders hunched as she gazed at the television in the corner.

'Hello,' she said wearily. 'How was the meeting?'

'OK.' His own voice too was colourless. 'The dinner?'

It seemed like a hundred years ago. 'Boring. Your drink's in the saucepan.' She turned then and watched as he went across to the kitchen, his feet dragging as if he were intolerably tired.

'Mark?' She scrambled up and stood in the doorway

behind him as he lit the gas, nerving herself. 'There is something we must talk about. I can't put it off any longer.'

He looked round. He knew she was right; they had to talk. He could not pretend with her, or let things drag on. She deserved far more than that and seeing the pain and doubt in her face he knew that she must have guessed something at least of the conflict that had been going on inside him for the last three days. He swallowed hard and for a moment he glanced away, unable to meet her eyes. He couldn't bear to hurt her and yet he knew it would be more cruel to deceive her. They had never lied to one another; never hidden anything.

Bewildered by the emotions within him, not certain suddenly what he should do or what he was going to say he forced himself to look at her again. There was a long pause. Then impulsively he held out his hands.

'You're right, Annie; we must talk.' He hesitated.

She swallowed. Now that it had come to it she was afraid. He might think she was going to use the baby as a lever to make him marry her; he might try and force her to get rid of it. Suddenly she knew she wanted to keep it more than anything in the world.

Why, when she loved and trusted him so much did she have this strange feeling of foreboding? Why, now that he was here, had she begun to feel so very cold?

She took a deep breath, but before she had time to say anything he had rushed in ahead of her.

'Annie, as you've guessed there is something you have got to know. There is something I must tell you. I wasn't at a meeting this evening at all . . .'

Unnoticed by either of them the milk stirred and began to rise in the pan on the stove.

She looked at his face and suddenly she knew. The anguish, the uncertainty she saw there were not because he had guessed her secret; they were there because he had one of his own. Her mouth went dry and she began to shiver uncontrollably.

The boiling milk hissed angrily over the sides of the saucepan and put out the flame. Automatically she released her hands from Mark's and pushed past him to turn off the gas. She was still shivering as she stood with her back to him, looking at the puddle of milk on the enamel round the gas burner.

'What do you want to tell me?' Her voice was tight with fear.

'Annie, we've lived together a long time. I've always thought – well, assumed – that we'd go on like that, but . . .' He stopped, fumbling for words, his eyes on her tense narrow shoulders. He wished he could see her face.

'Annie, we've never thought about marriage, either of us. We've always agreed that we're free. It's been a good relationship . . .'

He broke off again.

There was a moment of silence.

'It's over, is that what you're trying to tell me?' To her horror Annabel could feel unheard-of tears welling up into her eyes. She gripped the edge of the cooker until her knuckles whitened.

'There's someone else, Annie. I never meant it to happen. I still don't know how it did. But I feel so much for her. So suddenly. It's as if she's been waiting there all the time; I don't understand it. I've been so happy with you. I care for you so much, but this – this is different. I can't explain.'

He pressed his hand to his forehead in despair.

'How long have you known her?' Still she didn't face him.

'We met at the office on Saturday.'

'Saturday! That's three days!' At last she turned and her large grey eyes seemed enormous in the pinched whiteness of her face. 'We've been together five years, Mark. Doesn't that mean anything?'

'We're not married, Annie.'

'Not married!' She still looked stunned. 'That doesn't mean there is no commitment! It doesn't mean we don't belong to each other. I love you, Mark.' Her voice had begun to tremble suddenly.

He turned away, unable to face those enormous eyes.

'Mark.' She followed him into the sitting room. 'Have you slept with her?' Suddenly it was terribly important to know.

'I want to *marry* her, Annie.' Absently he bent and switched off the crackling blank screen of the television.

Slowly she walked to the window and pushed back the curtain; the narrow strip of lawn was bathed in moonlight. She knew she had only to tell him, now, about the baby, but something stopped her.

'I suppose you want me to move out?' She took a deep breath to steady herself. 'Have you fixed a date for the wedding?'

'Annie, Annie.' His voice was gentle. 'I haven't even asked her yet. I'm the one who must move out. This is your flat as much as mine. More perhaps.' Unconsciously his eyes went to the half-repapered wall. They never had finished the room. He bit his lip unhappily.

'I don't think I want to talk about it tonight, Mark. I can't face it.' Annabel ran her finger along the lower edge of the window frame. It came away dirty, but she didn't notice. 'We'll sort it out tomorrow somehow.' She faced him slowly and tried rather feebly to smile. 'It's all come as rather a shock, I'm afraid. I never guessed. I'll be able to think better, later.'

She walked numbly past him, ignoring his hesitant outstretched hand, and went into the bedroom. He turned to follow her automatically and was brought up short as gently she pushed the door closed in his face.

He didn't go home the next evening. He went to Susie. He was late and tired. All day at the office he had found his thoughts straying back to her – never once to Annabel. Once or twice he had broken off in mid-sentence with a puzzled colleague, unable to remember anything but the ash-gold glints of Susie's hair or the grey green of her eyes. Then at last he was at her door and she was standing there smiling and he could forget everything but the touch of her lips and the faint haunting scent of her perfume.

'I'm sorry I'm so late.' His arms were round her at last, as slowly the door swung shut behind them. It was a long time before he pushed her away.

She glanced up, half shy suddenly, and smiled. 'I'm so glad you're here, Mark. I was afraid that perhaps you weren't going to come back.' Since the night before she had been going over in her mind the scene in the bedroom, unbelieving, hugging to herself the memory of what had happened and of the things he had whispered to her as they lay in each other's arms on the bed. Still she could not bring herself to believe that this was really happening to her.

'Susie,' he whispered. 'Would you mind if we didn't go out? I'd rather have a snack here this evening.'

'That's a lovely idea, Mark.' She had to stand on tiptoe to kiss him unless he bent to meet her. 'What about a salad and some cheese? And as it happens, I've a bottle of wine.' She was very happy.

When at last he went home again the following evening. Annabel was sitting at the desk, a cup of cold coffee at her elbow, gazing in front of her with unseeing eyes. Mark frowned. Her hair was unbrushed and she was wearing an old pair of threadbare jeans.

'Annie?'

She turned to him, her face unmade-up and white. 'I've been trying to sort out our finances, Mark. They seem to be a bit entangled,' she began tonelessly.

'Annie, I rang you at your office. They said you hadn't gone in.'

'I didn't feel like it. I . . .' she hesitated. 'I was a bit sick this morning. I think I must have a touch of gastric flu.' Her eyes gave a flash of defiance.

'I came to collect my things. Don't worry about the money, Annie. I'll go on paying my share of everything for the time being.' She heard his words, but they were one dimensional; impersonal. She wanted suddenly to hit him.

'Don't be so bloody reasonable, Mark!' She got up, pushing the chair so hard it crashed into the wall, marking the new wallpaper behind it.

She wanted desperately to touch him, too. To feel the reassurance and comfort of his arms. But he, now, was the last person she could turn to. She wrapped her arms around herself defensively and went to stand by the window. 'You'd better pack. Don't worry, I won't smash up the place after you've gone. Anything you can't take now will be perfectly safe.'

'Oh, Annie. You know I don't think anything like that.'

The phone rang. Automatically she put out her hand and lifted the receiver.

Mark watched her answer and saw her face tighten with pain. 'It's for you,' she said quietly. 'A lady.' She put the receiver down on the table and walked past him into the bedroom, closing the door behind her.

*

'Who was the woman who answered your phone?' Susie asked curiously when he arrived at her flat.

Inexplicably he was angry with her.

'It's none of your business, Susie. How did you get my home number?'

'I'm sorry.' She was puzzled and then afraid. Suddenly she didn't want to know who it had been.

He sat down heavily on the edge of the kitchen table. 'Please, Susie, can I have some coffee? I've brought all my cases up and I'm tired.'

She wanted so much to do as he asked, to trust him, to forget the sadness of the voice she had heard on the phone. She bit her lip. 'Please, Mark. I have to know who it was, don't you see?'

He sighed. 'She's my sister. Who gave you the number anyway?' Strange, how he found it easier to lie to her than to Annabel.

'Your office gave it to me this afternoon. I wanted so much to hear your voice so I rang; I knew you wouldn't mind. Or at least, I thought you wouldn't . . . But you haven't got a sister, Mark. You told me, remember?' Her words tailed away. She could feel herself beginning to panic and desperately she tried to steady herself.

'All right, Susie. I suppose it's better for you to know the truth.' He ran his fingers through his hair. 'I have been living with someone; sharing a flat if you like. It was she who answered the phone.'

'Have you known her a long time?' She forced herself to speak steadily as she turned away from him and picked up the kettle, filling it automatically, her fingers fumbling with the plug and switches.

'We were together about five years, I suppose.' He spoke quietly, his eyes on the floor. 'She and I, well, we were different. We were very good friends and,' he hesitated, conscious suddenly of his enormous disloyalty in dismissing Annabel so casually, 'and, yes, we loved each other, of course we did, but we never thought about marriage. I've never thought of marrying anyone before. Not until I met you, Susie.'

She wanted to cry.

'I'm sure she must have thought of marriage, Mark.' Her hand was on the handle of the kettle, feeling it grow warm beneath her fingers. 'If you've been together so long she probably half thought of herself as married to you already.'

Slipping off the table he began to fiddle uncomfortably with a spoon on the dresser. 'All right, if it makes you feel better to know, Susie, I think she did.' He was silent for a minute. 'But what can I do? I want you. I love you. I want you to have my children and I've never felt that way about Annabel. I'd never even thought about it before.'

Susie pushed past him out of the narrow kitchen and went to stand in the middle of the sitting-room floor, looking down at his cases. 'Oh, Mark, why did this have to happen? It's all spoiled somehow. I never wanted anyone to get hurt by our love. It's too perfect for that.'

'Sweetheart.' He was behind her, his hands on her shoulders. 'Forget about her, she's my problem. I will be as kind to her as I can. She must have realized though, deep down inside her, that our relationship was going nowhere. If she's honest with herself she'll see that. She might be glad of the chance to meet someone else now, who will marry her and make her happy.'

Susannah glanced round at him hopefully. 'Do you really believe that?'

He smiled a little desperately and nodded.

'Will you see her again?'

'I must, Susie. I've still got a lot of stuff to collect and I can't – ' he hesitated, 'well, I can't just walk out on her. Not after five years.'

'No, of course not.' She shrugged off his hands with an impatient little gesture and went to turn on the electric fire. 'Funny,' she said in a strange high voice. 'It's cold suddenly; I thought it was supposed to be summer.'

Annabel had tried to eat a boiled egg but the runny yellow yolk congealed on the spoon and made her feel sick again. She felt hungry; empty inside and a little light-headed. Glancing round there were already signs that he was going from her life. Pictures; the hammer which for some reason lived on the bookcase, the clothes scattered untidily over every room in the flat – all had gone. A lot of the furniture would too, she imagined, eventually. Her mind skidded sideways at the thought and she found herself clutching the table as though it were about to get up and walk of its own accord out of the door.

She stood up and immediately flipped open a cigarette box on the desk. It was empty. It was months since she had smoked, but tonight . . . She began to bite her thumbnail. If she had the right change she would go to the machine on the corner. But there were practically no coins in her purse.

'Oh, Mark!' She found herself sobbing his name suddenly into the silence. She took a deep breath trying to steady herself.

The clock struck ten. She forced herself to go and turn on the bath and stood watching the water, eddying beneath the steam. She pushed her hair out of her eyes and glanced in the mirror. She was as slim as she had ever been. She supposed it would be a long time before it started to show.

For the first time in months she slipped on her nightdress afterwards. Then she lay in bed trying to read, but the print danced and blurred before her eyes.

*

'Annie.' When she heard his quiet voice she froze, her fingers clutching the book till it warped in her grasp.

'What have you come back for?' She refused to let the tiny whisper of hope surface.

'I thought I would get some more things.' He came in. He was frowning, his face was strained and sad. He stood for a moment looking at her and then he sat down at the edge of the bed, groping for her hand.

'Annie, I'm sorry.'

'So am I.'

'Can we still be friends?'

She raised her eyes to his and tried, not very successfully, to smile. 'I expect so. Later. Not yet.'

He nodded dumbly, not releasing her hand. 'We've had some good times.' There was a long silence. 'I haven't seen that nightie before. It's pretty.' He grinned a little.

'I didn't often wear them, did I?' She tried to smile again. But it was no good. Then suddenly his arms were round her and his lips were on her hair as she flung herself sobbing bitterly against his shoulder.

Susannah was pacing up and down her room, her mouth dry with fear, at every turn going to the window and peering out behind the curtain. It had begun to rain. There was an ominous roll of thunder and the street lamp in the forecourt below blurred and crystallized through the streaked glass. She walked across the room, pausing at the kitchen door, staring unseeing at the kettle for a moment, then she turned and retraced her steps, skirting the suitcase with a sudden pang of misery. She shouldn't have made him go back tonight. She shouldn't have *let* him go back. She wasn't sure if she had ever had Mark's love at all, not his real love and now she might never know. It had seemed so sincere, so real and yet how could he have done this, lying to her and to this other woman, this Annabel? But no, she comforted herself. Some instinct told her that his love had been genuine. His eyes could not have lied.

She glanced at her wristwatch. It was twenty to twelve. She couldn't expect him yet anyway. He had to drive there, talk to her, load the car, drive back . . . She went to the window again and lifted the curtain as a flash of summer lightning lit the sky.

'I must go, Annie.' Gently he pushed her back on the pillow. 'Please, darling, don't make it more difficult.'

She sat up and reached for her thin dressing-gown as a distant rumble of thunder broke the silence.

'You're right,' she said. 'I'm being silly and hysterical. Not at all me.' Her voice sounded cold, quite unlike herself. 'Shall I help you pack or something?'

'No, thank you.' He went to the window and pushed back the curtain. 'It's raining so I won't take much. If you don't mind, perhaps I could come back tomorrow after work.'

'If you like.'

'Annie . . .'

'Please Mark, stop it. It would be so much easier if you were just plain nasty to me.' She was pleating the skirt of her dressing-gown with shaking fingers.

'But I . . .'

'Get out, Mark. Please.' She had her back to him. 'I can't bear this hypocrisy another minute. Take your cases and go back to her.' She paused. 'You really only came tonight to appease your conscience, didn't you?' She faced him at last. 'There's nothing in those cases you could have needed that badly.'

'I couldn't bear to think of you on your own. I had to make sure you were all right.'

'Well now you've seen. I'm fine.' Her voice was trembling a little.

'Annie. We never . . . Well, we never discussed marriage or anything, did we? It's not as though . . .'

'Goodnight, Mark.'

'What I mean is . . .'

'Goodnight, Mark.'

She heard him hesitate and then go, as she stood by the window, her arms protectively across her stomach, watching the silhouettes of the rooftops against the flickering sky. Not until the front door had banged behind him did she move. Then slowly she reached up onto the wardrobe for her own big suitcase. One by one she began to drop her books and her clothes and bits of make-up into the case. Wherever they went, she and the child within her, they would have each other. One day, perhaps she would give Mark her address; he had the right to know. But not yet.

'Oh Mark, darling, you're soaked through. Here let me help.' Susannah had been waiting for him at the open door of her flat and her face, so recently white and strained, was suddenly happy in its relief. 'You've been such a long time.'

He smiled wearily. 'It didn't take long, Susie. I've just been driving around in the rain.'

'Oh.' She was chilled by his tone. 'Well, come on; I've got a stiff drink poured for you. You must be exhausted.'

He sat down on the edge of a chair, his drink clasped loosely, his hands between his knees. His face was grey with fatigue and she knelt quietly down to be near him, not daring to say anything.

'I can't do it to her, Susie,' he said after a long silence.

Susie climbed to her feet and walked away from him, determined he shouldn't see her face. She went to the window and threw it open. The rain had stopped. There was already a grey lightening of the sky in the east.

'You and I have known each other such a short time, haven't we?' She tried to keep her tone light, although she suddenly felt sick with apprehension. 'If only we had met years ago.'

'We could have been happy, Susie. You're the only woman I've ever really wanted to marry.'

She knew he meant it.

'We still could, Mark?' Her voice, trembling with hope was so quiet he could hardly hear it.

His knuckles whitened on the glass as he shook his head. 'It's not just that; there are so many reasons it couldn't work. Life's not that simple.' He took a gulp from his glass as the first cautious notes of a sleepy bird echoed across the room. In a moment it was silent again. 'Love like this, that we feel for one another, it is self destructive. It must be. It would devour us, Susie, in time and devour itself too.'

'Don't decide too hastily, Mark,' she whispered. 'Please think a little longer.'

But he had thought. For that hour, driving round peering through the rain-streaked windscreen at the black sky he had thought again and again. And realized with an unexpected feeling of relief that real though his sudden infatuation with Susie had been he could not, could never, change the love he felt for Annabel; the protectiveness which Susie had first aroused in him had now strangely transferred itself to Annabel, wrapping her round, making her safe, wanting so much to comfort her for the hurt he had caused her. It was strange to think of her as vulnerable and fragile and alone, but this evening he had realized that she was all of those things. He could not think how he had not seen it before. Susie had known him so short a time she would, he hoped, soon forget, without too much pain. Annie was different.

He had known then that he had to go back. Nothing had really changed. Annabel was the woman he loved and she needed him. Suddenly and inexplicably she needed him.

He drove home in the pale green dawn, the car window down so he could hear the full-throated roar of the birds greeting the day. The roads sparkled from the night's rain and the heavy trees bowed under their frosting of raindrops. He parked, climbed stiffly out of the car and quietly shut the door, taking a deep breath of the clean air. For the first time in an age he felt light-hearted.

He ran up the stairs three at a time and slotted his key into the lock. The room was as he had left it a few hours before; a few boxes and cases still piled by the wall ready for him to collect. He crept over to the bedroom door, picturing her lying there, her dark hair a blackbird's wing across the white of the sheets. He would wake her with a kiss and beg understanding and forgiveness.

But the bed was empty and neatly made. The room was unnaturally tidy, the dressing table bare and dusted. It was as though she had never been.

He sat on the bed, kneading his eyes with his knuckles while the joyous chorus of birdsong flooded through the window; mocking him.

Slowly, he stood up. He took off his jacket and walked back into the sitting room. Behind the sofa she had stacked all the wallpaper. Sadly he picked up a roll. At least he could finish the decorating for her.

Two weeks later Mark let himself into the flat after work and glanced round wearily. The room looked good now that it was finished. Annabel would have liked it so much.

Wandering rather aimlessly into the bedroom he flopped down onto the unmade bed, his arm across his eyes. The silence and emptiness of the place oppressed him and he hated being there in the evenings. Later, perhaps, he would go out and find himself something to eat. He lay there for a long time, his mind a blank, and then at last as the light slowly faded he dozed.

He was awakened by the ringing of the phone. For a moment he lay still listening to the insistent sound coming from the room next door, tempted not to bother, then suddenly something made him throw himself out of bed. He ran, fumbled desperately with the door knob, wrenching it open and grabbed the receiver, his heart thumping, afraid the caller would hang up before he could answer.

'Mark?' Her voice came from a long way away. She had not dared to hope he might be at the flat. 'Mark, I had to talk to you; are you alone?'

His relief and happiness were so great that for a moment he couldn't reply and in the long silence he heard her again. 'Mark, are you there? Mark? . . .'

The Indian Summer of Mary McQueen

'Mary, Mary, quite contrary,
How does your garden grow?'

Mary McQueen murmured the words to herself languidly as she stood at the veranda door, gazing through the mesh out to the barren, puddled lawns and the dripping maples. The rain was pouring straight down, a heavy curtain, never once slanted or scattered by the wind. She could hear the parched gardens gasping with gratitude beneath the weight of it.

Inside, the house was as hot as ever, humid and so uncomfortable that in another five minutes she would have to go and change her dress. She glanced back into the living room with its freshly laundered drapes and pretty summery chintz and she could not face the thought of dragging herself up the stairs.

If she did not look at the driveway where the gravel was rapidly disappearing beneath a sheet of slate-coloured puddles, for five whole minutes – not cheating – then, as she raised her eyes, surely she would see the biscuit-coloured Buick she had expected since breakfast, nosing in off the highway. She sat down on the rocking chair, her wrist dangling heavily across her knee. She immediately felt even hotter and more uncomfortable, but that way she could watch the tiny hands of the watch with the minimum of effort.

Dan McQueen had given it to her on the plane after they got married, as he took her up to the house in Vermont for their honeymoon. Then they had returned to live in New York. Fifteen years later, after deciding to make their home there in the soft woods and hills of New England Dan had inexplicably walked out. Mary had never suspected another woman.

'I have my English Mary,' he used to say, with nauseating frequency, at dinner parties. 'She's just about the greatest!'

Just about.

She had resented his work and his devotion to golf as did all the other wives at the Garden Club. But never had she suspected Dan, sidesman at the local church and co-organizer of the Lake Falls Arts Festival, of hankering after another woman.

Once, they had gone up to Tanglewood to listen beneath the great north American moon to Beethoven and Mozart. He had sat beside her on the grass holding her hand, trying to sneak little kisses like a boy of twenty. She had been so embarrassed. Dan was a man of fifty-six. But Dan did not like serious music – it was the organizing side of the Arts Festival he enjoyed, not the art – and they had not gone again.

She glanced at the watch once more. Two minutes more and she would look up at the rain-swept drive.

It was six weeks now since Dan had driven off with his bags to collect Sarah Walton. Mary could keep the house, he said. He would pay a regular allowance into her account.

He had been as excited as a kid going on holiday with his cases and, of course, his golf clubs. He had worn his new shirt and the silk cravat she had given him. She had had it sent from Fortnum's in London and she knew the label alone would have pleased him. That hurt as much as anything else; that he should wear her present when running away with another woman. It was as though he expected her to share his excitement, help him pack, even prepare the two of them some sandwiches.

'Don't you want to know where we're going, honey?'

He had sounded quite hurt and when she shook her head, wordlessly miserable, he looked upset and worried and took her hand rather as an anxious mother takes the hand of her child to feel if it has a fever.

She had waved him goodbye though.

That night, inevitably, Cyrus Walton had driven up complete with Californian wine and barbecued chicken. As inevitably after they had eaten he had expected them to go to bed together. Even in Lake Falls it seemed wife swapping could be viewed with equanimity if it salved one's hurt and avenged one's pride. But she proved contrary and Cyrus at last went home, hiccoughing and unfulfilled to his empty bed. She had sat a long time after she had locked up that night, considering whether she had been foolish and should have accepted his offer. Perhaps if he had been different she would have. But she had always found Cyrus the worst type of boorish male. She preferred her loneliness. Then.

The hand on the watch had traversed its full five minutes but she was reluctant to look up now and break the spell she had woven.

She could hear the rain pounding down onto the leaves and the roof and the gravel outside, but no scrunch of car tyres. She would wait another two minutes, she bargained with fate, and then go in if he hadn't appeared and fix herself a cold fattening drink.

After all, it had not been such a definite arrangement that he arrive this morning. She pictured again the square jaw, the fair untidy hair, the piercing eyes which seemed to see her soul, of the man with whom she had shared martinis and lunch on the plane down to New York three weeks before.

They had got talking, as people do on planes. He helped her with her seat belt and adjusted the air conditioning. Then they had a drink and relaxed.

By the time they had reached cruising altitude they had been chatting like friends; by the time they approached LaGuardia they had both felt, she was certain, that they *were* friends.

They were both pressed for time, but parting had seemed inappropriate and too hurried. Then she had remembered the new car, a biscuit-coloured Buick, which he was to pick up on this trip and drive back north. 'Come by, won't you?' She had asked and he had agreed. They had held hands for a moment and exchanged glances, she had thought, of significance and promise.

The two minutes were up. At last she raised her eyes again to the dripping garden. It was curtained by the falling rain, scented, beautiful. It smelt, she thought, like every beautiful smell there had ever been, but it was empty of life.

Getting up from the rocking chair she went through to the kitchen. Ice cream in the freezer. Maple syrup in the cupboard. Soda somewhere. To hell with the inches.

Then abruptly she slammed the carton back into the freezer. No. Bravado aside, she wanted a cup of tea, however hot it would make her feel.

Then she would go up and change her dress. And if she had a quick shower as well, he would probably arrive then. People so often call when one is in the shower.

She snapped on the radio as she waited for the kettle to boil. A phone-in show was on, as always, with lonely women pouring out their hearts in the seclusion of their kitchens to the public anonymity of the air. American women have such shrill voices, she thought suddenly with a shudder, and they are always complaining. But that, after all, was the purpose of the programmes. Suffering in silence may be dignified and English but was it any better for one's peace of mind? She thought not.

She switched off and looked instead out of the back window over vistas of dripping bushes and trees, down towards the lake. She and Dan used to keep a boat down there. Then, two years before, he had suddenly announced he was too old and sold it. It was the first time he had done anything like that without consulting her and she had been heartbroken, both for the boat itself, which she loved and for the precedent which, she had felt somehow even then, might bode evil for the future.

She made the tea with a teabag in her cup and carried it, steaming, up to her bedroom. It looked out over the front of the house, so she could see him if he came.

If he came?

So she was having doubts now. She sat down at the dressing table and wondered for the first time whether he would come at all. She had been so certain. She had even bought a new dress for the occasion. She glanced sadly at the bed where she had thrown it, crumpled and damp with perspiration.

If only the rain would stop. If only she dared run down to the garden, naked. If only there would be a premature frost.

As she did every day of every summer she thought nostalgically of the summers at home in England with the cool fresh winds and early morning mists and felt homesick once more for her happy girlhood.

If I had stayed at home, she thought again, where would I have been now? And what would I have been? Not, certainly, a middle-aged American matron, husbandless and hunting for a man.

She gazed up at herself in the mirror, suddenly appalled. Is that what she was? Is that what she, who so despised the other man-hunting women she had met, had become?

She scrutinized her image carefully. She certainly looked the part. Her hair showed no thread of grey and every strand was immaculate, her hairdresser saw to that. Her tights came from Lord and Taylor, her dresses from only a few select couture shops. Even in that boat she had not been really casual. Her slacks were tailored cleverly to conceal any broadening of the hips which might have shown and her jackets were without exception long enough. She had always been careful not to chip her nails gardening or on the jetty.

She stood up. Why in a temperature of over 100° and with the humidity unbearable was she wearing heavy make-up and tights at all? To impress a man she had picked up – oh yes, Mary, face the fact, that's what you did, she thought – picked up, three weeks ago on a plane ride to New York. For three weeks she had been living in a breathless pause like a teenage girl with her first infatuation. It was shameful, shallow and childish.

Looking back at the mirror she caught herself blushing with embarrassment and she felt suddenly more contrary than she had ever felt in her life before.

Falling on her knees in front of the highboy in the corner she pulled open a heavy drawer. There, neatly packed away in tissue and lavender were some of the old clothes which she had never brought herself to give away to the Garden Club bazaar. Pulling them out she heaped them on the floor around her, searching through the well-remembered garments.

She couldn't make up her mind between the dark blue cotton shift and the slacks and cotton shirt. Both were a little shabby and badly needed pressing. Both had been hers when she had first come to the States so very long ago.

She showered and removed her make-up and slipped at last into the shift, unwilling to try the test of time and her constant slimming by putting on trousers which she had worn as a girl.

Then she stood bare-legged and barefoot before the mirror. The dress was creased and faded in the creases and shabby and the wrong length for today's fashions but her legs, she decided critically, were perhaps not too bad. Her hair was all wrong. It was formal and stiff and, she suddenly realized, the colour was too hard for her face.

She brushed it hard, trying to dislodge the careful style, but it would not be disarranged.

Ten minutes later she was in the rain, her feet delightfully chilled in the cold grass, her shift black with absorbed water and clinging to her skin, her hair bedraggled, untidy and quite styleless. She cut armloads of roses, the raindrops still on their petals and watched the gentle curves of their leaves fill with more rain as they lay in the basket on the grass at her feet. She wondered if Sue Beckstein could see her across the lawn from her kitchen window. If so she would probably call up the local sanatarium.

She laughed aloud at the thought, shook her head so the raindrops flew, then picking up her basket she almost danced back to the house.

Her hair dried into tight little curls, with wisps and loose ends around her eyes. She stripped off the dress and threw it in the tub. Recklessly she tried on the old slacks. They still fitted after all those years.

She rummaged in a drawer and found a copper-hammered pendant which went with the throbbing green of her shirt, then still barefoot she ran downstairs to arrange her flowers. Dan had always discouraged flowers indoors because he reckoned they gave him asthma and hay fever.

The biscuit-coloured Buick arrived at ten after three. Mary was lying reading in the hammock on the veranda and hardly looked up as she heard the tyres on the drive.

The rain had stopped at last and he stepped out on the wet gravel to a fitful sunshine. All around the sky was still heavy with black thunder-clouds.

'Hi,' she called. 'I wondered if you'd turn up.'

He hesitated and then came towards her, at first slowly and then sprinting up the veranda steps.

'Have a cold drink,' she said with a smile. 'I'm sure you can do with a rest. My husband gets back about four. Perhaps you'd like to stay and meet him?'

They drank soda together on the veranda, he uncomfortable and formal with tie and shoes and she relaxed and happy and untidy. The seam on her left hip started to go a little as she hitched back up into the hammock but she didn't think he noticed. She saw him eyeing her unhappily as he laboured with polite conversation and remembered how he must have pictured her. Cool, friendly, immaculate and sophisticated. A rich woman on the make.

A little giggle escaped her and she tried to smother it within her glass.

'What's the joke?' he asked, embarrassed, suspecting her.

'Me,' she said and sipped her soda demurely.

He stayed only half an hour, anxious, without seeming so, not to risk meeting her phantom husband.

She waved him goodbye and then stood for a long time gazing after him.

That night she fell asleep on the couch by the open window, listening to Brahms' *Requiem* on the hi-fi. The next morning she drove downtown and made a reservation for a fourteen day round trip to England.

If they'll have me back, she thought, I'll stay.

She bought Levis and sneakers and, studying herself in her mirror at home, decided she looked good in them. Not mutton trying to be lamb, but artistic and intelligent.

She had the piano tuner come by and dug out all her old music and classical records. She read Walt Whitman and Emerson, Salinger, Burroughs and Mary McCarthy and replenished the tubes of paint in her paintbox. She had always meant to paint the fall; that after all had been the reason she had first come to visit the States as an art student way back. After she met Dan she had painted less and less as his social interests took up her time. Besides he thought her Bohemian and although he had said nothing she had felt herself discouraged.

She threw all the garbage and accumulated junk out of one of the guest rooms, set up her easel and began to paint again. She took her records up there and the kettle and wondered how she could have wasted her life for so long.

Slowly, by a fraction of an inch at a time as though not believing the chance she gave it, the grey began to appear in the roots of her hair. Bravely she ignored it and began to plan her trip to England.

Then with the first frosts Dan returned. He drove up beneath the reddening leaves sheepish and alone.

'I guess she and I didn't gel, honey,' was his only comment.

She was glad to have him back.

He noticed her hair, but said nothing. For two days she braved his puzzled looks and then she fled back to her hairdresser, who thought she must have been ill and congratulated her on her recovery.

Slowly she packed away her paints, brought the hi-fi back downstairs and forgot to practise the piano.

One day he said, 'Hon, I don't go much for those pants.

They don't suit the more mature woman.' Sadly she packed away her Levis, neatly washed and pressed, into the highboy. It was almost a relief to slip back into her smart clothes. She felt clean again, confident and immaculate. Her feet had had so much hard skin from going bare that she had laddered her tights when she first put them back on.

She missed the music and the painting. When Dan found her reading poetry he teased her; when he found flowers on the table he looked pained and sneezed. He said nothing, but she did not replace them when the petals dropped.

Arm in arm they attended parties and dinners as though nothing had happened. At first she tried to discuss things she loved and had rediscovered: poetry, music, the latest novels. But she met incomprehension and boredom. She remembered now why, so long ago, she had given up.

As though conscious of some loss in his wife which he could not name Dan suddenly promised her a trip to Europe in the spring. Quietly she slipped downtown and cancelled her own flight to England. With her returned reservations went the rest of her dreams.

The summer had been fun. But it was over. She knew the chance would never come again.

The day before the Garden Club winter bazaar she emptied the bottom drawer of the highboy, threw her paints and brushes on the top of the box of clothes and took the whole lot across to the jumble stall.

Her books she kept. That one small part of her, redeemed that summer and hidden in the guest room, she kept. That was all.

The Magic of Make Believe

She put the phone down and stared sadly down from the window thinking of Christmas things. Snow. Mistletoe. The hot chestnut man. Red noses. Mince pies. Noise. Quarrelling. Home . . .

'. . . We knew you wouldn't mind, Sue darling, as you'd be with Tony this year. Imagine! Christmas in New York with your sister! It's so exciting for us. And it's not as though you'll be alone, otherwise you could have come too . . .'

Her mother's tone was so apologetic, so guilty, so desperately hoping she wouldn't say the unthinkable – yes, I do mind. Yes, I'm hurt and lonely and miserable because Tony has left me and you're my parents and I need you.

When the phone had rung she had had the usual impossible hope which came with every call at home or at the office that it would be Tony. That, repentant, he was coming back to her, changing his mind as he did over so many things, suddenly and overwhelmingly, expecting to be hugged and forgiven and welcomed like a lost dog running home.

Slowly she covered her typewriter and picked up her tote bag. She smiled at the other girls. Her lips said the right words as she put on her coat and followed them into the lift, but her mind was whirling in a spiral of lost misery.

For the first time she was thinking: supposing he

doesn't come back. Ever. What shall I do? She had all this time been expecting him to appear in time for Christmas. She had known in some sealed, stubborn part of her that he had to come back. The certainty was as complete as the knowledge that her mother would be digging out the box of decorations and hanging them on the little spruce tree in the hall at home. But there would be no Christmas tree at home this year. And suddenly she realized that there would be no Tony either. This time he had meant it.

'I may be a while, Sue.' Tony had been standing in the hall of their flat, his raincoat shucked forward on his shoulders, the collar up, like Philip Marlowe after a particularly heavy night. She had grinned and raised her hand half heartedly, intent on what she was doing, not even standing up to give him a hug. Afterwards she remembered how he had hesitated, half turning back towards her. A thousand times she had asked herself what would have happened if she had jumped to her feet then and run to him and flung her arms around his neck.

But she hadn't. She had said, 'See you tonight.' Taken him for granted. Dared to be sure. Known, because she had an engagement ring on her finger, that he had to return . . .

But he hadn't. That night she sat up till one o'clock, watching and waiting, agonizing over what awful accident had happened, wondering when one rang the police and if one did what did one say . . .

She woke on the sofa, cramped and very cold, his last words ringing in her ears: *I may be a while*.

That was six weeks ago. He had sent a note.

'. . . I'm sorry but it wouldn't have worked. Forgive me and find someone else who will make you happy . . .'

Two days later when she came home from the office all his things had gone.

She pushed out into the noisy dark street, staring up at the coloured lights strung between the tall lampposts. Behind them the sky was never black in London. It was dun coloured. Muddy. The cloud reflecting the colour below it, mixing it and killing it with leaden overshadows. The sleet glittered on her eyelashes as all round her people rushed past elbowing one another in their rush to get home.

'*Sorry*!'

A particularly hard push sent her reeling towards the gutter, her boots slipping on the wet pavements and she fell, knowing suddenly that the wetness on her face was not sleet. It was tears.

'Oh Lord! Are you all right?' The man who had pushed her stopped and fought his way back against the crowd. He was tall, his collar also up against the wind.

He grabbed her arm and pulled her to her feet, swinging her back against the railings out of the way of the crowds.

'I'm . . . I'm all right,' she gasped, feeling stupid. Not wanting a fuss. Not wanting him to see her tears. Just wanting to crawl away and be alone. But impossibly he had gone down on one knee before her, raising the hem of her coat a couple of inches and looking at her muddy knees. She glanced down, her cheeks reddening with embarrassment and saw her tights were torn and a trickle of blood was oozing slowly down into the top of her boot.

He rose. 'That must be cleaned at once,' he said authoritatively. 'We'll find a chemist . . .'

'No, please. It doesn't matter.' She glanced up at his face for the first time. He had a tanned, rubbery comfortable sort of face. Youngish. Very young. Well, not much older than hers. A nice face.

He smiled at her. 'I don't often pick up strange women,' he said. 'But when I do, I do it properly.' He looked rueful. 'I was in such a hurry to get home.'

She felt absurdly left out and lonely suddenly.

'So was I,' she lied. 'There's no harm done, really. I'll see to it when I get home.'

'Bacillus *Clostridium tetani*,' he said absent-mindedly.

'I beg your pardon?'

'Tetanus. You must be careful and deal with that quickly. It's quite deep . . .'

'Are you a doctor?' She felt absurd standing there near the busy underground station, her knees bleeding like a child's, but she couldn't bring herself to leave. She had nothing to hurry home for now and he had a pleasant warmth, a kindness she wanted to be near for a moment longer.

A Salvation Army band was taking up its position near them. If they began to play carols she knew she would cry. She had to go. Now. She took a determined step away from him and let out a quite genuine yelp of pain as her left knee stabbed and throbbed as she put her weight on it. He caught her arm.

'A taxi is what we need,' he said decisively. He led her to the kerb and looked out into the road. She watched impressed as a cab appeared as if by magic from the almost stationary jam. Tony, for all his presence and *savoir faire* would never have managed to do that.

'Jump in,' he said. He climbed in beside her and leaned forward to slide open the glass portion behind the driver. The windscreen wipers were drawing refracted coloured arcs in the crystals of the sleet.

'Where shall I tell him to go?' he asked.

She gave him her address after only a second's hesitation. After all, he didn't look like a rapist or a murderer and Mrs Green would be in downstairs . . .

'What would you have said if I had lived the other end of London?' she could not resist asking.

'I'd have taken it on the chin, paid up and taken out a second mortgage on my flat.' He grinned and she found herself smiling back.

'You didn't tell me if you were a doctor,' she said as he sat back beside her, with a comfortable sigh. There was at least a foot between them on the hard slippery seat.

He grinned. 'Would that make it all right?'

'Make what all right?'

'Me, taking you home.'

'Probably not.'

'Then I can admit I'm not. My acquaintance with bacilli is purely passing, at the moment.'

She giggled. 'Are you going to tell me what you do do?'

'Must I? I'll tell you my name. It's Richard.'

'Mine is Sue.'

The taxi still had not moved a foot. Up ahead the lights changed from red to green and back to red. The driver glanced over his shoulder. 'I hope you're not in a rush, guv,' he commented.

'We've got all the time in the world,' Richard said.

Sue glanced at him accusingly. 'I thought you were in a hurry to get home.'

'I was. I hate being in limbo, between places. But now I'm here, which is somewhere. So I'm not in a hurry any more.'

He came up to the flat and poked around her drinks cupboard while she took off the torn tights in the bathroom and dabbed at her knees with cotton wool.

'One inch of decidedly-cooking sherry,' he said as she

returned to the living room, her elastoplasted knees safely encased in jeans, 'even less Sainsbury's whisky and a can of lager. I can safely say, either you are a dipsomaniac down to your last ten minutes' worth, or you are not a drinking lady.'

She laughed. 'I haven't felt very sociable lately. I'm sorry. Would coffee do instead?'

He shook his head. 'I don't feel I've made full reparation yet. I saw an off licence on the corner. I'll go and get something.'

He would not listen to her protests.

She stood and stared at herself in the mirror when he had gone. Her face was very pale and there were dark circles under her eyes, but there was a small sparkle in the clear blue irises which hadn't been there that morning.

He came back with two bottles of wine, a Chinese takeaway and a huge bunch of holly.

She stared.

'What on earth is that?'

'I thought you might get the wrong idea if I brought mistletoe.'

'But you didn't have to bring either!'

'I did.' He put the bottles down and stacked the paper carriers on the table. 'I've decided I've got to come clean and tell you what I do. Otherwise I'm here under false pretences. First, I'm not a doctor but I am a medical student, so I'm almost qualified to swab your knee myself. Next summer I shall be, exams permitting, and yours will be the first knee I touch professionally, I promise.'

'If the bacillus hasn't got me first.'

'Exactly.' He had found a corkscrew by himself and expertly drew the cork.

'Second, as this is the vacation and I am, in common with most of my species, hard up-ish, I have a temporary job. Namely, I am masquerading as one F. Christmas Esq. at the local big store.'

She stared at him. Then she burst out laughing. 'You're not serious!'

'Perfectly. I had only hung up my robe ten minutes before I met you. It's a jolly good job – with luncheon vouchers!'

They were half-way through the chow mien when the phone rang.

Sue climbed to her feet from her cushion in front of the coffee table near his and went to answer it, still laughing, unsuspecting.

It was Tony.

'Sue? Can I come and see you?'

She felt her stomach muscles clench uncomfortably. The receiver grew slippery in her hand. *Come home. Please come home.* The words screamed in her head, but she managed to control her voice with a supreme effort. 'Of course, Tony. What about tomorrow?'

'I had thought perhaps now . . .'

'I'm sorry. I'm busy tonight. Come tomorrow.'

She stood staring at the wall as she hung up, her hands shaking violently. Richard closed her fingers round the stem of her wine glass. 'Sip it,' he said quietly.

She obeyed and the world stopped spinning.

'That was my ex-fiancé,' she said after a moment.

'Don't tell me unless you want to.'

She went back to her cushion with a grimace. 'I think I do. Do you mind?'

She and Tony had met at a squash club in the City. She was swept off her feet by his handsome attentiveness, by his charm and his easy confidence and soon she was going with him everywhere, her blonde, blue-eyed prettiness set off by his dark hair and permanently tanned skin. He drove an MG and her parents had approved of him utterly. They had become inseparable and Sue was besotted by him, physically and emotionally obsessed by her first real affair.

'You still haven't told me what he does for a living,' Richard put in quietly.

Sue looked down. 'He hasn't actually got a job.'

'There's nothing wrong in that.'

'No, I don't mean he's unemployed. I mean he doesn't work.'

'Oh.'

There didn't seem any more to be said.

Tony took her to parties and dances and brought her first not-too-expensive presents, then expensive presents and moved in when her flat mate moved out and finally presented her with a sapphire surrounded by tiny diamonds as they chose the day three months hence when they would be married.

She looked down at the pile of empty cartons on the coffee table and laughed ruefully. 'Tony would have made me put this on plates in the kitchen and seal the cartons into a bin liner so they didn't spoil the ambience,' she said, gently self mocking.

Richard grinned. 'Why didn't I think of that? It sounds eminently sensible.' He reached for the bottle and filled her glass.

'My mother has started making lists,' Sue said quietly. Suddenly there were idiot tears in her eyes again.

'Mothers do.' Richard grinned, carefully not looking at her. 'My mother even listed how many hole-less socks I had when I started medical school.'

'How many were there?' She looked up, smiling through her tears.

'Three, as I remember.' He slipped off his shoe and stared reflectively at his protruding big toe.

She let out a gurgle of laughter. 'You'll have to do better than that when you get to Harley Street.'

It was nearly midnight when he got up to go. He walked slowly to the door. 'Can I ring you sometime?'

She nodded. 'Thank you for the holly and everything.'

He slipped back the lock and walked onto the landing. Then he turned and almost absent-mindedly dropped a kiss on her forehead. 'Don't forget to bathe your knees again,' he whispered. 'I realize I am probably too late to join the queue of your admirers, but I'm damned if I'm going to lose you to a bacillus.'

Tony arrived at seven-thirty precisely. He was carrying a sheaf of red roses.

'I've booked a table for dinner,' he said as he came in. He put his hands on her shoulders and gazed into her eyes. Then he kissed her. She felt her legs begin their customary descent to soggy cotton wool, but already he had backed away staring at her hand.

'You've taken off your ring.'

'I assumed our engagement was off, Tony,' she said. To her surprise now that he had let her go she felt perfectly calm. 'It's in the bedroom in its box if you want it.'

He bit his lip, crestfallen. 'Can't you put it on again?'

'I don't know.'

'Please. I want you to.' He took her fingers in his. 'Sue. I know I have behaved badly. I panicked. I needed space. Suddenly I saw the future all spread out before me like a long carpet. The wedding. The honeymoon. Bridge with your parents. Croquet or something with mine. Kids. Having to sell the car and get something sensible. Getting middle-aged. Going bald – what's so funny?'

Sue steadied her face with difficulty. 'I'm sorry, Tony. It just all sounded so unromantic.'

He grinned hopefully. 'Not really. The wedding will be nice and the honeymoon. And then. Well, it'll all be nice, I expect. Put the ring on again. Please.'

She shook her head. 'Not yet. Let's give it a bit more time. I think I need space too.'

'Sue. My parents have asked us to go down for Christmas. They'll expect to see you wearing it. Dad was furious when I said we'd quarrelled. He said I was spineless.' Suddenly he looked like a dog that had been kicked.

'We never quarrelled, Tony.' She bit her lip. 'Is that why you came back?' she went on in a whisper. 'Because your father told you to?'

'No, of course not. I'd have come anyway. Of course I would. Sue . . .' He reached out for her again. 'Come on, sweetheart.'

She gave him her hand. She went out to dinner with him and let him bring her home. Then she told him it was over and gave him back his ring.

The toy department was crowded. Children were everywhere, on and in and under the displays, evading harassed parents, screaming and crying and laughing with excitement. Sue looked at the lavish cardboard castle stuck with sparkling cotton wool at the end of the huge department. There was a queue of mothers waiting clutching the hands of their children. Had she really thought she would dare queue with them, without a child?

She paid for the small presents she had chosen and stared towards it again wistfully. Father Christmas might as well be in Snowland for real, she would get no nearer to him than this.

He hadn't phoned. Why should he? They had met once, passed a pleasant evening, laughed a lot and gone their separate ways. As far as he knew she and her fiancé had made up their quarrel and her life was once more complete. If he had thought about her at all.

Sadly she walked towards the escalator and let it carry her down back to reality and the office.

When she got home that evening a small packet had been wedged into her letter box. She gathered it up and let herself into the cold flat. The silver bells she had tied onto the holly in the vase glittered as she drew the curtains and turned on all the lights. She shook the sleet out of her hair and snapped on the TV for company and then turned the parcel over in her hands.

It was wrapped in white tissue and tied with ribbon. She wondered if it were from Tony to make up, but somehow something about it was not his style.

Puzzled she tore it open and stared. Inside was a tiny doll's first aid box. There was a note attached.

'I saw you through the windows of my castle and thought you might be looking for a bacillus-bashing kit. If you think a strong drink would be more effective, I'll pick you up about nine. F.C.'

She laughed out loud. Suddenly the evening had lost its bleakness.

The sleet had turned to snow since she had come home. She stood beside him on the front doorstep and stared out in wonder. In the street lights the air was magical. The treacly slush vanished beneath a crisp white crust which squeaked satisfactorily beneath their shoes and the air was a whirling net of cold.

She could not resist running her hand along the top of a car, watching the powdery whiteness caking and crumbling on her glove.

'You brought Snowland with you!'

He raised his eyes towards heaven. 'I'm never going to live that down, am I? Come on.' He caught her hand and dusted the snow off it. 'I'm going to be able to practise on your chilblains too at this rate. You're turning into a walking case book!'

The pub was crowded. Squeezed behind a small round table near the dartboard Sue sipped a shandy watching Richard play. He turned to her and raised his glass. 'Only one game, I promise. Is your fiancé waiting up for you?'

She was surprised by the suddenness of the question and looked down miserably. 'There is no more fiancé.'

He handed his darts to the man next to him. 'No more squash and Pimms and souped-up MGs?'

She shook her head, suddenly afraid she was going to cry as he sat down beside her, his burly figure squashing her on the narrow bench.

He put his hands on hers. 'The way you told it, he didn't sound right for you, Sue.'

'I know.' She sniffed hard, groping for a tissue.

'Come on. I'm taking you for a walk.'

They walked across the park in the whirling snow, his college scarf wound round and round her neck, his arm linked through hers as the dark disappeared before wave after wave of splintering whiteness.

'It doesn't often snow like this before Christmas,' she said, trying hard to be cheerful.

'It does when I'm in charge.' He smiled.

He took her home at last, exhausted, feet soaked through and numb, her nose and cheeks glowing.

On the doorstep he stamped the snow off his shoes. 'I'm coming in for five minutes only,' he said. 'I'm going to run your bath, prescribe you a night cap and, if I'm allowed, I'll kiss you goodnight.'

He was as good as his word, turning on the bath taps, then producing from his pocket a small bottle of whisky which he had bought in the pub. He put it on the sideboard. 'A slug of that with honey and lemon against the cold,' he said firmly. 'Then I must go. I've to be in my grotto again by nine in the morning.' He grinned.

He put his hands on her shoulders and drew her to him gently. 'Don't be afraid to cry, Sue,' he said softly as his lips came down on hers.

It was a warm, solid, comforting kiss, a bit shorter than she would have liked, she realized, as soon as it had stopped and quite definitely more-ish.

But he was fumbling in the cupboard for a glass. He made up her drink and carried it into the steamy bathroom.

'It's Christmas Eve tomorrow,' he said.

She nodded, feeling suddenly sick and empty.

'I won't have had my last sticky hug from my last toddling admirer till five.' He sat on the edge of the bath, testing the temperature of the water.

Firmly banishing the thought of Christmas Day Sue concentrated instead on wondering, since he was in such a masterful mood, if he were going to undress her as well. She rather hoped he was. The thought sent a small interesting tingle up her spine.

But he stood up again and moved towards the door.

'Get into that water before it gets cold. I've got to go now, but I'll pick you up at six with my tame reindeer. Unless you've got other plans of course?' He raised his eyebrows impishly.

There was a huge lump in her throat, but she could feel herself smiling blindly. 'I've no plans at all,' she said.

'Good. Don't bother to buy any food for the holiday. You won't need it,' and with that he was gone, leaving her in the warm bathroom with a glass of hot whisky in her hand. Behind her the flat door banged and she was alone.

She had to buy him a present, but how could she? She knew so little about him. In the end she bought a bottle of good wine – he seemed to be keen on drink and she suspected he probably knew about wine and on inspiration a pair of terrifying red, white and blue socks. He would never wear them, but they would bring his average of hole-less socks up a bit.

He was very prompt. She answered the door rather hesitantly, wondering if it were him, afraid he might have forgotten or changed his mind. But he was standing there in the same shabby coat, a broad grin on his face. 'I was tempted to borrow my red costume from the store, but I thought you might run if I did,' he said as he came in. 'Are you packed and ready?'

'Packed?' She stared at him with a small quiver of doubt.

'Of course. My mother would think it a bit odd if you turned up without a toothbrush. That's all you need though. We're very informal.'

'Your mother?' She was dumbfounded.

'That's right. The one who lists my socks.' He grinned. 'I've told her I'm bringing a girl home for Christmas.'

Sue looked down at her feet. 'But won't she assume we're . . . I mean, won't she think . . .' Her voice trailed into embarrassed silence.

'She'll assume nothing. She knows me better than that,' he said firmly. 'Now come on. This is all part of the therapy. A few days in the country.'

He drove a battered red MG. She stared at it in silence. Then she turned an accusing eye on him. 'You might have told me you had one too. And you were being so rude about them!'

'I'm never rude about Rudolph.' His eyes were gleaming maliciously.

'And since when has it been called Rudolph?'

'Since last night.' He tucked her case in the boot and helped her in.

The old house was already deep in snow as the car slithered its way up the drive. Sue loved it on sight, as she did Richard's mother, whom he introduced simply as Maggie and who greeted her with a kiss and a hug and pushed her into a rocking chair by a roaring log fire.

The ceilings were so low that the Christmas tree had to bend its head as did Richard when he waded through the two cats and three dogs sprawling before the flames to bring Sue her drink.

He grinned at her. 'No strings,' he whispered. 'Just enjoy yourself.' He winked.

While he was fetching logs from somewhere in the garden, logs that spluttered and hissed and exploded and smelt like summer nights by the Mediterranean, his mother sat down beside her.

Like her son she was tall, with deeply caring eyes and a warm smile.

'I'm afraid I haven't brought you a present,' Sue said awkwardly. 'Richard only told me we were coming here an hour or so ago.'

Maggie laughed. 'How like him. He told me a week ago.'

'A week ago?' Sue stared. 'He can't have. I've only known him a few days.'

'That's right. He rang up the night he met you and said there would be one extra for Christmas. "I'm bringing the girl I'm going to marry," he said.' She smiled. 'That's present enough for me, my dear, a thousand times over.' She stood up. 'I've been in a ferment of curiosity to meet you. But now I have, I'm so happy. Welcome.' She dropped a kiss on the top of Sue's head.

That night she had snuggled beneath the huge old-fashioned eiderdown and given up the struggle to evict a fat and very determined cat from the end of the bed when she was awakened by the door opening. A tall figure tiptoed towards the bed. She lay still watching as, with some difficulty it pinned a bulging stocking to the end of the counterpane with a huge safety pin. She heard a smothered curse as the pin must have driven into his finger and silently she managed to stifle a giggle.

Richard had turned back towards the door and was tiptoeing back towards the dim crack of light thrown by the landing lamp when she sat up. 'I never believed in Father Christmas before this year,' she whispered. 'Or since I was very very little. But I do now.'

He turned and came towards her. 'Go to sleep,' he said sternly. 'You're not supposed to have seen me.'

She held out her arms. 'Can I have a Christmas kiss?'

He sat down on the eiderdown and put his arms around her. He had just shaved and his cheeks were smooth and smelled of cologne.

'You invited me here under false pretences, didn't you?' she murmured, her lips against his. This time the kiss was of a very satisfactory duration.

She felt him smile.

'That would be against my principles,' he said softly.

'But you let your mother think you were going to marry me.' For some reason her chest had gone very tight and she couldn't breathe properly as she tried to see his face.

'Mother and I are always straight with each other. That's why we get on so well.' He smiled.

'But you didn't even know you were going to see me again.'

He smiled, touching her hair gently. 'I knew,' he said.

Several minutes later he started to stand up. 'I must go, Sue,' he said softly. 'If I stay any longer I may find it hard to leave.'

'But we're going to be married.' She started the sentence as a joke, but by the time the words had been said, spinning out into the silence of the old room beneath the thatch she knew they were true. The shortness of the time they had known each other did not matter. Tony, with all his show and his attraction did not matter. This was something so different, so right, that she was sure as she had never been, deep down, with Tony. Sure and content and very, very happy.

'Don't go yet.' She put her arms around his neck. 'Besides, haven't you noticed how unprincipled I am? I am already sharing my bed with one gentleman.'

In the distance, as Richard took her in his arms, the midnight bells began to ring, far away in the village. He kissed her gently. 'Do you think the other gentleman would move up if I asked him nicely?' he said softly.

And they both laughed quietly as, as if on cue, there was a deep contented purr from the end of the bed.

Destiny

On bitterly cold days I often went to the Palm House to warm up. Those heavy double doors were a passport to a tropical climate where hibiscus and bougainvillaea trail among the palms. My hands would come frozen out of my pockets, my chin out of my collar and I could walk tall and relaxed, breathing more easily after the paralysing cold outside.

Two lovely wrought iron spiral staircases lead up through the jungle towards the dome. One is marked 'up' and one 'down' and it was there that I met him. He was walking slowly, meditatively, down the 'up'.

Had I taken notice, had I had my wits about me, I would have been warned; I would have seen the danger signals within myself, but as it was I was unprepared and so somehow it happened.

I saw the shoes first as I climbed with my hands on the curving rail. They stopped about four steps above me and automatically, because they were facing me, I stopped too. I lifted my face slowly, my eyes travelling up the jeans, clean but washed-out, the T-shirt – no rude or meaningful messages emblazoned in those days – with behind it a hint of muscular chest, a heavy lumber jacket and then a face. Automatically my eyes prepared themselves to slip sideways and simultaneously I sidestepped to pass him, putting out my hand to grab the central newel post. Of course he, at the same moment, did the same, and we both clung precariously on the narrowed end of the wedge-shaped steps, my chin nearly touching his knees.

There was a moment's silence, then as we both moved back to the outside edge of the stairway there was a muffled snort from above me.

'Say – do you tango too?'

I could feel my colour rising. I hate sarcasm in any form.

'This is the "up" staircase,' I muttered stiffly, my head now level with the furry edge of his jacket.

There was a soft slither of snow far above our heads on the glass dome and somewhere to my left a sparrow started cheeping plaintively in the frondy palm tops. I raised my gaze reluctantly – our relative positions on the stair left me at a neck-cricking disadvantage. He had brilliant blue eyes and a ski slope tan. His face was very serious. Not angry; just concerned and really very pleasant.

'You know, you shouldn't always follow instructions so blindly,' he said conversationally. 'Had you looked up you would have seen me already on my way down.'

'If you deigned to follow instructions at all I should not have needed to,' I retorted. I took a deep breath. 'Anyway. It is perfectly possible for us to pass. There is plenty of room for two.'

'Ah,' he said. 'So this has happened to you before?'

'Frequently. But usually people manage to pass without making an international incident of it!' It had not escaped my notice that he had some sort of mid-western accent.

'OK.' To my amazement he proceeded to sit down on the wrought iron steps. He reached into his jeans pocket, extending a long muscular leg past me in order to reach down into it. 'Let's settle this in time-honoured fashion, as when two heads of state confront on a battlefield!'

I fully expected him to draw a gun, but it turned out to be a coin. 'Heads I go back; tails you go back, OK?'

I gave a helpless sort of tolerant smile – the kind of smile one gives to a child when indulging it disgustingly – and watched him flip the coin. It disappeared into the sea of greenery around our feet.

'You're supposed to catch it,' I said acidly.

For the first time he grinned. 'I'll go and get it,' he said. He stepped lightly past me and proceeded to run down the stairs.

I stared at him, speechless. He couldn't be serious. But he was. He was coming right back up again, dusting soft black leaf mould off the coin.

It was his turn to look up at me and he did so shrugging. 'I guess you think I'm nuts.'

'Something like that.'

'Can I buy you a cup of coffee to make up for it?'

It was a tempting thought. I hesitated, and I was lost.

'All right, why not!' I laughed and solemnly we both turned and made our way down, passing straight-faced two hapless visitors meekly climbing up the 'up'.

We met twice more after that, by appointment – once by the frozen lake where the ducks skidded ridiculously with much complaint on the blue ice and once in the museum in front of a case of grotesquely ugly wax vegetables and we talked and laughed and I felt we had known one another all our lives. He was outrageous and irritating; irrational and domineering and I found myself liking him more and more until I knew that I could never live without him.

The third time he did not come. I walked for nearly an hour, my feet frozen, looking at the spiked fringes of frost which had turned every growing thing into silvered gorse and my heart was inexplicably heavy. I knew so little about him. His name was Peter and he came from St Louis and he was working in England as a journalist. I didn't even know his second name. It had seemed too conventional a thing to ask him. And he didn't know mine.

What I did know was what he liked to read: Walt Whitman and Donne; what he liked to hear: Al Jolson and Britten; what he liked to smell: wet earth and burning leaves; and that his favourite place, like mine, was Kew Gardens. And I knew that inexplicably his absence had left an empty place inside me.

I resisted the urge to go more often, to walk melancholy down the paths I had walked with him, to stand as the thaw loosed the water on the lake and watch the ducks or, ever, to climb again up the spiral stair towards the forest ceiling where I knew that now the spring had come a blackbird would be rapping with its beak against the glass. After all, what was he but a passing nod of the head, a smile in my loneliness?

Defiantly I put him out of my mind, this intruder into my consciousness and my calm. And I filled my life so I was no longer lonely and I was even happy, ignoring that strange unjustifiable emptiness which had settled somewhere below my left ribs.

The man with whom I spent my evenings now was a tolerant conformist Englishman whose names I knew – not only the first and the last but the middle three as well. We fitted comfortably together without rasping at each other's corners. I met his parents and he met mine. We ate strawberries and cream at Wimbledon and fish and chips in Leicester Square. We laughed tolerantly at one another's jokes and did not always have to interpret our deepest thoughts. Our taste in films was similar – and music. I gave him Brandenburg 1–3 for his birthday; he gave me 4–6 for mine.

And yet still that sneaking emptiness, that flickering,

subliminal vision as I woke at dawn that made me think I must have been dreaming of the spiral stairs at Kew.

We went to the Proms and twice I suggested concerts with Britten. The music was elemental; untamed. It reminded me of Peter. In the queues outside I found myself gazing, staring, probing the crowds with lonely eyes and I cursed myself for an ungrateful benighted fool of a woman; only a woman would be so crazy.

And of course he knew, my lover of the five names – yes, we were lovers by now – he knew there was something strange about me. Delicately he probed around the fringes of my secret and equally delicately I rebuffed him. There was after all nothing to tell. But I saw him watch me watching and I saw the heavy burden of uncertainty in his eyes and I hated myself even as I turned in the cinema queue and let my gaze wander over that sea of animated faces. All the wrong faces. And he was always there afterwards to comfort me, my lover, his arm almost apologetic around my shoulders and I would turn and stand on my toes to kiss his cheek.

I married him as the first coloured leaves pattered down onto the hot dusty streets. But still I could not tell and still he could not ask outright. Perhaps we both forgot. It was unimportant after all – a casual meeting in the cold of the winter when the blood was thin and vulnerable, a passing of strangers whose chemistries apparently fused for a time but who then were separated and lost to one another for ever.

I had a child, and then another. I took a part-time job which I turned into a business and I was fulfilled and satisfied. That empty gap was so infinitesimal now I did not realize it was still there. I was full of love – for the man I had married, my children, my home, my work, even for my dog. I had no time to think; no time to dream or brood upon my dreams and that was good save for the fact that time passed so very fast and I did not see it passing.

They went to school and I employed a staff to run my business. Their father and I talked and laughed: our faces made expressions over the breakfast table; our mouths formed words. We did not hear one another any more but we were content as in a stupor, lulled by our own narcotic dream.

So it was strange that after all the years I should have thought again of Peter – suddenly, yearningly thought of him with such an urgency that it could not be denied.

There was nothing to keep me at home; nothing to stop me going to Kew on that first day of snow, of a new, another, winter.

I walked slowly along the paths, not looking especially for him, not thinking, my mind an emptiness as, hands in pockets, I passed down the line of white queen's beasts, passed the iced fountain and climbed the steps towards the Palm House.

He was sitting on the iron staircase. I did not raise my head as I approached, climbing methodically step by step towards him. Then I stopped. My heart was beating fast like a girl's and I could feel the colour burning in my cheeks. Slowly I raised my head until our eyes met.

'Last time we tossed a coin,' he said. His face was a network of lines but the tan was the same, the blue eyes as intense, the costume the same too, though nowadays of course everybody wore it.

'Why didn't you come, that last time?' I said quietly.

'I had to cover a story in France. There was no way I could let you know.' He made a rueful face. 'I left a note for you later, pinned to the stairs here. I was so sure you would come back and find it. But I guess you never did. I came here every day too, after that, but I never saw you.'

He had come each day. And I had nursed my little pain

and refused to succumb and turned my back on him. I swallowed.

'I did come. I walked by the lake.'

'You're married now.' There was no ambiguity about the plain gold band on my left hand that rested on the white railing by his head.

Was that sadness I could see in his eyes? Suddenly my own were full of tears. 'I'm very happy.'

'I'm glad.' He did not say that he was too. 'And you still go up the "up" and down the "down"?' A glint of humour lit his eyes.

I nodded. 'You didn't quite have time to convert me – not completely.'

I wanted to touch him, to reassure myself that he was real and as if he understood he slowly reached up and put his hand over mine. 'I somehow knew you would come today.' Slowly he stood up. Still holding my hand he guided me down through the drifting summer fronds and out of the giant hot womb of the place into the whispering feathery snow and the tiny forgotten scar beneath my ribs opened, as his arm went round my shoulders, into a raw throbbing cavity and deep inside I could hear myself moaning as we walked through the empty silent gardens.

This time we did not speak. Perhaps it had all been said in the silence of the long years. He guided me beneath the heavy blue arms of the cedar and there he kissed me – the long slow kiss which had lingered unacknowledged in my dreams and I forgot at that moment my husband and my children; I forgot my past and my future – everything but this man for whom I had waited here by the lake for a hundred years as the frost made spikes of silver on the willows over the water. We lived a lifetime in that afternoon before I fled.

My courage was not enough to walk blindly out of the gates into the anonymity of the whirling snow. Now I knew his name and he knew mine and one day, I knew, he would call me to him once more and I would have to tear myself apart to heal the wound he had reopened in my breast.

Meanwhile, cowardly, I sought the comfort of my husband's arms and I knew at once that he understood again, as he had always understood, and our tears mingled in the darkness.

A Summer Full of Poppies

'. . . The surface of the moon must look like this. Imagine the chaste huntress engirdled with barbed wire! It is hard even to imagine it as it was before I was wounded and went away. I remember it all mud and rain and cold and smelling of mould and decay, and now it is a parched desert with, where the fields used to be, behind the lines, a scattering of poppies . . .'

Maria raised her eyes from the crumpled letter to the dusty golden haze of the corn stubble which stretched down the slope before her, across to the woods and foothills in the far distance. There were poppies here, too, along the hedgerows; great splashes of blood-red colour in the dusty green and gold, and corn thistles, yellow patches in the hedge, with (too delicate and thinly growing to be seen from here) the pale blue of scabious and teasel.

The sun beat down on the shoulders of her thin embroidered blouse and on the chestnut plait of hair carefully wound round her head but her hat, thrown carelessly on the grass beside her, lay unnoticed.

'. . . Poor old Tom Kennedy has had a bad time. He's lost a leg. They think he'll be strong enough to come home by the end of the month and I've told him to look you up. Do you remember I told you he has no family of his own at all and I owe so much to him. Even now in that terrible hospital he manages to be cheerful; the nurses all adore him; I bet he gives them a bad time – teasing them I mean . . .'

There had been a photo of Tom Kennedy in James's wallet. He had shown her time and again the tall dark young man with widely-spaced light-coloured eyes and the new, so proudly borne uniform. 'I wish I could be like him, Maria,' James had said so wistfully as he sat, the healing arm still supported in its sling across his chest. 'He's such a good person, so gentle, yet so strong and always happy and cheerful.'

Maria had smiled at her young husband, her throat tightening at his vulnerability, his own unassuming and unrecognized gentleness. What business had these boys in a war?

She watched the shadow of a cloud race across the stubble towards her. It touched her with a finger of shivering cold and passed.

They had married when the corn, this same corn, was green in the field, she and James, he fumbling with the still-bandaged arm to slip the gold band onto her finger and smiling so bashfully in the neatly pressed uniform. She had been one of the lucky ones. She had married in that year of 1916; married the man she loved, known him for those few short weeks of bliss as his bone knitted and the shattered muscles drew together and slowly healed beneath the puckered white scar and then she had waved him goodbye, standing on the station platform, her arm aching as the small white handkerchief fluttered above her head. She waved long after the train was out of sight and only the smudge of smoke hung over the line in the still air.

'I'll try and be back for Christmas, my love,' he had said, as he bumped his bag into the carriage, his blue eyes twinkling down at her mischievously from the step. He was happy to be returning to his regiment, tired of the old men and the women and endless talk of war. They had no concept of what it was like out there and, though he sweated sometimes at night with the fear of returning and put his hands over his ears to block out the mind-breaking roar of guns, and the sound of screams, screams that had become for ever trapped within his own head, he could not bear any longer the inactivity; the knowledge that he, at home in England, no longer knew what was happening at the front.

He was sad to leave Maria. She was soft and golden and smelt of the new mown hay. He laughed with her and buried his face in her long chestnut hair, letting the scented weight of it run through his fingers like slippery water. But he never showed her the slim notebook in which he had scribbled his poems, those words from his own aching guts, twisted and moulded till they screamed like the sounds in his head and echoed the horrors of the trenches and the poignancy of those who prayed to come home and then knew as soon as they were there that somehow they could not escape; that they must return to the depths of hell of their own free will just as soon as they were able.

'. . . So many of the faces are new here, Maria, although a few of the old ones remain. Jones is here and Freddie Haytor and Timpson and Stuart, but I do miss Tom . . .'

Somewhere beyond Square Acre Field a column of smoke was rising straight up into the air, dissipating in the whiteness of the hazy horizon. Perhaps it was a rick burning, or a cottage chimney. She watched lazily, not registering curiosity or concern. Just watching and waiting as the shadows lengthened across the field. A wood pigeon began to coo, the soothing notes slurring into one another in the echoing woods. One by one slowly the stray yellowing leaves had begun to fall, accidentally, from the trees: the first unbelieved messengers of autumn.

She folded the letter into its worn creases and slipped

it back into the pocket of her skirt, brushing off the dusty grass. Already the sound of hooves from Patterson's wagonette had passed briskly on the road below. It was four miles to the station from the cottage she shared with her grandmother. James had lived there too for those weeks of their marriage. Maria smoothed the folds of her skirt and wedged the straw hat on her head, half listening for the whistle of the train, which when the wind was from the west, would echo across the country as it pulled out of the town and headed across the hills towards them.

The door had slammed as James rushed in from the road that day when he found out. He ran into the parlour where Maria's grandmother was sitting knitting socks for the men at the front.

'They've told me she was Richard Week's girl,' he shouted at the old woman, his eyes red-rimmed from the sun. 'That she was his long before she was mine. That she still loves him.'

The old lady laid down her needles and peered up, noting the hands gesticulating, the arms hanging free, their strength regained. His eyes were wild with grief.

'She's a pretty girl, James. You must have known she had boyfriends.'

He gestured impatiently, dismissing boyfriends as unimportant. 'I hear Richard was different. He was everything.' His face crumpled suddenly and he sat down beside the empty hearth, the line of unsunburned skin showing white where the folds of his cravat had loosened. 'I can't bear to think of her in another chap's arms . . .'

She smiled. 'She's yours now, James. That's all that matters. Richard has been in Flanders some time now. I believe he had already gone when she first met you.' She looked suddenly vague. Her eyes refused to meet his, slipped sideways and back down to her arthritic fingers and the tiring dark grey wool.

James understood then. Richard was away. She had wanted a man and as the one she loved was not there . . .

The quarrel they had that night was as unforeseen as it was unkind in its bitterness. Neither understood the passions that allowed them to hurl such insults at one another. They forgot the fears, the strains, the pent-up emotions with which they had been living and blamed one another.

That night alone in her bed, Maria lay crying herself to sleep as James, slamming the door, had walked out to stride until dawn over the fields towards the hills, his boots soaked with dew, his fair hair blown back from his face, his brain seething with an unforeseen jealousy which appalled him even as he recognized its force.

By some unspoken agreement neither spoke of Richard again. It was as though they both sensed a power to be released by his name which could tear them and their newly won marriage apart, and though James was often moved to do just that he refrained and forced himself to trust and love again.

As he turned to her on the step of the train she wanted to shout: 'It's not what you think, James; we never did anything; it's you I love now,' but her pride forbade it. If he really thought so badly of her, let him. She didn't care.

But she had written it down. Three times she had begun the letter; three times thrown it aside in her writing case until at last she had found the words to explain what there had been between her and Richard and what had passed. Nothing with him, however dear the memory, could equal the waves of happiness with James and the knowledge that she was his wife. And this although she had heard now that Richard had won himself a medal and promotion at the front.

It was only when her letter was posted at last that she stopped tormenting herself about what she might have done to James. His own to her, the letter in her pocket, had arrived some time later. She had read it again and again for signs of anger or remorse, unbending pride or forgiveness but the letter contained none. It was natural and friendly and being about other people was curiously impersonal.

She walked briskly down the lane towards the station, her skirt stirring small whorls of dust at her feet, her boots gathering a strangely matt film on the soft polished leather.

The wagonette would be there before her but it didn't matter. It could pick Tom Kennedy up with the luggage and then collect her on the way back from the station after the train had pulled out. In a way she was glad. She didn't want to have to see him climbing into the wagonette with his crutches and his stump and his wide-apart eyes, this man whom James had liked so much.

Tom Kennedy's letter had arrived only a few days after James's. '. . . I would so like to meet you, Maria, (may I call you Maria?),' he had said. 'I know James means to write to you himself but my transport has come more quickly than I expected or dared hope so I must risk my letter arriving unannounced. I have nowhere to go immediately and I would so like to stay with you and your grandmother. James said he was sure you wouldn't mind. How I envy him, lucky old Jim, going up to where the action is. But then I always envy Jim. For the last few weeks I've been envying him his lovely bride . . .'

I hear the thunder in my ears
And weep aside
For here there is no place for tears.

It had been a surprise to her, the notebook. Of all the

scanty belongings they had returned to her it had been the most personal, that and her own unopened letter which had arrived too late. She had not known that he wrote poetry or how he felt about the war. Beyond a vague almost nameless terror for his safety she had not thought about the icy mud or the broiling sun or the guns. It was all beyond her comprehension, or was it just too terrible for her to try and comprehend? She could not decide which.

'You're one of the lucky ones, my dear,' her grandmother had said to James over the breakfast things the morning before he left. 'You've had your terrible wound and God be thanked you've recovered. You'll not be asked to suffer any more. I feel it in my bones.' He hadn't suffered any more of course. He could have known nothing of the shell that exploded at his feet, nothing at all.

He had left a trunk in the outhouse for them to store for him, 'until we find our own home when the war is over'. There had been four days of blank misery as she realized she would never see him again and then suddenly on a morning of misty warmth and falling scented apples she remembered that trunk. Perhaps there was a message for her there. Perhaps part of him lingered, something, some way of recapturing him for herself. The key was in the drawer of the table in their room.

There was a powdering of dust in the black tin lid and she knelt in the rubbish of the shed and blew it off, gently polishing it with the sleeve of her blouse, tracing the initials of his name J. O. N. His middle name was Oliver. She had not known it until the moment they stood together before the altar in the little Norman church and exchanged the age-old vows, 'Till death us do part.'

She brushed the back of her hand across her eyes and inserted the key in the lock. It turned with ease and the lid lifted without any resistance. Inside, beneath a neatly spread newspaper were dozens of books. She pulled them out looking curiously at the titles, wondering why he had hidden them, not put them proudly on the shelves in their room next to her own.

Then she found his notebooks. Poems and stories, diaries and long descriptive passages penned in the rather careful sloping hand which she saw had not changed very much since he was a boy at school for there were some school books there as well. But after all he *was* still practically a boy. For ever.

She shut the lid of the trunk.

She had grown to hate the idea of Tom Kennedy. He had no wife, no parents alive to mourn him. His death would have hurt no one, while James's . . . James's death was intolerable. And she would have to tell Tom that he was dead.

She had put James's hairbrushes back on the small dressing table next to her own. There were one or two hairs caught in the bristles and somehow the brushes still smelt of him. She took his best shirt, the one he had left behind next to her dresses and skirts in the narrow cupboard, to bed with her and cradled it in her arms.

'Why, Maria, I'd have known you anywhere.' Tom beamed down at her over the wheel of the wagonette. He stretched down a thin brown hand and hesitating she shook it. 'Forgive me for not jumping down. I'm not quite up to gymnastics yet.' He gestured at the crutches tucked beside him and laughed. 'Oh God, but it's good to be home and here.

Come up beside me.' He swung her up to the seat without any difficulty. She tried to avoid looking at the leg of his breeches, neatly pinned above the knee. His eyes were grey not blue as she had imagined. But they were dreamy, like James's.

'James was killed, you know. The day after he got back to the front.' To her surprise she could say it quite without emotion.

His face folded and trembled for a moment like a girl's and he gripped her hand so tightly she felt the bones of her knuckles crack. She kept her eyes fixed on the rhythmical swing of the pony's rump beneath the long reins held so loosely in Patterson's hands.

'He was my best friend.' That was all he said.

He sat in James's chair by the empty hearth and took his place at the meal table and slowly he won them over with his charm and gentle humour. Maria's grandmother watched and nodded at him as she knitted and glanced from time to time at her granddaughter, noting without comment as the girl smiled and relaxed; hoping.

It was Richard Week who came home for Christmas to the manor, leaving the war for well-deserved leave modestly to display his medals and the attractively ugly shrapnel scar across his cheek.

Maria met him beneath gnarled apple tree branches white with frost in the orchard behind the mill. He seemed taller than she remembered, self-assured now, bronzed.

'Did you wait for me, my love?' His hand beneath her chin, his lips pouting towards her were too sure, too certain of their welcome. She raised her hand to push him away and he saw the wedding ring. His eyes widened and he whistled. 'I see you didn't. Too bad.' His breath came in frosty clouds to her face.

She lowered her eyes. 'My husband is dead, Richard.' She felt nothing any more for this young man. He was a stranger to her. Sadly turning away she retraced her steps towards the village leaving him staring after her, shaken. They had hardly spoken.

Tom Kennedy was waiting for her by the post office, leaning on his crutches, his face flushed with the effort of the walk in the icy air. He glanced at her keenly and meeting the gaze she blushed uncomfortably.

'Did you go to see this Richard Week?'

She didn't ask him how he knew but nodded miserably, wishing his hands were free so that he could put his arm around her. She had grown used to seeking comfort from Tom.

'I didn't know if I still loved him. I had to go and see him.'

'And do you?'

Shaking her head she turned her face towards the display of yellowing calico and linens in the post office window so that he shouldn't see the tears which threatened to spill over. She wasn't sure whether they were for the old Richard whom she thought she had loved, or for James.

'He told me all about it when he visited me in hospital, Maria.' Tom's voice sounded suddenly unlike him. She heard the tap and squeak of the crutches as he swung himself closer to her. Then she felt his hand, heavy, supporting his weight, on her shoulder. 'I am glad, Maria. I couldn't bear to think that you were deceiving him.'

Somehow she didn't resent the remark. Tom had the right to reproach her. He had been James's best friend.

'I wrote telling him the truth, Tom. He never got the letter; they returned it to me unopened.'

He nodded, understanding and squeezed her shoulder. Then he rebalanced himself upon the crutches and smiled, suddenly cheerful again. 'Come on, I'll race you home!'

In spite of herself she laughed.

I hear the thunder in my ears
And weep aside . . .

Together they read James's poems in the long evenings after her grandmother had gone to bed.

'I promised James I'd take care of her if anything happened to him,' he had told the old lady. She was concentrating on turning the heel of the current sock and did not look up, but nodding quietly she had smiled and approved and Tom, seeing it, had taken courage. He could not remember his own grandmother.

He brought in the dusty trunk from the shed and helped her unpack it in her room, balancing against the tallboy as he stacked the volumes side by side on the shelf, frowning to himself in the concentration of getting the spines neatly in line.

On the last day of his leave Richard Week came to the door. Maria received him in the parlour while Tom helped the old lady in the kitchen.

Standing awkwardly by the window with the line of budding geraniums in their pots on the sill Richard asked her to marry him. She thought she could hear in the silence that followed the tiny squeak of rubbers in the passage outside the door.

'I am sorry, Richard.' Her voice was clear, a little high pitched from nervousness; too loud. 'But I shall never marry again.'

In the shuffling and flurry of Richard's flustered protestations and reluctantly disbelieving goodbyes she did not hear the small sounds of the crutches in the hall as they retreated to the kitchen.

'Oh, she doesn't mean it.' The old lady was cutting the scones in half with a thin-handled knife, the blade polished grey with age and scouring. She looked up at the crestfallen young man and smiled fondly. He was more of a grandson than ever James had been. She had known him much longer now, for one thing. They both had.

'She said that to Richard to ease his going. You'd not grudge the boy that? There's many may never come back from this war; he may be one of them. But I think if you give her time she'll maybe think again, Tom. For you. Just give her time.' She leaned over and patted his arm encouragingly.

He grinned. 'I'll give her all the time in the world if she wants it.' He swung himself round and out of the kitchen. This house was his home now. He had nowhere else to go; no one else to go to. For a moment he felt panic sweep over him. There was so much at stake. Then she was there looking at him from the parlour doorway, smiling, the copper lights in her hair high-lighted in the sun from the window behind her.

She held out her hand. 'Let's go for a walk, Tom, shall we? It's such a beautiful evening,' and her face lit with a gentle, reassuring smile.

Had he had a cap Tom would have thrown it into the air. He followed her out into the garden whistling and they were already half-way down the lane which led towards the mill before he remembered that the old lady had their tea ready in the kitchen.

A *Face in the Crowd*

Behind the bony silhouettes of the trees the sky was a limpid aquamarine; a crystal bowl carrying the reflection of a thin moon lying on its back.

Leaning on her elbows on the windowsill, gazing out, Jill shivered. The air was chilled and pure as it lay against her face and she welcomed its icy touch. Downstairs the clock in the inn parlour chimed again. Another hour had passed. Three more hours till dawn, she supposed, then the interminable wait until she could decently order coffee, then the whole morning, perhaps the whole day.

And if he didn't come? Supposing he had no intention of keeping their rendezvous? Supposing he was still 4,000 miles away and had never thought of her again? A breath of wind tiptoed over her flesh. She shivered and turned to pad back across the polished oak boards to the double bed. Climbing in she lay against the pillows and stared up at the dark ceiling, pulling the blankets up beneath her chin. She knew she would not sleep again that night.

'Jill?' Andrew had stopped her one day in the street outside Oxford Circus Underground. 'It is Jill Forbes, isn't it?' He had sleepy grey eyes and dishevelled hair which made her think he had overslept and rushed out without his breakfast. Later she discovered that he always looked like that.

'I'm sorry?' she stammered, confused by the grimly hurrying crowds and the relentless rain which blew in their faces. They were forced to circle each other as she kept slowly moving, late already and unwilling to stop for a stranger.

'You don't remember me?' He wasn't hurt or indignant; just amused. Then he reached out and took her arm and guided her away from the centre of the pavement into a wide doorway out of the rain.

She looked at him again, helplessly, glancing at her watch as she tried to recall his face.

'I'm sorry,' she said again, 'but I'm terribly late; I've a day off and I have things to do.'

'You have nothing to do,' he said laughing. 'You're spending the day with me . . .'

At least, that was how she remembered their meeting. Probably it hadn't been so simple. He had had to explain who he was – he had been a student at the same college as her brother Ted, years before – and he had had to go with her to take her passport photos, waiting outside the kiosk, laughing as she sat solemnly inside, then on to do some shopping. Only then, unable to shake him off, had she relented and they had gone out into the rain once more and had coffee together at a stall beside some park railings. She had still not remembered who he was; the circumstances where they must have met, yes, but his face? No.

She had cupped her hands around the thick grimy china of the mug beneath the awning which deflected the rain into a noisy stream and stared at him, disconcerted by the complete absence of memory. He had such an attractive face, such an attractive personality. Surely she would have remembered this . . .

'What are you doing now, Andrew?' she asked at last.

He grinned. 'You still haven't a clue who I am, have you? You really ought to ring Ted and check my credentials. I might be an impostor.'

She sipped her coffee. 'I'll chance it,' she said.

'I'm a marine biologist,' he said.

She stared. 'But Ted is a historian!'

'Such unexpected meetings!' He shrugged expressively. 'I live in a hut by the sea. Literally. I'm only in London for four days collecting equipment and working at the library. Then I go back to Scotland.'

So that was it. He was clutching at straws. A face he recognized in the metropolis; someone to talk to in a city of strangers.

They had lunch and they walked and she went with him to collect various weird and wonderful pieces of gadgetry from his college. They left them at the hotel and then she took him back to her flat so she could change before they went out to dinner.

On her bookcase was a photograph of Jerry. Andrew spotted it at once as he waited. 'Your fella?' he asked, holding it to the light.

'My fella,' she agreed.

'Will he object to your going out with me?'

Strangely it had not crossed her mind, but now she paused, staring over Andrew's shoulder at the familiar face of the man she loved. She hesitated. Then she said softly, 'Yes, I think he might.'

She felt even more guilty on Saturday when she had to put Jerry off, cancelling their usual supper-and-film, because it was Andrew's last day. But why should she feel conscience-stricken? After all, Andrew was going back to Scotland, to his deserted beach where his only neighbours were terns and crabs and kittiwakes and where his whole life revolved around the study of the tides. It was not as though this was the start of something serious.

She went with him to King's Cross, to help him find his sleeper. They had to stand very close in the narrow compartment.

'I wish you were coming with me, Jill,' he said.

'So do I.' She realized her eyes were filled with tears and turned away hurriedly. He was, after all, still a stranger.

Hands in pockets, her collar high against the wind, she walked back up the Euston Road; oblivious of the broad double tide of traffic which roared past her. In her imagination she was with him on the train, or already there in his shack on the edge of the rolling Atlantic.

Jerry called for her at six the following Wednesday. They were going to the Opera and in the Crush Bar in the first interval they met some friends of her brother Ted.

'Andrew Hamilton?' the tall thin young man who had been Ted's house captain at school and had then gone on to the same college, turned his pale blue eyes on her curiously. 'I'll say I remember him. Extraordinary chap! why do you ask?'

She explained, vaguely aware that Jerry was beside her, his knuckles white around his glass.

'Good Lord! Well, all I can say is you're well out of that encounter, Jill, old girl.' He paused to acknowledge someone in the crowd, his glass held above shoulder level to prevent it spilling. 'As far as I remember he broke a trail of hearts from Oxford to John o' Groats, then in the end he married some foreign lady, French or Italian or something!'

Andrew had not mentioned a wife.

As Jerry led her back to their seats he looked at her carefully. 'Sure it's only casual interest?' he said.

'Quite sure.' She smiled at him as she opened her programme at Act Two. 'After all, I'll never see him again.'

But he came back to London at Christmas. And she found out that she was in love.

When Jerry phoned she made some excuse not to see him and walked with Andrew through the noisy decorated streets, staring up at the huge tinsel snowflakes suspended from their wires between the tall office blocks. Then they bought hot chestnuts outside Foyles and wandered round the British Museum.

It was afterwards in a restaurant off Long Acre that he reached across the table and touched her hand.

'I'm staying at a friend's flat this time, while he's away.'

When she looked up and met his gaze thoughtfully, he smiled. 'Come back with me tonight, Jill,' he said.

She knew that if she accepted it would be a commitment; one she could not easily break, but her feelings for Andrew were so different from those she had felt for Jerry; deeper, more sudden and more painful, and she acknowledged at last, more real.

She looked up and found he was watching her closely. 'You know what I'm saying, don't you?' he said softly.

She nodded. 'I'd like to come.'

That afternoon she phoned Jerry from her own flat. 'I can't see you any more. I'm sorry, so very sorry,' she whispered.

There was a long silence. 'I suppose I've been expecting it,' he managed to say at last. 'I've known a long time. I think since that evening at the Opera.' There was another pause. 'Are you going to marry him?'

She gave a shocked little laugh. 'Jerry! I've only known him a few weeks.'

'It only takes a few minutes, love,' he said on the other end of the phone. 'Be happy, Jill. I'm always here if you want to talk.'

She stared at the receiver in her hand for several minutes after he had rung off. Then slowly she replaced it. Only then did she remember that Andrew already had a wife.

He was waiting for her in the next room. Sadly she took Jerry's photo up and looked at it, then she slid it into a drawer. 'Shall we go?' she said.

He understood her mood, not hurrying her, not even suggesting they go back at once to the friend's place. Instead they walked along the Regent's Canal, watching the raindrops digging pits in the slate grey surface of the water, shrugging into their coats against the wind, promising themselves crumpets dripping with butter before the gas fire as soon as it grew dark.

She liked the tiny flat in a house off Camden High Street. It was full of pictures and books and lit by impractically angled spot lights which threw shadows over the rugs so that she tripped and nearly fell on a hidden pile of magazines. The divan was covered by a faded dhurrie.

He kissed her long and hard before he began to unfasten the buttons of her blouse. Then, turning off the spots, he led her to the bed, lit now only by the gentle hissing flow of the gas fire and pushed her gently down among the heaped striped cushions, his arms around her, his lips warm as they sought her breasts.

It was daylight when he took her home.

In the car outside her place he took her hand and held it.

'I've promised to spend Christmas with my parents in Edinburgh, Jill. I can't disappoint them,' he said.

She looked down, not daring to let him see her face. 'Of course.'

'But I could come back a few weeks from now,' he went on. 'There's a little pub I know, in the Sussex Downs. I'd like to show it to you . . .'

She wasn't sure she could bear it that they must part so soon. The packing and the trail, almost familiar on this occasion, to King's Cross. He gave her a tiny Victorian pearl pendant for a present; she gave him the Grieg tape he wanted for his lonely evenings by the sea.

'You don't mean you're going back there for the winter?' she had exclaimed aghast. She had seen the photos now of his hut in the wild sea grasses and the dunes and the little boat beached high on the wet sand. His only light came from oil lamps; his music from an old battery driven cassette player.

'It's a two year project, Jill,' he said, 'and I'm only allowed away for a few days at a time. There are too many measurements to take, notes to make, things to do. You wait till you see it . . . You'll understand then.'

She remembered that conversation as they stood together in the sleeper saying goodbye and she thought again of the cold little shiver which had crept down her spine at his words.

'But I hate the sea, Andrew,' a little voice had cried deep inside her. 'I hate the sea and everything to do with it . . .'

The inn was old and rambling, snuggling in a fold of the hills, its thatched roof gold against the frost blue sky of winter. In the hall the grandfather clock ticked the centuries away in peace, to the gentle scents of burning applewood and baking.

Lying awake in his arms she heard the clock chime in

the warm darkness and she felt the tears come to her eyes at the pain of her happiness.

They spent their two days walking hand in hand across the sheep-cropped turf, feeling the icy wind in their faces, running sometimes for sheer joy, their feet hollow on the chalky soil, and the two nights they lay together on the huge goosefeather mattress lost in the wonder of their love.

As she nestled against him, her fingers tracing the line of his shoulders, holding him close, trying to see his face in the dark she prayed that the night might never end. The sharp ecstasy of their love and the tenderness which followed it had left her wakeful and she lay, listening to his even breathing as he slept in her arms and she wanted to hold him for ever.

There was no choice, though. He had to go, wrenching himself away from her, refusing to let himself see her tears. But on Valentine's day he sent her a pale yellow cairngorm set in a Celtic silver pin. 'I've booked us into the inn again for Easter,' he wrote on the card. 'Until then I'm counting each day. We won't waste a moment in London. Meet me at the station . . .'

It was a cold wet Easter, the buds still tight on the trees, the daffodils the only brave defiant challenge to a reluctant departing winter. Jill didn't care. The agony of the long wait was over and she was once more in his arms. To her the colour of the sky, the full gurgling muddy ditches were an irrelevance beside the man who was sitting opposite her at dinner at the table near the huge inglenook fire.

'Nine and a half whole weeks since I saw you,' she said.

They both laughed as though it were something funny she had said. He was watching the firelight flickering reflected in the smoky golden brooch at her throat. It set off the tawny colouring of her hair and eyes.

'We must always come back here,' he said. 'For our anniversaries and special occasions. It will be our home from home. When is your birthday?'

She smiled happily, picking up her glass of wine. 'Not till August. We'll have to think of something to celebrate before then. When is yours?'

It seemed strange that she didn't know.

'June,' he said.

Cancer and Leo she thought later. Fire and water. They can never mix. And she pictured again the pounding cruel waves and the desolation she had stared at in the photograph of the shore which he called home and wondered if she could ever bear to leave the city.

Something to ask him; something to tell him. And either or both could end their relationship; before it had really started. Was either worth it, she wondered? Was it really worth it for the sake of truth?

It was August, and she stared at him across the breakfast table near the open window. He was buried in the Sunday paper as unconscious of her presence as were the other men in the room of their table companions. The stamp of a husband perhaps?

'I know about your wife, Andrew,' she said softly.

For a moment he did not move. He did not hold his breath. His fingers had not tightened on the paper. Then carefully he folded it back at the page he was reading and put it down on the vacant chair between them.

She tried to read his face, feeling a cold sick fear settling into her stomach. Defensively she reached for her cup and sipped at the coffee scalding her tongue so that the tears came. But it did not matter; he was not looking at her.

'How long have you known about that?' he asked. He

was staring at the ragged torn fragment of toast on his plate.

'Someone told me just after I met you,' she whispered.

'And you never said anything?'

'I never said anything.'

'Why?'

'I was afraid of knowing for sure.'

He looked up at last. 'And now you are no longer afraid?'

She reached out her hand, tentatively, scared of being rebuffed. 'And now I no longer care, Andrew. I love you too much.'

His fingers had closed tightly over hers, but he was no longer looking at her. His face was troubled as he stared past her out of the window.

'Life never is simple, is it?' he said at last. 'We think because we ignore something, because we pretend it isn't there, because we leave it behind that we are free of it. But somehow, somewhere it is going to catch you up.'

'I said I didn't care, Andrew,' she persisted gently.

'But I care.' He stood up violently, pushing his chair back so that it rumpled the worn carpet. At the other tables there was an infinitesimal shocked silence at the interlude, then a studied refusal to allow it to ruffle the calm surface of breakfast time.

'I'm sorry you had to know about her.' He waved his arms in the air helplessly. 'As long as you didn't know that I had had a wife I could pretend I had not been through it all; pretend everything with us was fresh and new and real . . .'

'Andrew!' Jill protested, but already he had turned on his heel. He walked stiffly past the other tables and out of the room closing the door with a sharp click behind him.

Jill remained where she was, painfully conscious of the questioning stares that were being directed at her, clutching at one pitiful straw as the misery of their first quarrel descended on her.

'*Had* had a wife,' he'd said. Had, not have . . .

She forced herself to pour another cup of coffee and sat before it, not touching it for five more minutes. Only as the other residents rose and made their way out of the room did she too push back her own chair. She stood for a moment looking out onto the rose beds then resolutely she went up the stairs.

To her surprise he was there, lying face down on the bed.

'Andrew, it's our last day. Can you forget I mentioned it? Please?' She sat down before the dressing table and reached for her brush. 'I don't want to know about your past. All I want now is the two of us together.'

It wasn't quite true, but she would settle for it.

He rolled over and lay watching her, his arm across his eyes as though he was dazzled.

'You say that, Jill, but it will always be there in the background.'

'It always was, for you, Andrew,' she reminded him gently.

He gave a sheepish smile. 'I'd better tell you about it anyway. She was too young and I was too idealistic. We both expected fairy tales and found a grim reality we couldn't cope with. End of story.'

She swivelled on the stool until she was facing him. 'End of story?'

He shrugged. 'You're right. Except for this residue of bitterness and disillusion. That stayed. I'm sorry. I love you, but I'm afraid of trying to make it permanent for us. Can you understand that? Like trying to trap a sunbeam. It's there till you make a move to hold it then wham, the world is dark.' He turned his head away. 'I shouldn't have led you to expect anything more from me, Jill. I can't give it.'

Later they walked, but no longer hand in hand. Somehow it was easier to put their hands in their pockets as if to ward off a cold wind. At lunch, though, the curious stares directed at their table by their neighbours anxious to know how the quarrel had progressed made them giggle. And suddenly the tension had gone. Jill felt the pressure of his knee against hers beneath the white starched cloth and, meeting his eye, felt her heart leap with relief.

They spent the afternoon in bed, both resolving drowsily that it would be best to say nothing more as they lay in one another's arms, realizing, after this their first argument, how fragile a thing love was; how easily it could be destroyed and how doubly precious it was for that reason. And for that brief afternoon and night their love reached a new height of passion and tenderness.

At King's Cross the following afternoon Jill knew, however, that things would never be the same again and she cried as she clung to him. 'Andrew! Oh Andrew!'

Firmly he unclasped her hands. 'It won't be long, love,' he said, 'I'll be back soon.'

But would he? Desolate she stood on the platform watching the long train snaking into the distance and she realized suddenly that she had not even got round to telling him how she felt about the sea.

Weeks later she was meeting her brother Ted for lunch. He was tanned and handsome, his hair streaked by three months of Kenya sunshine and she was proud of him as he escorted her to their table. He ordered for them, then he leaned across the cutlery and grinned. 'I met a friend of yours at Heathrow when I arrived.'

'Oh?' Unsuspecting she sipped the white wine she had asked for as an aperitif. 'Who?'

'Andy Hamilton.'

She became very conscious of the buzz of conversation around them, frozen as she was in a bubble of sudden silence. Cautiously she raised her eyes to Ted's.

'Oh?' was all she said.

'Nice chap. I haven't seen him for years. We had time for a quick drink and he mentioned he'd seen you.'

'Yes?' Her bleak answer was too quick; too casual.

He had been in London and he had not told her.

Ted was preoccupied with the arrival of their order and had not noticed her silence as she watched the waiter shuffling dishes onto the table.

Taking a deep steadying breath she said, 'What was he doing at Heathrow then?'

The plate of crudités gave her something to concentrate on so he could not see her face.

'He was off to some conference, I gather, on the west coast of America. High powered stuff. He won an award three months back for his research. Did you know?'

No, she didn't know. How could she? He hadn't told her.

The vegetables tasted like wet cardboard in her mouth, but she forced herself to swallow. It wasn't fair to Ted to spoil their reunion by crying. That she managed to contain in a short interlude in the Ladies' Room, dabbing her cheeks hard with her handkerchief and wishing it were still the fashion to wear thick concealing face powder. Ted did not look up when she returned. Instead he busied himself with the menu. When he spoke it was so casually she hardly for a moment heard his words.

'I rather gathered he felt he had messed things up with you,' he said quietly. 'A pity that. He's a good bloke, Andy.'

She found she could not speak.

He glanced up for a second and seeing her expression, hastily turned back to the menu.

'We all knew he'd made a mistake when he and Katya married. They were much too young. It only lasted about eighteen months, you know.'

She nodded, conscious that she couldn't hold the tears back much longer and that she was going to make a fool of herself in public. 'I didn't care about her, Ted. I don't care now.'

'What then?' This time when he looked up he held her gaze, forcing her to answer.

She shrugged helplessly. 'It's lots of things.'

'You never told him how you felt about the sea?'

She shook her head. 'The opportunity never came,' she whispered.

Ted frowned. 'Do you still get the nightmares?'

'No. Not for ages.' Her knuckles were white around the spoon she held. 'Anyway, it didn't matter. I'd have followed him across the Atlantic in a small boat if he'd asked me, Ted. But he never did. I told him I loved him. It was he who went away.'

'I told him about your dreams.'

She stared. 'You had no right!'

'I think I did, if your silly phobia came between you. But he said it hadn't. He said he knew there was something, but you had never talked about yourself. He assumed it was a man.'

'Oh.' Dully she slumped back in her chair. 'Is that why he never came back?'

Ted's eyes narrowed. 'He didn't say. It seems to me you never had a chance, him in Scotland, you in London. Why don't you go up to see him when he gets back?'

When he gets back? But how would she know?

*

She didn't want to phone Jerry, it seemed unfair. But he had said 'call me' and she was so lonely. He took her to the Chelsea Kitchen and was kinder than she had dared to hope he would be, listening to a story which she knew must hurt him if he still cared for her, yet unable to stop herself once she had started talking.

'How long is he away for?' he asked at last, picking unerringly on the most salient question.

She shook her head helplessly. 'I don't know.'

'Not even a post card?'

'No, nothing. Nothing for months.'

'But it's still on as far as you're concerned?'

She shrugged. 'How can it be? When he's so far away.'

Jerry couldn't help of course. All he could do was listen and buy another carafe of wine and offer comfort in his own way, taking her in his arms at her front door and kissing her gently on top of the head. 'Can I come in, Jill?' he asked.

She shook her head, but the knowledge that he still cared comforted her.

Later she crossed to her mirror and sat down staring at her face. How was it possible for her to love anyone so much? What strange chemistry had made her yearn for someone like Andrew when Jerry, sweet, kind Jerry who understood her, was there, loving her, waiting in the wings for a word?

'Stupid!' She said out loud to her reflection. She meant herself; her love; the whole world.

Three times she started to write letters to Andrew. Three times she tore them into little pieces and threw them out. What anyway was the point? She did not know where he was. His hut by the ocean was, she supposed, empty; perhaps abandoned for ever. She did not even know his parents' address.

Her only hope was the inn in the Downs and the

anniversary of their first visit a year ago. She clutched at the hope, writing to book the room because she did not have the face to phone with the lie that he would be with her.

A week before the date the snow began, falling overnight in a blanket on an unresponsive London, muffling the tyres, drifting for a few hours of beauty across the filthy pavements. The news carried hourly reports of the chaos in the country; the smothering and then the blocking of the roads and she knew she had the perfect excuse not to go. She listened to the weather forecasts, half willing the weather to grow worse to make the decision for her, knowing she would not have the resolution not to go.

She went.

The countryside was breathtakingly beautiful, the trees bowed down beneath their veil of white, the inn with a wraith of smoke from its chimney scenting the clear blue sky as it nestled into its fold of the Downs.

She was the only guest to arrive. 'I've put you in your usual room, dear,' the landlady said comfortably. 'Your husband coming separately, is he?' They had signed the register in their two separate names the first time. The next it had been easier just to use Andrew's.

The woman's face was kind and she produced tea and oven-warm scones and slid a hot water bottle into the huge double bed.

Jill forced herself to smile. 'I only hope he's coming,' she said. 'He's flying back from the States and with the weather as it is . . .'

At least the snow would cover her shame when he did not come.

She ate in their private parlour by the roaring fire and knew they were trying to cheer her with television and mulled wine while outside the icicles were daggers against the moon. She dreaded going upstairs alone.

Crawling back at last into the huge lonely bed she hugged the almost cold hot water bottle to her miserably, drawing her chilled feet up till she lay in a tight knot and finally allowed her tears to fall. He wouldn't come. She had known it all along. Their whole affair had been in her imagination, for him just an interlude to be ended as soon as he had realized she was serious, an encounter in the street that had led to a year of fun; for her a love which would stay with her for the rest of her life.

The cold dawn was filtering in at the window before she drifted off into an uneasy sleep listening to the sharp cry of an owl hunting over the snow-covered moonlit fields.

She was awakened by the landlady shaking her shoulders. 'It's your husband, my dear. Quickly! He's come through on our private phone. From America!'

The fire was out in the parlour and the room looked cold as she picked up the receiver with a shaking hand, her bare feet icy beneath her blue dressing gown. 'Andrew?'

'Jill. You are there. How are you, darling?'

Suddenly she couldn't speak. His voice from so far away sounded as though it were in the next room. 'I never let myself believe you'd be there,' he was saying. 'I told myself to forget you, but I couldn't. I decided a week ago to phone the inn. If you were there, I'd know you still loved me, if you weren't . . .' He left the sentence unfinished.

'I still love you, Andrew,' she managed to say at last. 'I had to come here . . .'

'Jill? Jill, love, don't cry. Oh God, I wish I were with you. Listen darling, listen . . .'

She could hear his voice repeating her name. Desperately she tried to pull herself together.

'Andrew, about the sea. It's only a dream I get. It doesn't matter. I'll learn to live near it – on it, if you want, I promise . . .'

'But Jill, that is what I keep trying to tell you!' There

was a crackle on the line and she heard his exclamation of annoyance. 'Ted told me about your dreams. I've had time to think. I've been a fool. And, oh so much has happened. Listen, darling, when it comes to it I can't live without you. I've been lost these last few months not knowing where you were or what was happening, not planning another meeting . . . Listen, Jill. I've been offered a research fellowship here in the States. I know we never discussed it, but would you be prepared to live over here–' his voice faded for a moment and distractedly she held the receiver away from her and shook it.

'Andrew? *Andrew!* . . .'

'Jill, listen darling. If you don't like the idea I'll turn them down. Can you hear me? Wait there! Don't move. I'm getting the first flight . . .'

She listened for a long time to the empty crackling on the line, staring around the room, then at last she hung up. The landlady had withdrawn discreetly and left her alone with the cold smell of the dead wood ash and the chill of the early morning still frosting the windows. But suddenly the room had lost its gloom and as she watched, in the earthenware jug on the windowsill, a bunch of winter jasmine caught the first tentative rays of the sun and turned to gold.

A Woman's Choice

It had happened after they went back to the States.

'No, no, no, Dan! It's just not on!' Maggie slammed her open hand down on the table in front of her, her eyes wide with anger. 'I knew you were going to suggest this and I won't do it. It's not fair to ask me.'

Dan looked up at her over the cup he held in both hands and gave a sheepish smile. 'OK, OK, so I'm sorry. I guess I knew it wasn't on. But hell, I had to suggest it. It might have worked.' He shrugged. 'Suzanne is – ' he hesitated imperceptibly, ' – was my sister, after all. And those two kids are family.'

'I know and I'm sure that they're great kids. But Dan, we don't want kids! We've no time, no room for kids, that's why we didn't have any of our own, remember?' There was something like despair in her voice – and guilt.

'Sure, honey, sure.' He stood up and pushed his stool back from the table, meticulously folding his newspaper so that it fitted into his briefcase. He stooped and kissed the top of her head lightly. 'Don't worry about it. Ma and I will have to do something of course, what with poor old Roger having no family that we ever met – and, I don't know, I suppose they'll have to be taken care of back in Carson. Perhaps a neighbour or someone might take them in; I understand they're with one at the moment.' He was frowning as he straightened his tie at the mirror next to the kitchen window.

'Can't your mother have them, Dan?' She began to pile up the dishes and refold the foil in the cereal packet.

'You know she can't.' For the first time he snapped. 'She's too frail. Not that she wouldn't want them. She's always spoiled those two when she got the chance to see them but Carson is so far away. That's the trouble. Too far to know what to do for the best.'

He opened the door. 'I'll call you from the office, Maggie. Bye for now.'

She heard him walk through the hallway and then the front door slammed.

The kitchen was suddenly very empty and quiet. She dumped the cups and plates in the sink and left them so that she would have time to put on some make-up before leaving the apartment. Glancing at her wrist watch she groaned. Late again.

In front of the bathroom mirror she stopped and looked hard at her face in the cold unflattering glare of the strip light. Her skin was sallow and tired from lack of sleep and there were dark hollows beneath her eyes. She grabbed a bottle of moisturizer and began to pat it on with quick impatient strokes of the finger tips, trying to flatten out some of the lines.

Then as she watched she saw her eyes for no reason at all suddenly fill with tears, brim and overflow. 'Oh hell.' She groped for a tissue and dabbed at the little creamy rivulets on her cheeks, trying to stem the flow. 'Oh damn poor Suzanne and Roger; damn their poor bloody kids! Why did it have to happen now?' She sat on the edge of the bath tub and blew her nose.

It was two days since the midnight phone call from the hospital which told them the news of the car crash; barely thirty-six hours since Sue had died, twelve since hearing that, though Roger might recover consciousness, he would almost certainly have irreversible brain damage. Ever since, she had been haunted by the vision of the two small children waiting with the baby sitter for their Mummy and Daddy to come home. She dabbed at her face again and stood up, sniffing, reaching for the matt foundation she kept for disguising the dark rings. It wasn't as if she knew the kids. They had been babies of – what? – eighteen months and three months respectively when she and Dan had last gone to Carson on a visit. She shuddered remembering suddenly the horrible baby smell in the house – the buckets of soaking diapers, the sweet clinging scent of regurgitated milk. But what a happy close family they had been, with Roger over the moon with his little son and his pretty daughter and Sue, in her usual dream world but ecstatic over her bouncing babies.

She dabbed again at her make-up and drew an angry red outline round her lips, blocking in the lipstick. It was then, on the way home in the car that Dan had finally agreed with her about no family of their own. 'You're right, Maggie,' he had said, groping for her hand in the dark as they waited at a red light, 'I don't think I could face all that hassle and noise in our home. My God, those buckets and all those hours feeding them!'

She hadn't said that many houses were cleaner and more efficient than Sue's, half out of loyalty to her sister-in-law and half out of relief at his words; instead she had returned the pressure of his fingers and given a quiet sigh of relief. It had bothered her in the past that perhaps Dan really did want kids; that he had said he didn't just to make her happy and because he knew her career meant so much to her. He had always been so good with children, instinctively good, while she shrank from them, resented them as a threat to her independence.

Her career! She looked back at the mirror with a sigh.

She wouldn't have a career at all if she didn't hurry up, finish her face and leave the house!

She took a cab downtown to the studios and crept into her office via the coffee machine. Minutes later the phone rang. It was Dan.

'I'm going up to Carson tomorrow with Ma; I've fixed it here so that I can be away for two or three days. You'll have to make my excuses to Bet on Thursday.'

Bet, wife of one of the senior producers, and her dinner party, to which so many important TV people would go. Maggie hadn't given it a thought. 'Are you sure you wouldn't like me to come with you to Carson?' she said stirring the coffee aimlessly with the end of her ball point. She didn't want to go; to see those two small faces, the large eyes. At the thought the blotter on her desk blurred and went out of focus suddenly and she shook her head angrily – 'Sorry Dan, what did you say?'

'I say there's no need for you to come. They know Ma best of any of us, she's seen them each year at least and she was there only a few months ago; they wouldn't remember you – or me for that matter.'

Remember her? How could they? She had held each child gingerly, at arm's length, for a token few seconds before returning it thankfully to its mother's arms, and that had been how long ago? Five years, which meant that the children were now five and six respectively.

With a sigh she picked up the internal phone. 'Hi, Bet. I'm afraid we're going to have to take a rain check for Thursday. Dan's going to be out of town . . .'

At lunchtime she ate a yoghurt, then she slipped out to the supermarket for a bag of groceries. The humidity had built up unbearably in the streets as the sun blazed down on the glaring sidewalks. On the corner some kids were splashing round a hydrant; little kids, perhaps five and six. She stopped still and looked at their laughing little faces. Behind her a woman came out with a bag of groceries, saw them and screamed furiously at the children. 'Sal, Tony, you come out of there!'

Two sheepish faces turned towards her and, tee shirts dripping, they slowly approached her. She set down her carrier on the sidewalk and dragged a handkerchief from her purse to dry them. Then laughing she suddenly hugged them both to her, soaking her thin dress.

Maggie turned away, a lump in her throat and walked blindly back up the street.

Dan was away three days. When he came back he looked pale and strained, his handsome face wretched as he threw his case on the bed and opened it.

'I saw Roger for a few minutes,' he said as Maggie sat at the dressing table, pretending to brush her hair. 'He's still in a coma. The little ones are still with the neighbour but she can't keep them much longer; they're all in one room with her kids and they keep looking through the fence at their house and saying, when can we go home? . . .' His voice broke suddenly and he sat down on the bed, pressing his knuckles into his eyes. 'Ma wants to move down there, take over the house, keep it as a home for them, but hell, she can't. She was knocked out by all this. She started getting pains in her chest again.'

Maggie slid the brush to her other hand and went on brushing methodically, her eyes fixed blankly on the mirror.

'I spoke to Jim Baines at work today,' she said at last as Dan opened the cupboard, rummaging for a coat hanger. 'I asked him if I could work half time or at home if I had to. He said there shouldn't be any problem.' She went on brushing.

'So?' He sounded guarded, but she saw in the mirror that he was looking at her suddenly.

'So we've got a spare room with two beds.' She flung down the brush and turned on the stool to face him. 'We can't let them go, Dan; we can't let them be separated. I don't know anything about children; I don't have the first idea where to begin, but we've got to try, haven't we? We're the only hope they've got.'

The relief he felt at her words was apparent in every line of his body as in two steps he was across the room, his hands on her shoulders.

'Do you really mean it, Maggie?'

She nodded wordlessly and he drew her gently to him and cradled her head on his chest.

The airport was crowded. Maggie had arrived early to find a place to park and give her time for one last fortifying coffee before the flight arrival was announced. Then they were there. She could see Dan walking towards her, holding in each hand the hand of a child. For one terrible moment she felt a total paralysis take hold of her. What had she done? What about her job, her future, all her plans? What did she know of children and their problems? She didn't even like children. She had no experience of children – not even of nephews and nieces of her own. And now they were here and Dan had stopped walking and three pairs of eyes were regarding her – all solemn – all waiting for her to speak. Her mouth had gone dry.

'Hi,' she said.

Dan grinned. 'This is Mary-Sue,' he said, 'and this is Hal. Say hello to your Auntie Maggie, kids.'

The two pairs of eyes looked sullen and hostile. Neither child said a word.

*

She had made the new drapes for their bedroom herself and lined the cupboard shelves with pretty paper. On each bed lay a new toy. A doll for Mary-Sue and a truck for Hal. Sure it's bribery, she had said to herself as she had written out the cheque for them. Sure, but how else can I get them to like me?

Dan brought in the cases and together they unpacked the children's toys and clothes. The little boy soon forgot some of his reserve in the interest of seeing his toys revealed, arranging them himself in a row under his bed, but Mary-Sue sat on her pillow and watched, her thumb securely in her mouth. She had not said a word.

The first three days weren't so bad. Dan stayed home from the office to help and Maggie, who had to go to her own office at the studios in the morning for one more week before starting to work from home, found things not at all too bad. In the apartment the children played in their bedroom or sat in front of the TV. They came to the table when they were told and allowed her to put them to bed without protest. Dan took them to the park and bought them ice-creams and took Hal on his knee and told him fairy stories to which the boy listened with enormous round staring eyes.

Dan was a natural with the kids, Maggie saw at once with a little pang of jealousy. He seemed to know what to say to them, what to do and they took to him easily, showing none of the shy reserve they kept for her, instinctively sensing her own.

It was not until Monday that Maggie first had them on her own. Breakfast passed without a hitch. Neither child ate much at any meal, which worried her, but at least at breakfast they could be persuaded to take a bowl of their favourite cereal in milk. Then Dan kissed her goodbye as so often in the past, folding his paper, picking up his case, going to the mirror to check his tie.

'I'll call you later,' he said. 'See how you're surviving. 'Bye kids.' And he had gone.

She swallowed. 'Right. Hal and Mary-Sue, do you want to go and play while I do the dishes?' Her voice sounded too brisk, too hearty.

She turned to stack the plates and cups in the sink, ignoring the two small faces which turned to watch her. They were still sitting there when she had finished.

'Right kids, run and play now. Auntie Maggie wants to do some work.' And she walked out of the room leaving them still sitting on their stools at the breakfast table.

She had commandeered a table by the window in the living room as a desk. On it she had put the reading lamp and a coffee mug full of pencils and ball points. Briskly she unfastened her case and brought out the pile of scripts she had to read. As she pulled up the chair she heard the door opening quietly behind her.

'Hi,' she called, without turning round. 'Want something?'

There was silence.

She went on sorting the scripts for a few moments, then turned. They were standing in the doorway holding hands.

'Mary-Sue wants to watch television,' Hal announced in a piping voice.

With a sigh Maggie glanced at the blank screen in the corner. 'Must you, darling? Auntie Maggie wants to work just now. Could you go and play, just for a little while? Please. You shall watch it later, I promise.'

The children looked at each other. She waited for the words, 'Mommie let us watch it,' but mercifully they never came. Reluctantly the two withdrew in total silence. Maggie turned to her work. Or tried to. She found she read a page – then read it again. But even the second time she could not remember what she had read. Her attention kept wandering to the two little waifs at the other end of the apartment.

She threw down her pen and got to her feet with a sigh.

The children's room was ominously silent. She pushed open the door and looked in. Mary-Sue was sitting on her pillow her thumb in her mouth, her legs curled up defensively under her, watching Hal who had found one of the suitcases and was industriously stuffing all his toys into it.

Maggie stood watching them for a moment. 'Well, well, Hal, you're busy. That's a nice tidy boy.'

He looked at her solemnly. 'Me and Mary-Sue want to go home,' he announced clearly. 'We don't like it here.'

'Dear God, Dan, what was I to do?' Maggie sobbed that night after the children had gone to bed. 'They kept looking at me with those great sad eyes. Children shouldn't look sad. They should be laughing. I tried to tell them that their home would be here now, but they didn't understand.'

'It's hard, Maggie, I know.' Dan got up and shook an empty cigarette pack hopefully. 'Ma told them the whole bit about Mummy going to heaven, and Daddy being too sick to look after them any more, but I don't think it's sunk in at all. They cried. Of course they cried, especially Hal, but,' he shrugged, 'it's so difficult knowing what to say: to reassure without raising any false hopes.'

'I don't know how to cope with it, Dan. We shouldn't have said we'd take them. We could do more damage than good.'

He shook his head slowly. 'I don't think so. I think unobtrusive love and security are what they need now. We've got to give everything we've got, Maggie and expect nothing in return. That's the only way.'

She stood up and went to unplug the percolator. 'Pretty thankless task that is for me. It's not you that's had to give up your job – as good as. No, sorry, Dan. I didn't mean that. I guess I'm just so mixed up myself about it. I'm sorry for them; I want to cry every time I see them; I want to cuddle them and protect them and make the world go away and yet I don't dare. I'm not like you. I can't do it. I know they'll reject me.' There was a sob in her voice and she sniffed angrily, as he started to protest. 'Oh yes I do resent them, Dan. I don't want to. I know I shouldn't, but because of them I've almost certainly lost that producer's job I was after and they've put me on to wading through lousy scripts. And I can't even do that properly because the kids distract me. They distract me if they're there and they distract me if they're not there because I think they'll start packing again and leave or something.'

She ran her fingers through her hair in agitation, pushing it back from her hot face.

Dan's blue eyes were very sober. 'I didn't realize, honey. I thought you were a hundred per cent behind me in this. Maybe we shouldn't have done it.' He got up and took the percolator out of her hands, pouring two mugs of black coffee. 'It's not too late, Maggie. We can send them back, honey. It's not as though they're settled here yet.'

She shook her head violently. 'No, no. We must keep them. I want to keep them. I do really.' Accepting a mug from him she sipped it, quick gasping sips, blowing the steam from the nutty black liquid. 'I suppose I'm just tired and depressed after the strain of the first day on my own.' She smiled wanly. 'I'll get used to it. We've got to win through with them, Dan, somehow. Make it up to them for what's happened. That's all that matters now.'

Next day was easier. She worked in the kitchen while they watched TV for half an hour. Then she called them in to help her with the baking. Hal was full of enthusiasm, kneeling up on a stool, one of her aprons tied under his armpits and was soon merrily covered in flour. She glanced at Mary-Sue who was sitting next to him toying listlessly with a spoon. The little girl had great dark circles under her eyes as if she hadn't slept, although each night when Maggie had looked in at the children both had been lying still, breathing evenly in the little yellow-draped room.

'What would you like to do, Mary-Sue?' she asked, racking her brains. 'I tell you what. If we let Hal make the buns – he's good at buns – why don't you make us some peppermint creams and we can all eat one while the buns are cooking.'

She turned away casually to the cupboard, praying she had some peppermint essence as, over her shoulder, she saw the child watching her, interested for the first time.

That night when she went in to check if the children were asleep she found Hal had crept into bed beside his sister. She gazed at them quietly for a minute and then tiptoed out of the room without a word.

The next day was quite good. After TV Maggie suggested they each have one of Mary-Sue's peppermint stars and she was rewarded with a shy smile. Then they went to the supermarket and the children pushed the trolley for her and chose the food they liked best. Then they all went home for a hamburger lunch.

It was the first night that Dan wasn't there to help bath them and put them to bed. He was going to be out till late at a business dinner and Maggie planned to catch up on her scripts. As she towelled each thin little body dry and powdered it and pulled on the patterned pyjamas she longed to put her arms round the children and hug them.

Why can't I? she thought miserably. What's holding me back?

She dropped a quick kiss on each head. 'Run to your beds now and I'll come and tuck you in and read your bedtime story.'

Wearily she stooped to pull the plug and watch the foaming water run away. A small blue plastic dolphin grounded nose first in the soapy dregs and she picked it out with a wistful smile, shaking a gobbet of wet fluff from its snout and setting it in the soap dish, then she walked slowly into the bedroom.

Later she poured herself a large Martini and sat spread-eagled on the couch, her head thrown back against the cushion. The room was airless and she was tired out but she had to start reading the scripts. Half of them were due back – with verdicts – by the next morning. Hauling herself to her feet she put on a record, then she went reluctantly to the table by the window and sat down, the ice-misted glass in her hand, sipping as she flipped open the first folder.

Slowly it began to grow dark. She didn't notice; reading hard, the lamplight reflecting in the polished wood, she worked on, finishing one script, writing her report and opening the next. Outside the hot air beat up towards the windows from the sidewalk, reverberating with the distant noise of cars. In a minute she would get up, make herself a sandwich, fix another drink . . .

It was several minutes before she became aware of the small figure standing beside her just outside the circle of lamplight.

'Hello, Mary-Sue,' she said quietly, dropping her pen and stretching her cramped fingers. 'Can't you sleep, honey?' A surreptitious glance at her watch told her it was after ten.

The little girl shook her head wordlessly. Her face was haggard.

And then suddenly it was so easy to know what to do.

Maggie pushed back her chair and held out her arms and the child threw herself into them sobbing miserably. Maggie drew her up onto her lap and hugged her tightly rocking to and fro, overwhelmed by the wave of emotion which shook her as she felt the thin little body pressed against hers, the arms clinging round her neck for comfort.

It was a long time before the storm of crying passed. Then came the moment Maggie had dreaded for so long. The little girl, her voice muffled in Maggie's shoulder murmured, 'My Mummy's never coming back, is she?'

Maggie's voice was surprisingly steady as she hugged Mary-Sue close. 'No, sweetheart. She can't come back. That's why she's asked Uncle Dan and me to take care of you and Hal for her.'

They sat for a long time in silence – so long that Maggie thought the little girl had fallen asleep in her arms from sheer exhaustion, but when she cautiously straightened Mary-Sue sat up, yawning, her face still pink and crumpled from the tears.

Maggie gave her a reassuring smile. 'Was Hal still asleep when you came in, love?'

Mary-Sue nodded.

'Good. Then I tell you what. Why don't you and I go and get ourselves a midnight feast. I'm hungry and I'll bet you are too. What do you say to a sandwich and some ice-cream soda. A secret; just the two of us. Not telling Uncle Dan.'

'Or Hal?'

'Or Hal.'

Mary-Sue nodded without another word and reluctantly she slipped from Maggie's lap still clinging to her hand as they went through into the kitchen.

It was the strangest midnight feast. They sat cross-legged on the rug on the floor on either side of a fat red Christmas candle, dug out from the back of the closet, eating peanut butter sandwiches and brownies and drinking from tall icy glasses with coloured straws.

Across the street the neon signs flashed reflections on the dark wall of the kitchen behind the child and Maggie could see her clearly in the opal glow, her face solemn, her shoulder length silver hair hanging over two pathetically narrow shoulders in cotton pyjamas covered in pale blue elephants. Somewhere in the distance a police siren wailed, and always far below was the roar of traffic.

With a sigh she thought of the unread scripts on the table next door. They would never be done in time now; she felt a little twinge of regret. Then she remembered again the warmth and longing in the child's arms and she felt that perhaps after all they weren't so important. They could wait their turn.

She found Mary-Sue was looking at her suddenly and she smiled gently in the candle light. 'What shall we do tomorrow, eh?' she asked in a whisper.

'Make peppermint creams again, Auntie Maggie,' was the sleepy reply.

Flowers Shouldn't Make You Cry

The sun glittered on the water, refracting a thousand facets of diamond light as the river tumbled towards the west. It was very cold. Jane shrugged herself deeper into her warm coat and glanced up at the man at her side.

They had pulled up in the layby and kissed and then while Ian felt in the glove pocket for a packet of cigarettes Jane had climbed out to stretch her legs and peer over the hedge. The sight took her breath away. The meadow, nestling in the elbow of dazzling water, was carpeted with daffodils. There must have been acres of them, of the palest yellow and their rich, delicate scent was everywhere in the wind off the mountains behind her.

The sound of her delighted cry brought Ian to her side in a moment. He smiled at her and reaching down broke off a bloom and gave it to her.

'They're wild, you know,' he said. 'Quite wild. You'll see, there are acres of them near the farm.'

She looked down at the single perfect flower and suddenly her eyes were blinded by tears.

She shook her head quickly, gazing away into the distance so that he should not see, should not realize that she could still think with sadness about the man whom this time last year she had been about to marry.

*

Edward had bought the bulbs, string bags of them, all daffodils and together they had knelt in the sooty earth of his small back garden and planted them, brushing away the dusty dried sycamore leaves which had drifted over the fence from the road at the back. She scooped out pockets of soil, setting the bulbs in place and firming back the earth and after a while she sat back on her heels, brushing a strand of hair from her eyes with the back of a grimy hand. She watched him working, as carefully he dug out a line of neat holes down the edge of the path and she frowned slightly. She had been planting the bulbs in big, bold clumps, visualizing the blaze of colour when they bloomed. His would be regimented and orderly, a thin yellow line.

He was a tall man, older than she, with a cynical shadow at his mouth and eyes which intrigued and tormented her. It was there, even now, while he bent concentrating to firm in the bulbs. She knew that she would do anything for him in her love and forgive much if he should ask it, but there was a strange centre of aloneness in him which chilled her sometimes. It was a place she would never reach, a place completely apart, a place that belonged to the days of the week she did not see him, the evenings he spent away from her.

Perhaps she suspected then that somehow his destiny might not lie with her; that soon her hopes and her world might begin to crumble even as the soft earth crumbled between her fingers. She shook her head to rid herself of her thoughts. She must not allow herself to build things up, to allow them to assume too much importance. She must wait.

The bulbs planted at last, she had watched from the kitchen door as he darkened the soil with water before he kicked off his boots and together they had washed off the earth, watching their fingers trailing black eddies down the sink.

Then his arms were round her at last and his lips on hers and for a while she forgot her fears and the bright rushing autumnal sky and the gently creaking door which swung to and fro in the wind.

In the end they went out for tea, walking hand in hand down the tow path before turning up the alley beside the pub and looking for the teashop by the church.

Their hands met on the checked gingham tablecloth and they had stared into each other's eyes, mesmerized, oblivious of the knowing looks of the three old ladies at the next table; that night she dreamed about him and the next, and then they met again to sit in the flickering twilight of the cinema, conscious only of each other and she feared again that the emotions were too strong, too sudden, their love too tempestuous. She knew she was obsessed and in her obsession the daffodils assumed a strange importance. They were a part of him; a part of her, planted by them both together as a promise of a future spring. The brooding bulbs in the earth of his garden became a symbol for her of their whole relationship.

In other gardens as winter began to release its hold she saw the hard green shoots hafting their way out of the frosted ground. But in the frozen space outside his kitchen door there was no sign. It had begun to matter tremendously that there should be one, the result of their joint efforts, a commitment for the future, something of hers which belonged in his world, something which was theirs together. And then it came. A first small spike, a second, thrusting up from the grip of the whirling snow which turned to water as it hit the path.

Edward was as attentive as ever, as loving, but somewhere deep inside there was still a core of separateness which made Jane uneasy. Her commitment was total. Surely his should be the same?

When it came, the moment she had so often feared, it was as if a lurking shadow had suddenly grown and darkened around her.

It was in the park where the buds on the trees and bushes were beginning to fill and the whippy gold green sallows by the lake were erupting into silver and pussy willow. She saw them across the water, Edward and the other girl. He was holding her gloved hand, gazing down into her eyes as she talked.

Jane stopped and watched them for a moment. Then, sick, she turned away.

'I saw you in the park today,' she said, her voice carefully unemotional as she climbed into his car that evening.

'Not me,' he said. 'I was in the office.'

She almost made herself believe him.

It was cold late spring. The pale green dilations which were the daffodils seemed to hesitate for an eternity before they began to swell at last into buds. She helped Edward decorate the kitchen and as they worked they left the back door open to take away the smell of paint. She could see the clusters of nodding points, the green shimmer above the dead earth and she planned to buy some tubs for geraniums later. If there was a later. And she ached with the fear that it might not happen, that the shadow might return. But for Edward there were no shadows. He was happy then, not suspecting her secret unease and it was while they were both working close like this in companionable silence that he threw down his brush and took her in his arms and kissed her.

'One of these days,' he said, 'I think I'm going to have to marry you.'

She hugged her happiness to her as she went on painting, not daring to show her joy too much.

His flat was big enough for two and slowly she found herself looking at it anew. He never suggested that she live there with him and somehow she never left any of her possessions there but secretly she dreamed. Here would go her grandmother's little chair, here her favourite mirror. She planned a colour scheme for the small dark bedroom with its ugly basement outlook and already in her mind's eye saw white trellis draped with clematis around the dustbins outside the window.

Once she crept into the bedroom alone and sat on the bed, looking around, thinking of colours; and it was then she saw it. A lipstick down behind the bookcase in the corner; she stared at it for a long time before she picked it up and then reluctantly she opened it. It was long and red and moist. A colour she would never use.

She left it on the table, swallowing her misery, inventing good reasons why it should be there, not daring to face him with it for fear of what his answer would be and later, after he had been in the bedroom to collect a book she saw that it had disappeared. She knew his swift action compounded some sort of guilt, but she loved him . . .

She would have preferred it if he had sprung the ring on her as a surprise – bought it or inherited it to place on her finger by moonlight or by the flicker of a candle. As it was he stopped suddenly as they walked down the High Street to collect her shoes from the mender and said 'What about it?'

She was embarrassed, unprepared, excited but flustered as the man behind the counter reached out a flock-lined tray.

On her finger the ring kept catching her eye as they

walked on to collect the shoes, a reminder that life can be very ordinary in its magic.

That evening she cut the first few daffodil buds and deliberately when he took her home she left her comb behind, her mended shoes and her jacket on the back of his bedroom door. It was a gesture of possession.

In the warmth of the flat the golden bells opened and filled the room with their fragrance. She came there every evening now and cooked on his stove and together they listened to his records, the bottom half of the dirty sash window thrown open onto the back garden so, from the tree in the road, they could hear the ecstatic carolling of a blackbird as the dusk fell and the flowers nodded palely in the dark.

She was very happy.

At last she dared to accept their love; she wanted to be with him all the time. She lay in his arms dreaming of the future, relaxed, confident, at peace.

But he leaned across her and turned on the lamp and looked at his watch, frowning.

'It's time you went, Janie.' His lips touched hers for a second. 'It won't be long now, before you're here, properly, for good, but now you must go.'

She sat clutching her knees as she watched him dress, feeling in some way betrayed, wanting him to stop, to turn back to her and take her again in his arms.

He found the car keys and then he turned to her. 'Come on, Janie. It's late. Don't forget I have to go to the office in the morning.'

So did she of course.

As she grew more confident in their relationship, so she felt more at home in his flat. She chose the material for the bedroom curtains in the lunch hour, secretly measured and made them and hung them while he was out buying some beer. They changed the room completely, making it bright and warm and now, a little, hers. But his polite admiration on his return, as he stood for a moment in the doorway looking, barely hid his anger at her presumption, and crying quietly in the bathroom later she realized she had taken too much for granted. She was still a guest, despite the promise implied by the ring she wore.

Edward spoke of getting married in the summer and, learning perhaps a little of his ways now, she knew better than to press him for a date. He would tell her she supposed when he so wished and she frowned, a tiny seed of rebellion taking root at last at her own passivity.

'We haven't decided yet, there's no hurry,' she said airily when her friends admired her ring and asked the obvious question. When she went home to her parents she had to take it off altogether – Edward had not agreed to go with her to meet them, although he had kissed away her hurt.

The back yard glowed with gold – clumps of dazzling colour and lines of waving heads along the short pebbled path. She thought again of her tubs and suggested them, laughing to Edward, expecting to be snubbed, but he agreed. They bought them that very weekend, humping sacks of soil to fill them and planting out the seedlings together. The garden was very pretty now but she knew, deep inside, that they were only playing house.

The other woman's name was Linda. If Jane hadn't gone to try to buy some ballet tickets and called off afterwards for a coffee near the box office she might never have known. They were sitting at a corner table.

Edward smiled, his eyes narrowed in the way she knew so well which usually made her heart turn over with love.

'This is Linda,' he said.

'I'm Jane. Edward's fiancée,' Jane repeated, putting out

her hand. She had recognized the brightness of the lipstick, the coat of the walker in the park.

They drank coffee, the three of them and laughed and joked and were at ease in their small talk, but something deep inside pained Jane so much she could scarcely swallow the hot sweetness of each sip.

He did not insult her with excuses. He kissed her later till her coldness stood no chance at all and told her he had fixed the date. She smiled and kissed him back but her happiness was chilled with apprehension; the game was spoiled.

There was no row, no scene when it happened. They had been working together in the garden, she showing him how to knot down the straggle of dying daffodil leaves to plant the summer colours between. Then they decided to go for a walk in the park.

The trees were heavy with new leaves rustling, as they walked hand in hand to the lake to watch the swans.

'I can't marry you, Edward,' she said quietly, gently easing off her ring. 'I'm sorry.'

'Is it because of Linda?' His face was stricken.

She shook her head. 'I can't explain. There is something wrong, my love. It wouldn't work.' The sleek white profile of the swan before her blurred and shimmered for a moment in her tears. She hadn't planned to say it; the decision had been quite impulsive and yet, now that it was made, she felt a strange sense of release.

Edward gazed out across the lake, his hands thrust deep into his pockets. He looked completely lost.

'Think again, Janie. Please don't decide just like that. Let's talk about it. Let's go home.'

But she had walked away across the park alone.

*

He sent her back the ring. 'Even if you still feel you could never marry me, Jane darling, keep it please. To help you remember the good times – and there were good times, weren't there? . . .'

She smiled faintly and kissed the cold stone and put it into the back of a drawer. She wouldn't need his ring to help her remember.

She had met Ian when she had been at her lowest ebb in the arid, empty days of the summer. Somehow she had accepted the loneliness, the separate oneness of existence and she had gone on living. Slowly she had found again her friends from the time before she had met Edward, but somehow their kindness, their understanding only touched the surface of her being. Inside she was alone and crying.

The memory of the daffodils comforted her even then. They remained. Deep in the earth they were drawing strength back into themselves from their dying leaves and next year they would come again, renewed and beautiful. They would comfort Edward and give him pleasure and perhaps remind him of the good times they had had together. She had not guessed then that she too would take strength from the dying of her love and that it would come again.

It was in the picture gallery that she had first seen Ian; he was standing gazing at a painting of some wild flowers and they remained side by side for a while, rapt in the painting, unconscious of one another.

Then slowly he had turned and looked at her and seen the expression in her eyes.

'Flowers shouldn't make you cry,' he said gently and strangely she had not been embarrassed that he should have seen. They had walked on slowly together, pausing before some paintings, passing others, companionable even then when they were strangers and she had not thought it odd that he should buy her a cup of coffee. Later she had even smiled again, her tears forgotten.

She had agreed to see him occasionally almost against her will, resenting the involvement, determined not to risk unhappiness again. But there was no need for unhappiness, no need for reserve. Ian was the kind of man who possessed an essential quietness and kindness which reassured but did not demand.

'Remember the good times, Jane,' he had said to her with a sad smile when she had told him everything. 'Every beautiful woman needs memories like those. Don't try and forget. Build on your dreams.'

They returned to the gallery often and the flower picture became special to them. Each time they would go and look at it first and then they would smile and he would take her hand.

Ian was watching her twisting the crisp green stem between her fingers. He put his arm round her and pulled her gently against his shoulder. He had seen the tears at once as she looked at the daffodil, but he did not say anything. She would tell him what she was thinking in her own time if she wanted to. He had known from the start that he could never push her and he had never tried.

She dropped her head to the daffodil in her fingers and sniffed it sadly. She was picturing again the little back yard with its brilliant blooms. Was Linda there to cut them this year? Somehow she didn't think so.

Poor Edward. She hoped he was happy. One day perhaps she would meet him again and she realized suddenly that it would be without bitterness, without sadness for what might have been, for how could she be sad when she had found Ian and his love for her? With him there was never sick apprehension, never fear, nor hesitation. There were no doubts at all.

'You're the woman for me, Janie,' he had murmured once as they walked together through the early dusk. 'I'm only waiting till you recognize it, darling.' She did not tell him, then, that she already knew it.

Ian glanced at her sideways. 'Come on, it's getting late. My parents will be wondering where on earth we are. You're not shy of meeting them are you?'

She pulled up the collar of her coat against the wind. 'A little perhaps.' She hesitated. 'It's a big step, meeting someone's parents.'

A step that Edward had refused to take.

Ian laughed. 'You'll love mine, you'll see. Come on. Let's go home.'

When Edward had said those words, she had walked away.

They climbed back into the car and set off again slowly down the winding lane. She glanced at him, watching his fair hair blowing in the wind from the lowered window and found suddenly that she was smiling.

Footsteps in the Attic

They both heard it at the same moment. Somewhere upstairs a door banged and there came the sound of running feet.

Mike stood up quietly and picked up the poker. Glancing at Tessa he put his fingers to his lips. 'Wait here,' he murmured. 'I'll get them this time.' He tiptoed to the door and opened it.

The hall was in darkness. Cautiously he made his way to the stairs and crept up, stopping abruptly as the treads creaked beneath his weight.

Her face white, Tessa followed him as quietly as she could into the hall. She waited breathlessly, peering up into the darkness after him and it was several moments before she noticed that the front door swung gently ajar.

With a click all the upstairs lights came on. 'All right, come on out. I know you're there,' Mike roared.

Tessa gasped, but his challenge was followed by a complete silence.

A moment later he appeared above her and leaned over the banisters. 'No sign,' he called. 'Not a bloody sign. I don't understand it.'

'Did you look on the top floor?' She found that her voice was trembling.

'I've even looked in the airing cupboard. There is nothing there. Nobody.'

'The front door was open again, Mike.'

He ran down, the poker still in his hand and examined the lock, clicking it open and shut and running his hand down the door jamb. 'I don't understand it. I suppose it must be local kids playing around. One of them could have got hold of a key, I suppose, but whoever it is it's got to stop. I'll fix the door now and get some bolts tomorrow. And this time I'm going to ring the police.'

Tessa stood behind him, gnawing at her knuckle while he phoned.

'You're probably right, sir, about it being kids,' the duty officer agreed after listening to Mike's explanation. 'We have a lot of trouble with them and if, as you say, your house has been lying empty for some time they've probably found a way of getting in to play there. They could have been doing it for months and no one's spotted them before.'

'What did he say?' Tessa asked as Mike hung up.

'Pretty sure it must be kids,' he repeated. 'They're going to send someone out tomorrow.'

It snowed again in the night so any footprints the intruders might have left were obliterated and the CID men who arrived as Mike and Tessa were finishing their breakfast found nothing to give any clue as to who they had been.

'It gives you a funny feeling, doesn't it?' she said later with a shiver. 'To know there's someone wandering around your house. I don't like it.'

'You're not regretting moving here are you, Tess?' Mike had brought an armful of logs in with him after seeing off the policemen. He threw them into the basket in the corner and stamped the ice off his boots.

'Of course not. I love this house. It's not really so isolated – it's only the snow that makes it so quiet.' She opened the window to throw out the crumbs from the breakfast cloth. 'Mike! There's someone out there now. By the gate,' she hissed suddenly. 'Come and look.'

He was behind her in a second, peering over her shoulder. Two men stood by the gate. One of them was pointing at the roof of the house.

'They look more like prospective buyers than burglars,' Mike muttered meditatively. 'Perhaps they haven't heard that it's sold. This is your chance Tess. We could resell quickly at a vast profit.' He grinned at her teasingly.

'Never!' She folded the cloth and put it in the drawer. 'Come away from the window, Mike. They'll think you're watching them!'

'I am watching them.' He opened the window again and leaned out. 'Hello! Can I help you?' he called, his breath smoking in the frosty air.

The taller of the two men raised a hand and tramped across the frozen lawn, his face reddened with cold above the upturned collar of his sheepskin jacket.

'When did you folks move in? The house was empty last time I saw it.' In spite of the irritation in his tone his face had a naturally friendly expression which Tessa found reassuring.

'Only a week ago,' Mike told him. 'I'm afraid you're too late if you wanted to buy.'

The man laughed. 'Not buy. Borrow maybe. Can we come in and explain?' Mike raised an eyebrow. 'I think you'd better. The door's round there.' He jerked his hand towards the side of the house.

Three minutes later their visitors were seated at the kitchen table and Tessa had the coffee on again. The red-faced man introduced himself as Pete Sanders. 'We're looking for a Georgian house like this for location shots for a film – part of a TV series. This one is just right. Beautiful, old, neat and surrounded by nothing – no telegraph wires that show from the front and, as I thought, empty!' He grinned expansively.

The other man was staring round the kitchen. 'Isn't it very big just for the two of you?' His abrupt question was curious rather than rude.

Tessa smiled. 'We're hoping to run it as a guest house next summer – or at least bed and breakfast.'

Sanders nodded. 'Perfect place I should think. Now. The thing is, I'm in a hurry. The shots I want require snow. If you'd agree I can get everyone up here today as soon as possible, because this snow's not going to last, I hear and my budge won't cover the synthetic variety. I usually give people a lot more warning than this when we want their house, but this is special.' He smiled winningly.

Mike glanced at Tessa. Her eyes were shining.

'Go ahead,' he said. 'It'll be fun. As you said, we're isolated and in this weather the neighbours haven't been falling over themselves to call. At least . . .' He hesitated. He had been on the point of talking about their visitor of the evening before – the third time they had heard him in the house – but he changed his mind.

Sanders had brought out some notes. 'All I shall want from you is that you keep out of sight. The house is supposed to be completely empty and our hero, played by Jim Dixon,' he glanced at Tessa knowingly, 'will walk up the front path – we'll have to brush out the footprints – he'll knock, walk round a bit, looking up at the windows, knock again, go back to the lane, get on his horse and ride away. OK?'

'Is that all?' Mike sounded disappointed.

'That's all.'

'The TV studios are only about twelve miles from here, apparently,' he said after he had escorted the two men back to their car. 'That's how Pete knew the house. He's had his eye on it for ages and he's been waiting for snow.

The rest of the series is more or less finished, I gather and it's due to go out quite soon. And – they're going to pay us!'

Tessa sat down opposite him. 'It'll be fun seeing ourselves on TV . . . Good advertising when we start the B&B . . . Mike, where are you going?'

He was reaching for his jacket.

'I said I'd clear away the empty crates round the side and shift the car into the barn. They'll be back in less than two hours. He said his men would do it, but I'd rather get it tidy.' He dropped a kiss on her head and hurried out.

The kitchen was suddenly very silent. She stooped and threw a couple of logs onto the fire and it blazed up, spitting frost up the chimney, filling the room with the scent of old dried apple. Upstairs she could hear Mike walking about, squeaking the boards, pushing furniture.

But Mike was outside. Only a moment before he had gone out of the back door.

Her heart hammering suddenly with fear she ran to the door into the hall and opened it. The front door was standing open, allowing the blinding snow-light to flood in across the floor and up the stairs. Mike must have let himself in and gone up for some reason.

'Mike?' she called, her hand on the banister. 'Mike, is that you?'

The house was completely silent again. She pushed the door shut and then cautiously she began to mount the stairs.

'Mike?' She stopped at the top and peered down the passage. There was no sign of him.

Then, distantly, she heard the car start, the engine coughing reluctantly as it was revved into action. Looking out of the landing window she could see Mike sitting at the wheel, the driver's door half open, his foot playing on the accelerator as clouds of blue smoke billowed round the car. She watched as he turned it and backed it into the barn, closing the heavy double doors before he walked back across the yard towards the front door.

She glanced round uneasily. 'Is there anyone there?' she called, her voice shaking a little, but the silence in the house had already told her that the bedrooms were empty.

She ran back down the stairs. 'You left the front door open, Mike and you know we want to conserve all the heat we can.'

He was riffling through the drawer in the kitchen table. 'Never touched it. I've just been putting the car away. A hinge is nearly off one of the doors on the barn. Have you seen my big screwdriver?' Exasperated, he slammed the drawer shut and went to peer at the clutter of tools on the windowsill.

'Mike, the front door was open again just now. And I heard someone upstairs. If it wasn't you, who was it?' Tessa swallowed nervously.

He turned to her at last. 'Upstairs. Are you sure?'

'I just told you.'

'Damn cheek! And in daylight too.' He picked up a heavy pair of pliers from the tools and went purposefully to the door.

Tessa followed him. 'I closed the front door,' she whispered. 'It was wide open.'

He went up two at a time and flung open the first door on the landing. The room was empty. So were all the others.

'No one here,' he commented as he closed the bathroom door.

'Look upstairs,' she whispered. The second, attic floor was dark and as yet empty of furniture.

Mike ran up, leaving her on the first landing peering after him. Minutes later he was down again. 'No, not a thing. It must have been the wind. Perhaps when I opened the back door, the front blew open.'

She followed him down, unconvinced. 'I heard furniture being moved.'

'Boards creaking? All old houses are full of strange noises. We're just not used to our own yet. Perhaps all the noises we've heard have just been that – noises.' He shrugged. 'Look, Tess, I must get on shifting those boxes and tidying the yard. Sanders will be back with his camera crew or whatever they're called and we won't be ready for him.'

Tessa stood at the door for a while watching him, then she went to the phone.

'Mr Forbes? This is Tessa Gordon. Do you remember? You sold the Old Rectory to us. Did you by any chance give the keys to anyone else to come over, anyone who didn't return them?' The line crackled and she could imagine old Mr Forbes drawing himself up indignantly at his desk.

'Naturally the keys were given to any prospective buyers, Mrs Gordon. But they were always returned to my office. And after your husband bought the property naturally all the keys were given to him. May I enquire why you are asking?'

She smiled quietly in spite of her worry. 'Well, to be honest, Mr Forbes, we think someone has been in here a couple of times, coming quite openly through the front door. They must have had a key from somewhere.'

There was a moment's silence on the line and then the quavering voice asked, 'Have you actually seen anyone, Mrs Gordon?'

'Well, no, why?'

'I just wondered. Have you told the police?'

'Yes. They were out here this morning.'

'I see.' He cleared his throat. 'Mrs Gordon. I don't

think you should make too much of these incidents. I . . . er . . . well, I seem to remember the vicar, old Mr Somerset, mentioning to me once or twice that a similar occurrence had happened to him. He . . . well, he seemed to think there was a perfectly natural and . . . er . . . happy explanation.'

'What do you mean?' Tessa was frowning. 'You mean he gave the keys to someone? Told them they could come in?'

'Well, no, not exactly. Look, Mrs Gordon, you must excuse me now, but I have a client waiting. Perhaps I might call on you one day next week when I'm over in your part of the world. I might just be able to explain.'

She stared at the receiver in her hand. He had hung up.

'Sounds as though he knows what it's all about, though,' Mike commented as they had a quick sandwich in the kitchen later. I hope it's not something he should have told us before we decided to buy. He's a funny old geezer, Forbes. He was very thick with the Rev. Somerset, too, I gather.'

They watched the arrival of the television crew with great interest, astonished at the number of people who seemed to be involved in the afternoon's work, their enthusiasm slightly dampened by the fact that they were expected to douse the kitchen fire at once, but mollified by an invitation to the mobile canteen which had followed the cars, vans and horse box into the lane.

'Now, no peeking,' Sanders instructed as a camera was being brought into position by the gate. 'In fact, why not watch from out here. You'll be able to see everything much better.'

They stood and watched as beneath the skilled hands of his men their house took on all over the lonely derelict appearance which they had been at such pains for the last week to dispel.

Then at last when all was ready and every footprint banished from the lawn, a hush descended on the assembled company.

'It really is a pretty house, isn't it?' Mike whispered softly as they watched Jim Dixon, nattily dressed in Regency costume, mount the rangy black cob which had been backed out of the horse box and ride up to the gate as the cameras started to whirr.

The sun sparkled on the snow, winking in the windows. Suddenly Tessa stiffened. 'Mike, look! At the top. The end room. There's somebody there!'

Mike frowned up at the house, screwing up his eyes. 'Where?'

'There. There.' She pointed. 'Quick, stop them filming. It must be him. We must catch him.'

Her voice had risen sharply and she saw Sanders and Dave, his production assistant, frowning at her. The camera stopped and Jim reined in his horse.

'Problem?' he said, smiling down at her.

'There's someone there. Up there.' She pointed at the house.

Everyone turned to look but the windows were blank.

'Do you want a couple of the boys to take a look with you?' Sanders turned to Mike. 'Only, for Pete's sake, go round the back! Don't make any more footmarks, OK?'

Tessa bit her lip. 'I'm sure I saw a face,' she said as they watched the three men making their way cautiously round behind the barn.

'Could be a trick of the light, the windows are full of reflections.' Jim grinned at her reassuringly. 'Don't worry, if there is anyone there, they'll find him.'

There was no one and Tessa, scarlet with embarrassment, subsided behind Mike to watch the proceedings in silence.

It was growing dark when the last of the equipment was packed up and the cars and vans eventually rolled away. Tired, Mike and Tessa went back into the house and set about relighting the fire in the chilly kitchen, drawing the curtains against the twilit lawn which was now crossed and recrossed with slushy footprints.

'Tea?' Tessa filled the kettle at the tap and plugged it in as Mike knelt at the hearth, feeding kindling into the small new fire.

They heard no more from the film people until one night the phone rang. Mike went to answer it. He was gone a long time and after a while Tessa looked up from her book, gazing into the fire listening. She could hear him wandering up and down upstairs.

When at last he reappeared he was looking rather odd.

'What is it?' Her book fell unnoticed in her lap.

'That was Pete Sanders,' he said quietly. 'He wanted to tell us when the film was going to be on.' He paused. 'There was something else too. He said that the film showed quite clearly the face you saw at the window.'

Tessa gasped. 'You mean the burglar?'

'No.' He shook his head. 'No. Our other theory seems to be the right one. It was a child. A little girl.'

Tessa stared at him. 'A little girl?'

He nodded. 'In the end room on the top floor. That's where you saw it, wasn't it?'

'That's right. What bloody cheek! How on earth does she get in? Oh, Mike,' she suddenly thought of something, 'does that mean they'll have to do the film again?'

'No. There's no time. They can edit her out,' he said. 'Strange isn't it, though, that we found no one?'

He sat down beside her again. 'I suppose we ought to go and have another look round. I was thinking in terms of rowdy teenagers smoking pot up there or something, not a little girl.'

'I thought you were up there just now.' She reopened her book.

'Just now? No, I was on the phone.'

They stared at each other in silence for a second. Then reluctantly he hauled himself to his feet again. 'I just checked the door too. She must have got in some other way this time. Come on.'

The hall light revealed the solid oak door still securely shut and bolted. The house was completely silent. They stood looking upstairs for a moment, then side by side, they began to climb.

Systematically they searched the first floor and then they stopped, looking up the narrow attic staircase. 'Go on, you've got to look,' Tessa whispered. For some reason her voice had gone husky.

Mike walked up slowly with Tessa close behind him and pushed open the first door, clicking on the light. The naked bulb swung gently, reflecting in the back window panes. But the room was empty. As was the next.

'This is the one,' he whispered outside the last door.

He pushed it open hard and threw the light switch.

The room was empty. They both went in and looked around. The room was small with one square window in the eaves. Like the others it had a deep window seat and a wall cupboard in the alcove beside the empty fireplace and it smelled of damp and disuse.

They looked round carefully.

'This must have been a nursery,' Tessa whispered. 'Look at the wallpaper.' She pulled open the warped cupboard and peered inside. A few bits of broken china lay on the dusty shelf paper and on one top shelf a heap of material. She reached up.

'Mike, look!'

Mike had been examining the window latch. He turned.

'Look. A genuine Victorian doll. Oh, isn't she beautiful?'

The waxen face was delicately painted and the dusty ringlets tied with threadbare blue ribbon.

'How on earth did she get here? I'm sure she wasn't here before.' She took the doll to the stark light and peered at her.

'Perhaps she belongs to the little girl at the window,' Mike said laughing. 'Come on, it's cold up here. Let's go down. There's no one here now.'

Tessa turned to follow him. Then she glanced down at the doll in her hand and she shivered.

She took it to the window seat and gently propped it in the corner. 'I think I'll leave her here,' she said.

She followed Mike to the door and then turned to glance back at the room, her hand on the light switch. The doll had fallen sideways on the window seat.

The house was very quiet. Mike had taken the car into town and Tessa was sitting at her sewing machine in the dark kitchen, the only light falling from the table lamp on the folds of the deep red curtain she was making. Outside it was snowing again. Standing up stiffly at last she turned on the radio while she made herself a cup of coffee. Then she sat down again to her curtains. The cheerful hum of the motor and the little warm patch of light which centred around her guiding fingers took all her attention and slowly she relaxed again.

The child must have been peering through a crack in

the kitchen door. She heard a smothered giggle and as she pushed her chair back in fright across the flags the sound of feet running up the stairs away from her.

She flung back the door and peered into the hall. The front door was closed and bolted.

Tessa went up the stairs two at a time. On the landing she stopped. There was complete silence from the top floor. She went on up, not giving herself time to think, heading straight for the nursery.

The room was empty. She hesitated, looking round. The doll was lying on the floor now, in the corner.

'Are you there?' she called. 'Come on. I won't hurt you. I just want to talk to you.'

She went over and picked up the doll. On its flaxen curls was a little wreath of daisies. They were real, the delicate petals tinged with pink. She carried the doll to the window and looked out. The garden was still inches deep in snow.

And then she understood. She glanced round and suddenly her hands were shaking. 'You live here, don't you,' she said out loud wonderingly. 'You're not one of the village children at all.'

She glanced down at the daisies in her hand and then gently twined them back in the doll's hair. Behind her the room was silent.

Below, in the lane, she saw a car drawing to a standstill. She frowned, wondering who it was and then she saw Mr Forbes, the house agent, climbing stiffly out. He stood for a moment gazing up at the house.

Carefully putting down the doll Tessa turned to go out and meet him.

She knew now why he hadn't mentioned the vicar's secret visitor to them before – and what he was going to tell her. She hoped he would know her name.

She wondered suddenly if Pete Sanders had kept the

edited bit of the film showing the face at the window. She hoped so. It might be the only chance she would ever have of seeing the dead child properly.

Someone to Dream About

How she came to fall from the horse she never really knew. She was galloping alone across the moors, her hair streaming out behind her, exhilarated by the huge, building masses of clouds on the horizon, feeling the electricity in the air, when suddenly she was conscious of a car travelling fast on the lonely moorland road some distance away from her. For a split second it distracted her attention – an intrusive, twentieth-century jar on her nerves as the sky was torn by the first wishbone of lightning – and in that second Moonlight swerved and, stumbling on a branch of wiry heather, threw Margot clear before falling heavily to the ground.

For a moment Margot lay stunned, feeling the first of the rain on her face, then, slowly, she began to climb to her feet, the exhilaration of the ride knocked out of her by the fall; her dream shattered.

Scotland had always brought out the dreamer in Margot. She would forget the image which was the Margot of London. Behind a desk as personal assistant to a high-powered financial director she was a competent woman, at ease with office technology, her hair bound sleekly to her head, her clothes businesslike, her shoes immaculate. There she was independent, seeking to taste everything the city had to offer: theatre, concerts, galleries, meals with carefully-selected men who shared her taste in food and wine – which often she would choose, not they. The men were purely decorative, to be kept at arm's length; her liberation total because she had allowed herself no possibility of involvement. That was how she saw it; commitment meant loss of freedom and to her, freedom was life itself.

At Inverglen she shed that image, as a snake sloughs its skin. There she found true freedom. She would put away the heels and the narrow skirts, let her hair loose and run wild. Then the thing she loved most, riding, became her obsession, every penny of her savings going to the hire of a horse for the whole of her holiday, while her London friends went skiing, or lounged on beaches in France and Portugal. And it was on the horse – a beautiful silver mare named Moonlight – that she would relive, secretly, all the fantasy lives of her childhood. She was Rob Roy, Flora Macdonald, Robin Hood, Boudicca, hero or heroine as the mood took her. Free. Alive.

If anyone had guessed about her secret life she would have died of shame. But there was no one to see her wild rides across the moors towards the high granite cliffs where the sea crashed onto rocks, slick with spray even in the gentlest weather. If her grandmother, Thea, guessed what went on in Margot's head, she never gave a sign.

It was a moment before Margot realized that the car had stopped a few hundred yards away and that a figure was loping over the heather towards her.

But he went straight to the struggling horse, his hands gentling the animal's fear, calming it as sweat poured off the satin coat, his strong, slender fingers feeling the animal's shoulder and on down the leg, not even glancing at her.

'Is her leg broken?' Margot heard her own voice, astonishingly calm, as she staggered towards the mare.

He looked up at her then, for a fraction of a second. His hair was plastered to his face, his jacket and shirt black with the now driving rain. The swift, dismissive glance told her that his eyes were violently blue and that they were blazing with anger.

'Small thanks to you if it isn't!' he snapped. 'Are you crazy or something? Riding at that speed over this ground – and in this light? Have you no common sense?'

'I'll ride my own horse on my own land how I damn well please,' she cried furiously. It was quite unlike her. She would never talk like that to anyone; it sounded absurd, arrogant and callous and she was none of those things. But for him now she would be all, and worse. 'What were you doing here, anyway?' she went on, her voice rising in the wind. 'That is a private road. If you hadn't been there and distracted me, it wouldn't have happened. She'd have been all right.'

Shock was beginning to hit her now. She could feel herself beginning to shake. Furiously she dug her hands deep into her pockets of her jacket. 'I'm sorry. I suppose I should thank you for stopping.' Her voice sounded ungracious and harsh.

'And walking on your land.' He was still bending down, his back to her, but there was no mistaking the mockery in his voice.

'That's right. On my land!' She suddenly wanted to cry. She ached all over from the fall, she was soaked through and very cold.

As if reading her thoughts he stood up abruptly and turned to face her. 'Are you all right?' he asked at last.

'Perfectly.' To her relief, her tone was remarkably steady.

'Good. Because this horse can't be ridden like this. You'll have to lead her.'

'I realize that.' She put her hand tentatively to the mare's muzzle.

He did not relinquish his hold. 'If this is your land – ' was there a slight emphasis on the words? ' – you live presumably at Inverglen House. That's a couple of miles. You'll have to take it very slowly.'

'I'll manage.' She gritted her teeth and in spite of herself hesitated. It was the arrogance about him which made her hackles rise – but it was an arrogance which matched her own. Obviously and perhaps rightly, he despised her. That interested her.

'You still haven't told me what you were doing here,' she couldn't resist saying over her shoulder as she turned the mare.

'Correct,' he said. And for the first time he grinned.

'It sounds like Alan Macdonald,' Thea Locke said with a laugh when Margot told her grandmother about the incident. She was kneeling before the fire drying her long hair after the rain. 'I believe he's Canadian, in Scotland in search of his roots.' She smiled. 'A pleasant man, so I've heard.'

'A male chauvinist,' Margot muttered.

Thea suppressed a smile. 'Oh? What makes you say that?'

Margot hesitated, looking up through her hair. 'His manner.'

'And the fact that he is, I believe, good looking and, dare I say it, sexy?'

'Grandma!' Margot looked up with a grin.

'I may be old, but I have ears! And my memory's good.' The older woman smiled wryly. 'I am so sorry for you children today. So possessive of your feminist honour that when a knight in shining armour jumps up and down in front of you, you turn your backs with a sniff. You need a man, my dear.'

'I do not.' Margot was furious.

'But romance?' Thea's voice was gentle. 'What do you do for romance?'

'I don't want romance! That is the point.'

As if conscious suddenly of the incongruity of her long, gleaming auburn hair, she swept it up on the top of her head and began stabbing at the untidy, still-damp knot with large hairpins. 'Is he on holiday here?' she went on, off-handedly.

Thea shrugged. 'Does it matter, dear?' she said.

A week later Margot was back in London and behind a desk, her eyes riveted to the screen of her word processor.

'How was Scotland?' Paula, her colleague, sat back in her chair with a sigh. 'I don't know how you can bear to come back here after all those acres.'

Margot grinned. 'One and a half acres, to be exact! The rest belongs to the National Trust for Scotland and other worthy bodies.'

On my land. Her own voice echoed in her head for a moment. What had possessed her to say it? He must have known. No wonder he had been so scornful. She punched at the keyboard indignantly. Why think of him? Who cares what he thought anyway? She certainly didn't.

He was waiting for her in reception. The soaked shirt was gone and he was wearing a tweed jacket. His hair, now that it was dry, was a sort of dark honey blond. But the eyes were the same. Piercing, direct, quizzical. And very blue.

'Miss Kinnaird?' He stood up as she pushed through the swing doors near him.

She froze.

'Perhaps you don't remember me?' He held out his hand. 'Alan Macdonald. We met in Scotland . . .'

'I remember where we met, Mr Macdonald.' She cut him short, trying to keep her voice coldly steady.

He lowered his hand, unruffled, taking in her smart skirt and jacket with a swift glance and then he reached into his pocket. 'I called on Mrs Locke last week, to find out how you were after the accident and when I told her I was coming to London, she asked me to give you this.' There was an envelope in his hand.

Margot looked down at it. 'I'm sorry you were put to so much trouble,' she murmured, suddenly at a disadvantage. 'I'm sure she could have posted it just as well.'

'She said not.' She could see the open amusement in his eyes. 'I don't know if you have any plans, Miss Kinnaird, but I was hoping you might let me take you to lunch.'

She could hardly refuse. If she did she would look ungrateful, even rude. 'You must let me pay for myself . . .'

'You can pay for me, too, if you like.' That was not what she had meant at all, but before she could draw breath he had stepped forward and, taking her hand, closed her fingers around the envelope. 'Come on. Take me somewhere nice and hugely expensive. I'm hungry.' Ostentatiously, he held the heavy glass door for her, then followed her into the street. She hadn't noticed the mischievous expression in his eyes.

The restaurant was packed and the tables smaller than Margot had remembered. She was intensely conscious of the proximity of his legs beneath the cloth.

'Did the horse recover?' he asked.

'She was fine, thank you,' Margot replied stiffly.

There was only the slightest trace of some transatlantic intonation in his voice, as he said to the waitress, 'The *entrecôte*, I think, with broccoli, beans and potatoes. And soup to start. The lady will have the same.'

Margot was silent for a full minute, trying to control her anger. By the time she was capable of speech the waitress had gone.

'I never eat steak,' she managed finally, with commendable restraint.

'It shows. With your colouring you should have glowing cheeks and shining eyes without dark circles round them.' With a raised hand he traced a line above her cheekbone, not quite touching her face. 'You are what our Scots compatriots call peelie-wally. Good hot soup and a steak is what you need. Why do you work in London?'

His directness was unnerving. 'Because my job is here.'

'Your family is in Scotland?'

'My grandmother is in Scotland.' She could feel all her muscles tighten warningly. The conversation was getting too personal, to the point where she usually began to withdraw; to raise the barriers. 'I go to see her as often as possible.'

'Which isn't often enough. She is very lonely.'

'How could you possibly think that?' She stared at him, genuinely astonished.

'Because she told me. I suspect that note of hers,' he looked pointedly at her bag lying on the table, where the envelope lurked, still unread, 'was an excuse to have me speak to you. And I think she wanted me to tell you that. I could think of no way of saying it covertly. I don't know you well enough yet. And I was never very subtle.' He grinned.

You can say that again, Margot thought. With a hard look at him she extricated the letter and tore it open: '*Forget all that feminist nonsense and hang on to this one. He's perfect.*'

Her grandmother had written it in bold black letters across the page.

Blushing furiously Margot glanced up. He could easily have read it from where he sat.

'I think you are mistaken, Mr Macdonald,' she said coldly, when at last she had recovered her composure. 'My grandmother could not possibly be lonely.'

He looked at her for rather longer than necessary. 'And you?' he said. 'Are *you* lonely?'

'Of course not. I have London.'

She wasn't sure how he had managed to get hold of the theatre tickets. The play had been sold out for months. That was the only reason she went, of course.

It was in the rustling auditorium, expectant and hushed with excitement before curtain up, that she remembered to ask him the question that had been bothering her. She turned to him as the lights dimmed. 'Were you on holiday in Scotland?'

He closed his programme slowly, his eyes on the heavy red curtain with its swags of gold. 'Not a holiday,' he said slowly. 'I've taken over as manager for the trustees of the Inverglen estates.'

My land.

As the house lights went down she put her face in her hands.

'Perhaps we can go for a ride together next time you come up north,' he said quietly in the darkness. 'I know somewhere I can hire a horse, too.'

It was nearly a year before she went to Inverglen again. And Moonlight had been sold.

Miserably she went for a walk, hands deep in the pockets of her jeans, down the lane, over the burn and on to the moor where it led towards the cliffs. A westerly gale was bringing the long, white-tipped breakers rolling into the bay where they crashed onto the rocks. White horses, she thought sadly as she turned away.

Alan Macdonald had gone, too. Thea had told her that before she had even unpacked her case the night before. To a desk job in Glasgow. She felt oddly bereft. Part of her had, she secretly admitted, been counting the days until she saw him, until they could go riding together over the moor. Purely for the company of another rider, of course . . .

But the dream had gone with the horse, and these were no longer her woods, her moors, her cliffs. She was just another Londoner now, on holiday, on foot and lonely.

She spent the days walking, feeling the heavy Highland sun baking her pale limbs brown, fighting off the vicious horseflies which lurked on the moors, staring down from the cliffs and walking on the rocks at the sea's edge.

Then she found his number. It was written in large figures on a card beside the phone, with the Glasgow code beside it. It hadn't been there the day before. Slowly, she dialled.

'I just wondered how you were,' she said.

'Fine.' There was a pause. He wasn't going to make it easy.

'How do you like Glasgow?' She was furious with herself now for having rung.

'Very much.' There was another silence. Then he relented. 'You are up until the end of the month, I hear.'

'That's right.' So Thea had told him she was coming.

'Good. The course will be over long before that.'

'The course?' she echoed.

'Didn't Mrs Locke explain? I've been on a month's course here.'

'No. She didn't explain.'

'Ah.' She could hear the smile. 'I'll ring you as soon as I get back and we'll go for that ride.'

She had no heart to tell him Moonlight had gone.

But when he arrived it was on horseback, a second animal beside him. They were both bays. She met him at the door. 'So you know.' Miserably, she stroked the horses' soft noses.

'About Moonlight? I'm sorry.' He leaned down and handed her the spare rein.

Her horse was smaller, naturally.

He rode well and fast, but for the first time even on horseback she found she was her London self still; prickly, inhibited, resenting him. Resenting the fact that he had arranged everything without consulting her; taken the bigger horse; led the way.

When he reined in at last near a clump of larch and turned to wait for her, she found she was seething.

'Sorry. Did I go too fast?' He slapped his horse's neck gently. She could see the amusement in his eyes as he provoked her and suddenly she was laughing, too.

'You should know. You chose the faster horse.'

'And the bigger?' It was as if he could read her mind. 'I was always brought up to believe the lady rode the more delicate, the more beautiful, animal.' He raised an arm quickly as if to ward off her blows, mocking.

They both looked at the sturdy cob she was riding and laughed again.

'I *am* taller,' he went on conciliatorily. 'You have to concede that, Ms Kinnaird.'

'This animal could take ten times your weight.'

'Do you want to swap, then?' Already he was dismounting.

Suddenly, she didn't want to any more. She didn't want him to mock her. She wanted him to like her and she didn't want to see him on the ungainly cob.

He had tethered his horse to a tree and now he came to stand at the cob's head. 'Come on, get down.' His eyes were on hers, challenging. No longer amused.

Behind them she could hear the crash of waves at the foot of the high cliffs. The wind tore at her hair and the two horses had begun to fidget restlessly, mouthing their bits. The humour and banter had gone. Now there was real tension between them.

She didn't know what to do. If she obeyed her instinct and rode away from him she would look childish and spoiled. If she obeyed him and meekly changed horses, it would be not the victory she had intended, but some kind of defeat.

She met his gaze as squarely as she could and knew he was reading her thoughts, enjoying her dilemma. His expression spurred her into action. She slid quickly from the saddle, then, leaving him standing there, she took the path down towards the rocks where the sapphire water creamed in from the west, casting clouds of spray against the wind. She knew he was following her, but she didn't stop. Suddenly she was afraid of what would happen if she did.

But she had to. The narrow cove was beneath the tide, and at the edge of the rocky path she could go no further. Slowly, she turned. He was standing several feet from her.

'OK, point taken.'

'What do you mean?' The spray was cold on the back of her shirt.

'The choice of horses is yours.' He gestured back up the path.

'It doesn't matter. It doesn't make any difference.'

'Oh, but it does. It makes a lot of difference to you.' He took a step towards her. 'Just what exactly is bugging you, lady? Why the need for all this independence?' He was very close to her now. 'What are you trying to prove?'

Suddenly, his hands were on her shoulders and he was pulling her against him. Instinctively, her arms went round his waist. She could feel the warmth of his body beneath the plaid shirt, the hard muscles of his back as she looked up into his eyes. She was paralysed by the conflict of emotions which seized her. Longing, fear, desire – and panic.

More than anything, for a moment, she wanted him to kiss her – then it was over. Her fear and resentment returned and, pushing him away, she stumbled past him over the rocks and began to run back to the horses. This time he didn't follow her. He stayed staring out at the sea.

The office manager approached Margot's desk a week later. 'Miss Kinnaird? There is a visitor for you. I've put him in the conference room.' She was obviously impressed.

He was sitting in one of the leather-upholstered chairs, staring out of the high window at the distant dome of St Paul's. Rising as Margot appeared, he inclined his head slightly.

'I am here in my accustomed role of courier.'

'Courier?' she stared at him. Her heart had begun to beat faster.

'Your grandmother asked me to bring something for her.' He lifted his case onto the large oval table and opened it.

Margot swallowed. 'I'm sorry. It's unfair of her to bother you . . .'

'Not at all.' He smiled at last, his eyes brilliant in the tanned face, as he handed her a large envelope. 'I wonder if the advice is still the same as in her last note.'

She could feel her cheeks going scarlet as she looked up at him. 'My grandmother has a very strange sense of humour,' she said stiffly.

'She is also a very shrewd lady,' he retorted.

Margot snatched the letter from him and turned away towards the window. Tearing open the envelope she drew out a single sheet. Once again, the large, black felt-tip letters confronted her.

This is your last chance.

In spite of herself, Margot smiled. Shrugging, she held it out to him. 'As you obviously read the last one, you'd better see this.'

He scrutinized it solemnly.

'What do you think I ought to do?' she asked after a moment.

'Why don't you ask me out to lunch again, then we can discuss it.' He grinned.

'I can't afford to take you out to lunch again,' she said sharply. 'Not the way you eat.'

He laughed out loud. 'Then may I take you? It's quite fair that way. One round all.'

'Now you're making fun of me.' Strangely, she didn't mind.

'What on earth makes you think that?' he answered.

She was out of her depth. Disorientated. He was not a London man, he was part of Scotland, part of her fantasy world. But this – the briefcase, the dark suit, the assured way he ushered her into the expensive restaurant and commanded a prominent table – none of it fitted. Nor did the meek way she found herself deferring to his opinion as he ordered the wine – he did, she noted, know about wine.

'So.' Settling back into the chair he looked at her at last. 'What are you going to do about me?' She thought there was a smile behind his eyes.

'Is there anything I *should* do?' She managed an ascerbic tone.

'Oh yes. A great deal. You must try and relax. Enjoy my

company.' He grinned. 'I'm quite safe, you know. House-trained. Good with animals. Some people even like me.'

She found herself smiling. 'I'm sure they do.'

'And I'm very persistent.' His eyes were fixed on her face. 'Will you come riding with me again?'

The sudden swing of subject nearly threw her. 'If I do, do I get the choice of horses?'

'You can ride a bicycle if you wish. I don't care.'

She looked down. 'I did quite like the old cob.'

He grinned. 'I suppose we could draw up a rota,' he said, half-serious. 'Then we'd know where we stood.' His hand was on the table, very close to hers.

On the defence at once, Margot glared at him. 'I hate it when you patronize me!' she cried and he let out an infuriated groan.

'I am *not* patronizing you! For God's sake, stop being so prickly, I am trying to accommodate your every whim.' His hand hadn't moved. She stared at it.

'Are you?' she whispered.

He leaned forward. 'I know how important your dreams are to you,' he said gently.

She stiffened. 'Dreams are stupid!'

'No!' His eyes were on her face. 'Dreams are important. I don't want you to lose them. They are part of you. But only part. Reality must count as well. Even if it means compromise.'

'Compromise?' She looked up.

He laughed then. 'Not a word you tolerate with ease, I know. But it's one you must learn to use. I'm real, Margot. But I want to be part of your dream as well, if you will let me. You must find a way to make the two worlds come together. You must if you want to be happy. But only you can make it work.'

'But I don't know how.'

'Yes you do,' he said firmly. 'But if you get it wrong

now and again, I shall be there to help you, if you want me.' Gently, he put his hand over hers. 'It's up to you. You must decide.'

For a moment she didn't move – tensely waiting for the usual emotions to swirl round her, building the barriers which would keep her safe from the world. But nothing happened. To her surprise she found she was smiling.

Without a word, she returned the pressure of his fingers.

'We'd better draw up that rota,' she said at last.

A Fair Revenge

The *Lady Bird* swung easily to her moorings. I knew he wasn't there, for no dinghy bobbed behind her and all was quiet. Gently I rowed closer and tied my painter to the rail. It was Friday but still early. Practically no one was about on the estuary. I doubt if anyone saw me climb aboard.

The cabin door was padlocked. That was new. In the old days he never used to bother. I hadn't wanted to do any damage – not to the boat – but there was nothing for it if I wanted to get in. I found a screwdriver and levered off the lock with a horrible splintering noise which echoed across the placid evening water.

The cabin was untidy. That too was different. 'Leave her shipshape, Zoë,' always used to be his final comment every time we left.

There were signs of this new moll of his everywhere. Clothes; make-up; cheap novelettes; a tin of scented talcum powder standing on the chart table. Poor, poor Alec. What I was about to do was undoubtedly for his own good!

It took me about ten minutes to make a really good job of it. Every darn thing went into that canvas sail bag of mine. Bikinis – three of them, would you believe; shorts – the skimpy kind Alec always said showed just what a girl was bad for; sun tan oil – Alec never bothered with that; talc; books; everything I could be sure wasn't his. Carefully

I tied the neck of the bag and stood back to survey my handiwork.

The boat was a little tidier, but not tidy enough. Shipshape Alec used to like her. Shipshape I would leave her, just to show him what he was missing!

That took me a lot longer. The tiny galley was filthy and some of the pretty coffee mugs I had chosen as a present for the boat were chipped. 'Silly cow,' I muttered. 'Can't she do anything properly?' What the hell did he see in her anyway?

It was just as well I had found out what he was up to. If I hadn't seen him with Patricia a couple of times and someone hadn't told me he was bringing her down here for weekends I might never have suspected. I might have gone on believing his story that he had sold the boat and was studying in every second of free time.

With a cautious look round from the cockpit I lowered the bag into my dinghy and climbed in after it. I had half a mind to chuck the bag overboard, but thought better of it. For a start it might float. I tied up to the jetty and humped the bag up onto it. Where could I hide it then? I glanced around. The boat house? The churchyard? The bushes round the pub?

'Hello, Zoë!'

I leaped round and saw Alec watching me from behind a pile of timber.

'Hi.' I could feel my face colouring.

'I didn't know you still came down here,' he said. I could see him looking at me closely, puzzled. He knew damn well I had never been without him before.

'I like to keep an eye on the old place from time to time,' I murmured. 'I miss it.'

To do him justice he did look a little bit taken aback at that.

'Where's the lady friend?' I went on sweetly. 'I hear you have a new crew for the *Lady Bird*.'

He glowered. 'I told you, Zoë. I sold that boat months ago.'

'Oh yes,' I said, 'of course.' The sail bag was resting solidly against my legs. I shaded my eyes in the evening sun and looked across towards the moorings. I could see the boat clearly.

'Can I buy you a drink?' he asked casually, obviously trying to distract me.

'Why not?' I grinned, humping the bag up onto my shoulder. 'Can I dump this junk first? It's going behind the tomb in the crypt. A friend of mine is going to collect it – sometime.'

He raised an eyebrow. 'Strange place to leave it?'

I nodded gravely. 'I'm not sure when she'll be down again. No one will find it there.'

He waited in the church as I felt my way down the worn steps and stuffed the bag down into the dark corner behind the cold stone tomb of the duke of somewhere or other. Then we went to the pub. I felt enormously happy and not the least bit guilty.

We had a super evening. The drink became several, followed by dinner at the bar.

'Well, Alec,' I said at last. 'You haven't told me why you've come down here if you've no boat.'

He glanced at me sideways. 'I didn't say I had no boat, Zoë,' he said, chuckling. 'I said I'd sold the *Lady Bird*. I bought another – a Folk Boat this time. Do you want to see her?'

I went cold. 'You really sold the *Lady Bird*?'

'Yes. I told you.'

'And she's not yours any more?'

'What's the matter with you, Zoë? I sold her to some people called Gill and Harry. In fact they're over there.'

He waved across the bar and a man and woman came over. She was tall and slim and attractive and now, did she but know it, without a stitch of clothing to her name.

'Are you going out to *Lady Bird* later?' I asked casually as a new round of drinks arrived.

Gill nodded.

'Oh God,' I said.

Alec looked at me. 'Are you OK?' he asked.

I smiled. 'Too much to drink,' I said and I ran for the door.

He caught me up in the churchyard. I wasn't being sick. I was trying to break into the church.

In the end I had to confess. He laughed and kissed me. 'Pat never liked it here; and I haven't seen her for weeks,' he lied, but nicely. 'You know, Zoë, I was missing you. I'm glad you thought I was worth fighting for.'

He helped me hump the bag back to the quay. The tide had dropped and he had to kneel to reach their dinghy. As he was lowering the heavy bag the rope that held it must have slipped. It fell gently into the dark water, floated for a second and then disappeared.

Harry must have been close behind us and he must have wondered what we were up to as we struggled, horrified, to our feet, but he just grinned. 'We're off now,' he said, helping Gill into the dinghy. Then he piled their luggage in around her. They seemed to have rather a lot.

Alec and I stood speechless, watching. Then as Harry reached for the oars Gill turned and smiled at Alec.

'By the way,' she called, 'that charming friend of yours, Patricia, has been here all week waiting for you. She couldn't get into your boat, so we said she could stay in *Lady Bird* as we weren't there. I hope she's left it tidy,' and she raised her hand as they rowed away.

Milestones

It was a stupid place to meet. Why had they chosen it? The enormous soft sofa so discreetly placed beneath walls hung with dark damasks was too deep for her; she knew it before she sat down. Either she would have to perch on the edge, nervily uncomfortable, or she would have to sit so far back that her legs would stick out in front like a child's. She stifled a nervous giggle and glanced around. On the far side of the hotel lounge, acres of ankle deep pile away, another woman had solved the problem by reclining elegantly sideways. In her hand she held a martini, her glossy fingernails displayed talon-like round the glass.

With a slight shock Elizabeth realized the waiter was now standing, obsequiously patient, in front of her, the white napkin as stiff on his arm as his paper shirt front. His face was carefully bland, though she was sure he had noticed her suppressed hilarity. She was going to order, automatically, a pot of tea. Then she checked herself.

'Champagne cocktail,' she commanded and defiantly she sat down, drew up her legs and crossed her ankles on the cushions.

'Very well, madam.' He bowed and amazingly he disappeared registering neither amazement nor disapproval. Perhaps respectable middle aged females put their feet up on his sofas at teatime every day and ordered champagne.

Then she saw him. He was standing on the far side of the room. Only just in time she prevented herself from jumping to her feet. She pretended not to notice him, reaching for a copy of *Vogue* from the glass-topped table in front of her, opening it nonchalantly, glancing at the glossy improbable women who prowled across its pages.

The waiter arrived with her drink and she brought it behind the magazine with her. Why wasn't he coming over? Had he changed his mind? Could it be that he didn't recognize her? Covertly she glanced round a double page spread of exotically languorous net clad legs and watched him.

He was undoubtedly the handsomest man she had ever seen. Tall, tanned; middle-aged undeniably, but without an ounce of surplus weight on his frame; green eyed, fair haired – not enough white yet to touch the gold – with the bearing of a soldier as he stood there, his hands clasped behind him, scanning the room. Unbelievably he hadn't seen her. She saw his gaze flicker over the martini drinker, halt and return taking in, Elizabeth saw, those bloody talons and also undoubtedly the plunging breast-line of her dress. After a moment the woman was dismissed and his gaze began methodically to travel once again. Slowly it was coming towards her.

With an unexpected, almost fearful tremor of excitement somewhere just below her diaphragm Elizabeth slowly lowered her magazine and waited.

She had been a girl of seventeen, small, slim, a little too leggy perhaps to be pretty but with a mass of untameable auburn hair which carried only reluctantly and for the shortest time her studied attempts at the styles of the latest film stars, and she had been brown, brown from the sun and wiry with the farm work at which she was as good any day as the two land girls she worked beside; better, grandfather often said. And sometimes she had been glad to get away from the girls and from her grandparents and from the farm, up to the north woods on her own, watching the sunlight dapple through the leaves onto the soft beech mast and there she would retreat into a world which school had so recently opened to her and which the sudden irrevocable necessity of leaving had so abruptly closed. Sometimes it was Wordsworth or Byron, but most often it was Keats she had carried in the pocket of her dungarees, the flimsy edition in the cardboard leather covers which she had sneaked from the bookcase in the cold locked dining room. She would sit, leaning against the five hundred-year-old oak by Hereward's Pond, and recite the lines to herself slowly, fixing them in her mind. Sometimes the words had come aloud and the trees had mocked her embarrassment and dared her to repeat them more loudly still until in the end she had done so, proud of her gentle expressive voice in the echo of the deserted forests all around her.

He had been sitting on the other side of the water, his khaki uniform a perfect camouflage in the duns and shadows of the clearing and she would never have known he was there.

I cannot see what flowers are at my feet
Nor what soft incense hangs upon the boughs . . .

she had intoned slowly to the trees, her eyes filling with tears as she felt the beauty of the words and quietly, across the pond another voice had taken up the verse:

White hawthorn and the pastoral eglantine
Fast fading violets covered up in leaves . . .
And the coming musk rose full of dewy wine . . .

She sat up, scarlet-faced and saw a young man climb reluctantly from the shelter of the trees, brushing the dried leaves from his uniform. He walked towards her round the pond, stopping only when they were close enough to see one another's faces.

'We learned that one at school; I think I got it right,' he had said, and then, awkwardly, 'sorry, I shouldn't have intruded.'

She blinked away her tears and smiled. 'It doesn't matter.'

'It does. You were crying.' Closer now, she saw how young he was. Not much older than she, but still old enough to be in and to have lieutenant's pips on his arm. And because he was there and because he had caught her crying, she had told him everything. How her father had died at Comines just before Dunkirk and how her mother was a VAD in London and how she ached sometimes with the unhappiness and the unbearable beauty of life, and he had understood. And he had walked her slowly back to the farm at last as the time for milking drew near and by then she was laughing. At the gate she turned and looked up at his face. 'You didn't tell me your name,' she said quietly.

'Hugh,' he said. Touching her hand lightly with his own, there on the top of the sun-warmed five barred gate, he winked and turned away.

She watched him until he was out of sight in the lane and then she walked slowly to the farmhouse door.

She went on going to Hereward's Pond but she never saw him there again and slowly hope of doing so died. Perhaps he had been a dryad of the woods himself, conjured out of her imagination. Then, one day walking round the market, her grandmother's basket on her arm, she heard her name called and it was he. His face now was more tanned than ever hers had been and his blond hair was bleached almost white. His grin was the same though, warm and infectious.

She did not ask him where he had been or how long a leave he had this time. She lived for the moment, savouring his company. Ten days later he was gone again.

Everyone assumed they would marry. She assumed it herself, clinging in his arms below the stars, feeling the warmth of his skin through his shirt. She did not know why he did not ask her and it was not a subject she could raise herself. Nor did she let her grandfather or grandmother mention the matter on the rare occasions he sat down at their long table under the blackened farmhouse beams.

The last time she saw him was on a beautiful autumn evening in 1943 when he gave her, for no reason that she understood then, a bracelet, a gold charm bracelet, clipping the links around her wrist himself, raising her hand and kissing her palm and then for a moment holding her hand tightly in his. Only when he had gone did she have the chance to examine the charms. There were four: a silver threepenny bit, set in gold; a St Christopher; a tiny cat and a fish made from little links so that it lay, limply realistic, across her finger, its scales glinting like frost-touched leaves in the sunlight. When she looked up again her eyes were full of tears.

Two years later she married and moved away from the farm. Her husband was an architect and when he joined a partnership in London they moved to Holland Park.

In her heart she had never believed that Hugh was dead and yet she knew that had he lived he would have come back to her; two years was a long time to wait to a girl who had been barely nineteen when they had kissed goodbye that last lingering time; a lifetime to wait and a lifetime to mourn.

Gareth was a strange choice; a prickly difficult man who felt the world against him and the war a personal affront to his plans. But he loved her and she, receptive, lonely and romantic, saw him as some sort of crippled god who with her care and adoration would rise again to Olympian heights. Holland Park was the first step on that ladder.

Fourteen months after the marriage Michael was born and Gareth brought her a tiny golden cherub to go on her bracelet. She had, after they were married, told him a little about Hugh, partly because she needed still to say his name out loud to ease the pain of his going, partly because there had been so little there to make Gareth jealous; just a romantic dream and a bracelet with all the links, but four, empty. It touched her that Gareth was sensitive enough never to try to buy charms for the bracelet in his own name, only in those of her children who were part of herself and through her of Hugh.

Michael was followed a year later by the twins Margaret and Alexandra and two years after that by Colin; Colin, the only one to take after Gareth in every way – a haunted, unhappy child, sensitive to every nuance of life, suspecting always its worst conspiracy against him, clinging to his mother, jealous of his brother, resentful of his sisters but not, as his father was, clever enough to temper his torments with the fulfilment of a creative drive.

And yet strangely Elizabeth saw in him the reflection of herself and recalled through him, after years of forgetfulness, the agonies and beauties of growing up to feel in the very core of one's being the anguish of the world's pain.

She had never been unhappy with Gareth. Perplexed, often; numbed a little more each day by the repeated need to extinguish herself in the need to tend constantly the fire of his demands; tired, frustrated; but she had learned too, not because she wanted it that way, but because that was the way it happened, to live vicariously through her children.

Their careers were predictable. Michael did well at school and went on to university, a stable, handsome, charming boy. The girls both went horse mad and Mags, who cared little for learning, left school early and became a lad at a racing stable, while Sandy, who though not as clever as her brother was something of a plodder, vowed at the age of five to become a vet and twenty years later was in her final year at veterinary college, having looked neither to the right nor to the left of her chosen career.

Colin had followed his father and elder brother to Harrow. Two years later he ran away. Two more schools followed in quick succession. From the first he fled; from the second he was expelled for smoking cannabis and it was then that Gareth, taut, neurotic, consuming forty cigarettes a day, announced that his patience was at last at an end and withdrew all financial support.

Colin, and through him Elizabeth, reeled under the blow, unable to understand either his crime or the withdrawal, as he saw it, of love, and Elizabeth was powerless to help him. She had no money of her own to give. Her intercessionary powers with Gareth had grown fewer as his inner tensions had increased and the other three children closed ranks as siblings do against the outcast, sensing in him perhaps the cuckoo who given any chance at all would a long time ago have humped each of them over the rim of the nest.

And so he had drifted away. Elizabeth saw him sometimes and he rang her from time to time when he knew she would be alone – which was often now. Once or twice she dreamed about him; hard, unpleasant dreams which frightened her and left her in the morning with a splitting headache and a sense of doom not-quite-perceived around the corner of her consciousness, but there was no way of checking that he was all right and slowly she would forget the dream. Even when she had neither seen nor heard of him for several weeks, long schooled to silent waiting by his scorn when quite young when she had rung, worried, around his friends, she would resist now the urge to flap. They would, Gareth callously assured her, hear soon enough if anything happened to the boy. Colin was not one to submerge himself in anonymity should extremis come upon him. Elizabeth's worries about drugs she kept to herself. She knew Gareth's views and she had no wish to hear them attached to their son.

Time passed. Slowly the other children grew away. Sandy qualified and went to join a practice in Herefordshire, Michael married and Mags moved slowly from stud farm to stud farm around Newmarket, coming home once every month or so with enough dirty washing to fill her mother's washing machine four times over and Elizabeth resigned herself to becoming an observer viewing life, or so it seemed to her, through a sterile bubble through which once in a while she was allowed to push her hands. Gareth smiled at her now and then and swore when she forgot to get his new bottle of Maalox and resigned from several of his committees and became, much against his will, something of a TV pundit, discoursing on the architecture of modern Europe and flying off to Paris and Bonn.

And Colin it appeared still read the papers, for scarcely had his father's jet climbed out of the cloud-hazed spirals above Heathrow bound for a much heralded conference in Vienna, than he was tiptoeing across the lawn of the house, their third, still in Holland Park, and knocking urgently at the french windows.

Elizabeth let him in, guiltily glad to see him, hugging him to her for a moment as though she could give him by transfusion of will power alone a little of her strength.

Colin returned the hug and each for a moment was struck by the other's thinness.

'Hi, Liz, how are you?'

'Better for seeing you, Col.' She forced herself to release his hand, to walk away from him, wondering at this urge to cradle him which, even though he was a man, her youngest son stirred within her. Instead of looking at him she stared down at the Afghan rug, rippled a little by their feet, its lineny fringe tangled and flaccid, its colours warm only where the watery sun slanting through the front window touched it. She longed to pour herself a gin. 'Where've you been lately?' She tried to sound casual.

He had thrown himself down on the leather Chesterfield, all knees and elbows, and glancing cautiously at him she saw his shirt had lost a button and there was a dull shine of grease around the inside of his collar.

'Here and there.' He grinned wearily and sat forward, his fists locked, swinging down between his shins above the carpet. 'I need some bread, Liz.'

She sighed, hearing Gareth's voice echoing in her head: 'Not another penny until you get a fucking job,' and knowing she would not refuse walked, an automaton, programmed by mother love, to where her handbag lay on an armchair. She knew there was about forty or so pounds in it and she knew she would give him everything, even the loose change in her purse.

She knew he would be grateful; would return warmth for warmth and stay with her perhaps for a while. If she could get him to eat a few square meals while his father was away, that too would comfort her. She smiled down at him as he looked at the wad of notes in his hand, counting them between finger and thumb like a teller at the bank. Then he tucked them away into the top pocket of his shirt and buttoned the flap. His eyes, so like Gareth's were a brilliant cornflower blue. 'I need a hell of a lot more than that, Liz.' There was no smile on his face, only the hard, weary lines of a man twice as old as he.

Drugs? Gambling? Crime? The possibilities flashed through her mind as she faced him, not believing the hard shine of the eyes, the new cynical twist to his lips as he waited.

'Oh come on, Liz, don't tell me you haven't been salting away the housekeeping all these years. You must have thousands stashed somewhere.'

He didn't believe her. He didn't believe she had no private account, no hoard waiting to be spent gluttonously alone when his father was gone or divorced or dead, and there was no warm sympathy when, worn out at last by his browbeating she broke down and sobbed, only a calculating silence as he stared at her, knowing he must believe her.

But still he had not relinquished hope. He cast around the room, eyeing porcelain, the carriage clock on the mantelpiece, the rug itself and rejecting them in the knowledge that his father would miss them instantly.

'Your jewellery! There must be some jewellery you could sell.'

'No Colin, no . . .' Her voice came from a thousand miles outside her head, distanced by fear and disbelief. But already he was bounding up the long curving flight of stairs, his hand skimming the banister, and bursting into the bedroom.

Her jewel box lay on her dressing table, unhidden in spite of Gareth's oft repeated warnings about burglars, each piece inside warm from her skin, loved. She had never accepted much from him in the way of gifts but with each piece there was a memory, or an agony of its own.

With an exclamation of triumph Colin took the box and emptied it on to the bed. Pearls, lockets, rings, lay tangled on the sprigged pale duvet, and among them Hugh's charm bracelet.

Never, in all her twenty-five years as a mother had Elizabeth struck one of her children, but now as she saw those thin pale hands picking avariciously over the milestones of her life something inside her seemed to snap. In a quick sweep of her hands she had gathered up the things and thrown them, all jumbled, into her pocket and she faced Colin her eyes blazing. The slap she dealt him across the face sent him reeling backwards, the imprint of her fingers first white and then red across his cheek and mouth.

'Your father was right about you all along,' she shrieked at him, her voice dumb, the sound coming from her mouth belonging to a stranger. 'You are ungrateful; you are a scrounger; you're no good. No good at all. Get out! Get out! Get out of this house before I call the police!'

And he had gone. Later, when the tears had stopped, she realized how nearly he had hit her back. The cold fury on his face had been almost insane as he looked at her, but he had said and done nothing and with that sole scrap she would comfort herself in the months and years to come. He had done nothing. One deep shuddering breath and he had turned and walked from the room, leaving the house by the front door which reverberated defiantly behind him from the slam.

On 28th March Colin was arrested and taken to Marylebone Police Station charged with conspiracy to defraud and Gareth put up bail for his son. Three weeks later as he chaired a meeting at the RIBA Gareth had collapsed with a massive stroke. Forty-eight hours later he was dead.

Elizabeth saw the next few months through a pale veil of valium, surrounded, as Colin was convicted and sent to prison for five years, by a warm protective trio of children who treated her like rare Dresden, sharing her out between them in a layer of impenetrable cotton wool. Once or twice she tried to fight her way to the surface, sensing sunlight through the mist which swam above her head, but each time she sank again, drowning in depression.

She stayed with Michael the most. He had married and had a little boy and when all else failed to reach her she warmed to those tiny clinging trusting hands. It was in this house, at the long untidy happy dining table where breakfast lay in a shower of toast crumbs and splattered groats, that she had nerved herself to reach for the *Telegraph*, wearily unfolding it to face a further instalment of the enquiry into Colin's money-making débâcle, and seen a photograph of Hugh.

Stunned she stared at it. The hair, the eyes, the mouth – each had been sculpted and hardened and worn, but it was the same face. She glanced up guiltily at her daughter-in-law who was spooning scrambled egg into Crispin's mouth.

'If you'll excuse me, Ann dear, I'll take my coffee and the paper out on the porch for a while.'

She was quite unconscious of Ann's stare; of the excitement which had been betrayed by her voice, of the fact that her movements, which for months had been slow and dreamlike, were suddenly electric with trembling.

On the straw chair on the porch she arranged her skirt with care and, turning to the side table, poured the slopped coffee back from the saucer into the cup. Then, cautiously, she looked again.

The photograph stared out at her from the page, the eyes direct and challenging. Her heart thumped a little with fear and she lowered her gaze to the caption.

'*Major General Sir Hugh Denniston*,' it said, and below it: '*Army Representative to join Whitehall Committee*.'

Strange, that in all these years she had never known his full name, never known he was a war hero, a holder of the VC, that he had been repeatedly parachuted into

France, had been captured, had, dear God, been tortured by the SS, was married, divorced, the father of two children, had headed this committee, that committee, been in Kenya, in Northern Ireland, in Rhodesia . . .

A gentle hand on hers made her realize suddenly that she was crying.

'Liz? Liz, darling. What is it?' Ann was kneeling at her feet.

Those tears, floodgates of misery and happiness, had released the straitjacket which had held her for so long and, sitting there on the porch with the sunlight slanting through the dew-wet plane trees, her arms around her daughter-in-law and her warm sticky grandchild, she relived those moments by the pond in Hereward's Wood and looking up at the clear autumnal morning sky saw again the defiant crippled squadrons limping home, and progressing, knew that Gareth was dead and Colin was in prison.

It was Ann who rang him. His number had all the time been in the telephone directory.

She had waited until Elizabeth, newly alive, had gone to the hairdresser and then, her heart quaking a little lest the baby wake up and cry or the milkman call or Liz change her mind and return, Ann had picked up the receiver in her bedroom and begun to dial.

The phone was answered by a woman. Disappointed, Ann hesitated, then she asked for Hugh and he came to the phone. The woman was his daughter.

Somehow she had expected to be speaking to a dreamer and the incisive voice unnerved her. She began to feel a little foolish. Perhaps Liz had been right after all to dismiss laughing the notion of contacting him. Perhaps it was all much too late.

Floundering, the receiver slipping as her palm grew moist with embarrassment, she began her story. She began at the wrong end, with Gareth's death, when all the time she had planned to say 'Do you remember Hereward's Pond and a girl with red hair?', and the polite silence in the receiver rebuked her.

But he did remember. When at last she managed to say the right words the quality of his silence changed. She felt his stillness.

'Elizabeth?' The word sounded stiff and painful from his lips when at last she stopped gabbling and waited for a reply. That was all he said, 'Elizabeth.'

'Would you . . . that is, do you think you and she should meet?' she asked tentatively after yet another silence.

'Does she want to?' he asked, and she could sense the piercing interrogation of his eyes on the other end of the telephone line.

'She doesn't know I've rung you,' she confessed.

'She didn't want to ring herself, of course.'

'No, she didn't want to ring herself.'

It was Ann who suggested the hotel – the public place, the neutral ground – and who wrote the date in her own diary and then for three days was too appalled at her own temerity to confess to Liz just what she had done. And as she told her she knew at once she had been wrong. If Hugh and Liz should meet again, it should have been at the behest of fate in the cool secret thickets around Hereward's Pond, or perhaps it should never happen at all, allowing each to remember a young golden image of the other and a dream to treasure in their heart.

'I won't go,' she thought as she sat alone on the autumnal golden terrace at the back of Michael's house. I'll be ill. Or go away. I'll go abroad.

She had stood before the mirror inside her wardrobe door for a long long time, staring hyper-critically at herself: the hair still auburn but a glossy darker colour now than it had ever been naturally; the figure neat, slim, good legs – legs are always the last part of a woman to 'go' Gareth always used to say, and she had gone around for weeks studying the thin elastic-controlled limbs of old ladies. Her eyes were still clear and needed glasses only for reading and television and her skin was good, pale now and no longer tanned. It was inside that she had not changed. Inside she was still that dreamy, vulnerable girl of seventeen, but would he know it? Would he recognize her at all?

Hugh's picture was folded inside the lid of her dressing case and she took it out again and looked at it. They seemed to have worn well, he and she, but how much had they changed, really?

The *Vogue* lying open on her knee, she watched him approach her across the room. He had shown no visible sign of recognizing her but unerringly now he was threading his way towards her through the chairs and tables. And then at last he was standing before her.

'I thought you might not recognize me,' she said at last, looking up to meet his eyes.

'Why not?'

She shrugged. 'I must have changed. I feel different sometimes.'

'Better or worse?'

'Some of each. Won't you have a drink? I don't like drinking alone.'

He smiled, sitting down on the edge of the chair opposite hers, in the same movement beckoning the waiter and in some mysterious way conveying his order without even speaking.

'I tried to find you, you know,' he said. 'But your grandparents had gone. No one seemed to know anything about you.' He gave one small shrug which to her betrayed more eloquently than the most poignant speech the agonized months he had spent searching for her when at last he had returned to England after the war. He gave a sheepish grin. 'This is one hell of a place to meet. I take it you don't normally frequent West End hotels.' He pronounced the word without an 'h'.

'It was Ann's idea, remember?'

'You get on well with your daughter-in-law?'

'Very. She's been very kind. Did she tell you my son, my other son, is in prison?' She had to say it quickly, to get it over with, to stop Colin's shadow hovering between them.

He leaned back slightly, reaching into his jacket pocket for a silver cigarette case.

'What for?' He tapped the cigarette on the case before returning the latter to his pocket and half turned to the waiter who, having set a double whisky down on the table before him, had produced a lighter.

'Fraud.' She sipped defensively at her champagne. 'It was all in the papers. It killed my husband.'

'I'm afraid I haven't seen the papers much. I've just come back from Zimbabwe.'

The gentle look he gave her told her he didn't mind. Not about Colin. He was part of her as were Gareth and Michael and little Crispin and the girls and all the last forty odd years.

'Your husband, what did he do?'

'He was the architect Gareth Sullivan.'

He frowned then, his glass half-way to his lips. 'But I met him. I met him several times. He was on a committee with me once,' and sitting forward, his elbows on his knees, he stared at her. 'All this time, Liz, and I never knew.'

Knew what? That she had married Gareth? That she was in London? That she was alive at all? All three perhaps.

He was watching her closely, reading her thoughts. 'Come on. This place is ghastly. Knock that back whatever it is – ' he was looking at the glass in her hand ' – and let's get out of here. I've got a car outside.'

She had forgotten he was so much taller than she. He made her feel delicate and feminine, almost girlish again as she followed him across the carpet. Behind them the woman with the glossy fingernails lowered her glass and stared after them.

She found a car outside, on the double yellow line, in the care of the doorman and affecting not to see the fiver which changed hands as the man opened the door for her she slid into the seat, waiting for a moment in that strange encapsulated silence for Hugh to come round and climb in behind the wheel. As they pulled effortlessly out into the traffic she leaned back and closed her eyes. She did not ask where they were going. She knew it would be the woods behind her grandfather's farm, now owned by strangers but mercifully preserved, where, at this time of year, the beeches were a cloak of gold.

As soon as she had got into the car she had spotted the tattered wartime copy of Keats in the glove pocket in front of her and quietly she smiled at the message. She wondered if he had remembered too the bracelet he had given her and gently as he guided the car into the traffic of the Cromwell Road she began to ease it down her wrist past the tightly buttoned cuff which had been so carefully fastened to conceal it.

The Magic Carpet

The day started badly.

'Why didn't you go into that first car park? There was loads of room.'

'Because it was so far from the fête. You know you hate walking.' Malcolm's voice had the patient note in it which always drove Ginny wild.

'I do like walking in the country, it's different, and look at this queue. We'll be here all day.'

The line of overheating cars crawling over the sticky tarmac was radiating heat beneath the blazing sky, while the procession of people strolling from the village kept safely, sensibly on the grassy verge in the black shadow of the heavy walnut trees. Ginny eyed them enviously. Her dress was sticking to her back.

'I've a good mind to get out and walk.'

'Why don't you, if you're going to be so grumpy?'

'All right. I will.'

She grappled for the handle of the door. Only when she was standing, slamming it shut, did she feel a twinge of conscience.

'Are you sure you don't mind me walking?'

'I don't mind. I'll meet you there, OK?'

The shade of the trees was heavy with bees and pollen and thick, humid heat. Her toes, bare in sandals, were pricked and stung by the grass vergey things which grew there. But at least it was better than the imprisoning seats of the car. Poor Malcolm. He was stuck there till he reached the car park. So much for an afternoon in the country. The idea of the little church fête had seemed such fun at the time – they hadn't dreamed there would be such a crowd. Distastefully she eyed the crawling vehicles, their heavy fumes polluting the country air.

A surge of excitement hit her as she came round the corner and saw before her the white marquees in the field, the khaki ex-desert army tents, the lines of booths with, in the centre, a tiny roped-off ring and everywhere the smell of drying grass with the sweetness of hay. Over a loudspeaker somewhere came music and as it was outside and a bank holiday she wanted suddenly to dance. She paid her ten pence at the entrance and then stood still uncertain what to do. How would she find Malcolm again? She walked cautiously in the direction of the car park. She could see the sun reflecting on the lines of windscreens behind a hedge.

Balls thwacked against the canvas backing to a coconut shy and she stopped to watch. 'Three goes for ten pence, love. Go on. Have a try.'

Why not?

Hitching her bag on her shoulder she took the three heavy balls from the man's hand and hurled the first one down the field.

'Bad luck, love. Two more goes.' Distracted, he was giving change to someone behind her. Her next go went wide. And the last.

She made a shamefaced grimace at the man and walked on. And then suddenly he was there, grinning, his camera in his hand.

'Malcolm! Did you come in by another entrance?' She was hoping he hadn't been watching.

'I saw you. Three bosh shots. How much did that little effort cost you?'

He was laughing at her and she blushed a little. 'I bet you couldn't do better.'

He couldn't.

They were even, now. Together they walked slowly into the white elephant tent. 'We might get something for the flat, Malcolm. There's so much we still need.'

'Like a dented warming pan or three chipped Victorian teapots, I suppose?'

Indignant she punched him in the ribs, then she began to push her way to the front of the gossiping women to where piles of exciting things were laid out on lines of flat trestle tables. All round the smell of trampled grass was very strong in the creamy twilight of the tent.

Strange, how two people with so much in common and so much in love could disagree so violently about decorating their first home. He wanted it light and airy; modern and functional. She had pictured it cluttered with Victoriana, draped and decorated, the windows festooned with lace.

'My goodness, Ginny, you need one of these.' His voice, mocking gently, was at her elbow. He had picked up a grimy watercolour in a fractured gilt frame. 'What is it?' He peered in the dim light. '*The Relief of Mafeking*, I think . . . Still it doesn't really matter much.'

She ignored him, her hand straying over the spines of a pile of books, glancing at the titles.

Reluctantly he relinquished the picture and followed her. 'Look, a novel by Mrs Radcliffe,' he exploded with a laugh. 'Ginny, my darling, that's for you . . .'

She was getting hot again, fed up with his teasing. In the distance at the far side of the table she could see a neatly folded embroidered tablecloth. As she pushed her way towards it, a gently determined hand reached out from the crowd and it was gone.

'That's your fault,' she flashed at Malcolm, suddenly. 'If you hadn't been fooling round distracting me I would have got that cloth. It would have looked lovely on the little round table.'

'Not my table with the melamine top.' His voice became suddenly threatening. 'No squalid cloth with somebody else's gravy stains is going on that. It's simple and perfect as it is.'

'It's not; it's . . . it's bare.'

'That's right. Bare.'

A woman came between them for a moment. When she had gone he was smiling again. 'Come on, Ginny. Don't let's quarrel. Let's go and see what else there is outside. This tent is getting too hot.'

They fought their way back to the entrance. Ginny was scowling. The tablecloth still rankled. 'That table needs something,' she muttered at his broad back as he pushed his way ahead of her into the sunshine.

'A pot plant, possibly. That is all,' he flung over his shoulder. 'Now forget it.'

A small child, red-faced and screaming, ran in front of them, the picture on its T-shirt grimy with melted chocolate.

'Come on, Ginny. I'll buy you an ice-cream.' He groped for her hand and together they made their way towards a booth with a long queue at the far side of the ring where two ladies, hot and dishevelled, unused to the problems of melting ice-cream and soggy cones, were battling manfully to supply the queue.

'What kind of pictures *are* we going to put in that room, Malcolm?' Her mind was still on the flat as they shuffled slowly over the browning grass.

'Perhaps one big one, over the couch. I haven't decided.'

'*You* haven't decided.' She repeated it just to make sure she'd heard aright.

He grinned. 'I know, Ginny. But if it was left to you we'd have fifty tatty old prints.'

'Better that than one painting on acres of white wall. With white furniture. Malcolm, it's going to look like an operating theatre!'

'Rubbish. It'll look very nice.'

They shuffled forward another place in the queue.

'It won't. Oh come on. It'll look terrible. It'll have no warmth. It'll be uncomfortable. Who'll want to sit in a room like that, on a cold winter's evening. No one.'

'I will.'

'Oh!' Exasperated she stamped her foot. 'Well, I won't. You can bloody well sit there alone.'

'Good. I will.' He grinned at her. 'Come on. We're nearly there. Do you want a pink one or a white one?'

'I don't want one now. I want a cold drink.' She pursed her mouth deliberately aping a small spoilt child. 'Come on. I don't want to stand in this silly queue.'

'Well I do.' The patient voice again. It snapped the last of Ginny's control.

'Well bloody well stand there then. I'm not going to!'

She was conscious of the shocked faces turned to her and the people hastily moving out of her way. Then she was alone, in the quiet green no man's land between the tents. She looked round for Malcolm following, but there was no sign of him. He had stayed stubbornly in the queue.

She stood for a moment, her hands absent-mindedly strumming a taut guy rope, examining the woven skeins of hemp. Behind her she could hear the music and the excited shouts of children. In front there was a narrow strip of grass and then a high hawthorn hedge silent except for the occasional sleepy note of a hedge sparrow.

As always her temper was gone as quickly as it had flared. She walked slowly back to the queue, her head held high. Malcolm had gone. She glanced round wildly, conscious of the interested glances of others waiting their turn for ice-cream, but there was no sign of him anywhere. In the ring a group of children were lining up for a race. 'Are there any more boys, seven to eight years old?' a megaphone boomed near her. 'Your race is starting next. Boys seven and eight years old, please . . .'

She began to walk slowly round the ring, her eyes scanning the crowds searching for Malcolm's blue shirt. Suddenly every other man there seemed to be wearing a blue shirt, but each time she looked again, heart thumping a little, for his face, she found another.

'Oh Malcolm, you beast. Where are you?' She felt suddenly angry. He had no business to walk out on her like that. None at all. She stamped her foot.

'Roll up, roll up. Come and try the hoopla. Roll up! Three hoops for fifty pence.' She was standing right in front of a stall. Behind it the vicar himself, his round face flushed and perspiring a little peered at her anxiously, his dog collar restricting, over shirtsleeves. 'Only fifty pence a go,' he said again, almost pleading. He was looking straight at her. Glancing round, embarrassed, she realized that there was no one else near the stall.

She grinned suddenly. 'What the hell,' she murmured and then clapped her hand, embarrassed, over her lips. She groped in her bag for the coin.

The vicar watched eagerly as she stood poised, the hoop ready to flick from her wrist. It skittered across the table and rolled drunkenly and uselessly away. 'Oh bad luck, my dear.' He sounded really quite upset for her. She aimed better the next time. The hoop fell neatly around a small packet of sugar cigarettes. She shrugged helplessly as the vicar handed them to her and slipped them, trying to keep her face straight, into her bag. The third hoop teetered, wavering towards the edge of the table and fell, half encircling, on the saucer of fifty pence pieces – the hoopla takings. They both laughed. 'You can't have that,' he said.

She had another useless go at the coconut shy and then wandered on down the rows of stalls, only half looking now for the blue shirt. She was beginning to enjoy herself. It was the turn of the little girls, five to six, in the ring.

A roar of laughter from a corner stall caught her attention and she wandered over. An old dresser, standing in front of draped sacking, was set up with old bits of chipped crockery. A man was hurling wooden balls at the plates and every smash was greeted by a cheer. She stood and watched for a while. It looked fun.

'Come and have a go. Come on,' the proprietor of the stall shouted, rattling the heavy balls in his enormous calloused hands. 'Get rid of all your frustrations, ladies and gents.' But the crowd was moving on, bored. In a moment they had gone and the stall was deserted except for Ginny. The man's shoulders slumped. He turned away, letting the balls roll from his palms into the box. Then he caught sight of her watching. 'Come on, darling. Want a go? Four for the price of three, seeing as it's you.' His shrewd eyes had spotted her new shiny wedding ring. He glanced left and right. 'Had a spat with your old man, have you? I've just the thing for you. See?' He bent and picked up a hideous jade green vase. He waddled over to the dresser and, sweeping a pile of broken china off with his arm, set up the vase on the middle shelf. 'There you are darling. That's him. Now. Take a good swing at it. Arm right back.'

Grinning she took the balls from him and hurled. The first smashed a plate on the edge of the shelf. It was the fourth ball which caught the vase full on its plump shiny belly. It rocked forward twice and then plunged from the shelf, smashing into a dozen pieces on the top of the dresser.

The man chuckled. 'Made you feel better, didn't it? Want another go?'

Ginny stood there, stricken. She hadn't meant it. She was shaken with guilt. Supposing she had harmed Malcolm in some way by smashing the vase. She hadn't really been pretending it was him. Oh please, please, Malcolm darling, where are you? She began to look round, lost again, searching desperately for his face in the crowd.

Puzzled, the man watched her for a moment. Then he shrugged. He waded through the broken crocks to the dresser and began to set up new plates and saucers, sweeping the debris from the shelves onto the old carpet laid on the grass below. Near the carpet was a sign. 'Carpet for sale. Five pounds.'

She walked quickly away, scanning the crowds again, searching everywhere for the blue shirt, aching to have Malcolm beside her.

In the ring it was the toddlers' race. Half of them were going the wrong way, but no one seemed to notice. The field was crowded. There were so many places he could be. In a tent, at a booth, walking like her in the crowd. Perhaps he had gone home without her? She was stricken with terror. Then she pushed away the thought. How silly. Malcolm would never do that, however angry with her. She set out to walk again, slowly, round the perimeter of the field, methodically glancing into every marquee and stall. It must be tea time, there were so many people clutching paper cups and sticky pink-iced buns. Wasps hovered over the litter bins.

She saw him at last back where she had started, standing arms folded, his feet slightly apart, watching two boys hurl wooden balls at the china on the dresser. There was a bemused smile on his face. The man had spotted him.

'Here you are, sir. Three balls for fifty pence. Small price to pay to get rid of your inhibitions, sir. Pretend it's your old woman, sir. Really put some beef into it.'

Ginny flinched. Surely he wasn't going to? She watched as Malcolm fished in his pocket for the money. Then he took the balls from the man. The first thwacked into the dresser back with such force that three saucers fell. The other two followed rapidly, shattering bowls. Malcolm was grinning. 'Thanks, chum. I needed that.' Then he was wandering off. He never looked round once.

Malcolm.

She stood and watched as he disappeared into the crowd and suddenly she found she was fighting back tears, screwing up her handkerchief in her fist. She felt desolate and abandoned as she was jostled out of the way by a big bouncing woman who had spied the stall.

'Come on, George. You've always wanted to smash the china. Come and have a go at this then.' The husband, equally big and bouncing, pushed after her and squealing with laughter the pair of them threw their balls at the dresser, hurling cheery insults after each shot.

Miserably Ginny gazed at the ground as the cascading china fell on the dim red design of the grubby carpet. It was a bit like the carpet in her parents' dining room. The kind she had thought would look so pretty in their flat, under the white melamine table . . .

She sniffed and blew her nose. Then, cautiously, she edged a bit closer trying to see the carpet better. Actually it was little more than a rug. But five pounds? It seemed too good to be true.

'Want another go, love? Come on, get it all out of your system. Four balls for you, wasn't it? Four for fifty.' He had spotted her at once.

She smiled at him uncertainly. 'Actually I was looking at the carpet.'

'Ah, I could tell you was a lady of discernment.' He slipped the balls into a capacious pocket. 'Real Persian that is. Woven in the desert and brought across the sands on the back of a camel I shouldn't wonder. Here, have a real butchers.' He held up the rope which held back the throwers so she could duck underneath and come closer. She walked with him to the dresser, feeling suddenly very exposed, blushing at the interested faces lined up behind her. Now that she was close she could see the carpet was horribly threadbare and torn. It was stained too beneath the piles of china. He stopped and with a flick of the wrist pulled it clear, pouring the crocks into a heap on the dusty grass. 'Look at that. There's real quality there. It's an antique you know. That's why it's a bit worn. It's an antique.' He glanced at her sharply from beneath his sandy brows and she found herself smiling suddenly.

'I can see it's old,' she murmured, seriously.

Her finger traced the pattern of little square stylized birds round the borders. She wanted it badly, however worn. She hesitated. Malcolm would kill her of course.

'Come on, darling. Make up your mind. There's people waiting to throw.'

'I'll have it.' She gulped a little nervously, wondering suddenly if she had five pounds in her bag.

Solemnly he began to roll it up, carrying it effortlessly under his arm. He threw it down on the grass just beyond the rope as she scrabbled in her purse. Four pound coins and a pile of odd loose change. He counted it carefully and then he grinned. 'Want another throw for luck? On the house?' But she shook her head.

The rug was surprisingly heavy. She heaved it up into her arms and then stood still. Malcolm had the car keys. She wasn't even sure where he'd parked the wretched car.

She couldn't wander round the fête carrying a carpet. What on earth was she to do? The trouble was she couldn't stop smiling. She was so ridiculously pleased with the thing.

She carried it away from the crowds to an emptier corner of the field where two oak trees stood, isolated from the woods behind the hedge. Nearby three girls were giving pony rides, leading the patient animals whose heads drooped lower and lower in the heat with a succession of breathlessly excited small children clutching their manes.

She set down the rug and carefully unrolled it on the grass, brushing off the bits of splintered china and goose-grass which still clung to it. It had a skimpy fringe on one side – at the opposite end the fringe seemed to have been shaved off. She stood and gazed at it proudly for a few minutes and then, experimentally, she knelt on it, brushing the threadbare pile with her hand. It was the first Persian rug she had ever owned.

'Don't tell me. It can fly!' Suddenly Malcolm was standing behind her, a coconut nestled in the crook of his arm. He was laughing at her.

She stroked it again. Protectively. 'For all I know it can. This is the sort of place one finds magic carpets.'

'What, at an Aunt Sally shy?' He snorted with laughter. Then he came and knelt beside her, reverently putting the coconut on the rug in front of him. 'Come on then. Ready to wish? Where do we want to go?'

He glanced at her sideways. 'I saw the rug too. I had a little bet with myself that you'd spot it. You know he's got another one down there already. Even more tatty, if that's possible.' He put his arm round her suddenly. 'Oh my lovely Ginny. You'll never learn will you, sweetheart?' He grinned again. 'Right. I'm waiting. Where are we flying to?'

'Just home? I want to see the rug down, in the flat.'

She couldn't keep the slight note of bravado out of her voice.

He was sitting cross legged now, palms down beside him on the rug, feeling the pile. 'I suppose we could mend it. If it were backed in some way it might not look too bad. Funnily enough these rugs can be dreadfully shabby and yet still look nice . . .'

She looked at him, her green eyes wide with astonishment. 'But Malcolm, it's old!'

He grimaced at her. 'I don't dislike old things on principle, love. I jut want to keep our flat in one style. As it happens I think a Persian rug or two would fit. It would look lovely under my table.' He glanced at her sideways. 'Perhaps you're right about that room. Perhaps it does need a little more colour to give it warmth. This would provide it, wouldn't it?'

'Oh, Malcolm!' She flung her arms round his neck and kissed him; 'Oh Malcolm, I do love you sometimes.' A thought struck her suddenly. 'I saw you at the stall, breaking china. Did you really think of me when you were doing it?'

'Of course. Every shot.' His eyes were twinkling mischievously. 'I'll bet you had a go too. And thought of me. Didn't you?'

She bit her lip, trying not to laugh. 'Well, there was this hideous green vase. And the man did say "pretend it's your old man".'

'Did you hit it?' he asked casually, lying back and putting his arm across his eyes.

She giggled. 'A bull's-eye.'

'But you're usually such a bad shot!' He sounded quite indignant.

'Ah, but I was provoked beyond endurance.'

'Just because I wanted an ice-cream?'

'That's right.' She lay back beside him and stretched

her arms ecstatically above her head. 'I am always provoked by ice-creams, especially pink ones.'

'And by white melamine tables?'

'Those too.'

He nodded sleepily. 'As long as I know,' he said. 'By the way. Did you see I'd won a coconut?'

The Proposal

'Have you time for a wee crack, Aggie?' Betty Anderson popped her head over the privet hedge and watched critically as her neighbour pushed two more tulip bulbs into the soft black soil.

Aggie Cameron straightened her back and wiped an earthy hand on her apron. 'What is it now, Betty? Have you yet more gossip for me, hen?' She didn't mean to sound impatient but she had been enjoying the peace of the crisp cold afternoon.

She knew, however, that Betty meant well and there was always the chance that the story would be about someone Aggie had actually met. Gossip lost its enjoyable edge if you did not know the people concerned. 'Come away in now and I'll put on the kettle while you tell me,' she said more softly.

She listened as Betty, her shoes rustling through the drifting leaves, made her way down her own side of the hedge out of the little gate and in through the identical one next to it. Then she turned and led her guest into the house.

Betty had at last learned not to offer to help. Aggie was not concerned that Betty would have made the tea in any one of a dozen kitchens. In hers, where everything had to be kept just so, no one touched anything. She did not like to be helped.

'Can I ask you something, Aggie?' She heard Betty's voice, slightly diffident, from the fire-side chair. 'How is it that you take so much care of the garden when you can't . . .' She hesitated, suddenly embarrassed.

'Can't see the flowers I'm planting?' Aggie finished for her. 'Och that's easy, Betty. I can smell, can't I? I can touch their soft petals and I can feel the green leaves trembling with the sap. I know you'll think I'm foolish, but I can almost hear the flowers sing as they hang their heads and rustle in the wind. And I can remember their colours you know.' She smiled gently, as she set the kettle down on the gas. 'I haven't always been blind. I can remember fine what a garden should look like in the spring.'

She groped for the other chair and sat down, waiting for the expected piece of gossip. For a moment there was silence and she sensed that her companion was inexplicably uncomfortable.

'What is it, hen? What's the matter? What is it you want to say to me?'

'Aggie. I've been keeping company with Roddy Mackay. I think you know that?'

'Aye. He's a fine man.' Aggie nodded sagely. She waited, her hands quietly folded in her lap.

'I think he's asked me to marry him, Aggie,' Betty went on in a rush. 'What am I to do?'

Aggic sat for a moment, her blue eyes fixed unseeing on the kitchen fire. Then she smiled. 'He's a fine man, Betty, as I said. But if you only think he's asked you and you're not sure what to do, then I think you'd best do nothing.'

Betty blushed a little and leaned forward. 'I think I love him, Aggie. I go weak-kneed and foolish as a schoolgirl when he comes to the house. It's ten years since my man died. I've not felt like this since I was courting him.'

Aggie rose stiffly and went to the kettle, her hand going without hesitation to the handle.

'Have you made up your mind what to say to him then?'

There was silence. Then Betty said. 'The trouble is Aggie, I'm not minded to leave my house. I've lived here too long. I've no desire to go up the mountain to Craigbeg.'

Aggie nodded. The two of them lived in pleasant little cottages and the gardens were beautiful. It took someone young and agile to live in the hills. Someone like her niece Alison and her husband. She remembered how they had gone for a drive up the glen and come back thrilled with the beauties of Craigbeg. They had even wanted, dreamily, to buy the place for themselves. How wonderful it would have been if they could live near her, close at hand. But Mackay had rudely refused their tentative offer for his cottage. And why not? He lived there himself. Now, if only . . . But Aggie firmly put the thought behind her.

'You'd best think about it, Betty. Don't say anything to the man, till you've made up your mind properly.'

It was four days later that Aggie, weeding by feel among the last blooms on the rose bushes by the garden gate, heard the deep cheery voice of Roddy Mackay above her.

'You're doing a fine job there, Mistress Cameron. I haven't seen such a garden in ages.' She heard her gate click and his step on the gravel path.

'May I have a word with you,' she heard him go on, his voice suddenly confidential close to her ear.

'Of course you may.' Aggie turned to him, wiping her earthy fingers on her apron. 'There's nothing wrong I hope, Mr Mackay?'

'Nothing indeed, Mistres Cameron, it's just that I have a wee bit of a problem and I'm no very sure how to solve it.'

There was a moment of silence. In the warm autumn sunshine, Aggie could hear the wistful song of her robin.

He was waiting for the stranger to leave so that he could hop back to the newly turned earth at her feet.

'The thing is, I think I've offended Betty Anderson. I've been going to see her fairly often, two or three times a week and then last time I went over there I must have said something to upset her. She's not said a word to me since. When I called yesterday and the day before, she didn't open the door to me, though I've an idea she was in.' Aggie could hear an aggrieved note slipping into the voice.

'That's strange,' she replied very cautiously. 'I know for a fact she has a great regard for you, Mr Mackay. Can you not think what it is you might have said?'

He kicked the gravel on her path and she heard him scratch his head noisily. 'I cannot and that's a fact. I mentioned to her that maybe her garden could do with a bit of a dig. That could have been it, I suppose. She said she wasn't strong enough to do it herself now she hadn't a man to help her. Well, I said, perhaps we could come to an arrangement. It doesn't do not to have a man to take care of your garden.' He paused.

Aggie smiled. 'There's no man to take care of mine either.'

'Och woman, but you do fine. You've no need of anyone. Betty now, she's not got the fingers for gardening. Such a fine patch it is, but her flowers are thin and poor and they're in all the wrong places and she hasn't a vegetable in the place.'

Aggie had always suspected as much. 'I know how you must miss gardening, Mr Mackay, living on that rocky hill yourself. I wonder, did you suggest some kind of permanent arrangement to look after her garden for her?'

'Well, I did and I didn't.' He shuffled his feet again. 'To tell you the truth I told her that I'd be happy to take care of the matter for her, if she'd allow me. Then she went all foolish and giggly and said she'd have to think about it. Silly woman. I know she's enough money and I'd not charge her over much.'

Poor Betty. So it was as a gardener he had offered his services, nothing more. In spite of herself Aggie could not hold back a sad little smile.

'Did you mention money, Roddy Mackay?' she enquired innocently.

'I did not. I thought it should come from her.'

'Do you not think that maybe that's what embarrassed her?'

Again he scratched his head. 'Has she no money then?'

Aggie saw her chance. 'Aye, she's got money. She's got a fair bit tucked away and of course there's the house that's worth a lot too, with that good land. But can you no see man, it's an insult for a bonnie woman like Betty Anderson to have to pay a man to work in her garden. There are many as would do it for nothing.' She paused, waiting for a reaction.

'Are there so?' He was pondering.

'There are indeed. I know for a fact she would rather you were the one to help her and she knows how you love the garden but there she is, widowed, healthy, lonely.' Aggie emphasized each word carefully. 'It's my opinion she needs a man to look after her, Roddy Mackay. The garden is only one of the things that need taking care of.'

She broke off a stray tendril of weed and twiddled it between her fingers.

'She's wealthy, you say?'

'Aye, she is that.'

'And there are men, shall we say, courting her?'

'There are a few more than a wee bit interested.' Aggie smiled to herself.

'Is that so?' Roddy Mackay's voice was thoughtful again. 'Well, I'm glad I had this wee chat with you, Mistress

Cameron. Will you mind and not say a word to Betty about this please?' The gate clicked open. 'I'll come and have another word with her this evening.'

Aggie stood and listened to his footsteps as he walked purposefully down the lane. Then she bent once more to her roses.

The next morning Betty Anderson knocked on her door as Aggie was washing up her egg cup and plate.

'You know what I told you the other day, hen, about Roddy Mackay asking me to marry him?' She was breathless with excitement.

Aggie nodded quietly and began to dry a knife.

'Well, I wasn't sure what to do and so after I talked to you I thought I'd follow your advice and do nothing, to give myself the chance to decide, you understand and I avoided him, and I even hid behind the curtain when he knocked on the door.' She giggled excitedly. 'Well, last night he came over again. Straight in he came, without knocking even, with a great box of chocolates. He fair swept me off my feet. He said he thought I'd probably misunderstood his intentions, and that I should know he meant to make an honourable proposal. Oh, Aggie, he declared himself really well.' She stopped and waited expectantly.

'And what did you say, Betty?'

'Oh, I said yes. Och, Aggie, he's a really fine man!'

Aggie nodded thoughtfully and put away the last of her china. 'So will you be going to live up at Craigbeg now?'

'No, he says he'd like us to go on living here. He likes the garden, you know. It's always been his great weakness, gardening and there's no land worth the name at Craigbeg, he says.'

Aggie took down her tea caddy. 'Will you take a cup now you're here, Betty, to celebrate? When will the great day be?'

'Oh, soon, soon.' Betty was ecstatic. 'He said he'd bring down his gardening things in the van this week. He's no real use for them up there and he can make a start on the beds, he said.' She giggled coyly.

That evening Aggie sat down at her telephone and carefully dialled her niece's number.

'Is that you, Alison? Now listen. The cottage you liked so much at Craigbeg, I happen to know that it's coming on the market fairly soon. You'd be wise to make an offer at once.'

'But he said he'd never shift.' Alison's voice on the phone was indignantly puzzled.

'Well, something's happened to change his mind,' said her aunt quietly. 'He decided he couldn't live without a garden.' Smiling to herself contentedly, she hung up.

Spaces

The front door clicked behind her and she was outside in the quiet street. Above her the stars were crackling with frost as she walked resolutely into the darkness.

'You won't be too late, Faye?' Marta had said anxiously as Faye shrugged on her coat and Faye had turned to look at her, her eyes vague as she frowned, trying to listen.

'Don't wait up. I've got a key,' she managed to say as she groped for the door handle.

Outside she paused. Those were more or less the very words that Paul had used. She had not waited up but he had not used his key; not until three days later when he returned, collected a suitcase and packed nearly all his things.

'It's not working, Faye,' he said gently as she watched, too frozen to protest or to cry out. 'Better this way. We both need space to think.'

Space: the enormous, echoing emptiness which was the flat; the cold silence inside her heart; the beating of her quiet pillow against her ear drums.

In the end she had gone to Marta who knew the whole story and only then did she cry. At home she had not dared. Marta, always uneasy with emotion, resorted to practicality and made hot whisky and lemon and looked for her aspirin. Love at its nadir is a lot like flu. One aches;

one cannot bear to be touched; one shivers and longs for death.

'But it will pass, you know it will,' Marta whispered kindly as she tucked her into the spare bed and Faye wondered briefly if her friend was after all a little glad it had happened.

But now time had passed and she had thrown off the initial fever of misery. Her need was to be alone with the dull ache which had stayed with her.

In front of her the road led curving up the hill, the pale street lights flickering in the sharpness of the air. There were fewer of them now. Soon there would be none. She walked steadily, listening to the echo of her own footsteps and, in her head, to the echo of her life with Paul.

They had met in the dark; in a garden, escaping the heat of a noisy party where the disco threatened to bring down the walls and the smell of the wine cup and the cigarettes and the reefers sent waves of nausea across her shoulder blades.

'Too much for you?' the voice had said softly as she leaned against the moss-covered wall and breathed the scented silence.

He had materialized out of the shadows, a tall thin silhouette, slightly stooped at the shoulders and he stood several feet from her. There had been a long relaxed silence before they felt the need to speak.

She had not asked his name and only later, separated by a surge of dancers who spilled out of the french windows to the terrace and across the grass in a flood tide, did she realize she had not even really seen his face and she knew herself bereft.

It did not matter. He found her once more with calm certainty, took her hand and guided her over the gravel drive, through the parked cars, to her own which was up on the grass. Only in the pale interior lights as they opened the door did she at last see his face.

Weeks passed. At first he would not move in. 'You must be sure,' he said quietly. But the touch of his hands on hers and the touch of his lips left no possibility of doubt. She had fallen headlong through love to infatuation and worship.

It worried Paul. 'No one should love another person like this,' he said, holding her face between cupped hands, looking at her as if he wanted to memorize every detail. 'It is not right; the gods will become jealous as they did in stories.'

She did not believe him. She had laughed at first, secure in her shield of certainty and at last so was he, taking her in his arms and burying his face in her hair.

It was not as though she were a starry-eyed teenager. She held a responsible job; people relied on her judgement and skill. She had to be strong. But how, when her heart began to pound uncomfortably and her mouth went dry the moment he entered the room and all she wanted was to go down on her knees and serve him? Watching herself, her joy turned to apprehension and a strange amorphous dread.

She told Marta in despair and Marta stared at her.

'For goodness' sake, Faye! You are the one who went to the Equal Rights Commission to win your promotion! You can't let yourself down like this. You can't let *us* down.' She brought their coffee and sat opposite Faye, her pale face earnest and affectionate. 'You know as well as I do that it's only chemistry! Rationalize things. It's the urge to procreate and that's the last thing you want to do, for God's sake.'

She looked hard at Faye for a moment then passed her a cup. 'I bet *his* work isn't suffering,' she said softly.

Faye coloured in indignation. '*My* work isn't suffering!'

'Not yet. But you are. You are being torn in two. And why? You've got him. You're not fighting a jealous rival, are you? He loves you from what I gather. Why the hassle? You were so happy at the beginning.' She shook two sweeteners into the palm of her hand and glared at them before tossing them into her cup.

Faye lay back in her chair and closed her eyes.

'But he won't marry me.'

'Oh Faye, come on. Since when did you want to marry?' Marta slid forward to kneel on the floor and put her hand on Faye's knee. 'What has happened to independent womanhood? Independent equals un-dependent, remember?'

Faye gave a small shrug. 'That was before.'

'You really are in a bad way!' Almost admiringly Marta folded her arms and stared. 'There's no point in chaining yourself to the railings outside your front door and picketing him then?'

Faye laughed. 'No point at all. I'm a lost cause!'

'But you're frightened of him!'

There was a long pause. Then at last Faye raised her eyes and looked at her directly. 'No,' she whispered. 'I'm frightened of myself.'

The gods were jealous of course and one by one they began to load the dice. Little things at first, like working overtime – first Paul, then Faye. They tried not to mind.

'We both need an evening to wash our hair,' he said, teasing. But she knew his assistant was eager and beautiful and she sat watching the hands of the clock tick round till midnight, eaten up with anguish, unable to understand her own reactions. What had she to be afraid of? He had eyes, she knew, for no one else. Never before had she felt like this; she was vulnerable and scared; a little girl lost in the dark, groping for the hand which had been holding hers until it was wrenched away.

When her night to work late at the office came she sat at her desk, her eyes on the dark rain-streaked windows and thought of him at home, bored and lonely, and she had to stay an hour longer than she intended, just to correct what her straying thoughts had set wrong.

Then they were both at home again and it was daylight and as the sun shone she felt happy and reassured. The shadows belonged only to the lonely darkness, she thought.

It was her own mother who brought that darkness back, arriving with her matching Gucci suitcases and her aura of Givenchy to spend the weekend.

'Good heavens, but it's Paul Sandford!' she said. 'I remember you from when you were so high! But surely, you were married to Josephine Stapleton?'

'It didn't matter any more. That is why I didn't tell you,' he kept repeating, later. 'It is as though it had never been. We've been divorced for five years, Faye. She is of so little importance I had all but forgotten her. Besides, I didn't know you'd care.'

And she had thought they could read each other's souls!

They made it up of course, but the scar tissue was tender. The slightest touch was going to leave it raw and bleeding.

Spring turned to summer. As her nerves drew taut her body became thin and circles of exhaustion appeared beneath her eyes.

Paul traced them with a gentle finger. 'You're wearing

yourself out,' he said. 'I can't let it go on. For both our sakes.'

But he did. No more than she could he tear himself from her. They clung to one another, fending off the intrusions of the world which seemed to have become hostile and intent on hurting them. Once or twice at a weekend he pulled the curtains and drew her back into bed, knowing the front door was bolted and they would lie there tensely in each other's arms listening to the knocking of their friends.

The first autumn gales sent leaves cartwheeling down the gutters and they went away together for a week. By the sea, with its relentless grey pounding, like the beating of a heart, Faye felt a little reassured, as she did in the almost empty guesthouse where the landlady hid her curiosity beneath a layer of professional uninterest. Paul had agreed to call her his wife for that week only; for the sake of the good lady's susceptibilities and Faye clung to the pretence, letting it salve her wounds and gently fingertip soothe away the circles beneath her eyes.

The shingle beach tired their legs and the wind whipped colour into their cheeks and they both began to eat again, slowly savouring the food.

'I wish we could stay here for ever,' she whispered, her head on his chest as they listened in the dark to the metronome sea through the open window. 'Those gods of yours couldn't reach us here.'

His arms tightened momentarily as he stared up at the ceiling. The tiny pattern on the wallpaper had faded to a dusky shadow crossed by the black framework of the beams. It hung over them like a trap about to fall.

He could feel the prickle of icy perspiration in the small of his back suddenly; the terror as he counted the days they had left.

'What is it, Paul?' she had raised her head and was

looking at him, though she couldn't see him clearly. He clung to her, drawing her head down so she couldn't guess at his tears.

'Nothing, sweetheart. Nothing,' he murmured.

It had come between them for so long he had thought he could live with it for ever. Knowing that it was too late to speak he had kept silent. He had thought their love strong enough to smother his pain. But the unspoken truth inside him had grown and festered and had bred this claustrophobia which surrounded them. This was the cause of Faye's apprehension, though she could not know it and for Faye's sake it could not continue. The barrier between them had grown too high.

He told her when their train reached London, in the railway café over cups of grey coffee.

'When I divorced Josephine it wasn't just that it had never worked; it was so I could marry again. Her name was Clare. I thought I loved her, but I never really knew what love was, Faye, till I met you. You must believe me. She left me after a few months when we both realized what a mistake I'd made and I never saw her from that day on. I kept it from you because I thought I'd lose you. Because I lied to you . . . Because I love you . . .'

He did not look at her; did not watch as she stood up and walked numbly through the swing door and out onto the teeming concourse of the station.

When she got back to the flat at last it was after eleven. He was there, sitting in the darkness, his head cradled in his arms on the edge of the sofa. She turned on the light and stood looking down at him.

It had taken so long to find out what was wrong between them that for a while she had not realized that at last the problem was lying there in the open, naked, like the canker in a split apple. There had been no trust between them.

Ever. He had not trusted her with the truth. She perhaps sensing it had not trusted him at all.

'But it doesn't make any difference,' she said at last. 'It mustn't. You know that, don't you.'

That night was the only time he ever hurt her. Bruised and bleeding she dragged herself to the bathroom and was sick. Then she locked the door and huddled on the floor till dawn. When she awoke he had gone.

'He did it because he loves you?' Marta stared at her in amazement. 'My God, Faye, he could have killed you!'

But Faye knew the anger had not been directed at her. And she knew that her life would be a desert without his presence.

'All right, so I'm a doormat,' she said to Marta, later, and she managed to laugh at the disgust and disbelief on Marta's face. It had been harder to laugh at herself, to let her head make mockery of her heart, but she had forced herself to do it. It made her feel no better, but at least she knew she was still fighting.

Strangely it was to Marta that Paul went eventually.

'Go on, say it,' he invited her, sitting at her kitchen table as she turned a frosty back on him. 'You can't think of any names to call me I haven't called myself already.'

'Then I won't waste my energy,' she retorted, not bothering to turn from the sink where she was peeling potatoes.

'Are you expecting guests? Can I have a drink?' He picked up the half bottle of wine beside him and poured some into a mug.

'That's for cooking, it's yesterday's. If you want me to speak to her for you I won't.'

'Do you think she'd take me back?'

Marta turned, the peeler dripping starchy water onto the floor from her hand. 'You know damn well she would. You've bewitched her.'

'Somehow you make that sound obscene.'

'Perhaps it is.' She stared at him for a moment. Then she turned back to the sink. 'She told me about your second wife.'

'I've found her,' Paul said softly. 'I hired a private detective. I've found her and I've initiated divorce proceedings. There will be no problem there.'

Marta continued peeling. 'So. Should I be pleased?'

'I want to marry Faye.'

'Third time lucky you hope, eh?' She ran the tap into the colander and then ripped off her rubber gloves.

'Faye is my destiny, Marta.'

'Oh my God, Paul. Now you sound like a third rate movie!' She came over to the kitchen table and reached for a dishcloth, staring at him. There was a moment's silence. 'But you're serious, aren't you?' she went on in astonishment. 'You and Faye, it's as if it were something different from other people. Deeper.'

He grinned sourly. 'Romeo and Juliet didn't have a monopoly, you know. It can happen amongst the filing cabinets just as easily.'

Marta laughed. 'Touché. But tell me, why have you come to me?'

He glanced at the glass in his hand. 'Dutch courage perhaps? I never meant to hurt her, Marta. I've never struck a woman in my life.'

Marta sat down and poured herself some wine. 'Funny isn't it? People like me scream for equality, yet when a man hits a woman we act shocked as Victorian maidens, just because she's a woman. I told her she should have hit you back. Hard.'

He shrugged ruefully. 'Unfortunately men usually pack

a better punch.' He paused. 'Perhaps if she had, she'd have brought me to my senses sooner. I would have stayed. We could have talked it through eventually, now everything is in the open. As it is I can't blame her for not trusting me.'

'Nor do I.' She leaned back in her chair and scrutinized him closely. 'You look awful. When did you last sleep?'

He picked up the wine bottle and held it up to the light. 'Last night, in theory. Shall I go round and see her now?'

He split the dregs meticulously between them.

'Not now,' she said. 'Soon.'

Two days later Faye let Paul back into her flat. She gave a rueful smile. 'Have you lost your key?' she said.

'I didn't like to use it without your permission. I forfeited that right. Did Marta ring you?'

Faye nodded. That was odd. To use her of all people as a go between. 'I thought you knew she hated you.'

They were standing facing each other, not touching.

'She cares for you though.' He was taking in every detail of her appearance, feeding on her nearness. 'She must have thought you should see me. Either that or she was so adamant that you shouldn't that she made you angry and you did it as a dare!' He smiled at last and she felt her mouth go dry.

'Something like that, yes,' she said.

She had already decided not to tell him what Marta had said: 'For God's sake marry the guy and give us all some peace,' was the censored gist of what she had advised.

He stepped forward and took her hands gently. 'She told you that I'm divorcing Clare. As soon as I'm free . . .'

'No, Paul,' she interrupted him. 'Don't say any more. Wait until you really are free and then we'll think what to do next.' Gently she disengaged her hand from his. 'Come in properly. We can't stand here in front of the door. I'll make you some coffee.'

He watched as she walked to the kitchen door, her head high, her shoulders a shade stiffer than he remembered and he felt a pang of fear. Perhaps not till that moment had he realized just how much he had hurt her. But obediently he sat down and waited while she brought the tray with biscuits laid out carefully in the brown earthenware bowl as if he were a visitor. He didn't recognize the mugs at all, they had been bought as a gesture of defiance together with a dress and shoes and a large bottle of plonk to drown her sorrows alone. None had worked, but he was not to know that.

'May I not come back then?' he asked at last. He did not look at her face.

'I don't know, Paul. I want you to, but . . .'

'To hell with all the "buts", Faye. If you want me I'll come!' He put the mug back on the tray, then he leaned forward and took her hand, holding it so tightly that she winced and tried to pull away. 'Don't you understand, darling. Clare and I are getting divorced! There is nothing to come between us any more. Nothing. No more reservations; no more secrets and nightmares haunting us from the wings.'

Nothing, except her months of pain and her resolution to be strong so that never again would he – or any man – make her feel the anguish and humiliation to which such complete surrender had left her open.

She wavered. She raised her eyes to his at last and half unwillingly allowed herself to go to him.

Her resolution spun and dissolved. With him she was complete. More than anything she wanted him and she agreed that he could come back. But the pain was still there. She was hurt more deeply than even she had realized. However much she wanted to, she found she still did not trust him; she could not let herself believe that the gods had finished their teasing and turned away to find another prey.

'Faye, you must believe me,' he pleaded. 'I only lied to you because I loved you so much. It will never happen again. The instant I'm free we can be married.'

She knew he was sincere and that his love was genuine, just as she knew her love for him had not changed. But she had no power to overcome her fears. They were involuntary and unwanted. She just had to hope that time would heal the bruises.

And time was what Paul did not give her.

'She's throwing my guilt back at me all the time,' he said to Marta one evening in despair. 'She doesn't even know she's doing it but it's coming between us like a brick wall ten feet high.'

'You've got to take him back unreservedly, or say goodbye to him,' Marta told Faye later. 'You can't go on turning this into a five act tragedy. It's making both of you unhappy. It's very unfair.'

'Unfair? To him?' Faye swung round on her.

'Yes, unfair to him. And to yourself.' Gently Marta hammered the point home. 'You are punishing him for something he had already punished himself for enough.'

Faye threw herself down on a chair. 'So, you're on his side now!' she said bitterly.

'I don't take sides. I watch from a safe vantage point. But I can see you losing him, Faye and it would break you up.'

For a moment they sat in silence. Marta searched desperately for something to say which would help, gave up and went to find some alcohol. It turned out to be the dregs of a whisky bottle. 'A snifter each,' she said triumphantly. 'Take him back without reservation, Faye. You can trust him now,' she said softly, 'and you can afford to trust yourself.' And she raised her glass.

But it was already too late. It was two days after that he got up as he and Faye were listening to a record in the dark sitting room, their eyes staring into the fire and dropped a kiss on the top of her head.

'I'm going out for a breath of air,' he said. 'Don't wait up. I've got a key.'

She sat unmoving for a long time after the sound of the music had died away. Then sadly she went to bed.

In the morning she was still alone.

And now, even staying with Marta she was alone and frozen in the spaces of her anguish. She walked on doggedly up the hill, feeling the cold wind lifting her hair about her ears, feeling the slight skim of ice forming on the pavements beneath her feet, her eyes used to the dark now, picking out details of sleeping houses, a wraith of pale smoke hanging still above a chimney and a holly tree, the berries glistening beneath a lamp, the red washed out of them by the pale light.

It was the first time she had allowed herself to think back to the day she and Paul had first met. They had not needed to speak then. What had gone wrong? Why was there this awful gulf between them now?

Slowly she turned and began to retrace her steps. Even if she had found the answer to her question it was too late. She had lost him a second time.

Marta has left one light burning on the table. The flat was very quiet. Dropping her coat on the chair by the door Faye made for the gently hissing flames of the gas fire and held out her hands to the warmth.

'Faye?' Paul was sitting in the shadows, so still she had not even seen him. 'Marta called me. She said I should come,' he said softly.

'Where is she?'

'In bed.' He held out his hands to her, smiling. 'I've done so much thinking, Faye. And each time I come back to the same answer. I still want you.'

She did not move. The shade of the lamp was angled so the light fell in a pool on the table. She could not see his face.

'I want you too, Paul.' She meant it.

'I'll give you time, Faye. I won't come back until you're ready. Just tell me when.'

'You're so sure?'

He chuckled. 'Destiny. I once told Marta you were my destiny.'

'She must have laughed at you.'

'No, funnily enough she understood. That's why she rang me tonight.' He stepped forward at last and took her gently by the shoulders. 'I'm going now. But I'll be waiting every second to hear from you. When you're ready, tell me.'

He didn't move to kiss her. He just stood looking down at her face and she felt herself strangely at peace for a moment, the pain and the doubt drained out of her. Giving a hesitant smile she put her hand on his arm. 'Don't go yet. Have some coffee, Paul.'

'If I stay, I'll find it harder to go later,' he said quietly. 'My self discipline is strained to the limit as it is.'

'I'll risk it,' she replied. Her mouth had gone dry just as it always had in the past and her heart had begun to pound uncomfortably below her ribs, but it was not with fear. For a moment longer she stood looking at him, realizing what had happened, then she turned away. She had been given a third chance; the gods had removed their veto. This time she could, and would, trust him with her life. She went into the kitchen and turned to the light, smiling.

An extra place had been laid at the table around a token cornflakes packet. Beside it was a note scrawled in red felt tip:

I shall expect there to be three of us for breakfast! M.

Faye laughed quietly. 'Just this once, Marta,' she whispered. 'I think we really will do as you expect.'

Marcus Nicholls

I was fourteen when it happened. But the memory still gives me nightmares, even after all this time. And still, when I go back to Camber, I avoid the stables if Duncan and Cathie are at home.

The summer had been unspeakably hot that year, with heavy thunderheads building up towards evening day after day, to deluge the countryside with humid storms which did nothing to clear the air.

I suppose if Aunt Flavia had been with us then, she would at once have said that the atmosphere was right for psychic activity; as it was, the three of us, Duncan, Sandy and myself, concentrated on staying in the neighbour's swimming pool as much as we could and on riding of course. We got up at six in the morning to ride before it became too hot and then turned the ponies out each day in the old orchard where there was plenty of shade.

Our parents felt the heat even more than we did, I think; our father worried about what the rain was doing to his standing corn and mother was worried about her mares – she breeds Welsh ponies. For us, although we helped on the farm and worked till we dropped, it was still the long summer vacation and we revelled in it. My brother Duncan was reading accountancy at university and Sandy was studying music. I was still at school, but there were weeks and weeks before I had to go back.

It was on Mother's birthday that Jan Fleming arrived to stay. She was Sandy's girlfriend – a lovely slim redhead whom I worshipped and hated and would have given my right arm to look like! And with her came a stranger.

'I do hope you don't mind, Mrs Nicholls, I really hope not; I knew you have lots of room at Camber Court and you've often said I could bring someone, so I wondered . . .' Jan's voice petered out, embarrassed and the stranger stepped forward. She too was tall and slim but dark haired, with enormous hazel eyes. Her mouth was rather large and her skin gypsy dark and I, standing in the shadows, saw Duncan's face as he watched her and I knew he had fallen for her on the spot.

'I'm Cathie Steuart,' she said in a low, musical voice. 'I'm a friend of Jan's from London and when she said she was driving down to the West Country I begged a lift. I certainly don't want to impose on you though . . .'

Duncan pushed past Mother hastily. 'We've plenty of room, Jan's right. Of course you must stay. Are you on holiday?'

She laughed. 'No. Believe it or not I'm here to work. I'm a photographer and I've got to photograph various houses – including yours – for a book a colleague of mine is writing about historic old houses in the west.' She glanced around. I could see her eyes taking in the carved oak staircase with its lovely half landing and the leaded windows which open onto the rose gardens at the back of the house. 'It's so beautiful here,' she said. 'I couldn't believe it when Jan said she was actually going to stay in the house. I just had to make her bring me . . .'

'You realize she's probably a burglar or a con woman or something,' Sandy said later to father, 'tricking her way into the house.'

But we all liked her immediately and it wasn't long before my parents had suggested that she make Camber her headquarters for the three weeks she would be in this part of the world.

I had already transferred my allegiance from Jan to her. After all, she was dark and so was I.

It happened about a week later. The day was overcast and the temperature up in the nineties all day. They were harvesting in the back meadow and the last of the corn to come in was being cut. Jan and I helped prepare the food and lay the long refectory table in the dining room for a large party for all the farm workers that evening. It was growing dark long before they arrived, hot and dusty from the fields, but soon the house was noisy with laughter and shouting.

Cathie had borrowed Jan's car again that day and gone over to Pincton Manor. Watching from my window I had seen her drive in at about nine and climb wearily out of the car with her bag of cameras. I heard her come upstairs and go into her room, then I heard the bath running. She came down to supper a bit late but looking very refreshed in pale red jeans and a cream linen shirt and I saw several eyes besides Duncan's on her.

Outside the window lightning flickered on and off and there were occasional low rumbles of thunder.

'Perhaps the weather will break properly this time,' my father was saying to someone down the table and I saw him wipe the back of his hand across his forehead. The enormous jugs of cider on the sideboard were already nearly empty. There was a burst of laughter from the far end of the room and the chink of cutlery and china – it was all very comforting and ordinary and happy.

The storm broke immediately overhead. One moment there was laughter and conversation and the heat coming through the long low windows which had all been thrown open onto the garden and the next with a terrifying crash the heavens opened and the rain began to empty itself onto the house and fields. I saw more than one person look scared for a moment, at the sheer ferocity of that storm. It was hard to talk because of the noise of the thunder which was almost incessant, but after the initial shock of the noise most people went on eating and drinking as before. We didn't even have to close the windows, I remember, because the rain was coming straight down; it looked like silver green needles in the lightning flashes which lit up the lawn.

Then there was an extra bright flash, accompanied by a sizzle and a crack and the house seemed to rock on its foundations.

'That's a strike,' I heard my father say calmly. 'I'd better see what the damage is.' He walked out into the hall and pulled open the front door.

Mother rushed after him shouting, 'Henry, don't go out, you'll get hit, don't go out!' and Cathie, who had been standing near the door, ran after her.

I still don't know quite what happened. We could see straightaway that the east end of the stable range was on fire. It had a hay loft over it and it was very very old – about 300 years, nearly as old as the house. Mother screamed, 'My horses!' and everyone started to run.

Cathie was in front. She tore across the courtyard with Father and Sandy and Duncan just behind her, pulling open the stable door and disappearing into the smoky darkness.

Minutes later as the other men raced for buckets and ran round the back of the stable to reach the hay loft, which had great double doors opening away from the yard, two horses released from their stalls appeared at the door and careered panic-stricken across the courtyard towards the orchard. Then Sandy appeared, leading another which he had blindfolded with a length of old rag. He pulled off the blindfold and sent the terrified horse off out of danger with a gentle push which sent it galloping into the darkness.

'One more,' I heard my mother saying, anguished. 'There's one more; Suki is in the box at the end, under the loft.'

Father was still inside with Duncan and Cathie as Sandy dodged round to help the men tackle the blaze from the rear. The rain was pelting down, bouncing off the cobbles, soaking our clothes and hair, turning shirts transparent against the skin.

And then I heard the scream. The most terrible sound I've ever heard. It went on and on.

The men running with buckets of water and Jan and Mother and I all stopped dead for a moment and looked at each other. I felt suddenly very sick.

The figure of a horse appeared at the stable door, lit up in a flash of lightning, her black coat gleaming in the wet, her hooves striking sparks of light as, ears back, she galloped half crazed out of the stable and away down the drive out of sight. I remember, even in my fear, vaguely hoping that the gate into the lane was shut.

Behind the horse I suddenly saw Father and Duncan appear at the door of the stable half carrying Cathie. She was sobbing uncontrollably. Father was ashen: he looked dreadful; so did Duncan. And Cathie was hysterical. Leaving her clinging to Duncan, Father came over. 'Beth, you and Jan take Vicky to the house quickly,' he said urgently to my mother. 'No one is to go into the stable; something's happened. The fire's out – they've pitched out all the hay now; there wasn't much in there luckily – but I don't want anyone going in there; not anyone, understand?' Already he was going back to Cathie.

'What is it? What's happened? Where's Sandy?' I could hear the fear in Mother's voice as she ran after him.

'It's all right; Sandy's round the side with the men. Go inside, please.' I could hear the strain in Father's voice as he snapped at her.

Duncan had his arm round Cathie. She was still crying brokenly as he tried to urge her towards the house. Another flash of lightning tore the sky open and I saw her face for the first time. I'll never forget the horror and anguish I saw there.

'Oh my God; oh my God! That poor man; oh God! Oh God!' She kept repeating it over and over. 'That poor, poor man. How could anyone; how could they? How could they?'

I stood still, shivering in the rain. What man? What was she talking about? Father had his arm round her too now and he and Duncan were half carrying her between them.

'Beth!' Father yelled after Mother. 'Ring Doctor Armstrong. Tell him to get here at once. And get that child inside!'

That was me!

I took one more look at the stable range and turning, ran after my mother.

Everyone else was still at the back of the stables, dealing with the fire, so the sitting room was deserted. Father carried Cathie in and laid her gently on the couch by the empty fireplace.

'Get the brandy, Vicky, please,' he said, seeing me standing nervously in the doorway, my eyes fixed on Cathie's limp form; her jeans and blouse were dark with rain and streaked with soot. In the hall I could hear my mother talking to Doctor Armstrong.

Cathie clung to Duncan and my father in turn. She was shaking so violently I thought for one minute that she must be putting it on, but one look at her face told me she wasn't. My own hands had started to shake as I poured out half a tumbler of brandy and took the glass to Duncan. He had his arm round her shoulders and raised her gently, putting the glass to her lips. She took a sip and then pushed it violently away.

'Christ! I could do with some of this myself.' Duncan took a drink from the glass and passed it on to Father. 'What do we do, Dad? He . . .' he hesitated, 'he wasn't alive, was he?'

Father shook his head and took another gulp of brandy. He held out the glass towards me and I ran forward with the bottle.

I felt sick. I was scared. Anything that could shake my father and my twenty-year-old brother like that had to be bad. And what had Duncan meant, 'He wasn't alive?' Who wasn't? Nervously I looked again at Cathie. Her normally tanned face was white. She clutched at Duncan convulsively.

'It was so awful,' she cried. 'The lightning came and I saw him there – three feet from my face. His eyes were open. Oh God. Oh God!' She was getting hysterical again, clinging to Duncan till I saw the skin of his forearm whiten beneath her grip.

'I know; I know, darling. I saw him too.' He was rocking her backwards and forwards in his arms as Mother came in with a rug.

'Keep her warm,' she said. 'The doctor is on the way. Now, tell me what's happened.'

For a moment there was silence as Father and Duncan looked at each other. Then Cathie, her voice rising desperately, sobbed: 'In the barn. In the barn. They've hanged someone. He's dead and his hands, oh God his hands . . .' Her voice had practically risen to a scream.

Mother reeled backwards as if she'd been hit and looked at my father.

'It's true, Beth. Duncan and I were right behind her. They've used the beam in Suki's stall; I'm surprised the horse didn't break out earlier. When we got there she panicked and flattened the wooden partition in the box. I was going to go after her when I saw it; we all saw it. The lightning showed everything for a moment. As soon as Armstrong gets here I'll get on to the police.' He sat down and put his head in his hands. 'Dear God. I went right through the war and I never saw anything so barbaric; never.'

It was a strange sight. The group of frightened, shaking people in their wet clothes, their hair flattened and blackened on their heads from the rain, their faces staring. Each time the lightning flashed the lights in the house dimmed for a second and flickered and then shone brightly again.

The doctor arrived in about fifteen minutes, roaring up the drive and swinging round to the front door where he left his car on the cobbles. He jumped out bag in hand and pushed through the open front door.

It didn't take him long to size up the situation. He gave Cathie an injection and ordered Jan and Mother to undress her and put her to bed with a hot water bottle. Then he went with Father and Duncan into the study. They shut the door.

I had been forgotten.

My curiosity got the better of me and I tiptoed out into the hall where I could hear them talking quite clearly as I sat on the bottom step of the stairs, shivering in my soaking shirt and jeans.

'I don't think he'd been there very long,' I heard my father's voice. 'The neck was obviously broken though. But to cut off a man's hands like that – ', his voice broke, 'words fail me, Armstrong.'

'Have you rung the police?' The doctor's voice was professionally calm.

'Not yet. Cathie was so hysterical and I wanted to get the women away.'

'Quite so. Well, if I may suggest, I'll go and have a look myself. No – you needn't come with me. I'm probably more used to these things than you; although, in this case . . .'

I could hear them opening the french windows, which overlooked the courtyard at the front of the house, and then their voices grew fainter and disappeared. Obviously Father and Duncan had decided to go with him.

I got up and slipped out of the front door. What I had heard nauseated me, but I was far too curious to be left indoors. I had to follow them. I saw the three figures striding through the rain towards the stable. The high loft door on this side was open too now and the bales of charred hay had been pushed down onto the cobbles. A man was standing up there with a pitchfork and I saw him raise his hand to my father in a thumbs up sign. The fire was well and truly out. Wisps of curdling steam crawled up through the loft doors and through the old red tiles but that was all. I could see the three horses from the stable standing on the far side of the courtyard by the orchard gate, sheltering beneath the old crab apple tree which overhung the wall. Beyond it our ponies were pale shapes in the dark.

I suddenly realized that there hadn't been any thunder or lightning for several minutes now. The storm was moving off towards the north east at last.

I wondered briefly what had happened to Suki. There was no sign of her. It scared me that my mother hadn't gone frantic with worry about her precious championship mare; everything was frightening that night and unreal. I shivered again in the dark. It was still raining hard.

I tiptoed across the wet cobbles to the stable door and waited, my heart thumping with terror. They had left it open and I could see the strong beam of Father's torch as he walked slowly down the line of stalls, followed by Duncan and the doctor. I knew the stable so well. The eight stalls and the old loose box at the end, Suki's box, with its blackened warped oak beam about ten feet off the ground.

Nothing could have made me take another step into that stable. The light stopped moving and I saw the three shadowy figures of the men stop. The torch beam raked up and down, roof to floor; I imagined it illuminating every wisp of hay in Suki's box – and anything else that was there. I shuddered at the thought. Then the light was joined by another. The doctor too must have had a torch on him. The two thin beams crossed and recrossed flashing up at the walls and roof; then all three men moved out of my line of vision into the box itself. I could feel the sweat standing out on my forehead as I stood there in the doorway, just out of the driving rain.

At first I didn't even notice the sound of hooves on the cobbles behind me. Then I heard a nervous whicker and turning, I saw the black pony standing, nostrils flaring, near the doctor's car. It was almost a relief to have to do something. I reached for one of the head collars on the rack inside the door and made my way out into the rain again.

To my surprise she came to me, pushing her head into my hands, almost begging for the head collar to be buckled round her ears. I stroked her rather nervously – Suki had a wicked nip and only my mother usually handled her – and discovered that she was trembling from head to foot.

I started to walk slowly towards the house and she followed without my having to pull on the rein, her head pushed hard into the crook of my arm and it dawned on me that she was probably as scared as anyone else by what had happened and that she was seeking reassurance, just as I was.

I met my mother at the front door. She had at last done the sensible thing and having put Cathie to bed and left her with Jan, she had put on a mac and gumboots and collected a torch. 'Vicky, you've caught her!' She reached out for the head collar. 'Is she hurt?'

'I don't think so.' My teeth had started chattering.

'Mummy. She's scared. She really is scared. Whatever happened in there – it's terrified her.'

'I know.' My mother was crooning gently into the pony's ear. 'I'll put her into the back paddock. And the other ponies with her. They'll be safe in there, and well away from whatever must happen.'

Whatever must happen? For the first time I thought of stretchers and police cars and ambulances racing up the long gravelled drive from the lane and I bit my lip as I watched my mother lead the trembling pony away round the corner of the house.

Then I turned to look back at the stables. They were still in the dark. I wondered suddenly why the lights weren't on. The fire presumably had fused the switches or something. Then I saw the thin beam of torchlight crossing behind one of the windows; then the next. Someone was walking back down the line of the stalls towards the door.

The three men reappeared, crossing slowly towards me, talking earnestly together. I waited in the hall, kicking off my wet shoes, idly inspecting my toe prints on the scrubbed flags.

The door opened and the three men appeared. 'I'll give the chief constable a ring, Armstrong,' my father was saying. 'I think this ought to go straight to him. Go on in and give yourselves a brandy. I'll be with you in a moment.'

Duncan and the doctor passed me, going into the sitting

room, and I heard the chink of glasses as I followed Dad to the study and stood in the doorway as he dialled.

'Hello? Bill?' He sat down on the edge of the desk and then realizing how wet he was stood up again hurriedly. 'Sorry to call you so late, old man, but I've a bit of a puzzle on my hands.' There was a pause, then he gave a short tense laugh. 'Yes. No, worse actually. Well, yes it was the storm in a way. No, I got the last of it in today, thank goodness. Listen, Bill. We had a bit of a fire in the hay loft – lightning struck a tree just behind it. We rushed over to get the horses out as fast as possible of course and we found something in there, Bill. A man has been hanged in there. What? Yes. In the loose box at the end. No, he was quite dead; no doubt about it I'm afraid. Three of us saw him: my son Duncan and myself and a girl who is staying with us. No, no idea who it was. No Bill, it wouldn't have been suicide; there's no question about that; someone had hacked off both his hands at the wrists. Yes.' There was quite a long pause as the voice at the other end spoke agitatedly into the phone. I could see the beads of perspiration standing out on my father's forehead.

'Yes, there was a lot of blood. But listen, Bill. He's gone. Yes – there's no trace of him now – nor of any blood. Armstrong is here and I took him over to see what he could do, but there is absolutely no trace of the body now. No trace at all. We were indoors for, I suppose, perhaps half an hour. But it's disappeared.'

I gasped and my father noticed me for the first time. He frowned and motioned me away, but I stayed where I was.

'It did cross our minds,' he went on into the phone, 'that the stables could have been fired deliberately to destroy all trace of everything – but then the tree was definitely struck. No question of that. Yes – so you'll come up yourself then? No, nothing's been touched. We've sent everyone else home now; they don't know what's happened. OK.'

He hung up and turned to me. 'The chief constable is bringing up a forensic team. He's getting them all out of bed if necessary.' He gave me a watery smile. 'I suppose it's no good telling you to go to bed, Vicky?'

I shook my head vehemently. 'I'd have nightmares, Daddy,' I said in a small voice and suddenly my eyes were full of tears.

I ran to him and he put his arms round me comfortingly. 'I know, love,' he said gently into my hair. 'I wish you hadn't heard – but there's nothing to be done till the police get here. Come and have a sip of brandy. It'll buck you up. Where's your mother?'

'With the mares.'

He nodded. 'Just as well to keep busy.' He frowned. 'She shouldn't be out there on her own, though.' He stood up, releasing me abruptly. 'I'll go and fetch her. Go through to Duncan, Vicky, and stay with him, understand?'

'You think they're still here, don't you, the people who did it?' My voice quavered childishly.

'Not for one moment. Don't think about it. Look darling, Dr Armstrong is going to give poor Cathie another shot before he goes. To make her sleep through into tomorrow. Would you like him to give you something?'

I shook my head and swallowed hard. 'No, I'm all right. Go and find Mummy, and I'll go and have a drink of brandy.'

I went into the sitting room and accepted a minuscule dose of brandy from the doctor and then I sat shivering on the edge of the sofa while the two men talked until my parents came in together. Then of course my mother took one look at me and packed me upstairs for a hot bath and a change of clothes, although she didn't insist that I go to bed.

The police arrived about half an hour later with searchlights and a large alsatian dog. They quartered the farm and nearly dismantled the stable block but it appeared that the rain, which hadn't eased for hours, had been heavy enough to remove any trace there might have been of tracks of any kind.

It must have been in the early hours of the morning that they eventually packed up and went. I had given in to my exhaustion at about midnight and crawled into bed, but I can't say I slept awfully well. My bravado, what there was of it, had left me completely in the loneliness of my bedroom, with its pale chintz curtains blowing so innocently in the open window and I left my bedside light on all night, pulling the thin single sheet up over my head. Somehow I still couldn't get the sound of Cathie's terrible screams out of my mind.

She came down next day at about mid morning, looking pale and shaken but otherwise more or less her old self. It was a glorious sunny day. The early morning had been white with low-lying mist as I looked out, but later it heated up again, until the temperature was as high as ever.

The farm returned to normal very quickly; or nearly so. The stables were searched again by daylight, but nothing was found. The hayloft was swept and repaired. It was as if nothing had happened at all. It was hard to believe by the next day that there had ever been a storm, or a fire – or a dreadful, insane murder. Except that no one was allowed to go out by themselves any more; there had to be at least two or three of us – even the farm men went about in pairs and we locked the doors and windows as dark approached, in spite of the heat. And the horses remembered. When my mother tried to lead Suki back into the stable she laid her ears back, her eyes rolling in terror and reared up with a terrified snort. They didn't try and make her go back in there again.

Cathie stayed with us another week and managed, with Duncan at her side constantly, to complete the rest of her photographs before she got ready to leave. She and Duncan arranged to meet in town as soon as his term started, and apart from the fact that it meant parting from him so soon, I suspected that she was very glad indeed to leave Camber Court. I was very sad to see her go. I liked Cathie enormously.

Nothing was ever found to give any clues as to what had occurred that night. There was no trace of any body; the poor man's description, as far as my father and Duncan managed to provide one, fitted no one who had been reported missing and as far as the police file went the murder went completely unsolved.

No one would ever have been any the wiser had it not been by the most extraordinary coincidence that we found out who the victim was. It was more than a year later when Father's Aunt Flavia arrived on a Christmas visit home from Canada. She was a tall, very upright old lady of, I suppose, about eighty, with brilliant blue eyes in her tanned face and a strong Canadian accent. It was tacitly understood by the family that no one would mention the horrible happenings of the summer before last but one night about three days after she had arrived when we were all sitting round the fire after supper, the incident was mentioned after all.

'Well my dears,' said Aunt Flavia, looking round with bright inquisitive eyes, 'have any of you ever seen the ghosts of Camber?'

She seemed disappointed that no one had, although we were all to varying degrees excited at the idea. I had often wondered if there might be a ghost or two at Camber but no one seemed to know. The house had belonged to our family for four hundred years although my father himself had been brought up in Canada and had only inherited it during the war when his uncle John and John's only two sons had all been killed, and although he loved it and felt it to be in his 'blood and bones' as he put it, he knew comparatively little about its history.

'There are two ghosts actually,' said his aunt, seeing that she had our attention. 'A lady who walks in the rose garden on summer nights and a little boy who runs about the upstairs corridors sometimes.' She looked round hopefully but none of us could claim to have seen either of them.

'How on earth do you know all this, Aunt Flavia?' my mother asked suspiciously. Aunt Flavia laughed.

'Very old books, my dear. My father left me lots of books which mention Camber. I don't know why he ever brought them out to Canada because they rightfully belong here. You shall have them all back when I die.'

'There must be a lot of history attached to this house,' Duncan commented lazily. He was sitting on the window seat, one leg up on the cushion in front of him. 'Cathie's book will be out soon; there's a whole chapter on Camber in that. I know Charles II came here once. Did anything else exciting ever happen here, Aunt, I've often wondered?'

She frowned. 'There was one time. At the time of the Monmouth Rebellion, against James II – do you remember? Judge Jeffreys and his ilk. There was a terrible fight here a bit later; young Marcus Nicholls, the son of the house, had fought for Monmouth at Sedgemoor and they captured him here in his own home. He was given a summary trial by some of the King's officers in the dining room here at Camber according to my book and they sentenced him to be hanged.' She paused, frowning for a moment. 'I believe he is supposed to have stood up and shouted defiantly at his accusers something about giving his right arm to serve King Charles's son and one of them said that in that case he would give Marcus the chance to give both.' There was a long pause. Then she went on. 'They cut off both his hands before they hanged him – somewhere in the outbuildings to the Court, I gather. According to the story he cursed King James and all his followers and said that if any of them or their descendants ever set foot in Camber again he would haunt them. They say he died very bravely, poor young man.'

She looked round. I don't know what reception she expected for her story but certainly not the stunned incredulity which showed on every face in the room.

My father stood up and reached uncertainly for a cigarette. 'When did you say this happened, Flavia?'

'1685 dear, after Sedgemoor. Why? What's the matter with you all?'

'This young man, Marcus. What did he look like?'

'I don't know. How could I possibly? There's probably a portrait of him in the house somewhere. Why?' She suddenly sat up, looking from face to face. 'You've seen him, haven't you?' She went pale.

I had suddenly begun to feel terribly cold. I moved nearer the fire and catching my mother's eye I saw she had begun to shiver too. The fine pale hairs on her forearms were standing straight up on end suddenly. I watched fascinated.

Father told Flavia the story from beginning to end and she listened, nodding slowly from time to time. When he had finished she looked up and gave a faint smile. 'Obviously this poor girl Cathie was the catalyst. She must be a descendant of one of the murderers – even of James himself – you said that her name is Steuart? What an awful thing.'

'I can't believe it.' Father relit his cigarette which had gone out while he was talking. 'I can't believe that that was an – apparition. I saw it. Duncan here saw it, it wasn't only Cathie.'

'But it disappeared, Dad.' Duncan spoke at last from the dim corner on the window seat. 'It disappeared without trace, without blood.'

'And it's still there.' Mother's voice was strangely flat. 'That's why Suki and the other horses still won't enter the stable, after all this time.' I hadn't plucked up the courage to either.

'The police dog knew,' Sandy added suddenly. 'Its hackles were all over the place and it growled and growled in that loose box and yet there was absolutely no scent for it to follow.'

'Are you going to tell Cathie this story?' Father suddenly turned towards Duncan.

'You must tell her,' Flavia said. 'She has the right to know. And the poor girl can't exactly have forgotten an incident like that. I don't know if it will help to put her mind at rest at all, knowing that, but she should know; she's part of the destiny of Camber.'

I wondered if anyone besides myself noticed the violent blush which coloured Duncan's cheeks as she said those words.

'Does it mean she won't be able to come back here without it happening again?' I asked quietly. She never had come back to Camber, although we had all been to visit her in London and gone to her parents' house in Bedfordshire.

Duncan frowned. 'Surely not?' He looked at Flavia, but she shrugged.

'What about an exorcism?' Sandy said suddenly. 'You know, bell, book and candle, the lot!'

'No.' Flavia rose slowly to her feet. 'No. Whatever happened here that night, has not, as far as we know, happened in 300 years before. It may not happen again for as long.

It may be that the thunderstorm and the fire had something to do with it; generating psychic energy or something. Leave it alone. That's my advice; leave it alone.'

'And the police?' Father stubbed out his cigarette and went to stand with his back to the fire. 'What do I tell the police? That the murder I reported witnessing happened 300 years ago and they'd better close the case?'

Flavia frowned. 'No, dear. Don't say anything to the police. They'll think you were drunk or something. It will have to go down on their files as unsolved. Leave it at that.'

And leave it at that we did. Except for one incident.

There was a portrait of Marcus Nicholls in the house. We found it hanging in a dark corner on the top landing where it had hardly been noticed before. It showed a tall, slim youth in riding breeches, one hand on the neck of a bony bay mare. He was a bit like Duncan to look at, I thought; the same nose and gently humorous mouth, but he had my eyes. Sandy pointed it out first. 'I say, look at that. We all wanted to know where Vicky got her big green eyes and dark hair. Well, there's your answer.'

I went back later to look at the portrait by myself. They were right. He did have my eyes. He looked friendly and kind and I could swear that he was watching me.

Everyone was busy in the garden that afternoon, gathering holly and ivy and mistletoe to decorate the house, so no one noticed when I slipped away.

The stable was deserted; the stalls swept and empty. Hardly anyone went in there any more as far as I knew. I took a deep breath, screwing up my courage and stepped inside. There was the age old smell of sweet hay and horses and dust and still a suspicion of the tang of burning.

Cautiously I made my way down the line of stalls watching the sunbeams slipping in through the high windows in the wall. I nearly didn't go as far as the loose box. My courage was ebbing fast.

Then I stood there, by the repaired partition which Suki had splintered. The door was still off, leaning against the wall. I looked in. The box was quite empty and absolutely quiet. A little patch of sunshine lit up the stone floor under the old blackened beam. Was it my imagination, or was there a brooding atmosphere about the place?

I swallowed. Then I went in. I produced from behind my back the small bunch of winter jasmine and frosted rose buds which I had cut in the bright cold of the garden and I knelt and laid them on the stone. Then I looked up. 'Please don't hate any more,' I said out loud. Was it just because we shared the same green eyes that I knew Marcus would listen to me? 'Please forgive. Go in peace and let Cathie come back to Camber. Please.'

I waited for a minute and then, feeling a little foolish, I scrambled to my feet and dusted the knees of my jeans. But somehow I felt better. I knew I wouldn't be afraid to come in there again.

The strength of the winter sun had woken a butterfly, which was trapped against the dusty window in the passage. I could hear it fluttering against the glass as I turned to go. Reaching up I pushed open the window and watched it soar up into the ice blue sky, then I walked out of the stable and made my way back towards the house.

Salesmanship!

Sylvia would insist on coming to the door and peering in as he worked. He didn't turn, but he could feel her eyes boring into the canvas, analysing the brush strokes, quartering the painting for new details. The sureness of his touch would falter and slow until he laid the brush down and waited, teeth clenched, for her to go away.

'Coffee, Sammy?' She was aware instantly that he knew her to be there.

'Thanks.' He bit the end of his palette knife and grimaced at the bitter stickiness of the paint on it.

'It's nearly finished, isn't it?' Her voice was breezy, encouraging, even patronizing.

'That's right.' Grudgingly he admitted it, stepping back to survey it himself.

'It's the best you've ever done.'

She always said that, silly bitch. If his paintings were so bloody good, why didn't they sell?

He'd asked her that once and she had looked at the ground and waved her hands apologetically, her cigarette shedding ash over the spare room floor. There was no carpet; a carpet would have been a concession to its spare-roomness; boards confirmed its status as his studio.

'They'll sell one day,' she had affirmed and he had snorted.

'When I'm discovered, I suppose,' he commented sarcastically.

She brought him the coffee and he laid down his palette and sipped it. It was real. Sylvia refused to use instant and that irritated him too; real coffee upset his stomach. Mercifully she went away then and he heard the ting as the phone receiver was raised from the cradle. He relaxed. He had often wished there was a lock on the spare room door. Then he could have ensured his privacy. To put one on now at this late stage would be too hurtful for Sylvia, but if he had established a precedent for painting behind locked doors from the start it would have been all right. And it would have been so much better.

The painting was good; he gazed at it, critically, just bathing himself in his achievement. The brush strokes were sure; the composition controlled and interesting, the colour and subject . . . He smiled. The subject was exquisite. He closed one eye to get a better look at it and his joy survived even that test.

Later he went out. Only for a half. It wouldn't take long and, after all, it was Saturday.

When he returned Sylvia was in the studio and with her were two strangers, a man and a woman. All three were standing before the painting talking in hushed voices.

Sammy stopped abruptly, suspicious. He had never suspected her of bringing in her friends to gloat. He felt a suppressed fury that the woman should be so disloyal and took a deep breath, summoning up a scathing remark which would without being overtly rude, send them chastised on their way. But Sylvia forestalled him.

'Here *is* my husband,' she exclaimed turning as if she hadn't realized that he was there.

The two with her turned in unison and smiled uncertainly, almost guiltily, at him.

'These are Paul and Joy,' Sylvia gushed. That was

unusual for her. It meant she was unsure of her ground. 'They run the new art gallery in Chichampton.'

Inwardly Sammy stiffened. Outwardly he bit back his remark and smiled instead, holding out his hand.

'Your wife kindly asked us over to look at your work, Mr Korner.' Joy was obviously the spokesperson. She was tiny and slim, in apple-green jeans with a muted blue shirt knotted below a token bust line. 'And I'm so glad we came. They're fantastic.' Her expansive gesture taking in the whole room, including the windows he noted, nearly knocked her colleague on the nose. Paul dodged expertly, then he nodded long sufferingly, presumably seconding her opinion.

'We'd certainly like to take two or three for the gallery, wouldn't we, Paul?' She rushed on.

Again he nodded.

'This one on the easel; it's powerful. We must have it. Do you have a framer?' In the fascination of watching her bobbed hair flopping enthusiastically in time with her speech, Sammy missed the question. Then he noticed Sylvia looking worried. It was an unusual sight and he pulled himself together rapidly to find out why.

'I'm sorry,' he smiled, he hoped with all his charm. 'I missed that question.'

'Your framer, dear,' Sylvia hissed. 'She was asking about your framer.'

'I haven't got a framer,' Sammy commented candidly, still distracted by the hair. 'I've never sold any of the paintings and for ourselves we've always made do by just hanging them up as they are.'

He saw from Sylvia's black look that he had said the wrong thing. Of course he should have implied that he sold lots of paintings and that he had a tame framer. They could always have found one later. But it was too late.

Joy did not seem worried by his naivety. On the contrary, she seemed even more delighted. 'It is so exciting to make a *discovery*!' she pronounced earnestly. 'Our very own discovery. I am glad you came in and asked us, Mrs Korner. We might never have seen your husband's work otherwise.'

Sylvia looked contrite. As well she might, thought Sammy. But he couldn't help being pleased with her. So she really had had faith in him. She hadn't just been flannelling all this time.

He listened in a daze while Joy named dates and discussed, apparently with herself, the technicalities of mounting and presenting the paintings she wanted. She wrote down the name of a framer for him – strange, he thought, she had close-bitten nails like a little girl – and then she and Paul had gone.

He and Sylvia stood looking at each other in the hall.

'I hope you don't mind, Sammy.' Sylvia sounded rather scared. 'I knew they'd be interested. It seemed so silly not to try to sell some of your paintings. We could do with the money.'

Sammy winced at the last remark but on the whole he was prepared to forgive her even that. After all she was the one who had dared. Half shyly he put his arm round her and planted a hesitant kiss on her cheek. She giggled and after a second moved away.

He went back up to the studio later, clicked on the light and drew the cheap cotton curtains. The painting on the easel stared at him reproachfully. Was it really finished? Under normal circumstances he might have pottered around adding the odd touch of paint here and there for days, but now . . . 'Don't touch it, Mr Korner; I forbid you to touch it; it's *perfect*.' The sound of Joy's high-pitched voice echoed for a moment in his head. Don't touch it! His own painting! He wandered restlessly round the room looking at other pictures; thinking, staring. Unconsciously he picked up the afternoon's palette and dabbed at a still life leaning against the wall. As the paint made contact he jumped back guiltily. After all it was going to be framed. It couldn't go with wet patches on it. He put down the brush miserably.

Then with resolution he went to the easel and lifted down the painting. It was finished and that was that. The time had come to prepare another new, virgin canvas.

Half an hour later he sloped downstairs and sat down on the sofa next to Sylvia. She was concentrating on the television and didn't look round, but after a moment or two her hand, crawling hesitantly across the cushion, sought his and held on. Her eyes remained glued to the screen where unbelievably a large coffee jar appeared.

'That's it; that's what I wish you'd buy.' Sammy was momentarily stirred to enthusiasm. 'Look, look!' He tugged at her hand.

'I am looking!' She sounded cross and Sammy scanned her profile anxiously.

'I do like real coffee, love.' He hated the apologetic note in his voice. Why couldn't he just tell her? 'It's just that it doesn't like me.' He shrugged helplessly and impassively she watched the screen which was now promoting with equal vigour the nutritional properties of a well-known chocolate bar.

He sighed.

When he wandered into the kitchen to boil the kettle she didn't seem to notice. He left a cup of tea, a peace offering, on the table beside her and crept back up the stairs.

Ten minutes later the painting was back on the easel, a corner wiped clean and a new idea under way. What the hell did Joy know about it anyway? A painting was a living, breathing, changing thing until it was actually sealed under varnish and left to hang in the dust.

His tongue protruding a little between his teeth he worked hard. Occasionally he hummed a little. His tea grew cold; the top filmed over unnoticed.

At closedown Sylvia looked in and watched in her accustomed manner over his shoulder for a while; but she was gone, yawning, before his arm had a chance to falter this time. He was relieved. If she had spotted what he had done she might have come right in and given an opinion. That would not have been welcome; not at the moment.

He worked hard, concentrating on every brush stroke. By two o'clock the painting was perfect; Joy would never have recognized it.

Sammy stood back as he cleaned his brushes and smiled. He was a satisfied man.

By half past two he was in despair. The realization had just dawned on him that he could never part with it; no, nor any of the other paintings which had suffered those rummaging critical hands. They were part of him; a very sensitive part of him. Supposing someone bought one and then became so used to it they never even saw it any more? Sammy groaned out loud.

He crept into the bedroom and fumbled for the light switch beside his bed. Sylvia always awoke in a fury when he crashed around in the dark, trying to be quiet. With the light on she merely awoke indignant.

'I'm sorry, love,' he whispered automatically as she stirred. 'I'll only be a jiffy.' There was paint on his shirt cuff. Guiltily he rolled it up, sleeve innermost and pushed it under a chair.

'I'll bet you altered that painting.' Her voice was sleepy, but her eyes peering over the duvet at him were intense.

'I had to, Syl.' He sat on the bed to take his socks off. 'The balance was all wrong. I've got it right now, though.'

'I'll bet you something else too.' She pulled herself up on one elbow.

'Oh?' He felt foolish sitting there with one sock on, one off.

'You won't let her have it in the end. Nor any of them, will you?'

To his surprise she was grinning. 'I never said that, Syl.'

'You didn't have to.' She leaned across and put her arm round him affectionately. 'It's written all over your face, you poor booby.' She kissed him and then lay back on the pillows watching as he removed his other sock.

'I'm going to tell you something, lover.' She never called him that except when she had overspent the housekeeping money or broken one of his mother's best crystal glasses.

He wished he'd got his pyjama trousers on. He felt too vulnerable sitting there in his pants.

'What?' he asked cautiously.

'You never noticed that one or two of your paintings – well, six actually – were missing, did you?'

He sat up straight, frowning. 'Missing?'

She nodded. 'I sold them. Oh, I kept the money for you. I just never dared tell you, somehow.' She looked miserably hard at her finger nails and took an absent-minded bite at one of them.

'You what?' He had grown cold.

'Sold them. I've watched you, Sammy. You look at them and fiddle with them and alter them and talk to them even. Then, wham! They're leaning against the wall. You look at them twice then they're turned face in and you forget them. It's criminal. They're forgotten. And they're begging to be hung up somewhere to be looked at.'

To his astonishment a great tear welled up in one of

her eyes. It teetered on the rim for a moment and then overbalanced, splashing down onto her cheek.

Sammy swallowed hard. 'I never noticed,' he whispered. It was the most terrible treachery. 'I never even saw that they had gone.' He was silent for a moment. 'I remember every painting I ever painted.'

'Of course you do.' She sat up again. 'But Sammy love, they're four or five deep round the walls, some of them. Oh Sammy. They deserve better. They deserve to be seen.'

'You sold them through Joy?' His voice was still hesitant.

She shook her head. 'I only met Joy this morning; well, yesterday morning now.' She corrected herself. 'The others I took to a gallery in London.' She took another bite at her nail and Sammy winced.

'How much did you get?' He couldn't help asking.

'Fifty each for the two little ones. Seventy-five for three others and £150 for the *Forest Fire*.' She looked at him sideways to see how he was taking it.

'I was fond of the *Forest Fire*.' He was mournful.

'It's nearly five hundred pounds, Sammy.'

'I always thought I'd change it so that the trees were silhouetted against the sky more.'

'Well four seventy-five anyway.'

'I suppose you sold the *Marionette*? I was looking for her the other day. I thought the strings ought to be tangled.'

'She fetched seventy-five pounds, Sam.'

'She'd have been so much better if I'd had a chance to work on her some more.' He got up at last and found his pyjamas. 'I suppose you want commission for handling the sales?' He turned round suddenly and appeared to be quite serious.

Sylvia smothered a giggle. 'I wouldn't say no, lover.'

She waited while he disappeared into the bathroom.

When he was sitting next to her she turned to him. 'I do care about the paintings, Sam. I'm sure they went to good homes, you know.'

Biting his lip Sammy lay back and switched off the light. 'Of course they did. I'm just being silly, I know it. But that's the way I am.'

'And Joy can have the pictures she wanted?' She was almost wheedling.

'Sometime, I suppose, yes.'

Sylvia gave a big sigh of satisfaction. 'As long as it's sometime, Sammy, there's no hurry.'

She turned over and settled herself for sleep contentedly. She knew exactly how long it would take! And this time she would claim her commission. She had already worked out just how much it would cost to buy a smart portfolio for carrying Sammy's paintings. Not for him of course. She was the salesperson in this family. She smiled in the darkness. Poor Sammy. She really must try and remember to buy a jar of instant coffee for him. First thing on Monday morning.

A Quest For Identity

When Katherine was seven she wanted to be a nun. She fingered her mother's coral beads lovingly, as a rosary, and threaded to them the cross she bought with her pocket money and chose herself from the black flock tray in the window of the second-hand shop on the corner. It was of chased silver, wafer thin and very holy. At the bottom of the garden, deep in a most secret place among the sooty privets, she had made from an old orange box an altar and there she played at churches, her head draped in the mantilla of an old dressing-up shawl.

At boarding school there was a chapel; stark, serviceable and compulsory. She threw herself into the daily service with fervour, mouthing the hymns in a reverent whisper, half disapproving when her friends heartily shouted the well-worn verses and screwing up her eyes during the prayers in an effort of concentration.

Confirmation classes begged from a reluctant father – 'You're not serious are you, Kate? All that mumbo-jumbo!' – were a bitter disappointment. Held in the cold chapel when other less dedicated people were at prep, the only sound save for the chaplain's bored voice, was the agonizing embarrassment of her own stomach rumbling.

But the day of confirmation itself was a success. The pretty white dresses and veils, the beautiful illuminated postcard from matron, mother in her best hat; and the bishop. The bishop was quite beautiful and she almost fainted with excitement to feel his hands upon her head. She accepted the glow of happiness within her as a genuine inspiring experience and knew that at last the mystery she sought had come to her. Her first communion in the cold spring morning, light-headed from lack of breakfast, excited and half-afraid, maintained the wonder and the exhilaration.

But as the months passed so did her resolution. Getting up early on Sunday was all very well in the summer but on foggy winter mornings it was a different matter. By the time she left school she had stopped going to church in the holidays altogether.

At university she read philosophy and deliberately abandoned the one religion in the quest for the truths of many. The search left her interested, well-read and with a BA, but without faith. And she no longer felt the need for it. Her life was full of material things; of work and play; of friends and men; of parties and books and fun. There were no more long evenings leaning elbows on sill, gazing from her bedroom window at the infinities of heaven. She shared her bedroom at the flat with three and peace was a non-existent commodity even in the depths of night. The agonizing soul-searching quest of the teenager had been replaced by the complacent confidence of a healthy young woman. If her soul still cried out for succour she firmly ignored the call. She rejected faith now as consciously and outspokenly as she rejected her parents' standards and values as being bourgeois, old-hat and faintly ridiculous.

George was an atheist. And at first everything that George said and did had the ring of absolute truth in her ears. She gazed into his eyes and hung adoring on his every word.

'It's ourselves that count, Kate. We are what we are and life is what we make it. No rational person can believe our course is dictated by a bearded old man in the sky.' He put his arm round her waist and squeezed her playfully.

'You're right, it's up to us.' Dazzled by his smile she followed him to parties and dances. She entertained for him and ended up darning his socks when she moved into his Notting Hill basement. Her parents threatened to wash their hands of her but both secretly came, each not telling the other and swearing her to complicity in their guilt, as they looked around the two dingy rooms with the stuffingless sofa, the clothes horses draped with towels and the uncompromisingly small double bed. Her mother brought her a bunch of chrysanthemums and michaelmas daisies the colour of the smoky autumn sky and the scent of her tweed skirt was of bonfires and new-mown grass.

Kate cried when her mother had gone. Her free-thinking independence hinted suddenly of squalor.

Then came Mary Thomas with whom she had been at school. Sweet angelic Mary, whose gym tunic had never been creased and stained was exactly the same, if a little plumper. She was not, as Kate had secretly expected, impressed and envious of *la vie bohème*.

'Oh Kate, how awful.' Mary looked round with blatant and sincere horror. 'That dreadful man. How does he expect you to live like this? Oh Kate, can't you leave him? Why do you stay?' She turned over the dusty books on the mantelpiece with fastidious fingers and touched by accident a mouldy piece of cheese which Kate had put down a few nights before and unaccountably lost.

'I love it like this,' Kate countered indignantly. 'This is the life I've chosen. I meet interesting people; I read interesting books. We save our money to go to the theatre and concerts. George is not interested in material possessions and I agree with him.'

'I suppose he'd think I was a bourgeois old hen then.' Mary smiled gently, but the expression in her eyes made

Kate think again. Mary was laughing at him. She saw his ideas as ridiculous and silly. 'It must be just like being a student still,' she went on, and Kate was confirmed in her opinion. Mary was quietly confident in her own way of life and in her eyes she and George were irresponsible children. The idea shocked Kate very much.

'What a boring cow she must be!' George shouted with laughter when Kate told him of the visit. 'I'll bet coming to see us is the most exciting thing she's done since she left school.'

'She's had a baby, George.' Kate did not mean to sound reproachful. It was wonder she felt for the experience her best friend had had which she could not share.

'Well, there's no great virtue in that. She's just adding to the population problem.' Unimpressed George threw himself down in the chair and put his feet on the table. He had brought the *New Statesman* home and was at once immersed in it.

'But George, she's happy. Really happy, and . . .' Kate groped for a word, rejected it as trite and cosy and then unable to find another, reluctantly produced it. 'She's fulfilled.'

There was another snort of derision from behind the paper, but no further comment.

Kate retreated to the kitchenette and began to open tins. Mary would undoubtedly by now be preparing a nourishing and wholesome meal for her family, made with real food; her saucepans probably matched and her kitchen would have come entire and co-ordinated from the pages of a glossy magazine.

Kate looked up at the greasy grey wall behind the cooker. Once she had begun to wash this corner and her efforts had ended sharply and distinctively in an uncompromising black line. The shiny road safety poster disguised nothing. She had given up not even half-way through the job and it showed.

Depressed she poured the contents of her saucepan into two bowls and carried them to the table where George's feet still rested, side by side, showing a hole in the shiny sole of one shoe.

'Has anyone ever told you that you behave like a peasant?' she said with unexpected venom. He peered over his paper and slowly removed first one and then the other foot from the table.

'Yes, you, honey, with boring repetitiveness. But you've never told me how you're so sure the nobs don't stick their plates of meat on the Chippendale.' He picked up his spoon and started eating ravenously. 'Or did *mummy* tell you?'

She hated the way he emphasized the word, debasing it to sound cheap and silly by a mere flicker of inflection. His occasional bitter sarcasm, always aroused if he thought she was getting at him through his background, usually reduced her to tears. His tone was too acrid not to be genuine.

Turning unhappily from her own food she rummaged under the cushion for a packet of cigarettes. She had given up giving up. 'I'd like to go out for a meal, George. Somewhere nice, just for once. Could we?' She blew a cloud of smoke in the air and pushed her hair back from her eyes. It was unwashed and stringy. Mary's had been immaculately styled. She checked her thoughts abruptly. It was almost as though she were jealous, which was unthinkable. She renounced her parents' way of life absolutely and that, after all, was the style Mary followed. It might work for Mary, but not for her. 'Please, George.'

He looked up suddenly, hearing the note of desperation in her voice. 'Katie, love. Of course we can, if it means that much to you. Candles, wine, dancing – the lot if it will make you happy.' He scraped his bowl and eyed hers speculatively. 'Aren't you hungry?'

'You have it.' She ground out the cigarette and threw herself down on the sofa. 'I'll have some coffee in a minute.'

'She really got under your skin today, didn't she?' He got up at last and ruffled her hair gently. 'Are you having regrets about living here?'

'No, of course not.' She reached for his hand and pulled him down on the sofa with her. 'It's just that I miss some things . . .' She broke off helplessly, looking round at the torn wallpaper, the shabby furniture, the threadbare rugs. It was as though for the first time she had seen them through her own eyes. Before she had always seen them through his. When her parents came she had been consciously on the defensive, but Mary's open criticism had caught her unawares, unguarded.

'It's not very nice, George, is it? Be honest.' She gazed at him intently. But he just shrugged.

'To *be* honest, Kate, I never notice. It suits me fine. It's cheap and it's warm and it's convenient. What more do I want?'

What more indeed?

On her way back from work the next day Kate hesitated in front of the greengrocer by the station. On the pavement lay ranks of potted bulbs, houseplants and buckets of golden daffodils. She eyed them longingly, trying to ignore the exorbitant price tags pinned to them. A florid young man came out of the shop wiping his hands on his overall.

'Can I help you, love?'

He stood in front of the flowers as if to prevent her even looking at them unless she meant to buy. Wordlessly she shook her head and turned away.

Three days later George had to go away to attend a conference. It was the first time she had had to sleep alone in the flat and she found herself lying gazing up at the ceiling in the dark, listening for all the strange city noises which now suddenly seemed hostile around her. The flat itself was hostile. It was George's, but for the first time since she moved in it was not a vehicle for George's dominating personality and without him there, without his belongings scattered to the four corners it was dead and dull. Of her own personality and her dreams it reflected nothing at all.

She sat up in bed suddenly and turned on the bedside light. What were her dreams? Where was her personality? Wrinkling her forehead to think better, she gazed at the paisley design of the old eiderdown. A sharp quill was sticking through the material near her hand and absentmindedly she pulled at it, watched as the delicate white feather drew through the tiny hole and opened like a flower in her hand. It was soft and pure and rather poignant.

At school she had dreamed of being a grown up. When she had stopped wanting to be a nun she had wanted to be a nurse, then in turn a riding instructor, a vet, a secretary with beautifully manicured nails, an artist and a concert pianist. But when the careers mistress, realistic, short of time and possibly of insight, intent on actualities had probed into the subject she had had to admit, even then, a lack of any real purpose.

It was taken for granted she would go to university – her grades had always been good – but her choice of subject, philosophy, had been a surprise to everyone. Kate could explain neither the origin nor the depth of her interest, but her examination results proved that this was indeed her subject. Graduation had brought the return of reality. Decisions could no longer be deferred. Or could they? Her contemporaries hoped for a career in TV or publishing or journalism and she had half-heartedly drifted with them. But of course she had failed her interviews; the keen young men saw at once through her veneer and spotted her lethargy and indecision. So she reverted to a quick course in shorthand typing and then as she had been at last about to face up to some half-hearted self analysis she had met George. Unbelievably he too had been doing a typing course, although his was part of a master plan for his career. They had compared their speeds and later mockingly their legs and agreed that hers were the more likely to turn a boss's head.

But her job at last was very ordinary, undemanding and boring. While her social life was an exciting and exhausting round of parties she had not minded this. Work was somewhere she could surreptitiously relax. She had usually completed her day's quota of letters by lunchtime. She was never stretched. Lately she had begun to question the point of it all. She adored the theatre and concerts. She was fascinated by some of George's friends, although more and more she was finding them pretentious and opinionated. But she had to admit to herself at last that, when she had time to think about it, like now, she found her home life boring and squalid.

She had, however, no complaints about sex, and that in itself was beginning to bother her. Was she hanging on to this life merely because George was good in bed? She hugged her knees and gazed thoughtfully at the washed-out amoebic shapes on the quilt. Where was it all leading? Was she going on like this for years, dragging at George's heels? And another thing: she missed the solitude of being an individual, even while amongst a crowd. George was too possessive to allow her that freedom. He didn't do it intentionally. It was just his way, but it was stifling her, that and the boredom at work.

She awoke next morning in a state of rebellion. She rang the office and said she had flu. (She still, childlike, crossed her fingers when she told a blatant lie, however expedient.)

Then as soon as the shops were open she went to the greengrocer. Before he had even set his wares on the pavement she had bought two large earthenware pots of hyacinths. They were half opened into lush heavy white heads and already their scent as she carried them home was overpoweringly exotic. She set them down near the phone and then reached for her address book.

Mary seemed astonished at her request, but agreed quite amiably to meet the 10.50. Kate felt guilty as soon as she hung up. She wanted to impose herself on someone else's life. She wanted to borrow some of Mary's serenity. She wanted quite simply to steal a day for herself; and that day had to have the essence of perfection within it. It had begun with the new treasured feeling of aloneness and with white hyacinths. It continued with a taxi: the plutocrat's barouche, as George called them, she remembered defiantly as she settled herself back on the broad seat. The bus queues lined the road as they went past and she had an irresistible urge to thumb her nose at them. But she did resist. She had stood dirt-splashed on the edge of the gutter in the nine o'clock queues too often herself to fling insults in their poor resigned faces.

Victoria was a palace of promises; the train, as it fled into the spring countryside, a magic dragon, a princess's carriage, a mystery tour. She gazed at the tiny pale green buds on the trees, the yellow whip-lash branches of the stirring willows along the line and ignoring the other passengers began quietly to hum to herself.

The train, a conspirator in her list of happy things, was on time as was Mary with her mud-splashed estate car with the silky spaniel in the back, the baby in the baby seat and shopping next to it. She leaned across and opened the door.

The set had fallen out of Mary's hair, Kate noticed as she climbed in and she felt a ridiculous sense of being let down. The immaculate clothes had been replaced by stained jeans, and a broad kimono top, beneath which she might or might not be pregnant of a baby elephant, lacked even a suspicion of the Harrods' account which had so shocked Kate before. Kate had a horrible suspicion suddenly that perhaps Mary wore her best clothes for 'going up to town'.

Mary put her foot flat. 'Got to get home before the washing machine stops,' she said apologetically. 'Otherwise Gerry's shirts will crease. If you'd rung last night I'd have done them then.' She swung the car off the main road into a narrow high-hedged lane.

Kate raised a deprecating hand. She wrinkled her nose. There was a mingled odour of dog and regurgitated milk in the car which filled her suddenly with nausea and she closed her eyes wearily. The *joie de vivre* which had given her the impetus for the day had gone. She was suddenly limp and drained. She followed Mary into the house, loaded with shopping and therefore unable to fend off the inquisitive spaniel from her white trousers.

Basically the house was all she had hoped and expected. It was pleasant, detached, attractive, with a gnarled fruit tree on the lawn and mossy grass sprouting through the paving stones of the drive, but her call had obviously caught Mary unawares. The hoover lay in the hall surrounded by looped flex. A duster and tin of polish sat on the hall table and she glimpsed baskets of washing in the kitchen.

Mary straightened up from putting the baby in its bouncing chair. 'I'm sorry about the mess, Kate. It's lucky it was you. I knew you wouldn't mind. If you had been Sally or someone like that I'd have told you not to come.'

Who was Sally? Kate groped back in her mind to school days and vaguely pictured a tall girl with buck teeth and freckles.

'She's married a baronet, you know.' Mary puffed slightly as she bent to collect a squeaky toy from beneath the sideboard. 'He's very nice; they came to dinner last week, but I could see her looking round to see if I'd dusted on top of the pictures.' She giggled and Kate relaxed a little. That giggle made her feel more at home. So did the sight of the kettle going on. But Mary's remark rankled a little. I wanted you to bother for me, a little voice cried out inside her somewhere. I do care what it looks like. I wanted it all to be perfect.

'And had you?' She didn't mean her voice to sound quite so weary.

'Had I what?' Mary was putting hot milk in the coffee and Kate shuddered. She had imagined the steaming saucepan contained some concoction for the baby.

'Dusted the pictures.'

'Sugar? – Yes, of course I had.' Mary giggled again. 'I even dusted the cat that evening.'

Kate spent the rest of the morning as a bystander feeling very much in the way but constantly being reassured: 'I know you won't mind, Kate; I must get it done. Just let me finish this then I can sit back and relax. No, no. I don't want you to help when you've come for the day.'

The baby's lunch was dreadful. Mary spread sieved apples liberally all over its face then to Kate's horror she sat down on the kitchen chair, and heaving her shirt up to her chin, proceeded to expose a heavy blue-veined breast. The baby seized hungrily and painfully, Kate saw aghast, at the raw nipple. My God, I'm a prude! she thought to herself. She was not sure where to look. There was nothing beautiful in the sight of mother and child. The one seemed ungainly, the other obscenely greedy and the expression on Mary's face, if totally unembarrassed, was anything but placid.

'The dog's trying to get into the cupboard, Kate. Clout him for me, will you? And turn down the peas while you're up, there's a dear.'

But at last it was all over. The baby was put to sleep in its pram after its nappy had been changed, mercifully out of sight and not on the kitchen table as Kate had gloomily expected. The dog was put out, the housework at last seemed to be if not finished, then suspended, Mary produced some expensive sherry and the lunch began to smell as though it were nearly ready.

Mary sat down and smiled with relief. 'All under control at last, so we can talk.' She eyed Kate with disarming directness. 'How's George?'

'Away for a few days. I was browned off alone in the flat. I hoped you wouldn't mind me coming.'

'Of course not.' Impulsively Mary leaned forward and put her hand on Kate's. 'I thought perhaps there was something wrong. You looked so lost and unhappy when I saw you in London.'

'I did?' Kate was shocked. 'Well, I'm not, or at least . . .' She hesitated. 'I'm not unhappy, Mary, and I love George dearly, but perhaps you're right about being lost.' Shrugging, she held out her glass for a refill as Mary uncorked the bottle again. 'I feel sort of empty; purposeless.'

'Have you and George ever thought of getting married?'

It was strange, thought Kate, how married people so often leaped on that idea as being the true panacea. She shook her head violently. 'He doesn't believe in it and I, well, I don't think I believe in it either. Not with him.'

Mary glanced up shrewdly. 'Keeping your options open? That doesn't sound to me as though you're wildly satisfied with him, or it would be "George for ever, right or wrong".'

'Is that how you feel about your husband?'

'Gerry?' Mary laughed. 'I'd never really thought, but I suppose I do in a way. I'm very happy here. I have a good man to live with, a lovely child and a nice house. I'm awfully lucky.' She stopped for a moment, frowning and then went on. 'But it's more than that. I've stopped striving after impossible goals. Most of my dreams are realizable – perhaps not now, but one day.'

Kate was pleating the tablecloth between her fingers. 'At least you still have your dreams. That's my problem. I seem to have lost all mine and my ambition. But not because I'm content. I've given up or lost interest; I'm not sure which.'

She glanced up under her eyelashes and saw Mary absently studying her finger nails.

'Perhaps that's part of growing up; what they call maturity.' Mary, getting up to strain the peas into the sink, was enveloped in a cloud of steam.

'No, it's not. There's something else wrong. Something deep down inside me. I think it is George in a negative sort of way. When I'm with him I don't bother about things; nothing seems to matter.' She noticed what she was doing to the tablecloth suddenly and tried to quickly flatten out the creases.

'George dominates you too much; he's killing the real you.' Mary put a plate before her. 'I told you before, you ought to leave him. Now stop worrying about it for a bit and eat.'

After lunch they walked in the fields, Kate in borrowed gum boots, the baby in a kind of back pack on Mary's shoulders.

'Do you still believe in God?' Mary asked suddenly, in the companionable silence as they watched the spaniel running figures of eight in the meadow grass.

'I'm not sure.' Kate answered without thinking and then stopped short. Two weeks ago she would have said no. Two years ago she would have said no.

'I do. It helps you know. One is no longer so terrifyingly alone.'

They climbed the stile and set off up the edge of a field.

A delicate shadow of green lay across it; spring stirring deep in the soil.

The route Mary took led them back over another stile into the ancient churchyard. Rooks were busy in the budding beeches behind the belfry and the sun was slanting through the lichened stones, showing up eroded inscriptions.

'I often rest here for five minutes.' Mary sat down squarely on a tombstone. 'It's peaceful here. A good place to collect one's thoughts. You ought to look in the church. It's got a beautiful medieval screen.' She sat and watched, the panting dog at her feet, as Kate wandered to the door and lifted the heavy latch.

The church was shadowy and very cold. The thin spring sunlight was filtered by the windows to throw ice-diamond facets onto the worn pavings. Slowly she walked up the aisle. She hadn't been inside a church since Mary's wedding. She tried to remember when she had last prayed. It had been a selfish prayer; a please, please, make it all come right prayer and it had got nowhere. It was illogical to pray to a God in whom one did not believe. It was not even permissible as a safety valve, just in case He might exist. But what if one had genuine doubts?

She raised her eyes to the agony of crucifixion in the east window. For six hundred years men and women had knelt in this church before that image. She could feel their prayers and their peace around her. She could almost smell the incense which had not been burned there for four hundred years.

Thoughtfully she slipped into a pew and, half-embarrassed, knelt. But her mind was still empty of prayer. She searched for the long-familiar words, hesitating as her lips fumbled silently and then gave up. There was too much turmoil still inside her.

Mary was wandering around reading the tombstones

when she came out at last. They made their way back to the house in silence.

Only when they had drunk their tea and were watching the baby kicking happily on the rug before the fire did Mary allude to her long wait in the churchyard. 'Did it help at all? I often go there to be alone.'

Kate smiled. 'I suppose it did in a way. It's a long time since I sat on my own to think like that. I've got as far as recognizing that it's not intrinsically my lifestyle that's at fault, although that is depressing me too. It's something inside me.' She picked up a rattle and shook it tentatively. 'You're right. Being with George is suppressing my will to live as an individual. He scorns faith in God; he denies the old standards and while I'm with him I agree with him. But I think deep down inside perhaps I've been yearning back towards them all this time. I've been allowing him to think for me and act for me. I've let him make all the decisions, even for my conscience, just as I let him decide what music we're going to listen to.' She looked up at Mary and grinned. 'You know that's why I came to see you today. I think I'd already made up my mind, but I needed someone to tell me I was right.'

That night when she walked wearily up the dark streets from the Underground back to the flat she found she was thinking deeply about her childhood again. She recalled with envy that early burning certainty in things which had so guided her daily life.

She paused by the phone to sniff the hyacinths and then, going into the bedroom fell on her knees beside the bed. In the trunk wedged beneath it was a carved sandalwood box. She pulled it out carefully and gazed for a moment at the design on the lid. Then she opened it. Nestling in a bed of cotton wool were her few pieces of jewellery and beneath them all she found the little silver cross. She held it in the palm of her hand for a moment, remembering the glow of security and otherworldliness it had always given her. Surprised, she found a little of the feeling remained.

Inexplicably, George brought her back a delicate Indian silk scarf when he returned and even more inexplicably he admired the hyacinths without once commenting on her extravagance in buying them. He even offered to help paint the flat but she still told him she was going.

'Kate, why?' He took her hands and gazed at her, shocked and horrified.

She shrugged. 'It's hard to explain. There isn't anyone else or anything like that. I just feel terribly restless.' She felt her resolution wavering at the sight of his anguished face. She had not really thought that he would mind much beyond the first irritation at the inconvenience of losing her.

'Will you come back?' He was beginning to look lost. 'Please Kate, will you come back?'

Again she shrugged. She turned away, hating herself for the pain she was giving him. 'Shall we just say I need to be alone for a while. I've chucked the job. I'm going down to Cornwall for a couple of weeks.'

'And then?'

'And then I don't know.' She turned back to him and smiled, a little sadly. 'Don't worry about me, George. I'll keep in touch.'

Standing high on the cliffs above the grey seas, her hair tangled by the wind, she realized fully at last that she had been right to seek her freedom. She missed George dreadfully, but she was free to make her own decisions and formulate her own plans.

'What are you going to be when you grow up?' They had asked her at school. Well now at long last she was about to find out the answer to their question.

Such A Silly Thing

Molly drummed her fingers on the breakfast table, looked at the clock on the mantelpiece, compared it with her wristwatch, and with an impatient sigh threw her paper on the floor.

From the window she could see the garden, flattened and sodden with the endless pouring rain. The thunder had passed. It had gone with the darkness and with it some of the humidity, but the room was still airless, in spite of the slightly open windows. There was a puddle on one of the sills she noticed vaguely, where the rain was being driven in. She let it stay.

When the doorbell rang at last she jumped. The house had seemed so empty, so quiet save for the rain on the paving outside.

Bill was grinning widely. 'Sorry I'm late, Molly. The car wouldn't start.' He shook himself like a dog and stepped into the porch. She could see a line of droplets running down his unruly forelock. One dropped onto his nose. She resisted the temptation to touch it with her finger.

'I'll fetch my bag, darling. Hold on one minute and I'll be with you.'

'Better bring your brolly!' She heard his voice echoing up the stairs after her as she ran to her bedroom. She stood looking round, her heart pounding. Her handbag was downstairs on the hallstand; her case too. She had packed last night after James had gone to bed. She looked down at the two identical beds, virginal beneath their white candlewick.

James had kissed her goodbye this morning as usual, about three inches in the air somewhere above her head as she sat over her coffee, passed her *The Times* – he took the *Financial Times* to the office – and strolled, humming gently, into the hall. She heard him mutter something about the rain and rattle the walking sticks in the stand, trying to extricate his umbrella. He swore gently, very unusual for James, and then from the sudden silence she knew he had gone. He always managed to shut the front door without a sound. There was nothing else to hear but the rain dripping down onto the terrace outside the window. She had poured herself another cup of coffee, a thing she seldom did and opened the paper to the Court page as though today were just like any other day.

'Come on, Molly, where are you?' Bill's voice broke through her thoughts and she jumped guiltily.

Poor James. He was going to be very upset in his own quiet way when he found she had gone. She took the envelope from her dressing table drawer and laid it gently on his pillow. Poor James.

Bill was waiting in the hall, her handbag in one hand and her umbrella in the other. He proffered them, one eyebrow slightly raised. 'Better bring a coat. It won't always be as hot as this.'

'Oh, I forgot.' She turned towards the stairs again, but he grabbed her hand.

'Never mind, sweetheart. Come on. We're late as it is. I'll buy you a coat.'

She slammed the front door and followed him across the soaking gravel to his car. The morning smelt of roses and grass and wet, wet earth.

In the car he turned on the radio. Then he leaned over

and kissed her. 'Mine at last,' he muttered, taking her hand. 'Dearest Molly. I've waited so long for this moment.'

She wormed her hand out of his grasp. 'Not here, Bill, please. Someone might see.' She patted her hair nervously.

She should have left the note downstairs on the mantelpiece. The bed was too personal; too pointed. What if Mrs White came today instead of Friday? She would see it and guess. The wretched woman might even read it. Perhaps she ought to go back and move it – but already the car was driving away. She sat back and closed her eyes. It was too late to go back. She must stop thinking about James. It would probably be days before he even noticed that she had gone.

She opened her eyes and watched the road through the labouring windscreen wipers.

Bill glanced across at her. 'I know how you feel, darling. It's a big step. Are you scared now you've done it?'

'If you know how I feel, why do you ask?' She didn't mean to snap.

Don't look so hurt, Bill, she thought to herself. You're supposed to be carrying me off on your charger, remember? You're taking me away from all this to a new life. You've swept me off my feet, remember?

She groped in her handbag for cigarettes and then remembered she had given them up. How strange. She hadn't made that mistake for weeks now. James had made her do it. 'I can't bear to hear you coughing like that, Moll,' he had said. 'Please darling, for your own sake.' He had taken her hands and looked into her eyes with such tenderness.

She shook her head angrily. Why did she keep remembering the good things about him?'

'Have you got a ciggy, Bill?'

''Course.' He changed gear expertly. 'In my left hand pocket.' He raised his elbow so she could reach.

Didn't he care about her health then? She lit one and took a long draw on it. It left her convulsed with coughing and she stubbed it out angrily.

'Let's stop for coffee somewhere, Bill, please.' Her voice was more urgent than she had intended and he looked at her, quickly anxious.

'Can you wait five minutes? There's a roadhouse about four miles further on. A good place.'

A roadhouse! James always took her to the best hotels for coffee so she could use the powder rooms in comfort. She wondered suddenly whether Bill would expect her to use public lavatories on their long drive north and she shuddered.

The roadhouse was red brick, impersonal and crowded. A coach had just discharged its occupants outside the door and Bill and Molly had to wait half an hour before they were served with their coffee. Then at last they were on the road again.

Bill sensed he had made a mistake. 'I've planned a really good stop for lunch, Molly, in Grantham. Then I thought we'd stay tonight in a pub about ten miles further on. We don't want to drive all day on our first day; or be too tired on our first night, do we?' He felt for her hand and squeezed it gently. 'I'm sorry about that last place. I've never seen it crowded before.'

'It doesn't matter.' She smiled at him. She must make some effort. Poor Bill.

Lunch was good. The restaurant was small and intimate and the food delicious. Molly relaxed at last, gazing into Bill's eyes across the brandy he had insisted on buying her.

'I shall fall asleep drinking like this in the middle of the day,' she murmured. He had lovely eyes. They were what had first attracted her. An intense blue of the kind that usually faded in middle age, surrounded by thick black lashes.

'Your ancestors must have been Irish,' she had said to him once, but he had laughed.

'As far as I know none of them have ever been further west than Hertfordshire,' he had teased her. And she didn't ask any further.

She wondered briefly why she had never wanted to know about Bill's family or his past. She should be curious about everything to do with the man she loved. Was it that she was afraid of what she might discover? Not that he was bad, but that he was good; too good. She wanted to imagine without being sure that there was something disreputable about Bill. It was not such fun being carried off by a respectable man. James was a respectable man.

Bill had started well. He had brought her flowers and chocolates and a tiny filigree pendant and stolen her glove and her hanky. He had carried her to the summer house at the Barnabys, that first time they had made love, gently ignoring her half-hearted protests and he had stopped her conscience with kisses. He had phoned her and written and played games of hide and seek to meet her in London when she went up with James, giving her an orchid as her prize when she had found him.

But now?

He had suddenly become diffident. Nervous. Almost half-hearted. Now that she was here with him she could sense all was not as it had been. He was not dashing any more.

She glanced at his profile. 'Let's do something foolish, Bill. I want to be mad this afternoon.' She put her hand on his knee, willing him to smile and mock and change his sober Rover into a rearing, bit-champing white stallion.

'Careful, Molly. You'll distract me while I'm driving. Wait till we get there.' He was frowning through the windscreen. The rain hadn't stopped.

She slumped back in her seat, disappointed.

They were registered as Mr and Mrs at the inn. It was a pretty room with pink chintz curtains and a wide bed. The ashtray on the dressing table had been emptied but not washed. Molly wrinkled her nose at the black film on the china. She threw herself down on the bed and kicked off her shoes. Bill came to her and kissed her tenderly. Then he brushed her hair back from her forehead. There was something slightly possessive about the gesture which she resented. He smelt of garlic from the lunch.

'I want to run naked in the rain,' she whispered to him, testing. 'When it's dark I'm going to explore the garden.' She giggled.

But he looked serious and kissed her again. 'Silly Molly. You can't possibly do such a thing. When it gets dark we'll be here together.' His deep blue eyes were close to hers. They were pleading and unsure.

She turned her head away. 'It's not working, Bill, is it?' Her voice was so soft she wondered if she had spoken aloud at all.

'You haven't let yourself make the break, sweetheart, that's all.' He stood up and walked away from her, hiding his face. 'It's not too late to go back, Molly. If that's what you want.'

She felt a tear roll down her face and brushed at it in surprise. She had not realized she was crying.

'I think I do, Bill. I'm sorry.'

He was looking out of the window, the chintz curtain partly obscuring his shoulder and his face. He turned and looked at her, his expression carefully impassive.

'Think about it, Molly darling.' He blinked several times, quickly like a child trying not to cry and she felt a wrench of love and pity. 'If you want to get back before James finds your note we ought to leave pretty soon.' He glanced at his watch although she knew he couldn't see it. 'I'll be downstairs having a drink.'

She sat for a while after he had gone, gazing at the pink and orange floral pattern on the carpet. Then suddenly she stood up.

Bill was in the lounge looking at a paper. 'I've squared the hotel,' he said without looking up, his voice dull and subdued. 'We can leave now.'

'You knew, didn't you, Bill?' She stood before him. 'Is that why you booked in here; why we didn't go all the way?'

'I had a feeling I might be driving you back, sweetheart.' He threw down the paper and stood up. 'You're not the type to run out on your husband. I knew it before you did. I was resigned.' He dropped a gentle kiss on the top of her head.

'And you don't mind?'

'Hell! Of course I mind.' He kicked savagely at some ash on the carpet. 'If I could I would throw you over my shoulder and take you away and keep you locked up somewhere safe, just for me . . . But I can't do that, Molly. You know it and I know it. You belong to James, I thought perhaps you could break away; I hoped you could, but . . .' he broke off shrugging his shoulders and turned away.

She followed him out to the car and climbed silently in beside him. He started the engine and then turned to her suddenly, the familiar grin once more playing round his eyes. 'Cheer up, Molly love. I don't like drama scenes. We've had a lot of fun, you and I.' He took her hand and kissed it gently. 'We didn't know when to stop, that's all. No harm done.'

He drove back very fast, retracing the journey of the morning. The rain had stopped at last and the afternoon sun turned the road into a ribbon of glass as the wet tarmac stretched before them. Trees, telegraph wires and fence posts were strung with diamond droplets.

Molly was thinking of the house. Supposing it was too

late. Supposing James had come home and found the note. Supposing Mrs White had been in and seen it? She found her hands were shaking in her lap. Bill was gazing ahead. Glancing across at him she saw his jaw set in a hard line.

The house looked strangely empty when the car at last drew up by the gate. Bill didn't move, so she opened the car door and slipped out herself, reaching over for her case.

'Will I see you again?' Her voice sounded timid, uncertain. She saw him swallow. Then he turned and smiled.

'If you want to, Molly; I'll be there. See how it goes, darling.' He raised his hand and then he had gone.

She went into the house quickly. She knew in her heart she wouldn't meet him again. It was over.

She put down her case in the hall and ran up to the bedroom. The envelope still lay on the pillow where she had left it. Clasping it to her thankfully she tore it slowly into a hundred tiny pieces, letting each bit drift into the waste paper basket.

She was still in the bedroom when she heard James's key in the lock. Her heart gave a little extra bump and she glanced in the mirror anxiously, patting her hair, then she ran downstairs. He was standing in the hall, looking blankly at her case.

'Oh James,' she held out her hands to him. 'James, darling.'

'Hello Molly.' He opened his arms as she ran to him and gently he kissed her hair.

'Oh James, I nearly did a silly thing today.' She buried her face in the breast of his pin-striped suit.

He held her away from him and gazed into her eyes. Then he smiled and kissed her again. 'I'm so glad you didn't, Molly. So very glad.' He stopped and handed her her case. 'Unpack, Molly. Then come and have a drink with me. I'm going to open some champagne.'

'Unpack?' She looked at him shocked. 'You knew? And you didn't say anything?'

'I've known about Bill for a long time. You had to make the choice yourself.' He laughed, suddenly boyish. 'Oh God, Molly, I'm so glad you chose me.'

The Heart Will Understand

'Unless you give me the authority to attend to these . . . matters, your father's business will undoubtedly fail and you will be able to look no further than to yourself for the blame . . . Sincerely, Philip Dane.'

Helen looked up from the letter on her desk and gazed out of her office window at the London street below, where the dank grey morning teemed with traffic and people.

It was already three months since her father had died, three months since she had made her way to Leabrook and stood with strangers in the snow and looked down into the open grave. One of those strangers must have been Philip Dane. She must have shaken his hand and murmured something to him as, one by one, her father's former employees made their way past her and stammered their condolences. Each one must have been wondering about her, wondering what she would do now that she owned the nursery, wondering about their future, their livelihood, their jobs. And she had said nothing. She had returned to the city.

Philip Dane's first letter had reached her three weeks later. She read it and put it aside. He could cope. He had been her father's manager. He must have been running things for those last months of her father's illness. He could continue to look after the place for the time being.

Someone knocked on the door behind her. 'Your coffee,

Helen – and there was a telephone call for you while you were out.'

Helen looked back into the room, still thinking of the fragrance of the formal gardens in which she and her father used to sit sometimes as it grew dark, listening to the last bees bumbling their way through the clumps of melissa and she frowned. 'Thank you, Sally. Who was it?'

'Mr Spencer. He was wondering if you could meet for lunch.'

After all these months of knowing him the mention of Stephen Spencer's name still made her heart do a quick somersault beneath her ribs. She sighed. Then slowly she stood up. 'Tell him I can't will you, Sally? Tell him I've been called away unexpectedly to the country for a few days. I'll contact him when I get back.'

The bank of elder trees by the gate was full of half-opened sooty green buds. Below them the stream ran red and muddy after the rain, the gurgle of water providing an accompaniment to the pure whistling of the blackbird which sat on one of the top branches of the still leafless ash.

Helen stood for a moment and looked around her in the twilight. The air was clean and strong after the city. And it was quiet. In spite of the bird and the water, it was quiet.

She glanced towards the house. Smoke rose from the chimneys and she could see a figure bustling around in the lighted kitchen window. Someone must have gone in to light the fire after she had phoned, to try to provide some kind of a welcome in the cold empty house.

She glanced across at the glasshouses and the buildings beyond them. Behind the high box hedge lay the long terrace of herbs, sloping away towards the south. Her father's whole life was represented by those buildings and the plants they contained. It had been a quiet, peaceful rewarding life as far as she could see. One which she had almost envied and sometimes despised.

She took a step onto the bridge which spanned the stream and looked back at her car. Leaving it there in the car park under the trees, its windows tightly wound up against the damp, its lights off, its engine quietly ticking as it cooled, she was leaving her link with the city behind her. And the link with Stephen Spencer.

When he had rung back that afternoon she had made Sally take the call. There was no reason to speak to him herself. There was nothing left for them to say to each other now.

She began to walk slowly up the path towards the house. It was warm and welcoming; womblike; clinging. It was so easy to feel at home there. Later, in front of the open fire she slowly unzipped her boots and sighed. The place would stretch out its arms and clutch, octopus-like, around her neck given half a chance. But she wouldn't give it a chance. She would sell it and return to her job in London. Sell the sentiment and the memories. Sell the millstone. Sell the worries which had been her father's life and which had eventually chased him into his grave. Sell her father's pride and joy. Leabrook had no claim on her. None at all.

The knock on the door took her by surprise. She glanced at her watch. She must have been dozing, for it was getting on for midnight. She padded barefoot into the hall and peered through the glass of the front door.

'Who is it?'

'Philip Dane.'

Her hair was untidy, her skirt rumpled and her boots still lay flopped by the fire.

'It's very late, Mr Dane.'

'Not for you, surely.' His voice behind the door was deep, with just a hint of the soft inflection of the hills.

She could see through the glass that he was tall.

Angrily she pulled back the bolt and drew open the door. 'It is late for me, Mr Dane. I had a long drive down this evening.'

He stepped into the hall without hesitation. 'I hadn't thought of that. But I won't keep you.' No word of apology. 'I merely wanted to welcome you to Leabrook and find out if you would like to come on a tour of the place with me in the morning.'

She looked at him. He was tall, broad shouldered, not handsome but ruggedly attractive in a weatherbeaten way, with a mat of untidy, straw-coloured hair.

She met his gaze steadily. 'I know the place, Mr Dane. It was my home once.'

'But not for some time, I think. Had I known you were coming, I should have been here to greet you properly.' He leaned his shoulder against the wall. 'You've come to sell up, haven't you?' He had not moved his gaze from her face. It was not a question. It was as if he could read her mind. She stepped back a little resentfully.

'I haven't decided what to do yet. There has been too little time.'

'It has been nearly four months since the old man died. You've had time to make up your mind.'

She felt herself beginning to seethe beneath his stare. 'There are many things to consider, Mr Dane. But I hardly think this is the time or the place to discuss it, do you?'

She reached for the door again, pointedly, opening it a little further, wanting him to go. He did not move.

'He said you'd sell. He said you were too much of a town girl ever to come here to live. And he's right. You wouldn't fit in here.' He swung on his heel and went towards the door. 'I'll collect you at nine, if that's all right with you and we'll walk round the whole nursery together.'

At half past eight she was already in the shop watching the staff sorting through the books and seeds, tidying the sachets of dried herbs, stirring the scents till they filled the old wooden building, carrying out the boxes of mints which were to be stacked outside on the nearly empty wooden benches. It was a misty morning, which hinted of sun later. Helen had dressed in jeans and a thick sweater against the cold. The ladies who helped in the shop were in large floral pinafores.

She could see Philip Dane through the window, making his way to the front door of the house and she watched out of the corner of her eye as he knocked and waited at the front door. It gave her considerable satisfaction to see him shrug and walk away. No doubt he expected her to lie in bed until mid-morning.

His expression as he saw her confirmed her suspicions.

'Good morning, Mr Dane. Forgive me for not waiting in the house, but there was a great deal to do this morning. I couldn't wait until nine to begin.'

He inclined his head slightly. 'When you're ready, I'll take you round.'

The ladies were watching them. Helen suddenly wanted to giggle. 'I'm ready now, thank you.' Meekly she followed him out of the door and towards the propagation beds.

'I handed in my notice this morning, Stephen.' Helen looked up into his face and forced herself to smile. 'I'm going to live at Leabrook. It's all arranged.'

He stared at her, his lean features suddenly nakedly

miserable and she felt a lump come to her throat. 'We've had fun you and I, Stephen, I know, but it wasn't working, was it?' She looked away from him, studying the menu in her hands as though her life depended on it.

'And everything there has been between us? It has meant nothing to you?' He spoke stiffly, his voice lowered as though he were afraid someone would hear.

'Of course it meant something to me. It meant a great deal.' She swallowed hard. 'Stephen, you and I have had a lot of good times. I'm . . .' She hesitated. 'There is something missing between us. There always has been. You know it as well as I do. I don't know what it is, but I've always sensed it and I think you have too. This is the right moment to finish it. I'm going away. For good.'

Suddenly she had a vivid picture of the last time they had gone out together. They had been to the theatre and after it had eaten in a little restaurant in Covent Garden. Then they had gone back to Stephen's flat and, gently, he had taken her in his arms and kissed her and later they had lain together, their arms around one another, their heads side by side on the pillows and she had been happy. Almost.

They were too tense together; too conscious of themselves. She knew that he was holding back. It was almost as if he were acting a part and she had felt a little chill of misery creep over her, an uncertainty which should not be there and she had wondered if he sensed the same in her. She did not know how to reassure him.

The silence in the room had been broken that last time by the sound of a car drawing up in the echoing street below. She heard the doors being opened and banged, voices and then, slowly, the silence again. But it was too late. Their aloneness was broken. She had not found out what was wrong. And now she never would.

She looked at him again now and was relieved to see

that he was once more in complete control of himself. His handsome face was impassive above the stiff collar, the discreet silk tie, the dark city suit.

'You've obviously made the decision, Helen,' he said quietly. 'I can see that there would be no point in trying to dissuade you.'

She bit her lip. There would. Of course there would. If he were to shout and rant at her, or hit her and drag her out into the street, or hurl the wine bottle across the room so that it smashed against the plate glass mirror on the opposite wall and splattered the decor with the musky Lambrusco – that would dissuade her. All or any of that would dissuade her and she would know that he cared.

She forced herself to smile. 'No, Stephen. There is no point in trying to dissuade me,' she said.

She saw him only twice after that before she moved. Both times they were like business acquaintances rather than people who had once been lovers. There was no acrimony, no heat; no terrible sorrow. Just a strange, deep regret. As a parting gift he gave her a Hermès scarf and a tight, distant kiss on the cheek. 'Let me know how you get on, Helen,' he said. 'I'll always want to know.'

And that was that.

She piled the last of her things into the back of her car, posted her flat key through the letter box for the landlord, slammed the lower door and climbed into the car. Stephen's scarf still in its glossy wrapping was in the glove pocket in front of her. She did not put it on.

Philip Dane came over that evening, not long after the van which had brought her few pieces of furniture from town had pulled away up the lane. He was carrying a bottle of wine.

'I thought you might like to celebrate or drown your

sorrows. Now that it's all over and there is no turning back,' he said. 'Tomorrow perhaps we can go out to dinner. They do a good meal at the White Swan.'

She stared at him. Then she smiled. 'It's been one hell of a day,' she said.

'No regrets so far?'

She frowned. No regrets. Not for the job or the flat or the people. Just one aching memory. Stephen. He was watching her closely. Seeing the doubt on her face. But she shook her head. 'No regrets. None at all.'

At her invitation he sat on the sofa beside her, stretching out his legs towards the fire.

'You know, I thought you were going to give me the sack.' He squinted down at her. 'You were, weren't you?'

'It crossed my mind.'

'That's what you came down here for, wasn't it, originally? To sell up and collect the money and go.'

'I suppose it was.'

'And instead you're going to take over and make decisions above my head?'

'And you don't like that idea?'

'Not one bit.' He grinned. 'I've run this place too long to have some pint-sized town girl lording it over me.'

'Not so much of the pint sized!'

He chuckled. 'You're not such a bad businesswoman from what I've seen so far. You must have been pretty good at that job in London.'

'I was.' It was her turn to smile. 'And I'll be good at this one too. And I'll lord it over you if I have to.'

'I realized that weeks ago.'

'Philip, did my father really say I was too much of a town girl to fit in here?' She twisted herself round so that she could see his face.

He laughed. 'Of course not. He said you could never

resist a challenge. So I made sure I presented you with one. And you rose to the bait beautifully!'

She and Philip worked well together, his training and skill with the plants combining with her flair for business. They recognized one another's strengths and of necessity grew close in the lengthening hours of daylight as the spring matured into early summer and grew warm. In the evenings they would inspect the herb beds walking slowly back towards the buildings as the last of the daylight lingered. And as they walked together, sometimes their hands would touch and she would glance at him and feel the strength of his attraction reaching out towards her. When at last he kissed her by the dew-wet sundial in the formal gardens where she used to sit with her father, the action had a kind of inevitability she could not resist. She was not prepared, however, for the wistful longing which came with the kiss and the thoughts, not of Philip, his strong arms round her in the dusk, but of Stephen.

It was weeks before she brought herself to write to Stephen and longer before she posted the letter. It was brief and defiant and though she didn't realize it, it was a little wistful too, as she thought of Philip's kiss which she hoped would blot out all memory, in time, of the man to whom she wrote.

Stephen read it in the tube, wedged shoulder to shoulder in the morning rush hour, scanning her writing with the same care he usually gave the City prices. Inside, he felt sick.

From the page came a shutter-speed glimpse of the countryside emerging into summer; of lavender beds and pots of rosemary, of the worries of small but growing mail order sales and the drying sheds. And the picture of a woman who had already changed, relaxed and grown in confidence. And at the end the casual mention of her manager. 'Philip is marvellous. Dad was lucky to find him and so am I.' No more.

Stephen closed his eyes, his hand automatically reaching up for the jointed handhold above his head as the train jolted across the points. He wondered why that morning's investment meeting had seemed to be so important – and why he'd let her go.

At first Helen found Philip's possessiveness refreshing. It was exciting to have someone to escort her with such obvious pride. She relished his admiration, but always at the end of the day she hesitated and drew back.

'Let me stay, Helen,' he would múrmur in her ear as they sat before the log fire, which they still lit for company in the cool of the darkness, and she would close her eyes and whisper, 'Not tonight, Phil. Not yet.'

It had been too easy. Too obvious. She did not trust herself. Her excitement when he came near was real, as was her intense longing for him to efface the memory of Stephen and take over her life and yet, at the same time, she began to resent him a little. He was too possessive. Twice now he had countermanded her orders in the nurseries in front of the men and had laughed at her when she tried to argue. A nice laugh, but nevertheless a laugh. The last time it happened she asked him back to the house for a coffee and they had a blazing row.

Two days later she was in the White Swan with a couple of the men at lunchtime and she saw Philip in there with someone else; a pretty dark girl whom she had never seen before. He had his arm around her.

She didn't say anything and very soon she was able to

leave. The misery and jealousy she felt surprised her. Could she really be in love with him after all? He was fun and attractive and there was no doubt she was very strongly drawn to him, but this was not what it had felt like before.

But had she been in love with Stephen?

For several days she scarcely spoke to Philip as they met in the sheds or in the office over the account books or as she walked slowly down the lines of staging in the greenhouses, watching the seedlings turning to sturdy plants beneath his care. Then she knew she had to say something.

He looked down at her gravely as she approached him in the sunny privacy of the box hedges. Then he smiled. 'When you first came here, Helen, you said you had no regrets. That wasn't quite true, was it?'

She stared down at the grass. 'It was true, Phil. It's just I need longer than I thought, that's all. There's been so much to adjust to – so much that is different. Don't hurry me, please. Give me a little space.'

He shrugged. 'I'll give you space, Helen. However much you need. But don't take too much time, if you can help it.' He touched her gently with his finger. Then he turned away.

She watched him go without moving. Suddenly she felt like crying.

The next day it rained, and the day after. The stream gurgled and creamed an angry red brown and the trees scattered their leaves into the rushing flood waters. With a shiver Helen turned her back on the scene and closed the door. She had just seen Philip drive away for a weekend she might have gone on too, the tyres of his car throwing muddy spray into the air. She felt bleak.

Summer though it might be, she lit the fire to cheer herself and knelt before it, feeding it wet, spluttering twigs and she almost did not bother to go to the door when she heard the knock.

It was Stephen.

They stared at each other in silence, her initial incredulous joy at seeing him damped almost instantly by their mutual hesitation. His reserve, his tight, careful restraint as he kissed her forehead and followed her into the sitting room were unchanged from the last time she had seen him. He did not fit at Leabrook. He never would.

They talked. They even laughed. They ate together and drank the wine he had brought with him. But something still held them apart and at last she slipped onto her knees on the hearth rug to feed the fire with logs and stare miserably into the flames.

He watched the shadows leaping on her hair. It was softer, more natural than he had ever seen it; prettier. She looked good without make-up, dressed in her old jeans. She seemed relaxed. Happy.

They talked some more and she began to sense a change in him. Puzzled she watched his face, yearning to reach out and touch the taut lines which ran from nose to mouth. Outside the rain battered the windows and they heard a gust of wind in the chimney and for a moment she thought of Philip.

'I'll show you to your room, Stephen,' she said at last and he did not argue. On the landing he took her hands for a moment and held them in his. Then he turned from her and closed the door behind him.

She lay awake a long time, thinking about him in the dark.

It was dawn when she was wakened by the distant sound of shouting. She lay staring at the ceiling, listening to the endless rain still beating down outside, then alerted by a sudden unexplained tremor of fear she got up and ran to the window. In the faint light she could see the stream spilling over its banks into the garden and car park, glittering across the lower fields. In the distance she could see several men working in the mud, piling sandbags, trying desperately to hold the water back from the greenhouses and the terraces. Frozen with horror she stared. One man was directing the others and with a moment's anguish she thought it was her father, his boots, his tattered raincoat, even his old hat which had still hung downstairs in the hall. Then she realized that it was Stephen.

Throwing on her clothes she ran downstairs, grabbing her own boots, her own raincoat and running outside into the rain.

He had heard the urgent shouts of the men while she had slept, it seemed and had let himself out into the dawn, sizing up the situation and taking charge, in Philip's absence, of the rescue operations. The taut lines had vanished from his face. The restraint had gone. Suddenly she could see the man behind the image she had always known.

By mid-day the level of the water began to fall back. It had come to within an inch of the top of the bank near the greenhouses.

Philip returned at half past twelve, leaping from his Land-Rover and running across the bridge to the shop. Helen smiled at him wearily. 'It's going down, Phil. We seem to have escaped the worst of it.'

He gave a grim smile. 'If we have then we're the exception. There's been bad flooding down the valley. I came back as soon as I heard, but the road is impassable in places. I had to go round – ' He broke off suddenly, staring out of the window. 'Who's that?'

Helen did not have to look. 'Stephen Spencer. A friend of mine from London. He arrived at just the right moment.'

Philip gave her a sharp glance. Then he was striding out of the door. Helen stared at the ground. The sunlight had broken through the clouds suddenly and struck blinding reflections from the wet ground where he had been standing.

His coat over the back of the old chair, the sleeves of his guernsey rolled up to the elbow, Stephen was sketching a map of the property at the work bench among the trowels and dibbers and the old pots of twisted thyme when Helen brought in the tray of coffee and sandwiches. Philip, with a couple of the men, was peering over his shoulder.

'Raise the bank here, and here,' he was saying, the pencil stump clutched between the mud-caked fingers, 'and take a bit out of the corner here, to allow for a faster water flow and you'll be safe in future. See?' He glanced up at Philip, who nodded thoughtfully.

Helen slid the tray in front of them. 'Since when have you been an expert on water engineering?' she asked softly.

It was Philip who answered, glancing up at her with the wistfulness of a man who knows he has already lost. 'I'll bet he has talents you never even suspected,' he said.

Helen laughed. 'I'm beginning to think he has,' she agreed. She held his gaze for a moment and then she looked away, blushing. It was obvious he knew and, somehow, she thought he understood.

It was Stephen who walked with her that evening as the sun set in a blaze of stormy red.

He did not speak. For a while he watched with her the bats flitting out of the darkness, then he turned and took her in his arms. There was no hesitation this time; no reserve as he brought his face close to hers. For a long time they were silent, clinging to each other, in the dark. Then softly he spoke.

'I was a fool in London,' he said, 'and I almost didn't find out in time.'

Party Games

'I often think,' someone was saying in the strident tone of a person who wishes their opinions to be heard, 'that James is a perfect fool to continue having these parties. They are so deathly boring.'

With pre-judged malice the owner of the voice leaned across and tapped her – it had to be a her – cigarette on the arm of one of James's more beautiful bronze nudes. The ash fragmented into the crook of the curved elbow and lay dusty.

Had she not seen me, this malicious woman, or was she deliberately trying to provoke me into defending my brother? Perhaps she didn't care, or more likely, didn't know me. Why should she?

'Meet my beautiful sister, Laura,' James had said to the first few guests to arrive. They had looked, smiled, accepted their drinks – and turned away. Soon James had grown bored with introducing me. I was obviously no ace to palm before this glittering troupe. As they moved slowly round his studio, delicately touching this, ostensibly averting their eyes from that, James turned to watch them, anxious, frowning behind the eyes, although his outward manner too was arrogant.

'For God's sake put some fig leaves on some of those figures, James,' I had said at dinner, still confident then, still excited.

He laughed and ruffled my hair. 'This is London, sweetheart; you don't have to pretend men don't have balls here.'

I blushed. I was mortified, angry and embarrassed. Was I then so provincial?

The studio was hot and crowded now and smelt of perfume and, strangely from the so glitteringly arrayed, of sweat. Smoke and drink fumes mingled and spiralled towards the high skylight windows. The gentle murmur of conversation had grown to a steady roar as story competed with story, joke capped joke.

'Smile, Laura; who's going to want to talk to you if you look so miserable all the time?' I could hear my mother's words echoing down through the years. She had said that to me sometime at nearly every children's party I had attended. And she would have said it at every teenage party too had she not then been left at home.

Her advice made no difference. Other people seem to acquire some strange charisma at parties which I cannot find. Parties leave me cold, claustrophobic and embarrassed, both for myself and for those I see around me. I am too detached and with the best will in the world, even with a serious attempt to get drunk, cannot lose that detachment.

I dangled my glass, empty already, from nervous fingers and watched the owner of the malicious voice as she circulated out of earshot. She was very beautiful: hair, jewellery expensive and tasteful, her dress a masterly combination of chic and casual. I envied her. Almost. Why, though, I thought sadly, does she accept James's invitations if she despises him so much? I wondered if James knew how she really felt. Perhaps it was a game they played: he asked her, although he knew she didn't want to come, hoping she wouldn't; hoping she would: I didn't know which. And she came, afraid perhaps to miss out on a Social Occasion, or knowing that James didn't want her there; or knowing he did. I sat down, thoughtful.

There were several chairs in the studio and they were all empty but mine. No one dared to sit; if they did that they might miss something. Or they might see themselves as I saw them, dispassionately; packed, noisy and rather silly.

I decided to play a game. I would pinpoint the best-looking man in the room and follow him with my eyes until he turned and saw me. If I could entice him towards my chair I would buy myself a present tomorrow; if I couldn't I would offer to wash the glasses after the last guest had gone. It was a daring game for me; a London game.

I sat up and began to survey the room.

'Hey; would you just move your chair a bit, gorgeous? You're right in the way there.'

Instead of retaining my cool and telling him to go to hell I leaped to my feet guiltily. Gorgeous indeed! The tall, handsome noble lord had not even looked at my face. He and I had been introduced. I remembered the purple satin of his shirt. I watched as he moved away, conscious only of the décolletée blonde at his side. As far as he was concerned I was just another statue.

Start the game again.

I looked around carefully, determined not to be shifted or put off again. It was strange that there should be so unattractive a selection of men present. Or was I suffering from sour grapes because none of them were mine? I tried again, leaning a little to get a better view of the far side of the studio.

'It's Laura, isn't it?' Someone was standing over me again. At least this one knew my name. I peered up at his face.

He grinned. 'We met yesterday at Solti's preview, d'you remember?'

I did not. 'Really?' I borrowed my mother's most withering tone. One day I'll buy myself a lorgnette; that will, I am sure, keep the whole world at bay. The young man looked suitably crestfallen and I was immediately repentant. 'I am sorry,' I said. 'I'm hopeless at names.' I shrugged, hoping he would forgive the commonplace insult which we all hand out so often.

Amazingly he seemed to, as people do, anxious to give a second chance.

'I'm John Divers,' he commented modestly. I should have been immediately on my guard, but I was past caring. 'Good,' I said. 'Please could you get me another drink?' I handed him my long-empty glass.

I watched him push his way through the people, purposefully elbowing them aside with an enviable offhandedness. I saw Madame Malicious totter slightly to his thrust and felt myself grinning. I hoped he would come back.

'You look a bit happier at last,' James was momentarily above me, hovering, anxious. 'For God's sake circulate, Laura. A fine hostess you've turned out to be.'

Hostess! It was the first I'd heard of it. To have heard James curse when I arrived on Thursday with my suitcase you would have thought I was the last person on God's earth he would have allowed to act as his hostess.

'Where did you dig up all these dreary people from Jimmy?' I asked a little too loudly. I was beginning to sound like *her*.

He shushed me, looking, scandalized, over his shoulder. 'Someone'll hear. You've had too much to drink.'

'I haven't. I've only had one glass and now I've lost that.' It's true I was acting a little drunk and it wasn't entirely deliberate. Perhaps some strange defence mechanism had come into play to give me courage or comfort.

'Well, for God's sake keep your voice down,' James hissed and he had gone.

I was stung by the injustice of that, as I had scarcely spoken a word all evening, but I was still enough in awe of big brother James to feel chastened and subside, miserable again, onto my chair.

To my amazement John Divers reappeared with my glass. 'You don't happen to know who that ravishing dark girl over there is, do you?' He leaned down confidentially, close to my ear. So that was it. The inevitable bucket of cold water.

'I gather she's a handful,' I murmured sweetly, sipping my wine. 'A nympho; I shouldn't try your chances there unless you're pretty hot stuff.' It wasn't true of course; I had no idea who the poor girl was.

The room was becoming unbearably hot; the pale chiffon of my dress clung to me uncomfortably. I wanted to pick the skirts up round my thighs, rid myself of the horrible cloying tights and kick my shoes up towards the smoky glass skylights. High above them the summer sky was at last growing dark. For a wild moment I contemplated actually doing it. I would have to jump on a table of course; such dramatic gestures could not be practised in a dark corner, or discreetly behind a marble nude.

What were the chances of getting away with it? Tights are not a garment one can strip off gracefully. One is too liable to fall flat on one's face.

I should have taken James's advice. 'Don't bother with tights and don't wear a bra with that dress,' he had said coming in, to my acute embarrassment, as I was dressing. 'Don't be silly, Laura. I am your brother, so you needn't cover up your tits. Don't be such a prude. Nude women are my job.' And when reluctantly I took away my hands he had been quite approving. 'I must get you to sit for me while you're here.'

But in spite of his ridicule I had insisted on my bra and tights.

I compromised now by kicking off my sandals and closing my eyes for a minute, allowing the party to revolve around me.

'You know, he's really quite talented.' Strange how words sort themselves out and emerge from the general babble when your eyes are shut. 'I think James is a fool to allow all these people into his studio. They might damage his stuff.'

'And they're not really interested in him as a sculptor, you can tell.' Another voice.

So I had two sympathizers in the room. I opened my eyes and looked around but in the tide of coming and going the owners of the voices were lost. I picked up my sandals and walked slowly across the floor.

People were sitting on the spiral stair which led up to the small gallery bedroom, with its curtain wall. I thought of the quiet oasis I would find up there among the coats and climbed purposefully upwards.

I had drawn back the curtain and was inside the little room before I realized there were people on the bed. Two people. One of them was Sandra, my brother's lady. The other was not my brother. It was too late to withdraw; too late to pretend I hadn't seen; too late for them to hide. The three of us stared at one another in stark embarrassment for a moment and then Sandra began to pull the bedspread up around her shoulders. Her dress lay tangled on the floor at my feet.

'Don't tell James,' she said.

I backed away, drew the curtain again and went to sit with the others for a moment on the spiral stair, resting my head against the wrought iron newel post. Below me the party raged like a forest fire. Automatically my eyes sought out James. He was standing alone for a moment, watching. Perhaps he was watching for Sandra. I pulled myself wearily to my feet and made for the kitchen.

There too were people. Someone was bleeding profusely into the sink. 'Can I help?' I asked distantly, half of me still upstairs, an invisible, sick voyeur. Several pairs of eyes turned towards me.

'Do you think it's an artery?'

'He did it on a glass.'

'I hope James doesn't mind; there's blood all over the tea towel.'

They greeted me with relief, like children who, when the game has stopped being fun any more, turn for reassurance to the nearest adult. I knew at least where the plasters and antiseptic were because James had stuck a chisel into his thumb the night before.

'Apply pressure to the wound,' I directed, as he had done then, bringing out the first aid kit.

They obeyed.

'Sit down so I can fix it.'

He did.

It was really quite a bad cut. 'It might have to be stitched.' I recognized the purple shirt and felt foolishly even spitefully pleased. So his lordship had to recognize me in the end. 'You really ought to see a doctor, you know.' I glanced up and met his eye.

He grinned, his face a little pale. 'You're doing fine. Thanks awfully. Silly of me.' He laughed uncomfortably. 'Always get a bit nervous at do's like these.'

You too, I thought. I would never have guessed.

'Damion, darling, are you all right?' I was elbowed out of the way by a vision in frothy lace. But Damion was now concerned more with the spillage of his blood than with dalliance with his lady. 'Shut up, Sue. Let Laura get on with it. She's patching me up beautifully.' So he had even remembered my name.

The circle of admirers watching my every move with the antiseptic was still there, morbidly curious.

'Make some coffee, someone,' I directed without looking up. 'Damion could do with something hot.'

Amazingly I heard the kettle being filled. Then James was there, fussing and apologetic that one of his glasses should have perpetrated the damage. I left them to it.

Slowly the party thinned. I saw Sandra, dressed and hair immaculate, go to James and take his hand and stand on her toes to kiss his chin. For the first time that evening his face relaxed and he smiled. Then she looked across and saw me watching.

'I wondered if you'd come and have some dinner with me one day.'

I remembered his name this time: John.

'Thank you,' I said. 'It might be fun.'

My eyes still followed Sandra and James. He had his arm around her and was talking to her with pathetic eagerness. 'Yes, John, that would be nice.' I smiled at him, knowing I was second best, but still happy. I rather liked his face.

He grinned. 'You were right about the nympho lady,' he whispered confidentially. 'Much too hot for me to handle.'

'God, I do hate parties,' James said when the last guest had gone. He threw himself down on the studio couch and stretched his arms high above his head. Dawn was breaking and high above the skylights tiny puffs of pink-tinged cloud were floating in the blue-black of the sky. Cigarette smoke still drifted beneath the high ceiling; the smell of it clung everywhere.

'Why do you give them, then?'

He rubbed his eyes slowly and then looked hard at his knuckles. 'I often ask myself that.'

'Do you think anyone enjoys them much?'

He laughed. 'I sometimes wonder. I know I used to. But now . . .' He sighed.

'It's a sort of ritual, isn't it? Everyone comes, even when they don't want to; everyone pretends to enjoy themselves, even when they aren't; everyone talks to the people they'd rather never see again and miss the chance of meeting the people they want to see because no one remembers, or knows, to introduce them. Relationships are made or broken and next day no one can remember why.' I looked at him sadly.

'Perhaps I give lousy parties.' Wearily he bent to collect the glasses round his feet. 'Do I gather you didn't enjoy it?'

'It was another party.' I knelt to help him. 'Sandra didn't stay then?'

He shook his head. 'She often doesn't. She has to be at work early tomorrow, poor love. I'm surprised she stayed so long.'

'I expect she was enjoying herself.' I rose, my hands full of glasses and went through to the kitchen. The bloody tea towel still lay on the table; plasters, antiseptic, coffee cups heaped anyhow around it. In the sink the tap slowly dripped, etching more deeply the groove in the stained enamel.

'I'm glad you met Sandy tonight.' James came in behind me. 'Did you like her?'

'I hardly spoke to her.' I knew my voice sounded guarded but I couldn't help it.

'She's a super person, Laura; one of the best.'

'I shouldn't let yourself get too fond of her, Jimmy.' I spoke very quietly, gathering up the towel to rinse in the sink. 'I'm sure she's nice, but . . .'

'But what?' He flared up at once in her defence. 'You know your trouble, Laura. You're a cynic.' His hands shook as he pushed a trayful of glasses onto the table. 'You always look for the worst side of people. You never take them at face value.'

I watched the red stain flowing out into the running water and gurgling away down the sink. 'I'm sorry, Jimmy,' I said. I thought of Sandra's surprised face and tousled hair as she sat up from the arms of another man in James's own bed. 'I'm sorry. I suppose it's just the way I'm made.' I went and gave him a quick kiss on the cheek. 'Take no notice of me. You're right. I am a cynic and I'm afraid I always will be.'

I went slowly back into the studio and looked around. After all, for all I knew James was well aware of what Sandra was like. Whether he did or not I had to let it rest there. I could say no more to James about it.

I wandered over to the beautiful bronze nude and gazed at her serene expression. It was Sandra, of course. I should have recognized her. Gently I blew the cloying ash from the angle of her elbow and went to turn out the lights.

A Stranger With No Name

Sally paused to pick up another piece of driftwood and throw it into the bag she had dropped on the frozen sand nearby. Her back ached and her eyes were sore with the icy glare from the sea and for a minute she straightened and gazed back along the beach. Far away near the dunes she could just make out the distant figure of a man.

Her heart leaped. Forgetting the bag she ran a few steps towards him, pushing her hair out of her eyes as the persistent stinging wind blinded her momentarily, hiding him from her. Then she stopped and waited.

His was the first figure she had seen on the beach in three days, the first in fact since she had watched him walk away. It had to be him. She had known he would come back . . .

They had been walking along the edge of thc sea in the rain, watching the pock marks hammered by the shower into the heavy slate of the tide, picking among the seaweed for shells, slipping them, sandy and wet and cold into their pockets, staring out across towards the distant rocks where the smoothness of the sea humped itself into an uneasy swell. It was a lonely place, a place of solitary wheeling seabirds and infinite wind-torn skies, a place where one could dream and think; a place where one could feel free.

She had been happy and at peace, linking her arm through Oliver's, savouring the salty rain on her lips, the sting of the cold clean air on her cheeks and she had not guessed what he was thinking; there was no warning, no premonition, of the outburst which was suddenly upon her.

'I can't stand this any more, Sally! When are we going to stop coming to this dreadful place?' He had pulled away from her, his gesture angry and impatient. 'Don't you ever long for company and lights and sunshine?'

She stood for a moment unable to say a word, stunned into silence by her total surprise. Then reproachfully trying to refocus her thoughts, to understand what he was saying, she turned to him. 'I thought you loved it here.'

'I do.' He hurled a pebble at the water. 'It's just that sometimes I would rather go to other places; do other things. I feel trapped in this place . . .'

'I'm sorry. I didn't realize.'

She couldn't have said anything worse.

'No, that's your trouble. You don't realize. You think everyone else is the same as you. You don't bother to try and put yourself in their place. You adore it here, so everyone else must. You revel in introspection so you think it must be good for others too.'

'Oliver! That's not fair; you said you liked it here. You said you loved the quiet . . .'

'Well, I've changed my mind. So let's go! First thing tomorrow. Right?'

And then, as though at a signal, it started; the flying words, the recriminations which had led to the bitter analyses of their oh so short marriage, both of them saying things they didn't really mean, hurling the insults into the face of the rain.

At least Sally hadn't meant them . . .

When they regained the cottage at last Oliver had heaped the driftwood onto the fire till it blazed and ostentatiously made himself a bed on the sofa in front of it and Sally had crept into the cold bedroom alone.

The next morning she had been watching the cool early light slanting across the sands from the sea. She had leaned on her elbows and taken a deep breath of the salty air, watching the darting swooping flight of the terns as they skimmed the green water. They had not spoken since the night before.

Behind her Oliver was stirring the coffee in an old saucepan on the stove, filling the kitchen with the pungent bitter smell of it.

'Well, have you made up your mind? Are you coming?' His voice, coming out of the silence, had sounded politely casual. She could hear him picking the strainer off the draining board, carrying the saucepan to the table, pouring it into the two cups.

'I'm staying, Oliver.' She did not turn.

'OK. I'll leave you the car. I shall walk up the shore to the village and pick up a bus.'

'Fine.'

They might have been discussing their plans for any day of the holiday.

'Your coffee is on the table,' he said softly and she heard him pick up his own cup and walk away into the other room. Then, at the door he hesitated. 'I'm sorry, Sally.' His voice was slightly muffled. 'It's probably not your fault.' And the door closed behind him.

But she had not believed him. Her knuckles were white on the edge of the window and her eyes blurred with tears as she stared at the dancing terns and still she did not move or make any attempt to call him back. What had happened? What had gone wrong? Why should last night's row more than any other have led to this? Of course it was her fault. It had to be.

She had watched him later, striding up the beach until

he was a tiny speck in the distance. Then with a sick knot of misery tightening in her stomach she saw him turn up into the dunes and he was lost to sight.

She stayed on at the cottage on her own. At first she was sure he would come back and she waited for him, never going out of sight of the pretty white-washed building which had turned so swiftly for him from dream to prison, trailing disconsolately near the cold sea's edge, gathering driftwood for the fire, sketching the sunsets, the fingers which held her pencils numb with cold, uncertain what to do. She could not go home. Without him it would not be home – and her only certainty was that he would not have gone back there either.

They had chosen the Victorian cottage of their dreams the day he had asked her to marry him, walking down the street arm in arm, pointing at the terrace of little houses, deciding without argument that they would choose the one with the white front door. When days later they had seen the agent's board go up it had seemed like a special omen and Oliver had bought the cottage, selling without hesitation the flat he had owned for fifteen years. Half his furniture had had to be sold too and some of his books, to fit into so small a house, but they were happy and in love and he did not seem to care.

And when she told him of the sea where she had gone so often as a child he had agreed to come, loving her shy eagerness and he had said he liked the empty shore, liked it enough to come again when the November gales were lashing the coast and they had huddled together before a fire of wood which he had chopped all afternoon and they had laughed and planned. And one of their plans had been to come again. And now it had all gone wrong as if he had awakened from his dream and, looking round, had hated what he found.

And yet he had come back.

After a few minutes watching she began to run again, afraid he might stop and turn or, like a mirage on the sand, shimmer and dissolve as though he had never been.

There were only the two of them on the whole beach. It was too far from the village to encourage trippers, even in the summer and the fishermen kept away except for the occasional boy digging for worms. She ran a few steps more and then she stopped uncertainly trying to get her breath, her hands defenceless at her sides, her shoulders stooped with disappointment. It was not Oliver at all.

He came on at the same steady pace; tall – taller than Oliver and much younger, nearer her own age perhaps; his blond hair longish and windblown, his jeans bleached white by the sea, rolled to the knees.

'Hi,' he said when they were close enough to speak.

'I'm sorry.' In her confusion she was staring at him angrily. 'I thought you were my husband.'

'I'm sorry to disappoint you.' He bowed gravely, giving a strange old-world courtesy to the otherwise obvious reply.

'You didn't pass him, I suppose?' she was floundering now, trying to conceal her embarrassment. 'I was expecting him back any moment.' Why was she so uneasy in the face of his politely distant manner?

'I'm afraid the beach was deserted.' He resumed his walk slowly and she found herself turning to walk beside him. In the distance the tide was licking gently round her bag, nudging the pieces of driftwood, teasing them free of the canvas.

She gave an exclamation of annoyance as she noticed

and he saw too, following her gaze. 'I'll get it,' he called and before she could protest he had broken into a loping run, splashing carelessly into the ice cold water and scooping up the precious fuel.

He was laughing when she came up to him. 'Making a camp fire?'

She felt herself blush. 'No. It's for the cottage. There's a load of logs in the shed but I can't chop them so I'm stuck with driftwood.'

He looked at her gravely, the wet bag in his outstretched hand. 'Does your husband not chop wood?'

She bit her lip. 'He . . . he forgot to do it before he went. He had to go away for a couple of days, but he's due back anytime . . .' her voice trailed away.

He nodded, glancing at the white-washed cottage set back against the grassy dune. 'I'll come up and chop some for you if you like.'

'Oh but I couldn't let you.'

'For the price of a meal?' Again the easy grin.

And suddenly she found she didn't want to refuse. She was sick of her own company, sick of collecting firewood, sick of the smoky damp flame it gave in the lonely little room while she went over all the things that had gone wrong, the mistakes she must have made, the disappointments he must have known during the short time of their marriage; as she wondered what had happened to the wonderful closeness she and Oliver had shared in the first few carefree weeks. How could it so suddenly have turned to such bitterness? Whatever it was that had happened she did not want to think about it any more. Not for a while. For a while she would let herself forget if she could.

She found she was grinning back at the young man. 'OK. It's a deal.' And she turned up the beach and led the way.

Throwing down the bag on the doorstep he went

straight to the wood shed heaving out the heavy logs and reaching for the axe. She stood for a moment in the doorway watching as he lifted it high above his head and brought it down with a crash onto the first up-ended log, splitting it cleanly and evenly with one blow and then she went into the cottage.

She threw open the kitchen window and reached into the cupboard to see what she could find. She had not bothered to walk up to the village store for food; she had not been hungry. But she found eggs and suddenly she found she was looking forward to cooking again. She reached for the heavy iron skillet which hung on the wall above the cooker and began her preparations to the steady sound of chopping outside. By the time the food was ready he had laid her fire and filled the log basket and there was a neat stack of wood piled in the woodshed.

She could hear him whistling merrily as he washed in the little lean-to bathroom and then he was at the table, his tall frame dwarfing the room. The omelette was succulent and rich, full of herbs and she saw his look of appreciation as he took his first mouthful.

He raised his glass. 'To the cook. My compliments.'

She acknowledged the gesture with a grave nod. 'Thank you, sir.'

'Your husband is mad to go away, even for two days with food like this at home.'

He meant it gallantly, making conversation, but her mood was too fragile to cope with the pretence any longer. She stared hard at her plate.

'I don't think he's coming back,' she said quietly. 'He's left me.' It was the first time she had really admitted it even to herself.

He stared. 'Why?' he asked quietly.

She shrugged. 'So many reasons. So few. I don't understand. We were happy I thought . . .'

Glancing up he saw that she had laid down her fork and was biting her lip.

He frowned, staring at the top of her head, at the curtain of honey blonde hair and the golden slightly freckled complexion. Her knuckles were white beneath the taut skin of her hands clenched on the edge of the table top.

'How long have you been married?'

'Only a few months.' Her voice was a whisper. She glanced up. Her lips were smiling but her lashes were salty wet. 'Sorry. Ignore me. Women get so emotional.'

'So do men,' he said, very quietly. He put his hand lightly over hers. 'Tell me about him.'

'He's older than me, you see. A lot older. He's tall and fair, a bit like you, but his eyes are grey and he's older . . .' She was looking past him out of the window of the small low-ceilinged room. It was very quiet suddenly. He had not moved his hand. 'He had never married before. A lot of women wanted him, but he was so independent, so free . . . He didn't want to be tied down.'

'Until you came along.'

She looked directly at him for the first time. 'Until I came along. But why? Why me?'

'You're very beautiful.'

She seemed to be considering for a moment. The colour rose imperceptibly in her cheeks and she gave a faint smile. Almost reluctantly she slid her fingers out from beneath his.

'That would not matter to Oliver. I think he believed I was deeper than I was – someone else, some dream he had conceived of the ideal woman. Perhaps he thought he could mould me to be her. But he found he couldn't do it. And it's my fault.' She pushed back her chair and stood up abruptly. 'I'm sorry. Your omelette is getting cold.'

'It's fine.' Picking up his fork he grinned, his blue eyes

sympathetic and gentle. 'Can you make coffee as well as you cook?'

She grimaced ruefully gathering up her own plate, the food untouched. 'Oliver always made the coffee.'

'Then let me. I'm good at coffee. It's man's work.'

She watched him as he ate and stood aside unprotesting when he waved her away from the sink to rinse the plates and fill the kettle. He made the coffee in a jug and they carried their cups outside into the frosty sunshine and stood looking at the water as it lapped gently up the beach.

'I'm sure you're not right to blame yourself alone, you know,' he said tentatively after a long silence. 'If he really did want to change you he must have been mad, but I doubt if that was it. Not really. How long did he know you before you were married?'

'Two years.' She did not resent his interest. It was a relief to talk.

'Then he must have known you as you really are. I wonder . . .' he paused for a moment. 'I wonder if it was himself he was running from? People do you know. Sometimes. I did myself once.' He stared thoughtfully out towards the rocks.

'But why? Why should he want to run at all? I don't understand.' A little of her anguish escaped the tight grip of her self control. It deepened and matured her voice.

He turned and looked at her. She was totally self absorbed. She had not noticed the wistful longing in his voice as he remembered for an instant his own pain; the problems he had faced when he had lost the one person in the world whom he had loved. She was overwhelmed with her own desolation. He felt a quick rush of pity. Suddenly he wanted to touch her, to comfort her and reassure her and show her she was not to blame, but resolutely he kept his fingers linked around his cup. The steam from the coffee was white in the crisp air.

'You can only ever be yourself,' he said gently. 'Anything else would be a betrayal of him as well as yourself. Always remember that.'

'I know.' It was a whisper. 'He asked me to go with him and I refused. I couldn't do it. Not like that.'

'Then you did right.' He bent and picked up a fluted sandy shell, hurling it towards the rippling tide. They both stared at the place where it had disappeared. A streak of red weed hung and breathed back and forth below the curve of the beach. It could have been blood on the surface of the sea. She gave an involuntary little shiver.

'When did he go?' He was watching the tiny gold hairs on the back of her wrists stir and rise and he thought it was the icy wind which combed the grasses behind them in the dunes which made her shiver.

'Three days ago.'

'What would you do if he didn't come back?' he said gently.

He thought she hadn't heard and glanced sideways at her face. It was bleak.

'I'll wait for him.'

'You can't wait for ever. Won't you go home?'

She shrugged. 'For ever is a long time, I suppose. Perhaps when the storms come, then I'll go. I don't know.' She gave a wan smile. 'Perhaps he won't be that long.'

He found himself staring at her. The smile had transformed her face. Instead of a cold shuttered prettiness she had for a second betrayed a shadow of vibrant beauty. Then the sadness returned.

He had to bite his lip to force himself to keep from reaching out to take her in his arms to comfort her, to stop him from begging her to forget this treatment and lose herself instead in him. He swallowed hard, staring into the depths of the empty cup in his hand. After all, he was a stranger; she had not even told him her name. He had come here to forget his own unhappiness not become involved in that of another.

'It won't be long,' he said with resolution. 'Take my word. He'll be back.'

'Do you think so?' Her eyes were full of hope. She set her cup in the sand and stood up again, staring along the beach as though she expected to see Oliver that moment, striding towards her.

'I think so. After all, you are here for him to come back to.' He looked away from her sadly. When he had gone back his love had gone. She had not waited as this girl was waiting. She had left him without compunction, or so it seemed to him.

He followed Sally slowly to the sea's edge where the cold white dribbles of water nudged at the heaps of stranded weed; her narrow shoulders were taut beneath her heavy guernsey and there was pathos in the angle of her neck.

Without knowing he did it he slowly shook his head. He had to leave her now. If he did not go now, then he would never go.

He held out his hand to her and unquestioning she took it. For a moment more they stood in silence. Then he let her fingers drop.

'Time's getting on.' He said it very gently.

She seemed to understand. 'Of course. Thank you for chopping the wood.'

'Thank you for cooking me the omelette.'

He turned away towards the village and took a few paces along the tide line. Then he stopped and looked back. She had not moved.

'You'll be all right?'

'Of course.'

'Is there anything else I can do?'

'Nothing. Thank you.'

'You're sure?'

There were tears on her cheeks as the cold wind blew her hair across her eyes. She did not look at him.

He stood for a moment undecided and then he was beside her again and his hands were on her shoulders. Gently he turned her to face him and he pulled her close. Her skin tasted of salt. He kissed her cheeks, her eyelids, her hair and then last of all her lips. They parted a little without protest and they were soft. But they were cold. For a moment he did not move, feeling the comfort of her presence within the circle of his protecting arms, knowing that somehow he was comforting her, then sadly he pushed her away. He began to walk without a word. And this time he did not look back.

She stood at the edge of the tide watching as slowly the leading ripples hesitated and lost their purpose and drew back, leaving the sand wet and clean and smooth. Only then did she turn and look into the distance. He had gone long since, just as Oliver had gone, along the beach towards the village out of sight. It was as though he had never been but there was deep inside her a small new warmth.

Slowly she wandered back to the cottage and hardly knowing that she did it she went round to the little lean-to woodshed and glanced in. The neatly stacked pile of split logs was real enough, as was the axe, newly-honed and in its place. Weakly she leaned against the wall and closed her eyes and thought about the stranger.

Much later as the moon was rising silver over the frosted dunes she lit the fire and watched the cheerful clear crackle of the logs in the hearth. She made some coffee as he had in a jug and then leaving it on the table she pushed open the door. The tide had gone out so far it was only a sliver of light on the shining moonlit sand and she ran down towards it feeling the cold bite of the wind in her face.

Strangely she was happy, her doubts and miseries resolved into a quiet confidence and resignation and the knowledge that Oliver would return and that when he did, however long it took, she would be there waiting for him.

She stood for a long time at the water's edge watching the trail of moonshine in the tide and then she glanced along the beach towards the village. For a moment she held her breath. She thought she could see a figure striding out of the dunes. She stared and then she started to run; then she stopped. It was too far away to see – perhaps it was just the shadow of a cloud thrown on the rippled sand. Her heart was beating fast as she waited, her shoes sinking into the softness of the wet silver at her feet. And then she saw the brightness of his hair and the tall, easy stride, and she began to smile. This time it was, it had to be, Oliver.

'You waited for me to come back?' he said as he came up to her and put his hands on her shoulder. His face was pale and strained in the moonlight.

'I waited.' She smiled up at him.

'I'm sorry I went away. I didn't mean to hurt you but I had to think. I had to be alone.'

'Is everything all right now?'

'Everything.' He kissed her lightly on the forehead. 'It wasn't your fault, you know.'

'I know,' she said quietly.

Hand in hand they walked back to the cottage and he sat down beside the fire and she brought him the coffee and watched him while he sipped it. She never mentioned the stranger who had chopped the wood and taken her so briefly in his arms. It did not seem important.

Just An Old-Fashioned Girl

It had happened the night before. She had worked late and was tired after the long walk back through the cold rain-washed streets. Neal had been home before her, letting himself in with his key, lighting the gas fire, straightening the room with, she was sure, a look of mild reproach.

Guiltily she had dropped her two heavy sodden shopping bags on the carpet and fumbled for the wet knot of her belt.

'I didn't expect you back so early tonight. I haven't had a chance to tidy up.'

He grinned. 'I've done most of it for you.' The room certainly looked very nice. There was a pot of nearly-hatched hyacinths on the table which hadn't been there that morning. Obscurely she felt irritated.

'Well, I've still got to get the meal and do something with my hair!'

But he shook his head. 'No need. I've booked us a table at the Captain's Bistro and your hair – ' he took a step towards her and taking a lank wet strand of it in his hand gave it a gentle tug, 'will look fabulous once you've had a drink.'

And that was how it so often was. She, agitated, late, scatty; he always calm, organized – and punctual, soothing her ruffled feathers and her ruffled ego. And she had, she decided, always found it irritating. It made her want to stamp her foot like a spoilt child, instead of receiving his influence with the gracious calm a woman of her age should accord it.

And as always, he was right. Her hair piled on top of her head, swathed in a soft towel, an inelegant tumbler of sherry on the edge of the bath at her shoulder, she lay back in water liberally sprinkled with Boot's best and she could feel the tight spring inside her beginning to uncoil and the weight of her day at the library slipping from her shoulders.

She put on a simple dress that night and twisted her hair up into an exotic confection of clips and stars. By the time they had walked back down the cold High Street the wind had pulled most of it down, but the effect, even dishevelled was, she knew, attractive to Neal.

Just as some men were supposed to be bosom men and some bottom men, Neal was a hair man, making almost a fetish of it, burying his face in it, holding the weight of it in his hands, winding it gently round her throat till it formed a silken glowing collar.

The bistro was half empty as they forced their way in out of the gale, the night lights on the tables flickering and dipping in unison as the door closed behind them on the evening darkness.

Captain Ferguson was there to usher them in, to take their coats, to bring the menus and then at last they were alone, facing one another across the table, the small clear flame between them.

'Have you decided yet, Emma?' Neal's eyes were steady on her face, his voice low. Neither of them had opened their menu and she knew he wasn't talking about the food.

'Give me a little more time, Neal, please. There is so much to think about.

He scowled. 'There is nothing to think about. Either

we get married, or we go on as we are. Surely that's not such a difficult question!'

But it was. Surely he could see it was.

They had lived together on and off for five years, sometimes as now, sharing her flat; sometimes camping in his, sometimes apart for months on end when his job as an engineer took him away, but always returning in the end to one another.

Of course she had wanted marriage once. All young women dreamed of marriage didn't they, even in this age of emancipation? Surely the most hardened female libber had the occasional aberration and pictured herself in a swirl of white and orange blossom, but that had passed.

As she moved on into her late twenties life became real, and dreams were tempered with, not bitterness exactly, but resignation and, she supposed, maturity. Neal was part of that maturity.

They had met in the library where she worked now as head librarian. She had been an assistant then, when he had come in searching for some esoteric books on early music – his passion – and a friendship had developed.

Within three months there was more than that. They were living together and within six she knew Neal was thinking of marriage. Then it had been too soon to talk of it, but afterwards she realized there was more to her reluctance than that. She valued so much her independence; she valued her privacy.

Somehow she had evaded the issue for a long time, but lately Neal was becoming more persistent, hinting darkly that they would soon be too old to start a family . . .

Marriage or stay as they were was the choice he had offered, but there was always a third possibility. One he hadn't mentioned. That they part.

She swallowed, staring hard at the candle behind which his face had become a hazy blur. The thought of parting had sprung unbidden into her mind without warning; it was the last thing she wanted; the last thing in the world.

'Would you like to order now, sir?' The waiter's voice cut through her thoughts and she looked up. Neal was watching her across the candle. Visibly he pulled himself together, dragging his eyes from her face to that of the waiter.

'We'll both have steak.'

'No!' Rebellion flared again as the waiter raised his pad to write. 'No, I'll have the chicken.'

Neal shrugged. 'White wine then?' he queried, this time hesitant and, knowing that he preferred red, she nodded.

Neither of them spoke until the waiter had disappeared.

'All right, go on, say it. I'm a cow!' Guilt made her angrier.

He shrugged. 'If you say so.' Then suddenly he grinned. 'You're trying to be, anyway. Why Emma? What's wrong? I'm not the enemy, you know.'

'I know.' Crossly she reached for a piece of bread from the basket and began to break it up.

And then it had happened. Her hair, still precariously coiled had begun to slip and Neal, leaning forward, had hooked his finger into one of the long heavy tresses. Gently he pulled. 'You're going grey, Emma,' he said.

Later outside in the beating sleet she walked head up, her coat blowing open, alone. She followed the High Street winding down between the houses and turned across towards the quay. The light outside the harbourmaster's office burned solitarily through the streaks of wetness, reflecting in a shivery rippled line in the water at her feet. For a long time she looked down, then stiff and frozen she turned and slowly walked home.

When she got there all Neal's things had gone. He must have left the restaurant almost immediately after her and loaded his car without a second's thought. Head high, eyes blazing in her wind-pinked face, she stared at herself in the mirror. Then reluctantly she reached for her brush. At nine o'clock the next morning she was at the hair salon.

She met Chris four days later. He was in his forties, divorced, tall like Neal but very fair and broad shouldered and though he was outwardly quiet he had a tough rough streak in him that appealed to the Emma in her which had emerged as her hair fell to the salon floor. He took her tramping over the moors and, with feet and hands aching with cold, to watch rugger matches and once or twice to a point to point where she backed a horse and won herself five pounds.

Her flat without Neal was untidy now, defiantly untidy and she had put away one by one the things he had particularly loved. One especially, the patchwork quilt so lovingly worked by her great grandmother out of minute squares of coloured silk. Even Chris had admired it, but it did not suit her new image of herself: cool, sophisticated, modern and ageless.

Instead she bought a black satin bedspread by mail order and secretly, for sewing too was for the birds, she appliquéd on it a huge scarlet 'EM'. She almost wished when she had finished it that Neal could see it. She wanted to watch his reactions.

'Come on, Em. Let me stay.' Chris had his arm around her shoulders, his right hand firmly anchored over her right breast. She squirmed uncomfortably.

'Chris, I've told you. I'm not ready. Not yet.'

'And how long does it take for you to be ready?'

She smiled and edged a little further away from him

on the sofa. 'Not long, I promise. Come on, have some more coffee. Then you will have to go. I must get to the library early tomorrow.

He was frowning this time as he stood up and she knew that he would not take her excuses much longer. Either sleep with him or break up with him. Chris would not waste time on a relationship that was going nowhere.

She ran her fingers through her hair, exasperated, after he had gone. Why did men always want something more? Why when there was so much to a relationship besides sex did they reduce everything to that one denominator and threaten so much else that was good?

Of course she knew her reaction meant she did not love him. How could she love him when at night, alone, shivering beneath her black and scarlet satin, her thoughts always came back to Neal. Neal who was gentle. Neal who was strong and understanding and patient with her.

Next morning she rang Chris from her tiny private office behind the book stacks. 'Chris. Tonight. Come to my place for a meal. We won't go out anywhere, OK?'

'You mean it, Em?' From his voice she knew he understood.

'I mean it, Chris.' She stared down at the phone for several minutes without seeing it after she had hung up. Then, with a shrug she turned back to her desk.

Chris went to considerable trouble with his appearance that evening. And on his way to her he stopped off at the florist and bought, for a small fortune, one single hot house rose. Somehow it seemed right for Em.

For her part she had bought two bottles of red wine. Only one bottle, all to herself, would bring her to it and if Chris wasn't going to drive home that night he might as well have one too.

Rain was lashing the windows as she pulled the curtains closed and turned up the gas fire, listening for a moment to the reassuring purr as the flame licked across the cold elements. She laid two places at the low coffee table before it and set the two cushions in place. Then she searched out a record to match her mood.

The bedroom was perfect. Small, intimate, the huge scarlet letters writhing across the swell of the pillows. The room had none of the warmth and love which Neal had known but then, she swore at herself sharply, it wasn't Neal she was expecting.

She was in the kitchen when the bell rang, a wooden spoon in her hand, dabbing ineffectually at a creamy mushroom sauce which was sitting on the cold burner waiting only to be poured over the chicken and put into the oven. Her bottle of wine was already a third empty.

She stared at Chris, her stomach suddenly contorting into a cramp of apprehension as he stood in the doorway, his hands behind him. He looked different, strange; scrubbed and almost shy, like a schoolboy on his first date as reluctantly, even awkwardly, he produced the rose. 'Do you want to stick this thing in some water?'

She took it, more embarrassed than he was, ridiculously touched at the gesture and fumbled in a kitchen cupboard for a tall glass to hold it while he stood in the doorway behind her watching. Then, all at once, they were laughing. The strain had vanished. They were no longer circling teenagers, awkward because of the contrived situation. They were adults again. He poured himself a tumbler of the wine and hauling himself up onto the worktop he sat and watched as she anointed the chicken with her sauce and put the dish into the oven.

They ate, they talked, they sat lounging on the cushions before the gas fire listening to records which almost but not quite drowned the sound of hailstones lashing against the windows under the heavy curtains. Chris made no move to touch her, watching her from time to time from beneath his heavy brows as she talked and laughed, her face a little flushed from the fire.

She was, he thought, more beautiful and more vivacious than he had ever seen her but quite unlike herself. Surely she knew that he had guessed she was playing a part, wearing a pretty social mask. He had realized from the moment he set foot through the door that he would never sleep with her now.

The little clock on the mantelpiece ticked round to one o'clock and she was still talking hard into every silence when at last Chris leaned forward and put his hand on her wrist. She stopped, electrified by his touch.

'It's late, Emma,' he said gently. 'We've both got to work in the morning.'

She nodded and clutching the coffee table to steady herself she stood up.

'I'll make some more coffee, shall I, before . . . ?' Her voice trailed away.

'Before I go. Yes, please, Em. I've drunk a bit more than I should.' He smiled. In fact he was stone cold sober. It was Emma who was a little tipsy.

'Oh but you can't go, Chris. I don't want you to. I want you to stay. Truly.' She waved vaguely towards the bedroom door.

He put his hands on her shoulders and pulled her towards him, staring down at her. 'Thank you, Em. But no. I'm not blind. I can see how it is with you. I understand.'

After he had gone she sat down again in front of the fire and stared into the hot depths of the flames.

But how is it with me? she thought miserably. I just don't know.

*

She still saw Chris; they were too fond of one another to part, but their relationship had steadied into a warm friendship which contained no demands. She had never mentioned her past to him. He knew there must have been other men, but she was a creature of mystery, a strange old-fashioned type of person inspite of her efforts to be different and he respected her for it. He was even pleased with himself now for taking her the rose. It hadn't been such a silly gesture after all.

Neal saw her several hundred yards away, threading her way towards him up the crowded Saturday High Street, her duffle hood pulled forward around her face, her hands deep in her pockets, a basket hitched onto her elbow.

He stopped and stared at her for a moment, then he turned away towards the nearest shop to avoid her. In the doorway he stopped abruptly, his eye caught by his own reflection, by the acute misery he had surprised on his own face and he felt a surge of anger. Pride had kept him from her all these weeks, but now she was there a few hundred yards from him and he would stay away no longer. Swinging back into the thoroughfare he pushed his way through the crowds and caught her arm.

'We're going for a walk.'

Emma, dreaming, had not even seen him coming and she bit back a cry of surprise as she found herself being pulled round into the teeth of the wind, but after only a second's hesitation, she went.

Stormbound, the fishing fleet clustered into the shelter of the sea wall and down river the slate water blended with a slate sky heavy with unshed snow. Side by side they stood and stared down at the restless decks jostling against the quayside. Then slowly Emma raised her head and grinned at him.

'You know, I think I've missed you.'

'And I think I've missed you.' His eyes narrowed. Her hair whipped from beneath the hood and was flailing around her eyes. He raised his hands and pushed the hood back from her face.

She waited, defiant.

He shook his head. 'You cuckoo. Why?'

The gesture seemed so empty now. 'I wanted to change my image.'

He laughed. 'And have you?'

'Of course. Can't you tell?'

'Not yet. But then I haven't seen much of you. Come and have a coffee.'

Thankfully she followed him into the warmth of the coffee house near the church where they found a corner table and faced each other free of the blinding wind at last. He stared at her critically as she slipped back her duffle coat.

'You've lost weight, but so far you're the same Emma. Say something, then perhaps I can tell.'

She grinned. 'Pearls of wisdom fall from my lips these days. And I'm called Em.'

'Why not Fred, it's more feminine. To me you're Emma and always will be.' He sounded sterner than she had ever heard him, almost schoolmasterly, and she resisted the answering urge to stick her tongue out at him and chose instead a large Danish pastry from the trolley.

He watched amused. She was different. More confident perhaps; more mature; calmer and more ordered.

'I hear you've been going around with Chris Foster,' he said after a moment's silence.

She met his gaze squarely. 'For a couple of months or so now.'

'Serious?'

'Depends what you mean by serious.' She stared

beyond him towards the window where the snow was again feathering down; a sign, back to front on the glass read, *Order Your Valentine Cake Now* and there was a picture of a thick creamy chocolate heart. Suddenly her eyes were full of tears. She blinked them back angrily. Grown women do not cry in public at the sight of a piece of romantic tomfoolery aimed at teenage children.

She groped in her bag for a handkerchief and blew her nose hard, still not looking at him.

'Could he spare you one evening, do you think?' His voice sounded husky against the usual coffee house squawk of women.

Squaring her chin she looked at him at last. 'That's for me to say, not him.'

She chose a date a week away so as not to seem too eager and they met, impersonally, at a pub they had never visited together before.

But he had a present for her – a tiny silver pendant – very modern in design. Not once did he mention her hair.

She ached for him to touch her, but he was strangely distant and formal with her, meticulously polite. But for the pendant which grew slowly warm against her skin as she played with it nervously on its chain, they might have been strangers as they sat facing one another across the table, their hands a few inches apart. There was no candle between them, but she felt as though there might have been a hundred miles.

And then suddenly he pushed back his chair and relaxed and laughed. 'You know, Emma, you haven't changed one bit. You're still the same delightful old-fashioned girl at heart, for all the sculptured haircut and the space age dress! I'm glad. I wouldn't have you any different for anything.' And his hand reached out at last and covered hers.

She grinned, thinking suddenly of the black satin bedspread. The day she had met him again she had put back her patchwork quilt. The effect had been devastating. She felt calm and reassured; back home; undeniably herself once more. But perhaps it was too late. Perhaps Neal no longer wanted her. Perhaps after all she no longer wanted him.

'How can you tell I'm the same?' she asked him, her fingers lying easily in his.

'The way you talk, the way you sit. Even the way you do your hair.'

'But – '

'But it does suit you, you're right,' he went on critically, his head a little to one side, 'although of course it makes you look older . . .'

She had spotted the glint in his eye. 'I could grow it again if you really thought I should,' she said. 'But it would probably take fifteen years.'

He looked thoughtful. 'As long as that?' Then he was smiling again. 'OK. I'm prepared to wait. I'll hang around until it does. If you want me that is?'

It was what she had been hoping he would say and yet now she hesitated. 'I'm more changed than you think, Neal. It might not work, us being together again. I want it to, but . . .'

The grip of his fingers tightened for a moment. Then he released her hand. 'I won't push you, Emma. But think about it, won't you?' He smiled and picked up the menu. 'This was where things went wrong before and I'm not going to make the same mistake again. You ordered chicken and white wine, remember?'

She grinned. 'I'll promise you this much, Neal. If I walk

out on you this time I'll wait around long enough to pay my half of the bill, does that seem fair?'

His eyes met hers and held them. 'Very fair,' he said.

All This Childish Nonsense

Richard. I've done something dreadful. Pat looked in the mirror, screwed up her face and tried again. *Richard, darling, I've done something rather wonderful*. That didn't work either. Not at all. Better to say it straight out. *Richard, there's someone coming to stay. For two weeks.*

The mirror was steaming up. Her palms were growing sweaty. *Richard, I know I should have told you a long time ago, but I never plucked up the courage. Richard, I know you'll want to throw me out . . . but the child was alone and it is Christmas. Richard, please . . .*

'You've done what?' His voice was too quiet. Pat looked hard at the floor and explained again. This time it was easier. She just told him; straight.

'They'd have had to put her in care or something. Richard, she is a relation of mine, sort of. I couldn't say no, could I?' Could I? Just as when Sarah had said: 'I know you and your husband won't mind, just while I'm in hospital.' She hadn't dared say: 'He's not my husband.' She had looked hard at the wall, above the white radiator and the telephone receiver had hurt her ear it was so tightly pressed. 'He's not my husband, we're only living together. Something like this could ruin everything. He says I'm taking him for granted . . .'

'How old is this child anyway?' Richard's voice was still enigmatically cool.

'Six, I think.'

Richard stood up and threw down the paper. 'That's all I need; a child of six, in a flat this size! I don't want anyone else here upsetting things. We're fine as we are.'

He went to look out of the window. Pat could see his knuckles on the green and white print curtain. She winced, waiting for the rip. Those curtains had been her first bad mistake. Attractive, light, airy, hand-made. By her . . . 'I hope you're not going broody or something,' he'd muttered, instead of thank you. Then he had ignored them. And they did look so lovely once she'd tidied the room a bit.

Of course later, in bed, he had murmured in her ear, his voice so soft and dreamy she wondered if she had heard right: 'Those curtains make the room, Pat. It might be nice to have new ones in here, one day,' and she knew it was his way of saying sorry and thank you. His way; in the dark.

'She won't be any trouble, Richard. Her mother says she's a very quiet, obedient child. She's used to going to stay with people.'

'Good, so let her go and stay with them again.'

'It's difficult, Richard. It's Christmas.'

'All the more reason for them to have her.'

He went into the bedroom. She followed him, hovering. He went back into the living room. She followed again. She knew she was irritating him. She wanted to disappear. She felt sick.

'What shall I do?'

He had picked up his jacket. 'Do what you like, but don't expect me to entertain her if she comes here.' He was at the door and going; then for a moment he was back. 'And don't,' he said, his chin set in the way she knew so well, 'expect me to dress up as Father Christmas.'

In the morning Richard ate the breakfast she prepared

and went to work with a smile and a kiss. She liked that; like it must be with real married people. Neither of them mentioned the child. She wished suddenly she was going to work, too. It had seemed fun to finish a job the last week before Christmas, start another in the New Year; have those two or three weeks free.

Then Richard had said: 'I hope you're not going to waste money buying me presents, all that childish nonsense.'

'I like childish nonsense,' she had wanted to wail, but hadn't the courage. What if he despised her for it?

So the cards she sent had been secret, although she'd written, defiantly, 'from Pat and Richard' and the ones they received had been gloated over and loved and then reluctantly put in a drawer. She went cold suddenly. The child would expect a tree.

She gazed round the room. Nothing was ready. The spare bed was still folded behind the door.

When the time came to meet the train she was there at the barrier and her face was smiling, but inside she was terrified and resentful. Suppose Richard never came home again? Suppose he threw her out? Suppose the child was uncontrollable? Even delinquent?

She saw the child at the other end of the platform. With it was an adult, responsible for the length of the journey only, who exchanged names and addresses and vanished into the crowd, not seeing or guessing Pat's panic; leaving a suitcase and the little girl to Pat.

Pat licked her lips nervously and tried to smile. 'Hello, Annabel,' she said, experimenting.

The little girl had enormous blue story-book eyes and was solemn. 'Hello, Aunt Pat,' she said. 'My name is Bel.' She put her hand in Pat's and waited expectantly.

My God, thought Pat, what now?

Somehow they got home. The little girl was enchanted

to have a bed which wasn't ready and which folded up behind the door.

'It's like a horse,' she exclaimed and mounted it, pretending to ride. The floor began to shake and Pat bit her lip. She was thinking of Richard's reaction. *Please let him like her*, she prayed silently, *please*.

'I'm hungry,' said Bel and Pat looked at her watch. What do children eat for lunch? Not yoghurt, crispbread and cottage cheese, that was for sure. She had better ask.

'Chips,' came the reply. 'Chips and sausages and fishfingers and chocolate pudding. Where's your Christmas tree, Aunt Pat?'

Richard looked for a long time at the small green fir, wedged with newspapers into his wastepaper basket. The whole flat was full of the scent of resin and pine needles. It was fragrant and beautiful.

'Uncle Richard, Uncle Richard, will you help us decorate it?' The child was already in her nightie with furry-bunny slippers.

Pat peered furtively through the kitchen door. She was hiding; she admitted it. But surely the pretty child could manage Richard better than she could? She breathed a quick prayer as Richard set down his papers and slowly began to unbutton his jacket.

'You fraud!' she whispered in the kitchen later. 'You utter fraud. All that silver tinsel in your briefcase; and baubles! How did you know I'd buy a tree? How did you guess?'

He grinned. 'I knew,' he said.

They had to bring the TV and the table lamp and their books into the bedroom so that the child could sleep. Pat saw Richard frown and she cursed silently. She hadn't thought of that, as she hadn't thought of the pools of water cascading from the bath onto the floor, the piercing giggles and screams, the enthusiastic assault on Richard's typewriter, or the scribbles in his books. ('It's not scribbles, it's my bestest writing.')

Bel found Pat's photographs in a box and scattered them, delighted, on the carpet, making patterns. 'Look, look,' she squeaked. 'You – on a pony. What's he called, Aunt Pat?'

Pat looked. She had been about fifteen. 'Black Beauty?' she hazarded hopefully.

'But he's not black, Aunt Pat.'

He wouldn't be!

'Oh, look! Here's Uncle Richard.' The child held out another picture, her head a little to one side. 'I like Uncle Richard.'

So do I, thought Pat. Lots. She reached for the photo. It was of them both. He had his arm round her shoulder and was smiling down into her eyes in that gentle, intense way of his which she loved so much. It had been taken the summer she had first met him, two years before. Was it really two years?

'Why are you smiling, Aunt Pat?'

She had met him at a friend's party. Both had gone alone, both planning to leave early. They had left early, but no longer alone. From the moment they started talking Pat had realized that she could never be alone again. Not as long as Richard was any part of her life.

It had taken a long, long time, though, for Richard to ask, half diffident, if she would move in with him. Scarcely believing it, she had arrived, suitcase and pot plant in hand, before he could change his mind and, laughing, he had found a saucer for the plant. 'You've brought your family, I see,' he'd said.

The pot plant was still there, on the windowsill.

'What are we going to give Uncle Richard?' Bel asked, confidingly, on Christmas Eve.

How could Pat say 'nothing'?

So they went shopping together and bought him some aftershave and some socks and a paperback. Then Bel had a brainwave.

'I'll pretend to be Father Christmas.' She gave a high-pitched giggle. 'Won't that be a surprise for Uncle Richard? We'll hang up the stocking for him and when he's asleep I'll tiptoe in and fill it with presents like the real Father Christmas does for children.'

The real Father Christmas?

Well, Pat had thought of it. She had managed to keep a few small things hidden besides the little girl's present from her mother which Pat had found tucked in the suitcase. But what would Richard say? Pat licked her lips nervously. *All this childish nonsense*. But there was a child.

Pat and Bel listened to carols on the radio while they made a Christmas cake. Not a rotten old cake, with currants and things in ('Yuk,' said Bel), but a chocolate sponge with thick squidgy icing. Pat hadn't made a cake before.

'My mummy doesn't need a book,' said Bel with peals of laughter. 'Books don't tell you how to make cakes.'

They'd better, thought Pat . . .

The amazing thing was, she found she was to have a stocking as well.

'Hang it up; hang it up,' the child shouted, dancing with excitement. Pat was embarrassed. There would be nothing in her stocking. She hadn't thought of it and of course Richard wasn't in on this conspiracy. She wildly wondered what she could put inside the woolly sock she was handed.

'Uncle Richard says people hang their stockings round the biggest radiator when they live in flats,' said Bel.

Doubtfully.

'Oh he did, did he?' said Pat. She felt warm inside as she realized Richard must be entering into the spirit of things, that he wanted to join in, to belong even.

She filled her own stocking, quietly, with a couple of unopened packets of tights and some perfume she had been given for her birthday. Then, lump in throat, she filled the other two and crept back to bed.

Richard seemed to be asleep. She had hoped he might help her wrap Bel's presents, but he hadn't offered. He had sat in the kitchen reading the paper. But she suspected he was taking an interest, his eyes glancing now and then at the lumpy packages.

Bel woke at half past five with shrieks of excitement. Sleepy and half apprehensive, with a wary look at Richard, Pat allowed herself to be dragged from the bed. She gasped. The stockings which she had left limply stuffed were bulging. Bel's had overflowed onto the carpet.

'I . . . er . . . think we must have duplicated.' Richard was sheepish as he peered around the bedroom door.

She looked at him. His hair was rumpled; his bathrobe torn. Looking down at the child, he was smiling, watching expectantly as her stocking was carried, bulging, to the sofa.

Bel stopped. 'Aren't you going to open yours?'

They smiled at each other, catching the little girl's excitement and reached, each a little embarrassed, for the grossly swollen socks which lay on the floor. Pat's heart began to beat a little faster.

The packets in hers were carefully wrapped in gold and black paper. 'Nothing very exciting,' Richard grinned. 'I'm afraid Father Christmas was a little rusty.'

Nothing very exciting! A silk scarf; a pendant; a tiny teddy bear.

'For me?'

'Look, Aunt Pat. I've got one, too!'

Pat went down on her knees to grope inside the stocking. A paperback. The sequel to the one she'd bought him! They held them up together and laughed.

'It proves we must be compatible after all,' he teased. 'We'll have to live together long enough to read each other's.'

She made mountains of toast and they ate it all sitting on the big bed getting butter and honey on the duvet and giggling. Then Richard lay back, contented and began to read aloud the story of *Thomas the Tank Engine*.

'Well, I liked it when I was six.'

'But, Richard, she's a girl.'

'I do like it, Aunt Pat; I *do*!'

The flat lay beneath a drift of coloured paper. She put on the chicken and wished she had risked a Christmas pudding. In the end they stuck five-pence pieces into the chocolate cake. ('You know, love, if you don't mind me saying so, it's really more like a pudding in the middle anyway.') But she knew he liked her attempts at cooking. It was one of the things on her side.

'My God,' said Richard in despair. 'Look at me. The picture of a happy family man.' He ran his fingers through his hair and groaned as Bel bounced onto his lap. 'This would put you off marriage for life, this would.'

He had meant it as a joke but the air was suddenly electric. He saw Pat, her eyes brimming, turn away to put the kettle on. Damn, he thought, damn, damn, damn!

Pat sniffed and shook her head as she filled the kettle. I knew it was all pretend, she thought, furious with herself. He's always told me he's not the marrying type. So why am I worrying? I never expected it. It's a lovely day and I'm not going to spoil it. She blew her nose angrily, then she plugged in the kettle.

But Richard was there behind her. His arm was round

her shoulder. 'Happy Christmas, lover,' he whispered and gently he kissed the back of her neck.

Bel was watching solemnly from the doorway. 'Have you given her your special present yet, Uncle Richard? I know where it is.' The child was clutching the doll ('Look, Uncle Richard, she wets her nappy!') which her mother had sent for her. 'Shall I fetch it?'

Pat turned. 'What special present?'

Richard shook his head in despair. 'Don't I have any secrets any more? Fetch it, then. Carefully.'

The present was wrapped in the same stripy paper. It was so tiny the sticky tape enveloped it. It was a very little box.

'I thought it might get lost if I put it in that great hairy stocking,' he muttered as he took it.

The kettle was clouding the room with steam but Pat took no notice. Shaking, she held out her hand and he gave her the box. A ring box.

'And besides,' he went on, 'I didn't want you to get the wrong idea. I expect Father Christmas is married already.' He grinned mischievously.

'I'm the one who wants a wife . . .'

A Love Story

'Chérie, je t'aime.'

I nestled into André's arms, his soft whisper so close to my ear that I couldn't tell if I felt the warmth of his breath or the brush of his lips on my hair.

'My Suzie, we must go.'

Reluctantly I allowed him to push me from his knees and I stood up, conscious of my crumpled skirt and unbuttoned blouse. I was a mess. I could never look glamorously dishevelled as I imagined his French girlfriends would have looked under similar circumstances. My make-up would certainly have run and my tights had snagged on the cushion zip as we sat down. I felt overwhelmingly depressed.

I had met André three months before at my niece's graduation party. He was twenty-three and I was nearly forty. At first I had been amused by his attentions, and flattered of course.

'But *chérie*,' he had said, gently teasing. 'The Frenchmen are always fascinated by older women. Surely you know that?' And I laughed and accepted first his compliments and then his invitation out to dinner.

But that one evening together had led to more and before I knew it I was falling in love with him. It was no use my telling myself every morning as I gazed in the bathroom mirror that I looked old enough to be his mother.

I didn't. I had a good skin and as yet the crows' feet were minimal, but even so I found I was spending far more time and money on my appearance than I had before I met André. I had the notion that Frenchmen expected their women to be chic and feminine and I intended to live up to André's every expectation. Even in bed. When he first made it clear that he wanted so sleep with me I had objected, in a real panic that once we had slept together there would be nothing left to attract him, but I did us both an injustice. When at last I gave way unable to hold out any longer against something I wanted so much, he proved a superb lover and his attentions became more marked and more loving every day.

As an assistant lecturer in French at the university he had a room in one of the men's hostels and acted as assistant warden there. At the weekends we would make toast in front of his electric fire and lie on his narrow bed together listening to tapes. But it was difficult there. We could never be sure that there wasn't going to be a knock on the door at any moment. The best times were when he came back to my flat and we knew we would be alone.

You may ask why I wasn't married. Most people did, in their usual tactless way. When I was twenty-two I had become engaged to a young man whom I worshipped. But our engagement grew longer and longer. Each time I tried to persuade him to fix a date he would find an excuse. At last after five years I had realized what my friends and family had probably known all along, that he was not the marrying kind. It broke my heart, but ours had not been the stable relationship which can last without marriage. After we parted I avoided any serious affairs, nursing my wounded pride beneath a stout campaign for the independence of women. Until I met André.

Now, in his cosy bed-sitter, in the dim light of the shaded lamp I looked up at him as he stood before the mirror combing his hair and I knew I loved him as I had loved no one before and I was afraid.

He turned and smiled, holding out his arms. 'I wish you did not have to go, Suzie.'

I loved the way he pronounced my name. He made it sound exotic and a little wicked. Other people just called me Sue.

We kissed long and passionately and then reluctantly we went out into the dimly-lit hall, tiptoeing so as not to disturb any sleeping students. From behind some of the doors came the muted sounds of music, but most were quiet. The lines of light beneath the doors showed that few were asleep. It was only a week from the exams and I suspected that many a set of brains was being cudgelled that night to try and make up for lost evenings earlier in the term.

André and I sauntered down the moonlit road, breathing in the heady summer air. My flat was about two miles from the hostel through the peaceful sleepy suburb and on fine nights I loved the walk back there under the stars, with André holding my hand. I was entirely happy.

We reached the bridge across the river and leaned over the parapet, looking down into the dark water rushing far below. Only the occasional flash of white showed in the gloom as a wave hit the rocks.

André put his arm round my shoulder. 'Suzie, there is something I must tell you.' His tone was ominously serious. I turned to him and waited without a word.

After a moment he went on. 'I have been offered a job in France, Suzie. It is one I want very much.'

That was all he said.

I looked down at the water again, trying to bite back the tears. After all, I had known it could not last, but I had not expected this. I had thought he would grow tired of me and find another woman and that my own cynicism would be there to comfort me, but no. He had said the words as though his heart too would break.

I glanced sideways. He was looking down as though the river would hold his attention for ever and in the luminous night I could see his profile with its firm nose and chin, the high forehead, the irrepressible curly hair. Somehow I stifled a sob. He must not know that I was crying.

'Come on,' I said. 'It's late.'

He didn't come in for a coffee and as I shut the door I felt as though my whole world was shattered. He had gone off without another word.

In my living room which was really more of a studio – I was a painter as well as a teacher at the art college – my portrait of André stood on the easel, nearly finished. I gazed at it for a long time, pleading silently with those warm brown eyes as if he could really see me. I felt empty; dead. Then I blew a sad kiss towards the glistening oils and turned for my lonely bedroom.

The next two days were busy ones as a rule for both of us and we had agreed not to meet until the Friday. I don't know how I prevented myself from ringing him in the interval, but I did.

As the hour approached when André would be picking me up at my flat I grew more and more nervous. Tonight I would find out when he was to leave and whether I would ever see him again. I grew increasingly depressed as I dressed in one of my prettiest summer dresses, one which I knew he particularly liked, but to my surprise André himself looked anything but depressed when he had at last appeared at the door.

'Bring a coat and scarf, Suzie,' he commanded. 'I have borrowed a car.'

We were swiftly in the country and as we roared through the fragrant evening with the roof of the car folded down I lay back and closed my eyes. Wherever we were going I was not really looking forward to it. There was too much talking to be done over the meal.

When we at last drew up in the forecourt of an old pub my cheeks were burning from the rush of wind and my hair, in spite of a scarf, felt tangled.

'Wait, I have something for you.' André put his hand on my arm as I leaned forward to open the door. From the glove pocket in front of me he produced a single white rose, its petals creamy against the tissue paper in which it was wrapped. 'I hoped you would wear that dress,' he said quietly. 'It is for that dress that I chose the flower.' Gently he tucked it into my bodice.

Our table was in the corner by the windows which opened out onto a mossy lawn, bordered with sweet smelling heliotrope.

André ordered with his customary efficiency and as the waiter poured out our wine I sat bemused, unwilling to break the spell of silence. Then André spoke.

'I have given in my notice at the university; next year I commence my job at Toulouse.' He waited, looking at me hard, but I refused to meet his eye, too bleak and miserable to make any pretence of being glad for him.

'Suzie?' He took my hand. 'What is the matter?'

I shook my head, not trusting myself to speak.

'You are disappointed it is not Paris?' He closed my fingers around the stem on my wineglass. 'But that may follow after a year, or maybe two or three.' He looked at me hopefully.

At last I managed to say something. 'I am glad, André. Truly glad. I know it's what you wanted.' I took a sip of wine.

'You are not glad, Suzie.' He sounded hurt and reproachful.

'Yes I am.' I took some more wine. 'It's just that I shall miss you, that's all . . .' My voice cracked as I spoke the words and I fought to hold back the tears. I would not spoil a beautiful evening by crying like a teenager. I clenched my fists.

'But, *chérie,*' André looked amazed, 'aren't you coming with me? I thought you had said so often you would love to live in France?'

It was my turn to look amazed. I hadn't thought; I hadn't understood.

We were silent as the waiter brought the vinaigrettes, but as soon as he had gone André pushed away his plate and took my hands in his. He looked so earnest, his brown eyes pleading.

'Suzie, I had not meant it to be like this. I had planned it to be so romantic, later. But I have decided. You will marry me. We will be married next month before we leave, then we have the rest of the summer to find a flat in Toulouse. See,' he fumbled in his breast pocket, 'I have brought you the ring.'

On his palm lay an exquisite little circle of sapphires and diamonds in a red gold Victorian setting.

I was speechless.

He smiled happily and took my hand. 'Let us see if it fits.'

He slipped it on and I gazed at it, enchanted. I was still looking at it when the waiter came to take our plates. He reappeared a few moments later with a half bottle of champagne and bowed in front of André.

'The compliments of the manager, monsieur. We could not help noticing the little ceremony just now and he hopes you will accept this with our congratulations.'

Amazed, we looked at each other and then round the room and to my intense embarrassment I found that everyone at the other tables was looking at us. They had been watching the whole thing. One man raised his glass in salute. 'To the happy couple,' he said smiling and one after another the other people followed suit.

It was I think the happiest evening of my life. It passed so quickly, in a haze of wine and food and good wishes. Then there was the scented moonlit drive back in the early hours of the morning.

It was an anti-climax to realize that I was to spend the next afternoon with my parents and my sister and her family at home. They had met André only a couple of times and knew nothing of my relationship with him.

Before I left to go to them reluctantly I took off my ring. I wanted to break it to them gently that I was going to live abroad and I wanted to be able to pick my moment.

I was still walking on air when my father opened the door to my knock. 'Come in, Susan darling,' he said cheerfully. 'Tea's all ready. Your mother is just bringing it through.'

I bent to fondle the little Jack Russell which had bounded out to greet me and then followed my father into the sitting room. My sister Gwen and her husband Phil were already there, curled up on a sofa by the fire.

'Hi,' Gwen said when she saw me. 'I hear you've got yourself a gigolo, Sue. I can't think how you managed to tear yourself away.'

'Gwen.' Father automatically stepped between us, but I saw at once from his amused face that it would only be minutes before he joined in with the teasing. With Gwen I could cope. We had been at each other's throats all our lives and I was used to her catty remarks. I put them down to jealousy – but Father – that was too hurtful.

My cheeks flamed. 'I can't think what you mean,' I said as repressively as I could and to forestall any further remarks I headed for the kitchen.

In the hall I stopped in front of the mirror. My face was flushed and my eyes suspiciously bright. How stupid not to be able to hide my feelings at my age. If only I hadn't known what Gwen meant. I wondered who had been gossiping.

Taking a grip on myself I went into the kitchen and kissed my mother fondly. One look at me told her something was wrong of course and before I knew it I had poured out the whole story. She listened quietly and then put her arm round my shoulders. 'Poor Susan. It must be dreadful for you to take such a decision.' She turned to the kettle. 'But I think you are right to turn him down. It might seem hard now but in ten years you'll be glad you did it.'

'But I didn't turn him down,' I sobbed, anguished. 'Mother, I love him. I want to marry him.'

'But dear, think.' She put the tea things down and looked at me hard. 'Think very carefully. There is not only the difference in your ages, as if that wasn't enough, but he's foreign. He wants you to leave this country and all your friends and go off with him heaven knows where. Oh Sue darling, you can't do it.'

In my heart I wondered if she was right but at the same time I was indignant and angry. How could she talk like that about André? He was mature well beyond his years. He was responsible. He would not ask me to do anything that would leave me unhappy.

Eventually I dried my eyes and gave her a watery smile. 'I'll think about it a bit longer,' I said as steadily as I could. 'Let's not talk about it any more now.'

Obviously Gwen and Phil and my father had reached the same conclusion because nothing more was said on the subject the whole afternoon. We just chatted about various things and I tried very hard indeed to ignore the deepening depression which was hanging over me.

My mother's words had reawakened my own terrible doubts about the difference in our ages. It was something I had tried to forget, but as I walked slowly home from my parents' house I remembered all the little things. André was still childishly optimistic and irrepressible and in some ways yes, he was a little irresponsible too, while I was cynical and inclined to be weighed down by cares. Possibly these were differences of character rather than age but to me they pointed to one thing only – my approaching senility, his carefree youth. I thought of his hard lean body; his cheeks and eyes, young and bright and I remembered the way I had to throw my shoulders back and pull in my stomach when I appeared before him naked. He told me that my body was beautiful, but I never quite lost my self-consciousness before him and dared not relax for one second.

We were not going to meet that evening so I let myself into the silent flat and went straight to bed, worn out with misery.

I knew I looked pale and haggard the next day when I met André for coffee after his last tutorial. I saw him give me a sharp look and then as we sat down he let out a sharp exclamation.

'Suzie, where is our ring? Why are you not wearing it?'

I jumped guiltily. That morning I had slipped it on, tried to recapture the joy of having it on my hand, had worn it all the time I was making my toast and coffee and then just before I left for work I had taken it off, kissed it longingly and placed it in the drawer.

'I didn't want to wear it to work, darling,' I lied hastily. 'I was giving pottery lessons and I didn't want to get it covered in clay, or take it off and have to leave it lying around.'

He accepted my explanation with a smile and a squeeze of the hand, but he still looked crestfallen. Like a disappointed schoolboy . . . I stopped myself abruptly. There I went again, harping on his youth. I forced myself to smile.

'Where are we going this evening, André?' I said, trying to change the subject. 'What about that French film you wanted to see?'

But he shook his head. 'Suzie, I know something is wrong. You must tell me.'

I glanced up at his anxious face and sighed. 'All right. But not here. Can we go back to my flat?'

'What is wrong with here?' His chin suddenly took on a stubborn set and he gestured round the dark café with its intimate little tables. The atmosphere was fragrant with coffee and cigarette smoke and there were only two other couples there.

'All right,' I said quietly. 'I'll tell you here. Darling, I love you more than I can ever say, but I don't think I should marry you.' To my surprise the words sounded very calm and reasonable.

André's expression did not change. He had obviously been expecting this. 'Can you tell me why, *chérie*? Is it that you don't want to live in France?'

His hand was trembling as it held his cup and I felt a lump come to my throat.

'No, no. Of course not. It's because I am so much older than you. Don't you see? I don't think it would work.'

He gave a pained sigh. 'But we have been over this so often, Suzie.' He sounded a little impatient. 'I told you that for me this is not a problem. It just does not matter.' He accentuated the words by striking the table with his fist. The cups rattled on their saucers and there was a moment of silence at the other tables. Then the muted murmur of conversation continued.

I looked down at my coffee, embarrassed. 'It doesn't matter now, but in ten, fifteen years' time, what then? When you are forty and I am nearly sixty; how will you feel about it then, André?' My voice cracked as I spoke and immediately his hand caught mine. It was reassuringly firm.

'In France a woman is considered to be at her most attractive in her fifties and sixties, *chérie*. That is when she has the experience to please her man. She is mature. She is no longer just pretty and frivolous; she is *beautiful*!'

He gazed deeply into my eyes and smiled suddenly. 'Look at Deneuve. She is fifty!' He shrugged his shoulders in the very Gallic way he had.

I had to laugh. 'But I do not have quite the same advantages as her.'

'No,' he snorted. 'But for me you are much better. Listen.' He captured my other hand and leaning across the table gazed at me earnestly. 'You are worrying about what will happen in twenty years' time. My love, if we have so much as twenty years happiness we shall have a great deal to thank God for. Do you not think that to ask for more is being greedy? You are saying, "I want a promise of half a century perhaps of perfection" – but who knows what will happen then? Let us take our happiness now, while we have it. We will leave the future until it comes, eh?'

He was silent for a minute and then abruptly he released my hands and began to drink his coffee.

I sat for a while unable to think of anything to say. I wanted so much to be convinced, but somewhere deep inside me there was still a niggle of doubt. His argument sounded so reasonable. I was facing problems which might, probably would, never occur.

'What would your parents think?' I said at last, cautiously.

André's face broke into a beaming smile. '*Enfin*,' he said triumphantly, 'she has seen how foolish she is. They will love you. I have already written to *maman* and she is longing to meet you.'

He stood up. 'Come on. Let's go to see that film.'

He was irrepressibly happy for the rest of the evening and eventually I cheered up too. We laughed and much later as we wandered back through the warm night towards my flat, we began to make plans. Once more he left me at the door. He had a few more essays to mark, he admitted with a grimace. He blew me a kiss from the corner of the street and was gone.

I opened the door of my flat and was amazed to find my father sitting there sipping coffee.

'Your mother lent me the spare key,' he explained lazily. 'Where's young André got to?'

'Young . . . ?' My heart missed a beat. 'he's gone back to the hostel. Why?'

'Just as well.' My father heaved himself to his feet. 'Your mother told me all about it, Sue. You know it just won't do, don't you?'

'Why not?' My hands were suddenly terribly cold. 'We have discussed it a great deal. I'm going into it with my eyes open.'

'Yes, but is he?' He put his arm round my shoulder. 'Listen, Sue. The last thing I want to do is hurt you; but think of him. He is young and in love. He sees you as some perfect English dream he's thought up for himself. But when he takes you home, what happens? His friends are married to girls fifteen years your junior. Are *they* going to be your friends? He is bound to make comparisons. He will be too loyal perhaps to hurt you if he can help it, but one day you can bet he will take a little mistress . . .'

'Father, how *can* you!' I was furious. 'How can you be so horrible and unkind? You make me feel ugly and old and *unloveable*.'

He held me close. 'Sue, Sue. I'm sorry. It's because I'm trying to save you from being hurt later.' Sadly he looked at me and then he smiled. 'But of course, it is for you to make the final decision, my love. Whatever you decide we'll stand by you.' He dropped a quick kiss on my forehead and then said, unbelievably, 'Have you ever thought of having an affair with this chap, Sue? Just to get it out of your system.' He looked embarrassed. And I felt suddenly horribly ashamed. I had been having 'an affair' as he meant it, with André for months now and here he was suggesting it! Putting aside all his principles and suggesting something which would shock him so profoundly. I wanted to cry and after he had gone I did. I cried myself to sleep.

Next morning I sat for a long time at my dressing table gazing at the mirror, my fingers gently trying to coax the lines of exhaustion from beneath my eyes.

I had considered André. I had considered my mother and father. I had even considered Gwen and Phil. Now at last wasn't it time to consider myself? Wasn't André right to say think of today? Who could tell what the future would bring? What did I want? Now.

Slowly, deliberately, I reached into the drawer, found my precious, beautiful ring and slipped it onto the fourth finger of my left hand. I stared at it for a long time then I stood up. Today I would wear it. Tomorrow could take care of itself.

A Window on the World

Mrs Benton was old and very frail and she seldom went outside her house, relying instead on Mr Folkestone, the 'paying guest' who lived upstairs to do her shopping for her. But she didn't feel cut off from the world for she had her front window. For hours at a time she would sit in the rocking chair which had been her mother's gazing out at the road, occasionally moving the net curtain aside so that she could get a better look.

It was a lonely life, but Mrs Benton never complained for she had one especial interest, and this was the young man who lived in the house directly opposite. He had lived there with his mother for about six months now and his name was Jeremy. She had persuaded George, the postman, to tell her that much. Jeremy Hall. He was tall and good looking with soft floppy chestnut hair and green eyes. George thought he lectured at the technical college three miles away, but he could not be sure. Certainly Jeremy left nearly every morning at about twenty minutes to nine on his blue scooter and more often than not he had a stack of books with him which he strapped behind his seat. Some days he came home early, at about three and others not until after six.

Mrs Benton had made up a story about Jeremy. She pretended to know all about him and his family and his work and in her imagination he would come across and see her and tell her his troubles and his plans. And she would listen and nod and stroke the cat which purred on her knee.

That cat was all the family Mrs Benton had now. Once she had a daughter and a son-in-law and a little grandson, but they had all gone to live in Australia. There had been letters at first and then just cards and then nine Christmases ago even they had stopped. Her grandson must be about twenty-eight now, she thought wistfully. Sometimes in her dreams Jeremy would call her 'Grandma'.

One afternoon it was raining particularly hard. Mrs Benton saw Jeremy come home, the rain streaming from his hair and coat, his books carefully wrapped in a polythene bag. She knew his mother was still out shopping for she had seen her go half an hour before. Jeremy dived into the house, beginning to take off his coat even before he shut the door. Mrs Benton nodded. Sensible boy. It would not do to catch cold. She wished she could afford to buy him a proper briefcase for those poor books.

She rocked back and forth a couple of times and then leaned forward again in astonishment, for someone was coming to her own door. Or to be exact an umbrella was coming. A pretty pink and red floral umbrella. Mrs Benton raised the corner of the curtain expectantly. Yes, it was definitely coming up her front steps.

Suddenly deciding that she must answer the door herself and not wait for Mr Folkestone to do it she heaved herself slowly to her feet and groped for her sticks, waiting impatiently for the ring on the doorbell. But it didn't come. Disappointed Mrs Benton hoped whoever it was would not go away before she got there and she shuffled as fast as she could in her floppy slippers out into the hall and groped for the door latch.

Standing on the doorstep was a girl, dressed in a tightly-belted blue mackintosh, the umbrella daintily twirling around her head. She had long fair hair, darkened into streaks by the rain, and enormous grey eyes.

'Hello,' she said, startled because Mrs Benton had opened the front door before she had plucked up the courage to ring. 'I am sorry to bother you, but I wonder if you,' she hesitated a moment looking at Mrs Benton's arthritic hands and then went on, blushing prettily, 'I wonder if there is anyone who can help me? It is silly really, but I can't get the top off this jar.' She held out an enormous bottle with a screw top lid. 'There isn't anyone else in the house I've moved into round the corner and I must have this open.'

Mrs Benton smiled. 'Of course, dear. Come in and I'll call Mr Folkestone. I am sure he can help you.'

Then she stopped suddenly. How silly. What did a lovely girl like this want with a couple of old fogies like herself and Mr Folkestone? No, she had a better idea.

'On second thoughts I don't think he's in.' She frowned and leaned a little more heavily on her sticks. 'But I know who can help you, my dear. You run across the road there and ask Jeremy. He's such a nice boy and I am sure he's very strong.'

She stood watching as the girl turned back down the steps and made her way across the wet pavement. Then she closed the door. She did not want them to see her watching. As fast as she could Mrs Benton shuffled back to her chair, lowered herself painfully into it and twitched back the curtain.

The beautiful girl was knocking on Jeremy's door and after a moment or two he opened it. He had put on a thick rust-coloured sweater, Mrs Benton could see, which went beautifully with his hair.

She watched the girl explain and hold out the jar and she saw Jeremy laughing as he took it. He opened it with one quick tug and handed it back to her. Then they stayed talking for several minutes before the girl turned and waving, set off home. Jeremy stood and watched her go out of sight round the corner before he shut the door.

With a sigh Mrs Benton let the curtain fall.

Soon after that Jeremy's schedule began to change. Often he came home much later than before and his scooter would turn into the road from the opposite end to the college, from Mrs Benton's end. She wondered whether he had changed his job and day-dreamed excitedly about the day when he would come and tell her all about the new people he was meeting and especially about the girl in the blue mackintosh.

Twice she saw her go back to Jeremy's house. Once she went in. It was teatime on a Saturday and his mother was there. And once she just collected him at the door and together they walked off up the road, talking excitedly and holding hands.

Mrs Benton's pleasure and happiness in seeing them together like that would only be bettered by one thing and that was the piece of excitement of her own which was coming. One of her rare expeditions outside the house. Mrs Carnaby who used to lodge with her before Mr Folkestone had written to say she had bought a car. She was coming to town for the day especially to take Mrs Benton to see the Christmas decorations in Hartleys and help her do her Christmas shopping.

Leaning heavily on her two sticks, but with her eyes sparkling with delight, Mrs Benton walked slowly and determinedly down the aisle between the scarf counter and the gloves. Mrs Carnaby tactfully leaving her on her own for a while knowing there were chairs for her to sit on here if she got tired. She paused now and then to look at the lovely squares of chiffon and silk, hanging her sticks on her arm as she gently touched the cool beauty of the fabrics.

Then she looked up to see which counter she would visit next and there, almost next to her, stood Jeremy and with him was a tall dark-haired girl wearing a scarlet coat. Mrs Benton had never seen her before. He had his arm round her. 'Choose, Angela,' he was saying quietly, in a deep pleasant voice, very much as she had imagined he would sound. 'Choose which you'd like, my dear. I think this one suits you.' He held up an emerald green silk scarf studded with tiny black stars. Mrs Benton glanced up at the maker's placard over that section of the counter and gasped. Had he any idea how much that scarf would cost?

Evidently Angela at least did have, for at once she said, 'No, Jerry darling, I can't let you. It's much too expensive.'

Then the most terrible thing happened. Mrs Benton, turning from the counter, saw *her* coming towards them across the shop. Still wearing her blue tightly-belted mac, her hair swinging beneath a black velvet head band. Her face was radiant and for the last few steps she almost ran. 'Jerry,' she called breathlessly. 'Jerry, love, I thought it was you.' Then she stopped dead. She hadn't seen Angela who had been hidden by Jeremy's broad shoulders and now suddenly she was face to face with her. Uncomfortably Jeremy let fall the green scarf. He unwound his arm from Angela's shoulders.

'Pam, I didn't know you'd be here.' His voice was uncertain and Mrs Benton, now unashamedly staring, saw an uncomfortable flush spreading to his cheeks.

'No, I can see that.' Pam's eyes blazed. 'Please, Jerry, don't stop your transaction on my account.' She leaned forward and plucked the scarf from the pile again. 'It suits the lady perfectly I should say!' She pushed the scarf into his hands creasing the silky folds. 'They do hold football matches in strange places nowadays, Jerry, don't they? I never dreamed you'd be playing here when I rang you yesterday. And with such a lovely opponent. No wonder you couldn't come to the cinema with me.' The girl's voice was taut with grief as she rushed on. 'I suppose fields get so muddy don't they and men are so boring to play with . . .' She turned and walked quickly away, her head held high, but not before Mrs Benton caught sight of the tears in her eyes.

Jeremy and Angela looked at each other, then Angela suddenly gave a nervous giggle. 'Jerry, what have you been doing? I didn't know you ran a harem, my darling. How intriguing.' Her smile was suddenly frosty. 'I didn't think simpering blondes were quite your style though. You've never shown any interest in them in college.'

Mrs Benton's blood was boiling. So that was it. A girl from the college. Pam wasn't a simpering blonde. She was beautiful and sweet and . . .

Placing her sticks firmly on the carpet she began to walk forward, intent on saying her piece, but already the two young people had turned away.

'There's no need to be vicious, Angela,' she heard Jeremy's voice, suddenly loud in the discreet hush of the shop. 'Pam is a lovely person. She's hardly a harem. She's a very dear friend and I won't have her hurt.'

'You mean you'd rather hurt me?' Angela's voice, though as low as his was loud, came surprisingly clearly across the thick carpeting.

'No, but you're better at taking care of yourself. You're tough, Angie and Pam is vulnerable and lonely. She knows no one here.'

'It sounds to me then as though you ought to rush after her to console her, Jerry dear.' Angela dropped the hushed voice and faced him suddenly beneath a shimmering Christmas mobile. 'And don't worry about me or that lovely Christmas present. As you so rightly imply I have others to turn to for comfort,' and she swept away, leaving him standing on the carpet.

He hesitated for a moment looking after her uncomfortably then he shrugged and, suddenly seeming to make up his mind, he turned and almost ran after Pam, disappearing into the crowds of afternoon shoppers.

Mrs Benton breathed a sigh of relief. He had made the right decision, of that she was sure.

The next few days Mrs Benton could hardly bear to leave her chair at the window in the evenings; but there was no sign of Pam. Jeremy came home at his usual time, went in and uncompromisingly slammed the front door. If he went out again it was not until after Mrs Benton had gone to bed.

Then one traumatic evening Angela turned up. Mrs Benton clenched her fists angrily, twitching the curtain in her anxiety. He let her in, but she stayed no more than ten minutes. When she left she paused for a moment on the doorstep to hurl abuse at the figure inside the door and then she ran down the road.

'Good, that's finished.' Mrs Benton sat back satisfied. Then she stiffened. Jeremy had come out on his freezing doorstep to look after Angela. He gazed for a moment then as he was about to turn away he looked straight at Mrs Benton's window. It was too late to let the curtain fall and pretend she wasn't watching. She felt herself blush, but to her surprise he didn't seem to be cross at being spied on. He gave her a friendly grin and a wave. Then as if suddenly realizing that she must have seen everything he jerked his thumb in the direction of Angela's retreating back and with a heavenwards glance of exasperation gave a dramatic shrug of his shoulders. Then with another wave he had gone.

Mrs Benton let the curtain fall gently. He had let her in on his secret. She was an accomplice and he knew she was there. She was so happy that evening she didn't know what to do. In the end she treated herself to half a glass of sherry in celebration.

Three days later she was watching some damp wintry flakes of snow nose down past her window at lunchtime when Jeremy came home unexpectedly early. He had no books on his scooter. She watched him undo the strap on his crash helmet and, leaving the helmet on the seat of the bike, he ran indoors. He had not even glanced in her direction. She could not suppress a tiny feeling of disappointment, but this was soon forgotten as she saw Pam. The girl walked slowly hesitatingly down past Mrs Benton's house, and then almost reluctantly crossed the road. She hesitated so long on Jeremy's doorstep Mrs Benton almost got to her feet in anxiety and then miraculously, before she rang, the door opened. She stood for a minute on the doorstep before she disappeared inside. Mrs Benton's fingers were not so arthritic that she could not still just cross them in an emergency.

She was so intrigued about what would happen she forgot to go and make her own lunch. Instead she sat and rocked and watched.

Forty-six minutes later, by her watch, the door opened and Jeremy and Pam both appeared on the doorstep. He slammed the door behind them and together they stood for a moment by his bike. Then at last, gently, he gave her a long, lingering kiss. He watched as she turned away and walked quickly round the corner. Then he reached for his helmet and strapped it on. As he was about to mount his machine he seemed to remember something. He paused and glanced across the street towards Mrs Benton's window. She hadn't moved the curtain today, so he couldn't possibly see her, but even so he gave that cheery grin and waved and then this time, just for her, he gave the thumbs up sign.

She never saw Angela again.

Christmas was getting close now and the evenings grew dark so very early but from the lights of the street lamps she could see Jeremy and Pam come and go. And now they both waved, and once Pam, her face radiant as her hair blew free of the blue crash helmet she wore as she went pillion on the scooter, looked up and blew her a kiss.

Then one Saturday morning came the awful news. Mrs Benton had opened the door for George who had brought a large exciting parcel. It was for Mr Folkestone.

'I see your young Mr Hall is leaving us then,' he said cheerfully. 'Got himself a new job, I hear and leaving home.'

Mrs Benton felt the tears rush to her eyes. He couldn't. He couldn't go and leave her. Not now. She clutched at the door, swaying suddenly.

'Hey, ma, are you all right?' Dimly she heard George's voice, and felt his strong hand under her arm. 'Here, let's go and sit down. Where's your chair, ma?' He helped her back into the front room. 'Hadn't he told you then? I'm sorry; I shouldn't have said anything.'

Mrs Benton sniffed loudly and groped for her handkerchief. 'No,' she gulped. 'He hadn't told me; I didn't really expect him to.'

She sat for a long time after George had gone not even bothering to look out of the window. No more Jeremy; nothing to look forward to in the afternoons when he was due to come home. No more of the cheerful puttering of his scooter engine and waves from him and Pam.

She dabbed at the tears which insisted on running down her cheeks and did not even hear the doorbell. Mr Folkestone must have opened it for the next thing she knew there was a tap on her own door. She looked round to see it being pushed quietly open.

'Excuse me; can we come in for a moment?' The girl, still dressed in her blue mackintosh, was peeping round it.

Mrs Benton hastily blew her nose and smiled, her heart

giving little irregular bumps of hope and excitement. 'Come in, my dear, of course.'

Pam came in and she was closely followed by Jeremy. Hand-in-hand they crossed over to the rocking chair. The girl knelt down suddenly and in a spontaneously happy gesture took Mrs Benton's wrinkled hand in her own. 'I wanted you to know that Jerry and I are getting married. You really introduced us, you know. We have you to thank for everything.'

'And we would like you to come to the wedding,' Jeremy added. 'Please, will you? And here:' he thrust a small parcel into her hand, 'a small Christmas present to say thank you.'

Mrs Benton could not answer him. She was crying again. But this time with happiness.

It was not until a little while later when Pam had made them all some tea that Mrs Benton felt better.

Then she could not stop smiling. She made Jeremy sit next to her on the old sofa which she found so hard to get out of with her legs and listened as they told her of their plans.

They had found a small house on the northern edge of the town and they asked her to come and see them as soon as they were settled. Jeremy was anyway planning to sell his scooter and buy a second-hand car, so he would be able to come and fetch her.

By the time they had left Mrs Benton would have called herself the happiest person in the world. Slowly, after they had gone, she opened the small present. It contained a bottle of cologne and two exquisite lace handkerchiefs. She went back to her chair, holding them tight and sat down slowly gazing out into the sunny frosty street. Pam had brought two lengths of yellow ribbon with her and with them Jeremy had tied back her old net curtains.

'We like to see you sitting here, Grandma,' he said

gently before they left. 'Not only us, but the whole street love you, you know. They'd miss you dreadfully if you ever skipped a day.' He dropped a quick kiss on top of her head and with that cheery wave of his hand she had come to love so much, he had gone.

A Promise of Love

There was misty sunshine in the distance now, sending shafts of pale light over the sea. Louise stood motionless, her hands gripping the cold rail on the promenade, watching each wave crash up the steep beach and ebb again, sucking hungrily at the pebbles below the barnacle-encrusted concrete. Her hands were blue with cold, covered in little salty droplets of spray. She had forgotten to bring any gloves.

A heavy shower swept across the empty roadway behind her, soaking her hair, her coat, her shoes. But she ignored it. Her eyes were fixed desperately on a sea suddenly slate-black beneath the rain, save for far out where the light remained. On her cheeks the raindrops mingled unnoticed with her tears. Why, oh why had she come back? What was she seeking from this same cold, cruel water?

The top of the tide had left piles of seaweed, dead and ugly, heaped on the road. It didn't matter though. There were no cars; no people. The town in February was dead. It didn't seem possible that she was looking at the same element as the sleek blue summer sea when the world had been happy and perfect and she had quite wilfully ruined everything.

They had been going to stay in a cottage at the end of the town, where the old fishing village was, where the pebbly beach and the harbour gave way to sand dunes which stretched for miles, shifting and changing shape in the wind, so that they, like the sea, were never the same.

John had seen the advertisement in the paper; end of season let. And on the spur of the moment they had decided as the days were still warm, to go.

'Are you pretending we're married?' she had asked as he sealed the letter and he had laughed. 'Whatever for?' he said and he kissed her fiercely.

Whatever for indeed, after all this time? She had gone to the long narrow kitchen of the flat they shared and beaten the eggs for the omelette until they frothed angrily, spluttering in the iron pan.

'It'll do you good to go away, Lou,' her boss had said. 'If you don't mind my saying so you have been looking a bit run down. Going with your nice friend from the flat are you?'

She forgot to fold in the carbon as she scrunched it in her fist and her hands became all black. 'Yes, Mr Fielding. My nice friend from the flat. That's right.'

They packed and threw their cases in the car and left early to avoid the Friday rush. At the first traffic lights John turned and looked at her with a little smile. He drew his hand, electric, along her thigh. Then the lights changed and he reached for the gear lever, leaving her heart bumping a little at the message she had seen in his eyes. Resolutely she gazed through the windscreen; she hated herself sometimes for loving him still so much; for knowing herself to be so dependent on him while he remained so free.

The cottage was built of stone, sparsely furnished beneath its roof of slate at the edge of the sea. The only colour in the white-painted bedroom under the eaves came from the exquisite patchwork quilt on the bed. Dropping the cases John turned to Louise.

'At last,' he said, and held out his arms.

Outside they could hear the whistle and crackle of gossiping starlings somewhere in the heavy-laden apple tree on the lawn at the back.

'Stop!' she laughed. She struggled in his arms, pushing him away.

But already his lips were pressed urgently against hers; she felt the edge of the bed behind her and they fell, clinging together on the gaily coloured patchwork.

Then at last he allowed her to push him away. 'What's wrong?' he asked.

She sat up slowly, watching the dust dancing in the shaft of sun which shone through the window. If only she knew how to tell him what was wrong; tell of her fear and her insecurity; of the longing in her heart to hear that he needed her as much as she needed him.

As he got up and wandered over to the window she glanced down at the brilliant colours in the quilt she was sitting on. Some woman had spent hours, months even, of her life stitching the tiny fragments of cloth into this beautiful pattern. Surely the pattern of a relationship between two people who love one another and are prepared to declare their love to the world should be a little like that? Thousands of intricate multi-shaped pieces formed with time and caring into an enduring whole. Gently, wistfully, she stroked the patchwork.

'Louise?' He had been calling her name.

She looked up. She saw his hands and rose and went to him, as she knew she always would.

They wandered along the beach beyond the dunes, over the strip of flat wet sand collecting the fluted razor shells which lay nestling in among the scattered weed. The hazy September sun had been warm on Louise's shoulders as she glanced round the deserted beach. Then her depression vanishing as suddenly as it had come, she began to run, feeling the sand between her toes, the spurts of sun-warmed water beneath her instep. And she laughed as he began to chase her.

They walked for miles, not talking, as the sun sank lower in the sky, watching the tiny high, flecked, white clouds turn pink and gold. Imperceptibly the tide turned and the mother of pearl water crept once more slowly over the evening sand.

Near the point the beach grew steeper and the dry shifting dunes drew near the water. There were no other people in the world. At the water's edge an oystercatcher ran jerkily through the dribbling tide, thrusting its red beak ramrod straight into the sand. Then it flew arrowlike out towards the distant mistiness of the sun and they heard the eerie sad whistle of its cry.

The sound made Louise shiver suddenly. John looked at her, then he drew her to him, his arms strong. As he said her name there was no mistaking the tone of his voice.

High above them a plane flew straight and sure across the indigo arch of the sky, too high for them to hear it, its vapour trail a ruled line of silent gold. Slowly, his hands on her shoulders, he turned her to face him and kissed her. She closed her eyes and he kissed each eye-lid, his kisses growing more fierce and demanding, tracing the line of her lips with his finger. This time she didn't push him away. Her desire rose at his touch, a new warmth of love flooding through her as she felt the urgency of his love, unconscious of the warm wind which stirred the wiry marram grasses near her head or the thin mist of sand which had blown across her discarded crumpled dress.

They were roused at last by the gentle lapping of the water on the beach. John sat up and looked round him. Then smiling to himself he leaned forward, grasping a shell which lay near his hand and began to draw, watching the crisp curl of sand beneath his sharp strokes. With a sardonic lift of the eyebrow he drew an enormous heart.

Louise, pulling herself dreamily to her knees ran her finger through the crisp tangle of her curls. Then she reached for her dress. She laughed when she saw what he had done. 'You old Romeo,' she teased; 'who'd have thought you were a romantic!' Snatching the shell from his fingers she added a cupid's dart and put their initials, LM and JG. 'There you are. A Valentine heart!'

He grinned wryly. 'What else?' A deep haze was drawing in from the sea. The gold of the sunset was distant now, shrugging out of sight beyond the cloud. 'Come on, it's time to go,' he said abruptly. 'You've got to find the food and get us a meal, remember?'

Already the water was nibbling the edge of the heart.

'You know something?' she said casually, brushing the sand from her breasts as she buttoned her dress, 'I had always hoped, a little, that our first holiday would be our honeymoon.'

Seeing him frown she bit her lip. 'It would be nice, wouldn't it, John? To be married?' she persisted gently.

He hesitated, straining the sand through his fingers. 'For some perhaps. But not us . . .' He gazed out to sea, not looking at her.

A thin trickle of water was flowing round the heart in the sand, blurring the edges, gently smoothing away the J. She didn't notice. 'There isn't any reason we shouldn't get married is there? We love each other so much . . .' Her voice trailed away.

'No reason, except that I don't want to. We're happy as we are. Marriage would spoil it. I don't want to be labelled and slotted into the system . . .' He turned to her, narrowing his eyes and took her hands in his. 'I thought you felt the same. We don't need marriage. Haven't we proved it after all this time?'

The lapping water had washed the sand again. Both John's initials had gone. It was growing cold.

Louise leaned towards him, frowning a little; intense. 'John you did say a long time ago that we would get married. One day.'

He looked away, a little guiltily. 'Did I? Well one day perhaps we will. But not yet.'

But she couldn't leave it alone. Some demon had made her go on.

'John. I want to get married. Now.' She rose to her feet, her toes sinking a little into the soft sand.

'No.' He cut her short. 'No, Louise. I'm sorry.' He glanced down angrily.

The drawing had gone. The transparent tide rippled gently over the place where the pierced heart had been, a strand of sea-weed fluttering gently in the bubbles in the half-light.

John said nothing. Then slowly he turned to her. She was crying suddenly, blindly gazing down. 'It went so fast,' she sobbed. 'And you think our love is like that. You think it will disappear like a drawing in the sand . . .'

'No, of course I don't.' He was impatient. 'Come on, Louise, nothing stays the same for ever, you know that. What if the sea does take away the heart? We'll draw another. We'll come back on Valentine's Day itself, if you like. Come on; stop crying. You can't trap things. You can't freeze them and preserve them. Relationships change; love develops. It needs to be free, don't you see?'

She shook her head wordlessly as the evening breeze teased the blues and greens of her skirt in the dusk, thinking suddenly again of the patterned patchwork in the bedroom of the cottage. 'The sea knew. The sea knew it couldn't last. *Your love* couldn't last.'

'Louise, that's rubbish. Stop making a scene.'

'I'm not. How long have we lived together? *Years*, John. If you're not sure now, you never will be.'

He shrugged bitterly. 'Then you must look for someone else. If the security of my love isn't enough, you must look for someone who can give you more.' He turned away from her suddenly, his voice grating, and stood, his hands in his pockets, staring hard out to sea.

She took a step towards him, frightened by the bleakness of his voice, but the uncompromising line of his jaw stopped her. Her eyes were full of tears.

'All right then, I will.' Her voice broke on the words. She hesitated, but he didn't move and suddenly overcome with misery and hurt she turned and stumbled away from him up over the shifting sand of the dunes and half ran, half staggered back towards the lights of the town. She didn't look back. In any case he was soon lost to view behind the dunes. She didn't turn, didn't see the look in his eyes as he gazed after her.

The cottage was in darkness. She lifted the latch with shaking fingers and stepped in, her heart thumping. Then she picked her way slowly up the stairs, dashing away her tears and clicked on the light in the bedroom. Their two cases still stood side by side on the carpet where John had dropped them. She had never even unpacked. Listening for his step in the garden she ran to the window and leaned out, but the dunes beyond the hedge of osiers at the edge of the lane were silent and empty.

'I must go. Now. I must,' she had murmured.

She bent to pick up her case. If he came she knew she would weaken; if he took her in his arms and kissed her she would be lost.

She hesitated, praying he would come, knowing she must go.

Then at last, when she knew he wasn't coming she

carried the case down the stairs and walked out into the misty night towards the station.

John did not return home to the flat the next day, or the next, so she packed her belongings slowly and miserably and took a taxi to her sister's flat. There she waited, desolate, for him to ring her. A hundred times she picked up the phone herself and began to dial his number – the number which had been hers as well. But something stopped her. Pride? She supposed so. Rather desperately she began to go out with other men, but each date was a hollow meaningless pretence and not repeated. She grew thin and permanently sad. And almost every night she would lie awake thinking of that evening on the beach. If only John had turned and called her back. If only he had smiled. If only . . .

Christmas came and went without a word. Not even a card. And now it was February. Drawn irresistibly by the memory of the heart in the sand, masochistic, longing, she had come back. It was the fourteenth. Later, when the tide had gone down a little, she would walk back alone down the beach and look for the place where the heart had been and they had made love for the last time.

'Louise!' The voice sounded close to, but she dismissed it from her mind as she always did. Her hands had grown numb from gripping the ice cold railing so long. Shakily she raised one of them to brush away the tears which were hot on her cold face. The tide had withdrawn a little now, leaving a strip of shiny glossy pebbles. The sunlight in the distance had come closer too.

'Louise!' Again she heard the voice and again, 'Louise . . .' She could hear feet on the road behind her. Incredulously she turned. It wasn't a dream. It was John.

'Hello,' he said. He was looking down at her, his face

very close to hers, his dark eyes anxious, but warm and loving. 'It's Valentine's Day. I didn't dare hope you would remember.' Hesitating a little he held out his hands.

She smiled, biting her lip to stop it trembling. What did it mean, his being here like this? Suddenly she realized how much courage it had cost him to come at all.

She heard his voice again, as if from a distance. 'I was determined not to contact you. I knew you must have the chance to find out what you wanted.' He looked down at her with a wry smile. 'If you knew how many times I've picked up the phone.' Suddenly she felt his lips on her hair. His arms went round her, hard; hurting. Then he released her. 'Come on,' he said, taking her hand. 'Let's go to the beach . . .'

Excavations

The bulldozers and JCBs were already there, lined up by the high chain-linked fence. The excavation was a sea of mud. Frances felt her eyes fill with tears. Only a few more hours and the machinery would begin its destruction; two thousand years of history would be shovelled aside to accommodate an underground car park beneath a store.

People were picking their way across the duckboards over the mud, staring at the markers being pointed out by the rescue diggers.

'Don't call us archaeologists,' one woman had said bitterly to Frances. 'This isn't archaeology. All we can do now is throw things into boxes and run.'

She heard a child shriek with fright and excitement as it slipped off the walkway into a trench in the rain and her heart gave a lurch. It had sounded so like that other child. The child in her dream. She watched as a group of people gathered, retrieved it, wiped it down and moved on. Behind them the bottom of the trench filled slowly with water, the neatly cut layers of soil blending and turning a uniform mud colour, even the scorched red clay which showed the year the city had burned nearly two thousand years before obliterated now for ever.

She hadn't meant to come again. She had seen the temporary exhibition a dozen times, talked to the men and women working there, read up the accounts of the ancient city which was losing yet another piece of its history for ever and wept for a past she couldn't regain. She had tried to stop. Tried to beat the obsession, tried to control the need to return, but still she found herself walking through the gate and staring down at the neat square where two weeks earlier they had found the mosaic floor. It had gone now, rolled up like a carpet to be cleaned, relaid and set behind glass, never to be walked on or played on again.

'Hello.' The voice behind her startled her out of her reverie. 'Good to see you again. I'm afraid it's the last time, though, before the new precinct is finished.'

Frances turned. The tall, bearded man had been in the exhibition trailer last time she saw him, wearing boots and a waterproof coat, with his hands covered in mud.

She smiled. 'No more mud for you, I see.' He was wearing the same jacket but this time with clean cords and shoes.

'No more mud. Not here.'

'Even Boudicca's effort must have looked feeble compared with this devastation.' She tried to make her voice sound light and disinterested.

'I doubt if she was as systematic as this in her destruction,' he agreed. 'She burned the place but she didn't then bury it under a hundred million tons of concrete. On the other hand, I suppose we should be glad they're not putting the population to the sword.'

Frances flinched, but she managed a wry smile. 'You try standing in front of one of those diggers tomorrow,' she countered. 'You might find them just as bloodthirsty.'

He laughed. 'I don't intend putting it to the test. I couldn't bear to see it happen. Do you want to come and have a cup of tea? The kettle is on in the trailer.'

He had noticed how often she came to the site. He was not normally attracted to redheads, but this slightly built, beautiful creature had a strange grace about her which fascinated him. And her interest had been so intense, so painful as she watched the men and women in the trenches that he had stopped and watched her and then spoken to her, caught by the poignant droop of her shoulders. It was the second time he saw her that he recognized her. Then he had understood. Then he had known that he must get to know her; must find out if the stories were true . . .

She had a friendly smile, but the sadness was always there in her eyes. 'That would be nice,' she said at last. 'I should love a cup of tea.'

She followed him across the site to the exhibition van. It was closed today, exhibits already packed away. He unlocked the door and gestured her inside. 'We have to clear the site by five. Then they're putting in the security guards.'

'Then only the ghosts will be left.'

'That's right.' He glanced up as he put the kettle on the small Calor gas stove and lit the flame. 'I'm Charles Wentworth, by the way.'

She smiled. 'I'm Frances.' No surname. No catch.

She sat down on the stool by the table. Boxes of shards still lay there, hastily labelled. The dust of the site lay over everything. It had a strange sharp smell which caught at the back of the throat.

'Do you believe in them?' she said suddenly.

'Ghosts?' He reached down a tin of tea-bags from a locker. 'Sometimes.'

'Sometimes?'

'When a site is taken over by the developers like this, I'd like to think they'll be chased screaming from the excavations.' He kept his tone humorous.

'Has it ever happened?'

'Yes. But sadly never for long. Incentive payments usually overcome superstition.'

'What a pity.' She picked up a small square tile from a pile, stroking it with her fingertip to remove the dust.

'Those are Roman tesserae. Probably from the Boudiccan period. You can have them if you want.'

'Really?' She stared at him. 'Aren't they important?'

'Possibly. It's too late. The markers are about to be ploughed in, remember? All this lot is more or less rubbish now.' He sighed. 'There was so much left to do, but we ran out of time. I suppose we were lucky to get so much, given modern day priorities.'

She glanced up at him, sympathizing with his helpless bitterness.

'It is sad they couldn't have incorporated all these remains into the development and used them to bring in tourists,' she said cautiously. 'Every town in England has a shopping precinct. Very few have a Roman city.'

'They'll think of it. When it's too late,' he agreed. 'They'll say, "let's develop the town for tourists. Now what shall we show them." '

They both laughed wryly. He watched her closely as she took two of the small tiles in her hand and closed her eyes.

'I wonder who walked on these,' she said dreamily.

'Men, women, children. Much like us.' His voice was very quiet. He held his breath.

'I see a woman with a long blue gown, her hair bound up with ribbons,' Frances said slowly. She frowned, frightened by the force of the picture which had come into her head. Please God, don't let it happen here, not in front of a stranger. She gripped the tile till her knuckles whitened, trying to push away the images as they crowded in. But they came, as they always came, whirling out of nowhere, filling her mind.

He was watching her closely. He bit his lip, trying to

conceal his excitement. 'What else can you see?' he prompted quietly, hardly daring to breathe.

Frances sat for a moment, holding the tile. 'She's afraid.' It was too late to stop. She had to go on. Her voice strengthened and she began to breathe more heavily. 'She's lost Claudia! She's lost her child!'

'Claudia! Claudia!' The woman's voice rose to a scream. 'Where are you?'

She stared round frantically. The streets were teeming with panic-stricken people. Near her a cart overturned and she heard a horse shriek with fear. From the distant suburbs the sound of the watchman's horn echoed across the city again and again.

The child had been at her side only moments before, happily skipping down the gravel road between the shops, her new long red dress a small flame in the dullness of the misty morning.

Boxes of fruit fell from a stall near her as it overturned and the two men behind it vaulted over the planks which moments earlier had been their display area and ran. From the pouch of one fell a scattering of coins. He did not bother to stop and gather them.

'She's coming! The Queen of the Iceni is coming!' a man near Julia shouted. 'Save yourselves. Run!'

Run! How could she run without the child? Her daughter. Her little Claudia. Julia whirled round, confused and terrified.

Her husband, Claudius, had told them not to pull down the town walls. He had told them it was crazy. He had told them again and again. But no, it was the policy. This was a peaceful country now. This was a land of rich villas, wealthy retired men and their families. There was no danger, they said. No danger at all. That was before they had flogged the British queen.

At her side for a moment she recognized one of the servants from the villa. He was a tribesman, long Romanized. 'Save yourself, Lady. They will spare no one,' he shouted, momentarily sorry for the woman who had been kind to him. 'This is the day we throw the Romans out of our island. Your only hope is to get away!'

'I can't go without Claudia.' She was sobbing now.

'Then you will die. They will spare no one!' Already he had gone, running through the crowds towards the temple. In moments he was out of sight.

'*Claudia*!' She spun round desperately, trying to swallow the nausea which had risen in her throat. 'Claudia! Claudia!'

'Run!' The shouts and screams echoed down the narrow street. 'Run!' And now she could smell the smoke, acrid and thick; the smoke which drifted across the city from the villas which had been fired in the wealthy western suburbs of the town, the area where she and Claudius lived.

Tears in her eyes she flung down her basket. 'Claudia! Claudia, where are you? *Claudia*!'

The sound of racing hooves was coming closer. The echo of chariot wheels on the distant road.

'Claudia . . .' Her throat was dry, her stomach knotted with terror. She must run. But where? The crowds were panicking, screaming, milling in all directions. She tried to keep her balance as a man bumped into her, failed and fell on her knees on the tiled forecourt of a shop as he leaped across her and hurtled away up the road.

'Mama?'

She was there! Suddenly the child was there, her little hands outstretched, her eyes huge with fright. 'Mama! What's happening?'

Julia threw herself at the little girl and hugged her,

then frantically she set off, dragging her after her. In a second she and the child had disappeared into the crowded, panic-stricken streets.

Moments later the first of the wooden Iceni chariots hurtled around the corner, the driver carrying a burning torch which streamed flame and smoke in its wake . . .

Only the sound of sobbing broke the silence.

'Here. Drink this.' Charles folded her hands gently around a mug. 'Are you all right?'

Frances sipped the scalding liquid and spluttered.

'I put some brandy in it. We had some in the first aid cupboard.' He sat down opposite her and smiled reassuringly. His heart was thumping with excitement.

Frances put down the mug and groped in her pocket with shaking hands for a handkerchief. The sobs she had heard were her own. She blew her nose shakily. In front of her, on the table, lay a heap of dusty tiles.

'What did I say?' she asked at last.

'You described the sack of Camulodunum. It was as if you saw it all.' He tried to hide his excitement.

She bit her lip. 'You must think me such a fool.' She drank some more of the tea, grateful for its biting warmth. She was still shivering violently.

'No. I don't think you're a fool. I think you are a clairvoyant of some sort.' Charles leaned across and picked up one of the little tiles, holding it experimentally in the palm of his hand.

'No. Don't be silly. I have an overactive imagination, that's all . . .' That was what the judge had said. That was what she clung on to. It sounded normal. Explainable.

'Are you sure that's all it was?' He glanced up at her. 'I've met someone who did something like this before. She came to the centre. We gave her various things to hold and she told us about them – their history. Who they had belonged to. Things like that. It was uncanny. But she stayed quite detached. Purely an observer.'

'It was my imagination,' Frances repeated stubbornly. To her chagrin she found her legs were shaking so much she couldn't stand up. 'I ought to go.'

Charles glanced at his watch. 'We've half an hour before Tom comes for the trailer. There's no hurry.'

She smiled wanly and sat back, still fighting the panic, remembering the fire, the screams, the flailing swords.

'Did they get away?'

'Who?' She dragged herself back to the present with difficulty.

'Julia and her little girl.'

'I . . . I don't know.' She stared down at the tiles. 'I can't remember.' Suddenly her eyes filled with tears. 'I've never felt fear like that before – never in my whole life. Not even when – ' She broke off abruptly.

'Not even when?' he prompted gently after a few moments.

No, she mustn't tell him. She had told her husband and look what had happened. She touched the small tile with her fingertip gingerly, then abruptly she pushed it away. She stood up. 'I have to go.'

'Are you sure you feel well enough?' He didn't want her to go. She was a link, a channel to the past which was his whole life.

She tried to smile. 'I'm sorry. Have I shocked you?'

'No. I'm not shocked. I'm interested. Do you want to take the tiles?'

She shook her head vehemently. 'Put them in your museum.'

'OK.' He sat watching her for another few seconds. 'I think they made it, don't you? Julia and little Claudia.' He picked up the tesserae and tipped them into a cardboard box. 'I'm sure they hid somewhere until it was all over.'

She shook her head, biting back her misery. 'Claudia's father was killed, and her brother . . .' She stopped. She had spoken without thinking. 'He was only fourteen. Oh God!' She sat down again and put her head in her hands. 'And Julia . . . Julia was raped . . .' She was sobbing again.

'The link is still there, Frances.' Charles reached out and touched her hand. 'It's all right. It will break. That is what the psychometrist who came to see us said. She said sometimes it stretches and stays, like a spider's thread, then it breaks. It always breaks. Then you will be free. Let me lock up and I'll walk with you. Have you got a car?'

She shook her head.

'Where do you live?'

She didn't want to be alone. Not any more. When she was alone the memories flooded back; the memories of another woman, another time. 'I live in Lexden. Not far.'

He nodded slowly. 'Lexden burned first of course. I'll walk you home if you'll let me.'

She smiled. 'Thank you. I'd like that.'

Her eye was outraged and confused by the muddy site outside the van. She could still see the neat row of thatched shops, the entrance to the villa, the gravelled road – and the smoke; the smoke that had rolled over the city and obliterated it.

Slowly they began to walk. They left the site, glancing sadly at the huge machines of destruction waiting in the wings and began to walk through the streets.

Glancing at her he smiled. 'Each time you go up one of the escalators in the new store they'll build there you'll remember today.'

She smiled and shook her head. 'No, I'll remember that day nearly two thousand years ago.' She took a deep breath. 'I've seen her before, you know.'

'Julia? I thought perhaps you had.'

'She haunts me. I think she must have lived where our house now stands.'

'It's possible.'

'You don't think I'm mad?'

'No.'

'My husband did.'

The divorce had been in the papers the week before, with all the gory details of her unreasonable behaviour; her year-long obsession with a ghost. It had made the national headlines.

Charles smiled sympathetically. 'I confess I did recognize you from the photos. But all that proves is that your husband is a racist.'

'A racist?' She stopped and looked at him, astonished.

'He obviously doesn't like Romans.' He smiled. 'Does all this make you believe in immortality?'

'No.' It came out more harshly than she meant.

'You should.'

'I would have thought archaeologists would believe in the utter finality of death.'

'On the contrary. We're professional resurrectors.' He could sense her pain; real pain beneath the shock and fear. She had walled off the vulnerable wounded part of herself; the part which encompassed the mortal echo which was all that remained of Julia and her child. He should help her to try to forget it. He wrestled with his conscience and lost. 'Don't you want to know what happened to them?' he asked after a long pause.

She shook her head.

'If you knew the truth they might rest in peace,' he persisted hopefully.

God! How he wanted to know the truth. What he would give to listen to her describe the scene again; an eyewitness account of the sack of Colchester. It was unbelievable! He could imagine the paper he would present; the articles he would write; the books . . .

She stopped in the middle of the pavement for a moment, looking at him. 'Why me? Why do they pick on me?' Her question had the ring of desperation. Slowly she began to walk on.

He pulled himself together with an effort and followed her. The woman was suffering. It was unfair to encourage her – to encourage Julia – and prolong her agony. 'As you said, perhaps you live on the site of their home.'

She gave a tight half laugh. 'We used to dig up things in the garden. Bits of pottery. A coin. A little statue which we gave to the museum. Things like that. We were so excited.' She tried to bite back her tears.

Her house was large and grey, set back a little way from the road. The garden was full of blossom, the flower beds beautifully tended, the lawns neatly cut. Even in the rain it was lovely.

There was a house agent's board nailed to the front gate. Charles noted it and frowned. Part of the tragedy of divorce.

As they walked up the drive – the high privet hedges cutting them off from the roar of the traffic in the road outside – he stared round, trying to get the feel of the past which here was so close beneath the surface, trying to reach out as she must reach out to touch the minds of the dead. If only he could do it too. Why was it that she, with no particular interest in history could see it, touch it, feel it, while he . . . he must be content with books and shards and bones?

He put his hand in his pocket. The small tile lay there, abstracted from its fellows as he tidied up the van. Did it hold the key? Gently he closed his fingers around it. He closed his eyes.

They both turned in surprise at the sound of wheels on

the gravel. The gates behind them had been closed. For a moment he didn't understand; he didn't seem to be able to focus properly; the air was full of smoke.

Her scream turned his blood to ice. All he saw was the flash of the upraised sword, a glimpse of the eyes of the man who drove the chariot, then everything went black.

DISTANT VOICES

In Memory of
'Uncle Stuart'

STUART ERSKINE BIRRELL

1887–1916

a kindred spirit

CONTENTS

PREFACE

When my first collection of short stories, *Encounters*, was published in 1990 I did not expect to be asked to compile a second, so I was enormously pleased to find myself writing some new stories, and making a further selection amongst my old ones, for *Distant Voices.*

I still very much enjoy writing short stories. For me they are the sorbet between the courses of longer novels. They freshen and stimulate the palate. They indulge the writer's and the reader's whim with a quick glimpse into shadow or sunlight. They intrigue, they titillate, they frighten or they amuse.

As in *Encounters* those stories that are not new have been chosen from more than two decades of writing and are very varied in theme. To select a few for comment or explanation might help to put the collection in context. Three of the stories, for example, *A Test of Love*, *To Adam a Son* and *Flowers for the Teacher* are unsophisticated and sentimental, written in the early seventies for the so-called true-life market, while others like *Witchcraft for Today* and *When the Chestnut Blossoms Fall* depict incidents in an older world where romance has grown a little cynical.

There are of course ghost stories – two inspired by my own garden. The core story in *Frost* came from a sad tale told me about a greenhouse here, thankfully perhaps, now demolished; *Rosemary and Thyme* is based on an experience which I had myself whilst weeding in my herb garden one morning in early spring.

Catherine's Cat has laid to rest (or perhaps not?) a terror which haunted me for a while as a child and made bedtime a torment for many months – the suitcase on the wardrobe.

The Duck Shoot Man was based on an incident which happened to my mother and my grandmother and myself when we paused on a journey to Edinburgh and spent the night on Lindisfarne.

Dance Little Lady (purely imagination, this one!) was written in the brash eighties; *The Toy Soldier* (inspired by a toy we found in our cottage) in the more thoughtful nineties, a time of redundancy and re-evaluation.

There are many more, about different times and different places, depicting different moods and both the strange and the mundane.

Three of the stories are much longer than the others. *Dance Little Lady*, *A Family Affair* and *Watch the Wall* are almost novellas – two mini thrillers and one a historical romance – something to get your teeth into.

Whatever the length and whatever the subject, I hope you enjoy reading them as much as I enjoyed writing them.

Distant Voices

THE LOCK WAS STIFF and the door swollen. It was several seconds before Jan could force it open and peer at last from the bright sunlight of the porch into the darkness of the house.

As she had climbed out of the car, which was parked on the overgrown gravel of the drive, and looked up at the grey stone façade, she had felt a strange nervousness.

'Go and have a look round, my dear. Take as long as you like.' David Seymour had pressed the large iron key into her hand the day before, when she had met him for the first time. 'I want you to get a feel of how it was.' He smiled at her, his gentle face dissolving into a network of deep wrinkles, contradicting his initial wariness. 'Then we'll talk. Later.'

His grandson, Simon, had been with him. 'Simon's an architect. Clever chap.' The old man had introduced him fondly. The young man was tall and fair with his grandfather's piercing eyes. Where the older man had the look of a buzzard, hunched, predatory, the younger version was an eagle, right down to the aquiline nose. He had held out his hand to Jan, but his appraisal of her was anything but friendly. Clever he may be, she decided instantly, but also hostile, defensive, and summoned, she suspected, to guard his grandfather's privacy.

Of all the people there on that fatal night fifty years ago, David Seymour had been the hardest to approach. And without him she would get nowhere. He had been, after all, the husband.

She had looked forward so much to this part of her research. Interviewing the people concerned; comparing their memories; putting the pieces of the jigsaw together. But it was harder than she had imagined. Some of the people there had suppressed what had happened for over fifty years. The memories were painful, even after so long. To have an inquisitive journalist raking over the past was the last thing many of them wanted.

She took a step into the darkness of the house and paused. It smelled damp and musty. The floors were dusty and cobwebs hung festooned across the landing window. She peered along the corridor towards the staircase which swept uncarpeted up towards the light and then round and out of sight.

That must have been where she fell.

Behind her the door creaked. A wind was getting up. She could hear the rustling of the leaves on the oaks which grew on either side of the long driveway and she shivered, half wishing now that she had brought someone with her. 'This is silly.' The sound of her voice in the intense silence was an intrusion, but a necessary one. She reached into her soft leather shoulder bag and brought out her micro cassette recorder.

'Monday the fourth,' she said firmly, holding the machine close to her mouth. 'I have just arrived at The Laurels. I am standing in the front hall. The house is empty and has obviously been closed for a long time. No one lives here now and there is, as far as I can see, no furniture or anything here.'

She moved to a door on her left and put her hand out to push it open. The room inside was empty; pale light filtered through round the edges of the shutters, diffused green by the ivy which clung to the outside wall. The parquet floor was scuffed and criss-crossed with old, long-dried muddy footprints.

'This must have been the drawing room. It's large. Beautiful. Ceiling mouldings; candelabra, lovely carved mantelpiece,' she murmured into the machine in her hand. She sounded, she thought with sudden wry amusement, like a house agent preparing particulars for the sale of an especially desirable property.

The silence was intense. She turned off her little machine and walked slowly around the room, trying to feel the atmosphere. Had they all been in here, talking, drinking, smoking, when it had happened? Dinner was over, they were all agreed on that. And the ladies had withdrawn. But what had happened after that? John Milton said they had all gathered in the drawing room and that someone had agreed to sing. Sarah Courtney said the men were sitting over their port whilst the ladies were still upstairs, powdering their noses. Stella had finished and had gone on down alone. . .

Walking back to the foot of the stairs, Jan peered up. 'The staircase is shallow, graceful, curved elegantly around the wall,' she murmured into her machine. The banister, polished and smooth, was almost warm beneath the light touch of her fingers. 'Stella Seymour's body was found crumpled at the bottom by the other guests who ran from the dining room, and presumably from the bedroom, when they heard her scream. At the time her death was widely thought to be suicide. It was only four years later, after the war had ended, at the instigation of the man who claimed to have been her lover, that the first accusation of murder was heard.'

Slowly Jan began to climb. Half-way up she stopped suddenly. She could hear something. The intense silence of the house had gone and instead, she realised, she could hear a gentle murmur of conversation coming from somewhere quite near her. She was almost at the bend in the staircase. Frozen with embarrassment she looked up and then back. David Seymour had promised her the house was empty. She could feel her heart beating fast. This was ridiculous. She had permission to be here.

Squatters? Was that it? Could there be squatters in the

house? Uncertain what to do, she clutched her tape recorder more tightly as she tiptoed on up the stairs and peered along the upper landing. Several doors stood open up there; all the rooms were empty of furniture.

The sound of voices was louder now. She could hear the occasional chink of glass, of cutlery on china. It sounded as if a dinner party were in progress. Flattening herself against the wall she squinted back down the stairs where she could just see the door opposite the drawing room. It was closed. Why hadn't she looked in there? Had she not noticed it in her anxiety to see the staircase? Whatever the reason, she thanked God she had not gone barging in, for that seemed to be where the noise was coming from. Get out. That was what she must do. Get out now, without anyone seeing her.

Taking a deep breath she crept back down the stairs, intensely aware that this was where Stella Seymour had died.

The sounds were quieter again now that she was nearly down. Gradually the hall fell silent. The front door was still ajar as she had left it. She could see the wedge of sunlight thrown across the dusty floor. How strange that the noises had been louder from upstairs.

She stopped. She could smell cigars. Then, quite near her, she heard a man laugh. Spinning round, she faced the sound. There was no one to be seen. Her mouth dry, she switched off her tape recorder. Pushing it into her shoulder bag, she tiptoed towards the dining room door, holding her breath as she edged closer. She could see now that it was not quite shut. Cautiously she moved forward. She could hear the voices again. And subdued laughter. Smell the tobacco. There was a sudden crescendo in the noise and a shout of laughter as she brought her eye to the crack in the door.

They were sitting around an oblong table – some dozen people – no, she saw suddenly, just men, all at one end of the table. The air was wreathed in smoke. They were all wearing dinner jackets.

A sudden sound behind her brought her upright swiftly,

her heart pounding. She could hear footsteps on the landing.

'David, darling –' The voice was clear and high. Excited. There was a rustle of skirts, the quick patter of feet and then suddenly – horribly – a high-pitched scream.

Jan froze, her hand still clenched on the door-frame behind her back. She could hear it. The sound of a body falling, but there was nothing there. Nothing at all. The dust was untouched on the steps save for the scuff marks where her own shoes had been.

Whirling, she stared behind her at the door. Beyond it there was total silence. Her heart was hammering so loudly in her ears she felt sure it must echo all round the house as she pulled the door-handle and swung the door open. The dining room was empty. There was no table. No scent of tobacco. The room smelled merely of damp.

Only when she was sitting at last in her car peering back at the house did she start to breathe again. She flung her bag onto the passenger seat beside her and slammed down the door lock, then she sat for a moment, her forehead resting against the rim of the steering wheel. She was shaking all over.

David Seymour had poured her a cup of coffee himself, from hands which were considerably less shaky than hers, despite his ninety-four years. 'You've just come from The Laurels now?' He stood looking down at her, his expression curiously neutral. 'My dear Miss Haydon, I am so sorry you should have been so frightened. There is no one there, I can assure you. My grandson keeps an eye on the place for me. He went over there only a couple of days ago.'

'I shouldn't have come straight to you like this.' The black coffee was taking effect. This was an old man and his memories of the house must be bad enough without her adding to them with wild stories about ghosts!

He shook his head, sitting down opposite her. 'I'm glad you did. Who else would you go to?' He reached for the phone from the table beside him. 'I'm calling my grandson now. He can go over there straightaway to check that there are no intruders.' His voice was strong and alert, like the rest of him, Jan thought, as she leaned back against the cushions and sipped her coffee gratefully.

She realised he was watching her intently as he replaced the receiver. 'Simon is coming over here first.' He reached for his own cup. He paused. 'You are irrevocably set upon writing my wife's biography?'

Jan frowned. 'There are a great many people who would love to read it. She was a very great painter. She's been a heroine of mine for as long as I can remember.'

'And that is a reason for raking over her bones?'

The sharpness of the words brought Jan up with a shock. 'I'm sorry. I understood you had no objection to the book.'

'Would it matter if I had?' His gaze was suddenly piercing.

'Well . . .' She hesitated.

'No. Of course it wouldn't. In fact my opposition would whet your appetite. It would make you curious. You would want to know what the old buzzard was hiding!' He glared at her.

She smiled shame-facedly. 'I expect it would, if I'm honest.'

He nodded, seemingly satisfied with her answer. 'Good. You'll do. Now, do you believe that I murdered her?' The directness of the question was shocking.

'I – no – of course not.' She was embarrassed.

'There is no *of course not* about it, my dear. You must search the evidence. You must be a thorough and honest investigator.'

'But they never charged you.'

'No.'

'You loved her.'

The old face softened. 'Indeed I did. I worshipped her.'

'And she didn't have an affair –'

'Didn't she?' He seemed suddenly to be looking inside himself, searching for pictures which had long ago grown fuzzy and out of focus. 'She was a vibrant, sociable, lovely person and she was lonely. I had been away so long. It was the war.'

Jan bit her lip. 'Then the article in the American paper was true?' It had appeared only a few months ago, reviving old memories, claiming that the baby Stella had been expecting was the result of an affair.

'I did not say that.' She could see his pain. 'I didn't know if I could father more children; I had been wounded. But the American had long gone and Stella was above all honest. She said he had meant nothing and I believed her. I did not know he had taken so many of her pictures away . . .'

'Surely the pictures didn't mean anything.' Obscurely she felt she had to comfort him. 'He could have been going to sell them or exhibit them for her –'

'Perhaps.' He sighed. 'The fall was an accident. A catastrophic, disastrous, tragic accident. She would not have killed herself. I'm sure she wouldn't. And yet how can I be sure? And how will I ever know about the child?' He took a deep breath and looked up at her again, suddenly almost pleading. 'You will make your own mind up as to the truth of all this, and I think you will make the right decision.'

Was he asking her to decide? To find out the truth for him? Jan bit her lip as the old man sighed again, a bone-weary sound which tore at her heartstrings.

'In a way I'm glad all this has happened,' he went on after a moment. 'Simon has been trying to make me face the rumours and think about that house for years. It's an albatross; a Pandora's box. If there are people squatting there, which I doubt, then it's time to let it go. I hope Simon will get married, then he could live there, but it's too big for one person alone.' There was another short silence. 'Stella wouldn't have liked squatters. She loved that house, you know. All her best painting was done there.' He levered himself to his feet. 'Did you see her studio?'

Jan shook her head. 'I'm afraid I left rather quickly.'

The old man grinned. 'Ran away, did you? Can't blame you. I've always thought the house was rather spooky, myself, but Stella always filled it with people. There was never any silence. Only when she was painting, or when she said she was painting . . .' He turned away sharply. For a moment Jan wondered if he were sobbing silently. She could see the movement of his shoulders and she ached to comfort him. But as she watched he straightened himself and with a visible effort he turned and went over to the window.

Jan too had heard the car draw up outside. She waited, watching, as David Seymour turned to face the door.

Simon's first words were to the point. 'If you have been upsetting Grandfather – '

'No, Simon!' The old man's interruption was peremptory. 'She has been doing nothing of the kind. I gave the girl permission to go to The Laurels. And I want her to write Stella's story. It's all so long ago now. No one is going to be hurt . . .'

Simon swung round. 'But Grandfather – '

'Enough.' David threw himself back on the chair with a groan. 'I want you to tell her everything she wants to know. And go with her to check out the house.' He gave a short laugh which after a moment changed into a cough. 'She thinks someone is squatting there. She heard people in the dining room.'

They went in Simon's car. Jan had followed him out of the house reluctantly, sensing his hostility. 'I'm sorry to inflict this on you,' she said as she slotted her seatbelt into place. 'I'm sure you have better things to do than chase out to the country at a moment's notice.'

'If there are squatters something must be done about it,' he replied. Engaging gear smoothly he swung the car out into the traffic. 'How long were you in the house?'

'Only a few minutes.'

'But you saw no one?'

She hesitated. How could she tell him what she saw? 'No.'

'And the door was locked?'

She nodded. 'It didn't seem to have been opened for ages.'

'I have the back door key. I imagine that if there are intruders, they too have gone in that way. Only Grandfather still has the front door key, as far as I know.'

'Do you remember your grandmother?' Jan glanced at him curiously.

He gave a short laugh. 'Hardly. She died long before I was born.'

'I'm sorry. Of course.'

'You've seen her self portrait? The one in the town gallery?'

Jan nodded. 'She was very beautiful.'

'Yes.' He turned onto the bypass and accelerated away from the traffic. 'I suppose the idea is to bring your book out in time for the exhibition they're planning for next year to mark the fiftieth anniversary of her death.'

'It will be wonderful to have so many of her paintings together.'

'Even the ones in the States. Quite.' His voice was dry. 'We're almost there.'

He pulled the car around the back of the house and they climbed out, looking round. The house seemed as deserted as before. There was no sign of life at all as Simon pulled out his key and opened the back door.

'No one in here, anyway.' He walked ahead of her into the kitchen.

Jan looked round. Oak dresser, table, chairs, deep sink, rusty range. It was obvious that no one had cooked here since that day in the war when David Seymour had walked out of the house after his wife's funeral, locked the door and gone back to his squadron.

She could feel her stomach clenching with nerves. 'Perhaps they are camping in some other part of the house.'

'Perhaps.' Simon reached into his pocket and produced a torch. He did not switch it on however. Enough sunlight filtered through blind and shutter for them to see clearly as they walked slowly through the ground floor. Outside the dining room door he stopped. 'You heard them in here?' He had his hand on the knob.

She nodded. She knew what they would find. Only dust and cobwebs decorated the room which had glittered with such life. 'I suppose you think I'm going mad?'

He grinned. It made him look suddenly and unexpectedly approachable. 'No more than dozens of other people who have seen and heard it too.'

She stared at him. 'You mean you know about it – what I saw? You knew! Your grandfather knew?'

He nodded. 'Ghosts. Memories trapped in the walls. Who knows. None of the people in the village will come near this house. Which suits us fine.' He pulled the door closed. 'Come and see Stella's studio.'

He gave her no chance to say anything as he strode back to the kitchen and out of the house. She followed him, almost running, over the long grass of what had once been the lawn and through an overgrown shrubbery to a low, thatch-roofed building which overlooked a reedy pond. He reached for the key which was hidden beneath a moss-covered stone. 'I can't think why this place hasn't been vandalised. But it seems Stella's secrets are still her secrets,' he said shortly. He stood back and let Jan go in ahead of him. 'Did my grandfather not tell you about this place?'

Jan shook her head. She stared round.

The studio stood on the edge of the water, its large windows allowing the sky and the willows and the glittering ripples to explode into the room, filling it with light. All Stella's painting equipment was still here: easels, canvases, paints, sketchbooks curled with damp, the pages stuck together, an ancient sofa, draped in a green silk shawl, the fringe trailing on the ground, black with mildew, vases of flowers, long dried and faded beyond recognition, on the table a straw sun hat amongst the scattered brushes and pencils and dried-up tubes of paint.

Jan bit her lip, fighting the lump in her throat. 'It's as though she only left a few minutes ago.'

'He would never let it be touched.'

She picked up a palette knife from the table. The lump of paint dried on its tip matched exactly the colour in the foreground of the painting on the easel.

'What do you think really happened that night?' She was staring out at the water. A pair of mallard swam into view, the pond rippling into diamond rings around their gently paddling feet.

'No one knows for sure.'

'The article in the American magazine said that she was pushed. That it was murder.' She turned and looked at him. He was very handsome, Stella's grandson, with her colouring, if the portrait in the gallery was anything to go by, even if he had inherited his grandfather's nose. 'It said that she was pregnant by another man. An American.'

Simon's eyes narrowed. 'Grandfather should have sued them. But he didn't want to. He didn't want anything to do with the article. He thought everyone would forget, and her memory would be left in peace.'

'Instead of which I come along.'

'Instead of which you come along.'

'He told you –'

'To tell you everything. I know.' He had strolled over to the windows and was looking out, his shadow falling across the floor to the green shawl. He sighed. 'I expect you know about the letters. To the GI. And that he had sent so many of her drawings and paintings back to the States. That rather supports the gossip in a way.' He turned and faced her. 'What do you think you heard in there? In the house?'

'People? A tape? A radio? Echoes? Ghosts?' She could feel her skin beginning to shiver even though it was warm in the studio. The air was heavy suddenly with the scent of oil paint and linseed and turpentine.

'Did you hear a woman laughing?'

'Yes, I did.'

'And she sounded happy?'

'I heard her calling him. Your grandfather. She sounded ecstatic. And then I heard her fall.' She paused. She had heard the voice, but where had David Seymour been? Downstairs in the dining room with the others, or had he appeared suddenly on the landing next to her? She bit her lip. No. Surely it had been a happy voice. 'I think it was an accident. I think she wanted me to know that. You've heard her too?'

He nodded. 'I think at that last dinner party they were enjoying themselves. They were all deliriously happy. Stella and Grandfather and John and Sarah and the Daniels and Peter Cockcroft. It was wartime. There was rationing. So many of the fit young people were gone, so many of their friends had died, but Grandfather had been invalided out after being terribly wounded. He was safe. He had recovered. They were all there and they were happy. After my father was born Stella had hoped and hoped for another child but none came. Then suddenly Grandfather was back and she was pregnant again. They were celebrating. It was the happiest moment of her life.' Simon turned away from the window and looked at Jan. 'I'm guessing. No, it's more than that. I'm almost certain that's what happened. Grandfather trusts you. He likes you and I think that when he heard that you had seen something – heard something – in the house, he knew that she trusted you too. Only nice people hear her laugh – ' He stopped abruptly as Jan's eyes flooded with tears. 'Oh Miss Haydon – Jan – I'm sorry, I didn't mean to upset you.' He delved into the pocket of his jacket and produced a handkerchief. It was slightly painty.

Jan wiped her eyes. 'You are an artist too?' She was feeling rather silly.

'A bit. If I've inherited half her talent I count myself a very lucky man.' Gently he steered her to the sofa. 'Sit down a minute. Get your breath back.'

'How could he bear to think of selling the house?'

'He can't. Not really. He'd have done it years ago if he were going to. After the inquest he went back to the war even though he wasn't really fit – I don't suppose they asked too many questions – they needed all the men they could get. As far as I know he never came back here, but I think he must still love the house in a way. And the house must have happy memories as well as sad ones. They shared so much here. Besides, don't you feel it? She's still here –' He gestured at the easel. It was another self portrait, this time in Edwardian dress, unfinished, a few details completed: the face, which was vibrant, happy, glowing with life; the sparkling jewels around her throat and wrists; her hands, the ostrich feather fan. . .

As they sat down Simon had left his arm around Jan's shoulders. She was shivering. The sun had moved a little, and the studio was no longer lit across the water. It filled with weaving, drifting, green light.

'If only she could speak to us,' he went on. 'Give us a sign. Something to tell Grandfather that the baby was his. It's such a sad story, but at least then that last awful doubt would be gone and he would know once and for all that it was an accident; that she didn't, couldn't, have had any reason at all to kill herself.'

Jan smiled. 'What sort of sign?' This was scarcely objective research, but she was beginning to enjoy the feeling of his arm, so lightly draped over the back of the sofa.

'I don't know. Move something. Say something. I'll leave it to her. Anything.' He grinned. 'Listen, Grandfather asked me to take you back to tea. He wants to lend you her letters and diaries.'

'Then he really does trust me.'

Simon nodded slowly. 'I told you. He wants the whole

story of her life to be known at last. He said he was too old for them to hang him.'

'But that's admitting –'

'No. It's not admitting anything, except that he loved Stella more than life itself.' Simon stood up. He held out his hand. 'Let's go back to the house.'

For a moment she didn't move, then, reluctantly, she stood up. For a second she stood looking down at the face on the easel, then she followed him outside.

At the back door of the house she stopped. 'Can I go in once more? To see the dining room?'

'Of course.' He stood back so that she could go ahead of him through the kitchen and out into the corridor. The dining room door stood open, a wedge of light pouring from it across the floor.

They could both hear the music. Glen Miller. And the talk and laughter. The chink of knives and forks on crockery; they could both smell the cigar smoke, and through it all the faintest trace of oil paint.

Jan found she was holding Simon's hand. She was trembling, but she could not resist going nearer. Slowly, step by step, they crept towards the dining room as gradually the noise of the dinner party got louder. She could smell other things now. Cooking. Carefully hoarded coffee. Wine. A woman's scent. One hand firmly clutching Simon's, she reached forward with the other and gently she pushed the door open a fraction.

The room was empty.

In the echoing silence she gave a little sob of disappointment.

It was Simon who spotted the soft curl of an ostrich feather drifting on the bare boards.

The Drop Out

OF COURSE he wouldn't really come. The idea was too bizarre. But then, a husband is a husband, even if this one had hardly fulfilled his matrimonial duties to the letter.

Zara leaned forward and gazed into the mirror. If he did come he was going to see quite a change in her after all this time. She vaguely recollected that her hair had been not only a different style but a different colour then. Her figure had improved out of recognition and maturity had brought sophistication and confidence.

'I wonder if he's got a paunch?' she asked her reflection out loud. And giggled. Gerald with a paunch was unthinkable.

She looked at the letter again. It began, 'Darling,' – That too was unlike him. Gerald had never been one for endearments. He must be in trouble, she decided as she slipped on her elegant silk suit.

Money? She had always understood that he had plenty. He had been 'something in the city' when they married. She had never bothered to find out what. Certainly he had from time to time continued to pay handsome amounts into her account. For old times' sake and when he remembered, she always thought, rather than for any mundane idea that he should support his wife. Not that she had needed supporting for years, of course, thank God. But, come to think of it, there had been no money now for nearly a year.

She stood sideways to the mirror and ran a critical hand

down her flat stomach. No. She was the kind of woman who did well in business and thrived on it. Gerald's conscience money or whatever it was had brought her some nice little extras, like the small Mercedes in the driveway. It had in no way gone towards her upkeep.

Well. If not money, what? Women. She knew some wives were called on to extricate their husbands from the clutches of too-persistent girlfriends, but Gerald had never had that problem. She had heard in fact that he merely turned the latest woman onto the last with a cold-blooded delight which often shocked both parties into flight. She paused for a moment. Perhaps he wanted a divorce? No. It was unthinkable. He, like her, found the state of absentee matrimony far too useful and pleasant an arrangement to end it.

The police? She looked at the mirror for a moment, her eyes wide, and then shrugged the idea away. It was too ridiculous to contemplate.

Zara gave up the idle speculation with a glance at her watch, ran downstairs, collected the car keys from the mantelpiece and went to the door. She was not usually given to conjecture and certainly not to day dreaming, and she had made herself uncharacteristically late for the board meeting.

He was sitting on the doorstep.

In rags.

For fully two minutes Zara looked down at her husband without speaking. Then, bleakly, she stood back and motioned him into the house, wrinkling her nose ostentatiously as he passed in front of her.

He walked straight to the drinks table and poured himself a Scotch. Then he turned and looked her up and down. He was slim still, no sign of a paunch, lean and hard, brown and fit, and his eyes twinkled mischievously.

'Go and run me a bath, Za-Za, dear. Then you can stop holding your nose, and we can talk.'

'But, Gerald!' Her usually well-modulated voice had risen to a squeak. 'What's happened to you?'

'Fate hasn't been kind, lady.' He put on what sounded like a very professional whine. But still his face was laughing. 'Go on woman, before my fleas start hopping onto your Persian rugs.'

With a cry of horror she fled upstairs and, turning both taps on full, groped for the small bottle of Dettol in the medicine cabinet. It smelled very strong in the steam, but anything was better than Gerald's . . . aroma.

While he bathed she washed his glass assiduously, sponged the outside of the whisky bottle and then got out the vacuum cleaner and ran it over the carpet where he had been standing. Fleas indeed! She shuddered.

With a sudden pang of guilt that she could so completely have forgotten her meeting she went to the phone and called the office to instruct her PA. 'I don't feel too well,' she explained quietly into the receiver and was amazed to find it was the truth. She felt sick and slightly feverish.

He reappeared in half an hour wearing her bathrobe. Voluminous on her, it sat on him like an outgrown coat on a gangly schoolboy, exposing long muscular legs and arms, and an expanse of hard brown chest.

'No sign of a man up there,' he commented as he threw himself down on the leather sofa. 'I could have borrowed his razor.' He sounded faintly aggrieved.

'I suppose you're hungry?' Zara ignored his remark loftily. She was indignant to find that her heart had started to bang rather hard beneath her ribs as it had, she distinctly remembered, when she first knew him.

'I'm starving, lady. Not eaten since the day before yesterday.' He reverted to his whine. She ignored it.

'I hope you don't still expect oysters for breakfast,' she commented sarcastically from the kitchen as she filled the kettle, remembering some of his more extravagant tastes. Her hands were shaking.

'A crust will do, lady, just a crust.' He appeared immediately behind her suddenly, and put his hands gently on her shoulders. 'I suppose you want an explanation?'

'I think I do rather.' She gave a small laugh.

'You could say I'd been down on my luck.' He looked at her hopefully, then on second thoughts shook his head. 'No, I know. It's not me is it. Would you believe that I did it on purpose?' He paused. 'You'd never credit the things people put in their dustbins, Za-Za. Someone ought to write a monograph on it: *The world's great untapped source of wealth*.'

'I'm sure the dustmen tap it successfully,' she commented acidly, slipping two slices of bread into the toaster. 'Judging by the things they nail to the fronts of their vans.'

'Teddies,' Gerald said reflectively. 'Your dustman here nails teddies to his van. I saw him as I came up the road. How anyone could bear to throw their teddy out I shall never know. It's worse than homicide.'

'Gerald! You never kept yours!'

'I did!' Her perched on the edge of the breakfast table to take the toast as it popped up, snatched his fingers away and blew on them hastily. 'Didn't you even search my trunks and the things I left?'

'Of course not. They were private.'

Gerald stared at her. 'You are truly a wonderful woman Za-Za. I wonder why I left you?' He buttered the piece of toast thoughtfully. She was also, he noted, slimmer, taller, if that were possible, and overall a thousand times more stunning than he remembered her.

'You couldn't stand me, dear.' She smiled. 'It's a shame because I really rather liked you.'

'Liked?' He raised an eyebrow.

'Loved, then.'

'Still in the past tense?'

She smiled. 'Stop fishing Gerald and tell me what you've been up to.'

The black coffee had steadied her, and she sat down opposite him, elegantly crossing her legs, waiting for him to begin.

For a few minutes he ate in silence, giving every impression that he really hadn't eaten for days, then he sat back with a sigh and reached for his own cup.

'One morning on the way to office, I thought, Gerald, old chap, what does it all mean? You know, the way one does? I couldn't find a convincing answer. So I thought, Right. If there's no reason for doing it, don't.' He grinned and reached for the sugar.

'There's always the need for money, Gerald.' She tried not to sound prim.

'Money for what?' You earn a damn good salary, so *you* don't need it. *I* don't need it. You had a house, I had a flat, did we need both, for God's sake? Why should I risk a coronary for the sake of a subscription to a golf club full of bores and for the Inland Revenue?'

'Gerald, that's a very trite and short-sighted remark, if you don't mind my saying so. And how,' she flashed at him suddenly, 'do you know how much I earn?'

'I own your company, dear. No,' he raised his hand as she put down her cup indignantly, about to speak. 'No. You got your job on merit alone, and I am totally uninterested in policy. Now, as I was saying, I thought, Why don't I drop out like all those delightful chaps one sees singing in the underground. The trouble is, I can't sing. I expect you remember that. I can't paint, or pot or woodcarve, to earn enough money to subsist, so I had to resort to begging. More coffee, please.'

She poured it for him without a word.

'I told James to stop the car. I told him to take a month's salary in lieu, drive the car home, lock it up, turn off the gas and the electricity in the flat, stick the keys back through the letter box – oh and empty the fridge. I thought of that. Then I called the office and said, "I'll be away for a year or so," and gave my solicitor a ring, about power of attorney and that sort of thing. I bought a large cream doughnut, simply oozing cholesterol, and a can of beer, put all my loose change in the hat of one of those pathetic young men you see sitting leaning against walls with their dogs beside them and started walking. Right then and there, in my city suit.' He threw back his head and laughed. 'I bet you didn't recognise it when I came in.'

'Did you enjoy yourself?' Zara tried not to sound shocked or angry.

'Marvellously.' He reached for the breadknife, cut an enormous wedge of bread and began heaping butter onto it. 'I've been all over the south of England and right down to Cornwall, to all the little off the road places one misses in a beastly car. I've stuck it for eight months.'

'Why did you come back here then?'

'For one thing I was hungry this morning. For another, I wanted to see you again.'

'Gerald. How could you afford the stamp and the paper for that letter?' She was suddenly suspicious.

He looked embarrassed for the first time. 'Well, the trouble is Zara that I've begun earning money again. First it was only casual jobs: car cleaning, fruit picking, even potato lifting once – God! What a job that was. Then one night in a pub, I happened to recite one of the poems I'd been making up on the road as I walked along. They passed the hat round and I made about seven pounds fifty. A fortune! Well, I've gone on from there. Each town and village I visited after that I'd chat up the landlord and stick a notice in his pub saying I was going to give a recital. Then afterwards I'd pass round the old hat.'

'Gerald, you're not serious!' Zara looked at him with real admiration.

'Well, the truth is dear,' he looked down at the cup, half embarrassed. 'I think I need an agent or something. You see I want to have them published. I know it's silly, but I've got ambitions for them. I've found out what life is all about, you see. For me, it's poetry.'

'And you'd like me to act for you?'

'Would you?' He looked up eagerly.

'Of course.'

Zara enjoyed dressing her husband as a poet. She spent the morning buying him jeans and shirts and a rather expensive-looking leather jacket. She even debated whether he would wear beads or a necklace, or a thong around his neck with a bead on it, but decided finally against it. He had after all been in the habit of wearing a pinstripe suit.

She had left him before setting out on her spree, reciting his poems to her dictating machine. When she got back, her cleaning lady was standing open-mouthed at the drawing room door, listening.

'It's filth, Mrs Lennox, real filth,' the woman complained, jumping guiltily when she saw her employer. 'But it's beautiful. I could listen for hours, so I could.' She giggled skittishly.

Zara stood beside her and together they heard Gerald reciting. It was indeed beautiful.

After a moment he swung round, microphone in hand, and saw them. To Zara's amazement he broke off abruptly, blushing. 'I didn't know there was anyone there,' he murmured and then he laughed. 'They're not really for ladies' ears.'

'Nonsense. They're damn good.' Zara went in and reaching up planted a quick kiss on his cheek. 'I'll start putting them on the word processor for you this afternoon.'

They decided they would call him Noxel, which was Lennox inside out. No other name. It looked right in print, and would sound good, Zara thought, on the radio. She ignored his comment that it made him sound a little like a lavatory cleaner.

Gerald Lennox had been, they both agreed, a bore.

She took him round London, showing him off to her new, trendy friends, and she bathed in reflected glory as Gerald's exquisitely metred adjectives and highly coloured phraseology assailed their ears. She had always suspected they cultivated her acquaintance for her money and contacts. Now she had produced someone who belonged to their world. More than belonged. He actually did things. Most of them, she now discovered, claimed themselves passive rather than active participants in the arts. Zara felt herself to be one-up at last and was very pleased with her eccentric, wandering poet.

Together they giggled over the raised eyebrows of the neighbours. It seemed no one recognised him.

Then Zara's lover came back from two months in Cape Town. He let himself in half an hour before she was due home from the office and found Gerald sitting at her computer.

'My dear chap,' Gerald glanced up and then rose, his hand outstretched. 'I knew you must exist, but she never admitted it, bless her.' He grinned amicably.

The other's mouth fell open, and he felt uncertainly for the nearest chair and sat down heavily. 'I'm sorry,' he said at last. 'I don't believe we've met?'

Gerald leaned back in his seat. 'I'm Zara's husband, actually. But not to worry –' as the other man rose abruptly to his feet, Gerald lifted his hand to reassure him. 'I'm off. I've been wanting to move on for some time now, but I didn't like to leave her on her own. She's been a brick these last few weeks.'

He shuffled his papers together and collected the pages he had been printing. 'Give me ten minutes old chap. We'll manage the turn-round before she gets home.' He took the stairs two at a time.

The new arrival sat, looking rather stunned, for a moment. Then, a trifle wearily, he rose to his feet and went to pour himself a drink. When Zara came home he was in the bath with a large gin.

She saw the note from Gerald on the hall table and knew without reading it that he had gone. She considered for a moment and then breathed a deep sigh of relief. It had been an interesting interlude, but not one she had wanted prolonged. It spoiled her concentration at the office.

Moment of Truth

STEVE AND I had known each other since we were children, brought up in the same village, growing together, and at last, realising that we were in love, we became engaged on my eighteenth birthday. Then began our struggle to save enough money for a deposit on our own home. Steven didn't want us to marry until, as he put it, he could support me properly, or at least put a roof over my head, and in spite of my pleas that it didn't matter, our engagement stretched out for one and then two years. Steve was a mechanic at the local garage in the village and was hoping desperately to be offered a partnership by the owner, so the future looked good, if only we could save enough for that deposit. And then something happened which was to have a profound effect on our lives together. Steve's great aunt Irene who had looked after him when he was a little boy suddenly had a stroke and they said that she would never be able to manage on her own again; even when she was strong enough to leave the hospital she would have to go into a home for elderly people where she could be properly looked after.

As soon as she was well enough to have visitors she called Steve and me to her bedside. She could hardly speak, and her poor withered hand lay paralysed on the sheet but she made it clear, with tears in her eyes, that her cottage was ours. It was to be a wedding present.

Six weeks later we were married. The cottage was tiny, but

it was our own home at last and I adored it. The low oak-beamed parlour had two rocking chairs and a table and there was room for little else. The bedroom window opened out under the thatch and wisteria and honeysuckle climbed round it. I remember I leaned out of that window on the first morning after we moved in and took a deep breath of the fresh air and I could have cried for happiness.

I worked as a waitress at the local Tudor Tea Rooms before we married and I kept on my job. For one thing I enjoyed it; for another we were still saving all we could. The cottage needed modernising badly and we wanted to start a family of course, so it seemed sensible to work all the hours we could fit in, putting every penny we earned into the bank. Although we were both tired and strained more often than not, we stayed happy. Or I thought we did. But perhaps without our realising it, earning money had by now become for us both an end in itself, more important even than our love for each other.

The trouble started in the summer two years after we were married. We were always very busy at that time of year in the café, for hundreds of tourists crowded into our tiny Cotswold village to see its beauties and its famous manor house, and often I would come home too exhausted even to give Steve his supper before I tumbled into bed, falling asleep as soon as my head touched the pillow. I was much too tired to make love.

It was about then that Steve started working overtime in the evenings. 'I might as well, for all I see of you,' he said rather bitterly. 'And besides, I can't bear to see you so tired.' And he had weighed my heavy blonde hair – the same colour as his almost – in his hands, and kissed me rather wistfully on the cheek. 'If I work extra perhaps soon you can give up the waitressing altogether.'

I glanced up at him gratefully and tried not to feel guilty as I noticed, for the first time, that he too was tired, and his face pallid from lying all day under cars when everyone else in the village was deeply tanned from the summer sun.

And so it happened that we had hardly seen each other for the last three months or so at all. We were saving, yes; but without my realising it, our marriage was fading away.

I was feeling especially tired and depressed when one day, as I was serving at the front tables, the ones which looked out of the mullioned windows across the green, a young man came in. He was of middle height, not terribly good-looking, rather swarthy, but he had the most incredible eyes. Light grey, so light they were like silver streaks in his tanned face. He beckoned me over.

'What's your name, sweetheart?' he asked in an American accent.

I smiled at him easily, whisking crumbs off the table with my cloth. I was used to this.

'I'm Linda,' I smiled. 'What can I get you, sir?'

'Tea. An English tea with cream cakes and scones please, Linda my love, and later perhaps you can show me the town?'

'Sorry sir, my husband will be expecting me home,' I answered with a practised smile. I turned to get his order.

Usually I dismissed passes like this man's without another thought, but something about his eyes, and the way his face fell when his gaze rested on the wedding ring which I waved under his nose, tugged at my heart.

When I took the tray to his table I asked casually, 'You all on your own then?'

He nodded. 'I'm over from the States for a few months. I'm a photographer and I'm doing a series on beautiful old England.'

There was something so wistful about his smile that I felt my heart do a quick bump.

As I moved quickly round the tables with my tray I could feel his gaze following me and every time I re-emerged from the kitchen with a new plate of scones and clotted cream, there he was watching.

When I took his bill to him he grabbed my wrist. 'Honey,

wouldn't your husband spare you for half an hour – just to have a drink with me at the pub? I hate going alone.'

I felt my stomach lurch. I had told him Steve expected me. It wasn't strictly true, of course. He had told me that there was a rush job on at the garage again that night, and he might not be back until even later than usual. As I said, I was depressed, and bored.

I took a deep breath. 'Okay,' I said. 'Perhaps I could manage a very quick drink, but not here.' I thought of the prying eyes and quick tongues of the village folk. 'Have you a car?'

He nodded.

'Then pick me up outside the post office.' I glanced at my watch. 'I'm on till we close this evening, at six. I'll see you then.'

His name turned out to be Graham, and he told me at once he had a wife and two kids in Wisconsin. We spent a couple of hours driving round the leafy lanes and then went to the fifteenth-century pub in the next village. He brought me home and dropped me at the end of our lane before going back to his hotel.

It was a perfectly innocent and very enjoyable outing, and so was the next, three nights later when Steve was again especially late. After that Graham took to dropping in at the tea rooms every evening as we were closing and I would tell him whether or not I would be able to spare an hour or two.

Steve was more and more regularly late at the garage as they seemed unusually busy so I saw more and more of Graham. I never mentioned Graham at home. The first time, Steve had come home in a temper from work, very unusually for him, and I knew it had not been the right moment. Then after that it became increasingly difficult.

Then came the time, inevitably, when Graham kissed me.

It happened so gently, so naturally, I hardly noticed it coming and before I could help myself I had returned it, passionately allowing him to draw me against his chest till I could hardly breathe.

'Oh no Graham. No!' I pushed him away suddenly. 'No, don't. I love my husband.'

'Sure, honey.' Gently but firmly he drew me back again. 'He won't miss a kiss or two, for a lonely man.'

But I was scared. I turned my head away and pushed with my fists against his chest. 'Don't Graham. No. I want to go home, please.'

Reluctantly he released me. 'Okay Linda, if you're sure that's what you really want.' He looked at me closely and as those silvery eyes met mine I felt my heart give a disloyal little lurch. It wasn't what I wanted at all.

He dropped me off at the end of the lane as usual and I made my way through the fragrant twilight to the cottage. Steve wasn't home, so I let myself out of the back door and into the garden. I could smell a whiff of pipe smoke from next door. Ian Johnson and his wife were sitting on their porch chatting quietly.

I had kicked off my sandals to walk on the dewy lawn, so I suppose they didn't hear me. The cottage was in darkness so they must have assumed I was still out.

'It's that pretty little wife of his I'm sorry for,' came Ian's voice, low but clearly audible. 'She doesn't suspect a thing.'

' 'E deserves to be shot 'e does,' came his wife's voice. 'Such a lovely couple they were. And I was so pleased when old Irene said they could live in her cottage. Hoping for some little ones next door, I was, and now this 'as to 'appen.'

'She's bound to find out.' Ian again, and a fresh cloud of smoke wafted over the roses as he drew on his pipe.

As I stood, listening, I was shaking with cold. My hands gripped the skirt of my dress and crushed the fabric convulsively. I felt terribly sick.

What were they talking about? I wanted to run next door, to scream, to cry, to ask questions, but in my heart I already knew the answer.

Steve's boss had never been all that keen on overtime in the past, so why should he have started working till all hours this summer especially? Certainly not just to help us with our finances, and I had never bothered to go to the garage to check. I could feel a great sob, like a lump in my chest, and I turned and fled into the cottage before it could come out like a scream of misery.

I sat for an hour or more in the dark listening to the steady calm ticking of Aunt Irene's grandmother clock. Then I heard the front door open and close again softly.

'Linda, are you home?' Steve called quietly.

I couldn't say a word. I sat in the dark, my hands still clutching my skirt.

'Lyn?'

He pushed open the parlour door and clicked on the light.

'Lyn! What are you doing here?' He gazed at me in astonishment.

I hadn't actually been crying, but my face must have told him everything for he sat down suddenly on the edge of the rocking chair and ran his fingers through his hair. 'You know, don't you.' It was a statement, not a question.

I nodded dumbly.

'Oh Lord, Lyn. I'd have given the world for it not to have happened.' He stared at me miserably. 'What am I going to do?'

'You'd better tell me the truth,' I whispered at last. And I waited, my face in my hands, while he told me.

'Her name's Lauren. I met her a few months before you and I were married. She went to work in London, and then three months ago she came back. I serviced her car and we got chatting.' He shrugged. There was a long silence, then he raised his head and looked at me. 'She's going to have my baby, Lyn. I don't know what to do.'

'Do you love her?' I couldn't recognise my own voice, it was so cracked with fear.

He nodded. Then he shrugged desperately. 'Not as much as I love you. You mean everything to me, Lyn, you know you do, but . . .'

'But! While I've been working my fingers to the bone, struggling, saving . . . you've been spending money on someone else. The whole village knows except me. You louse! You hypocrite. You foul, beastly rotten dirty beast!' I was screaming at him now, and I saw him stand up, his face pale.

'Quietly Linda, please,' he tried to interrupt me, but I couldn't stop.

'You mean, unkind, disloyal bastard!' The tears were streaming down my face now. 'How could you! How could you? Well, if you don't want me, thank goodness there is someone who does!'

Blindly I pushed past him and groped my way out to the front door. I opened it and ran down the path between the hollyhocks in my bare feet.

I don't think he tried to stop me. I didn't wait to see.

I turned out of the gate and ran down the road. I had only one thought in my head. To go to Graham. I was so hurt and angry and miserable I didn't think at all beyond that one thing.

I ran most of the way to his hotel, not caring about the cars that flashed past me in the dark or the one or two passing pedestrians. My feet hurt terribly on the tarmac and my hair whipped in tangles against my burning face. The receptionist looked at me in horror as I pushed open the revolving door, but she rang through to Graham's room without comment and ten seconds later I was in his arms.

He helped me to his room and rang down for drinks and some coffee. Then he sat me down firmly on the bed.

'Calm down, Lyn honey. Tell me slowly,' he ordered. He reached over into his bedside cabinet and produced an enormous box of tissues.

Somehow I blew my nose and stopped crying. Then, gulping, I poured out my story to him.

After a few moments there was a knock on the door and a maid brought in the tray with the coffee and drinks. She stared at me curiously, then I saw her eyes widen as she noticed my feet. They were bleeding. At the sight of them suddenly I burst into tears again, and she was bustled off on Graham's instructions to get a bowl of warm water and antiseptic.

By the time they had finished fussing over me I had managed to stop crying and when we were alone again at last I gave him a watery smile.

'I'm sorry, Graham. Forgive me. It was all such a shock.'

'Of course it was, honey.' He took my hands and held them gently. 'The guy sounds no good to me at all. You're well out. Do you want to go back to London with me, Thursday?'

I nodded dumbly. I never wanted to see Steve again or our beautiful cottage which I couldn't even think of as home any more. All I wanted – was out.

Later, much later, I crawled into bed. Graham's bed. He turned off the lamps one by one, then he climbed in beside me. I was exhausted and still very tense and when he rolled over towards me and reached out I shrank away suddenly.

'Okay honey. No hurry.' He turned onto his back and lay staring up at the ceiling and after a few moments I heard his breathing grow deep and regular and I knew he was asleep.

I barely slept that night. Every time I dozed off I awoke with a start, clinging to the edge of the bed. As dawn broke I crept from the blankets, my eyes heavy with lack of sleep, and drew back the curtain to gaze out into the garden.

We breakfasted in the room, then as soon as I was sure that Steve would have gone to work I let Graham drive me back to the end of the lane. He had a day of appointments he couldn't break so he persuaded me that I may as well go home and collect some things.

Quietly I let myself in and not letting myself stop to think I ran up the stairs.

Steve was lying face down on the bed. I stopped dead when I saw him and turned to run downstairs again but he had heard me and he raised his head. His face was strangely red and swollen and it struck me suddenly that he too had been crying.

'Where have you been?' he whispered. 'I've been out of my mind with worry.'

'With a man of course.' I wanted to hurt him as much as he had hurt me.

'Oh Lyn.' He bit his lip, painfully sitting up and swinging his legs to the floor. 'What has happened to us?'

'Nothing happened to me,' I retorted. 'I trusted you; I was working hard, for us, and look what happened.' It didn't cross my mind that perhaps if I had been less preoccupied with Graham over the last few weeks, things might never have gone so far.

I stamped across to the window and looked out. Ian Johnson was cutting roses next door. I could see the curl of blue smoke rising from his pipe.

I heard Steve coming across the room behind me. Then his hand was on my shoulder. 'Linda, my love. Can you ever forgive me?'

I shrugged off his hand, and shook my head.

'I'm leaving you, Steve. Even if I wanted to stay, it seems to me you've got commitments elsewhere now.' I was so weary by now that my voice was quite unemotional and flat. I hardly cared what was going to happen.

We stood in silence for a moment, then Steve said, 'Who is this man?'

I felt suddenly dreadfully guilty. 'He was just a friend. Someone I met at the teashop.' I turned and nearly spat at him, 'He was just a friend to me, but I knew he loved me. He cares. I'm going to London with him. There's nothing for me to stay for, is there?'

As I felt the tears welling up in my eyes again I turned back to the window. 'Go away Steven, please.'

I held my breath. Would he go? I desperately wanted him to stay suddenly, but I heard his soft footsteps on the rug and then the sound of the door shutting behind him. Then I let the tears run down my face unchecked.

I don't know how long I stood there. Perhaps it was hours. Slowly my tears stopped and dried in streaks on my cheeks. I felt completely drained and empty.

I nearly didn't answer the knock on the front door. But then I slowly dragged myself down the stairs. There was a young woman on the doorstep. Instinctively I knew it must be Lauren. She was tall and slim with auburn hair. There were great dark circles beneath her eyes too.

'Are you Linda?' she asked bluntly.

I nodded, still clutching the door-handle.

She swallowed. 'Will you tell Steve I'm going back to London. I don't want to see him again.'

'But the baby!' I blurted out.

She blushed crimson. 'There isn't any baby, Linda. I made it up. I knew that was the only way I would get Steve, make him divorce you. But I couldn't go through with it. I'm sorry.'

She paused as though she was going to say something else, and then she turned and ran down the path.

I didn't know what to do. I just stood there for a while, looking after her, then I went slowly into the kitchen and made myself a cup of black coffee. It made me feel rather sick, but I hoped it might help me to think straight.

What was I to do? My brain raced in circles. Steve, Graham, the cottage, my beautiful little home. Steve, Graham, Steve . . . oh Steve.

I hardly know to this day what made me do it, drag a comb through my hair, collect my purse, and take the bus into Minster. The old people's home was near the bus station, set in a lovely garden.

Aunt Irene was sitting on the porch, gazing out at the rose beds when I arrived. She smiled at me when she saw me and gestured at the chair near her. Her poor hand was still paralysed but she looked much better than when Steve and I had last seen her.

I felt her looking at me closely as I sat there not knowing what to say. I didn't want to tell her anything; I just wanted the comfort of being near her, I think because she was Steve's aunt.

'It's good of you to come, my dear,' she commented at last. 'I've been thinking a lot about you and Steve.'

I felt myself blushing and I looked at my hands. Me and Steve. It seemed strange that she could still refer to us together like that, as if nothing had happened.

I looked up and smiled wanly, and I was quite embarrassed to find her looking at me so shrewdly. I felt it was almost as if she knew exactly why I was there. I suppose it can't have been difficult to guess that we had had a row.

'You know, Linda, I often think of my life in that cottage when I was young. I'm so happy to think that you two live there now, to fill it with happiness and laughter. I never told Steve this, but when I was a girl,' she paused and there was such a long silence I thought she had forgotten what she was talking about, the way old people do, but then she went on, 'I was engaged once, you know. To such a nice boy.' Her faded blue eyes twinkled at the memory. 'We nearly got married, then I found out that he'd done something very bad – he'd stolen some money. I told him I couldn't marry him. He went away to the war of course, in 1914, and he was killed in the first month.' There was a long silence. I could see that even now, after so many years, it still hurt her to think about it. At last she went on, 'If I'd stood by him, in spite of what he'd done, I often think perhaps he might not have been killed. I might have had children of my own . . .' Her voice tailed away again, and I felt my eyes fill with tears.

She smiled suddenly. 'You won't wait too long, will you Linda, you and Steve? I would so like to see your babies before I die, my dear.' Then she became suddenly brisk. 'Why not go and find the housekeeper and ask her if you can stay and have lunch with me. I'd like that. Don't look so sad, dear. Take no notice of an old woman's ramblings. After all, you do have Steve; and I know you love each other so much, that nothing could come between you the way it did between Robert and me. Nothing, however bad, should come between lovers. They must forgive.'

I got up and dropped a kiss on her head. 'I'll go and see about lunch,' I said, my voice catching in my throat.

Of course it was very hard to forgive and I could never forget, but somehow we managed to get through that summer, Steve and I. When Graham came for me that afternoon I told him I couldn't go to London after all and he shrugged philosophically. 'I'm sorry, honey; if you change your mind you know where to find me . . .' I think he was secretly rather relieved. After all, he was happily married in Wisconsin.

And I didn't change my mind. I loved Steve and I realised that whatever he had done I was prepared to give him another chance. I knew I had been lucky too. Graham understood and he had not taken advantage of me when I had, I now realised, been playing with fire. I might so easily have found myself in the same situation as Lauren.

And now, the leaves are blowing from the trees and I've lit a fire in the grate and the room is filled with the scent of burning apple logs. I've given up my job; somehow we'll get by on the money we've saved already, and by the time spring comes I shall have a baby and if it's a girl I shall call her Irene. Steve doesn't know the real reason I chose the name, but of course he's pleased, and he's thrilled about the baby. And I love him so very much.

The Duck Shoot Man

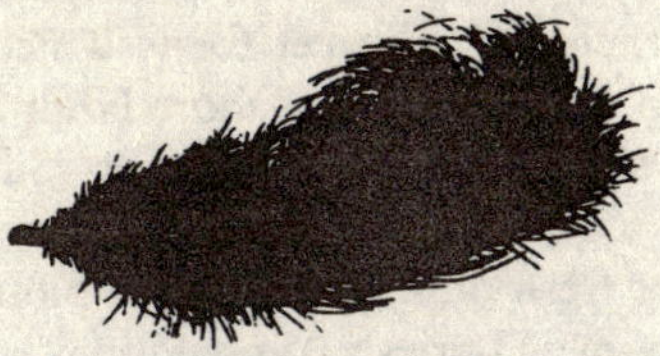

ALTHOUGH THE SUN WAS SETTING in a blaze of livid gold behind the distant hills Harriet Cummins had her back resolutely towards the sight. Instead she was peering doubtfully through the windscreen of her stationary car at the retreating ripples of water on the road in front of her.

'Extraordinary,' she murmured to her friend, Cathie Hamden, who was seated apprehensively beside her. 'You wouldn't expect that the last bit to be uncovered would be the nearest bit to us. The land must be lower than the sea or something.'

'I still think we ought to wait, dear.' Cathie was looking at the shining mudflats and the road which snaked across them. A flock of ducks was wading happily across the causeway, not pausing to discriminate between mud base and thin mud scum.

'Rubbish. I'm going now.' Harriet reached purposefully for the handbrake before she switched on the ignition. That way the car already had a little impetus before the engine spluttered into life. 'I wonder,' she went on, gently malicious, 'if there's enough petrol to see us across. Wouldn't it be awful to be caught by the tide and have to climb into one of those baskets!'

Cathie let out a squeak of fear as Harriet knew she would. She smiled to herself, but even she cast a slightly apprehensive glance upwards as they passed the first post with its plaited straw refuge.

She noticed that Cathie was sitting upright, clutching the top of the dashboard – the way she usually sat, in fact, when Harriet urged their old car over forty, which she was constantly trying to do, even in the short High Street at home – and spitefully she jabbed the accelerator. 'Silly old woman,' she murmured scornfully to herself. She always thought of Cathie, with her fresh pink face and still-blonde hair as old, although at sixty-five Harriet's companion was three years her junior.

The car coughed momentarily, a frequent occurrence from its bronchial engine, and Harriet clutched the wheel more firmly, ignoring the subdued groan on her left. The wheels were sending up a fine spray and in the strange slanted evening light it was sometimes hard to see where the road ran. The water flowed impartially before them disguising their route in a silver tissue of reflections.

They gained the upslanting firmness of the island with undisguised relief, stopping momentarily to gaze back over their shoulders at the winding road through the mudflats. Already the tide had ebbed away and in places the causeway was drying in the cool sea wind.

Harriet groped in the glove compartment, leaning without apology across her friend. 'Where's the address? I want to get to the guesthouse and have a bath.' Maps and books were rummaged unceremoniously to the floor.

Cathie tightened her lips a fraction. 'I think, dear, you'll find that you put it in your bag,' she murmured at last, half apologetic.

'Rubbish. Why should I do that?'

Cathie smiled bitterly. 'Because you said I'd be sure to lose it if you didn't.' She watched as Harriet turned to the back seat for the battered leather hold-all she was pleased to call a handbag. Sure enough the instructions were there.

'Humph!' That grudging snort was the nearest Harriet ever

came to apology, the glitter in Cathie's eyes the nearest to triumph.

The car shuddered forward again, and they began to thread their way through the network of lanes which led to the island's only village.

The guesthouse was not hard to find. It stood out at the end of a row of whitewashed fisherman's cottages, a modern bungalow with cream and red paint and ornamental scroll-work on the nameplate, *Castleview*, which hung on a gibbet by the front gate.

Harriet parked the car with its near-side wheels in the thick lushness of the hedge and sat back, squinting at the house.

'*Castleview* indeed.' She craned her neck to see if the claim were true. 'I do hope it's going to be all right. One can never tell, booking from so far away. Well, what are you waiting for?'

'I can't get out this side, dear.' Cathie moved round slightly and slid half an inch to the right to show she intended climbing across the handbrake, as soon as Harriet had herself moved. Beyond her the heavy greenery pushed against the car window.

Harriet gave a little smile. For a moment she considered making Cathie slide across. Then she relented. She made a great show of restarting the car, backing off the verge, waiting for her passenger to disembark, and then reburying the car in the hedge. Then at last she herself climbed stiffly from the driver's seat.

The air was strong: a combination of salt and honeyed ripeness from the heavy hedgerows and the evening breeze off the cool of the sea. She sniffed loudly and allowed herself to grin happily at the scarlet and golden remnants of the shrouded sun as it sank into heavy bruised cloud on the inland hills.

Then she turned her attention to the bungalow before them.

'I can't think why they were allowed to build such an ugly

house,' she commented tartly. She pulled her tweed jacket down neatly over well-padded hips. Her right eyebrow had risen an indignant half-way to her hairline.

Cathie, knowing the signs, licked her lips quickly.

'It does seem out of place,' she ventured.

Already Harriet had opened the gate and was making her way up the concrete path. Half-way to the door she stopped.

'Look at this garden,' she appealed, not so much to Cathie as to the limpid blue of the evening air. 'Geometric! Could have been designed by a town clerk with a ruler.'

Town clerks were for some reason one of Harriet's pet hates. She blamed them for most of the twentieth century's more uncomfortable problems.

She waved her hands at the neat beds of salvia and the short-haired grass. 'You know,' she confided over her shoulder in an echoing stage whisper, 'I shouldn't be at all surprised if they have flying ducks over the fireplace.'

'Ssssh!' Cathie glanced in agonised embarrassment at the heavy lace curtains, and then permitted herself the luxury of wondering quickly why they bothered with net curtains with such a large front garden and such a deserted lane which was in any case firmly hidden behind the high hedge.

Harriet rang the bell and smothered a giggle as the pretentious chime rang out in the silence. 'I wonder if we could transfer to one of the cottages,' she hissed, as somewhere in the distance a dog began to bark. Cathie smiled nervously. Someone was coming. She patted her fair hair into place.

The lady of the house, Mrs Cosby, was large and red-cheeked and determinedly jolly. She beamed benevolently at her guests as she led them across the house to show them their rooms. 'I've no one here now, but a gentleman come for the birds and yourselves,' she explained cheerfully. 'The season's more or less over, you know, once the kiddies are back at school.'

She threw open a door. Inside was a small room with a single bed, a blue straw-plaited chair and a dressing table.

Harriet glanced at the window. The lace net curtain reached only half-way up the window here, a gesture showing that this was the side of the house with, some fifteen feet away, a thick holly hedge blanketing the view. She did a lightning toss-up in her mind. 'You'd better have this one,' she murmured to Cathie over her shoulder.

Cathie nodded gratefully.

Harriet's own room was on the opposite side of the corridor. She breathed a sigh of relief as the door was flung open. Her gamble had paid off. The half span of intricate net showed a view over miles of mudflats, and at the end of the promontory, the castle reflected stilly in the low of the tide.

She carefully regulated the broadness of her smile.

'The gentleman is next door to you here,' Mrs Cosby was saying. 'And the you-know-what is opposite, there.' She coyly indicated a door on which was a small enamelled label bearing the inscription, *This is IT*!

Cathie saw her friend's mouth twitching and prayed she would be able to suppress whatever remark was about to burst forth.

'I'm afraid –' Harriet began, and then continued to Cathie's extreme relief, 'that we've left our cases in the car. I hoped perhaps your husband . . . when you get to our age, it's hard to carry things.' She eyed Mrs Cosby closely. The woman was probably Cathie's age – perhaps a year or two younger.

'Oh, I'm a widow. I thought I told you in my letter.' Mrs Cosby fell into the trap at once. 'But never mind, I dare say I can carry them for you. If there's anything too heavy I'm sure that Mr Danway will fetch them up later when he comes in.'

'Mr Danway?' Harriet had thrown her jacket on the bed – a gesture of possessiveness.

'My other guest. A strange one, he is, but very quiet. No trouble at all. Now, my dears, tea is at six as a rule, but as you were late arriving I've put it back today. Just this once.'

Her expression was suddenly threatening. 'It'll be ready in about ten minutes, if that suits?'

She did not wait to hear them agree.

Harriet watched the door close. At once came the expected outburst. '*This is IT* indeed! Do you think she ***knows*** there's such a word as lavatory?' She sat on the bed and gave a gentle experimental bounce.

'Hush dear. As a matter of fact it's a bathroom. I looked.' Cathie walked to the window and raised the net to look a little wistfully at the view.

'Have you got a screwdriver?'

Cathie jumped and looked round apprehensively. 'What for?'

'To unscrew the notice of course. No? I'm sure there'll be one in the car. Come on. At least help me get that net curtain down.'

'You can't.'

'Who is going to stop me?' Harriet stood and gave orders as Cathie struggled to pull the hook of the curtain wire over the screw which held it. At last she managed it, panting. The wire dropped to hang down the side of the window, the net a heavy bridal train, trailing to the floor. 'I hope Mrs Cosby's not offended.'

'Why should she be?' Harriet sat down heavily at the dressing table and began to rub her face with the licked corner of her handkerchief. 'Ought to be glad I've let some light in!'

Five minutes later they were summoned by gong to the guests' sitting room. Four tables stood regimented on the carpet, two by two. Only two were laid; one for one and one for two.

Cautiously they sat down. Harriet peered into the teapot and sniffed. 'I knew it. We should have brought our own tea. I wonder what she's going to give us?' She peered at the other table. 'She's made him wait to have it with us, old devil. I bet he's usually in the pub by now.'

Cathie had already helped herself from the loaded toast-rack. She was buttering enthusiastically as their hostess came in with a heavy tray. She was hungry and not even Harriet's scornful remarks about her weight – Cathie was the lighter by a good ten pounds – were going to put her off her food this evening.

'Is your other guest going to eat with us?' Harriet asked pointedly as Mrs Cosby began to unload her tray onto their table.

'Oh yes, I daresay,' she answered comfortably. 'I just heard him come in.' They waited in silence till she'd gone back to her kitchen, then Cathie leaned over the table. 'Do you think he's a boyfriend?' she simpered a little.

Harriet's eyebrows shot up. 'That woman must be your age if she's a day!'

Cathie looked taken aback. 'Well, even at my age, Hattie . . .' She broke off as the door opened.

A man came in. He was tall and sturdy, with rugged features and ruffled wiry hair – a man perhaps in his late forties. He stopped abruptly when he saw them, then he strode across to his own table in silence.

'Good evening Mr Danway.' Harriet's voice rang across the room.

He stiffened, then half turning he nodded in their direction. He chose a chair with its back to them, and sitting down leisurely moved his place setting round the table until it was in front of him.

'Well!' Harriet made no attempt to lower her voice.

Cathie frowned at her, embarrassed equally by the behaviour of both. She was relieved when Mrs Cosby appeared with a new tray. Obviously familiar with Mr Danway's taciturn nature their hostess made no attempt to talk to him as she put the plates on his table. It was to the ladies she turned at last.

'Got everything, have we? Is there anything else I can fetch you, my dears?'

A dog had bounded into the room after her and it ran to

Cathie, its tail wriggling obsequiously. She patted it, flattered that it should have singled her out.

'That's Rudie,' Mrs Cosby volunteered. 'I hope you don't mind. Soppy case he is.' She stood for a moment surveying him fondly.

'I think,' Harriet's voice was frosty, 'we'd rather he were kept out of the dining room. Wouldn't we, dear?' She shot a look at Cathie who guiltily snatched her hand away from the soft slobbering head which was lovingly pushing against her knee.

Dog and landlady vanished and the meal continued in silence. From time to time Harriet threw dark, meaningful glances at the man's back. She seemed preoccupied and Cathie, snatching at the opportunity, helped herself to more sausages from the serving dish. The room was quite silent save for the sound of knives and forks on china; the large clock on the mantelpiece had stopped at ten past eleven.

When Mr Danway pushed back his chair and threw down the newspaper he had been reading, both ladies jumped nervously. Cathie focused all her attention on the bowl of sugar from which she had been about to help herself.

He stopped beside their table for a moment, looking down at them in silence, then abruptly he strode from the room, slamming the door behind him.

Cathie found that her knees were shaking a little. 'What a *peculiar* man,' she commented and reached for her teacup.

'Did you see his eyes?' Harriet's voice was almost awed. 'The were yellow, like topaz. Weird.'

'Do you think he's . . .' Cathie hesitated a moment, hardly daring to voice her question, '. . . well, *normal*?'

'He certainly didn't look it to me. Remember to lock your door tonight, dear. I certainly shall.' The shudder which shook Harriet's sturdy frame was not entirely faked.

Cathie laid down her knife and fork. Her appetite had vanished of its own accord. Regretfully she eyed the sausage left on her plate and comforted herself with the thought that probably the dog would get it.

The two ladies made their way back to Harriet's room. By unspoken consent it had become their headquarters and neither woman had felt like sitting in the two formal armchairs before the defunct clock – no flying ducks, Harriet had noted with something akin to disappointment.

The door of the room next door was ajar.

'I must go to the loo!' Harriet announced loudly, intending to be heard well beyond the confines of her room. She advanced sideways across the hall, towards the bathroom door, her eyes glued to that of the opposite bedroom.

Abruptly she stopped. Cathie saw her expression change to one of horror before, after the briefest hesitation, she groped for the handle of the door marked *This is IT* and dived out of sight.

It was a nerve-racking five minutes. Cathie waited, not liking to close the bedroom door in case a rescue was needed, not liking to walk away from it, in case – well, in case. But supposing he came and saw her standing there? She trembled at the thought.

Then came the welcome noise of a cistern flushing and Harriet emerged. She closed the bedroom door behind her and leaned against it, breathing heavily.

'He's got a gun.'

'What?' Cathie's voice rose up in a squeak.

'He's got a gun. It's lying on the bed. I saw it.'

They looked at each other in silence for a moment. There was a strange suppressed excitement in Harriet's eyes.

'What shall we do?' Cathie breathed the words tremulously and Harriet, probably for the first time in her life, shrugged, at a loss.

'Do you think *she* knows? Do you think he's got some kind of a hold over her?' Harriet carefully left the door and went to sit on her bed. Her legs were trembling a little and she raised her chin defiantly to hide the fact from Cathie.

Cathie's eyes widened as she considered the possibility. 'He had an unpleasant face; thoroughly unpleasant.' It was as near as she ever got to being critical of someone's appearance.

'Capable of anything, I'd say.' Harriet forgot herself so far as to lick her lips. 'I wonder if he's escaped from somewhere?'

'We'd have seen it in the paper.'

'Not necessarily. They might not have wanted to spread panic.'

Somewhere close by there was the sound of a door slamming and both ladies jumped violently. Cathie ran to the window. The garden was dark and deserted. Beyond the low wind-flattened hedge at the end of it, the salt marsh and fields spread out towards the luminous sea. Dusk had closed in now and the wind was gathering strength. One or two leaves whipped from a stunted apple tree at the corner of the garden and flicked against the glass near her face and she flinched. She drew the curtains, making sure there was no crack between them, and returned to her seat on the bed.

It was then that they heard the heavy footsteps outside in the corridor. There was a loud knock on the door.

They clutched each other in fright. Harriet rose to her feet. With considerable dignity she went to the door.

'Who is it?' There was only the slightest quaver in her voice.

'Danway.'

She closed her eyes and swallowed. 'What do you want, Mr Danway?'

'I've brought your cases. You and the other lady. Leave them out here, shall I?'

There was an instant surge of relief on Harriet's face. 'If you please, Mr Danway. That is kind of you.'

They listened to the double crash of the heavy cases being dropped on the floor, the tramp of his footsteps and the bang of his door. Harriet cautiously opened hers a crack.

She hauled in the two cases and then shut it again. 'Now what?'

'I need my case in *my* room, dear,' Cathie commented. 'Surely he didn't think we were sharing?'

'I doubt if it crossed his mind.' Harriet was tart. 'Go on. Take it and run over. I'll cover you.' She wasn't too sure what the last phrase entailed, but it certainly seemed appropriate.

'I can't run. It's heavy.'

'Well, drag it then.'

'Should we go to bed, do you think?'

'Well, I'm not going to sit up all night. Lock your door.' Harriet was beginning to feel alarmingly tired. She had driven nearly two hundred miles that day and now, to find her room was next to that of a gunman – actual or potential – it would be surprising if she had not found the situation exhausting. She watched Cathie drag her case across the hall and disappear into her room, then with a sigh she closed her own door and locked it.

The rest of the evening was uneventful. She managed to reach the bathroom safely, then she regained her bedroom where she climbed into bed with a book and her little transistor radio to listen to the news. The news, when it came, was disappointingly lax in reporting any escapes from any prisons anywhere and she turned it off, half relieved, half disappointed, and opened her book. Hercule Poirot was hot on the trail; she began to gnaw her thumbnail avidly, her pages turning more and more quickly as the book neared its climax.

And then she heard it. In the silence of the room she could just make out the sound of a movement next door. She dropped her book on the counterpane and listened intently. Yes, there it was. A scraping and tapping. And then footsteps. A drawer being dragged open – quite distinct, that sound – and a low cough.

She pulled the bedclothes up to her chin and listened as hard as she could. The wind was blowing more strongly now. She could hear the hedgerows rustle and squeak, and the tapping, somewhere, of a twig against the window.

Suddenly she could not bear not to know what was happening. She slipped out of bed, turned off her side-light and tiptoed, shivering in the dark, to the window. She flung back the curtains and peered through. It was pitch black out there, save where the light from a neighbouring window, his window, streamed out across the pale grass.

She waited, hoping to see his shadow, but there was no sign of movement, only the methodical noises from next door. Then the light went out and there was silence. She held her breath.

Distantly she could hear the strange echoing, churring noise of a nightjar somewhere on the marshes. It was a very lonely sound above the endless sighing of the sea. She strained her ears again. There was no sound of bedsprings from next door. Had he gone to bed, or was he still up waiting, and listening, just as she was? Leaving the curtains open she turned towards her own old-fashioned iron-frame and climbed wearily in. She was still very tense and she found herself longing to be able to go and fetch some hot milk. That alas was not possible in someone else's house, even had she plucked up the courage to leave her room again.

Eventually she dozed.

The dog awoke her, barking furiously somewhere the other side of the house. She lay rigidly clutching the bedclothes, her heart pounding uncomfortably as she gazed up at the ceiling. Then, cautiously, she moved her eyes. A large round moon had risen. The pale colourless light flooded through the window illuminating her door and the far wall. Her eyes went without volition to the door-handle. Had it moved? Her hands flew to her mouth as she stared fascinated, hardly daring to breathe.

Then she heard it again. A stealthy movement from next door. He was stirring. She raised herself cautiously on her elbow and groped for her little clock. Half past three. Footsteps trod softly across the floor in the next room and she heard a creak and then a low clatter. He was up. He was walking about.

She put the clock down and lay back on her pillow, tensely listening to every sound. A bar of cloud drifted over the face of the moon and for a moment her eyes closed.

He had picked up the gun and was standing carefully behind his door listening. The dog was silent now and nothing in the house seemed to be awake. He checked that the gun was loaded and then, shouldering his haversack, he opened the door softly and listened again.

The old woman was standing in the hall in a patch of moonlight, waiting for him. It was the blonde, nervous one; the younger of the two. She stood there in her pink flannel nightdress, her hands stretched out as if to bar his way.

Harriet had opened her door a fraction. She put her eye to the crack and with a gasp saw Cathie standing there blandly smiling in her nightdress, her bare feet white in the moonlight. What was she doing? Why didn't she move? Was the silly woman sleepwalking?

She tried to call out as the man stood in his doorway, his face growing ugly with anger, but Cathie didn't seem to see that she was antagonising him, and no sound came to Harriet's dry lips. Her throat was constricted with fear.

Then it happened. The man strode forward. He tried to push Cathie out of his way but she stood firm, gazing at him gently, that irritating foolish smile still on her face. He pushed again and she began to struggle with him, the two figures circling slowly, soundlessly on the rag rug on the polished wood floor.

Then the gun went off. It wasn't a loud bang. Just enough to make Harriet jump, her heart leaping, thudding, into her throat. Then she saw the blood. Cathie was still smiling, but there was blood soaking through her nightdress. Drops fell darkly onto the rug and the polished floor, wet, black pools in the silver moonlight.

Slowly Cathie's hands went to the place and, surprised, she

looked down, and still looking surprised, she sank slowly to her knees. Harriet wanted to scream. She wanted to call out. She wanted to run.

She stood rooted to the spot for a moment, and then, terrified as the man turned to look at her, his face a blank mask, she moved at last, retreating into her bedroom, slamming the door, leaning against it, sweat pouring down her face. The key. Where was the key? Surely there had been a key?

Her fingers fumbled desperately at the lock and at last she managed to turn it. She ran for the chair which stood before the small table and wedged it under the door-handle, then she ran to the window and drew the curtains tight to shut out the cruel moon.

'Cathie!' she sobbed out loud. 'Cathie.'

She heard steps outside her door and she froze. He was listening at her keyhole. She turned to look but the room was pitch black without the moonlight. She dared not move to try and find the light-switch.

She waited for what seemed like hours, hardly daring to breathe, then at last, shaking uncontrollably, she groped her way to the bed and sat down. She dared not open the door to look. But supposing Cathie were still alive? Suppose she needed a doctor? She pictured again that swelling scarlet patch on the flannel nightdress, and miserably she closed her eyes. It had been right over Cathie's heart.

She must have dozed. When she awoke it was daylight. She lay, puzzled for a moment at the intense misery which gripped her whole body, gazing out of the window at the blue sky, light with high puffy clouds. Then she remembered. She dragged herself from the bed and went to the door and listened. The house was silent. She swallowed hard, then, suddenly resolute, began to dress as quickly as she could. She was stiff and her fingers were awkward and cold but she was determined to face whatever had to be faced from the security of her tweed suit. She even ran a brush briefly through her curly white hair.

Then she was ready. She listened carefully as very cautiously she turned the key. It took a lot of courage to open the door but she did it at last and looked out.

The body had gone. The floor was clean. Everything was as it had been the night before when she first went to bed. She breathed a sigh of relief. Mrs Cosby must have found Cathie. Perhaps the ambulance had already taken her away.

Plucking up her courage she went softly down the passage towards the guests' sitting room. A strong incongruous smell of bacon was floating up the passage. She shuddered as she pushed the door of the sitting room open. The same two tables were laid again, one for one, one for two. At the latter sat a figure.

'Hello dear.' Cathie peered round. 'I knocked on your door earlier, but you must have been sound asleep.'

Harriet's mouth fell open.

'Are you all right, dear?' Cathie looked concerned. 'Come and have some cornflakes. This sea air has already made me hungry.'

Harriet groped her way to the table and sat down. Her eyes were fixed on Cathie's bosom which was covered in a pale yellow jumper.

Cathie smiled at her benignly. 'Have some coffee, dear. That nice Mr Danway will be in soon. I was asking Mrs Cosby about him. He's here for the duck shooting, you know. He went out in the early hours this morning. I'm surprised you didn't hear him.' She leaned forward confidentially. 'Do you know, Hattie. It was so ridiculous last night. I dreamed he broke into your room and shot you! It really quite upset me this morning till I realised it was just a dream.' She gave a little giggle as Harriet slumped into her chair. 'I suppose it was the gun that did it. Silly me. Shall we go down on the beach later and look for shells, dear?' she went on happily. 'It's going to be a lovely day.'

With a shaking hand Harriet reached for her napkin, guiltily pushing away the whisper of treacherous disappointment which had touched her at the sight of Cathie's robust form. 'You must have eaten too many sausages last night,' she murmured with something almost approaching her usual asperity. 'Fancy dreaming a stupid dream like that!'

Frost

THE CHAIN-LINK FENCE gleamed red in the light of the rising sun. Looking down at it from her bedroom window across the bare square of earth and rubble which would one day be their garden, Amanda sighed. Turning from the window she sat down on the end of the bed and stared round the room. Small, functional and new, like the garden. So new it still smelled of paint and varnish and the sour tang of sawn deal.

Next door the baby was crying again as it had been on and off all night. The muffled protests and the distant sound of a radio somewhere across the road only served to emphasise the silence in her own house.

'We must live somewhere new; so new no one else has ever lived there before! I don't want a second-hand house! I don't want a house full of other people's dreams and nightmares.' Andrew's sweep of argument carried all before it as it always had and her own dream of an old cottage with a thatched roof and roses round the door crumbled before his enthusiasm, swept away as impractical and romantic and hopeless.

So here they were, newly married, newly moved, practical and down-to-earth and Andrew had left for work, early as usual, leaving her with the long day stretching out before her, empty, soulless and alone.

'You'll soon find a job; make some friends. Go and knock on some doors.' So easy for him. He had done it already and talked cars and sport and TV programmes and the relative qualities of the local pubs. Her knocks had been greeted with vague smiles, barely concealed impatience, screaming children, hurried uncomfortable exchanges in the frantic business of her neighbours' days.

Standing up at last she went to the window again. The sun was up now, the light outdoors harsh and unforgiving. Beyond the chain-link lay all that remained of the old suburban garden in which their small development of 'executive starter homes' had been built. The grey stone mansion had long gone, destroyed, so she had heard, by fire, but something remained to titillate her curiosity for there, beyond the long swaying grasses and the lichen-covered apple trees, she could see the reflection of the sun on glass. Several times she had walked round the neighbouring streets, trying to find the entrance to the garden, but with no success. It seemed to be a lost enclave, an unsold, unremembered plot amongst the neat geometric streets, the small red roofs and the manicured lawns. The lost garden beckoned. It was old; it was romantic; it was the focus of her dreams. One day she knew she would find the entrance and walk there on the old land beneath the new.

She had no premonition that today would be the day, no warning that suddenly the urge would become undeniable. One minute she was standing in her lonely bedroom listening to the baby's wails, the next she was running downstairs, knowing that she had to find what lay beyond the wire.

No one saw her. Glancing behind her at the rows of neat windows, most swathed modestly in ruched nets and fancy frills, she put her foot, without giving herself time to think, on the concrete stanchion which held the high fence in place, grabbed at the top of the wire and vaulted it. In the neat houses behind her, women got their children ready for school; they fed their babies and made their beds and looked for the car keys so they could go to a supermarket too far away to visit on foot. None looked out of the windows. There were no gardens yet to admire. Some had laid neat squares of grass bought by the metre; two had planted small whips of birch and miniature weeping willow. None looked beyond the chain-link fence. Those who did saw nothing but a wilderness of weeds and wondered, if they thought at all, why the plot had not been sold.

Amanda stood for a moment feeling the unexpected iciness of early morning dew soaking into the legs of her jeans. It made her gasp with surprise. Glancing back she saw how high the wire she had vaulted was from this side, with beyond it the blind windows, and she shivered. Ducking through the wet grasses she ran for the apple trees, suddenly afraid of being seen, feeling the catch of bramble and spear thistle, the slippery wetness in her shoes, the cling of burrs in her hair, then she was out of sight of the houses and wrapped in the silence of the garden.

She stopped, trying to steady her breath, willing the beating of her heart to quieten and steady, and at last, as the pounding in her ears subsided, she let the peace and beauty of the garden enfold her and soak into her soul. Walking slowly now, exploring, confident she could not be seen, she found that she was listening to the liquid song of a wren as it scuttled and hid in the ivy which swathed an old grey garden wall. On the top of one of the apple trees a blackbird eyed her suspiciously and then relaxed, ignoring her. Its throat swelled and it began to sing, the sound echoing gloriously round her in a cascade of liquid notes.

Enchanted, she listened without moving, conscious that in the distance she could hear the steady popping sound of ball on racquet from the municipal tennis courts in Celadon Road – surely once part of this same garden. She did not move until the blackbird stopped, flirted its tail and flew away. Then she plunged further into the undergrowth.

She saw the old man before he saw her. A trug laden with flowers on his arm, he moved slowly and silently away from her along the path and out of sight. Frightened and embarrassed she drew back into the shelter of the brambles and watched.

The half ruined, shabby greenhouse stood against a high brick wall. Most of the glass was broken; that which remained was smeared and furry with lichen. On the wooden battens the paint rose in blistered flakes to leave weathered broken frames for the surviving jagged triangles of glass which they clasped. This then had been the glass she had seen from her bedroom window; this the glass which had caught the rising sun. She crept closer, staring in. Where had he got the flowers? She could see the wild remains of an old vine, clinging to the glass; giant nettles, fat hen, avens. A few poppies splashed the only colour through the green; the staging was littered with broken clay pots and rotten splintered seed trays.

At the back door of the house he proffered the basket of blooms. 'The last of the chrysanths, tell her ladyship.'

'Her ladyship wants to see you.' In a flurry of white aprons and uncomfortable self-importance the cook beckoned him in.

He nodded, stamping mud from his boots, pulling his cap from his head. For special occasions she often asked him in, planned the flowers with him, consulted his expertise. She loved flowers, did her ladyship. With a smile he stepped onto the shining oak boards and made his way towards the morning room.

Amanda glanced through the door and then stepped inside the greenhouse. With a frightened squawk a bird flew up from the floor and beat for a moment against the glass before finding a gap and soaring out into the sunlight. She ran a finger over a work bench. The soil was dust under her hand. A rusty tobacco tin rattled as though it were full of nails. Another was full of empty, desiccated seeds. Keeping a wary eye out for the old man she wandered further in, savouring the warmth, the smell of dry earth, the buzz of a bee trapped beneath the glass. Outside the sun moved higher in the sky.

The shadows shortened. The dew evaporated. The day grew hotter.

A strange sweet smell assailed her nostrils. Unpleasant. She sniffed with sudden distaste. It was the smell of decay. Near her hand, as she picked idly over the rubbish on the bench she found a packet of cigarettes, half empty, the cigarettes inside as dry as the dust. She frowned. They must have lain there abandoned for years. Her fingers hovered over them, hesitated and moved away. Inexplicably she felt a shiver tiptoe across her shoulders.

'I'm afraid there can be no hothouse flowers this year, Bates.' She was sitting with her back to the desk, her pen poised, the ink already dry on the nib, turning to him for only a second in her busy day. 'We shall not be firing the boilers.'

'Your ladyship?' He could think of nothing to say.

'That will be all, Bates.'

'But the orchids, your ladyship. The frost –'

'I'm sorry, Bates. There will be no more orchids.' None of his business why; hide her fear and sorrow and rage from the servants at all cost. She could see it all in his face: first the bewilderment; then the realisation; then the sick disbelief. 'That will be all Bates.' She could say nothing else. Beneath the high frill of her silk blouse and the long strings of creamy pearls she too felt sick. In the drawer of the desk only a few inches from her hand the pile of gambling debts burned like a fire. Reginald was in the garden now. Sulking. She could see him if she moved her head slightly. 'I'm sorry, Mama.' That was all he had said. 'I'm sorry, Mama.'

She closed her eyes and took a deep slow breath.

'You may go now, Bates,' she said.

Suddenly she could smell tobacco. Amanda looked round, afraid, expecting to see him there, but she was still alone. The greenhouse grew warmer. She put her hand up to the neck of her blouse uncomfortably and turned back towards the door. A fork and spade were leaning against one another, dug into the earth. Around their handles a trail of bindweed had woven them together.

'She told you then.' Cook felt a twinge of pity for the white-faced old man. He stared at her blankly. 'She let two of the maids go this morning,' she went on as if it would be a comfort.

He shook his head blindly. 'The orchids. They'll die.'

She shrugged. 'They're only flowers.'

He had pale blue eyes, irises as clear as the sky. Unfocused now, they swam with tears. Shocked, she stepped back.

'The frosts are coming. I can smell 'em.' The old man's voice cracked.

She shook her head. 'It's the horses. Mr Williams heard them quarrelling last night. He owes thousands. This wouldn't have happened if his old lordship were still alive.' She shook her head and turned away. No point in telling him the rest, poor old man. It wasn't just the orchids which were going. Half the servants; her ladyship's jewellery; the silver; maybe even the house itself.

Leaving the greenhouse Amanda followed an overgrown track round towards the old kitchen garden. The walls which sheltered the neat beds had nurtured a tropical jungle there. She wandered over the paths and finding a bush of raspberries long grown wild picked some, sucking their sweet juice from her fingers as she remembered she had had no breakfast.

'No!' The shout behind her was full of pain.

She spun round, staring wildly towards the bushes. The birds had stopped singing. She could no longer hear the tennis balls. Nervously she retraced her steps towards the gnarled pine tree which towered over the glasshouse and dodged behind it, looking round. There was no sound of footsteps, no further cry. Her heart was hammering under her ribs and suddenly she was not enjoying herself any more.

She glanced over her shoulder. From here she could not

see the chain-link fence at all. All round her the overgrown shrubs and tall grasses pressed in in a thick wall. She took a deep breath. Backing away from the tree she glanced to her right. A pane of glass in the greenhouse had caught the sun, blinding her. Beyond it lay the stretch of grass which had once been a lawn and beyond that the fence and home.

To her left a shrubbery – leggy, thin-leafed rhododendrons, holly, smoke trees – scrambled over one another towards the light, above them a huge acacia.

Cautiously she made her way back towards the greenhouse. Behind her she could hear a pigeon. The soft coo swelled into the silence and then died again as she saw the old man hobbling towards her. She stood transfixed with embarrassment. There was nowhere to go; nowhere to hide in time. She bit her lip and stood waiting, expecting a tirade of abuse for her trespass.

He walked straight past her. His eyes, the clear pale blue of forget-me-nots, did not move to left or right. With them steadfastly fixed on the greenhouse he hobbled within two feet of her and on down the path. Behind him the air was cold.

There would be a frost that night. The evening was clear. The smoky bonfire spread the scent of burning leaves throughout the garden; the plume of blue rose straight up into the still air as he raked them higher and higher onto the pile. He glanced over his shoulder towards the glasshouse seeing the blooms basking in the warmth through the sparkling panes: creamy petals, tinged with pink – velvet, pampered, exquisite blooms fit for the show tent. There was no breath of wind. A huge moon hung like a wraith in the blue sky, lifting over the trees. By dusk it would be at the zenith and the first ice crystals would start to crisp the grass.

He rubbed his eyes with the sleeve of his jacket, raking harder. Behind the windows of the house mother and son were once more at war. Their voices filled every room now. He had taken her pearls, her diamonds, the silver flatware and sold it for a song. More than that. He had taken her pride.

Below stairs the Williamses waited, shocked and afraid. The others had gone: the last of the maids, the under gardener, his lordship's valet. This morning when Mrs Williams had brought the breakfast tray into the dining room her ladyship had sat there at the head of the table as usual but she had spoken no word; her face was white, almost transparent with exhaustion, the lines beneath her eyes blue-black. Staring in front of her she made no sign, spoke no word of greeting or command and putting down the tray Mrs Williams had crept away and cried.

Staring after the old man Amanda shivered. Perhaps he was blind? But surely he would have sensed her there so close to him on the path? She could see him now, pottering about in the greenhouse, bent, slow moving, deliberate in his movements as he groped amongst the rubbish on the staging.

Nearby the blackbird burst once more into song. With a sudden shock Amanda looked round. When she turned back to the greenhouse the old man was no longer in sight. She bit her lip, conscious of a rash of goose pimples across her skin and, hurrying now, tiptoed back the way she had come.

He banked up the bonfire as it grew dark, put away his tools and stood for a moment staring up at the sky. The first ice from the north was sharp. It would be a hard winter. Shrugging, he walked slowly back towards the greenhouse and went inside. Closing the door he stood for a moment in the soft darkness. The air still carried a trace of heat from the sun but already the chill was building. He lit his lantern and stood it on the staging, waiting for the flame to steady and the shadows to stop their wild jumping. The old wooden chair, where he used to sit to eat his piece and drink the tea one of the maids would bring him stood now beside his untidy workbench. He reached for the packet of cigarettes and drew one out with a shaking hand. The pull on the nicotine was good. It steadied him. Made him feel calm. Sitting there he watched the smoke drift up around his head as the temperature began to drop.

As the leaves began to droop and the brown touch of the frost claimed the first blooms, turning the plants to pulp, he threw down the cigarette end and climbed onto the chair. His long scarf made a gentle noose for the scraggy neck as he hooked the end over the curved nail in the roof support. He gave a wry smile as he pulled it tight. No more than an old turkey cock who must die at last. He shivered. Around him he could hear the plants dying. His own death, he thought, as he kicked away the chair, would be less hard.

Amanda stopped. She turned towards the greenhouse. From somewhere she could smell burning leaves. She frowned. It was an autumnal smell; aromatic and smoky, redolent of cold days and frosty nights. She shuddered again, violently this time, suddenly acutely aware of ice in the still, summer air.

The chain-link fence rose six foot in front of her, a barrier between her and home. The foothold which had hoisted her over was on the far side. For a moment she stood, defeated, aware that her neighbour was watching her from one of the upper windows of her house. With a smile and a shrug Amanda turned back towards the trees to look for something to stand on.

From the bedroom window she could see the reflections on the glass in the evening sunlight. A different angle, a different colour, it was as beautiful as in the morning, but warmer, richer, more textured.

As soon as she had dropped back onto her own square of bare earth and ducked into her house her neighbour had knocked on her door, baby on hip, and smiled conspiratorially. 'I saw you over there. You've got more courage than me. I've wanted to explore that garden since the day we moved in.'

She was, it seemed, a kindred spirit after all. And she knew the story. The fall of the family fortunes, the gambling debts, the frost and then at last the fire that destroyed the house.

'There is no entrance to the garden,' she said as they sat down over a cup of coffee, the baby, quiet at last, playing at their feet. 'My husband has seen the plans of the estate. They sold off all the land bit by bit after the fire – that was sometime between the two World Wars, I think – then the owners moved away. The son, or perhaps it's the grandson, still owns just that last couple of acres, but he never bothered or noticed that there was no access to it. It can't be sold. It can't be entered. It can't be touched by the developers or the council or anyone.' She smiled at Amanda. 'A secret garden – with no one to look after it. Safe. No one to spoil it.' She paused, and added sadly, 'No one to love it.'

'Oh, there's still someone to love it.' Amanda returned the smile and bending down she gave the baby a biscuit. 'The gardener's still there.'

Her new friend's eyebrows shot up. 'You don't mean –?'

Amanda nodded. 'He's still looking after it. He's keeping it safe. And I don't think he would mind if you and I go there from time to time. In fact, I don't think he would even notice.'

It was an irony that she would like to have shared with Andrew but probably never could: the new house in the ancient garden; the dreams and nightmares there beneath the untrodden floor and on the far side of the fence.

The Fairy Child

THE RAIN WAS STREAMING DOWN the office windows as I folded my letter booking the cottage, clipped Peter's cheque to it and pushed them both into the envelope. I looked again at the address. 'Ishmacuild.' The word was a magic spell in itself.

A magic spell. I repeated the phrase out loud, gazing at the orange carpet at my feet, but seeing only silver sand, rippled by wind and tide. Was that why I had chosen the island for our summer holiday; why of all the places in the guide book I had picked a tiny lonely spot like Ishmacuild: because of a magic spell?

'Your turn to choose where we go this summer, Isobel,' Peter had said with a grin. 'Don't choose the Bahamas though, will you? I don't think the family coffers will quite run to that.'

In the five years of our marriage it had worked out that way. He had chosen one year and I the next, each seeing places we might not have dreamed of otherwise, for our tastes were so different. I, the dreamer, seeking lonely places or sites steeped in history, and Peter, the energetic sportsman, choosing lively walking, sailing and exploring holidays. Such an arrangement could have spelled disaster for some marriages, but for ours it was a stimulus and an excitement. We both enjoyed the new efforts we had to make and learned, too, far more about each other than we ever would have done had we reached a dreary compromise each year.

The next time I was in the public library I crossed to the travel shelves and scanned the titles. I knew roughly what I wanted: the Scottish Highlands and Islands. I, with the maiden name of Macdonald, had never been there. My father had always said that our family came from Scotland years ago, and although we'd often talked about it we had never visited it when I was a child. This year, I was determined, I was going to remedy that. I reached down a volume and flipped slowly through the pages, glancing at the breathtaking photographs. There were so many places to choose from, so many lovely things to see. I took the book home and with it another of stories and legends. It was in this second book that I found Ishmacuild:

> Below the picturesque village, deep amongst the rocks, lies the magic fairy pool where countless generations of Macdonald women have gone by moonlight with a gift of gold to ensure the birth to the family of a son and heir. . .

I blinked and read on quickly. That was a very unhappy subject and one I tried to put out of my mind, but somehow over the next few days my thoughts insisted on turning back to that magic pool. After all I was a Macdonald woman, and I desperately wanted a son and heir.

The first two years of our marriage had been intentionally childless. The last three not so. Neither of us had worried at first and we had used the chance we had to go to concerts and theatres and have the kind of holidays our friends with growing families could not afford. But of late I had begun to wonder if anything could be wrong. I had not mentioned it to Peter but once or twice I had seen him glance broodingly into the pram of our baby nephew, and I knew that like me he was thinking about children.

The guide book recommended Ishmacuild for its peace

and silver sands and the beauty of the surrounding mountains. It listed several addresses.

When, tentatively, I suggested the place to Peter he laughed. 'So the famous Macdonald blood is coming to the surface at last.' He dropped a kiss on my forehead. 'It's a lovely idea, Isobel. We'll write for details at once.'

So it was all arranged. On a beautiful June evening we climbed onto the train which was to take us north. My heart should have been singing and my blood tingling with excitement but it wasn't, for something was wrong with Peter.

Peter was usually a cheerful, matter-of-fact person. Tall, strong, broad-shouldered with the clear grey eyes and tanned face of an outdoor man, he was everything a dream husband could possibly be. I could never quite get over my luck in having married him at all. His humour and optimism carried me along on the crest of a wave even when I was feeling a bit down. But now, for two days he had been moody and depressed. He had eaten nothing and snapped at me every time I spoke to him. His face had taken on a sunken grey look which secretly terrified me. I wondered whether to suggest he saw the doctor, never a popular idea with Peter at the best of times, and I wondered with a sinking heart whether I should suggest cancelling the holiday, but in the end, cowardly, I did neither and hoped for the best.

In the sleeping car which normally would have been an exciting adventure to share and enjoy we undressed in total silence. Peter hauled himself into his berth without a word and settled down, his face to the compartment wall. He never even said goodnight.

I lay awake for hours listening to the rhythmical rattling of the wheels over the miles of track, tense and unhappy. The further north we got the more I was filled with a dreadful sense of foreboding, and when at last I fell asleep in the early hours of the morning it was to a restless slumber tormented with formless nightmares.

The grandeur and beauty of the scenery and the excitement of the boat trip out to the island distracted me a little next day, I must admit, from Peter's mood. He seemed to have made up his mind to try and enjoy himself and he smiled and talked and gazed as I did at the scenery unfolding before us on every side. But I could see there was still something very wrong. The strange look haunted his eyes and though his mouth smiled and joked I could see that deep down inside he was in bleak despair. I shivered as, standing by the boat rail, feeling the hot salt wind blow the hair off my face, I turned suddenly and caught him looking at me with such an expression of bewildered resentment and hate it was all I could do not to cry out in horror. It was as if he had become a stranger. I turned back to watching the slippery silver waves and bit back my tears.

The cottage we had rented was tiny; no more than two rooms with a little kitchen and bathroom extension built on at the back. From the sink as I filled the kettle for our first pot of Highland tea I could see a vista of mountain peaks and valleys leading to the horizon and before them the silver sea lochs, glittering ribbons in the dusky twilight. Somewhere down there beyond the horizon lay the magic pool.

The next morning dawned bright. I lay for a long time listening to the shush of the sea in the distance and the weird, eery whistle of the curlew, watching the thin beams of early sunshine edge slowly through the undrawn curtains. Suddenly I realised that Peter was watching me. I turned to him, and leaned over to kiss him, but abruptly he turned his back on me and pulled the pillow over his head. Hurt, I drew back.

'What's wrong, love? Can you tell me?' I whispered, hardly daring to ask the question which had brought such fear into my heart.

'Oh, go to hell,' the muffled words sounded so desperate I didn't know what to do. I climbed out of bed and stood gazing down at him numbly. 'Go on; go away. Leave me alone.' Peter's voice was taking on an angry tone. Quickly, stunned with misery, I grabbed my dress and sandals and fled to the bathroom.

The path from the back door led across an area of heather bent towards the rocks and the loch. I ran quickly, wanting to get as soon as possible out of the sight of the cottage windows. Tears, half of fear, half anger, were running down my cheeks, and all I wanted was to hide my misery on my own by the shore.

I didn't see the small fishing boat, hidden as it was by the rocks, until I was almost on it and by then it was too late to turn back. A young man, tall, with a thatch of midnight-black hair and piercing blue eyes, was learning negligently against the stern pulling a net from the tangle at his feet. His lips were pursed in a soundless whistle. I turned away as soon as I saw him, wanting to be on my own, and headed up the beach but he must have seen me at once. 'It's a grand morning.' His voice, not raised above a half-whisper, arrested me where I stood. Seeing me turn back he gave a broad smile. His teeth were astonishingly white in his tanned face.

'You'll be staying up at the cottage. How are you finding it?' he asked casually, his fingers never ceasing to work through the tangled black mesh.

'Oh fine.' I rubbed the back of my wrist across my eyes, hoping he wouldn't see that I had been crying. 'We only arrived yesterday though. So I haven't seen very much.'

He grinned. 'Well, I'll take you out in the boat any day you want. Do you like the fishing?'

I shook my head, warming to the charm of his infectious smile. 'I'd like to go for a sail though. And one thing, I would like so much . . .' I hesitated, imagining he'd think me such a fool.

'You'd like to visit the fairy pool,' he finished for me. 'Aye, everyone wants to go there. I'll take you whenever you wish. Now, if you like.' He straightened hopefully, but I shook my head. 'I must go back and get some breakfast for my husband now. Perhaps later?'

He shrugged. 'Any time. You'll always find me round the boat if I'm not at sea. My name is Ross by the way. Ross Macdonald.'

'I'm Isobel,' I said. 'Once Macdonald too, now Hemming.'

He held out his hand. 'No doubt we're kin. I saw it in your eyes.' He grinned. 'Now, away to your food, Isobel Macdonald. You must not let your man starve.'

He turned back to his nets and I began to retrace my steps towards the cottage. My encounter with Ross Macdonald had cheered me and when I went back into the kitchen I was humming quietly to myself. I stopped abruptly when I saw Peter sitting at the kitchen table. He was absent-mindedly stirring a cup of coffee.

'There's more in the pot, Isobel,' he murmured and there seemed to be a note of apology in his voice.

The next three days passed quickly and without further incidents. I told Peter about Ross and we went out with him twice on fishing expeditions. I was beginning to like the tall islander very much. He had a calm, gentle sense of humour which did much to ease us over uneasy silences and the awkward angry moods which still came on Peter seemingly for no reason at all.

Then on Wednesday night came the most terrible moment of my life. I had had my bath and was sitting up in bed reading, wondering why Peter was taking so long. On the past two nights he had gone to bed early and had been asleep when I joined him. At last he came, turning out the light, and he stood looking down at me for a long while without speaking. I threw down my book and held out my arms expectantly. He went white and took a step back as though I'd hit him.

'No, Isobel,' he said, quite loudly. 'Never again, my dear. Never; I'm going to divorce you.'

'Peter!' I heard the anguish in my own voice, like the voice of a stranger. 'Peter, what's happened?'

'I don't want to live with you any more. That's what has

happened. There's no more to be said on the matter.' He walked deliberately to his side of the bed.

I flung myself up on my knees and caught hold of him. 'Peter, why? Peter, I love you. Is there someone else?' My eyes were burning with hot tears. 'What's wrong?'

Quite coldly and deliberately he flung me off. One minute I had my arms round him, clinging, the next I was lying on the cold, painted floorboards. He climbed silently into bed and turned his back.

Sobbing wildly I scrambled to my feet, grabbed my jacket from the back of the chair, and flinging it round my shoulders over my nightdress ran out into the translucent warmth of the night.

It was quite easy to pick my way down to the loch for although it was after eleven, it seemed not to get dark at all this far north. My heart was hammering against my ribs with fear and I felt very sick.

All I wanted was to be alone by the gently lapping waters of the loch. Alone to think.

It was almost as though Ross were waiting for me. One moment I was alone, sobbing desperately, and the next he was there beside me. With only the slightest hesitation he put his strong arm round my shoulders and pulled me against him.

'There, there, lassie; it's best to cry. No woman should be afraid of crying, especially one as beautiful as you. Why, your tears are like crystals, here on your cheek.' He raised his finger gently and brushed them aside.

'Oh Ross, what shall I do? Peter wants to divorce me.' I clung to him, thinking only of my husband and the terrible pain in my heart.

'I could see that there was something wrong between you.' Ross nodded, his lips very close to my hair. 'My dear, I'm so very sorry.'

Slowly, clinging to him for reassurance and comfort, I

walked beside Ross down the warm beach. We didn't talk at all after those first few words, then at last when we reached the barrier of fallen rocks which lay across the end of the sand he stopped and turning me to him he kissed me. Behind us an enormous moon was rising slowly from the circling mountains and somewhere on the waters of the loch a lonely night-bird cried.

I hardly know what made me let him do it. The magic of the night, the warmth of the sand, the ache of rejection in my heart which needed so badly to be comforted and stilled. All those things must have helped to enchant me as we sank slowly together to our knees in the moonlight, still kissing, and I let him slide the pale blue silk of my nightdress from my shoulders.

It was dawn when I finally let myself back into the cottage. I felt chilled and the hem of my nightdress was wet with dew, but I felt indescribably reassured and happy. It was as though Ross had imparted to me some of his own quiet strength.

I put on the kettle and groped in the cupboard for the teapot as the first red glow of the sun rose above the mountains.

Peter found me there. He stood for a moment in the doorway looking down at me and I saw with a hideous lurch of pity that he had been crying.

Without a word I pushed a cup towards him and began to pour out.

'Isobel, I'm sorry, darling.' He sounded hoarse and uncertain. 'I've been thinking about it all night. I must tell you the truth.' Nervously he clasped his hands around the cup, staring deep into the steaming liquid. 'I went to see Dr Henderson a week or so before we came here. No.' He held up his hand as immediately I tried to interrupt, full of anxiety. 'No. I'm not ill or anything . . .' He sighed and sipped the scalding tea, trying to find the courage to speak. 'I had to know if it was my fault we have no children, Isobel. I had to know.' He looked at me pleadingly. 'I'm sorry, love.' He seemed unable to go on and I waited, not daring to say a word. I could feel myself beginning to shiver.

'I'm sterile, Isobel. I can never father a baby.' He suddenly managed to find the words and they came out in a rush. Then he sat quite still, not looking at me.

I felt numb.

For a long time we sat in silence, neither looking at the other. I could sense his misery and shame and I wanted to comfort him but part of me was crying out in a shock of disappointment and yearning. Never have a baby. Never hold my own child in my arms. I could not bring myself to believe it. I wanted to argue; to say it couldn't be; to talk about specialists and further tests but one look at his face clamped the words in my throat.

At last I dragged myself from my chair and going round the table to him I dropped a quick kiss on the top of his head. However I felt about babies I still loved him more than life itself and I told him so, kneeling before him on the cold kitchen flags, my hands resting, pleading, on his.

'You can't divorce me because of this, darling. You can't.' My own voice was breaking. 'I won't let you. I love you too much. Babies don't matter so very much; perhaps we might adopt one, but the important thing is we have each other. That's all I care about.'

At last he brought himself to look at me, and I saw the anguish and uncertainty still flickering behind his eyes. 'I'm not a proper man Isobel. I can't be, I . . .'

'I've never had any complaints, have I?' I leaned forward and kissed him firmly on the lips. For a moment he stayed completely still, without responding, and then, almost unbelieving, he returned my kiss. We clung together for a long time as the sunlight slowly crept into the kitchen and then at last we went together into the bedroom.

We lay together, not making love, just lying quietly, for a

long time, in one another's arms until eventually, exhausted by misery and tension, Peter fell asleep.

Never once did I give Ross Macdonald a single thought. What he and I had done together on the warm moonlit beach had belonged to the magic of the Highland night. Save for the sense of calm serenity which he had left with me, our meeting might never have been. It would certainly never happen again. Strangely I felt no guilt, only a happy wonder when I thought of it at all and gratitude that he had comforted and reassured me in the only way that mattered – then.

The rest of our holiday passed in a daze. We were both stunned by the loss we were sure was ours, but our happiness in refinding each other in some way made up for that. We walked and swam and climbed the lower slopes of the mountains and went fishing with Ross. Ross never showed by word or sign that he remembered our encounter and I was grateful for his silence. I knew there was nothing cheap or easy in what we had done and I treasured the memory of it in secret.

But most of all I treasured Peter and our time together. We never mentioned the subject of babies again; at night sometimes after he had gone to sleep I found myself crying quietly into my pillow and my dreams were sad and lonely ones, but during the day I refused to let myself think about it at all. Time enough for that when we had both had the chance to adjust a little.

On the last day of our stay, deeply mysterious, Peter insisted on walking alone into the village three miles away. I guessed it was to buy me a present so I happily kissed him and after watching for a moment as he set off up the white stone road I turned and wandered slowly down to the loch to make my farewells to the mountains alone. Ross was leaning against his boat sorting out the nets very much as I had seen him that first day of the holiday.

'Hello there,' he smiled at me, his blue eyes clear and friendly and somehow understanding.

'It's our last day,' I murmured. And I stood still.

When he held out his hand I took it naturally and we stood for a moment looking at each other. Then gently he let my fingers fall. 'Shall we take a wee walk along the shore?' he said, and I nodded.

When we reached the rocks he led me this time between them. I followed up a steep path winding high into the cliff face and then back down among the rock pools at the corner of the island itself. Finally we came to a deep circular sheltered pool, hung with weed the colour of emeralds and garnets.

'There you are lassie,' he glanced at me and smiled. 'The magic pool of the Macdonalds. Will I leave you while you make your wish?'

I looked down into the opaque shifting water, suddenly overcome with misery and shook my head. 'I've no wish, Ross. No wish now. That is why I didn't ask you to bring us here. To have done so would have been the most tactless thing in the world.'

He looked puzzled. 'I thought you and your man were happy again?'

'We are, Ross.' I held out my hand to him, wanting to feel the comfort of his fingers as I fought back the urge to cry. 'We are happy; but there's no wish. Not now.' As I stretched towards him I felt a slight catch at my wrist. My bracelet had snagged on a corner of rock. With a little cry I tried to grab it as the fine gold links snapped but I missed it and it slid into the deep pool.

'Oh no, my lovely bracelet!' I cried. Ross scrambled over to my side and together we gazed down trying to see beyond our own reflections into the depths of the water, but it was impossible.

'It's bottomless, lassie; it goes right down through the island to the sea bed. That's why it's so magical.' Ross looked up at me. He smiled enigmatically. 'It seems the fairies were determined to have your offering of gold after all. So perhaps they know your wish already . . .'

I felt very sad as I walked back up the beach with him, overwhelmed by the end of the holiday, my beloved bracelet gone and my misery over Peter a blank pall. There seemed to be nothing left to look forward to. Nothing but emptiness.

Ross and I didn't say goodbye. He squeezed my hand when we got back to the boat and bent once again to his nets. I walked slowly back up the beach without looking back.

Peter was waiting for me when I reached the cottage looking very pleased with himself. In his hand was a box. I opened it and it contained the most beautiful carved silver brooch. The kind they made locally. In the excitement of putting it on I forgot to mention the loss of my bracelet.

Two months later I knew I was pregnant. Of course Dr Henderson must have known it wasn't Peter's child but he said nothing as he ushered me from his surgery, he just shook my hand and wrote a note for the office to get them to give me a few days off work as I was looking, so he said, so run down.

When Peter came home that night I was sitting on the sofa. He kissed me hello and I pulled him down beside me. 'There's something I've got to tell you, love,' I gulped. I had felt strangely calm waiting for him, but now the moment had come I found my hands were shaking.

He held them tightly and looked into my eyes, frowning. 'What is it, Isobel. What's wrong?'

'I went to see Dr Henderson today.' I swallowed hard and went on in a rush. 'I'm sorry Peter. I'm going to have a baby.' To my horror I could feel the tears welling up suddenly. I tried to blink them away but they spilled over onto my cheeks.

Peter let go of my hands. For a moment he looked so hurt I was stunned. Then he stood up.

'I never guessed there was someone else, Isobel.' He bit

his lip. 'I can't blame you, I suppose. I expect you want a divorce as quickly as possible to marry him?'

'Oh no. No! No!' I flung myself at him. 'Oh Peter darling. There's no one else. There never has been; not like that. It's just that . . .' I stopped.

His arms were round me and I was sobbing into his shirt front.

'It was the fairy pool. I dropped my gold bracelet. It would never have happened otherwise.' I burst into sobs again.

'The magic pool of the Macdonald women?' he murmured into my hair. 'You went and wished and the fairies granted you your heart's desire?' He didn't sound cross, it was almost as if he were smiling.

I glanced up at him through my hair. 'I know it can't really be that. It only happened once – that night you threw me onto the floor. I ran down to the beach and . . .'

He put his fingers on my lips. 'Don't tell me any more, darling.' He dropped a kiss on the top of my head. 'I'd rather think it was the fairies.' He took a step back for a moment and gazed at me steadily. 'This is something we would have had to discuss and think about sometime, Isobel. I know we never mentioned it but there are other things besides adoption when,' he hesitated, 'when there is nothing wrong with the woman. That way she can have a baby herself even when her husband . . .' he stopped and took a deep breath, 'when her husband is like me. Perhaps I would have preferred a more clinical approach,' he grinned, 'but on the other hand perhaps it's nicer to thank the fairies than a doctor.'

Our daughter was born two months ago now, a gorgeous child with eyes the colour of amethyst and a fuzz of soft black hair. Peter was there at the birth and if I ever had any fears that he might reject her they were dispelled when I saw him with her. He adores her and is as proud as any father I've ever seen.

We called her Faye.

Who Done It?

FLAKES OF SNOW blew in through the door with him as Jenkins pushed his way into the warmly lit bar of the Dog and Duck. It was early yet and only old Fred and Mr Denby were in.

'My usual, Sam,' said Jenkins. He was full of importance. Leaning his elbows on the bar he looked sideways at Mr Denby. 'Heard the news, have you?'

'No Jenks, what's that then?' Sam slid the pint glass expertly across the polished counter.

'They found a body up Highfield way.'

'A body?' Mr Denby straightened up sharply and looked at the newcomer for the first time. 'A dead 'un you mean?'

' 'Course I mean.' Jenkins was indignant. He took a long drink at his glass. 'Huddled up under Jeffrey's barn he was, in all the puddles and melting snow up there.'

'Who was it then, Jenks?' Fred spoke for the first time. His hand was shaking slightly as he raised his own glass to his mouth.

'Don't reckon they know yet.' Jenkins drained his beer and waited expectantly, his fingers casually nudging the glass across the bar. 'He was pretty soggy, so they say.'

'He would be.' Mr Denby nodded sagely. 'It's been thawing the last twenty-four hours.'

'Snowing again now, though.' Jenkins nodded towards the dark windows. The glass was as far as it would go without pushing.

Mr Denby noticed at last. 'Same again all round, Sam, please.'

'What do the police say, Jenks?' Fred was lighting his pipe, sucking the flame down into the encrusted bowl.

'They reckon it was murder.'

Fred dropped the match and blew on a burnt finger. 'Murder? What makes them think that?'

'He had a hole in his head, that's what. And blood all over him.'

'Poor chap.' Sam produced three brimming glasses. 'I wonder if it was old Everett. He used to sleep rough in the barn sometimes.'

'No, it wasn't him.' Jenkins clasped his glass happily. 'It was Everett as found the body.'

'Do they reckon he did it?' Mr Denby looked at him sharply.

'Nope. He's got an alibi.'

The four men were silent for a while, listening to the fire hissing round the logs in the hearth, then Fred slammed down his empty glass on the counter and turned for the door.

'Goodnight all,' he called and was gone.

'I think he knows something,' said Jenkins quietly. 'Did you see how his hand was shaking?'

'And he burned hisself on that match.' Mr Denby nodded. 'Do you think we ought to tell Constable Conway?'

'No.' Sam shook his head vehemently. 'If he did it he had good reason. Fred never does anything without a very good reason.'

Fred plodded slowly up the hill. The lights in Constable Conway's cottage were blazing as he went up the slushy path and knocked on the door. Mrs Conway showed him into the parlour where the constable, his blue shirtsleeves rolled up above the elbow, was sitting at the table, eating a large bowl of stew.

Fred sat down opposite the young man and waited until

his host's mouth was empty. 'That body you've got. Know who it was?'

Conway shook his head without speaking and spooned up some more stew.

'Did he have a red shirt and a townified tie?' Fred was twisting his cap round between his fingers on his knee.

Constable Conway choked slightly. 'How do you know that?'

'I seen him before. He was heading up Highfield way. Looking for hammer beams, he said.'

'Hammer beams?' The constable's mouth dropped open. 'What are they when they're at home?'

'Don't rightly know, but Jeffrey's barn's got 'em. He had a camera with him.'

Conway nodded. 'Yes, that was still there. There wasn't no robbery. The chap had quite a bit of money in his wallet.'

'Was it by the door you found him?' The casualness of Fred's question did not fool the constable. He had risen and, buttoning on his tunic was already reaching for his notebook.

'Now see here, Fred. You'd better tell me everything. What do you know about all this?'

'Nothing much. But a few days back I was up that way. I saw one of those great icicles fall over that doorway. Like a sword it was, three or four foot long. That would kill a man if he were standing underneath.'

'I reckon it would.' The constable nodded thoughtfully. 'Could have been that.'

'And the icicle would have melted long since.'

'I reckon it would.'

Fred left the cottage well satisfied.

There was no one left in the village now who would remember the slick fancy architect fella who had seduced and then abandoned Fred's pretty daughter. Only old Mrs Hennessy, and she was blind. And you can't fingerprint a puddle, now can you?

Watch the Wall, My Darling

PART ONE

WITH EACH SMART TAP of her foot on the sun-baked ground the swing arced higher. Above her the dappled shade of the oak tree cooled the air. Mercifully hidden now behind the high yew hedge the garden party was in full swing.

Caroline Hayward grimaced as, throwing back her head at the apogee of the swing's travel, she felt her long heavy hair slip from its combs. Her bonnet had already gone, hanging from its ribbons behind her like an unruly animal. Shaking her head she laughed suddenly, feeling her hair whip across her face. What did it matter how she looked? She was alone at last and for a few precious moments she was free!

'That swing was not designed for adults!'

The deep voice startled her so much she nearly released her hold on the ropes.

Dragging her slippers in the dust to slow her momentum she tried desperately to stop, suddenly acutely aware of the acres of petticoat showing beneath her light, blown skirt. Grabbing at what remained of her dignity as the swing slowed she curbed her first instinct which was to jump to her feet. Instead she smoothed her skirts, taking a deep breath as she saw who had addressed her. Dressed in sober black like all the men present at the bishop's garden party, the Reverend

Charles Dawson, her host's elder son, was standing facing her, his darkly handsome face showing uncompromising disdain; Charles Dawson who had spent the best part of the party surrounded by a cluster of his father's younger women guests.

'You obviously find our party boring, Miss Hayward,' he said with a humourless smile. 'I'm sorry, but I must suggest you find other ways to amuse yourself. That swing was not designed to take someone of your weight.'

'I am not that heavy, Mr Dawson!' Caroline retorted. To her chagrin one of her slippers had fallen off and she was feeling for it desperately with her foot, hidden beneath her full, long skirt.

He allowed himself another tight smile. 'I didn't mean to imply that you were.' He gave a slight bow, his eyes gleaming. 'Nevertheless, the swing was put up for my brother's children, who are aged six and seven respectively. When you have recovered your shoe –' he raised an eyebrow slightly, '– perhaps I can escort you back to the party and fetch you a glass of lemonade.'

She could hear in the still heat of the garden beyond the hedge the deep voices of the sober, assembled clerics, the higher voices of the women, the occasional constrained laugh. She and Mr Dawson were uncompromisingly alone.

No one had noticed when she had slipped away. Her father, the Reverend George Hayward, had been deep in conversation with his bishop, his daughter long forgotten, when she had glanced round the company, many of whom she had known all her life, and experienced her sudden, quite unexpected wave of rebellion.

The violence of the emotion which had swept over her had astonished her. She was overcome with anger and despair. She was still a young woman, wasn't she? She was still reasonably attractive, wasn't she? She was still full of day dreams and of hopes. So why was she here, at her father's side, faithfully accompanying him as ever on parish business, in the role into which she had slipped almost without realising it when her mother had died? Her sisters were married, her brother now lived in London. She alone was left. And it had been expected and accepted by everyone that she would fill her mother's shoes. All thoughts of her marriage seemed to have flown from her father's mind. The few persistent suitors who had called on her slowly slipped away. And no one seemed to have noticed but her.

She glared at Charles Dawson. She had not been one of the young women clustering round him with adoring looks and simpering giggles. No, she had been beside her father listening dutifully as he talked church business with the bishop! Not that she would have talked to Charles anyway, she reminded herself sternly. It was no problem for her to remain immune to his handsome good looks, behaving as he was like an extension of her father in his obvious disapproval of her. She had always detested him for his pompous ways. And he would never, ever, have been one of her suitors. Rich and well connected, he would look far higher than a mere rector's daughter.

The thought made her even more cross. She had never allowed any of the young men who had found their way to the Rectory door in Hancombe to arouse their hopes when they had come calling upon her and now it was too late to change her mind. She was old. She was destined to look after her father for the rest of his life. She was on the shelf. She was twenty-nine years old.

'. . . don't you think so, Miss Hayward?'

With a start she realised Charles Dawson had been speaking to her as he escorted her away from the swing and back towards the party. He was tall, broad-shouldered, and, oh yes, he was good-looking. As he looked down at her she realised she had been staring at him.

'Don't you think so?' he repeated.

'I'm sorry, I didn't catch what you said,' she murmured.

She caught the expression of impatience, quickly hidden, which crossed his face before she looked away.

'I said, that I fear there may be a storm later,' he repeated.

'Yes indeed, the air is heavy.' Now he would think her deaf as well as rude and stupid!

As they emerged through the gap in the hedge she noticed several pairs of eyes speculatively upon them. Her father's were not amongst them, she saw at once with relief, and suddenly she was overcome by an irresistible urge to laugh. Here she was, dishevelled, her hair down and her gown awry, appearing in the company of the most eligible man there, and quite unchaperoned!

As if reading her thoughts Charles Dawson stepped away from her rather too hastily. 'May I suggest, Miss Hayward, that you retire to the house to tidy yourself,' he said curtly, and with a bow he left her. For a moment she stood where she was, aware that she was still being watched closely, then slowly and demurely she began to walk across the grass.

Somehow she managed to reach the ladies' withdrawing room in the palace and there she managed to redo her hair and replace her bonnet. Outwardly she was docile and smiling. Inwardly, her moment of amusement gone, she was seething with resentment and anger. Of all the pompous, sarcastic men why did it have to be Charles Dawson who had followed her? He would tell his father what he had caught her doing and no doubt they would smile about it together over the port that evening, and then the bishop would tell her father! And her father would not find it amusing. He would be very, very angry. Oh, the humiliation of it all!

Leaving the shelter of the palace at last she ventured back onto the lawn and, in spite of herself, she found herself looking for Charles. She saw him at once, talking to a group of elderly ladies, and to her chagrin he looked up and caught her eye. For a moment she felt his gaze sweep up and down her body, as if checking her appearance, then infinitesimally he smiled.

Anger erupted in her once more and riding home beside her father in the carriage later she could feel her resentment still seething. But to her relief it appeared that nothing had been said to him about her escapade for he was in high good humour as they trotted through the leafy lanes back to Hancombe, nestling in its fold of the Downs.

'Tomorrow, Caroline, you and I shall visit the cottage up the Neck,' he was saying, sure as always of her obedience and her time. 'I should like to take baskets of food to Widow Moffat and the Eldron family. Poor things, it is two years since Sam worked . . .' He broke off suddenly. 'Caroline, are you listening to me?'

Guiltily Caroline turned to him. Her gaze had been fixed on the crest of the Downs where the golden haze of the afternoon had settled in a shimmering blur on the woods.

'Of course, Papa. I shall prepare the baskets myself.'

The shadows were running up the valleys between the hills, turning the green of the fields to soft purple beneath the haze. She could smell the rich drift of honeysuckle and roses from the hedgerows on either side of the lane. There was a beauty and a poignancy in the air which soothed her and at the same time unsettled her strangely.

She longed to be alone, away from her father's strident demands, but it was hours before she was able to escape to the privacy of her bedroom. With relief she closed the door at last behind the maid, Polly, and, drawing her loose wrapper over her nightgown she went to the window and leaned out, staring down at the dusk-shadowed garden. She still felt tense and unsettled; lonely.

It was very hot; the coming darkness was bringing no relief from the heat. If anything it was hotter now. Her mind turned back to the party and the cool freedom of the swing. If Charles Dawson hadn't found her she could have remained there all afternoon, with the breeze combing its untidy fingers through her hair. Unbidden, a picture of her host's son floated before her eyes; his tall, stern features, the arrogant smile, the quirked eyebrow when he saw that she had lost her shoe. Almost she had thought he was laughing at her, but then she realised that he must have despised her for being such a hoyden. His own white shirt and silk cravat had been immaculate; not a hair of his head nor his beard was out of place. No doubt he had never sat on a swing in his life.

Slopping some water from the ewer into the flowered basin on her washstand she bathed her face and neck. Then she lay down on the bed. There was no point in thinking about Charles Dawson; no point in thinking about men at all. Lighting her bedside candle she picked up a book and allowed it to fall open.

It was several weeks now since her sister, with a finger to her lips, and a stern warning not to tell their father, had given her the leather-covered volume of Lord Byron's works and from the day she had first opened it it had become her most treasured possession. Her favourite poem was *To Caroline*.

'Thinkst thou I saw thy beauteous eyes . . .'

She shivered as she read the impassioned words, words she knew by heart she had repeated them so often in the lonely darkness of her room. If only they had been addressed to her.

'Caroline!'

The abruptness with which her door flew open startled her so much she dropped the book. It slid to the floor with a crash. Her father, still fully dressed, stood silhouetted in the doorway, the candles on the table in the passage behind him streaming in the sudden draught. 'Caroline, where are my drops? I've been calling you!' His voice, usually so strong, dropped to a whine.

Caroline got up wearily, her feet bare on the cool boards. 'They are in your dressing room, Papa.'

'What were you reading?' His voice rapidly regaining its strength, her father approached the bed and, stooping, picked up her book, staring in curiosity at the gold letters on the spine.

Slowly the colour drained from his face. He held the book out towards her and shook it. 'Where did you get this . . . this obscenity?' he hissed. His voice was tight with anger.

Caroline had gone white. 'Please give it back, Papa. It is mine – '

'No!' He was beside himself with fury. 'This goes on the fire where it belongs. I don't believe – I cannot believe that you knew what you were reading! That a daughter of mine should dream of opening such a book – '

'Papa – '

'Enough!' His voice was strident, his need for medicine forgotten.

Caroline clenched her fists. 'Papa, I am a grown woman, old enough to decide what to read for myself.'

'No woman under any circumstances should be permitted to read anything that . . . that monster of depravity has written, Caroline.' He turned away. 'I would never have allowed your mother to do so, and I shall not allow you to do so, either.' At the door he stopped and looked over his shoulder. 'We shall talk of this again tomorrow,' he said ominously, and he closed the door.

For several moments Caroline stood still. Fury and indignation vied with sorrow for her beloved book and fear of what her father would do to punish her, grown woman or not. For a moment she blinked back humiliating tears, then galvanised into action by the same streak of rebellion that had driven her to seek refuge from the party earlier she began once more to get dressed.

How dare he!

He dared because he was her father and he knew best.

But he didn't know best! He had never read Lord Byron's work, of that she could be almost certain. He, like so many others, was reacting to the unnamed scandals to which her sister with a whisper had hinted. Terrible scandals. What they were she could not guess. And she did not care. Nothing anyone said about him made his poetry less beautiful. Caroline felt the heat of the night caress her languid body as she eased her wrap more loosely around her shoulders. The air had became almost unbearably humid. She pinned her long hair back off her neck in a heavy looped knot and still barefoot, let herself silently out of the room.

The Rectory was in darkness. She padded down the broad staircase and hesitated for a moment at the bottom outside her father's study door. All was silent within and she could see no light beneath it. He must have gone to bed. Turning she pushed through the door which led to the kitchens at the back of the house. The fire in the range was not damped down as it should have been. It was burning brightly. Peering in she could make out the blackened edge of the binding of her book in the heart of the coals. He had been as good as his word. With a sob she slammed the range door shut.

The key to the garden door was missing from its hook. For several seconds she stared at the empty place in the long line of keys, then again she rattled the door. It was locked fast.

With a sob of anger and frustration she turned and made her way to the front hall. The Rectory was completely silent save for the slow ticking of the grandfather clock in the hall. Cautiously she opened the door into the vestibule and putting her hand on the front door knob she turned it. That door too was locked. She was trapped in the dark, silent house.

Back in her room it was hours before she slept.

At breakfast her father was quick to tell her her fate. He had obviously spent at least part of the night thinking of a suitable punishment for his errant daughter.

'You have behaved like an irresponsible child, Caroline.' He put his hand to his forehead dramatically. 'Yet I cannot believe you knew what you were doing. If I did . . .' he paused, shaking his head sadly, 'I don't know what punishment would be sufficient, but as it is, I put your sin down to ignorance rather than the intention of knowingly reading such . . . such filth. Each evening from now on, child, you will read and then learn a passage from the Bible which I shall mark for you, to cleanse and purify your mind.'

Spooning some devilled kidneys onto his plate as he spoke he never looked at her face, never saw the anger and indignation in her eyes. Already he had moved on, to talk of their parish visits, of the Sunday school picnic she was to organise, and of the garden party the day before. It never crossed his mind that she might defy him.

Still seething with anger, she was putting on her bonnet, ready for the first of those parish visits when Charles Dawson was shown unexpectedly into the morning room.

'Mr Hayward. Miss Hayward. Forgive me. I see that you are about to go out!'

Caroline felt her mouth go dry. So this was it. He was going to tell her father himself about her unladylike behaviour at the party and that would seal her fate. Her father would be convinced of her utter depravity! She felt Charles's eyes on her, and defiantly she raised her own to meet them.

'Thank you for your hospitality yesterday,' she murmured. 'My father and I enjoyed our visit to the palace so much.'

'Did you indeed, Miss Hayward?' His tone was lightly mocking. 'I'm so pleased. It would have been so easy for one such as yourself to become bored.'

'Indeed not . . .' Caroline replied, flustered, but already her father was interrupting.

'Oh come, sir, my daughter enjoyed every moment of it, as I did. I have of course already written to your mother to thank her for her hospitality – Charles.' He hesitated slightly before using the younger man's first name. 'Her parties are renowned throughout the county, you know.'

'Indeed they are.' Charles bowed and Caroline caught the slightest quirk of his eyebrow. 'I shall however tell her that you enjoyed yourselves. Particularly you, Miss Hayward. I am sure she will ask you again.'

Was he deliberately taunting her? Trying to keep her intense embarrassment hidden, Caroline glanced at him angrily from beneath her lashes, but his face was bland as he turned back to her father.

'Forgive me calling so early, Mr Hayward, but I had to be in the area on business and I felt I must call in to say good morning.' He smiled. 'It did worry me that Miss Hayward did not seem to be herself yesterday.'

Both men looked at Caroline.

Her father frowned. 'She seemed all right to me.'

Caroline clenched her fists. 'Of course I was all right, Papa. I can't think what Mr Dawson means.'

He was enjoying himself hugely. She was sure of it now.

'You looked pale, Miss Hayward. Several people remarked upon it,' he went on solicitously.

'Did they indeed. How kind of them to comment.' She could feel herself growing more cross and agitated by the second. 'If so, it must have been because of the heat.'

'Indeed it must.' He bowed assent with a smile. 'And it is going to be hot again today. Already the hills are covered in heat haze. I suspect that storm is not too far away.' He smiled again. 'However, I must not delay you any longer.' He turned towards the door and snapped his fingers at Polly who was waiting in the hall. As she brought him his hat and cane he turned back and held out his hand to Caroline.

'Miss Hayward.' He bowed slightly over her fingers. 'How nice to see you again, Mr Hayward.' Then he had taken his hat from Polly and with another bow he had gone.

George looked after him with a frown. 'Charming young man. Such style. And showing such concern to come and ask after your health.' He sighed. 'A pity you could not have married someone like him, my girl, while you had the chance.' He shook his head. 'A great pity. And now it is too late. You won't marry now, I don't suppose.' Unaware of the cruelty of his remark he reached for his own hat.

'I have not looked for anyone to marry, Papa, since Mama died,' Caroline put in softly. 'It is my duty to look after you.'

'Quite so.' The rector picked up his gloves, either not hearing or deliberately ignoring the wistfulness of her tone. 'Young Dawson is likely to marry Marianne Rixby, I hear.'

Caroline was occupied with tying the ribbons of her bonnet, facing the mirror in the hall. For a moment she saw her face reflected in the glass – clearly showing still the traces of angry colour. As she watched the colour faded. Then she saw Polly's eyes were fixed on her face too. Bleakly she smiled. 'Shall we go out, Papa? Polly has already put the baskets in the trap.'

It was a long day and she was exhausted when they returned home. Her father had lost no opportunity of lecturing her about her reading habits and reproaching her about the potential husbands she had apparently thrown away through her selfishness and her arrogance. As the afternoon grew more and more hot and uncomfortable she found herself biting her lip in an effort not to scream. Desperately she wanted to get away.

The haze was pearly now over the Downs. The lanes shimmered with heat and the pony's coat was black with sweat beneath the harness as they drove slowly back towards the Rectory. She was dreading the evening. They had guests for dinner, amongst them Archdeacon Joseph Rixby and his wife and daughter, and she would be expected to play the radiant hostess yet again. There would be no escape.

Her room was cool as she changed into a green silk gown and looped her dark hair gracefully around her pale face. She longed to send a message to her father that she had a headache and could not come down to dinner, but her sense of duty prevailed as usual. She must be there as hostess to his guests. She must ignore his jibes and his sudden spite and be gracious to them.

Wearily she went downstairs into the drawing room. With relief she saw that the double doors into the garden stood open and the fragrance of the night drifted into the room. Calmly she greeted their guests at her father's side, looking with more than usual interest at Marianne Rixby as the girl arrived, beautiful and sylph-like in a gown of white lace at her parents' side. So this was the woman Charles Dawson had chosen to marry. She raised her eyes to Marianne's, forcing herself to smile a welcome as she took the girl's hand

and was astonished to find herself greeted with a look of undisguised venom.

She took a step back. Behind them Polly was moving around the room with a tray of glasses, and already the Rixbys had drifted off with her father to talk by the window. 'I saw you yesterday,' Marianne hissed at her. Her mouth was fixed in a narrow smile. 'What were you doing with Charles?'

'Doing?' Caroline frowned uncomfortably. 'I wasn't doing anything.'

'No? Coming out of the shrubbery, with your hair down and your dress all disordered?' Marianne's eyes spat fire. 'Did you think no one would notice?'

'I . . . I had been feeling unwell,' Caroline stammered, aware that her father's gaze was fixed on her suddenly from across the room. 'Mr Dawson . . . Charles . . . was kind enough to lend me his arm, that was all.'

'All?' Marianne's whisper turned into a small shriek. 'And how, pray, did your hair come down?'

'I had been sitting on the swing,' Caroline replied wearily. 'I thought the cool air might help my head.'

'And did it?' The other girl's voice was full of malice.

'A little.' Caroline's composure was returning. 'Your fiancé is a compassionate man, Marianne. He saw my distress and offered to help me, that is all.'

'Not her fiancé, Caroline, not yet.' Sarah Rixby's ears had picked up the end of the conversation and she sailed over to her daughter's side. 'Though we are expecting dear Charles to speak to her father at any moment, are we not, my darling?' From the rector's elbow the archdeacon inclined his head towards his wife and went on with his conversation. 'Dear Marianne,' Sarah continued, 'it will be such an excellent match, do you not think?'

'Indeed,' Caroline nodded, malicious in her turn. 'A very excellent match indeed.' She wondered briefly if Marianne had ever been subjected to the man's sarcasm and insufferable snobbery. She thought not.

The candles burned low over the dinner table as the evening grew even hotter. The ladies' faces glowed with heat and it was with relief that after they had withdrawn, the gentlemen retired into the gardens with their cigars and their glasses of port. And it was still comparatively early when they called for the carriages, all now aware that the long-promised storm was finally on its way.

By the time she had returned to her bedroom Caroline's head was splitting with pain. She sent Polly away as soon as the girl had brought up her hot water, not even allowing her to stay and help her undress, then, kicking off her shoes she threw herself onto her bed. Beside her a moth beat its way suicidally around her candle; beyond the open windows the night was humid and very still as if waiting with baited breath for the storm to break.

She must have dozed for a while. She awoke suddenly aware that the moth had dropped, its wings singed, to the floor beneath her bedside table. The candle had burned low. Her bedroom was shadowy as she made her way at last to the ewer and, dipping a corner of the towel into the rapidly cooling water, she bathed her forehead to try and ease the pain. It was then for the first time she noticed her book-case. It was completely empty. She gasped. Throwing herself down on her knees in front of it she ran her fingers over the hollow shelves. During dinner someone had come upstairs and removed every single book. No, not every book. Her Bible still lay there on the top shelf. Inside it was tucked a sheet of paper with a passage noted in her father's neat hand. Glancing at it furiously she saw that he expected her to read and learn by heart twenty-five verses by next morning!

'Papa!' Her fury and anguish were for a moment overwhelming. She was paralysed by the sheer frustration and anger which swept over her.

She climbed to her feet and paced up and down the floor several times before she stopped in front of the window to stare out at the night. The garden lay there cool and inviting, a haven of calm. Her headache, she realised, had miraculously disappeared.

It was then that her rebellion boiled over. Still wearing her evening gown she slipped her shoes on once more, and opened the door. The landing was dark.

Picking up her bedside candle Caroline crept downstairs and into the kitchen. The door into the garden was locked once more. This time she was not to be deflected. She had to get out. She crept into the dining room, still warm with the smells of food and hot wax from the candles, and found to her relief that the windows into the garden had only been latched. There was no key. Pushing them open she stepped out onto the moss-covered terrace.

She knew where she must go. Tiptoeing towards the gate she let herself out and began to walk swiftly up the lane. No one saw her. The windows of the Rectory were all in shadow.

The night was strangely airless. Above her the sky was sewn with stars and a quarter-moon hung hazily above the Downs, but to the south the night was thick and brooding and she thought she heard a distant rumble of thunder.

Buoyed up by her fury and her frustration she walked fast, holding her skirts clear of the dry ruts in the lane, and turned up the path towards the church. Behind it the hillside led up steeply to the ruins of the old castle, the place she went to sometimes to be alone, when she had to escape the claustrophobic atmosphere of the Rectory. The villagers seldom went there, and never at night, or so she had heard. They thought it was haunted. She herself had only ever been there during the day.

The lychgate into the churchyard squeaked as she pushed it open and she glanced behind her in spite of herself. But the lane was empty in the faint moonlight beyond the ancient yews. Reassured, she shut the gate and made her way over the dew-wet grass, threading her way between the mossy, moon-shadowed tombstones. On the far horizon lightning flickered faintly, but she ignored it.

The church was in darkness. She glanced at it warily, for the first time feeling a little nervous. The building looked somehow larger and unfamiliar, the well-known shapes and corners of the walls irregular, menacing. She bit her lip, for a moment wavering, then the thought of her empty bookcase and the string of verses from the New Testament, together with the memory of the tortured burnt remains of her poetry book simmering in the heart of the range returned and with it her anger and indignation. Gathering her skirts she began to run on towards the second gate.

The hillside was steep and shadowed. She could hear herself panting as she scrambled up the winding path, groping blindly where the shadows made it totally dark. She could smell the night-scented stock in the cottage gardens in the village below and the newly scythed grass in the churchyard. The smell of smoke hung on the air and she wondered bitterly if it was from the Rectory chimney.

She was panting when she finally reached the top of the hill and emerged from the wooded path into the clearing which held the castle ruins. Up here the moonlight was clear. She could see the black shadows of the crumbling walls hard across the grass. She stopped right in the middle of what had once been a courtyard and stared southwards at the sleeping countryside. Again the sky was lit by the flicker of summer lightning, and this time a low menacing rumble of thunder followed it. She ignored it. Panting slightly she walked across to a low, ruined wall and hitching herself onto it she started reciting the little litany she always repeated when she came up here. 'Papa relies on me. I have to obey him. He means well and I have to look after him. That is my duty . . .'

Duty, her soul was screaming, her duty! To suppress all her hopes and dreams; to give up all thoughts of having her own mind, all thoughts of any independence, all thoughts of a home of her own in order to look after a bigoted selfish old man? Yes . . . Yes . . . I am his daughter. It is my duty . . . Besides, I love him.

So often she had fought this battle within herself, up here, in the ruined castle, where long ago battles had raged. Each time her better self had won. She had firmly suppressed the rebellion, allowed the peace of the countryside to soothe her and returned to the Rectory, meekly ready to take up her duties once more as a dutiful daughter. But this time . . . this time she wondered whether she could ever bring herself to go back.

She sat there for a long time as the moon hazed and disappeared behind the clouds, watching the storm draw closer as it moved steadily inland from the sea.

The sound of a stone falling was very loud in the silence. She stared round into the darkness, forgetting her father and the troubles at the Rectory, as her mind flew nervously back to thoughts of ghosts.

In spite of herself she couldn't help remembering cook telling her once of the headless man who was supposed to run across the courtyard and disappear into the thickness of the wall and she shivered. The lightning flickered again, throwing the castle ramparts into eery relief and out of the corner of her eye she thought she saw something move. Her heart hammering, she slipped off the wall and crouched close to it. It was stupid to think about ghosts. No one of any education and sense believed in ghosts! What she had heard was a piece of masonry falling; the movement was a trick of the eldritch lightning. The thunder growled once more and she took a deep breath. She should return to the Rectory now, before the rain came.

As she stepped away from the loose rubble of the wall she heard from somewhere quite close the sound of a low laugh. For a moment her terror was so great she thought she would die, then relief flooded through her and she heard herself sigh. What she had heard was no ghost. It must have been one of the village lads, up here courting. Almost trembling with relief she frowned at the unexpected, miserable wave of loneliness and envy which fleetingly seized her as instinctively she moved back into the shadows again. Whoever he was he had come up here to be alone with his girl. It would embarrass them enormously to think they were being spied on by the rector's daughter.

Gathering up her skirts she had started to creep silently around the side of the wall when the sound of more subdued laughter pulled her up short. It was male laughter, strident for all it was guarded, and it came from several throats. Frowning, she glanced over her shoulder towards the sound, and was in time to see the flare of a flame. For a second it illumined a face as it was sucked down into the bowl of a pipe, then all was dark again. On the leaves overhead the first raindrops began to patter down.

Caroline flattened herself against the wall, suddenly afraid again. The face she had seen was no familiar village lad. It had been that of a stranger and there had been something furtive about his action – the fleeting way he had glanced round over his shoulder into the darkness. Whatever he and his companions were doing, they did not want to be seen doing it; and she did not want to see them.

Cautiously she stepped back, holding her breath, her heart thumping with fear. The path back down the hillside seemed a thousand miles away. Away from the trees the rain was harder. She could feel the drops cold on her head and shoulders. Praying that the lightning would not betray her she picked up her skirts again and ran towards the outer wall. Reaching it safely, she pressed herself against the wet stones, listening as she peered round. They did not appear to have seen her. Breathing a quick prayer of gratitude she stepped carefully towards the steps and flattened herself back as a brighter than ever flash of lightning tore across the sky. It was enough to show her that some dozen men were standing inside the ruined walls about twenty yards from her. A second flash showed her they were intent on piling some boxes beneath the rubble in the old castle moat.

'Smugglers,' she breathed to herself with a shiver of real

fear. She had so often heard her father talking about the men who avoided the excise by bringing in brandy, wine and tobacco all along the lonely Sussex shore and how they cheated the government and the people of the country. It was a favourite theme of his. These men had obviously met a boat down in the estuary, collected a load of some sort of contraband, and were hiding it up here in the castle. Suddenly she was seething with indignation, her fear completely swamped by her anger. All she wanted to do was to get back down the hill so that she could alert the authorities and they would be caught.

As she watched the storm surged on overhead. It was raining hard now and she was becoming drenched. Her hair pulled loose from its knot and hung down on her shoulders. Her thin dress and petticoats were soaked, the silk clinging to her body like a second skin. As each shaft of lightning tore the black sky open she cowered back against the wall. She was not afraid of storms, they exhilarated her, but the speed and power with which this one had finally driven inland from the coast was awesome. Another green flash split the night sky and as suddenly as it had come her anger and indignation had gone and she felt the excitement of the night. Her anger had been her father's, not her own. To her amazement she realised that she envied these men. They were free, able to sail on the wild sea, ride their shaggy ponies through the storms. Like all men, they were their own masters. What they were doing was exciting and dangerous. What did it matter if the revenue men lost a few guineas? Was that so very dreadful?

In that second, as she watched them, her heart beating with excitement, distracted by her romantic dreams, one of the men saw her in the next flash of lightning which lit up the sky.

She saw him turn towards her, saw his hand raised to point at her, then his warning cry was lost in the crash of thunder which followed.

Her exhilaration vanished and was replaced by icy panic.

Abandoning all caution she turned and fled towards the gap in the wall. Her wet skirts tangled between her legs; her hair whipped across her eyes and her thin shoes slipped on the wet grass. Her heart pumping with fear, she ran blindly to the left, her hands outstretched to feel the wall. Another flash of lightning betrayed her. In the long suspended moment of white light they all saw her now. Dropping their loads the men were after her. She heard their angry shouts as she dodged around the end of the wall and across the strip of old cobbled courtyard.

She did not stand a chance. They cut her off in seconds and when the next flash of lightning illumined the scene she was surrounded. She pressed herself back against the wall, trying to catch her breath, feeling the cold, wet stone against her shoulders. Her head high she looked defiantly at the men. One of them had produced a lantern, and he held it up towards her.

'Miss Hayward?' The astonishment in his voice as he recognised the rector's daughter was genuine.

Dazzled by the lantern light held so close to her face Caroline could see nothing of the men behind it. She was shaking with cold and fear.

'You know her?' A harsh voice queried near her, clear above the rumbling thunder.

'Aye, I know her. It's Miss Hayward – rector's daughter.' So one man at least came from the village. Blinded by the lantern, Caroline felt a desperate rush of hope. 'What are you doing up here, girl? Surely you know better than to come here at night?' His voice was hard with anger.

The first man swore obscenely. 'I don't care who she is. She'll talk. She'll have to be disposed of.'

'She'll betray us, Jake.' A third voice rose above the whispers of the men around her. 'There's too much at stake to let her go, you know that . . .'

'No!' Her voice sounded shrill and unsteady to her own ears as she stared frantically around. 'No, I won't betray you,

I promise. I'll say nothing. Please, let me go.' She could sense their fear and anger mirroring her own as the lantern hissed and smoked in the blinding rain.

'She'll get us all hanged!' The angry words were fierce and uncompromising. 'Better get rid of her. Take no risks.'

'Aye!' The voices of the men around her were raised in agreement.

'No – '

Her cry of terror was cut off as the man Jake turned on the first speaker and roared at him, 'Would you turn us into murderers, Bill Sawyer? Is that your game? This woman will not betray us. I'll vouch for her. She's been good to me and mine.'

Jake Forrester. Caroline recognised his voice now. His wife had been ill for most of the summer, and Caroline had day after day taken her food and medicines from the Rectory. Pushing the others aside Jake stood in front of her. 'Will you promise you'll tell no one of what you've seen here tonight?'

'I promise.' Her mouth was dry. The faces around her were hostile, shadowed in the lamplight, streaming with rain. 'I won't tell anyone. I'm . . . I'm on your side. I swear it.'

The excitement was gone. There was fear and suspicion all around her. She could feel them considering, weighing up the risks. Even Jake looked grim. They surrounded her, hemming her in. She was trapped. If they decided she could not be trusted there would be no escape. She bit her lip, feeling the cold rain trickling down her neck, soaking into the bodice of her gown.

'Go on, girl. Get back to the village, quickly now,' Jake said softly. 'You keep quiet and no harm will come to you or yours. But if you ever betray us by so much as a hint . . .'

The threat was obvious. She shivered. Without a word she turned and made her way towards the steps. The men parted. Blindly she walked between them, hardly daring to breathe, feeling their eyes following her. Somehow she forced herself not to run. With as much dignity as she could she walked across the wet grass and stones and out of the light of the flickering lanterns into the deep shadows of the trees.

Once she was out of their sight she began to run, her feet finding the way by instinct in the dark as she hurled herself down the slippery path towards the churchyard. Scrabbling with the latch of the gate she pulled it open and slipped through, her breath catching in her throat. A flicker of lightning, more distant now, lit up the churchyard as she made her way between the tombstones and down towards the road to the village. The rain was stopping.

As she let herself out of the lychgate into the lane she could feel her heart thudding beneath her ribs; she was gasping for breath, her wet hair falling across her eyes, blinding her so that she didn't see the tall hidden figure until it was too late.

She screamed as the hand reached out in the darkness and seized her wrist. Struggling frantically she was swung forcibly to face her captor and felt her arms gripped by fingers of steel.

'Don't make a sound!' The command was hissed at her viciously. Below them on the road she could hear now the sound of horses' hooves. A troop of horsemen were riding along the road from the direction of the village. So Jake and his friends were betrayed. Even if she screamed again they would not hear her, up in the castle ruins. And they would think it was she who had betrayed them. She struggled desperately to free herself. Somehow she had to warn them.

As if he read her thoughts her captor released her arm and clamped his hand across her mouth. With a little moan of despair she kicked out at him and she heard him swear quietly under his breath as her foot met his shin but he did not release her. He held her in silence as the horseman passed close below them. It seemed like an eternity before the riders disappeared into the distance and the sound of the hooves on the track faded into silence. A desultory flicker of lightning pierced the yew branches overhead. For a moment their faces were lit. The man's expression was grim as he looked down at her and at last, abruptly, he let her go.

'Miss Hayward!'

It was the Reverend Charles Dawson.

PART TWO

Beneath the dripping branches of the yew trees Caroline stood rigid with shock. She could still feel the burning imprint of Charles Dawson's hands on her body through the wet silk of her dress and the bruises from his merciless grip over her mouth. He stared down at her for a full minute in the faint moonlight, then his voice cut through the silence. 'What in God's name are you doing here?'

'I was going for a walk and I got caught by the storm.' She was unhappily aware of the way the thin material of her dress was clinging to her, making her feel vulnerable and almost naked under his glare.

'You were going for a walk!' He sounded incredulous. 'Another of your sudden whims, no doubt – this insatiable desire for your own company.' He sounded furiously angry.

'That's right.' She was defiant. 'As far as I know there is no law against it, sir, as there undoubtedly is against laying violent hands on someone as you have!' She steadied her voice with difficulty, fighting off sudden stupid tears of shock. How dare he! He was accusing her, trying to make her feel guilty, when she had simply been walking alone, minding her own business, in the churchyard of her father's church.

She was praying that the men in the castle would remain silent up there above them as she straightened her shoulders and looked as imperiously as she could at her captor. Behind them another cloud shrouded the moon. 'What exactly are *you* doing here, Mr Dawson?' She tried to see his face and failed. All she could see was the faint gleam of his eyes.

'That's my business.'

Caroline retreated a couple of steps and felt her shoes sink into the leaf mould at the side of the path. She could feel her small store of courage evaporating fast. 'In that case, there seems no further reason for me to stay here in the wet,' she said defiantly, keeping her voice as steady as she could. 'I think I should like to go home now.'

'I'm sure you would.' His voice was strangely soft. 'But first I think we have to find out just what you've seen on this midnight walk of yours.'

'I've seen nothing.' She had spoken too quickly, she knew it, and her voice was too high.

'Nothing?'

'It's dark. I was getting some air and when the storm came I sheltered beneath the lychgate – ' She broke off. In the silence of the churchyard behind them she heard clearly the sound of light, running footsteps. Her heart almost stopped beating with fear. Somehow she had to distract him; somehow she had to get him away.

'Please, will you take me home?' Until she spoke she didn't realise that there would be so much fear in her voice. She put her hand out and felt her fingers touch the rough linen of his shirt. He wasn't wearing a jacket, she realised suddenly. Behind them the footsteps drew closer.

'Please – '

But he had heard them. He caught her wrist and pulled her out of the streaming moonlight into the deep shadows once more. 'Don't make a sound.'

'But – '

'Quiet, I said!' His fingers bit into her wrist. Near them the footsteps drew to a halt and they could hear someone breathing heavily. Then, clear in the silence of the night, came a low cautious whistle.

Swearing under his breath Charles Dawson stepped out into the moonlit churchyard, dragging Caroline with him.

Jake Forrester stood clearly visible in the pale light.

'I thought you'd gone, girl.' He was staring beyond Charles towards her.

'You knew she was here?' Charles's voice was hard-edged.

Caroline looked from one man to the other uncomprehendingly.

'She was up at the castle, but I reckoned she could hold her tongue – '

'Hold her tongue?' Charles snapped. 'She had arranged to meet the patrol! If I hadn't stopped her she would have sent them straight up to take you all where you stood.'

'No! That's not true,' Caroline cried. 'I didn't know they were coming – I didn't know who they were.' She swung round to face Charles. 'I don't understand any of this. What are you doing here?' With dawning comprehension a slow feeling of dread was beginning to creep over her. Feebly she tried to pull her wrist free of his grasp.

He was looking at her thoughtfully.

'Whoever it was who rode by just now, I wasn't going to meet them, I swear it,' she cried again. 'You must believe me, I didn't know they were coming. And even if I did I would not have betrayed – ' She was going to say, 'you.' She fell silent, trying to come to terms with what was happening. She couldn't bring herself to believe that Charles Dawson, the suave, tight-lipped son of the bishop of Larchester, was in league with the smugglers. It was impossible. But his next words confirmed that that was indeed exactly what he was.

'Come on.' He addressed Jake. 'Back to the other men. The roads are alive with soldiers tonight. We must disperse quickly.' Already he was striding back towards the castle, dragging her with him.

'No.' Caroline pulled away from him. 'Please, let me go home.'

The two men looked at her. 'She'll not talk, sir,' Jake said quietly.

Charles looked down at her, his face hard. 'There is too much at stake.'

'There is nothing at stake, sir!' Caroline retorted, goaded into fury by his expression. 'I have given my word. That should be enough for you. I shall not betray you. Whatever your motives are in doing this it is not my concern. Now, please let me go!' She wrenched her wrist free of his grasp.

He frowned. 'Men's lives are at risk . . .'

'I am well aware of that, Mr Dawson,' she snapped. 'I can guess what you were doing, though why you should be involved in this I cannot even begin to imagine –'

'Then don't,' he said curtly. He hesitated for a moment then he stepped away from her. 'Go, then, Miss Hayward. Go back to your bed. But I shall expect you to keep silence. If you don't . . .'

'If I don't?' His threatening tone enraged her.

'If you don't it will not only be these men and myself who suffer,' he replied softly. 'Because you and your father will find yourselves implicated as well.'

'What do you mean?' she flared. 'That's not possible. We had nothing to do with any of this!'

He smiled. 'You need find out, Miss Hayward, only if you betray us.' He turned away and began walking fast through the churchyard towards the gate. Jake hesitated for a moment, then he followed him.

Caroline closed her eyes and took a deep breath. Her knees felt shaky and her mouth was dry with fear as she retraced her steps towards the Rectory. She was beginning to shiver. Her soaking dress clung to her and her shoes squelched uncomfortably in the mud. Softly she opened the gate and slipped into the garden. Avoiding the raked gravel of the driveway she tiptoed across the wet grass and round to the back of the house. The French window still stood slightly ajar. With relief she pulled it open and slipped through the curtains.

The candelabra on the sideboard had been fitted with fresh candles. Her father was sitting at the head of the table, swathed in his dressing gown. His Bible lay open on the table before him, the pages golden in the flickering candlelight.

'I have been waiting for you.' His eyes travelled up her wet form and she saw the lines on his brow deepen. 'I am sure you have an explanation for your absence.' He got up heavily and walking past her, he reached up to shoot the bolts on the windows. He closed the heavy curtains then he turned to face her once more. 'I am waiting.'

Caroline shrugged. 'I went for a walk in the gardens, Papa. When the storm came I thought I would shelter rather than try and run back.'

'Your shelter was obviously sadly inadequate.' He was staring down at the carpet where the sodden hem of her dress was seeping into a puddle round her feet.

'The rain was very heavy.'

He sighed. 'Indeed it was. Would it be too much to wonder why you felt the need to walk in the garden in the early hours of the morning just as a storm was breaking?'

'I had a headache, Papa, and I couldn't sleep. I thought the air might help it.'

'And did it?'

'Yes.'

'Then I suggest that you go back to bed before you catch cold.' He blew the candles out one by one, leaving a single flame burning in the candlestick by the door. 'We will talk more of this tomorrow. I do not like the thought of my daughter wandering alone, even in the gardens, at night. It is most unseemly.'

'I am sorry, Papa.' Gritting her teeth, she lowered her eyes. 'But there seemed nothing wrong in it, to me –'

There was mud all over her skirt – distinctive, chalky mud from the hillside, mud which could not possibly have come from the manicured beds and lawns of the Rectory garden. With a quick glance at her father Caroline clutched at the sodden green silk, trying to hide the tell-tale smears.

'Forgive me, but I am very cold. I think I shall do as you say, and go to bed.'

'Would you like a glass of ratafia to warm you?' As she reached the door, he stopped her, his voice unexpectedly gentle.

She shook her head. 'Thank you, no, Papa.' She took the candle from him and turned away.

As she fled up the stairs, the shadows leaping round her, she was uncomfortably aware of his eyes following her in the soft lamplight from the table in the hall, and of the streaks of dirt left by her swirling skirts.

There were dark rings under her eyes when she confronted her father over the breakfast table next morning. Her hair was tightly knotted at the back of her neck, her dress neat and irreproachable.

'I have not learned the Bible passage, Papa.' She met his eyes defiantly. 'There has not been time.' She held her breath, waiting for the outburst she knew would come, but to her surprise her father merely shook his head. 'Tonight, then, tonight. You are none the worse for your soaking?'

'None the worse, thank you, Papa.'

Her father was helping himself from a dish of eggs beneath one of the silver covers on the sideboard. 'I thank the Lord you were not tempted to stray beyond the garden last night,' he went on, not turning. 'The smugglers were out. My verger was here at eight. He said the excise men failed to catch them.' He sighed as he sat down. 'These rogues must be caught. They killed a man down on the foreshore last night.'

'No!' Caroline's distraught cry made him look up.

He frowned. 'I am afraid so. But don't distress yourself. They will be caught.'

All night her brain had been whirling with the events at the castle and in the churchyard. Each time she had closed her eyes she had seen Charles Dawson's tall figure – wet through, wild, dressed in shirt and breeches, his hair tousled by the storm, his eyes alight with anger. And her body had remembered the hard touch of his fingers with a strangely disturbing glow of shame.

She shivered imperceptibly again now at the thought.

'Is it known where they come from?' she asked cautiously as she sat down.

'Local,' he replied. 'It would surprise me if some of them didn't come from this village. The rogues! They deserve to hang!' He frowned at his daughter. 'Do you not wish to eat?'

She shook her head. 'I'm not hungry, Papa.'

'I trust you are not sickening for something. Take some hot chocolate at least. I am going into Larchester later this morning to consult with my fellow magistrates. There must be something more we can do to catch these men. It is a scandal that they are still free!'

Caroline watched her father ride away an hour later with mixed feelings. Half of her was relieved that he was so distracted by his anger against the smugglers that he had forgotten his indignation at her; the other half was eaten up with anxiety over what was to happen about the smugglers. How could Charles Dawson be involved with them? How could he, a man of God, be a thief and a murderer?

Miserably she paced the floor of the morning room, oblivious to the beauty of the day outside. Still his image rose before her eyes. The anger and hardness in the man, his determination, his ruthlessness. If Jake had not been there to restrain him, what would he have done to her? Her mind shied away from the answer to that question. But the truth remained. He or his men had killed that night. And if they had killed once, why should they not have killed again?

Suddenly making up her mind she ran for her bonnet and taking her basket, loaded with jars and packets, on her arm she let herself out of the Rectory. The lane was already drying in the hot sun, the muddy ruts hardening beneath chalky crusts as the hedgerows steamed, glittering with raindrops.

Jake Forrester's cottage was at the far end of the village, a tiny run-down hovel. She hesitated only a second before she knocked at the door. It was several moments before it opened.

Mrs Forrester peered out, blinking in the sunlight. She was

a thin, stooped young woman, her heavily pregnant figure obvious beneath her threadbare gown and flimsy shawl. 'Why, Miss Hayward!'

'How are you, Susan?' Caroline groped in her basket for her jars of calves' foot jelly, her honey and her loaves of fresh baked bread from Polly's oven. 'I thought I would come and see how you are. Is your cough still bad?' She followed a flustered Susan Forrester into the cottage and peered round the small dark room. It was empty. She could feel the chill striking off the walls. 'How is your husband, Susan? Is he here?'

Susan shrugged. 'Jake's all right, Miss. He's gone over the hills today and tomorrow to help with some droving.' She sat down heavily. 'I don't like him going so far and leaving me so long, but we need the extra, with another baby on the way.'

Another baby. Caroline had noticed the empty cradle by the window. Three babies had been born in this house in the last three years and all had been dead within six months. She felt a clutch of pity at her heart. 'He's a good man, your Jake.'

'Aye.' The woman's thin face broke into a smile. Then as swiftly as it came it vanished and Caroline saw fear and worry in the woman's eyes.

'What is it, Susan?'

'Nothing.' She made a big effort to smile again. 'I worry about the baby.'

'It will be all right this time, Susan. There's been no disease in the village this summer – '

'Not yet!' Susan could not keep the bitterness from her voice. 'Squire Randall said he'd improve the cottages, but he hasn't done it. He said he'd see we'd have the thatch patched; look at the damp in here after last night's rain.' She was racked with coughing again as she pointed to the glistening marks on the mud walls. 'And new wood for the door. They even talked about some kind of drains in the village once, but nothing ever came of it. Dr Styles says we'll never be free of the fever until they sort the drains.'

Caroline bit her lip. 'I'll talk to Papa again. I'm sure Mr Randall will listen to him.'

'He'll listen. And he'll promise. He'll promise the world. But he'll do nothing.' Susan put her hand to her belly defensively. 'You see if I'm not right. If anything's to be done it must be done by ourselves. My Jake's promised he'll do the roof, somehow. He's got some pennies saved, he reckons.' She smiled tolerantly, obviously not really believing it. 'Maybe that'll do to keep the place water tight this winter and keep the baby warm.'

Caroline frowned. 'I'll do all I can. I promise.'

'I know you will try.' Susan smiled wearily. 'You've been good to me.'

But not good enough. Caroline frowned as she walked slowly away from the damp cottage, still cold, even on such a warm day. It was not right that women such as Susan Forrester, who worked so hard and asked so little in return, should suffer so in the loss of her babies. Did Susan know Jake had turned to smuggling? She thought not. And could she really blame him for it, if it brought some money into that penniless household? Wouldn't she have done the same thing in his shoes?

Her thoughts were interrupted by the sound of hooves in the village street and she looked up to see Marianne Rixby and her brother, Stephen, trotting towards her. They drew to a halt beside her. Stephen raised his hat. 'It's a very hot day to be walking, Miss Caroline.'

Caroline smiled. 'I wasn't going far.' She eyed Marianne cautiously. The girl's riding habit looked cool and elegant, her hat on her bright curls throwing a delicate shade across her face. And she couldn't help making a comparison between this spoiled, cosseted young woman with her rich, elegant clothes and slim, daintily gloved hands and Susan in her threadbare home-spun. It was an uncomfortable thought.

She bit back a wry smile. What would Marianne think if she knew her precious Charles was out at midnight after the dinner party last night with a gang of smugglers; what would she say if she knew that, for a moment or two, admittedly in anger, he had been holding Caroline pressed close to his chest!

At the thought she felt the heat rise again in her cheeks. She put her hand to her face. 'Perhaps I should go back to the Rectory. I hope we shall see you again soon.'

'Indeed you shall.' Marianne simpered prettily. 'Charles has asked to speak to Papa this evening. When he has done so and we announce our engagement we shall have a party, and you shall be invited, dear Caro.'

Dear Caro! Caro! Caroline seethed as she walked on her way. Marianne had never, ever, called her that before. She swung her empty basket onto her other arm. No doubt Marianne would be less happy when she had sampled Mr Charles Dawson's vicious temper and found out what a hypocrite and a liar he really was!

The rector returned in time for luncheon very pleased with himself. 'Someone on the quay has talked. We know who their ringleader is!'

'You know?' Caroline stared at him, white-faced.

He nodded smugly. 'Not only do we know, but we know they've planned another landing tonight. The devils! They thought that would fool us – going out two nights running. How wrong they are! We'll catch them red-handed and we'll hang every one of them.'

'Papa –'

'No, Caroline. I know how soft your heart is. But they must be punished.' He turned as Polly knocked on the door to announce the meal. 'Come, my dear, let us eat, then you can learn your Bible passages this afternoon while you rest.'

He couldn't know about Charles. If he had learned that a man of the cloth, and the bishop's son, was involved in the smuggling surely he would not be so calm? Surely he could not keep something as terrible and shocking as that to himself? She glanced at him warily. He couldn't know the truth. He couldn't.

Later, in her room, Caroline stood looking out of the window at the garden. The heat of the afternoon lay like a gauze curtain on the countryside, making it shimmer like gossamer. Her Bible lay open near her on her desk but she had not looked at it.

Her mind was far away.

Jake Forrester, hanging on the gallows. Susan and her baby, due any day. And Charles Dawson. Would he be caught too? Would he hang? Or did he wait at a safe distance, his own cover still intact, directing these men to their doom?

Why? Why did he do it?

She paced back and forth a couple of times, the image of Susan and her pale, strained face, her hacking cough, constantly before her. When she had mentioned the cottage to her father at luncheon he had frowned. 'I'll speak to Joe Randall again about those hovels,' he had said. 'They are a disgrace to the parish. It wouldn't have happened in his father's day. He looked after his workers.'

And with that she had had to be content.

Twice more she paced up and down the room. She had to do something. She couldn't let Jake be caught. His companions might have killed a man, and they should be punished, but would more deaths solve anything? Weren't they all men driven to crime by poverty and despair? All except Charles Dawson, who had no such excuse. She was desperately angry. How dare he! How dare he send these men to their deaths?

Almost without realising she had done it she had slipped out of her muslin gown and reached for her riding habit. She would ride to see him. However much she detested him, she had to speak to him and force him somehow to call back his men; to warn them of the trap. She had to save Jake for Susan.

She paused outside her father's bedroom door and listened for a moment as she tiptoed down the stairs. Sure enough she could hear the faint sound of snoring. He had retired to rest in the heat of the afternoon.

The groom was asleep too, on a heap of hay. It was several minutes before he could bestir himself enough to saddle Caroline's pretty bay mare, Star, and lead her out of her cool shadowy box into the blinding sunlight of the stableyard. He offered to ride with her – part of his duties if she rode out alone – but with little enthusiasm and was obviously relieved when she turned down his offer.

Charles Dawson's parish was some five miles away through narrow lanes and across trackways over the Downs. It seemed a long way in the heat. Time and again she slowed the sweating horse, letting her walk in the dappled shadows beneath the trees which bordered the lanes. There was plenty of time. The raid would not take place till after dark, but he had to have time to send messages to his men. The closer she got, the more slowly she rode. Her anger had evaporated slightly in the heat and she had to admit that she was a little apprehensive. She was not looking forward to meeting Charles Dawson again.

The Rectory at Pengate was a large Georgian house, set between two graceful cedar trees. As Caroline rode up the long drive she saw the curtains in the main rooms were drawn against the sun and her heart sank. It had not crossed her mind that he might be out. Dismounting, she pulled the bell and waited, Star's rein looped around her arm. Her heart was thumping painfully now, and she found she was having to hold tight to her courage before it oozed away completely.

It was several minutes before the door opened and she found herself confronting the tall figure of Charles Dawson's butler. The rector, she was informed, was indeed out.

'He can't be!' she cried out in dismay. 'He must be here.'

'I am sorry, Miss. He is not expected to return until tomorrow!' James Kennet was eyeing her crumpled habit and the dishevelled wisps of hair flying from beneath her hat. He frowned.

'Then where is he? He was going to the Rixbys' this evening, but surely not already?' She knew she sounded desperate.

'I am sorry, Miss.' He tightened his lips in disapproval. 'I do not know where he is.'

And with that she had to be content. Disconsolately Caroline turned the mare's head back towards home.

The afternoon had grown hotter. The baked mud in the lanes was like stone; the air, as the horse left the shade of the deep lanes for the open downland, was stifling.

But she was not going to be defeated that easily. She would have to go to the Rixbys' and lie in wait for him. That was the only choice she had left. She had no idea how late he would be – perhaps too late – but what else could she do? She was not going to give up. Not yet. Kicking the reluctant Star into a canter before she could change her mind and cravenly seek the cool shadows of her curtained bedroom she took the road that led towards the archdeacon's house in the cathedral precinct.

The roads were busy and a pall of dust lay over the city of Larchester as she threaded her way through the streets praying she would not meet anyone she knew, trying to decide how to go about reaching Charles before he got to the Rixbys. Now that she was nearly there, the practicalities of the situation faced her squarely. She was in Larchester, unchaperoned, looking for an unmarried gentleman whom she was, to all intents and purposes, about to accuse of murder! She bit her lip. So what! It had to be done. Jake had to be saved.

She halted her mare in the shade of some trees near the cathedral. Charles was expected in the evening. That was all she knew. Early or late? She had no way of knowing. He might have cancelled his visit or be there already for all she knew. At the latter thought she kicked Star on. If he was already there she had to find a way of speaking to him now.

Star solved the problem for her. As they walked towards the precinct Caroline realised that the mare had begun to limp painfully. Slipping from the saddle she ran gentle fingers down the sweating pastern – then slowly she coaxed her forward.

'I am so sorry to intrude,' she said to Mrs Rixby. 'I couldn't think what to do when she went lame, then I thought I could ask your groom as you were so close.'

In the stables Star had been fed and watered and bedded down in deep straw to rest the sprained tendon. Caroline had been ushered into the huge, cool drawing room and given lemonade and a fan and already she knew that the archdeacon would be returning in an hour and his wife had been unable to resist telling her that Charles Dawson was calling on him at six.

At six. Surreptitiously Caroline glanced at the clock on the mantelpiece. She had over an hour to wait and she had gathered swiftly that her presence, if not exactly unwelcome, was certainly not timely.

'Our groom shall drive you home, my dear, as soon as you have drunk your lemonade,' her hostess said firmly as Caroline sipped from her glass. 'Your horse can remain here until she is better.'

Caroline smiled, her brain working like lightning. Above all she didn't want to be escorted off the premises. Somehow she had to make them let her leave alone. She put down her glass. 'Thank you, but I can go home with our verger. He drove into town this morning and I can easily get a lift with him.' She jumped to her feet. 'There is no need to trouble your groom. But I'll just say goodbye to Star . . .'

She smiled at Mrs Rixby's haughtily raised eyebrow, said a firm goodbye and made her way, alone, back into the stableyard. To her relief the groom was nowhere to be seen. It took only a few seconds to slip into an empty stall and sit down on some straw bales in the deep shadows, out of sight.

She heard the cathedral clock strike the quarter, then half past. Twice she heard footsteps nearby and once a horse rode into the yard at a trot. Creeping to the half door, her heart in her mouth, she peered over, but it was a stranger.

She did not let herself think what would happen if Charles went straight up to the front door. Instead she concentrated every bit of her mind on praying that he would ride into the yard and that she could catch his eye before he shouted for the groom. If not she – and Jake and all the others – were lost. What Charles would say when he saw her here, of all places, she did not dare to think at all.

It was nearly a quarter past six when a sturdy black cob turned into the yard and stopped. The groom was at its head before Caroline could reach the door. Heart in mouth she watched as Charles, a tall figure in immaculate coat and trousers, strode towards the house without once glancing in her direction. It was the groom who saw her.

'Oy! What are you doing in there? Come out of there!' His voice echoed round the stableyard as he caught a glimpse of her white face peering over the half door.

Charles stopped dead and looked round. Paralysed with fright and embarrassment, for a moment Caroline did not move.

'Why, Miss, I'm sorry.' It was the groom who recognised her first. 'What are you doing in there? Your mare is over here.' He seemed bewildered.

'Miss Hayward?' Charles strode towards her. He pulled open the stable door, his face full of suspicion.

'I . . . I had to see you,' she stammered. 'I couldn't think what to do . . .'

For a moment he stared thoughtfully down at her. Then he turned to the groom. 'You may see to my horse. I shall look after Miss Hayward.'

'I . . . I heard you were coming to ask for Marianne's hand this evening . . .' she floundered on. 'I went to your house, but you had already left.'

'I see. You couldn't bear to think of me wedded to another.'

The sarcasm of his tone belied the sudden amused gleam in his eye.

Caroline went scarlet. 'It's not that at all!' She exclaimed indignantly. 'I had to warn you –' she put her hand to her lips and as she glanced over her shoulder, her voice dropped to a whisper. 'Oh, please, don't you see? I had to find you. My father says you have been betrayed. The excise men will be waiting tonight on the coast. Your men will all be taken –'

He cut her short in mid-sentence with a sharp gesture of his hand. Behind them the archdeacon had appeared. He was staring at Caroline in astonishment.

Charles forestalled his questions. 'You will have to forgive me, archdeacon. Miss Hayward has brought me an urgent message. She has met with someone from my parish who needs my services. It seems to be a matter of life or death. Would you forgive me if I return to see them at once? Perhaps we could discuss our business tomorrow?' He smiled.

The archdeacon's brow had furrowed sharply. He looked far from pleased. 'If you feel you must, then of course, I cannot prevent you.'

'Quite so.' Charles's answering smile did not quite reach his eyes as he beckoned his horse forward once more. He turned back to Caroline. 'Is there more to your message?'

She nodded, aware suddenly of eyes watching them from the windows of the drawing room beyond the rose garden to the north of the stableyard.

'Then please excuse us, archdeacon.' Charles turned to their host.

At his imperious tone Joseph Rixby's expression froze. He was looking extremely angry. 'I won't detain either of you,' was all he said however and with a stiff bow he turned away.

'Well?' Charles turned back to Caroline, his horse's rein in his hand.

'They know. They know who leads them,' she whispered.

'They know?' he looked at her in astonishment. Then his face darkened. 'And was it your father who told them, I wonder?'

'I didn't tell him,' she flared. 'I don't break my word.'

She turned away sharply, aware suddenly that there were pieces of straw clinging to her skirt. She wondered if the archdeacon had noticed them and knew immediately that he had. 'I don't know how they found out, or even if they are right in what they think. Papa didn't tell me who it is they suspect. All I know is that you must hurry. You have to. I just pray you are in time to save Jake and the others. It's them I care about.'

'I don't doubt it.' He paused. 'Who else knows about this?'

'I don't know. The authorities. Papa came into Larchester this morning to meet the other magistrates – '

'And they told him I was involved?'

'I suppose so.'

'So, why am I still free? Why were the soldiers not waiting for me here?'

'Perhaps because they want to trap you all together. I don't know. Oh, please hurry. You must warn them . . .'

'If I am being watched I must avoid them – how did you get here?' He spoke sharply.

'On my mare. But she's lame.'

'Then we'll borrow one for you. Here, boy.' He shouted behind him into the yard. 'Saddle Miss Marianne's mare quickly – '

'But you can't – what will the Rixbys say?'

'Nothing if they think I want to marry their daughter.' He spoke with strange bitterness suddenly. 'You shall ride beside me. If they are looking for a man alone or a group of men they certainly won't stop a woman and a clergyman.'

'You mean I'm to come with you to warn your men?'

'Why not? It was Jake Forrester you were worried about wasn't it?'

'Yes, but – '

'Then you can help me save him.'

He turned as the groom led an elegant grey horse out of one of the boxes. There was a glint of silver as some coins changed hands. 'No word of this loan, my friend,' Charles winked at him. 'We'll have the horse back by dawn. I doubt if Miss Marianne will want it tonight. If she does you'll have to think of an excuse and find her another mount.'

Charles turned and with scant ceremony swung Caroline up onto the side saddle. The groom was grinning as they turned and rode out of the stableyard. Behind them the curtains in the archdeaconry twitched and fell into place. In the drawing room Marianne subsided into tears.

Charles set a fast pace south and the grey mare, fresh from her stable, kept up with ease. He glanced at the horse approvingly. 'She makes a good ride, I'll wager,' he shouted above the drumming of their hooves.

Caroline turned and glanced over her shoulder. To her relief the road behind them was empty. She had half expected to see the glint of the sun on bayonets and the glow of red coats. With an effort she reined in the excited horse. 'You don't need me now. We're not being followed. I must go back,' she called.

'Why? Don't you like the sound of our adventure?' He slowed down beside her and patted the neck of his sweating mount. 'I would have thought that a woman who walked through churchyards and visited haunted castles at night would enjoy such an excursion.'

She coloured. 'It's not that. But Papa will worry. He may even suspect –'

'That you consort with criminals?'

'Don't be silly.' Her retort was sharp. 'But I am not supposed to leave the house alone. He doesn't know where I am –'

'He will within the hour.' He laughed grimly. 'Do you think the Rixbys won't send after you to find out what you were doing in their stableyard? Your reputation may well be ruined when the world hears you rode off with me.' His expression was unrepentant.

'It may well be when the world knows you are a smuggler and a murderer, sir,' she retorted tartly.

Slowly he reined in his horse. 'I am not a murderer, Caroline. Nor are any of my boys out there. They are all good men, like Jake Forrester. The man who died last night was killed by one of his own comrades in the skirmish. None of my men had firearms. It was a tragic mistake, but not of our doing.'

'Not of your doing?' The wave of relief that flowed over her at his words did not stop her turning on him. 'Being a smuggler is a usual and acceptable second occupation for a country rector I suppose?'

'No.' He urged his horse on once more.

'Then why do you do it?' They were riding side by side now, their horses striding shoulder to shoulder in the narrow lane. 'Why?'

'I have good reasons.' He kicked his mount into a trot. 'Come, we must get on. We pass close to Hancombe soon. You can go home, if you wish. I'll go on over the Downs.'

'No!' Suddenly the thought of returning to the claustrophobic atmosphere of the Rectory was unbearable. Besides, she sensed a challenge in his words. 'I'll go with you. As you say, they are not looking for a woman.'

For a moment he looked at her closely, then he gave a tight smile. 'You know what you are risking?'

She nodded.

'Then you are very brave.'

Before she could think of an answer he had pushed his horse forward into a gallop and she found herself kicking the grey frantically to keep up with him.

They did not stop again until they could see the sea below them – a ribbon of brilliant blue, gilded and coloured by the westering sun. Charles was breathing hard as he slipped from his horse. 'It's early yet. The boys won't gather till dark.

There will be plenty of time to warn them then. The ship comes in with the high tide in the early morning. And the soldiery won't gather till late if I know them. A night spent getting drunk in Larchester to keep their courage up is more to their taste than a cold beach at dawn and by then we'll have signalled the *Marie Blanche* to return to France with her cargo untouched, and my boys will all be tucked up in their beds.' He turned to where she still sat on the high side saddle. 'You must go back now, before your father calls out a search party. Tell him the bishop's son asked you to do an errand for him.' He gave a ghost of a smile. 'If he questions it, send him to me. I'll pacify him. It's better if you go. There's no more for you to do here. I'll be better alone.'

She looked down at him. He still appeared immaculate, scarcely a hair out of place beneath his hat, every inch the elegant churchman, escorting his lady to a Sunday picnic. Only his eyes didn't fit. They were silver in the tanned face – alive, excited, seeing danger ahead, and, she realised suddenly, enjoying it.

'You didn't tell me why you do this,' she said quietly.

'No, and I'm not going to.' He smiled. 'Take care of the horse, Caroline, or we'll have the Rixbys after us. This will take some explaining tomorrow, I fear!' He did not look the slightest bit afraid. 'I will see to its return in the morning.'

'It was a matter of life and death, didn't we say?' she murmured. She didn't want to go. To ride alone through the dusk and go back to her stifling room and learn a passage from the Bible . . . it was unthinkable. Impulsively she pulled off her bonnet and shook her head, feeling her hair slipping from its combs. 'Will I see you again?' She meant: to get their story straight.

He grinned. 'Undoubtedly. You must come to our next garden party.' He was loosening his horse's girth, tethering it beneath the trees.

'Goodbye, then.' In spite of herself she felt strangely desolate.

He looked up at her again. Then he swept off his hat and bowed. 'My thanks, Miss Hayward.'

She gathered up her reins. 'Would you really have implicated Papa if I had betrayed you?'

He laughed. 'Indeed I would.'

'How?'

'I'd have told them about the four kegs of brandy hidden in your hayloft! Goodbye, Miss Hayward.'

He brought his hand down on her horse's rump with a smack and it leaped forward. Almost unseated, Caroline struggled for control. When she had at last brought the mare back to a halt and turned round he had gone.

She set off slowly with her back to the setting sun, following the lanes as best she could. She wasn't familiar with the country here and the horse was tired, so she did not want to take any short cuts.

It was two miles further on at the village of Ewangate that she saw the militia, a huge crowd of men and horses gathered outside an inn. There was no doubt as to their mood and there was no doubt that most of them were, if not local, then at least men brought in from along the coast. The women in the cottages were huddled defensively on the green, talking in low voices together, and their menfolk were eyeing the strangers with obvious hostility as the soldiers drank their ale and talked and laughed. Caroline felt herself grow cold; they were here already, and so close. Charles was wrong. They were not from the barracks in Larchester. They were men from the coast, men who knew the sea, men who, in spite of the ale, were far from too drunk to know what they were doing.

She slowed the mare, aware that every eye was upon her as she made her way up the village street. It was too late to turn back. She could only go on, conscious that an obviously well dressed young woman on a valuable horse, completely unescorted, would be noted and remembered by every single person who saw her.

Cursing her stupidity in riding so carelessly into the village she rode on, looking neither to right nor left, keeping her eyes fixed on the bend in the road ahead.

'So, where are you off to, my beauty? Why not stop and have a drink with us instead, eh?' She froze with horror as a gnarled hand clamped suddenly onto her horse's bridle, making the animal sidestep nervously. 'Too proud to look at the likes of us, are you?'

She found herself staring down at an unpleasantly scarred face with blackened teeth exposed in a leer.

'Leave her, man.' As if in answer to her prayer an officer had appeared from inside the inn. He saluted. 'I'm sorry. Captain Warrender, ma'am, at your service. Take no notice of these ruffians.'

Caroline gave him an uncertain smile. 'It seems strange to have an army gathered here, Captain. Are you looking for a war?'

Her remark was greeted by a growl of laughter from the men who had crowded around her.

'As good as. We fight the free traders, ma'am. There's bounty in it for these fellows, and the satisfaction of knowing that we aid the law.'

'Free traders?' Caroline stared at him.

'Smugglers, my beauty.' The man who had halted her horse grinned at her. 'A hotbed of them, this coast.' There was another growl of laughter which, Caroline suspected, meant that many of the men present could be found amongst the smugglers themselves from time to time.

'Smugglers?' she echoed. 'Are you going to catch them?'

'We are indeed.' The officer grinned. 'Down at Windell's Cove. We've left men on every approach to the coast and we'll be in position there ourselves before dark, and when the devils come we'll be waiting for them.'

She swallowed. 'I'm glad I shan't be there, then. Good evening to you, Captain.'

She rode on, aware that every eye in the village was fixed

on her back as her horse walked past the last cottage and into the leafy lane.

Somehow she had to get back to Charles. She had to warn him. He wasn't expecting this! Every one of those men had been armed to the teeth. She had seen the cudgels and staves, the knives and swords, and she had seen a pile of muskets outside the door of the inn.

Dragging the horse's head round as soon as she was out of sight of the village she skirted back across the fields, heading as fast as she could urge the tired animal towards the clifftop where she had left Charles. But where was it? Desperately she tried to remember the way. Shadows were lengthening now and the lanes were darker. Already the militia would be moving out. She glanced round but everything looked the same in the monochrone light. There were no landmarks. Her heart was hammering with fear as she pushed the horse on, threading her way through the trees, expecting at any moment to hear them behind her.

It seemed a long time before at last she had retraced her steps and found the clump of trees where, to her relief, she saw Charles's horse, grazing peacefully in the shadows. It looked up enquiringly as she rode up, then went on with its eating. She slid from her saddle and tethered the mare beside it, leaving her detested bonnet dangling by its ribbon from the pommel, then she turned towards the cliff.

'Charles?' Her whisper was lost in the taunting cry of a lone, circling gull. There was no sign of him. Hesitantly she stood on the cliff's edge, looking down at the cove beneath. It seemed deserted. The sea was calm and gentle, the dark gilded water running in gentle ripples up the sand.

'Charles, where are you?' She looked round desperately, pushing her hair out of her eyes. The place was deserted.

Biting her lip she looked at the narrow sheep track which wound its way down the cliff, almost sheer as it zigzagged between rocks and clumps of grass and clustered flowers. The sun was dropping now into the sea. A dazzling sunpath lay across the water, touching the wet sand. Slowly gathering the skirt of her habit in one hand she began to descend the path.

Charles was waiting behind an outcrop of rock at the base of the cliff.

'I hope you have a good reason for coming back.' His tall figure threw a long shadow across the sand behind them.

'I saw the militia – not two miles away.' Her words tumbled over each other in her rush to tell him. 'There were dozens of them, all armed, and they will be here before dark.' She was out of breath after her climb. 'They have blocked all the main roads. They mean to trap you.'

Charles let out an oath.

Caroline gave a rueful smile in spite of herself. 'That was the smuggler, not the rector speaking, I take it,' she said wryly.

He glared at her, then, unexpectedly he laughed. 'I fear it was. My apologies.' For a moment he was silent, considering the situation. 'It appears I am doubly in your debt. I would have sat here waiting for the trap to close. I have sent word to the men, and I pray the message will get through in spite of your road blocks, but a few of them may not get the warning in time.'

'How did you send word?' She stared at him. 'There was no one here.'

'Oh, but there was.' He was leaning against the rock, watching the clouds entwining themselves around the sun, changing it from gold to crimson as they dragged it down into the sea. 'I have a system which usually works. The two men here will each have told two more, and they in turn two more, on through the villages. As long as no link breaks they will all be warned.'

'And if the link breaks?' She was watching his face, fascinated, as the westering light threw the planes of his cheekbones and his nose into silhouette.

'That was why I stayed. In case.'

'And you would have stayed here all night?'

He nodded. 'All night, if need be.'

'You care about those men.'

'They are my brothers.'

'Of course.' She was silent for a while. 'I still don't understand why you do it.'

'For the money.' He seated himself on a slab of rock. 'What other reason could there be?'

In spite of herself she was disappointed. 'But you don't need the money –'

'They do.' His mouth hardened. 'You want to know why I do it, Miss Hayward? I'll tell you. Those men, every one of them, are ground into poverty by the way this country operates. And the two things working men have to alleviate their pain and their poverty, alcohol and tobacco, are taxed to a price where few can afford them and the taxes are frittered away by an administration that is uncaring and incompetent. I come from a class, Miss Hayward, which could help men like your Jake Forrester. But we don't. We watch them die. We watch them die in their babyhood and their childhood, in their teens and in their twenties of disease and deprivation. These men are old before the age of thirty. Well, I decided to do something about it. By exploiting one of the local pastimes.' He gave the ghost of a grin. 'I redirect some of that money to where it should go. To the poor. To the sick. To the deserving.'

'Like Robin Hood,' she said softly.

He laughed. 'Perhaps.'

'Besides which, you enjoy the excitement.' She had suddenly discovered that she liked Charles Dawson after all.

'I won't deny it. It beats spending the evening writing sermons.'

'No doubt you have already written your sermon for this week.'

'Of course.' He was mocking. 'How are we going to get you home, Caroline?' he went on softly. 'You can't ride in the dark.'

'I know.' She liked the way he used her name. Sometimes the acerbic Miss Hayward, sometimes the soft, almost caressing Caroline. 'I don't know the way through the countryside, and the roads are blocked.'

He frowned. 'It was unforgivable of me to bring you down here. Did your father have no idea at all that you were going out? He really will be worried now that it is dark.'

She laughed nervously. 'I was supposed to be in my room learning a passage from the Bible as punishment for my waywardness.'

'Indeed?' He raised an eyebrow. 'May I ask what dreadful deed you could possibly have perpetrated to incur such a punishment?'

She grimaced. It seemed so long ago since her father had burst into her room and snatched away her book. 'I was reading Lord Byron's poems.'

His crack of laughter was quickly smothered. 'My poor Caroline. So your soul is damned to perdition. Poor George Gordon. Is he still thought to be an ogre, then?'

'Not by me. I loved his book. But Papa put it on the fire.'

'One day I'll give you another copy, and you shall read it to your heart's content –' He broke off as the sound of a rock falling resounded above the gentle sighing of the sea. Silently he stood up and putting his arm around her shoulders he pulled her into the deep shadows of the tumbled rocks.

Straining her eyes towards the far side of the little cove Caroline felt suddenly very afraid. There were men out there with muskets ready to shoot on sight. If she and Charles weren't killed they could be captured and quite possibly hanged. What was she, after all, if not a willing accomplice of the leader of the smugglers?

She closed her eyes and took a deep breath, very aware of Charles's strong arm around her shoulder, of his tall figure so close beside her, comforting her, giving her a quite spurious sense of security. Then his lips were at her ear, almost touching.

'Up the cliff. Quietly,' he breathed. Taking her hand he turned and began to tiptoe back towards the path.

Behind them as the cove fell into darkness it remained empty. If there was anyone there they were hidden in the shadows, out of sight.

The horses were where they had left them. There was a quiet whicker of greeting from Charles's cob, then intense silence in the wood. It was as if the whole world were holding its breath. Soundlessly Charles untied the horses and helped Caroline onto her saddle. Just for a moment he went on holding her hand. 'You're a brave woman, Caroline Hayward.' Leaning down towards him she saw him glance up at her. He reached up and gently touched his finger to her lips. Then he had vanished into the darkness and she heard the rustle of hooves as he led his cob ahead of her.

She was about to turn her exhausted mare after him when the night exploded into noise. By the livid light of the powder flashes from a dozen muskets she saw the ring of armed men who surrounded the wood and she knew that they were trapped.

PART THREE

As the muskets exploded around them Charles span round. 'Get back!' he shouted. 'Get back into the woods. I'll head them off!' Leaping onto his horse he rode straight at the line of armed men.

Fighting to calm the panicking mare Caroline managed to pull her back into the darkness. Throwing herself from the saddle she dragged the horse deep into a thicket and tied it there with shaking hands before creeping back towards the edge of the wood.

Flares had been lit now and it took her only a moment to see that Charles had failed in his attempt to ride through the line of men. They had dragged him from his horse and as she watched he was overpowered and she saw them binding his arms behind his back.

Her mouth was dry with terror as she clung to the powdery trunk of the tree round which she was peering. In the flickering light of the flares she saw Charles, blood streaming from a wound in his forehead, dragged between two men back to his horse and pushed up onto the saddle. Already the ranks were closing round him. In the smoky light she saw the face of the officer who had spoken to her earlier.

'Half a dozen of you come with me,' he shouted. 'We'll take this fine gentleman back to where he can do no more harm. The rest of you, search the wood for the other horse. See if there is anyone hiding in those trees. Then wait at the cove.'

With a gasp of fear Caroline shrank back into the shadows.

'The other horse was mine.' She heard Charles's voice clearly above the shouting. 'And my men are far away, my friend, all forewarned about your trap. There will be no one there for you to find.'

'No?' She saw Captain Warrender look up at him and smile. 'I think we'll check anyway.'

With a little sob of fear she turned back into the wood, pushing her way through the undergrowth, feeling the branches and leaves whipping across her face. She groped her way frantically back to the mare and tearing free the rein somehow managed to scramble back into the saddle. Get away! She had to get away.

She turned her horse's head away from the flares and the shouting of the men and, blinded by tears, urged the animal up a soft ride at a canter, praying the horse could see better than she in the darkness beneath the trees.

It was a long time before she reined in and tried to listen for sounds of pursuit. There was nothing behind her. She had crossed meadow and downland in her wild flight and now she was in the forest. The trees around her were still.

Only an owl in the distance broke the silence. They had not followed her.

Go back.

She swallowed, trying to gather her wits.

Find out where they are taking him.

Go home, another part of her mind was screaming. *Go home and hide. Forget him. He brought it on himself.*

Go on. Follow him. After all, he was caught because he wanted to save you.

She leaned forward and rested her forehead wearily on the mare's sweating neck. It was the truth. He had ridden at the men in order to distract them from her. Had he ridden the other way, into the darkness, he might have got away.

She straightened and took a deep breath. She would go after him.

Turning the tired horse she began to retrace her steps, her ears and eyes straining for the least sight or sound of another rider in the darkness, but the meadows and woods were empty in the thin moonlight. She carefully skirted behind the cove, not daring to go near the cliffs where the soldiers were presumably hiding. Instead she headed west, making for the main road. Reaching the crest of the hill she stopped and cautiously surveyed the road ahead as the moon fought its way out of the haze and swam free, bathing the landscape in clear silver light.

She could see them clearly, half a dozen riders clustered tightly together – at that distance she could not make out which one was Charles. To her relief she realised that they were riding slowly now, making it easier for her to follow them safely.

It was half an hour before they reached the outskirts of the market town and port of Lakamouth and ten minutes after that before the militia escorted their prisoner into the castle. Reining in the mare at the foot of Market Street Caroline saw them disappear beneath the gatehouse arch and the heavy doors swing shut behind them.

Immediately she turned away. Now that Charles was out of sight she felt abandoned and alone. Up till that moment she had concentrated on keeping him in view and on not being seen herself. Now the sleeping city frightened her. She glanced sideways down the narrow streets where the moonlight never reached and she shivered. Somewhere she heard the sound of running feet and nearby a cat yowled.

What was she to do? She had no money, and anyway would never dare approach an inn at this time of night, and she was so vulnerable: a woman, alone, with nothing but her horse for protection. And the horse was exhausted. It would never carry her back to Larchester.

She took a deep breath and turned back towards the road. In the open countryside at least she felt safer, free from the spying eyes which seemed to her to be watching her from every street corner and alleyway.

In the end she found a barn on the outskirts of a village. Leading the horse inside she thankfully helped herself to hay and water from the trough for the horse, and curled up herself in a pile of sharp-scented straw, too exhausted to care where she was or who found her.

It was full daylight when she awoke, stiff and hungry. The mare was munching contentedly at the wisps of hay and sunlight streamed in through the huge open doors, evaporating the dew on the fields. Wearily climbing to her feet and dusting the straw from her habit she looked around. There was no sign of anyone about. Relieved, she splashed her face with water from the trough, tried vainly to smooth back her tangled hair – her bonnet had been lost long ago in the wood – and set about resaddling the mare.

It was still very early when at last she reached home and to her relief the roads were comparatively empty, for wherever she passed people she was painfully aware of their amused stares.

She went, not to the rectory, but to the Forresters' cottage. Susan was outside with two buckets of water she had drawn from the pump in the street. She straightened and stared at Caroline in astonishment as she threw herself wearily from her horse.

'Susan, where's Jake?'

'He's inside. He came home last night after all –'

She broke off as Caroline thrust the mare's rein into her hand and pushed past her into the cottage. Jake was lacing his boots. He straightened in astonishment at the sight of her.

'They've captured Charles – Mr Dawson,' Caroline began, with a glance over her shoulder to make sure Susan had not followed her in. 'They've taken him to Lakamouth Castle.'

'Dear Lord!' Jake stared at her. 'But I thought everyone got away. He warned us hisself –'

'He stayed to protect me!' Caroline cried in despair. 'We have to help him. What can we do?'

Jake sat down heavily on one of the two wooden chairs. 'As to that –' He scratched his head. 'Lakamouth, you say? Why so far? Why didn't they bring him back to Larchester?'

'I don't know.' She shrugged impatiently. 'Maybe the militia are based there.'

'Ay, that's more than likely.' He paused thoughtfully. 'Leave it to me. I'll talk to the others and see what they think is to be done. Your father's been looking for you.' He seemed to notice at last the state she was in. 'You'd best get back home –'

'But you'll send me a message? I must know what you're going to do.'

Jake shook his head. 'It's best you leave it to us now, Miss –'

'No! Don't you see?' She caught his arm. 'Jake, if it hadn't been for me he would have got away. I owe it to him to help him.'

For a moment he said nothing. Then he nodded. 'All right,' he said, 'I'll send you word.'

Leaving the mare in the rectory stable with strict instructions that she be rubbed down and fed and watered Caroline crept towards the kitchen door and pushed it open. Polly and the cook were seated at the table shelling peas.

'Miss Caroline!' Polly jumped to her feet. 'Dear Lord! Look at the state of you! Where have you been?'

'Where is my father?' Caroline collapsed onto a chair.

'He's ridden over to Pengate again. Such a to do there's been. Archdeacon rode over last night and demanded to know why you'd taken Miss Marianne's pony. Then when we couldn't find you anywhere and he told your Papa you'd gone with Mr Dawson your father went straight over there, and oh my dear, the servants there said they hadn't seen hide nor hair of either of you. Mr Hayward was all for scouring the country. And now, look at you! Did you have a fall?'

Caroline closed her eyes with a little prayer of gratitude. Of course, that was the perfect alibi. 'Yes. I fell. I'm sorry I frightened everyone. I must have knocked myself out. I felt too dizzy to ride so I stayed in a barn somewhere until morning.'

The two women threw up their hands in horror.

'But where was Reverend Dawson to let you ride home alone?' Cook was frowning at her closely.

'He had to stay behind. I wanted to get home. It wasn't his fault. I should have stayed with him, but I knew Papa would worry – and now I've made things so much worse.'

To her relief she was able to wash and change and eat something before Mr Hayward, summoned by the groom, returned to the rectory. His anger was only slightly mitigated by his concern when he heard that Caroline had fallen from the borrowed horse. Peremptorily he sent for the doctor, who examined her closely and professed himself surprised by the absence of bruises, before ordering her to bed for the rest of the day. She went gladly, relieved to escape her father's furious questioning which was leading her deeper and deeper into a tissue of lies.

Her room was cool and quiet. The house was silent. She

lay back in the bed, staring at the open window where the curtains stirred gently in the breeze. What was happening to Charles? Would he be tried? Surely he could not be hanged? She closed her eyes miserably, her fists clenched so that her nails cut into the palms of her hands. She couldn't stop thinking about him and unhappily she realised that she had come to admire Charles Dawson far more than she should.

Messages had been sent to the Archdeaconry and to the Rectory at Pengate confirming the safety of horse and rider and one had been received back from Kennet, Charles's butler, saying Mr Dawson had been detained – Caroline blanched at the word – and would not be home for several days. Who had sent that message, she wondered?

All day she waited for news – from Jake, or from her father – with the revelation that Charles Dawson had been arrested but nothing happened.

Then, on her supper tray she found a note:

Are you willing to help? If so, be at the Forresters' cottage at dawn. That was all. There was no signature. She stared at it. It was written in an educated hand on a sheet of heavy, good quality notepaper. Holding it over the empty fireplace she watched it burn, letting the last pieces of ash flutter down into the cold grave. Her heart was thumping nervously.

She barely slept. Long before dawn she was up and dressed in her freshly pressed habit, her hair bound up in a net. Holding her boots in her hand she crept down the stairs into the cold grey of the dew-soaked garden. It hadn't crossed her mind not to go.

She walked swiftly down the village street, flitting like a shadow past the rows of cottages until she reached the Forresters' at the end of the street. It was silent and in darkness.

Nervously she raised her hand to the door, but it opened before she knocked. There were several men inside. Of Susan there was no sign.

'I knew you'd come.' Nervously Jake produced a chair. Seated on the only other chair in the room was James Kennet,

Charles Dawson's butler. So, he knew all about it. Suddenly she realised who must have written the note. He half rose in acknowledgement of her presence then he subsided again. She could feel him eyeing her closely.

'Mr Charles and I had a plan worked out in the event of this ever happening, Miss Hayward,' he said formally. 'At the moment our luck holds. They are still holding him at Lakamouth but we have found out that they intend to transfer him to Larchester for the assizes. I hardly need tell you the scandal that would ensue once he was recognised. It is imperative that we rescue him before he is discovered, never mind before he comes to trial!'

'And how do we do that?' Caroline found that her mouth had gone dry.'

'Bribery, Miss Hayward.' He sighed. 'There is no garrison proper at Lakamouth, which should make things easier. The prison there is, so I gather, guarded by a very poor sort of person. With luck we should be able to spring him with no trouble.' His mouth turned down at the edges wryly at his use of what he obviously thought was the correct cant term.

'How much money will you need?' Caroline's heart sank as she glanced around the room. So this was why they wanted her. But she had nothing of her own.

Kennet smiled. He had obviously read her thoughts. 'It depends how much you can get. You'll have to go to the bishop.'

'The bishop?' Caroline stared at him. 'You mean he knows?'

'No, of course he doesn't know.' The man's voice was scornful. 'But Mr Charles left this letter.'

Caroline unfolded the paper he handed her. 'Father, I have urgent need of several hundred guineas for a cause which would I know, gladden your heart. Please, would you entrust the money to the bearer of this letter. I shall explain to you as soon as I may. Your affectionate son, Charles.' She looked up. 'He was expecting this to happen!'

'We all knew that it might.'

'But why do you want *me* to go to the bishop?'

'You are a more respectable messenger even than I, Miss Hayward.' Kennet allowed himself the ghost of a smile. 'You could wheedle more out of him. We'll need as much as we can get, and quickly.'

It was still only ten o'clock when James Kennet drove Caroline in the Pengate rectory chaise to the door of the Bishop's Palace in the close at Larchester. She had been released from her bedroom into Mr Kennet's charge by her father only when he knew that she carried a message from Mr Dawson to the bishop. Only half an hour after that she had left, having been regaled with a thimble-sized glass of sherry, a hearty handshake from the bishop, a bag of gold coins and a large, scuffed soft leather wallet stuffed with notes issued by the Larchester and Lakamouth Bank.

She had changed into her prettiest sprigged muslin dress and tied her best bonnet over her gleaming curls for the visit, and the bishop, his eyes twinkling, had been openly appreciative of his attractive visitor.

'Charles in a scrape again, is he?' he had roared at her as he filled her glass, having read the letter. 'No, don't bother to deny it. That boy was always in trouble. No different now he's grown. I just hope he's all right.' He had eyed her closely. 'A friend of Charles's, are you?'

'I hope so, my lord.' Caroline could feel herself blushing.

'Hayward's daughter, eh?' He seemed to be trying to place her. 'Good, very good.' And with that she was ushered out once more by the bishop's attentive chaplain.

They drove out on the Lakamouth road, the money lying in Caroline's lap.

'The others will be there to meet us in case we need any help,' James Kennet said after a long silence. 'They'll have seen to it that there's a boat ready to take him off on the afternoon tide.'

'And if they don't release him?' Caroline glanced at the man's profile.

'Then we'll have to think of something else. But I don't think we'll have any bother. Half those men are smugglers themselves. They join the militia for the bounty. If your money's better, then they'll take it.' He flicked the reins.

They put up the horses and chaise at the Angel Inn. Jake and three companions were waiting for them there, lounging around in the stableyard.

'We've signalled the *Marie Blanche*. She's standing off to take him to France.' Jake grinned contentedly. 'All we've got to do now is use a bit of gentle persuasion up at the castle.'

They all looked at Caroline.

'Oh no. Not me!' She stared at the five men in turn, horrified.

'Who better?' Jake grinned. 'Let your hair down and let them see your eyes red from crying. The sight of you would soften the hardest heart. Mr Kennet will go with you.'

She glanced round wildly. 'But I can't!'

'Of course you can. It's his only chance.'

For a moment she was tempted to turn and run, then her courage returned. Hadn't she wanted excitement? Hadn't she resented the boredom of life in the rectory? Well, her prayers had been answered. She had found herself an adventure. Besides, it was for Charles, and for him she realised suddenly, she was prepared to risk anything. Slowly she nodded. 'All right, I'll do it.'

'Good girl.' Kennet's slightly patronising, and certainly disrespectful accolade left her glowing with pride.

The whiteness of her cheeks was real however as she walked shakily under the great gatehouse arch and paused, her face hidden by her lowered veil, as Kennet asked the way. She followed him past the guards, across the rounded, slippery cobbles towards the far side of the courtyard.

The officer in charge of the prisoners was lounging at a desk in a small room inside the Edward Tower. He stood up as Caroline entered, hastily buttoning his tunic. 'Madam?' He glanced from Caroline to James Kennet and back suspiciously.

For a moment Caroline was struck dumb. She didn't have any idea what to do or say. She was no actress and she was very frightened. She looked up at the man piteously and unexpectedly and, perfectly genuinely, burst into tears.

It cost them every penny they had with them as well as the gold locket Caroline wore around her neck, but at last they found themselves making their way down long dank passages to the cells with a signed release form from the captain of the guard folded into Caroline's reticule.

Charles was sitting at a rough wooden table in a small cell. His jacket was torn and the cut above his eye had, before it crusted over, bled copiously into his shirt, but he was not, as she had feared, in chains.

Nor was he pleased to see her. 'What in God's name are you doing here? I was sure you had got clean away!'

Taken aback, it was a moment before she replied. 'We've come to release you. I would have thought you'd be pleased,' she said tartly. 'You are free.'

'Cost your father a pretty penny, too, Mr Charles.' Behind her, Kennet winked. 'We thought Miss Caroline could wheedle a bit more out of him than I could. And she did. Are you ready, sir?' He lifted Charles's torn jacket from the back of the chair and held it out to him.

'You fools!' Charles put on the jacket with a grimace. 'Do you want her implicated? Do you want me identified? How long do you think it will be before someone recognises her? Already they have her bonnet!'

The guards had taunted him with it that morning – crushed and sodden with dew as it had been when they found it trodden into the hoofprint in the muddy wood.

'All they know,' said Caroline, her dignity hiding her hurt at his ingratitude, 'is that there is a lady in your life who cares enough for you to pay her every last penny to get you out of here. Who is there to recognise me anyway? Besides, I have my veil.' She turned and walked out of the cell.

Charles frowned. 'Caroline, I'm sorry. I didn't mean to –' But she had gone.

With a glance at one another the two men followed her, and uneasily they retraced their steps back towards the courtyard. They were almost there when the door of the guard-room opened and a man stepped out. He stood barring their way.

'So, what is this? A rescue party?' His eyes ranged from one to the other, then came back to Caroline and his expression sharpened. 'Don't I know you?'

'I don't think so.' She kept her voice as low as she could. She had recognised him at once. It was Captain Warrender, the officer whom she had met the day before as he and his men mustered at the roadside. She wished the flimsy veil over her bonnet were thicker. Feeling his sharp eyes on her she lowered her head. But it was too late.

'I know who you are! The girl on that blood mare at Ewangate yesterday. By God! You were one of them! It was you who warned them –'

'This gentleman has his release, Captain.' Kennet stepped forward. 'It was all a case of mistaken identity. 'You must be mixing this lady up with someone else.' He reached behind him and firmly gestured Charles and Caroline on. 'If you wish we can check with your superior officer.'

Caroline felt Charles take her arm. They were moving on past the guard post. In another moment they would be outside.

'Wait –' the captain called. His cry was broken off as Kennet brought the edge of his hand down sharply on the back of his neck and he crumpled to the floor. Dragging him back into the empty room Kennet locked the door on him and pocketed the key. 'Hurry,' he breathed.

They walked as fast as they could without attracting attention across the cobbled courtyard towards the gatehouse, through it and out into the street. Threading their way swiftly back towards the Angel, they were, almost at once, lost in the crowd of horses and carriages and milling townspeople.

'The boat's waiting at the harbour steps.' Jake met them at the stable entrance with the horse and chaise. Within seconds Kennet had dived into the box beneath the seat and produced a shirt and coat from the change of clothes he had hidden there. He helped Charles strip off his bloodstained garments, wrapped them in a bundle and stowed them away. For a moment Caroline found herself staring at Charles's broad chest and muscular shoulders and she felt a strange twist of longing deep inside her. Then he was being thrust into fresh clothes. He saw her staring and gave a tight smile. 'I'm sorry. No sight for a lady. You should have turned away.'

She blushed. 'I'm . . . I'm sorry. Please. We must hurry.'

'Indeed we must.' Kennet was beside her again. 'Let me help you up, Miss, and here, if you'd remove your bonnet. I thought we might have need of disguises.' He had dived once more into the box and produced this time a crimson shawl. 'If you wrap this round your hair, Miss. Now you look quite different. See?' He pushed her bonnet out of sight beside the bloodstained shirt.

Moments later she found herself wedged between Kennet and his master in the two-seater vehicle. With a wave to Jake and his companions they were driving away from the inn.

Caroline was very conscious of the pressure of Charles's thigh against her own, his shoulder next to hers. 'I haven't thanked you yet,' she said. 'You saved me by riding at those men.'

'I did no more than you did for us,' he said curtly. He glanced behind them, through the small window in the hood of the chaise. 'You have put yourself in more danger coming here. That was foolish.'

'She was very brave, Mr Charles,' Kennet put in on her right. There was a hint of reproof in his voice.

'I don't doubt her bravery. I merely deplore her headstrong urge to rush into danger,' Charles retorted. Abruptly his face lightened into a smile. 'Not that I would have her any other way now I come to think about it. I must like obstreperous women!' He glanced down at her with a teasing grin. 'One of these days I'll come back for you, if you're not careful, and enroll you amongst my followers.'

Caroline didn't answer. Already they had reached the harbour. Kennet drove to the water's edge and stopped at the top of a flight of steps. A small rowing boat waited below. The man at the oars glanced up and raised his hand.

'The *Lucy* out there will take you out to the *Marie Blanche*. Good luck Mr Charles.' Kennet leaned forward slightly.

Charles leapt down. 'Thank you. Both of you.' He inclined a slight bow to Caroline. Then almost as an afterthought he reached up and taking her hand kissed it lightly. 'Take her home, James, and tell her father to keep her out of mischief.'

That was all. He did not look back. They watched as the small boat rowed out to the fishing boat anchored in the middle of the harbour. Already its sails were lifting.

'Where will they go?' Caroline asked sadly.

'They'll meet with a Frenchman in the Channel.' For a moment the butler sat still, staring after his master. 'Mr Charles will go to ground for a while in France while we see which way the land lies here. There will be a hue and cry for him when they find he's been released in error.' He grinned complacently. 'Nowhere along the coast will be safe while they look for him.' He shook the reins. 'No time to hang around for you, either, Miss. I must get you home. Once you're there, you'll be safe.'

She did not let herself look back and in seconds the chaise had swung back into the network of busy streets.

Her father was waiting for her in his study. 'I expected you back long since.' He frowned. Then he went on more eagerly, 'You saw the bishop?'

She smiled wearily: 'The bishop was very hospitable, Papa. I was able to carry out Charles – that is, Mr Dawson's – instructions.'

'And when are we to see Mr Dawson home?' He was watching her closely.

She shrugged. 'I don't know, Papa. No doubt he will contact his father when he returns.'

The rector was obviously dying to ask more, but something about his daughter's bleak expression stopped him short. He walked over to the window and stared out at the sunlit garden. 'The archdeacon's groom came over this afternoon and collected Marianne's mare. He says you can go and fetch Star tomorrow,' he said quietly. He turned and looked at his daughter. 'I understand Marianne is rather upset.'

'I'm sorry,' Caroline replied listlessly. 'I shall go and see her, of course.'

He sighed. 'I think you should. And now, perhaps you should go up and rest before dinner. It will give you the chance to catch up with learning the Bible passages I gave you.' He sat down at his desk and pulled a book towards him. When he did not look up again she understood that the interview was closed.

Marianne was tearful. 'But where did you go? *Where?*'

Caroline shrugged. 'I've told you. All I did was ride into the countryside with him. Somewhere outside his parish – I don't know where.'

'But why? Why you?'

'Because I brought him the message.' Patiently Caroline repeated once again the story she had decided to tell. It was after all, so near the truth.

'He hasn't come back, you know,' Marianne went on miserably. 'He said he would talk to Papa the next day. But he didn't.'

'I am sure he intended to. I am sure he will as soon as he can.' Caroline stood up wearily. 'I don't know any more than I've told you, Marianne. He didn't confide in me.' That last at least was true.

* * *

The Rectory was intolerable. Her days were as meaningless as before, boring, filled with the chores of everyday life – interspersed with learning the interminable verses her father set her. Firmly she suppressed her rebellious desire to escape. She had to help her father. But even he could not stop her dreams. And dream she did of her few stolen hours with the handsome rector of Pengate.

She couldn't stop thinking about him. Those last few words to her in the chaise: had he meant them? Had he meant he would come back? She lived again and again his quick kiss on her hand and the disturbing sight of him, naked to the waist, his muscular body so close to hers as he changed his clothes. Where was he? Had he reached France safely or had his ship been intercepted by an excise cutter in the Channel? She didn't even know that. Her father had spoken of the abortive raid with fury, and later he had mentioned that the ringleader had been caught and then allowed to escape. He gave no sign that he knew who the man in question was. Soon even those few mentions stopped and the smugglers were not spoken of again. Once she had gone furtively to the stable to see if any kegs were hidden there. If there ever had been, they were there no longer.

Caroline's only moments of real pleasure were her visits to Susan Forrester, whose tiny new daughter had, to her astonishment and pleasure, been christened Caroline. She knew Jake had no news; the smuggling had come to an end. No repairs had been started on the cottage.

Then came the invitation to the bishop's Michaelmas party. The reception rooms at the palace were as usual crowded. At her father's side Caroline stood looking around, still listless, her face pale and strained. She had not wanted to come. Almost at once she saw the Rixbys on the far side of the room and her heart sank. Marianne no longer bothered to hide her hostility to Caroline, or the fact that she blamed her for what she took to be Charles's jilting of her. She replied to Caroline's tentative smile with a scowl and a toss of her head, then she turned back to the young man at her side.

'Young Lord Wentworth.' Mr Hayward had noticed the direction of his daughter's gaze. 'It seems Miss Rixby is no longer pining for her lover's memory.' He noted his daughter's heightened colour with a sad nod. Just as he had suspected. The silly child imagined herself in love with Dawson. He sighed. How providential that the bishop's elder son had absented himself from his parish – for his health, the story from the palace went – and a curate left in charge at Pengate. George Hayward bowed absent-mindedly to a colleague. When he turned back, Caroline had gone.

The gardens were deserted. Her shoes crunched on the carpet of golden leaves as she made her way along the yew hedge and through into the garden beyond. There were leaves on the grass beneath the swing; leaves had drifted onto its seat in the still afternoon. She stood for a moment, her hand lightly caressing the rope. The only sound came from a robin sitting on a trellis nearby, trilling its song into the clear autumn air.

'I hope you remember that you are too heavy for that swing.'

For a moment she thought she had imagined the voice. She spun round. Charles was standing near the hedge watching her. He was dressed once more in sober black, his hair neatly brushed, his shoes spotless. He gave a slight bow. 'So, you still hate parties, Miss Hayward.'

'What are you doing here?' She took a tentative step towards him. To her annoyance she found she was trembling.

'I followed you. I guessed you'd come here.'

'I meant what are you doing back in England?'

'I am attending my father's party.'

'But it's not safe –'

'I had to come back, Caroline. I couldn't leave my parishioners forever.' He paused. 'I have something for you. Kennet told me you gave your locket as part of my ransom.

I can't replace it, of course, but I should like you to have this instead.' He reached into his pocket and produced a pendant on a thin gold chain. He held it out to her. 'Please. I should like you to have it.'

'I can't.' Caroline stared at the dainty thing lying in his palm. It was a wisp of filigree gold and pearls. 'I can't accept a gift from you. It wouldn't be right.'

'It's not a gift, Caroline, it's to replace the one you lost. Please. It's the least I can do. I owe you my life.'

She looked at him uncertainly. 'You know I shouldn't take it.'

He smiled. 'But you never do things you should, do you? Did you learn your passage from the Bible?' There was a teasing light in his eyes.

She nodded ruefully. 'There was no escape.'

'So, now you are the dutiful daughter of the Rectory once more? No more galloping round the countryside at night with criminals?'

She shook her head. 'I fear I am quite reformed.'

He must not guess how much it hurt her to smile and spar with him like this; how much she longed for him to touch her.

'Poor Caroline.' He took her hand and tipping the pendant into it closed her fingers over it. 'So, make this one last gesture of rebellion. Take my gift, with my thanks. I must go back to the house.' He gave her a long searching look and for a moment she thought he was going to say something else, but he turned away.

She waited at least ten minutes before she followed him.

She found her father where she had left him. This time he was busily engaged in conversation with the archdeacon.

'Papa! There you are.' Both men stared at her interruption and she saw her father frown.

Marianne, she noticed, was talking to Lord Wentworth again. Her fingers closed more tightly over the pendant in her hand and she slipped it regretfully into her pocket. She would never be able to wear it, of course. Her father would see it at once and ask her where it had come from. Already he had enquired where her mother's locket was.

'You look so pretty, Caroline, my dear,' the archdeacon said valiantly, eyeing her flushed cheeks. 'How are you?'

'Well, thank you.' Her smile froze as Charles appeared beside her father. He gave a slight bow. 'Miss Hayward, gentlemen. How nice to see you here.'

George Hayward gave him a searching look. 'I didn't realise you were back, young man.'

Charles smiled. 'Only yesterday. I decided my parish could not do without me another moment.'

'And did you have a good holiday?' the rector persisted.

'Hardly a holiday, sir,' Charles said cryptically.

'Last time we met you were going to come and see me, Charles,' the archdeacon put in forcefully. 'About my daughter, as I recollect.'

There was a moment's silence. Caroline's eyes were fixed on Charles's face. For a moment he seemed taken aback at the archdeacon's questions but he recovered himself fast.

'Indeed I was, sir. Perhaps I could come and see you one day next week? Then, maybe, I can explain my circumstances more fully.'

'I think you should.' The archdeacon's face relaxed slightly. 'And now George, there are things you and I must discuss.' He took Caroline's father's arm, leaving her standing awkwardly, facing Charles.

There was a moment's silence.

'Are you going to ask for Marianne's hand?' She knew it was none of her business. The moment the words were out of her mouth she could have bitten off her tongue.

He glanced over his shoulder. 'It seems I may have implied that I will.'

Somehow she made herself smile. 'And will you tell her of your alternative career?'

'I doubt it.' He smiled. 'I fear that career is over. I shall, however, have to think of other ways to help those who need money.' He hesitated. 'Caroline – '

'I'm sure you will have a strenuous helper in Marianne.' She stepped away from him, unable to hide her unhappiness for another moment. 'Forgive me, but there is someone I must speak to.'

She fled after the archdeacon and her father.

How could she have been so foolish as to dream for even a moment that one day he would think of her as anything other than useful at a moment when he needed help? He had not seen her as a woman – or if he had it was only because being a woman made her a nuisance. The pendant meant nothing. It had been exactly as he had said, a replacement for the one lost; nothing more.

She found that she was staring at the archdeacon. He smiled. 'You look a little distrait, my dear. Can I fetch you some lemonade?' She saw his eyes searching her face curiously. 'Has someone upset you?'

'Indeed, no.' She smiled desperately. Charles had followed her. She felt his presence as a sudden tingle down her spine.

'Your daughter, archdeacon, seems much taken up with Lord Wentworth,' Charles said thoughtfully. 'I wonder if she would have time for me now.'

The archdeacon's nose became a trifle more puce. 'If you are implying – '

'I am implying nothing, sir.' Charles gave an elaborate shrug. 'It was merely an observation.' Behind them they all heard clearly Marianne's throaty giggle and saw her coquettishly tap Lord Wentworth's arm with her fan. She had not given the Rector of Pengate a second glance and not once had she acknowledged his presence in the room.

The archdeacon frowned. 'My daughter is very young, Charles – ' He broke off as Caroline gave a horrified gasp.

Barely ten paces away from them, standing talking to the Mayor of Larchester, was Captain Warrender of the Lakamouth Militia. Before she could move he turned and saw her. His mouth dropped open and she realised at once that he had recognised her.

'What is it?' Charles stared at her ashen face.

Already the man was thrusting through the crowded guests towards her.

'Oh God! Hurry!' Not stopping to think, Caroline grabbed Charles's hand. To the astonishment of the archdeacon and the other guests around them she turned and fled, pushing her way through the room with Charles close behind her.

In the hall she stared round wildly. 'Hide!' she gasped. 'We've got to hide!'

'My father's study!' Charles threw open the door opposite them and pushed her inside. Closing it behind them he locked it. Then he turned to her. 'Who was it?'

'The captain of the militia. He recognised me!'

'And why, may I ask, should the captain of the militia recognise you, Miss Hayward?' The bishop's deep voice made them both swing round in alarm. Charles's father was seated at his desk near the window, having taken a few minutes' break from his guests.

Charles closed his eyes and took a deep breath. 'Father, I'm afraid I have to do some explaining . . .'

Behind them the door-handle turned and rattled. They all saw the wooden panels give as someone thrust against it from the other side. The bishop stared at the door over his gold-rimmed spectacles. 'May I suggest you both go into my chapel, my children, and pray that you can think up a good explanation for all this, while I see who is so anxiously waiting at my door.' The bishop stood up slowly.

Charles took Caroline's hand and dived towards a door half hidden by a curtain in the corner of the room. Inside, the bishop's tiny private chapel was dark, lit only by the small lamp hanging over the altar. Charles pulled the door closed softly. He turned to Caroline and raised a finger to his lips warningly. Silently they waited in the semi-darkness. There was no sound from the bishop's study. Caroline sat down heavily on one of the four chairs. She found she was shaking violently.

Going on one knee beside her, Charles took her hands in his. Neither of them dared speak. They stayed like that for a long time, clinging together in the shadowy silence, then at last the door opened.

They followed the bishop sheepishly back into his study and stood side by side before him as he sat down at his desk once more.

'I have told Captain Warrender that he was mistaken in thinking any guest of mine could have been involved in a gaol break,' he raised his eyebrow painfully, 'and an attack on an officer in the Royal Militia,' he said at last. 'The captain has apologised and left the palace. Charles, would you be kind enough to tell me exactly what has been going on. From the beginning, if you please.'

Charles did so.

Caroline listened. His voice did not waver once as he told his father the whole story, and not once did the bishop's face betray his feelings as he heard it.

When Charles had finished there was a long silence.

'You realise that your motives, however altruistic some of them may have been, cannot excuse your behaviour,' the bishop said at last.

Charles grimaced. 'I realise that, Father.' He looked for a moment like a chastened small boy.

'I could not allow you to remain in your parish, even if it were safe for you to do so.'

Charles blenched.

'And what of Miss Hayward?' the bishop went on relentlessly. 'She is in as much danger as you. She could be recognised anywhere. Quite apart from which it appears to me that she had been quite unpardonably compromised. Do you realise what you have done to this young woman, Charles?' He sighed wearily.

'I can at least put that right,' Charles said with an unrepentant grin, 'if I marry her.' He paused. 'And that could be my penance too, perhaps, to marry a rector's daughter?' He looked at his father hopefully.

Caroline's face burned miserably. 'I wouldn't marry you if you were the last man on earth,' she replied angrily. This wasn't how she had dreamed of him; this wasn't how she wanted it to happen. She turned to the bishop. 'Your son is already engaged, my lord. And I assure you, I do not feel myself compromised.'

The bishop looked at her thoughtfully. Then he turned to Charles. 'Do you think the Rixbys would have you as a son-in-law once they knew you were gaol bait?'

Charles laughed grimly. 'I doubt it. But the matter is resolved I think by Marianne herself. She has found more glamorous amusement than me! I am sure I shall find the Rixbys no longer hope for a proposal from me.' He turned to Caroline. 'I meant it you know. I was extraordinarily attracted to you from the first moment I saw you on the swing. Up till then I'd always thought you beautiful, but too quiet.' He grinned. 'Then later I found you were quite different from the average rector's daughter and I fell hopelessly in love. Given all the time in the world I should have pursued you with total single-mindedness and spoken to your father without delay. But as things are I must tell you now, without preamble, that I am absolutely certain that you are the woman I want for my wife.'

'As a penance!' Caroline retorted.

The bishop let out a snort of laughter.

'Some penance! Can't you see that he is in love with you, my dear? And I don't blame him. I would be myself if I were twenty years younger.' He stood up and came round the desk. 'Poor Miss Hayward. So public a proposal. And by such a reprobate. If he weren't my son I should advise you not to have him.'

He put his arm around her shoulders. 'I'm afraid deviousness runs in the family, my dear. You don't stand a chance against Charles and me together. You must accept. If you love him that is. You can leave the archdeacon to me. From what I saw earlier Marianne won't break her heart over Charles. And I think I can persuade your father to give his consent. I have been debating the replacement of poor old Canon Peters and it seems to me your father might be a very able successor to him.' He smiled. There was a moment's silence.

'I won't make you learn passages from the Bible,' Charles murmured in her ear. 'And you can have a new bonnet and your very own copy of Lord Byron's works.'

Caroline smiled in spite of herself. 'With promises like that, I confess I am tempted. I'll think about it.'

'Good.' The bishop nodded approval. 'But now to the other problem. You cannot go back to Pengate, Charles. Quite apart from any other consideration that man was no fool. He will lie in wait outside the close to check for himself that the young lady he saw really is someone else, and in so doing he is bound to see you. You will have to stay here, both of you, until we can think of a plan to get you away.' He frowned.

'In the meantime, you could marry us, father?' Charles took Caroline's hand.

The bishop looked at them thoughtfully. 'I think that would be a little premature, Charles. Ladies like months to plan things like weddings.'

'Not this one, father.' Charles smiled. 'This one is a rebel. There is nothing she would like more than a secret wedding in the cathedral at dead of night, followed by a honeymoon aboard the *Marie Blanche* on the way to France. Am I not right?' he appealed to Caroline.

She laughed. 'I'm afraid Charles knows me too well already, my lord,' she said. 'I do find that idea appealing.'

'And your day will be made if you are pursued by armed soldiers with warrants for your arrest, no doubt,' the bishop said dryly. 'I would rather your honeymoon were spent quietly in London while I find you a suitably quiet parish somewhere far from the sea!'

'Oh, Father – '

'That is my decision, Charles.' For the first time the bishop looked angry. 'And now, you may take Caroline into the garden for a while, while I speak to her father.'

Charles seated himself on the swing and gently pushed at the ground. He smiled up at her. 'You can wear the pendant now.'

She took it from her pocket. 'Would you mind a new parish?'

He shook his head. 'I have to remember that my father is also my bishop. I must obey him. Besides, it's a challenge! Think what we could do in a new parish together.'

She smiled. 'You could become a highwayman.'

'With you for my Moll?' He laughed. 'What a pair we should make. I can see life will never be dull with you!' He grew serious again. 'And what if I reformed and settled down to a life of hard work? Would that dismay you?'

She looked up at him soberly. 'If life grows dull, Charles,' she said, 'I can always ask Captain Warrender to tea!'

OBE

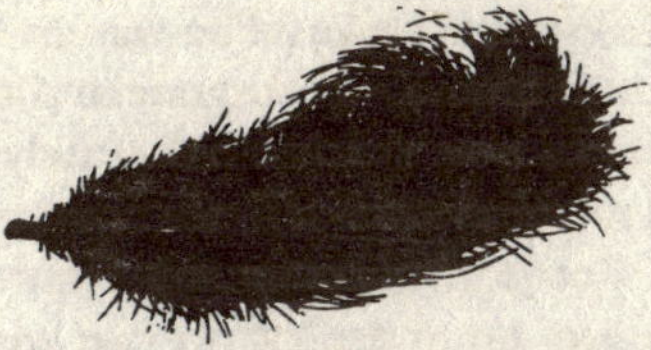

IT WAS THE FAULT of the books of course. She knew they said that the technique would work but she hadn't actually believed it. Not deep in her heart of hearts.

The thing was that she loved the theory. Who wouldn't? It was pure fantasy. And she loved the whole scenario that went with it all. The exercises, the meditation (an excuse to sit for twenty minutes twice a day without moving and feel self-righteously good, not guilty, about it), the props: the oil burner, the candle, the chunk of amethyst and best of all the feeling which she knew was probably wrong, not in the spirit of the thing at all, that she had a secret and one which would, if Desmond found out about it, shock him to the roots of his hair.

She had never joined in as much as she should with the parish work but it was becoming commonplace for vicars' wives these days to have a job (in her case boring secretarial) so the ladies of the parish had been given free rein to follow their inclinations for supporting good causes and she kept out of the way as much as she could.

This evening, for example, she had intended to go to the W.I. meeting. That was why she hadn't gone with Desmond to the school nativity play. The trouble was as soon as the door closed behind him she experienced such an incredible feeling of release. Poor darling Desmond. If only he wasn't so – so – Pi!

When they had married he had been a market gardener. Not garden centre material; not even really the specialist nursery type. But that might have come. With her pushing and her energy it really might have come. Instead he had suddenly got God. Badly. Within five years he was an ordained priest, the market garden and house had gone and they were living in an inner, well not city exactly but definitely urban environment, in a small modern church-owned cottage which gloried in the name of Rectory. She still wasn't quite sure why she hadn't left him. No, that wasn't true. She knew exactly why. She still loved him. Adored him actually. And he still adored her. Obviously. Otherwise how did she manage to entice him to do the things she still managed to entice him to do under the cover of the ecclesiastical duvet?

It was all his fault actually because he had given her the idea in the first place. After a particularly exciting interlude which had left him with watering eyes and distinctly out of breath, as he lay triumphantly on top of her, her wrists firmly held to the pillow where they could do no more harm (if that was what you called it), he had whispered the word. Witch.

Lying still, looking up at him with misleading docility Serena smiled.

The word appealed to her. It did not conjure up pictures of old crones and broomsticks and untimely bonfires. Not the way Desmond said it. Oh no. It had definitely been intended as a compliment.

It was as she was choosing a book for Desmond's father's birthday ('golf or gardening: they're safe') that she saw the book on Wicca. That's what they called witchcraft these days. She sidled nearer the table on which it was displayed. *New Age/Religion/Popular Psychology* it said on the sign hanging over the display and she flipped the book open. The photograph thus exposed (the right word, she thought, with a gasp and then an audible, half embarrassed, giggle) was of a woman, stark naked except for a beautiful necklace, facing an equally naked man who had no necklace, but whose wrists appeared to be tied together.

For a long moment she stared. She did, she had to admit, feel quite aroused. She glanced up and saw two tables away, thank the dear Lord with his back to her, Stan Eversley, a churchwarden from their parish. She slammed the book shut and wondered in sudden embarrassment whether this was a hot flush. Something exceedingly uncomfortable was certainly sweeping up her body and colouring her cheeks an unseemly hue.

'Mrs Perkins? I thought it was you.' He had seen her then. The hot flush was swiftly followed by a cold douche of dread. She picked up the nearest golfing book (had the assistant classified it under New Age/Religion or had a careless customer put it down in the wrong place?) and she left the shop with her innocent purchase, smartly wrapped, under her arm.

She didn't buy any books on Wicca of course. Of course not. Even though it did seem to have more scope for, well, fun, than the C of E. What she did buy was a book on personal development. Later. When no one she knew was in the bookshop. And even then she told the assistant it was for her nephew. Then she bought another, on yoga and one on meditation, both recommended by the first.

She drew the line at incense. Desmond, a low church man if ever there was one, would freak out at the first whiff, but aromatherapy oils were all the rage and – she studied a book on this subject as well – could with a judicious choice of oil be used in meditational settings. The amethyst cluster was actually being used to decorate a shelf in one of the local hand-made pottery shops. It wasn't for sale, but she knew by now that if a crystal calls you and wants to live with you, you cannot argue with it. Luckily the shop assistant had read the same books and knew this as well so a mutually satisfactory deal was struck and the amethyst too was presumably ecstatically happy.

There weren't often occasions when she could light her

beautiful ceramic oil burner and her candle and lay the crystal near them. She needed to be sure not only that Desmond was out but also that no one else knew that she was in. (The parishioners, even though they knew she worked, still felt they had a right to every second of time she was at home.)

Guiltily putting on the answerphone and switching off the lights she crept upstairs to the cupboard euphemistically called the sewing room (not by her, as she told anyone who would be interested) and closing the door behind her she stood still for a moment to centre herself.

It was growing increasingly easy to slip into the meditative mood. She was, she thought, quite good at it, although she wasn't sure how one judged such things. Certainly she was learning how to go more and more deeply into whatever it was that made her tick.

The first time she had what her book called an OBE (out of body experience to those of you who are unrehearsed in these matters – forget the Order of the British Empire) she nearly died of fright. One moment she was sitting cross-legged on the floor, her eyes shut, her mind alert but free, her hands upturned on her knees, the next she was up in the corner of the ceiling looking down. With a yelp of fear she tumbled back into herself, scrambled to her feet, tore open the door, ran down the stairs and into the kitchen for a very unalternative caffeine fix. Her hands were shaking so much she couldn't get the lid off the Gold Blend. For the first time in her life she wished she smoked. That would give her something to do to settle her nerves. She had actually been there, on the ceiling. Not imagining it. Not dreaming it. Not wishful thinking it. Actually. For real. Genuinely.

When Desmond came home she was curled up on the sofa watching an old tape of *Taggart*. He glanced at the screen, gave a slight grimace aimed in equal parts at the gory corpse in close-up and the unintelligible Glaswegian dissertation on methods of slicing through the jugular, and he dropped a kiss on top of her head.

'My roots need touching up, don't they?'

Serena didn't take her eyes off the green-clad figure in charge of the scalpel.

'Do they?' He squinted down. 'They look all right to me.'

It was amazing how much she had noticed in that split second of altered viewpoint: the greying roots and an unacceptably prominent, some might say slightly conked nose she had never noticed – never before seen from that angle, the spiders' webs festooning the light bulb and lamp shade and the worn patch on the carpet just inside the door which was barely noticeable from ground – or normal eye – level.

It was two days before she meditated again and of course she couldn't do it properly. She was too tense, and let's face it, too afraid.

A week later though it happened again and this time she found she could move around the ceiling. Two days after that she discovered that, unbelievably, she could fly through walls.

Practising sometimes twice a day she became proficient at manoeuvring. In fact all she had to do was think herself somewhere and there she was.

It was while she was skimming around Desmond's study that the thought of him transported her abruptly to where he was, sitting uncomfortably in the Eversleys' sitting room, a cup of coffee balanced precariously on his knees, a crumb from a lately-consumed biscuit stuck provocatively – or so thought his wife – to the corner of his lower lip. Oh Des. It would look so silly to anyone else. He would be mortified if he knew. Opposite him Jean Eversley was sitting on the sofa, her hands laced around her knees, her eyes glued to the crumb. Every now and then she brushed self-consciously at her own lips. He frowned, puzzled by her action, failed to imitate her body language, and ploughed on with what he was saying.

'Jean, my dear. I appreciate your confiding in me, I really do. I just wish there was something I could do to help.'

Serena thought herself onto the arm of the chair next to

him. Cautiously she reached out a finger to touch his lip. Desmond frowned. He shivered visibly and looked round. 'I'm sorry, Jean. Someone must have stepped on my grave.' The crumb was still in place.

Serena felt herself smile. She didn't dare try and touch him again. She still wasn't that good at this manoeuvre which was rather advanced. The technicalities were still a little vague and she wasn't convinced she might not suddenly materialise in person. In fact she wasn't convinced that Jean Eversley couldn't see her, for the woman's eyes had grown suddenly huge and her normally florid complexion had paled.

She had thought she was invisible – had been to herself when she hovered in front of a selection of mirrors at home, and was, obviously, to Desmond or he would have reacted to the vision of his wife floating neatly onto the arm of the chair in which he was sitting and arranging herself with provocatively crossed legs right there in the churchwarden's overheated sitting room – but her worst suspicions about Jean were confirmed a moment later when the woman's voice, a creaky, whispered, shadow of its former strident self suddenly said, 'Can you see it?'

'It?' Desmond frowned. Vaguely locating the area on which she was focusing he stared straight at Serena. 'See what?'

Serena breathed a sigh of relief.

'It. The ghost!'

Desmond shook his head sternly. 'Oh come now, my dear Jean. You're overwrought.' Standing up he put a fatherly arm around the woman's shoulder. To her relief Serena saw the crumb, dislodged by this sudden activity, release its hold on his lip and fall harmlessly out of sight onto the carpet. 'It's the thought of Stan playing you up, that's all. You're upset. Once things have settled down again you'll realise there are no such things as ghosts.'

'What about the holy ghost?' Jean was trembling visibly but not too shaken to be perverse. Serena scowled. How typical of the woman.

Desmond however handled it brilliantly. He gave a deep, world-weary sigh. 'That is not the same sort of ghost, Jean.' He smiled. 'As I'm sure you very well know . . .'

He was about to get boring.

Serena thought herself home.

When he got there himself by more orthodox methods (1987 Vauxhall) half an hour later, she was making biscuits.

'So, do I gather Stan Eversley is having another affair?' She smiled at him innocently.

'How on earth did you know that?' Desmond seemed genuinely shocked. After all Jean had only just found out.

'Village gossip.' Deftly Serena put the baking tray into the oven. 'The old hypocrite! How does he think he'll get away with it?'

Desmond threw himself down in a chair and pulling the teapot towards him he shook it experimentally to see if there was any tea left. 'He always does. Jean will forgive him. She adores that silly old man.'

Of course she had to be very firm with herself. Spying on parishioners was definitely not on. Nor was spying on Desmond. Not once she had checked that his relationship with the beautiful and frustrated Dawn Freeling really was the spiritual and healing challenge he said it was. But it was oh so tempting.

When Don French rang up to say he couldn't come to the vestry meeting because he had a migraine she couldn't resist running upstairs, locking herself in the loo and popping over to his house to see what he was really up to. Just to give some support and spread a healing thought or two, you understand. She found him in the sitting room, his feet propped up on the coffee table, sharing lager and a take-away curry with Joseph Porter, the tearaway brother of the Methodist minister. They were glued to a video of *Seven*. Apoplectic with rage she almost lost control. Luckily the sweeping gesture designed to hurl the already emptied, crushed, cans of Holsten to the floor had no effect at all other than to make her spin round and round in circles. But she saw Don give a shiver. He edged away from the table and put down his fork. 'Joe.' He had gone pale. 'Did you feel that?'

'Wha'?' Joe, the son of an Oxford scholar, was glotally disadvantaged at the best of times. After a chicken vindaloo he was virtually incoherent.

'Cold. Rather unpleasant.'

Thanks a bunch! Serena was fuming, but back in control.

'Na.' Joe lurched forward to grope with a wayward hand for his can.

With slit-eyed concentration Serena honed in on him. Putting her own hand firmly round his wrist she pulled.

Joe let out a scream. Curry and lager flew in all directions. He leaped to his feet, vaulted the back of the sofa and cowered behind it as Serena positioned herself next to Don and whispered, with gratifying effect, the one word 'Rectory'.

When she walked back downstairs to where Desmond and Stan and the others were holding their meeting the phone was ringing. Desmond returned from answering it with a smile. 'Don is feeling a bit better. He thought he would come over after all,' he said.

She knew she had to stop doing it. Her conscience was troubling her more and more and besides that, her character was changing and Des had noticed. She was becoming a know-all – she knew for example exactly when Stan Eversley had stopped dallying and returned to Jean's bed – and she was becoming insufferable. She had all these private jokes. She was like those poor souls one saw walking down the street chuckling to themselves at some hilarious unshared secret. Maybe this was what they were laughing at. Maybe they could all do it: leap from their bodies and whiz around the world. She had tried that as a change from the affairs of the parish. World travel. She would watch a programme on the TV about some distant, exotic and above all expensive place and then she would pop over there for a quick look. And no danger of malaria or funny tummy.

But secrets become burdens. There was no one to share her experiences with; her close friends had dropped away or become hostages to the Royal Mail when she and Des had moved to the parish – so far from where they lived before – and she had made only acquaintances since then. Not once did she meet some other out-of-body soul and only seldom did people see her and when they did they were nearly always afraid.

Except once. In France. She was standing gazing at the most beautiful waterfall she had ever seen, in a lush, narrow, deserted valley high in the Franche Comté when she heard footsteps near her. The man who stood there was tall and devastatingly good-looking in a particularly French way. Only a little out of breath after the climb, he sat down on some rocks to recover as he stared down at the rainbow arc of water. She studied him with interest, made brazen by her invisibility. He was definitely a dish.

'So, ***madame***, what do you think of the view, eh? Is it not beautiful?' He had not looked directly at her, but who else could he be speaking to? It had to be her. There was no one else there.

Startled out of politeness, she grimaced, ignoring this question. 'Can you see me?'

'But of course.' He smiled.

As well he might. It was hot at home now summer had come and she had retreated to the sewing room wearing only knickers and bra – for which small mercy she gave a quick prayer of thanks, she had so nearly succumbed to the urge to walk around the house naked!

Embarrassed, she tried to resist the urge to wrap her arms protectively and disguisingly around her chest, and failed. She could feel herself blushing.

'Are you really here, properly?' It was a dumb question, but she was feeling severely rattled.

'We are both here properly, ***madame***.'

She laughed. 'Not necessarily.'

He turned and looked at her at last. He had the most beautiful eyes. They ran swiftly and a little too professionally over her body, and then returned to do it again, slowly. Caressingly. She could feel her blush spreading.

Casually he stood up and walked to the edge of the chasm, staring down at the falls. The sound of water was deafening around them. 'So, are you suggesting that we are, or should be, improper?'

She could hear the laughter in his voice above the roar.

'No, I am asking if you are a ghost.' It sounded crazy, but it was a crazy situation.

He let out a huge guffaw of laughter. 'I am if you are.'

'I'm not a ghost!' She was shocked.

'No?' He turned to face her, his eyes sparkling with humour. 'But I think you may be a wraith, perhaps. Do you know the difference?'

She shook her head.

'Ah.' He reached between the rocks to pick one of the delicate bell-shaped flowers which grew there and stood looking down at it. 'I think it is a matter of relativity.' He chuckled. 'We must come here again to discuss it.' He paused. She saw his glance run quickly over her again and Serena was agonisingly aware of her faded, non-glamorous elastic, well past its sell-by date – the kind of thing no French woman would be seen dead in – probably no Frenchwoman *was* seen dead in. He did not seem to notice. She saw his tongue run fleetingly across his lips as, smiling benignly, he stepped forward and ran his finger over her shoulder, lightly, causing only the slightest frisson, nudging one of the offending straps out of the way.

His touch was only too real. But she was supposed to be out of her body. So what was her body doing here? It should be at home waiting for her. And it should not be showing or feeling the slightest interest in the presence of another man, however attractive. She did, after all, still adore Des.

Serena bit her lip. She knew it was time to go.

Before she lost all sense of reality.

And shame.

He was standing very close to her now. Smiling, he handed her the flowers.

And that was it. The next moment she was sitting cross-legged on the sewing room floor.

Her first thought was, 'Bother!' or a word to that effect. Her second was, 'I must buy some new underwear; how could I ever let Des see me like this,' her third was, perversely, 'I wish I could tell him all about it!'

But Desmond, she knew, would not understand.

He would probably have her certified.

He would probably have her burned at the stake.

Better to keep it a secret. Just between herself.

And the Frenchman.

Looking down she found she was still holding the spray of flowers he had given her and she wondered what they were. Perhaps he would know. She could always return to collect some more. But perhaps not. It wouldn't be fair to Des!

Smiling, she stook up and, still wearing only her underwear, she wandered slowly downstairs.

The Gift of Music

THE TENNIS BALL hung for a second in the sky, dazzling white against the blue, and then with a smashing hit Kim had driven it across the net.

'Ser-*vice*!' The note of admiration in Fel's voice was genuine. 'How come you didn't do that last time, honey?'

She laughed. 'Don't think I wasn't trying to!'

She crossed the court and held her ball against the racquet ready to serve again. In front of her the ground was almost bare of grass. Each time a ball hit little spits of dust shot up. It was uncomfortably hot. She thought with longing of the cool porch and the iced lemonade, made with real lemons, waiting in the kitchen, and distracted by the thought served a double fault.

'Deuce!' Fel called. 'Come on, I thought you were going to beat me.'

'I can't.' She threw down the racquet, rubbing the palms of her hands against her short skirt. 'Come on. I want a drink. I'll race you up to the house!'

She vaulted the net, laughing, as he collected up the balls. She knew it irritated him to leave the game unfinished and she liked teasing him by doing it. Fel was a meticulous man: that was part of his charm, but just occasionally he had to be shown that life could be unpredictable, as unpredictable as it had been for her when, in London, she had met the young

American lawyer and within months had married him and found herself living in New York.

They ran up the green lawn to the house and threw themselves down on two long chairs on the porch. 'Well, who's getting the drinks?' Kim asked. She pushed her dark hair out of her eyes and glanced across at him.

He groaned. 'I'm having second thoughts about marrying you, woman. Marry in haste, repent at leisure. At this rate I shan't have any leisure to repent!' Levering himself up again he stood looking down at her. From above, her small neat head with its pointed chin and long-lashed hazel eyes looked strangely vulnerable and childlike. He reached out to touch her, just for a second, protectively, unable to stop himself and she smiled up at him, reaching out with her hand in his.

Somewhere deep in the house the phone rang. Fel listened, distracted by it, then it stopped.

'Ma must have answered,' he murmured.

It had been a risk bringing Kim up to Connecticut to meet Ma. That was why he had waited until they were safely married. He glanced over his shoulder towards the shadowy door. His mother was a strong personality. She liked to interfere, to run her children's lives. His sister had escaped, and he had learned to negotiate from a safe distance. But Kim. Would Kim be able to cope with her?

He grinned down at her again. 'Ma likes you, honey. We did the right thing coming straight here to tell her ourselves that we've got married.'

'I like her too.' Kim stared dreamily across the rose bed towards the two great chestnuts which almost hid the next door house. 'She's nothing like I expected.'

He grinned. 'Nothing like me, you mean. That's because I took after Pa. You'd have liked him, Kim. He was a terrific guy. My sister Penny is more like Ma.'

Kim glanced up. Yes, there it was again, the troubled, preoccupied look she had noticed whenever he mentioned his sister. She wondered now if it was the moment to ask him about her, but already he was changing the subject. He released her fingers gently from his and went to lean on the verandah railing. He seemed to have forgotten about the lemonade.

'I told Ma about you last night, Kim. I mean about your wanting to go to the music school.' He frowned, scraping at the flaking paint with his finger nail. 'She wasn't too keen on that idea. She reckoned a wife ought to stay home and look after her husband.' He tried to lighten the remark with a laugh.

'Just as you do!' she flashed. 'What a coincidence! And I suppose she reckons that a wife should be kept barefoot in the kitchen. What is it? *Kinder*, *Küchen*, *Kirche*. That would be right up her street, I'll bet. Straight from the old country. How archaic!'

She swung her legs down and sat sideways on the chair, her face tight with anger and disappointment.

'Calm down, Kim. She said nothing of the sort.' Bracing himself against the railing, Fel looked at her. 'Listen sweetheart. Of course I'd like you at home looking after me. What man wouldn't? And I'd like kids – soon. I want a family and I've never made a secret of that. But you've never made a secret of the fact that you want to give up work to go back to school and train to be a professional singer. Okay. I knew the score when I met you and I asked you to marry me, knowing what you wanted.'

She levered herself from the low chair and came to stand beside him, picking a cluster of rosebuds from the climber which circled the pillar and sniffing at them. 'So why keep bringing the subject up? You make me feel a selfish louse.'

'Kim!' He put his hands on her shoulders and pulled her to face him. 'That's nonsense and you know it. It wasn't me who brought it up. It was Ma. It's natural she should care. She wants grandchildren.'

'She's got grandchildren, Fel.'

He stared at her. 'What do you mean?' Imperceptibly his grip tightened on her shoulders.

Astonished she saw there was anger in his face. 'You told me that your sister had kids – when I first met you.'

'I did?' He dropped his hands and stared at her for a moment. Then he reached into his hip pocket for a cigarette pack. 'I'd forgotten that,' he murmured. 'Did I tell you about her?'

'What about her?' She tried not to sound too eager. He had in fact told her practically nothing. But again he fell silent. He shook out the match and dropped it into the roses below. 'I'll get the lemonade,' he said briskly and he strode into the house leaving Kim staring after him, nonplussed.

She heard the tap of May Bernstein's heels on the polished floor of the dining room inside the shuttered windows. The windows were open inside the shutters, leaving the room beyond comparatively cool in the dim light. It crossed Kim's mind briefly that the woman had been eavesdropping but she shrugged. What if she had? She had to know the truth – that Kim wanted a career. And what business was it of hers anyway? Fel's yes. May Bernstein's – never.

She held the already drooping roses to her chin and sniffed them sadly. What if she did have to choose? Career or marriage? Which would it be?

She knew she could sing. Professor Bertolini had himself suggested she take lessons both from himself and at the music college. But what if after that she failed? No one could guarantee success. Would it not be better to choose marriage to the man she loved and who would give her a home and security and love?

It wasn't the fact of her working Fel hated. She worked now. It was more than that. He knew that music could become a rival if she were good; it could take over her whole life. And it was that which might threaten their marriage.

'And I am good.' To her embarrassment she found she had spoken out loud. She listened, but there was no sound from behind the shutters and then she heard Fel's voice from the depths of the house. 'Is that you, Ma? Come and have a glass of your lemonade. We're on the porch.'

They came together, their footsteps echoing on the polished wood floors and Kim heard May Bernstein's rather petulant voice quite clearly, echoing a little as they crossed out of the kitchen into the hall.

'That was Penny on the phone. Imagine! Suddenly she wants to know me again after all these years. And why? Because she wants help with those kids! And I told her. I can't have them. I can't Fel, can I? At my age? What would I do with two kids?'

'Ma, you'd love them.' Fel sounded distinctly uneasy.

'So? And they'd kill me! Why the hell can't *his* family take them? That's what I say!'

The screen door clattered open as Fel pushed through with the tray. On it were three tall frosted glasses and a jug of lemonade.

May Bernstein was behind him. She was a short, stout woman with hair unnaturally dark for someone her age, aggressively waved. Her face had heavy features which lightened into charm only when she smiled.

She smiled when she saw Kim. 'My dear, but it's so hot. I'm glad you stopped playing tennis. Have a drink. Fel, give the girl a drink, she's wilting.'

Fel had already poured out a glass. Tiny pieces of lemon pith floated in the cloudy liquid.

Kim took it gratefully and began to sip, the ice balls banging against her lips.

'What does Kim think I should do?' May asked suddenly. She sat down heavily on a chair and held out her hand to Fel for a glass.

'I haven't told her,' he said unhappily. 'I didn't want to burden her with family problems.'

'And isn't she family now?' May looked indignantly at Kim. 'You want to know, don't you?'

Kim nodded, dying of curiosity.

'Well, I'll tell you. My daughter left her beautiful home the first chance she got to go and live with a no good, weak-kneed drop-out of a man. Not marry mind you. Just live. And he's paid her back by going off and leaving her, dumping his two kids on her. That's all. And now she comes crawling home and she wants me to take the kids.'

Kim looked bewildered. 'You mean they're not hers?'

'That's right.' May's lips tightened imperceptibly. 'Their mother was a black girl.'

'And she can't have them?'

'She's dead, Kim,' Fel interrupted gently. 'The story is terribly complicated, but if Ma insists on dragging you in you may as well get it right.' He shot his mother a challenging look. 'Penny met Brad years and years ago, before she left here actually, and they had something really good going for quite a long time. Then things went a bit wrong. She went to Europe to work for a couple of years and when she came back she found he had married Val and they already had two babies. But she was very ill and the younger child was barely two when she died. She had no family to help and Brad turned back to Penny and of course she took on all three of them. But he started going to pieces. It was hell for Penny. All she heard about was his lovely dead wife and how he missed her. He never seemed to realise how much Penny loved him and how much he hurt her by talking about someone else all the time. Anyway, to cut a long story short he began to leave her – and the kids – for longer and longer intervals. He didn't seem to be able to bear the kids near him – I suppose they reminded him too much of Valentine. Then about six months ago he left. And he left a note saying that Penny could keep the children or put them in a home, he didn't much care.'

'But that's awful!' Kim stared from one to the other, appalled.

May opened her mouth to say something, but Fel got in

first. 'It sure is. Penny is at her wits' end. She's got a chance to go back to her old job and she's due to go abroad again soon; she loves the kids but she can't afford them or look after them on her own.'

'But can't the law make him –'

'She doesn't know where he is. Of course they could track him down, but meanwhile what happens to those two mites?'

'And she wants *me* to have them!' May tipped the last of her lemonade down her throat.

'Can't you?' Kim couldn't stop herself glancing at the big garden, thinking of the empty, echoing house behind them.

'Nope. I'm not sentimental and I'm not well. You can't hand over two children to someone, like two puppies and say, "Here, you have these, I don't want them any more." '

Kim bit her lip. 'How old are they?'

'Four and five.' Fel's voice was abrupt. 'Hadn't you better go and take a shower and change, Kim? If we're going to eat before we leave we'll have to hurry.'

She glanced from mother to son and nodded slowly. Fel's face was dark with disapproval and his mother's had become stubborn and malicious as her gaze came to rest on Kim's face.

With a sudden shiver Kim set down her glass. 'I'll see you later, when I've changed,' she said, and she turned and went into the house.

The water was like ice cold needles on her skin. She stood under it for several minutes feeling it beating on her closed eyelids, dragging her hair back from her forehead and cascading across her shoulders. Why doesn't Fel try to persuade his mother to take them, she thought as she reached for the soap. God, I hope he doesn't feel we ought to offer.

The thought was still with her later as they drove back through the evening traffic towards the city. She glanced sideways at his face. He was humming gently with the car radio apparently concentrating on the traffic.

'Does Penny want Brad back?' she asked suddenly, as they drew up at a red light.

'Do you mean does she still love him?'

Kim nodded.

'I think she does. But she must know it would never work even if he did come back. He's changed a hell of a lot.'

'You knew him?'

'Oh yes. I introduced them.'

Kim stared at him. 'Then for God's sake, don't you feel a bit responsible?'

'Why should I? People must work out their own destinies.' He shrugged.

'Not people of four years old, Fel!' To her surprise she found her face was flushed with heat.

'No.' Fel's voice dropped sadly. 'And they're lovely little kids.'

'You've met them?'

'Yep. I've known them since they were born. I kept in touch with Brad when Penny went away and I met his wife, Valentine. She was a lovely person. They knew she had cancer when they married. That's why I could never forgive him for letting her have babies. They both knew she wouldn't be there to look after them. Oh hell, Kim, the whole thing was a mess. She wanted children because that way she felt she could live on through them and of course he wouldn't refuse her anything. I've never told Ma this. As she says, she hasn't an ounce of sentiment. She wouldn't even try to understand. Valentine was a jazz singer. She sang like an angel and she told me once that she was sure that her talent would survive in her kids –'

His voice cracked as he spoke and Kim looked at him sharply. He was staring straight ahead, his knuckles white on the steering wheel.

She was silent for a moment.

She understood. She knew how Valentine had felt. She would have felt the same and suddenly she knew what her own choice would have to be if it ever came to it. And the winner would not be Fel. She closed her eyes tight and rested her head against the back of the seat.

'How long will Penny be abroad?'

'Three months.' The car crawled into a long line of traffic and stopped. From somewhere ahead the sound of music drifted above the murmur of idling engines.

'Three months isn't so very long.' Kim heard herself murmuring the words as Fel wound down the side window to rest his elbow. He gave no sign that he had heard.

It was late by the time they climbed the stairs to their door. Wearily Kim put her bags down and went straight through to the kitchen, groping in the icebox for a can of frozen orange.

'Come on, Kim, don't keep on brooding about it.' Fel followed her in.

'I'm not brooding.' She scowled at him and went to the kettle.

'There's nothing we can do, Kim. We can't have them here.' He gestured back towards the rest of their domain. Three tiny rooms.

'We could.'

He stared at her. 'Kim, darling. We can't afford it. You'd have to quit your job to look after them and we need your salary for a while. And anyway,' he added triumphantly, 'what about your singing career?'

'What about Valentine's?' Kim echoed in a sad, tight little voice.

'Oh God!' Fel hit his forehead with his clenched fist. 'I should never have told you that bit. Val is dead, honey. There's nothing we can do for her now. If the kids can sing – well, they'll sing. It makes no difference who looks after them.'

Kim gave him a withering look. 'I know you don't believe that, Fel, so don't say it. And I still think your mother should be the one to help. Why don't you try to persuade her? You could you know.'

'Kim, forget my mother. Leave her right out of this, honey.' Fel frowned grimly. 'I am not prepared even to try. I don't even want to see my mother again for a bit.'

Kim stared at him. Then she picked up her glass of orange and walked through into the bedroom. By the time he followed her she was asleep.

The next morning after Fel had gone she called her office and told them she was sick. Then she sat for ten minutes with a cup of black coffee beside her, staring at the telephone. On her knee lay Fel's address book. She had found the number under P – he had simply written Pen.

Taking a deep breath she dialled. The girl who answered had a pleasant throaty voice.

'Kim?' she queried. 'You mean Fel's new wife?'

'Yes, how are you?'

'Distracted! Did he tell you what's happening?'

'Yes, Do you have to go?'

'I can't get out of it. Hey, Kim, why don't we get together? I'm dying to meet you.'

Penny's home turned out to be a large untidy apartment on the West Side. Kim was distinctly nervous as she rang the bell but Penny soon made her forget that. She greeted her with a hug. She was a tall, big-boned girl, very like Fel but several years older, her long honey-blonde hair tied back in a pony tail which brushed heavily across her shoulders every time she moved. Kim liked her immediately.

'Excuse the chaos,' Penny said cheerfully, waving her arm around the room. 'The kids had a party yesterday and I was so dead after it I left the lot to clear up today. Come on through and we'll get some coffee.'

'Where are the kids?' Kim asked.

'School. At least Tad is. And Betsy Hen goes to baby school now, mornings.'

'Betsy Hen?' Kim giggled.

'Elizabeth Henrietta. She's the cutest little madam you've ever seen. On Lord, Kim, what am I going to do?'

Penny sat down on a stool and put her elbows on the breakfast bar.

'I love those kids as if they were mine and most of the time I can cope. I've a lovely woman who will come in and take care of them when I'm on an assignment – I'm a journalist, I suppose Fel told you? She's taking half the money she should as it is. But she can't do it for three months. No one could.'

'Can you keep the flat on?' Kim asked curiously.

Penny nodded. 'Their father put it in my name before he went, bless him. It's the only security he left us – but it was a lot. No, it's not the accommodation that is the problem, it's money. I've got to find the money to pay Annabel to come and take care of them.' Penny reached for a bag of coffee beans and poured some into the grinder.

'I was with your mother at the weekend when you rang,' Kim said. 'She thought you wanted her to take the children. That's why she said she couldn't help.'

'Oh she could help all right. With one hand tied behind her.' Penny pressed the button on the grinder viciously. 'There are two reasons why she won't help. One is they're half black. Oh yes, you've no idea how bigoted she is. And the other is to spite me. She wants to pay me back for walking out on her all those years ago. If she doesn't get her way with someone she'll hold it against them for the rest of their lives. Never cross my mother, Kim. Never.' She was pouring hot water into the jug.

Kim closed her eyes and sniffed appreciatively. 'Why did you leave home, Penny?'

Penny glanced up. 'Didn't Fel tell you?'

Kim shook her head.

'Because I wanted out. As I expect you've discovered for yourself, my mother is a self-centred, domineering busybody. She had my life planned out for me to the last second and my wanting to be a writer did not even figure in her calculations. I was to marry – a man of her choice would you believe – and raise her grandchildren for her and go to whist drives with her and plan little trips to town with her. I knew that she was clever enough to make it all happen too, so I fled before she had the chance. Since then she hasn't wanted to know me. I was a fool to ring her yesterday, but she's loaded and she has that big house, and hell – it was worth a try!'

Kim bit her lip. 'Fel said Valentine wanted them to sing,' she said quietly after a moment.

Penny smiled. 'I reckon they will too. Here, have some sugar.'

'I'm going to start training as an opera singer this winter.' Kim spooned some of the dark molasses sugar into her mug and stirred it thoughtfully. 'So I know how much the gift of music can mean.' Pride and sympathy and longing were all there, in her face.

Penny was watching her closely. 'I know you want to help, honey. But you can't. You concentrate on your own career and become a great success, right? My problem is something I've got to work out myself. Perhaps I'll quit my job and try to get another that doesn't need me to travel so much.'

'But that's so silly. Your mother has got to help,' Kim cried. 'It would all be so easy for her. She's so rich. Do you think if I tried to explain to her how much you love them – or Fel? Fel could speak to her.'

Penny shook her head. 'She's like a brick wall, Kim. Don't bother. And don't get involved for God's sake or you'll end up getting hurt too.'

But Kim did bother. She took the train that afternoon and rang May from the station to come and collect her.

May was delighted to see her. She drove her back to the house chatting amiably and ensconced her in a chair on the porch. But when Kim mentioned the reason for her visit her lips tightened.

'They are nothing to do with us, Kim,' she said primly. 'They must have some relatives who would take them. Some of *her* relatives I mean; their own people.' She flicked delicately at an invisible speck of dust on her silk shirt.

'You know they haven't.' Kim shook her head. 'Ma – you did say I could call you Ma?' She smiled pleadingly. 'I went to see Penny this morning. Have you been to her place?'

'It's not hers, dear. It belongs to that man.'

'It's her home,' Kim persisted gently. 'He's given it to her and the kids. It's such a happy place; it's full of love. I think you'd enjoy it there. And Penny would so like to see you. She misses you, you know.'

She was increasingly certain that Penny misjudged her mother. Underneath May Bernstein was as sentimental as anyone else. It was just a case of managing her right.

'Penny misses me?' May looked astonished. But Kim saw the little touch of colour that had risen in the heavily made up face. 'Did she say so?'

Kim crossed her fingers. Then she nodded.

'She was such a self-sufficient child,' May complained suddenly. 'She never needed me. It was Fel who demanded attention all the time. Penny has always gone her own way. She couldn't wait to get out of here and into the world on her own. It hurt her poor dear father so much when she left.'

'She was sorry too,' Kim said gently. 'She wanted to come back, but she was too proud. It's her love of the children which has given her the courage to swallow her pride and cry for help.' She was playing the sentimental bit as hard as she could, but she was sure she had read May Bernstein right. Behind the immaculate clothes and make-up, the money and the whist drives there was a very lonely woman begging for love from her children.

Behind them the house felt very empty.

May reached for the bourbon bottle which stood on a tray

on the table in the corner of the porch. She poured herself a hefty measure, then, on second thoughts she offered Kim some too.

Kim shook her head. She took a deep breath. 'I met the two children just before I left. They came home at lunchtime. They worship Penny, Ma, they really do.'

She couldn't put the thought of the two small faces out of her mind. They had inherited their real mother's dark skin and her curly hair, but there could be no mistake about who their mother was now. They had thrown themselves at Penny, burying their faces in her mane of blonde hair, talking nineteen to the dozen about what they had both done that morning. Then, shyly, they had kissed Kim too and she had lost her heart to them. It was then she had decided to go to her mother-in-law for help.

'I know Penny finds it hard to talk about her feelings,' Kim went on slowly. This was she decided an inspiration. 'For all she's a brilliant journalist, she's holding a lot of herself inside. And she's afraid of being hurt, afraid you'd reject her after all this time. But she needs you so much, Ma. She wants you to help her. She loves those two kids as though they were her own. And she desperately wants you to love them too, to tell her she's right to give them a home and security. To come and see them. They haven't got a grandma except for you.' She was putting every ounce of emotion she possessed into her plea.

May sat down heavily on a wicker chair. 'Penny thinks I'd reject her?' she repeated slowly. 'But she was so aggressive on the phone. She sounded as if she's become a real hard bitch.' She tightened her lips at the memory.

'That was fear,' Kim put in quickly. 'She was on the defensive. She expected you to say no.'

'And I did, eh?' There was a wan smile round the older woman's eyes.

Kim walked over to the tray and poured herself a glass of lemonade. The heavy cloud which had overcast the morning was thinning and a patch of pale sunshine shone down on the lawn.

'So you think I should go and see her?' May said suddenly into the silence.

Kim turned, her face bright with hope. 'Would you? Of course it's terribly untidy and everything but – '

'Penny has always been untidy. Her bedroom used to be a pigsty.' May put down her glass. 'Did this man leave any money at all to support his kids?'

Kim surreptitiously crossed her fingers again. This time it wasn't for a lie. It was for luck. 'Not a penny. Just the apartment. Penny's finding it quite difficult I think. But she's managing.'

'And you say she loves them?'

Kim nodded, holding her breath.

With a groan May levered herself up out of the chair. 'And you love them too? Why for God's sake? You don't even know them. All right. Tell me. How do I know she wouldn't slam the door in my face if I went there?'

'She wouldn't.'

'If she had the money could she find someone to take care of the kids? I wouldn't have them here. I meant what I said.'

'She's got someone. She just can't afford to pay her any more – and certainly not for three months.'

'Does Fel know you're here, Kim?' May turned suddenly and concentrated her stare on Kim's face.

Kim swallowed. She shook her head. 'He didn't want me to interfere.'

May grinned maliciously. 'And Penny?'

'No she doesn't know either.'

'I thought not. Come on. You're going to have to get back if you want that train. I'm going to write to Penny tomorrow.'

Kim felt her heart leap with happiness.

Putting down her glass she gave one last look out towards the tennis court. Already she could picture Tad and Betsy Hen playing out there; and then, running up to the house as she had done yesterday, into the music room. Perhaps they would be allowed to practise on that beautiful Bechstein with all the photos on it.

How wrong Fel and Penny had been. May was as sentimental and soft underneath as the next person. And so easy to manage.

She jumped as she felt a hand on her shoulder.

'I'm making some conditions for all this, Kim,' May said quietly. There was a strange harshness to her face. 'I'll help Penny with as much money as she needs, not only now, but to bring up those brats and give them a decent education. But only if she promises never to bring them here. I don't want to see them. Or her for that matter, as long as she's living like that. And you'll have to promise me something too.'

Kim's heart sank. 'Of course, Ma. You know I will. Anything.'

May's eyes were as green as the sea and she stared up into her daughter-in-law's face. 'You give up all ideas of having a singing career, okay. I want you and Fel to move in here. I mentioned it to him yesterday and he said you would never agree. Now that's not right, is it dear? You and I, we'd get on just fine. And I want you to stay home and look after my son and give me grandchildren. Unless you agree there's no deal. Those kids can rot for all I care.'

And she turned away and put her tumbler back on the tray, the gold charms of her bracelet clanking heavily against the glass.

Island Shadows

THE SUN REFLECTED on the tidal mud, turning it to molten silver. Blinded by the glare, Jill reached up onto her head for her dark glasses, extricating them from a wind-blown tangle of hair, and lowered them onto her nose. Ahead of her, the golden retriever trotted eagerly, nose up, pointing, plumed tail jaunty. She could smell it too now: coffee and something fried; uncomfortably powerful smells, activating pre-breakfast taste buds with painful precision. 'Collie, come here.' She had noticed the dog's quickening pace too late. 'Collie!'

But already the retriever had vanished round the low, wood-topped promontory and she was alone on the shore.

Reluctantly, lead in hand, she jogged after the dog, cursing it roundly under her breath. Wretched animal! Disobedient! Stupid! Idiot! Greedy! Her shoes slipped in the muddy sand and her breath caught in her throat, assailed by the icy wind. A small fishing boat chugged up the centre of the estuary, the engine sounding unnaturally loud above the wind and the sharp slap of the tide on the shore. For a moment she heard the distant piping of a bird, then the sound vanished, torn and shredded like the clouds.

Around the headland the cliff had collapsed and the woods, autumn leaves already nearly gone, dropped towards the water, giving a comparatively sheltered mooring. Several boats were still anchored there, and one, near the shore, had run a plank from its deck down to the sand. She was just in time to see her dog trotting purposefully up the plank, tail still waving, to disappear into the boat.

It was fairly large – an old wooden barge, two-masted with black, tarred cabin and brass-rimmed portholes. Smoke was coming from a chimney in the roof of the cabin, and whisked dancing into the sky.

She stopped in despair, waiting for the tirades of abuse which she knew must inevitably follow Collie's illegal boarding.

None came. The boat lay quiet, its reflection broken and jagged in the slapping water, festoons of brown weed floating round it like a streaming, frothy skirt.

'Collie!'

Her call was not as loud as it might have been. There was still a chance she could extricate the dog without their visit being discovered.

'Collie, come here.'

The gang plank was bleached and dry, split by sun and wind and water. It led up at a steep angle. The dog must have jumped without hesitation down into the waist of the ship. She bit her lip. 'Collie drat you! Come back!'

She was conscious suddenly that she could hear music from the boat – faint, distorted by the wind, hardly audible – the chanting of monks. Plainsong. Unaccountably the sound reassured her.

The tide was coming in. She stared at the end of the plank. It was stirring, carving elliptical patterns in the muddy sand around it as it worked loose, easing up and down. The boat itself, she realised suddenly, was beginning to stir. It had been firmly aground but now, soon, it would be afloat.

'Collie!' She shouted properly this time and almost at once she saw a head appearing over the far side of the cabin roof. A man's head.

She bit her lip, embarrassed and suddenly shy, rooted to the spot as he came to the side and looked down.

'The mutt eating my breakfast is yours, I take it.' The

voice was deep, musical, surprisingly unangry considering the content of his words. He was very tanned, with short grizzled hair and piercing light-blue eyes. The faded denim shirt he wore was threadbare and torn and covered in paint stains.

'I'm afraid so. I'm so sorry. She didn't hear me call.'

He still hadn't smiled. Looking down at her intently he didn't even speak for several seconds and she stepped back, feeling the intrusion of that intense gaze as an almost physical assault. Then at last his face lightened slightly. 'You had better come and collect her.'

'Thank you.' She hesitated. The plank was narrow and steep and her tatty trainers already muddy and slippery. She put her hand on the cold overlapping boards of the boat's side and reluctantly put one foot on the plank. Above her he was watching.

'It feels a bit wobbly.' She found herself saying it apologetically, conscious of her own inadequacies rather than the shortcomings of the gangplank.

'Take a deep breath and run,' he advised. He had folded his arms to watch.

'Couldn't you just send Collie down?' She gave a small laugh – a deprecating shrug.

He sighed. 'I doubt she'll come.'

She had realised by now that he was enjoying the situation and the realisation spurred her at last into action. Four quick steps and she too had jumped down onto the deck to stand next to him. He hadn't moved. His arms still folded, he had made no attempt to steady her as she arrived.

'This way.' He turned towards the steps which led beneath a hatch into the main cabin. For the second time she hesitated.

She had only ever really trusted one man. Their relationship had encircled and empowered her. It had given her all she needed in her life to be strong and secure and in her own eyes, a reflection of his, attractive. Then one day she had returned home unsuspecting, happy, confident in a future extending into contented companionable old age, to find a note. The enchanted circle had been no more than a smoke ring, puffed into non-existence by another who had sneaked in beneath her lack of suspicion. The certainties of life had no more substance than a house of cards and she found herself a naïve, worthless nonentity in her own eyes.

Only Collie sustained her, lying patiently across her knees, a six-stone teddy bear, with a warm flannel tongue to lick away the tears. Months passed. To outsiders she was herself again. Only the dog knew the nights of self-questioning and despair, the emptiness inside her and the shattering of trust. Blithely certain that she had got over 'it' he had called her a couple of times to check – big deal – that she was all right. He did not know or care that never again would she believe or trust another human being.

And another human being was staring at her now, standing on the steps which led down into his lair and in that lair was the only friend she had left in the world.

'Collie!'

Her cry was suddenly desperate.

He raised an eyebrow. 'Why, when the dog is patently a goldie do you call it Collie?' His tone implied a conversational level suitable for a three-year-old.

She smiled at last and he saw the thin pale face with its halo of dark straight hair and deep grey eyes spark for a moment into animation.

'She's called Colleen.'

'I see. An Irish dog. I should say that explained everything.' The humour, if it was there at all was so tart and spare as to be all but indiscernible. He turned and disappeared into the cabin.

She waited, conscious of the cold breeze lifting the weight of her hair on her neck, the shift of the tide and the loosening of the plank in its contact with the solid earth, although lashed this end, she noted, to the rail.

Seconds turned to minutes. The silence was unnerving. The tape which had still been playing when she first set foot on the deck had stopped and not been replaced.

At last she could bear it no longer. First one foot on the ladder then another, her knuckles white on the companionway rail.

The first thing she saw was Collie, traitor that she was, lying at the man's feet. He was standing in front of an easel beside a large glass window, let into the stern. Even from where she was standing she could see that he had been painting the birds. The rich colours of the shelduck and oystercatcher leapt from the canvas, vibrant and astonishingly real.

'Coffee?' He nodded towards the table where amongst a debris of paints and brushes and unwashed cups and saucers she could see a red enamelled coffee pot. She wanted to, but good sense prevailed. 'I don't suppose I have time. The tide seems to be coming in.'

He smiled. 'Another time then.'

And that was that. She slipped the leash onto Collie's collar, thanked, apologised, stammered, blushed and left. She doubted if he had heard any of it. He was still standing by his easel, his hands thrust deep into the pockets of his old jeans, his eyes fixed on the middle distance where the tide race and wind met to hurl white horses across the mouth of the estuary and out towards the island.

She went back of course. Not the next day, nor the next, but on Monday when the sun broke through the heavy cloud and brought an icy wind in from the Arctic she put on her jacket and scarf and, keeping Collie on the lead this time, went for a tramp down the beach.

The boat was there, but even from the distance she could see it was empty. It looked abandoned. There was no smoke at the narrow chimney and no dinghy bobbed from the stern. The gangplank had gone. She stood for a while, staring at it wistfully. It looked lonely now. At the weekend the other yachts had gone. Winter was coming fast and they had no doubt retreated to their safe marinas to await the coming of spring. Only the one boat remained, dark on the water. As the tide swung her gently to the mooring ropes she could see the name now. *Araminta.*

Without knowing why, she sighed. She turned away, head down into the wind, the dog's lead round her wrist, and plodded on, feeling the coldness of the wind now on her face, realising the evening would soon be there. She must turn back. Go home to the empty flat where she no longer bothered any more even to put flowers.

'Just to the end of the groyne, Coll,' she addressed the dog firmly. Collie looked back and wagged her tail. 'Then we'll go back and make hot buttered toast and get disgustingly fat, the two of us.'

The dog beamed. It had an uncanny knack of understanding when food was being discussed. Together they traced the edge of the tide, kicking and sniffing respectively at bits of driftwood and weed, then as one they turned and began to walk back.

He was trudging down the shore, laden with backpack and two shopping bags, his head down into the wind as hers had been. It was Collie who recognised him first. The lurch with which she set off to meet him dragged the lead out of Jill's hand.

He looked up and for a moment she thought she saw a smile flicker round his eyes. 'Well. The collie from hell.'

'Hello.' She found it was quite easy to smile after all. 'I thought you must have packed up and gone away for the winter, with the rest.'

'Wimps and townies.' He hauled the pack off his back and dumped it on the ground with his other bundles. The small tender, she noticed now, was drawn up well above the water line under the stark branches of the trees. He caught the painter and hauled the dinghy down towards the water. 'Do you want to go out to the island tomorrow?'

'The island?' Startled by the invitation, she stared past him out into the estuary.

He had begun to pack his things into the little boat, tucking the bags under the thwart. 'I'm going to take some photos. The forecast is good. Cold and bright. Should be calm. The mutt can come if she can sit very still.'

'You mean we'd go out in that?' Jill couldn't hide her horror as she stared down at the tiny boat.

He smiled properly this time. 'It floats.'

'Maybe not, with me and Collie in it.'

'Weigh more than twenty stone between you?' He raised a laconic eyebrow.

'Of course not!'

Her indignation pleased him. He nodded. 'Thought it unlikely. No problem then. I'm leaving about eleven. That way we can use the tide and minimise the effort.' He smiled again. 'Come if you want to. Don't if you don't.'

With that he turned his back, catching hold of the edge of the boat and dragging it down into the water. In seconds he had vaulted into it and slotted the oars into the rowlocks. He did not say goodbye.

Jill watched him for a moment – disconcerted to find he was facing her as he rowed towards the *Araminta*. He nodded, once, but that was all.

She turned away, knowing she wouldn't have the courage to go.

She was there at ten to eleven, dressed in jeans, a thick sweater and jacket, her hair tied up in a blue silk scarf, a thermos and some sandwiches in a haversack on her shoulder. Collie was excited, leaping about ahead of her, and Jill had serious reservations about taking the dog. Supposing they capsized out in the deep water? In this weather they would drown in seconds.

He was waiting for her with the boat, his arms folded, his eyes once again on the distance. Turning as the dog bounded up to him he gave that tight half smile she was beginning to recognise. 'I'm glad you came.'

His camera and drawing things were packed in a waterproof

bag, tightly wedged in the bow. Her haversack joined them and she followed, with Collie, grinning delightedly, at her feet. The boat seemed very low in the water with its load, but he rowed easily, heading confidently out into the waves.

'You haven't told me your name.' She had to raise her voice over the wind and water.

'Roger.'

She could see that was all she was going to get. 'I'm Jill.'

They didn't talk. Her hand firmly clamped round Colleen's collar Jill sat staring out at the water, revelling in the wind and the emptiness around her. To her astonishment she found her apprehension had vanished; she suspected that her own grin was as big as Collie's as she stared at the dog which sat motionless, ears streaming in the wind.

They beached in a small shingle cove, ringed with stunted pine trees, pulling the boat up above the tide while Collie gambolled happily round them.

She sat on a pile of stones and tried not to watch him as he unpacked his camera. The quick sure movements of his slim fingers as he slotted the lenses back into place, the powerful wrists, the intense concentration in the face fascinated her. He was the antithesis of Justin, who had smothered her with his shambling good humour, who had infuriated her with his vagueness and captivated her with his charm.

Looking away at last she stared out towards the sea, her eyes narrowed against the breeze. The island was strangely sheltered. The air seemed almost balmy. The trees, evergreen and resinous, had a spring-like quality which she found strangely relaxing.

It was Colleen, pressing nervously against her legs, who alerted her to the figure standing in the trees. Accustomed to the dog's unfailing sociability Jill frowned. She glanced at Roger but he was preoccupied with his camera, squatting on the shingle, rummaging in a waterproof bag containing his rolls of film. Collie pressed closer. The distinctive line of hackles on her back rose and she whimpered.

Jill put a warning hand on her collar. 'It's not our island, girl,' she whispered. 'Other people are allowed to be here.'

Roger heard her. He glanced up. 'Have you seen something?'

'There's someone standing watching us. In the trees.'

He raised an eyebrow. 'I thought there might be. He's probably from the monastery. Just ignore him.'

'Monastery!' Jill echoed. She couldn't resist a quick glance. The figure was still there, unmoving, and now she realised the slight oddness was due to the uncanny stillness of the man, who watched, arms folded, his silhouette made unusual by the habit, knotted at the waist. That was why Collie was growling softly in her throat. She had never seen a monk before.

'Should we be here?' She asked Roger at last as he straightened and slung the camera round his neck.

'We won't go near their end of the island.' He smiled that sudden revelatory smile which he dispensed so rarely. 'Come, we'll go down to the rocks.'

There were flocks of birds there, paddling along the tide line, probing the stones and mud with their bills. Jill put Collie on the lead and took her for a long walk along the top of the low sand cliffs while Roger set up his hide.

The monk was standing now at the edge of the cliff staring across the estuary towards the mainland. Jill froze, her hand tightening on the lead. She needn't have worried. Collie had dropped, head on paws, hackles raised in a crest all down her back. It was the same man, she was almost certain – or did they all look the same in that dark heavy robe?

He did not turn or acknowledge in any way that he knew she was there, and afraid that her presence might in some way compromise vows of silence and seclusion she crept away.

They walked in the pine wood, keeping a wary eye out for any further members of the brotherhood, and then eventually made their way back to the boat. There they sat in a patch of sheltered sunshine and shared sandwiches and Jill drank coffee and poured some water into a plastic bowl for Collie. Without being told she knew Roger would have lost all sense of time once he had crawled into that tiny hide out on the rocks. It was strange how soon the birds seemed to have forgotten the man who had disappeared inside it. Unconcerned they made their way up to and round it, plodding over the flat rocks and through the wet sand.

The sun began to drop in the west and Jill felt a shiver of cold. The shadows of the trees crept long and black across the beach. She was beginning to get worried about the darkening strip of water over which they had to row when at last she saw him emerge from the hide, dismantle it, roll it up and walk back towards her, accompanied by the alarm calls of the birds on which he had been spying.

'We saved you a sandwich.'

'Thanks.' He took it and ate ravenously.

'Did you get good pictures?'

He nodded. 'The best. The light was perfect.' He accepted a mug of coffee and absent-mindedly he patted Collie. In the distance a bell had started to toll.

'Is that for the monks?' Jill saw the dog's hackles rising again.

'Compline.' He shivered. 'Come on. We'd better load up. I don't want to be on the water in the dark with no lights.'

'I didn't realise there was still a monastery on the island,' she said half-way back across the water. She was sitting, her arms tightly wound round Collie's neck against the cold. Shivering she buried her face in the dog's thick ruff. 'I think I remember hearing that there was a ruin there.'

'There is.' He was rowing fast. 'One of Henry the Eighth's ruins. Beautiful.'

'So they rebuilt some of it?' She was peering over his shoulder now, looking out into the darkness. The water had a strange oily intensity in the distance. It was sinister; forbidding.

He didn't answer. He was pulling harder on the oars and

she felt a sudden frisson of nervousness. Supposing they became lost out here in the cold and dark?

He read her thoughts at once. 'Don't worry. We're nearly there. I'm not going to risk losing my cameras.'

'Thanks!' Her indignation was real.

He smiled.

On the beach she helped him pull up the boat and unload his equipment. It was almost full dark now. The water behind them gleamed with an eerie luminosity and already a sheaf of stars was bright in the heavens. He looked up.

'There'll be a frost tonight. You'd better get home.'

For a moment she was hurt. She had thought he would ask her into the boat – offer her dinner. But why should he? They were barely acquaintances. She nodded. 'You're right. It's a walk to the village. Perhaps I'll see you again?'

He smiled. 'Knock on the side of the boat when you're passing, and I'll provide some breakfast for you and the dog.'

She waited three days. Then he cooked them bacon and toast with free range eggs from the farm on the cliff and real coffee, perked on the black stove in the galley. He showed her the photos and she was astounded by their professionalism. It was as she was looking through his sketches of shelduck that he asked the question.

'Where's your husband?'

She looked down at her hand. She had taken the wedding ring off the day she found out that he had gone to someone else, but the tell-tale circle of pale skin on the tanned finger betrayed her.

'He left me.'

'Did you love him?' His voice was strangely hard. She glanced at him and saw he was staring out of the window towards the island.

'Yes.'

'And you still love him.'

'Yes.' She shook her head. 'I'm trying not to.'

'Don't!' He swung round and she was astonished at the

sudden intensity of pain in his face. 'Never try and deny love. However much it hurts, it is better than emptiness.'

He walked across the cabin and back, with quick restless steps, as though unable to contain his sudden emotion. He swung back to her. 'I'm going to the island again this afternoon. Do you want to come? Only for a couple of hours. I need a few more pictures; not birds this time – just general views of water and trees. Collie would like it.'

At the sound of her name Collie sat up, ears pricked.

Why not? There was nothing to return home for. No washing or ironing or cooking. As yet no job to fill the lonely hours.

'Okay. I'd like to.'

She let him wander off alone again, sensing that he needed no company; that she and Collie would interrupt his concentration. Instead she went once more down to the rocks and then up to the cliff where the monk had stood. It was almost no surprise when she sensed Collie cringing behind her and turned to find the monk standing near her. He was staring out again towards the sea. 'I'm sorry. I didn't hear you.' She backed away, embarrassed, the dog winding around her knees.

She was about to walk away when he slowly turned towards her. His face was shadowed in the cowl he had pulled over his head and his arms were folded. For several seconds he stood looking at her, then he took a step forward. Disengaging his arms from his long sleeves he reached out to a bush growing out of a crack in the rocks. He broke off a spray of leaves and held it out to her.

She put out her hand, and when he didn't move closer she took a step towards him. Collie whimpered. She took another step and accepted the sprig from his fingers. Their hands did not touch.

'Thank you.' She smiled. She could not see his face and she felt a strange nervousness tightening across her chest. He gave a small half bow and turning away he began to walk slowly back towards the trees. In only a few seconds he had vanished into the shadows.

Jill looked down at the sprig in her hand. It was rosemary. She looked round, surprised. How could a rosemary bush survive out here on the cold, exposed cliff? She walked over to the spot where he had picked it. All she could see was gorse, clinging in the crevices with sparse grass and brambles.

Thoughtfully she walked back to the boat.

The sun was setting when Roger returned. It blazed crimson across the water, from a sky laced with black and green.

'There'll be a storm tomorrow.' Roger narrowed his eyes, looking at the sun path.

'The monk gave me this.' Jill held the rosemary out to him. 'The same one, I think, that we saw last time.'

Roger looked at it for a moment. He made no attempt to touch it. He was silent for several seconds then he took a deep breath. 'There is something I have to tell you.' He walked down to the water's edge.

'I'd rather you didn't.' Somehow she knew this was something that was going to spoil whatever thin thread of friendship was developing between them. He frowned. For a moment he said nothing but as they stood where they were in silence, she could feel the distance stretch and spin out, pulling them apart before they had ever properly drawn together.

'I'm a murderer.' He didn't face her. Almost, the words were lost in the wind.

She didn't believe him. For a moment. Her disbelief made her laugh – a high, hard, insincere sound which rang emptily in the silence around them.

He turned then. 'You don't believe me? I find it hard myself. I did something out of love – the greatest love possible. I killed a woman – the woman I loved – to save her from pain so great it was driving her to despair.' He took a deep breath, finding the strength to go on. 'She had cancer, you see. It was inoperable. There was nothing anyone could do. At the end,' he hesitated, staring blindly at the ground, 'at the end, she knew what I was doing and she blessed me for it. I saw it in her eyes.'

He turned again and walked away from Jill along the edge of the tide, staring out at the sinking sun. 'In this country such an act is called murder. The police are looking for me. If they find me, I shall go to prison.'

'Roger.' She didn't know what to say. For a moment she didn't move. It was Collie who went after him; Collie who pressed herself against him, giving comfort.

He put his hand on the dog's head, gently. Then he turned back. 'I don't know why I told you. Because I was in danger of growing fond of you, I suppose. I couldn't do that to you, and I couldn't do that to her.' He looked at her for a moment. 'Are you going to give me away?'

She shook her head. 'You know I'm not.'

He nodded. 'I wanted you to come out here to the island. This is a special place; very special. I used to come here as a boy. I used to see the monks too, then.' He turned away from the sea and began to walk back up the beach. 'Come on. We must get going. It's growing dark.'

They did not talk on the way back. Not until they reached the mainland. 'If your man comes home, forgive him, Jill. If he doesn't, forgive him anyway. Hate and bitterness are corrosive. Her husband ran away with someone else and she let her anger and misery eat her up. When we found each other it was already too late.' He gave a strange, strangled sob. 'Who knows, if one believes in these things, perhaps we will have another chance in another life. Perhaps not.' He gave another of his deep, painful sighs. 'Come into the boat a minute. I've something for you.'

It was a painting of the estuary, with the island in the foreground. Amongst the trees she could see the ruined Gothic arch of the old abbey.

'It's beautiful, Roger. Thank you.' She reached up and gave him a kiss on the cheek. 'They won't find you here, will they.'

He shrugged. 'I hope not. I am not prepared to go to prison.' The way he said it had a finality which made her shiver. 'Come again in a few days.' He looked down at her fondly. Then, squatting, he took Collie's head between his hands. 'And you, mutt, look after your mistress. Don't go introducing her to any more strange men.'

She walked up the shore in the dark, turning at the headland to look back at the *Araminta*, a silhouette against the stars, lit only by the glowing light from two portholes. In two steps she was round the headland and out of sight.

She went back the following Saturday. It was no surprise to find the *Araminta* gone. She stood forlornly on the beach, staring out to sea. 'Where do you think he went, Collie?' There was no need of a lead today. There were no people or dogs on the rain-lashed sand, and no boats in the fairway.

It was not until April that she returned to the island. Justin had phoned and suggested hopefully that for old times' sake, maybe, they could go out for a picnic somewhere. If Collie had been a child he would have access, he pleaded, and it wasn't as if he were still with anyone else. The someone else had been a mistake, a disaster, a moment of madness he would regret for the rest of his life. When he arrived, he told her remorsefully that he had been an unforgivable fool and touched her hand and the voice she heard in her head was Roger's. 'If your man comes, forgive him, Jill.'

She took Justin into the flat and showed him the new picture over the fireplace. 'I want to go there.'

'The island? I used to go there as a boy.' Roger's words too. 'It's a wonderful, magic place.'

So they hired a boat and he rowed across, dog in the bows, Jill with the picnic in the stern. The day was beautiful, bright, tossing wind and small slapping waves, and they explored the island from end to end. He showed her the monastery ruins, the beautiful abbey church with its towering broken arch, the weed-filled herb gardens, the crumbling walls, the filled-in, useless well. There was no modern part of it, nowhere habitable at all.

She stood for a long time on the grass-floored nave of the old church, listening, half expecting to hear the plainsong in the wind, or the call of the bell. There was nothing except the carolling of a blackbird in the thicket. There were no monks there now; there hadn't been for four hundred years. Somehow it was no surprise.

Collie gambolled around, carefree and plainly happy. For a while Jill wondered if she should tell Justin what had happened. He had changed. He was more thoughtful; more mature. It was obvious that he too had been unhappy. It would be easy to confide. She thought better of it though. The monks belonged to her and to Roger and to the distant past of the island on which they stood.

And Justin himself? Well, maybe Justin belonged in her future. Forgiveness, with Roger's silent prompting and that of her own heart, was easy. Trust might be more difficult. She would have to see.

There was only one moment when her resolve not to talk about Roger and the monks wavered. As the evening drew on and they returned to the boat Collie, leaping ahead over the sand, stopped dead. Her hackles rose and she backed away from the boat, whimpering.

'What's wrong with her?' Justin, puzzled, released Jill's hand and went on ahead. There was nothing wrong that they could see. Only, on the thwart where Jill had been sitting, a small posy of rosemary.

A Test of Love

'MUM, YOU CAN'T MEAN IT!' I gazed at my mother aghast. 'I don't believe you. It's not true.'

She sat down and put her hand to her head wearily. 'I'm sorry, Holly, I've been trying to decide for three days whether or not to tell you. I don't want you to be hurt.'

'Well, I am!' I rounded on her. 'I'm very hurt. That you could believe such rotten malicious gossip. I thought you liked Mick.'

She sighed and looked up at me, shrugging her shoulders. 'I did. I do, Holly, I like him very much, but now . . .'

I had been able to see from the moment I walked in that there was something wrong. My mother was young and pretty and she and I had always been more like friends than mother and daughter. Sometimes I called her Carol instead of Mum, and we would giggle and she would borrow some of my clothes to wear. I knew men found her very attractive and most of the time I wasn't jealous because I was so happy with Mick.

Now as I looked down at her sitting in the kitchen at the battered old table I noticed for the first time the lines round her eyes and at the corner of her mouth. In her glossy hair there were several streaks of grey. And I was glad. Suddenly I felt really bitchy.

'You're just saying that because you're jealous,' I blazed at her. 'You're always been jealous of Mick and me, watching us, envying us. I've seen you.'

I flung the shopping basket I was carrying down onto the table, shot her a look of real hatred and turned for the stairs. Once in my bedroom I flung myself down on the bed and burst into a storm of tears.

The trouble was that for all my indignation, deep in my heart I was pretty sure that what she said was right. And I couldn't bear it.

My mother had just told me, quietly and matter-of-factly, that Mick, the man I loved more than anyone or anything in the whole world, had been in prison and that he had left his home town and come to live near us because he was in trouble again.

Gradually my sobs grew less violent and eventually I just lay there thinking about him, sniffing miserably into my pillow. I was numb with shock and unhappiness.

I had met Mick three months before at the end of term dance at the college where I was studying. From the very first I had known he was the man for me. He wasn't particularly tall or good-looking but he had something very special: a kind of style which made me feel a million dollars. Soon I was going out with him practically every day, but deep down, I just had to admit it now, I had had from the start a niggling doubt about him. He refused to talk about his past at all, or about Warpington which, he had once let slip by mistake, was his home town. He told me nothing about his family or friends. 'It's now that matters, Hol,' he would say if I pressed him. 'Now and us. I want to forget there was ever a time when I didn't know you.'

Being not entirely naïve I had wondered briefly whether perhaps he had run away from a wife and family or something, but I had put the thought out of my head straightaway. Mick would never deceive me. Of that I was sure.

There was a timid knock at the door and Mum came in. She was carrying a cup of tea.

'Holly, darling. I had to tell you. If I hadn't someone else would have.' She sat down on the bed.

I turned and looked at her, sniffing into my tissues. She seemed so tired. I felt very remorseful suddenly.

'I'm sorry I shouted,' I whispered. 'I didn't mean it.'

She smiled and reached for my hand. 'I know, love.'

'You don't know for sure it's true.' I looked at her desperately. 'Do you? Who told you?'

'Shirley Rhodes told me, Holly. Her aunt knows Mick's grandmother, who he used to live with. I'm afraid there's no doubt.'

I flung myself back on the bed and gazed up at the ceiling.

'What did he do?' I asked tonelessly.

'He went to prison for receiving stolen goods, Holly. He ran an antique shop in Warpington and I gather he bought several lots of jewellery and valuable furniture from various thefts and then passed them on.'

'And now he's in trouble for doing it again?'

My mother shrugged. 'She didn't know but there had been another wave of burglaries around the area and apparently the police questioned him straightaway. His grandmother said he left home without a word the same night. She hasn't heard from him since.'

'He kept the shop on then, after he came out of prison? What happened to it?'

Mum shook her head. Then she stood up and went to the window, looking out at the grey evening. Rain streaked the glass.

'I'm not going to ask you not to see him again, or anything like that. I know how much you love him, Holly. But please, promise you'll be careful. Don't get mixed up in anything.'

I could feel my stomach turning over sickeningly. At that moment I never wanted to see Mick again. I was heartbroken. I felt as though he had actually hit me. I had trusted him, loved him, secretly I had dreamed of marrying him and now – this. I could feel the sobs welling up inside me once more.

Turning from the window Mum glanced down at me, then she went softly to the door. 'Come down when you feel better,' she whispered, and she left me on my own.

Mick was supposed to be picking me up the next evening for a party. All day I tried to pluck up the courage to ring and tell him not to come, but each time I went to the phone there was someone in the box. I did not have the determination to wait. And I don't think I really wanted to put him off. That was too easy and too final. I had to be quite, quite sure. I had to see him just once more.

So when the time came for him to arrive I was at home, waiting miserably for him. I had not bothered to change.

Mum refused to go out. 'I'll be in the kitchen, Holly,' she said firmly. 'I won't appear unless you need me.' I think she had visions of Mick, suddenly revealed in his true colours, a furious gangster, pulling a gun on me, or at least a knuckle-duster.

Perhaps I did too, a little. I was shaking with fear, certainly, when I opened the door to him.

Mick took one look at me and put his arms out to me in concern. 'Holly, darling. Aren't you well? What's the matter?'

'Everything's the matter, Mick.' I led him into the sitting room and closed the door. I was terribly conscious of Mum across the hall probably listening for all she was worth in the kitchen.

'I know everything.' I looked at him sadly. 'I know the truth.'

He flushed and looked terribly guilty and my heart sank. I had prayed he would deny everything. I had hoped desperately that there was another Mick Woodfield somewhere. I had made every excuse possible for him. I had expected him to laugh or bluster, or just lie his way out. I couldn't bear that he just calmly admitted it.

He came and sat beside me. 'I don't know who told you Holly, but I doubt if you know the truth.'

'It was your grandmother. She told a friend of Carol's. That's how I know. Your own grandmother.'

I looked at him defiantly. To my surprise he grinned, obviously relieved!

'In that case Holly darling, I'm sure you've got it wrong. What do you know?' He reached for my hand, but I snatched it away.

'I know that you've been in prison. You were a fence for stolen jewellery and furniture through your shop, and now you've . . .' I could feel tears flooding my eyes. 'You've done it again and you're . . .' I could not go on. Suddenly I was crying openly.

He smiled gently and persisted in feeling for my hand. 'I'm on the run?' he finished for me. 'Is that what she told you?'

Softly he brushed the tears off my cheek. 'I'll tell you the truth, Hol. I was done for receiving, although I was innocent, as it happens. I should have known the things were stolen, or at least been suspicious. My shop hadn't been open long and I was so keen to make a go of it. I was pleased when I was offered the stuff. They more or less implied they wanted to help me because I was new. And green,' he added bitterly. He looked at me, pleading. 'Of course it was my job to find out whether it was okay. All the articles had been listed and descriptions circulated by the police but I hadn't bothered to look at the lists the police gave me. I was stupid and careless. I was given a short suspended sentence. I never went to prison.'

I could feel the relief welling up inside me. I raised my eyes to his. 'And now?' I whispered, hardly daring to believe him. 'Why did you run away this time?'

He flushed again. 'Yes, you're right. I did run away. Of that I am guilty, Holly. The first robbery there was the police were on to me like a ton of bricks. It suddenly dawned on me. From now on I shall be suspect, however innocent I am.

They will always be there checking on me till I begin to feel like a criminal. And I hardly dared buy anything for the shop after that. It was as though I had lost my nerve. I closed it. I gave the key to an agent to sell it for me, and I came through here to find an ordinary job.'

'But why didn't you tell your grandmother?' I stared hard at him, trying to read his mind, desperately wanting to believe what he said.

He grinned. 'My grandmother, Holly darling, is a wicked old lady. She loves to shock people. She told all the neighbours about my long prison sentence as though she were proud of my record and whenever she met a stranger she played up my activities until I sounded like one of the great train robbers.'

'But that was unkind. And stupid.' I was indignant.

'To me, yes,' he smiled fondly. 'But she didn't mean it that way, Holly. It was excitement for her; fame, in a way. She's very old, that was why I moved in with her, to keep an eye on her – not that she needed it, and she doesn't quite realise the significance of it all. I'm sure when I left she told most of the neighbours I'd fled to the greenwood, an outlaw like Robin Hood. She knows jolly well where I am and why I left.' He grinned again. I could see he was very fond of the old lady but she must have been exasperating to live with. I could see that too.

'Oh Mick, darling.' I threw myself into his arms suddenly. 'I was as bad as her. I believed such terrible things of you. I even let Carol hide in the kitchen to save me if you were violent.'

Mick roared with laughter. 'And she's there now?'

I nodded and giggled feebly. 'It was silly, wasn't it?' I was so relieved he had taken it as a joke. It suddenly dawned on me that he could have been very angry indeed at me for believing gossip about him. I had nearly wrecked our relationship completely. I closed my eyes and breathed a silent prayer of gratitude that I had not made that phone call from college.

As though he could read my thoughts Mick suddenly held me away from him at arm's length and gazed sternly down at me. 'You know I ought to be very angry with you, Holly. You shouldn't have decided you knew the truth about me on the strength of a little gossip. You didn't have much faith, did you?' Then he relented a little and I saw the old twinkle come back into his eyes. He planted a kiss in my hair. 'But thanks for giving me the chance to tell my side of the story. If I'd been in your shoes I'd probably never have wanted to see me again.' He kissed me again.

'I love you, Mick.'

There was a sudden burst of music from the radio in the kitchen and the clink of china. We jumped apart and then laughed.

'Carol is as relieved as we are,' Mick said quietly. 'I think we'll forgive her eavesdropping just this once, shall we, as she was there as a bodyguard!' He drew me to him again. 'After all, let's face it, I have got a record now, there's no getting away from it. And I should have told you about it.' He looked down at me, suddenly solemn. 'Does it make any difference? Would you rather we finished now you know?' He gazed at me so seriously that I felt my blood run cold. I couldn't bear the thought of losing him. Not now.

'Oh no, Mick, no, no.' I buried my face in his jacket. 'I love you so much. I think even if it had all been true I would still love you.' I suddenly realised that was true, and paused, as serious as he was. I don't think I had realised just how much I had loved him before.

'I think,' I said quietly, after a moment, 'I must always have had a secret longing to be a Maid Marion.'

We were still in each other's arms when Mum knocked rather too loudly on the door and brought in a tray. There were three glasses on it, and the bottle of sparkling wine Uncle Bill had given her at Christmas. We had been saving it for a special occasion.

'I think,' she said, handing the bottle to Mick to open,

'we'd better drink to you both and then we can decide on a date to summon Friar Tuck to perform the ceremony.'

'Carol!' Mick was laughing again. 'You were still listening?'

'Of course I was you silly boy.' Mum smiled at him, quite unabashed. 'How else would I have known the right moment to come in?'

How else indeed!

Witchcraft for Today

I HAD ALWAYS LIKED Sarah's kitchen. It wasn't fitted; every woman's dream of beautiful bleached oak fitments, hob and eye-level, spit-in-your-eye grill, Provençal crockery, Le Creuset casseroles did not feature at all. Instead it was a room, just like any other, a living, eating room, in which she happened to cook. The antique Welsh dresser and waxed oak table were kitchen equipment I suppose – although both were habitually lost under a drift of books and papers and magazines. And cats. There were cats everywhere. A litter of kittens which had somehow never been given away, had stayed around, much to their mother's disgust, until they grew into fat, sleek, contented moggies who only now and then remembered their kittenhood and rioted as a pack round the dresser shelves, scattering willow pattern, two-year-old invitations and even older bills which were then retrieved and carefully returned to their previous positions in the dust.

Sarah was my best friend. We had known one another since school and the relationship, sometimes close, sometimes distanced by the exigencies of husbands and jobs, had remained easy and relaxed. It was, I thought, a real pleasure for us both when destiny brought us to live within fifteen miles of one another. Our house was a pretty terraced cottage in a street of eighteenth-century symmetry in a small East Anglian town. Hers was a rambling farmhouse in a scattered village, once pretty, now blighted with the dreadful post-war housing for which Britain will be drummed out of the Pantheon of the Arts forever when the final great judge hands out prizes for architecture.

My first visit was a revelation.

'Sarah!' I kissed her on the cheek and gave her a hug.

'Belinda!' She kissed me back, her lips not quite touching my face and, drawing me into the kitchen, she ensconced me in an old armchair which was covered in an embroidered shawl. Judging by the state of my skirt later the entire family of cats had been sleeping there only minutes before.

She made coffee – thick, real, stomach-churningly delicious – in a heavy earthenware jug and produced some home-made biscuits. Then she pulled up her own chair near me. There was only one cat in the room at the time. A beautifully marked silver tabby, it sat on the back of the Aga staring at us with disconcerting intensity.

'Donald has left me.'

The baldness of her statement took me aback. She said it without any visible emotion, without a tremor in her voice, though now I noticed for the first time the dark circles under her eyes, the transparent unhappiness.

'When? Why?'

My response shocked even me by its crass inappropriateness, but my surprise was absolute. Their marriage had always struck me as being absolutely sound – one of the great love affairs of the kind which would endure until they were both in their nineties.

'When? On the seventh of May.' She smiled. 'About six in the evening to be exact. And why? Why do they ever go? They dress it up and justify it in every way possible, but when it comes down to it I suppose it is fear. Fear of growing old. Fear of responsibility. Fear of death. He is desperately trying to retrieve his youth.'

'There's someone else?' I asked it in a whisper.

She smiled. 'The younger model. Of course. And apparently she looks like me. Even sounds like me on the phone. I suppose I should be flattered that he wants a repeat prescription. He can't have hated our lives together so much if he wants to travel the same road again. It's her energy he wants, of course. He needs it to restore his own.' She crumbled a biscuit on her plate and stirred the crumbs into the shape of a star with a fingertip.

I didn't know what to say. If Keith ever left me I would die, and we are far less close in some ways, I had always thought, than Sarah and Don.

'Are you going to get divorced?' I knew as soon as I said it that it was probably the wrong thing to ask, but what do you say?

She shook her head thoughtfully. Standing up she went to look out of the window. Behind her the kitchen felt safe, warm, comfortable. I could smell our lunch cooking in the Aga. There was a bottle of Harvey's Amontillado on the dresser with two crystal sherry glasses, next to an old stuffed teddy bear. A vase of pinks and lavender vied with garlic and oregano to scent the air.

I jumped as a soft, delicate-pawed cat plumped into my lap and sat facing me, huge green eyes fixed on mine.

'I'm going to get him back.' She turned, and leaning against a fridge almost invisible beneath a cluster of magnetised posters and postcards, she scrutinised my face. Her gaze was for a moment uncomfortable, too intense, like the cat's. It invaded my space and filled it and I was shocked by the emotions which reeled around me. Pain, fear, longing, jealousy. They spun like living things in the room, circling, prowling, sucking energy from the air.

'Sarah –' My protest sounded strangled in my own ears and I actually put a hand up to my face as if to ward off something physical. The cat leaped off my knee and vanished through the cat flap.

She smiled suddenly and the atmosphere changed abruptly. 'Sorry.'

For a moment I thought she was going to say something else, but she changed her mind and reached instead for the sherry. Pouring two glasses she handed me one. I hadn't finished my coffee, but I put down my cup without comment and took the glass instead.

'Do you believe in magic?' She asked the question with such elaborate casualness that I felt myself stiffen. A shiver of goose pimples spread across my back. Somehow I knew we weren't talking Paul Daniels here.

'Do *you*?' I replied in a whisper.

She appeared to consider for a long moment then she nodded.

I should perhaps say, here, that Sarah had somewhat unruly grey hair, gardener's hands and the kind of gentle attractiveness you might expect from a grandmother of three – which she is. In spite of the bunches of herbs hanging in fragrant profusion from the ceiling beams – herbs at which I now glanced slightly apprehensively – she has never for an instant reminded me of a witch.

'What are you going to do?' I asked at last. My mouth had gone dry. I drank my sherry with unladylike haste and held my glass out towards her. She topped it up without seeming to pay any attention to what she was doing. All her concentration was elsewhere.

'Oh, I've already done it,' she replied.

I could feel my eyes rounding like marbles in their sockets and I found myself staring at the teddy bear on the dresser. The central seam up its stomach and chest had come unravelled and some of its stuffing was showing.

My hysterical train of thought was interrupted by a shout of laughter from Sarah who had evidently followed both my gaze and my train of thought. 'Oh, Belinda! Not that. Not Pooh!' She swooped on the bear and hugged it to her. 'He's here for running repairs, not as a moppet! Do you think I would stick a pin in *him*?'

There was something about her intonation which I did not

like. It implied volumes. 'So what do you stick pins in?' I asked dryly.

'No pins.' She turned to the Aga. The casserole inside was Le Creuset after all. Withdrawing it she lifted the lid and stirred the contents. Then, the casserole back in the slow oven, she put a heavy pan of water on a hot-plate.

'It's not difficult, you know. Magic. Once you've got over the initial distaste. One thinks of it as bad. Evil. I kept reminding myself that I was a member of the PCC.' She gave a small giggle. 'But all it is really is the controlled manipulation of events. You need little more than focused attention to achieve your goal.'

'You must need more than that,' I protested. 'Otherwise everyone's dreams and curses and hopes and fears would manifest all over the place all the time.'

She sat down, leaned back in her chair and reached for her own sherry glass, savouring the drink sip by sip.

'Who is to say they don't,' she replied quietly.

My mouth dropped open. 'Well, clearly they don't,' I said. I sounded, I suspect, a little bit cheated and that was how it felt. Surely it couldn't be that easy. If it was she would look happier, younger, triumphant! And I – well, my dreams and regrets are not part of this particular story.

'Have you any idea, Belinda, just how little of our brain we use?' She squinted at me sideways over the sherry.

I had heard that one often before. Nodding sagely I reached for the bottle. She didn't seem to notice.

'A fraction of its power. Not intellect. Sheer power.' She gave me that look again. 'Focused, it is capable of becoming a laser.'

I didn't altogether like the implications of all this. 'Are you saying,' I put in doubtfully, 'that magic is a way of focusing the brain?'

'Exactly!' She nodded vehemently. 'And if you can do it properly, you can do *anything*!'

'I suppose it's a bit like prayer,' I went on, hopefully trying for normality as I gazed into the depths of my glass.

'No.' She shook her head vehemently. 'No. No. No! Prayer is a plea. It is part of a one-sided bargain. Our side. It is a submissive thing, a begging thing. We grovel before our god and ask him to work everything out and then give us what we want. Magic is a command. We demand that the forces out there comply with our wishes. We are in control.'

There was a long silence. I didn't dare meet her eye. When at last I looked up she was staring at me fixedly. The expression on her face was quizzical.

'So, what have you done?' I wasn't sure I actually wanted to know.

'She is going to be sent abroad any day now.'

I didn't have to ask who 'she' was. 'How?'

She shrugged. 'I haven't worked out all the details. I don't have to. All I know is that it will happen.'

'And then Donald will come back to you.'

She looked at me enigmatically. 'He'll come back anyway. When I'm good and ready.'

That last bit was bravado. Even I could see that. It was obvious just how much she still loved the man. I stared out of the window for a minute. Would I want Keith back if he had gone off with someone else? I didn't think so. After all, how would I ever be able to trust him again? But perhaps she had already thought of that. Perhaps she had fixed that side of things as well.

As we sat down to lunch I found myself eyeing the plate she had set in front of me with some suspicion. She spotted it, of course, and let out a hoot of laughter. ' "Eye of newt, and toe of frog, wool of bat and tongue of dog," ' she quoted mischievously. 'Belinda, you are a fool. What do you think I'd want to turn you into?'

What indeed!

In fact, after that the conversation took a decided turn for the normal. We swapped family news (other than marital) and gossip and happily tried to cap each other's stories of our respective children's brilliant achievements. I put my suspicions aside and enjoyed her culinary expertise and the second jug of rich coffee which succeeded it and we did not mention Donald again until I was digging in my handbag for my car keys.

'Let me know how things go,' I said meaningfully, the way one does.

She beamed at me. 'I'll ring you when there's news,' she said.

She rang me four days later.

'You know the little project I mentioned,' she said with elaborate casualness. 'It appears Sandra has been offered the job of a lifetime in New York.'

I didn't really know quite what to say. In the event, I said, 'And she's taking it, I suppose?'

'Of course.' Sarah sounded rather modest under the circumstances. 'She realised that he was only playing with her. She was far too young and unsophisticated for him. She thought he would marry her once he'd divorced me. Apparently she was under the impression the divorce was only a matter of formality. Imagine it!'

'Imagine!' I echoed rather feebly. 'So, what happens next?'

I had to wait two weeks to find out. Although it was really her turn to come to me I accepted Sarah's invitation to lunch with alacrity. I had by now learned what the sign against the evil eye (the one they are always talking about in historical novels) is all about and how to do it!

I knew something had happened as soon as she opened the door. It wasn't just that she seemed to have lost about a stone and gone blonde instead of grey. It was something else. She was sparkling – even glowing – with happiness.

We didn't waste time with coffee or sherry. There was a bottle of Moët in the fridge.

'I suppose I needn't ask,' I said as I caught the froth in one of her cut-glass flutes. 'Donald has come home.'

She poured two glasses carefully and handed me one. Only

then did she shake her head. 'I'm arranging for Donald to go to New York too,' she said.

I stared at her. I didn't even bother to ask her what she meant by 'arranging'.

'But –' was all I managed to say. A large black cat was eyeing me from the dresser.

She giggled. 'I wasn't entirely frank with you last time, Belinda, because I wasn't completely sure it would work.' She sipped airily.

I waited in silence. I know a pause for effect when I see one.

Sure enough when she felt she had whetted my appetite sufficiently she put down her glass. She had, I noticed suddenly, taken off her wedding ring.

'I had been reading about Thought Forms,' she said. 'In another of those wonderful New Age books.' So, that was where she had got it all from. 'And, well, I thought maybe I might try and create one.'

'A Thought Form?' I was completely at sea.

She nodded. 'You visualise something. And you visualise it so hard and so often and so well that it sort of becomes real. It really happens.' Suddenly she was blushing.

'Sarah –?' It took a minute, but at last I had caught on. 'You don't mean . . . ?'

She nodded. 'I couldn't be sure Donald would come back,' she said, being, I thought, deliberately disingenuous. 'So I thought I would toy with a few ideas.'

With the emphasis on the 'toy', I thought. I continued staring at her, waiting to see what would happen. I had by now noticed that the kitchen table was set for three.

She picked up her glass and took another sip. 'Not too young,' she said dreamily. Okay, so not a toy boy, I revised hastily. 'But younger than Donald.' Poor old Donald. 'Tall. Handsome. Well off. A widower, I thought, but well over his bereavement.'

My God! Every woman's fantasy man. I waited, breathless.

'I used to visualise him and all the things we could do together.' For the first time she looked evasive. Even downright shifty. 'Things Donald and I haven't done for years.' She gave an embarrassed little laugh. 'It helped me so much, the day dreaming, the planning. It was like concocting the perfect recipe. Altering a detail here, giving a little tweak to the design there . . .'

A little tweak? All right. So my mind was boggling. Isn't yours?

She put her head on one side. 'I suppose, with my conscious mind, I didn't really believe that it would work but obviously I was doing all the right things.'

Obviously.

'But what about Donald?' I said at last.

She shrugged. 'I thought I would love Donald for the rest of my life. He thought so too. He thought he could come back any time he wanted and I would be here waiting for him with open arms. He was the one who spoiled it. It's always the men who spoil things.' She looked sad for a moment. 'Never mind. Even if Sandra doesn't want him there are loads of hungry women in New York who will.'

'And you?' I said.

'I am going to live in Tuscany,' she replied. 'With Antonio.' She stood up. 'Belinda, I want you to meet my Thought Form.'

He must have been waiting in the hall for his cue. The door opened and in he came. Everything that the recipe had specified. Tall. Handsome. Rich (well, he certainly looked it). Charming. Forty-something at a guess. As he took my hand and kissed it my first thought was, poor, poor Donald. But it was, after all, his own fault. My second was: can I learn how to conjure the spell?

The Poet

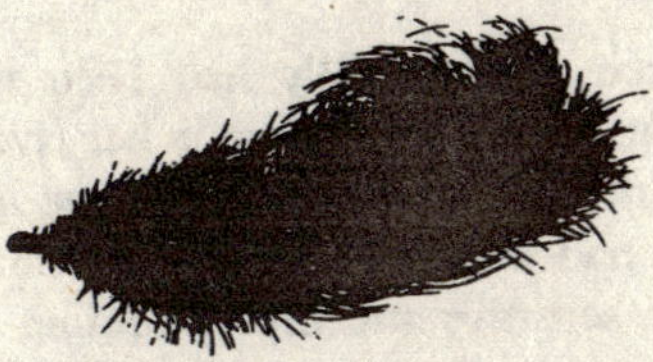

SALLY COULD HEAR the thunder of the waves on the beach through the open window and her heart beat with suppressed excitement. Hastily she finished unpacking, throwing the last of her clothes into the drawer. In the bottom of the suitcase lay her volume of Keats's poems. She took it out and looked at the faded limp cover. The dreaded A levels were over. For the whole glorious summer she could forget school and work, but still, with all its underlinings and pencilled notes she had wanted to bring this book. Keats knew exactly what it was like to be in love, to ache with feelings, and to dream.

She gave the book a little hug and put it on the bedside table. Time enough for reading when the great white moon was shining on the beach, and something – excitement, fear, her own beating heart? – kept her awake, watching the brilliant colourless light making a pool on the pattern of the rag carpet.

'Are you ready, Sal?' She could hear her brothers calling from the living room of the holiday bungalow.

'Come on Sal.' Her father added his voice. 'We're going shopping.'

She ran out to the car, tossing back her long hair. It was three miles to the village and each year that they had come to Farmingley-on-Sea the daily drive to the shop and post office had been a ritual for the whole family.

They did the shopping together, working their way through

the long list and then went on to buy some postcards. Three doors beyond the post office was Shore Cottage. Sally hugged herself with excitement as she looked at the neat white front door and the hollyhocks in the garden. He was due to arrive tomorrow.

For nearly ten months Sally had been writing to Nick Hamlen. He had published a poem in her favourite magazine and she had written to say how much she liked it. He had replied and she had written back. And so it had gone on. He wrote amusing, sensitive and understanding letters, and she had fallen slowly in love with this unseen man; her very own poet. Once she had asked for his photograph but he had ignored her request and she had not liked to mention it again.

Then, a few weeks back she had told him that they would soon be off to Farmingley for their annual two weeks by the sea.

'Surprise, surprise,' came the reply. 'You'll never guess where my dad and I are booked for a week!' He had not actually suggested that they meet but Sally read the letter over a hundred times and gloated, and dreamily planned their first encounter.

She knew Nick had left school the year before. He was a trainee reporter on his local paper. He had had several poems published in magazines and papers and was collecting enough of them to make up a little book. Sally pictured him as tall and thin and a little pale. He would be immensely attractive, perhaps a little like Keats, and she thought perhaps he too would cough a little now and then, discreetly, into his handkerchief, ill and exhausted from long hours at his desk. That, she was sure, was why his father was bringing him to the bracing sea air: for his health.

That night she sat cross-legged on her bed and read the *Ode to a Nightingale* softly to herself. She could hear the waves on the beach and smell the salt and the seaweed and the cool night air, and her window became a magic casement, opening on the foam of perilous seas in faery lands forlorn.

She waited three days – agonising wasteful days – praying Nick would come over. Then, unable to bear it any longer she took the chance while her brothers were in the shop to go to Shore Cottage herself. She stood for a moment outside, her hands sticky with nerves, trying to steel herself to go up the short path and ring the doorbell. Then she managed to do it at last. The door was opened by a middle-aged man with a pleasant face. He smiled down at her rather vaguely.

'Could I see Nick, please?' she enquired in a small voice.

'He's gone for a walk on the beach,' the man, presumably Nick's father, explained. 'I doubt if he'll be back before midday.'

The beach!

Sally fled back to the others in a ferment of impatience to get home, but her mother who was sitting in the kitchen poring over a new recipe book said there had been no visitors. Sally muttered something about a quick walk before lunch and ran out of the sandy front garden across the path and onto the dunes.

From the top of a great shoulder of sand, named Ben Nevis by her younger brother, she scanned the deserted beach. It was a grey unsummery day and the waves were being whipped into angry horses which leaped skywards and lost themselves far out at sea beneath the murky clouds.

A long way off she could see a lone figure walking slowly along the tideline. He stooped slightly and she could see his hands clasped loosely behind him. Every now and again a heavily crashing wave running up the beach further than the others would come up over his shoes, but he didn't turn aside. It had to be Nick.

She ran down the shifting dune, kicking the sand from her sandals, and fled towards him across the empty beach, her hair flying behind her in the cold wind.

He heard her coming and turned and waited. She had pictured this moment so often. He would hold out his arms as she, his life and his inspiration, came to him through a golden mist.

He didn't. He stood watching her, his shoulders rigid. He wore glasses and his face, with a stubborn upturned nose, was freckled. Sally stopped, breathless, a few feet from him and looked at him in blank disbelief. He was short, about the same height as she was, and his sandy hair stood up from his head even in the wind, in an unromantic bush. His mouth was too big and his eyes were small and rather close together beneath the heavy horn rims.

'I'm sorry,' she muttered, blushing. 'I thought you were . . . *are you*, Nick Hamlen?'

He nodded, looking rather puzzled. 'I don't think I know . . . ?' Then his face cleared and he grinned merrily. 'Why, you must be Sally.' Spontaneously he held out both his hands to her.

Involuntarily she took a step back. He had a nice smile, but he was so unlike her imaginary picture of him. Surely no poet could look like this? She knew she should smile back; she knew she ought to shake his hand, talk politely and smile. Don't show him your shattered dream, she heard a voice inside her head. Don't be rude and unkind.

Tears came to her eyes, and she shook her head blindly. 'It's the wind,' she said, brushing her arm across her eyes.

'I know, it's wild today. Superb.' He stood looking exultantly out to sea without speaking for a moment. Then he grinned at her again. 'It's good to see you, Sally, after all this time. You never told me you were so pretty.'

He said it matter-of-factly. Not like a boy chatting her up. He said it as though it were the simple truth.

Sally felt herself blushing again. But she couldn't help thinking: so he never bothered to imagine me as pretty. He has probably never bothered to think about me at all. She suspected now that he had probably never even been going to look her up. Bleak with disappointment she stood silently beside him watching the sea and wondering what to say.

He turned to her again suddenly. 'How did the exams go? I nearly forgot to ask.'

'All right.'

'You're not worried about the results? I was when I took my A levels. I nearly died of nerves.'

She looked at him astonished. He did not look as though he had a nerve in his body.

Suddenly he looked at his watch. 'I've got to get back, Sally. It'll take me half an hour or so to walk back to the village and Dad will be expecting me.'

She felt snubbed. But at the same time she was glad. Obviously he had not wanted to meet her. Their letters had been fun, but no more. His lovely romantic descriptions and his lively libellous passages about his employers: that was just the way he wrote. He himself was nothing like that. The Nick Hamlen of her dreams did not exist. This young man was totally unromantic, she was sure. Probably he was very practical. He looked as though he had never had a cough in his life and he was not even good-looking. She wished she hadn't come.

With a shy, sad little smile at him, she turned away to walk back up to the dunes.

'Sally!' He was still watching her. 'Will you be on the beach this evening?' His ginger hair was being blown ludicrously forward across his head and he kept brushing it back with his hand.

'I don't know, it depends.' Their words were being whipped away by the wind. 'It might rain.'

'It won't.' He grinned, and turning began to walk fast along the beach away from her.

He was right. The wind had blown itself out by early afternoon and slowly the clouds began to lift. By tea-time a watery sun had broken through. Sally sat for a long while after the meal, in her bedroom, looking through Nick's letters. Then she lay back on her bed, her arm across her eyes.

She had made up her mind not to go and meet him. Her

dream was shattered, and now she supposed he wouldn't even bother to write to her again. What was the point?

She ignored her father and the boys when they called her to go for an evening swim and lay, overwhelmingly sad and depressed, looking up at the ceiling with its cracked, crumbling plaster.

She must have fallen asleep at last for her mother woke her, knocking on the door of her room. 'Sally, there's a young man here asking for you.'

She scrambled to her feet, horrified. She had never dreamed he would come to the house.

He was standing grinning in the living room, one hand behind his back. He looked taller indoors and his smile was full of charm.

'Hi!' he said. 'You weren't there so I thought I'd come and collect you. Come and watch the sunset.' He seemed quite unabashed by her mother who was standing there looking at him.

'Go on, Sally dear,' she said. 'Some fresh air will chase your headache away.' With a smile of encouragement she disappeared into the kitchen.

'I've brought something for you,' Nick whispered.

Sally smiled uncertainly.

'Come on outside,' he went on. 'It's turned into the most beautiful evening.'

She followed him through the tamarisks, across the dunes and down onto the beach and still he hadn't given whatever it was to her. Together they walked away from the evening bathers, up to the west towards the rocks. The setting sun was staining the sea red and gold.

He stopped suddenly and looked at her with a shy grin. 'I hope you won't think I'm foolish, Sally, but I've written you a poem.' He held out his hand at last. In it was a piece of crumpled paper.

She stared at him. 'A poem. For me?'

'I know I don't look the part, Sally. Everyone tells me that.

They laugh if I tell them I write poetry, so I don't tell people any more. That's why I was so pleased when you wrote to me. You seemed to understand. I didn't want you to meet me because I knew you'd take one look at me and run.' He shuffled his feet in the sand. Then he looked up again, laughing at himself. 'Go on. Read it.'

She took the paper and read silently for a few moments, the light wind gently stirring her hair. Then she looked up at him, her eyes wide. 'It's beautiful, Nick. It's the most beautiful thing I've ever read. Thank you.'

He grinned happily. 'Will you come for a picnic tomorrow?' he asked suddenly.

Looking up at him she noticed for the first time what beautiful deep blue eyes he had, set beneath thick dark lashes. 'Try and stop me, Nick,' she said quietly.

The Toy Soldier

FOR THE FIRST TIME since they had arrived the house was completely empty. The removal van had gone and Joe had levered himself into Sue's small Fiat and driven down the road to the post office/general store to find some tins of food.

She was standing in the middle of the kitchen. Slowly she ran her hand across the cooker. It was rusty, disgustingly greasy and the enamel was chipped. It wasn't her cooker. Her cooker, her hob and oven, her beautiful fitted kitchen, belonged to the building society now, together with their house and garden. Joe's car had gone too, three days after he had had the letter. The letter which had destroyed their lives with that one word: redundant.

She sniffed and turned quickly towards the window, determined not to cry. Self pity would not help. They were lucky. Joe had found another job at once and a job which came with a cottage. It was little more than glorified care-taking really, looking after his uncle's house and supervising the running of the farm while he was away abroad for a year. The trouble was it was the sort of job where one isn't sure, as Joe kept repeating to himself endlessly, whether one has been done a huge favour, granted charity which could be withheld at any moment, or whether it was oneself that was doing the favour, working for less than the going rate, grateful for a house of less than acceptable condition and tied to both, as the donor fully intends, by guilt and gratitude.

Sue glanced round the room. Most of their furniture was being stored in the next door barn. They had brought in only enough to live. She touched one of the cardboard packing boxes. Her heavy iron saucepans, her wooden bowls, even the bunches of dried herbs, packed carefully, newspaper wrapped on the top. All she had to do was put them on the shelves and hang them up and it would feel like home. She smiled ruefully. Tinned spaghetti in one of her beautiful French dishes. It didn't seem right, somehow.

She moved towards the back door. A shabby curtain hung across the glass on a piece of wire, the angular blue and green pattern a busy cacophony of design. She screwed up her face in disgust. Turning the key she pulled open the door and caught her breath at the sight beyond.

The unkempt garden was separated by a skimpy thorn and beech hedge from a field that had been newly ploughed. The dark expanse of earth stretched so far it seemed to curve with the horizon beyond her sight, but above it the sky blazed with the setting sun. She stood and stared, forgetting the squalid kitchen behind her.

Crimson.

Magenta.

Ruby.

Opal.

Emerald.

Sapphire.

She tasted the words, breathless with delight.

In their suburban, tree-lined avenue she had never properly seen the sunset, never imagined a sky so vast and empty and – her mind groped for the word – pure.

'Isn't it stunning.' Joe was suddenly behind her.

She jumped. She hadn't heard him come back. Narrowing her eyes against the glare she found herself suddenly near to tears. 'It's the most beautiful thing I've ever seen. Better even than Cornwall.' It was the greatest praise she could bestow.

Behind them the shabby kitchen was growing dark. Putting his arm around her shoulders Joe pulled her against him fondly. 'Almost makes it all worthwhile,' he whispered. There was a hint of pleading in his voice which made her heart turn over with sadness.

'Almost,' she echoed. She was surprised her own whisper sounded almost cheerful.

They watched the sky turn at last to a pale aquamarine. One single star appeared low on the horizon.

'I've bought some grub,' he said after a long silence. 'And a bottle of plonk.'

'Oh, Joe, we can't aff — ' her words of reproach were cut off as she felt his fingers tighten on her arm.

'We can afford it. This is our first night in our new home, for God's sake. Surely we can stretch to a £1.99 bottle of wine!'

She swallowed. 'Of course we can. To wet the house's head.' She turned to him. A stupid phrase to use under the circumstances, but it had slipped out before she could bite it back. She reached for the light switch and clicked on the naked bulb which hung starkly on its cord in the middle of the room. Immediately the sky dimmed and with a sigh Joe shut the door.

'So.' He looked round the room bleakly. 'Where are the glasses?'

'In a box, I expect.' She stared round hopelessly at the closed cupboards. 'I wonder if there are any here we could use.' She stooped and pulling open a warped door beneath the draining board, looked inside.

A child's toy sat there in lone splendour on the shelf. A colourful plastic soldier. Instead of legs it had a rounded base so that when it was pushed it rocked sideways and stood upright again.

She lifted it out and stood it on the window sill. As she moved it, it gave out a soft musical chime.

'At least it's bright,' she said.

'Sue –'

'Let's look in these.' She pulled open the top cupboards now. They were empty. Bending over the cardboard boxes stacked in the floor under the small table she found some crockery at last, wrapped in newspaper, and carefully she extricated a couple of cups. 'These will do.'

'Sue, we have to talk about it.' Jim was staring helplessly at her exhausted face. 'You didn't have to give up work. I'm sure you can still keep the job. You can have the car. Your career matters.'

'My career existed fifty miles from here, Joe. My career couldn't, it seems, support us. Your career folds so we have to come to this Godforsaken place to give you a job and mine has to go.' She clenched her lips, her fists, and stared up at the ceiling in despair. Damn. Damn. Damn. She had to keep her bitterness inside! 'I'm sorry, love.' She turned to him and forced a smile. There was genuine regret in her voice, and sadness. 'Don't take any notice. This job is perfect for you. You are going to be really happy here, I know it. And so will I be, once I've found my feet.'

Once.

How?

She sniffed. 'I don't suppose we'll be able to find the corkscrew,' she said.

Joe came up behind her. Putting his arms around her he rested his chin thoughtfully on the top of her head, inhaling the smell of her hair: shampoo and dust and the sweet scent of her skin. 'No problem,' he said. 'You are presupposing a wine posh enough to have a cork. This is a screw-top bottle.'

And suddenly they were laughing. Putting down the cups she threw her arms around him and hugged him. Behind them somewhere in the garden an owl hooted.

She was down first in the morning. In spite of the worry she had been so exhausted she had slept like a log. Pulling her heavy sweater down over her hips with a shiver she unbolted the back door and peered a little apprehensively out into the darkness. It was only just growing light. The rank, weed-strewn garden smelled fresh and clean and she could see a few daffodils near her, their petals almost luminous beneath the cold sparkle of the dark.

She took another deep breath, savouring it, feeling the oxygen pumping round her body, then she closed the door and turned to face her lacklustre, grease-encrusted kitchen. On the window sill the toy soldier rocked gently back and forth, his big plastic grin cheerful against the peeling wood.

'What have you got to smile about?' she asked him out loud as she filled the kettle. Then she frowned. She walked across to the toy and pushed him with her finger. He was heavy. The weighted base needed a firm push to make him rock. A gentle chime rang out as slowly he rocked to a standstill.

The door. Of course. The door had caused the draught. Giving him a final push she reached into the packing case on the floor for cereal bowls and headed for the food boxes to find some cornflakes.

By midday she had scrubbed the kitchen, lined the shelves with clean paper and filled the cupboards, threaded a pair of old curtains onto the wire which served as a curtain rail and hung up an oil painting of scarlet nasturtiums which Joe's nephew had painted for them last Christmas. She had left the toy soldier on the window sill. He was bright and cheerful and she liked his smile. Some child must be missing him terribly, she thought as she caught herself glancing at him yet again. Or had they merely outgrown him and abandoned him to a lonely life of imprisonment in the cupboard waiting to see if he was going to be passed on to another child or merely thrown away?

Leaving the kitchen she started on the low-ceilinged, beamed living room, vacuuming, unrolling rugs over the worn patches on the carpet and unpacking the few cherished ornaments and books they had decided to bring with them. She looked in despair at the two armchairs, their covers torn and stained, and the sofa which seemed at some point to have been pulled off a bonfire. It had scorch marks all down one arm (on closer inspection she found several cigarette stubs down behind the cushions). Luckily for whoever had lived here before, the coarse old horsehair had smouldered and gone out. Wrinkling her nose she humped all the cushions outside onto the small front lawn. When Joe found her she was beating the dust out of them, her fists white on the handle of her broom. He watched for several seconds, then he called her. 'Hey, what did he do?'

She stopped, pushing the hair out of her eyes with the back of her arm. 'Joe! What are you doing home?'

He shrugged apologetically. 'I suppose I could have taken sandwiches . . .'

Her hand flew to her mouth. 'Oh Joe, I forgot. I'm sorry.' It was his first day at work. His first lunch break. Before, he had gone to the office, catching the ten past eight train and not returning until five fifty-seven, out of sight, out of mind while she immersed herself in her career, her life, her whole existence, as an advertising executive in their local market town. Today she had prepared nothing for him.

They shared a can of tomato soup and a cheese sandwich then, dropping a kiss on her head he went back to the farm office. She sat on at the kitchen table over a cup of instant coffee, too depressed and tired to move as she planned vaguely to swop all the furniture for some of their own from the barn. Nicely furnished, the old cottage would actually be very attractive. Behind her the sun moved round at last to the kitchen window and flooded into the room. On the sill the soldier smiled silently into space.

Finishing the coffee she forced herself to stand up at last, went to the phone and dialled.

'Robert? It's Sue. I know this is a long shot, but is there

any chance I could have my job back?' After all she could always commute. She disguised the urgency of her request with a small deprecating laugh but her knuckles were white on the receiver. She listened intently to the mellow even tones the other end, hearing the laughter, the rattle of keyboards, the sound of other phones ringing in the background, the sound of a large office in action – her world – and at last she nodded. 'Oh well. I knew it was a long shot. Keep me in mind, won't you, if she doesn't stay the course.'

She put down the phone and found that she was shaking. Slowly she walked back towards the kitchen and stood in the doorway, staring at the sun-filled room. More coffee? That, of course, would make her feel worse; jumpy; sick. It was only a job. There would be others; other things she could do. Something she could do from deep country. Perhaps she could go freelance? On the window sill the little soldier rocked back and forth, chiming cheerfully. As she watched the rocking slowed and ceased. The window behind him was open a crack. The curtains stirred a little in the draught. She smiled. For a moment she had thought . . . but that was silly. Reaching for her rubber gloves she went back to her scrubbing.

When Joe came back that evening she had a small fire lit in the narrow black grate, and a casserole simmering on the cooker. The rooms were fairly straight and she had found enough early spring flowers in the wild garden to deck the house.

They had saved enough of the screw-topped wine to have a glass each while the potatoes were cooking.

'If you really don't need the car I thought I might drive into town on Monday and see if there are any temp jobs going locally,' she said as she sat down near the fire. The cottage was cold now it was dark. She did not look up. She was staring at the burning fir cones she had thrown onto the flames.

'I see.' He sounded bleak; she was rubbing in his failure,

adding to his guilt. 'Are you sure that is what you want?'

She nodded. 'Just for a few months – to keep me occupied. And it would help to tide us over.' She straightened up. 'We're lucky to have this place, Joe, and we'd survive here even if I didn't work. It was brilliant of you to land this job' – the sop to his ego at last – 'but,' she hesitated, 'I'd go mad, here, on my own. I'd be better working.'

He sat down, rolling his glass between his palms. He looked defeated. 'Perhaps you're right.'

'I know I'm right.' She came to sit on the floor at his feet, leaning against his knees. 'We'll make a fortune yet, Joe, you see if we don't,' she said softly. 'You see if we don't.'

She awoke suddenly. The cottage was silent. Beside her Joe was sleeping flat on his back, breathing steadily, one arm thrown up across the pillow, the other hanging down to the floor.

She lay still, staring up at the ceiling. A half moon hung outside the window, throwing a wash of pale light across the floor. Then she heard it. From downstairs – a gentle chiming sound. She waited, her eyes on the moon, listening drowsily, then slowly she sat up. Glancing at Joe's sleeping face she pushed her feet into her slippers and padded towards the door.

Opening it silently she stood on the landing and listened. There it was again. The quiet musical chime. She ran down the stairs and tiptoed across the cold boards to the kitchen door. Quietly she pushed it open.

The kitchen was completely silent. Moonlight shone through the thin curtain casting a bluish glow into the darkness. On the sill she could see the silhouette of the little soldier. The toy sat unmoving, staring at her with large unblinking eyes.

She stood for several minutes waiting, watching the plump plastic outline, then with a sigh she turned and closing the door quietly behind her she went back upstairs. When she reached the top she was smiling. A dream; that's what it was. A charming, silly dream.

'Are you all right?' Joe was awake as she slid back into bed.

She nodded. 'Very all right.' To her surprise she found that she meant it.

'Good.' He moved towards her and gently he began to remove her nightdress. What with all the stress and worry it had been weeks since they had made love.

All the next day she found that when she walked into the kitchen her eyes went first to the window where the little soldier sat on his sunny sill. Each time he stared back, his eyes bland and expressionless, his eyelashes black cowlicks against his brow, his red plastic cap set at a jaunty angle.

After lunch she wedged open the back door and set to work on the flower bed just outside, pulling up the rampant weeds, exposing the poor smothered daffodils and finding to her delight lavender and marjoram and a clump of newly shooting chives. Every now and then she straightened her back and stood staring out across the field. Behind her the toy stared solemnly inwards, his back to the garden, his stance rigid, immobile as the curtain danced gaily around him in the afternoon breeze.

When Joe came home at dusk he had a box of groceries in the back of the car. Included was another bottle of screw-top. 'To think I used to worry about vintages,' he said cheerfully as he undid the bottle and slopped some into the two glasses she had put ready on the table.

'Joe.' She turned to stir the pan on the stove. 'Who lived here before us, do you know?' Her hand tightened on the wooden spoon. *Please, don't let it have been a child who died.* She closed her eyes for a moment, then she turned and took her glass.

'Funnily enough I was talking about it to one of the farm workers in the office today,' Joe said. He opened the back door and stood staring out at the sky. A band of black cloud bisected the colour of today's sunset which was a stormy scarlet damask. 'The same couple lived here for forty years. They stayed on a few months after he retired, and then went off to live with their daughter down on the south coast somewhere.'

'Forty years!' Sue echoed. 'Perhaps he belonged to their grandchildren then.'

'Who?' Joe shut the door. Taking the lid off he peered in and sniffed appreciatively.

'My soldier,' she said.

'Him?' Joe pushed the toy and watched as it rocked to and fro, the chime ringing around the room. 'Must have done. How long will supper be?'

That night she awoke again. She lay in the dark, her ears straining as in the distance she heard a rumble of thunder. Joe lay on his side, his head cushioned on his arm. They had made love again that night and she was glowing with happiness. It had never been quite so good when they were both exhausted after work. A flicker of lightning showed outside the window. Smiling to herself she snuggled down under the covers, feeling Joe's warm heaviness comforting beside her.

The chime was so quiet she barely heard it. Her eyes flew open again and she held her breath. Beside her Joe groaned and turned over.

For a moment she was tempted to wake him, then slowly she pushed back the covers and stood up. As she reached the foot of the stairs she heard it again – quietly plaintive as if the toy were rocking to and fro slowly, pushed by a methodical hand.

The kitchen door was shut. She turned the knob as silently as she could and eased open the door. She was groping for the light switch when a flicker of lightning illuminated the kitchen and she saw the toy on its sill clearly outlined against the window. There was no sign of movement. Not now, but she had the distinct impression that the expression in the soldier's usually bland eyes was one of guilt.

Clicking on the light she went over to him and after a second's hesitation she picked him up.

'What on earth are you doing?' Joe's voice was so unexpected in the silence she nearly dropped the toy.

Putting it down hurriedly she turned to face him. 'I'm sorry. Did I wake you? I couldn't sleep because of the storm.'

'Are you sure it was the storm? You're not still worried are you?' Avoiding her eye Joe went over to the kettle and plugged it in. 'We're not so badly off, you know, Sue. We have a roof and enough money to live. I know it's not what we're used to, but things could be worse. In fact you know,' he paused, and then went on, still not looking at her, 'now that you're not working, or not full-time, wouldn't this be the perfect time to think about starting a family –'

'No, Joe!' She cut him off firmly.

'Please, Sue, can't we at least discuss it?'

'No, Joe. We've discussed it a thousand times. You know I don't want a baby. I don't want children! You know it!' She swung to face him. 'I need a job, Joe. I need people. I'd go mad stuck at home with a baby, I know I would.'

'Lots of people do both, Sue. They work as well!' He took down two mugs from the shelf.

'No, Joe. I'm sorry.'

He nodded sadly. 'I know. I know. I just hoped.' He looked down at the empty mugs. 'I suppose with us both losing our jobs' (I didn't lose mine, Sue thought, anguished, I gave it up, for you) 'and the house going and everything, suddenly my priorities have changed. I've stopped being acquisitive.' He gave an apologetic shrug. 'It's as if money doesn't matter any more. We lost so much, but we still have what is important. We have each other; we have a home, however small. Any home is enough as long as you are there. That's important. That sunset the other night. That was important. And when I saw you standing there with that child's toy –' He shook his head and when he spoke again it was very quietly. 'For me, that was important too.'

There was a short silence. She looked up at last and he smiled. 'Sorry. Deep stuff. Philosophy lecture over.'

She grinned uncomfortably. 'You were being a bit pompous.' Taking the mugs out of his hands she put them on the table, then she threw her arms round his neck and held him close.

It was later – much later as she fell asleep – that she heard the chime of the little soldier again. This time she didn't go down.

'I cleared these cupboards out myself, my dear.' Julia Somerskill, from the end cottage, was staring at the toy soldier, perplexed. 'They were empty. And there's been no one else here since. No one at all.'

'So, where could he have come from?' Sue leaned forward and filled up the other woman's coffee mug. Joe had needed the car after all this morning, so she had not been able to drive in to see the job agencies.

Julia shrugged. 'There weren't any toys in the cottage. There haven't been any kids here for about thirty years.'

'None that died?' Sue bit her lip, wondering why that uncomfortable thought kept surfacing.

'Good Lord, no, my dear. They're a healthy bunch round here. It's the good air. Besides,' Julia reached for the toy, 'this is modern.' She shook it and the cheerful chime rang round the kitchen. 'I suggest you keep it for your little one.'

'I haven't got any children,' Sue put in quickly.

'No, but you're expecting, aren't you?' Julia reached across and spooned some sugar into her coffee. 'I can always tell.'

'I bloody hope not!' Sue was shocked out of politeness. She grimaced shame-facedly. 'Sorry, that slipped out. No, I'm not expecting and don't intend to be.'

Julia smiled comfortably, not in the least put out by the outburst. 'Maybe. Maybe not. You've already had a job, haven't you.' Did she sound a little bit pitying? 'Perhaps you never got round to thinking about kids.'

'Oh we thought about them. I just don't want them.' Sue scowled.

'And your Joe. Does he feel the same way?' The gentle voice was probing.

Sue shook her head. It was none of the woman's business, but she might as well know the score.

'This house is very special,' Julia said quietly after a moment's silence. 'To you it probably seems small and shabby and not very nice, but there is something about it. It's over three hundred years old you know, under the linoleum and the patches,' she grinned. 'And people in the village have always regarded it as a wishing house. If you spend a night under the roof and wish, you can make your dreams come true.'

Sue's mouth fell open. 'You're joking. There's no such thing!'

'Maybe, maybe not.' Julia, a small twinkle in her eye, gave a mysterious shake of her head. 'Children are a powerful dream.'

'My husband's, not mine.'

Julia met her eye. For a stranger she seemed to have assumed an air of unexpected authority. 'And you think his dreams are less potent than yours? You need to beware, my dear, lest his dreams are the stronger.' She smiled.

Sue stared at her. 'But we've agreed.'

'Then that's all right then.' Brushing biscuit crumbs from her skirt Julia stood up. 'I must go, my dear. Thank you for the coffee, that was nice. I'll see you soon.'

She was not pregnant! She would know if she were pregnant. She could not have been so careless. Sue put her hand to her stomach nervously as from the living room window she watched her visitor walk away up the lane.

When Joe came home she was still worried. 'She sounded like the village wise woman,' she said, surprised how much Julia's comments had unsettled her. 'I know it's silly, but it was as though she knew something.'

'Don't brood on it, Sue.'

'You don't think she could be right?' She couldn't hide the horror in her voice.

He shrugged. 'I doubt it,' he sighed. 'It would be a miracle if you were.'

She stared at him. The woman was right. Why should Joe's dreams be less powerful than hers?

They did not discuss it again, nor did she feel like making love that night and when she heard the little soldier's chime she turned over and pulled the pillow over her head.

She wasn't pregnant. Cursing the stupidity which had allowed her to turn her back on the job agency and instead, when at last she got hold of the car, to waste precious money on the kit from Boots, she binned the offending items and went out to hide her relief in the garden, ripping out nettles and dead thistles until it began to grow dark.

Pulling her boots off on the back doorstep, she went inside and hung up her jacket, automatically turning to switch on the kettle. It was not until she went to the shelf for the tea caddy that she noticed that the soldier was gone.

She stared at the spot by the window where he normally stood. It was empty. Turning round slowly on her heel she scanned every work surface and shelf. Then she opened every cupboard. He had been there when she went out, she was absolutely sure of it.

'Joe?' The second she heard his step in the hall she ran out to meet him. 'What have you done with my soldier?'

Joe shook his head. 'What do you mean? Nothing.'

'But you must have. He's gone.'

She searched the house from top to bottom, but there was no trace of him, and that night as she lay in bed the long dark hours, brightened by the moonlight flooding into the cottage windows, were completely silent.

* * *

She tried two temporary jobs and hated them both. When the second came to an end she did not go back to the agency. Instead she went to the garden centre and bought boxes of bedding plants, comforting herself that she and Joe could always forego the fearsome screw-top if they were really short that month. Joe was pleased, the more so when his uncle flew in from Nairobi and, far from warning Joe that his job might come to a premature end, asked him instead to agree to a five-year stay. 'He's offered us the tenancy of the farmhouse too.' Joe took her out to dinner on the strength of the payrise which accompanied all this largesse.

Sue shook her head. 'Let him rent it to someone else. I'd like to stay where we are.' In her head she had called it the cottage of dreams, though her own had not come true, and neither, as far as she knew, had Joe's.

Until now with the proper job.

He nodded. 'I hoped you'd say that. It's all those plants you've put in the garden. Awful waste if we moved again.'

'Joe.' She looked up at him, and put her hand over his as it rested on the table. 'Tell me what you want most in the whole world.'

He smiled. 'You really want to know?'

She nodded.

'To stay in this job. I love it. I really do. And to stay in the cottage with you – the new happy you.' His smiled broadened. 'I don't know if you've noticed, but you grin a lot these days, and I've even heard you singing over the washing-up.'

'Never!'

'Have so.' He turned his palm over and squeezed her fingers. 'Stay happy, Sue.'

'And that's all you want?' She glanced suspiciously into his face.

'For now.' He winked. 'You are happy, aren't you?'

She thought for a moment and then she nodded. 'I suppose I am.'

'What about the job?'

'I didn't like the jobs.'

'I meant your real job. The one you gave up for me.'

'I don't miss it so much now.' She looked down at her plate. 'In fact I think I'm quite glad to see the back of it. I didn't realise at the time how tired and stressed and hyped up it made me. And you're right I had a whole set of priorities which no longer seem to be valid. Even though I didn't want it for myself and I was always measuring myself against what other people had, what they did. Celie and Jane and Liz – with their children and their Volvos and their dogs and school runs. And Janet and Martina with their high-powered jobs and their mobile phones. They all seemed so much more competent and fulfilled than me. Now, none of that is important any more.'

'Perhaps you've proved to yourself that you are competent and fulfilled as well,' Joe said slowly.

'Perhaps I have.'

'So, do you feel properly settled in now?' Julia was walking her dog up the lane as Sue, puffing, was mowing the front lawn. 'I heard you were going to stay.'

Sue nodded. She walked over to the gate and leaned on it, twiddling her fingers at the old spaniel which sat down with relief to rest while they talked.

'And have your husband's dreams come true yet?' Julia grinned mischievously.

Sue laughed. 'Not all of them certainly.'

'It's only a matter of time.' Bending to fondle her dog's ears Julia shook her head.

'Silly woman,' Sue muttered to herself as she went back into the cottage. Going through into the kitchen she was about to wash her hands under the tap when a small sound caught her attention. Spinning round she stared at the window sill. The toy soldier was back in place, and he was rocking gently.

Shocked, Sue stood quite still. 'Where have you been?' she asked out loud.

The bland face beamed at her silently.

'I suppose you think you can just come and go as you wish?' Sue turned back, crossly, to the tap and finished washing her hands. Silence.

'And I suppose you think you've won? You and Joe between you. You think I'm going to provide you with hordes of screaming children to play with and spend the rest of my life vegetating in the country.' Reaching for the towel she turned round. 'Well?'

The hat seemed at a jauntier angle than before; the red-painted mouth more cheeky, the black eyelashes curved like birds' wings on the white plastic face. As she stood and watched the toy began slowly to rock again. And at last she heard again his cheerful chime.

To Adam a Son

PICKING UP THE handful of letters from the mat I threw them on the table while I fetched myself another cup of coffee. Paul, my two-year-old son, was playing happily in one of the kitchen cupboards, unloading saucepans all over the floor. Sitting down, I sorted through the post. Two were bills, two circulars, one a business note and one . . . I stared at the envelope in disbelief. It was Adam's handwriting, there was no mistaking the sharp black italics on the white paper. *Ms Claire Sutcliffe*, it said. I snorted at the 'Ms'. How like him!

I had heard nothing of Adam for over two years and now, this, out of the blue. Still not opening the letter I turned to look at Paul. He had Adam's black hair, his blue eyes, his smile, his charm.

I had tried so hard not to think about the old days that it was a shock now to find it all coming so vividly back to me.

Adam had known me since I was a child and from the time that I was about seventeen, he was years older, we had become more and more inseparable. Then there had been that terrible car crash which left me with a twisted leg and a limp for life and Adam with recurring headaches. We had never been lovers but I think there had always been an understanding that one day we would marry. I had treasured the hope, and planned secretly for the day that I would move into Adam's beautiful house as his wife. He was an important man in our town and his wife would have to be a superb hostess. I used to practise my cooking on all our unsuspecting guests with this in mind. How I longed to entertain in his elegant drawing room.

After the crash however it all changed. Although we still saw each other just as often it became increasingly clear that I would no longer be considered as a potential wife. It dawned on me eventually that a woman with a limp did not fit Adam's plan. I just could not really believe this of him, but no sooner had the idea crossed my mind than it began to torment me. At the first opportunity I challenged him with it. How badly I chose my moment! He had one of his headaches, and, as he had been doing more and more regularly, he had been drinking heavily. We had a dreadful row and I screamed at him, did he not think he owed it to me to marry me now; after all, the crash had been his fault.

I had never mentioned to him before that I knew or cared whose fault it had been – I didn't – but obviously I had struck a very exposed nerve. I remember it so clearly. He went white, even his lips, and then he hit me, hard, across the face. Gasping with shock I paused only a second before hitting him back and it was a matter of moments before we were rolling on the floor exchanging punches like two spoiled children. I suppose technically it would be correct to say he raped me. His anger turned to a passion before which I was helpless and then back to anger, and when eventually he had slammed out of the door, leaving me lying practically naked and terrified on the floor, it had been a long time before I could get up and dress myself and creep wearily home through the dark.

The next morning I left town, nursing my bruises and an unbelievable fury. I even contemplated going to the police, but my pride stopped me in time.

It was comparatively easy to pack up the flat where I had lived since my parents died, and make the journey to London.

I stayed quietly in a hotel for a while, living on my savings while I got my breath back, so to speak; then I found myself a flat and a new job.

Two months later I knew I was pregnant. A chance in a million but that's the kind of luck I had. I had been brought up a Catholic and although I never went to church now, I had enough beliefs left to know that I could never contemplate abortion. It took me nearly two months more to make the decision to go back and see Adam.

I don't really know what I had in mind; or whether I was even going to tell him about the baby. I think I hoped that when we were facing one another again I would know instinctively what to do.

Choosing a time when I felt fairly certain he would be home I drove my hired car up to his house. I felt really sick and frightened as I stood on the doorstep ringing the bell, and while I waited I turned to look at the bleak windswept garden with one or two rain-blackened roses still clinging to the bushes.

Eventually I heard footsteps. Adam's younger brother Colin opened the door.

'Claire!' He was plainly astonished to see me.

'Hello Colin.' I smiled brightly. 'Is Adam home by any chance?'

'Not yet.' He looked slightly puzzled. 'They've only been gone four days.'

'They?'

I must have looked a little bewildered for Colin suddenly invited me in. Leading the way into the living room – where it had all happened four months before – he poured me a glass of wine.

'We looked for you everywhere, Claire. Where on earth did you go? Why did you leave so suddenly?'

'Adam knew,' I said briefly.

Colin looked even more puzzled. 'But he said . . .' He stopped suddenly, obviously deciding not to pursue the subject and it was then, after taking a sip of wine himself, that he dropped his bombshell.

'Adam got married last week, Claire. He and Alison are away on their honeymoon.'

I remember the beautiful cut glass falling harmlessly from my fingers onto the soft white carpet, and the pale gold stain as the wine lay for a moment in a pool before it soaked away into the deep pile.

Then Colin was pushing my head between my knees and gradually the room stopped swimming.

After a fainting exhibition like that I could hardly pretend I didn't care, but I don't think Colin guessed the real reason for my weakness. I was fairly certain my pregnancy didn't show yet, and anyway I had dressed to make absolutely sure that it would not on this occasion!

Eventually I got away, without leaving any address, and I returned to London to work out my problem alone.

I was extraordinarily lucky really. I still had some savings left, and some money my parents had left me. I had a really super little flat, not too expensive, and found that my landlord would not mind a baby, and my job – I was a designer – was very easily changed so that I could work at home. I became a freelance, fitting out my bedroom as a studio. The tiny box room became the nursery and I spent many happy hours decorating it.

Paul arrived at last and I was thrilled to bits with him. It was the happiest moment of my life when I took him home and laid him for the first time in the little wicker crib.

Strangely enough I very seldom thought about the lack of a man in my life at all. Or perhaps it would be more truthful to say I never allowed myself to think. Sometimes in the evenings when I was tired and depressed I would lie on my bed and abandon myself to tears of frustration and loneliness, but as time went by and Paul grew older I had less and less time to myself for self pity. He became more active during the day and so I had to work at night, sometimes going on till one or two in the morning to get it all done. Then there was no time for tears. I would be asleep almost before my head touched the pillow.

The people I worked for were tremendously kind and all very sociable, so I was not really lonely, I suppose. Occasionally I had to take Paul into one of the offices with me if Mrs Martin next door could not have him for an hour or two and he was always spoiled outrageously.

I wore only trousers or long skirts now, so my twisted leg never showed, and I think my limp became far less noticeable as time went by. My hair had grown very thick and lustrous during my pregnancy and I was very lucky, it stayed that way. I grew it long and although I shouldn't say so, I think I became much more attractive over those two years, certainly more self-sufficient, more confident.

I made a point of never thinking about Adam and Alison, although once, at the dentist's, I saw a picture of them in one of the society magazines. I tore out the page when I thought no one was looking and kept it for months on the kitchen dresser. Then one day it got torn and I threw it away without a thought.

And now, here I was beginning to tremble as I looked down at Adam's letter in my hand. Slowly I tore it open and extracted the single sheet of paper. *Dear Claire*, I read. *I wonder if I could come and see you next Wednesday evening. I'll be there about nine if you agree. Adam.*

How on earth had he found my address? I gazed down at the two lines of neat writing, trying to see so much more than he had written. Of course, I couldn't guess what he wanted after all this time, but I knew a moment of crazy, idiotic hope.

The next few days passed in a whirl of uncertainty. I longed for Wednesday and yet I dreaded it even more. I was puzzled too about what to do about Paul. Did Adam know about him or should I try and hide all traces of him?

In the end I tidied all the toys out of sight into his bedroom, folded the pushchair which usually sat in the hall and put it under my bed in the studio and swept the bathroom clear of baby powder, potty and toy boats. Paul practically never woke up at night so I was fairly sure there would be no sounds from the nursery.

I was carefully dressed and made up long before nine and rapidly feeling more and more sick. I tried to get on with some work to kill the time but I got very little done.

The doorbell rang at three minutes past nine and I walked very slowly to answer it.

'Hello Claire.' Adam stood for a moment smiling before he moved to step forward. I was staggered by his appearance. He had aged about ten years. His hair had begun to go grey and his eyes were sunken and dull. There were premature lines around his mouth and nose and as he came into the living room I saw that he stooped slightly.

I was acutely conscious suddenly of his gaze on me too. That at least had lost none of its intensity. I was relieved that I had taken so much trouble to look nice; casual but elegant clothes, immaculate hair and nails.

I was about to pour two glasses of whisky – I had bought a bottle specially – but he stopped me with a raised hand.

'I'm sorry, Claire. Could I have coffee? I'm on the wagon these days.'

I put the bottle down, surprised. 'You don't drink any more?'

'I had too many warnings, Claire. Too many times when . . . well, when I didn't know what I was doing.' He glanced at me sideways and in spite of myself I felt a blush coming to my cheeks.

'Okay. I'll put the kettle on.' I screwed the top back on the bottle.

I had just whisked a small yellow car out of sight into a drawer when I realised Adam had followed me into the kitchen. I don't think he saw.

'Tell me,' I said as I filled the kettle, 'how did you get my address?'

He grinned wryly. 'There are ways of finding people if one has to.'

'And did you have to?'

As there was no immediate reply I turned to face him. He was frowning vaguely.

'You look very beautiful, Claire. You've changed a lot.'

'You mean I wasn't beautiful before?' I raised my eyebrow archly.

He smiled. 'Of course you were. I wouldn't have loved you otherwise.' He hesitated. 'But now you're . . .' he paused, 'you're quite lovely.' He seemed lost for words and I was suddenly embarrassed. I busied myself making the coffee and Adam carried the tray back into the living room. I knew he was studying me carefully as I walked in front of him – my limp had almost gone now – but he made no comment.

We sat stiffly opposite each other in silence, cautiously sipping the hot coffee. I kept a weather ear open towards the small bedroom, but there was no sound.

'You didn't tell me how you found me, Adam,' I prompted at last.

'There are firms which specialise in that sort of thing.'

'You mean a private detective?' I was scandalised. 'You haven't had me watched!'

'No, no.' He laughed at the rising note of horror in my voice. 'Only traced, Claire, not watched.'

Even so, he must have been told about Paul. I felt myself growing cold.

'Why have you come, Adam? I think you had better tell me.'

He leaned forward to the low table and put down his coffee cup.

'My divorce came through last week.' He said it so quietly, so flatly, I did not for a moment understand. He went on, 'You knew I was married? Well we separated five months after the wedding. The whole thing was a disaster from the start. I never should have married Alison.'

'Then why did you?' I kept my voice deliberately low.

'I suppose it was . . .' he fumbled for words and then with a wry smile at me he went on, 'it was on the rebound really. The night you and I parted was so terrible. I came to find you the next morning but you had gone. I searched everywhere.'

'But not with a private detective?' There was a touch of sarcasm in my voice but he ignored it.

'No, I didn't think of that then. When I couldn't find you I got very angry. Alison seemed to be everything I wanted in a woman; she was beautiful, sophisticated, intelligent . . .'

'And she didn't limp.' I could have bitten out my tongue after I had said it.

'Claire, Claire, you're wrong.' His voice was anguished. 'It wasn't your limp, my darling. As if that mattered. I thought that perhaps I would never be able to marry – not anyone – because of *my* injuries, injuries I didn't tell you about, not yours.' He glanced at me. 'I thought I was going to die, Claire.'

I was stunned into silence.

'Then soon after you disappeared I determined to marry Alison to prove to myself I didn't care, however long I had. To prove that all I wanted was a beautiful hostess just like you said.' He paused a moment. 'You had your revenge for what I did to you, Claire. We were miserable.'

We sat in silence for several minutes. Then he went on. 'They operated on my head. It wasn't as I feared.' He mustered a smile. 'Once they put all the bits back together I was as good as new.' He glanced at me again. 'I still love you Claire. I always did. Will you give me another chance?'

I was not the type to fling myself on his neck crying, but for a moment that is what I wanted to do. The flood of relief which swept over me brought home suddenly just how much worry and unhappiness I had had over the past two and a half years. And just how much I still loved him. I glanced up, fighting the pricking behind my eyelids, but he held up his hand.

'Claire, there is something else I must tell you.'

I waited, panic-stricken suddenly by the worried, sad look which had returned to his face.

'I have a little daughter. She was born after Alison left me, and my loving wife sent her back to me with her compliments. I have custody now. She has a nanny, but she needs a mother.' He looked at me pleadingly.

I couldn't help a little half-smothered smile. 'There is something, in that case, which I must tell you too. I have a little son, and he has no nanny but he badly needs a father.'

Adam stared at me, a smile slowly breaking across his weary features, and held out his arms. 'They told me you'd been seen regularly with a little boy, but I couldn't be sure he was yours.'

'Ours, Adam,' I corrected him gently and then I did go to him.

We were married three weeks later. Juliette, Adam's daughter, was a delightful little thing, only a few months younger than Paul, and the poor baby, who had known only a swiftly changing succession of nannies, clung to me eagerly from the start. Paul was a little disgruntled at first, at having to share his mummy with two new people, but this was more than made up for by the thrill of having two new playmates – Adam being especially popular.

I live in that beautiful house now, and I am learning to be a hostess, not that the idea appeals as much as it did before. I prefer to be alone with my family.

Writer

HIS MOTHER HAD called him Oliver after the boy in the film who had been one of Fagin's gang. He hadn't seen the film, but he knew the story. Oliver ended up being rescued by a nice rich family and living happily ever after.

Nolly, his mates called him. Only his mum in the whole world called him Oliver and then only when she was angry. And she had been angry this evening, angrier than she had been for a long time.

The lift had been out of order for a start and she had had to carry the shopping up the nine floors, heart thumping, face and body shining with sweat. Instead she would like to have stood looking at the graffiti on the inside of the lift doors, trying to hold her breath against the smell, but grateful not to have to face the echoing stairs.

The note was the last straw. *Nolly has a good imagination*, Mrs Peters had said. *When I get stories they are first class. But this is the third homework this week he has not handed in.*

'How many times have I told you, you silly little tyke!' Sheila Garnet stared at her son helplessly. 'What have I got to say to make you understand? If you want to get out of this dump, you've got to get your exams!'

Then, disconcertingly, she had burst into tears.

Nolly was dumbfounded. His mother never cried. She was tough and cheerful even when he could see nothing to be cheerful about.

He had no brothers or sisters, no dad, no grandmother or grandfather. The few times he had made tentative enquiries about these missing pieces of the jigsaw of his life she had frozen him off. 'We've got each other; that's enough,' she said firmly.

And, mostly, she was right.

He was a sturdy boy, strong for his twelve years though not yet very tall, his hair carroty, his face covered in freckles, his eyes a brilliant green, the colouring, though he would never know it, of a certain handsome squaddie in the Argylls who had been posted to Sheila's town a year before he was born and she had left for London. Also from that squaddie came his stubborn chin, his flashpoint temper and his incurably romantic soul.

He saw nothing wrong at all in the high-rise block in east London where he and his mother lived – and for one good reason. He never really saw it. He lived in a dream world, populated with imaginary friends. This evening however his mother's tears had catapulted him for a while into the present. Consumed with guilt and remorse he quietly began to put away her shopping for her in one of the small chipboard kitchen cupboards, carefully folding the carriers to use again, and then he reached for the kettle and put it under the tap. The pipes banged a little as the water ran and he was conscious suddenly of the smell from the rubbish can under the sink. Every day his mum made the trek down to the bins in the windy street below. Perhaps he ought to offer to help her. Carrying the mug of tea into the small living room of the flat which doubled as her bedroom – the other room she had given to him – he put it down on the coffee table in front of her. The coffee table was one of the things Uncle David had helped them get – taking them in his car to Texas and then putting it together for them. He wasn't a real uncle of course, he hadn't any of those, just the husband of one of Mum's friends. And he hardly came over any more.

He sat down next to her on a sofa that was blue and brown

and red in sort of squiggly patterns. There was a cigarette burn on the arm though his mum never smoked.

'Sorry.' His voice came out quiet and on this occasion genuinely contrite. 'I'll do the next one. The one tonight. Honest.'

She looked up at him. Her eyes were a brilliant blue and he loved them for their real beauty but at this moment they swam behind a screen of tears. The dam, which had been in place, firmly, for years, was beginning to crack.

'Please, Nolly. Do it. You could do so well.' She shrugged helplessly.

It was easy to slip away of course. He did it every night. After their tea she would sit down to watch *Neighbours* or *Home and Away* and after only a few minutes she would be asleep. Sometimes she didn't wake until it was really late and time for her to go out again, which was really boring, but although he was now beginning to realise a little just how exhausting his mother's life was with her two jobs, the shopping, the stairs and everything, mostly he didn't think about her at all. Checking that she didn't react when he stood between her and the screen he quietly slipped out of the front door, pushing the key on its piece of string back through the letter box after him. One flight down, running fast, he remembered the rubbish. For a second he hesitated, then shrugging he ran on. He'd do it for her tomorrow.

His favourite place at the moment was behind the train sheds at the end of Alma Road. If he ducked through the broken rusty wire fence and ran lightly over the railway sleepers he found himself in a piece of wasteland hidden completely from the road. Shoulder high with rose bay and buddleia the place had a special smell, a feel of its own. It was a quiet, hidden paradise. He had never seen anyone else there and he was careful not to tell any of his mates. This was special. It was a secret world and he didn't want it spoiled.

In a rusty old box hidden in the dry rank grass he had secreted a couple of books. Sitting down on the grass cross-legged he didn't touch them for a bit. Instead he stared round. On the far side of the no man's land in which he sat was a car dump. Rank upon rank the car bodies rose in the air, some flattened, some just tossed and abandoned like old dead leaves. Decaying and uniform in their rust they had a strange appeal for the boy. Each one, once, had been shiny and new. Each one had been cleaned and polished and loved. So when had things started to go wrong? Had their engines broken down? Had they been torn and flattened in some horrendous motorway pile-up (and was there blood still to be seen by a discerning eye?). Sometimes he would slide through yet more rusty wire and wander amongst the heaps of corpses, once or twice irresistibly drawn to touch, one small almost gentle hand stroking the disintegrating metal, not breathing, daring the great heap to fall. Never once had he been seen; never once reprimanded. This was a part of his secret kingdom.

Tonight, though, on this beautiful warm evening, he had come to sit and read. His mates would call him a suck if they knew so he did it in secret. The books he had nicked from the library.

One was on butterflies and moths. He wouldn't think where the butterflies here in his secret place came from but here they were on his little piece of paradise. Cabbage white and tortoiseshell and red admiral and even occasionally a beautiful peacock on the blue sugary plumes of the buddleia. The other book was on birds. Not the birds he saw here – sparrows and pigeons and starlings mostly with an occasional brave blackbird – but the birds of the sea and shore: gulls and waders and divers. Birds that would paddle on the sand's edge and probe the mud with their long bills; birds that would soar across highland lochs and plunge into the icy water to emerge with fish clutched in their cruel talons.

He had seen them on the telly of course, but mostly Mum wouldn't watch the natural history programmes. She would if he asked especially, of course, because it was educational, but he knew she thought they were cruel because they showed animals eating each other and she would rather be watching her soaps or a nice comedy to make her laugh and he'd feel guilty even as his stomach turned over with the excitement of seeing the wild beautiful places in front of him. *EastEnders* was too much like home, thank you very much.

Turning a page he ran his hand gently over the photograph of the osprey, absorbed, empathetic, feeling the wind in the great wings, the uprush of the cold water, seeing with those black gold-rimmed eyes the unsuspecting salmon gently cruising in the dim, peaty depths.

The librarian watched Oliver as he came in. Slouching casually, the scruffy haversack on his shoulder bulging with torn exercise books, his school tie hanging round his neck like a halter, one trainer lace dragging, he looked like most of his class-mates. She wasn't sure what had first caught her eye – the flaming red hair perhaps – but it was his behaviour which set him apart. To begin with he would joke and push and be a complete pain like the others, disrupting the silence, bringing as they did some undefinable sense of threat to the older users of the library. Then quietly he would slip away from the crowd round the book stacks to the natural history section or to the travel books.

When she saw the first book vanish into the haversack she knew she ought to jump on him but something stopped her. Instead she went to see what he had taken. And she wondered why he had not borrowed it openly. The answer was not hard to work out. To borrow a book was to set yourself apart. One or two boys had tried it but the jeers of their friends were cruel and the books were unceremoniously dumped back on one of the reading tables. She sighed, and wearily she stood up and moved away from her desk. Soon the security marking of the books would be finished. He had to be sorted before that.

'Excuse me.' Her hand on his shoulder was light. Startled green eyes looked up at her, first frightened then defiant then hostile. The last expression assumed by the small face was one of blank insolence. This one stuck.

'You were going to check that book out properly?' She smiled at him, careful to be non-threatening.

'Yea.' The universal and sometimes she thought the only word they all knew.

'There's a new bird book over there, on the acquisitions stand. You might like to borrow that too.' She moved casually between him and the other boys. 'Take a look.'

He glared at her suspiciously. 'Okay.' He sounded casual too now; in another age he might have put his hands in his pockets and started whistling.

'You have got your library card?'

'Yea.' He was uncomfortable. She had held him too long.

'Good. You can take them both out.'

'Might.'

'Tell your mates it's for an extra project. A punishment. Make you look well 'ard.' She winked conspiratorially and turned away.

When she got back to her desk her fingers were crossed.

The library was crowded. It wasn't possible to watch him all the time and she didn't see him leave. But when she passed the acquisitions shelf later the bird book had gone.

Jodie and Squill had seen him borrow the books and they had jeered and given him grief as he knew they would but he had taken the library woman's advice. 'It's for Mr Brent. Extra. Mega punishment.' He glared defiantly and to his surprise they accepted it. Just like that. No more hassle; she obviously knew a thing or two that library woman. He had glanced back at her as he pushed his way out of the heavy doors and in the gaze was the smallest hint of respect.

He didn't open the new book until he was ensconced in

his special place. Unwrapping the piece of gum he had jobbed off Squill he tucked it in the corner of his mouth and pulled the book onto his knee.

The glossy paper smelled cool and exotic, of grass and cream and brandy. He wasn't sure what cream and brandy smelled like, but he thought it would be like that, sort of hot and cold at the same time; peppery and smooth.

The book was nothing but pictures, hundreds of wonderful pictures of exotic colourful birds, flying and swimming and preening and eating against a background of brilliant skies and seas and jungles. He sat transfixed, turning each page slowly, relishing the crisp noise they made as they brushed his T-shirt, hearing in his head the crash of waves on the sand, the wind in the trees and the eerie call of the birds in the night.

He took the book home with him when it grew too dark outside to see. Fishing the key out of the letter box he let himself in and looked round. His mum had already left for work and the flat was empty. He went into the kitchen and looked in the cupboard. She had left him a can of beans and half a loaf of bread for his tea. Putting the book down on the work surface he opened the can and put the pan of beans on the gas ring. He toasted four slices of bread, slopped the beans over them and carried his plate through to eat in front of the TV. He flipped through the channels. All talk; newsy things about politics and stuff. No animals. No birds. No travel. No adventure. He frowned. Best of all he would like to have watched a film – Indiana Jones sort of stuff with jungle and exotic places and birds and animals and himself as the star.

He glanced at the kitchen door. From where he sat, his mouth smeared with sauce from the beans, he could see the book sitting on the side. The bloke who took those pictures must have travelled by boat and train and plane and jeep. He had visited all those places, like the birds.

Putting down the empty plate, he drew his legs up under

him on the sofa. 'Slinging the Pentax round my shoulders I climbed down from the cockpit and put my feet onto the burning sand,' he said to himself out loud. 'Around me I could hear the cicadas and in the distance the cry of an eagle. The shadow of the bird swept over me and for one second came between me and the cruel sun.' He paused, his head on one side and grinned. That had sounded real good. Just like a film.

Pushing himself off the sofa he went to the chest of drawers beside the divan his mum used for a bed and rummaged through the top drawer. Amongst all the women's stuff he found a ballpoint pen that worked. He knew there ought to be something to write with in his bag but there wasn't. But there were his exercise books. Turning one upside down he opened it and was confronted with the most exciting and frightening thing a writer can see. A clean (only slightly creased) page. He looked at it for a long time, almost paralysed by the thought of what he was about to do, then slowly, sitting at the table in front of the window, he began to write.

Outside the undrawn curtains the panoramic view of the lights of London lay like a carpet of sparkling stars. He did not see them. 'I could see the zig zag marks the snake had left in the sand. The heat was burning through my trainers –' he paused and looked up for a moment. A small smile touched the corners of his mouth. He had written himself a Pentax, why not some Reeboks? Crossing out the word trainers he wrote in the change, a small frown between his eyes, his tongue protruding from between his teeth as, on tiptoe, he crept from the sand into the edge of the forest, conscious of the flash of birds' wings high in the branches over his head. From somewhere in the distance, a half echo on the wind, he heard the sound of jungle drums. The small hairs stood up on the thin brown arms of the boy sitting at the table on the ninth floor of the tower block and he felt the skin on the back of his neck prickle with fear. Somewhere on the periphery of his concentration he heard the beat of music from the flat below him. He took no notice. His exercise book filled, he put it to one side and took another – on the front it said, 'French', but it was almost empty apart from a few one word answers, in columns, all marked with crosses. 'Raising the camera I squinted through the view finder and pressed the shutter. The click was very loud in the silence of the forest and I waited, holding my breath in case the head hunters had heard. They hadn't. They continued sharpening their spears as though nothing had happened. On the branch next to my shoulder a huge hairy spider began to move towards me, spinning a silken thread between its clawed legs.' He stopped. The images in his head were so powerful he wondered how he could ever find enough words to describe them, to keep up with the urgency of the story that was suddenly pouring out of him. Looking up he saw the reflection of his own face in the dark square of window. If he looked beyond it, beyond the light hanging from the centre of the ceiling, he could see the stars and the winking lights of a plane flying west towards Heathrow. Who knows, perhaps it had flown in from Rio or Buenos Aires. Exhausted, he put down his pen and stretched his fingers, then he picked it up again. 'I couldn't stay. Carefully I backed away into the shadow of the jungle, checking with my thumb the sharpness of my machetty – machety – masheti –' he couldn't spell it and cross and frustrated he scribbled over the word and wrote in 'knife'.

When his mother arrived home just before six she found him at the table fast asleep, his head cushioned on his arms. Exhausted herself after a night cleaning offices in the City her tired face relaxed into a smile. It had not been a bad night. The girls had remembered and clubbed together and bought her a box of chocs for her birthday and there was a strong rumour going round that there was a small payrise in the pipeline. She rested her hand for a moment on her son's head, wondering if she should wake him, then she caught sight of the exercise book beneath his arm, the page covered in his quick careless writing. Pulling it out carefully she closed it without looking at it and nodded. So the little tyke had decided to finish his project essay after all. That was the best present of all. Putting the box of chocolates down in front of his sleeping head she glanced once out of the window at the glorious dawn sky. A flock of seagulls flew across the window, their wings pink in the light of the rising sun. She smiled. Not such a bad old world, perhaps, after all.

The Fate of the Phoenix

This story, although complete in itself, was written as a short modern-day sequel to an incident in my novel Child of the Phoenix. *There the first part of the story of the jewel is told against a thirteenth-century background of love and passion, betrayal and treachery, emotions which echo through time, to be heard today by any who will listen.*

THE OLD MAN watched the golden cascade of the girl's hair as she lowered her head over her sketchbook and he heard her pencil scratch the paper. Outside, through the window, he could see her boyfriend's car. The old man examined the lines of the sleek Porsche. It lacked style in his eyes. It was aggressive and spurious, like the eighties age which spawned it, though the young man himself looked pleasant. He glanced at the girl again. It was as discreet as a widow's veil, this long hair of hers.

She had written asking if she could sketch the treasures in his collection, her enthusiasm and the freshness of her words leaping off the page at him. 'I heard so much about your things from Grandmama. She thought you might show them to me.'

Grandmama. The word echoed with mustiness and age. How could his beautiful Julia be a grandmama? If only he had married her when she had danced through his life, laughing. But he had been so wrapped in his studies he could not picture Julia Grant in his life of academe and so he had lost her. He could imagine her voice now, teasing, laughing with this golden child: 'See if the old buzzard is still alive. See if he is still in love with his stones and fossils.'

'I'm glad you decided to come.' He smiled. 'You are very different from your grandmother. I often wondered if she was still alive.'

'Of course she's still alive.' She giggled. 'She told me you were lovers.'

Ridiculous, but he was blushing. 'Not what you would call lovers,' he corrected gently, 'and it was a long time ago. I'm surprised she still remembers me. She was so lively, and I was such a fusty old bird, even then.'

The girl smiled. 'She loved you, you know. Poor old Grandpa knew he was always second best.'

To cover his embarrassment he stood up, gripping his stick. He looked past her to the young man. 'Let me show you something, Giles, while Vicky finishes her sketches.' He led the way up the staircase to the gallery where he kept more of his treasures. In the doorway he realised Vicky had followed them and he saw their astonishment. It pleased him enormously when people were impressed by the collection.

'It's like a museum,' Vicky whispered.

'I've always been a collector.' He led the way across the floor. 'Julia thought I was quite mad.'

He lifted the lid on a glass-topped case and stared down at the display of car badges. 'All over eighty years old,' he said proudly. He saw Giles bend closer and he smiled.

'Mr Fraser.' Vicky was examining a selection of carved stones. 'Grandmama said to ask you what became of the phoenix.'

'The phoenix?' He stared at her. Then slowly he nodded. 'So she did remember.'

'She said you promised to put it back where you found it.'

'I agreed to do it with her.' He shook his head. 'And I meant to, but she never came back; later I heard she had married; I lost interest in it after that and in the end I stored it away.'

'Can I see it?' There was a catch of excitement in Vicky's throat. 'You must see this, Giles. It is the most wonderful story.'

She could hear her grandmother's voice in her head now: 'John Fraser was an amateur archaeologist even then, and he and I had been going out for ages when I pestered him into letting me go on one of his excavating trips. I thought a few weeks camping in Scotland might finally persuade him to ask me to marry him. It was not just going to be me and John, of course. There would be archaeologists, labourers to do the digging and two other women who were going to share my tent, so it was all going to be very proper and I would be chaperoned. Don't laugh, Vicky! It was important then. We went to this old castle in the hills. I can see now why John found it so romantic and exciting, but then I was nothing but a silly little flapper, and I found it boring. I wanted to drive and picnic, I wasn't interested in exploring ruins. It was such a desolate place. And John thought it was wonderful. He used to tell me to listen but all I could hear was the silence of the mountains and moors, broken only by the sound of sheep and eagles.' She smiled wryly at Vicky's rapt expression.

'Anyway, the novelty of tents and uncomfortable camp beds soon wore off. As did the charm of the hot evenings. I was eaten raw by midges. John laughed at me and told me to wear a veil over my hat like the others. And something with long sleeves. He thought I would get used to it. But I didn't.

'Then, one evening when it was so sultry even I could feel the atmosphere of the place John told me about a siege hundreds of years before when everyone was killed or hanged and the women who were captured were put in cages.' She shivered. 'I didn't want to hear about it. We had a gramophone and some records back at the tents and I wanted to go and dance on the shingle at the river's edge but instead I sat smoking furiously to keep the insects at bay and waited while he finished some work. I was looking forward to the walk back across the fields with him. It was almost dark inside the castle walls and the others had all gone when John called me to him. He was in what used to be the chapel.' Vicky felt the hairs on the backs of her arms stirring. 'John had been working near a pile of stones and suddenly as we stood there a part of the wall fell in. We stood looking down at the rubble guiltily, you know, like children who had broken something – and it was then that I saw the shine of metal.'

There was another pause and Vicky found herself holding her breath. 'Was it treasure?' she whispered at last.

Julia nodded. 'It was an enamelled pendant. John picked it up and I remember the awe in his face as he asked me if I realised what we had found. I didn't of course. After the initial excitement I was disappointed. It was dirty and crudely designed. Some sort of bird on a nest. I could see that much. We decided to wash it so we climbed down the ravine behind the castle. It was spooky and I was afraid, as if I knew we shouldn't have touched it.' She fell silent. Vicky watched her. 'He shook it in the peaty water,' Julia went on after a moment. 'We saw the dirt dissolve and it began to glitter. It was gold and enamelled. It was a phoenix. Even I could see that.'

Her eyes seemed to be fixed on the far distance. Vicky waited patiently.

Julia shook her head at last. 'We decided to keep it a secret. It was very naughty. John was racked by guilt, but we wrapped it in my scarf and hid it in my tent. It was strange –' She stopped. Her voice had softened, and Vicky saw a wistful smile on her face.

'Strange in what way?' she urged.

'Well, that night a storm broke and we had to run for our tents, rescuing the gramophone and the chairs. We were all laughing and singing. For the first time it was almost as good as I had dreamed it would be.' She fell silent again, thinking back. 'John grabbed me and I felt his lips on mine. It was magical. Romantic. Wonderful. He had never done anything like it before. Then the moment was over and he had gone, leaving me at the entrance to my tent.

'As I got undressed I was walking on air. Then I found myself wondering about the pendant which was under my pillow. I climbed onto my camp bed and suddenly I found I was shivering in spite of the heat. The rain was drumming down on the canvas and the thunder rolling round the hills. It was all very dramatic. I can remember it so clearly. But it was all over. By next morning the excavation was awash. It was decided to abandon the dig for that year. Within two days I was back in London.' She sighed. 'To cut a long story short I decided to wear the pendant to a dance a week later. We cleaned it properly and John bought me a gold chain to hang it on.'

'And what happened next?' Penny breathed.

'I was sitting in my bedroom, getting ready. I picked the pendant up from my dressing table and put it on. It may seem strange, but I hadn't tried it on before. I think I was superstitious about it. It slipped down inside the lace at the top of my petticoat between my breasts. It was very cold.' There was a long pause. 'It was then I felt the hand.'

'The hand?' Vicky stared.

Julia nodded. She grimaced. 'I thought it was my imagination. I could feel this hand stroking my shoulder. Then it moved down my breast. It was gentle, seductive, like nothing I had ever felt before. It touched my nipple – then it stopped. Suddenly I could feel rage – anger – all round me. It was terrifying. And before I knew what had happened the phoenix had been wrenched from my neck. The chain broke, and the pendant flew across the room.' She smiled at the look of horror on her granddaughter's face. 'I was so frightened. I was hysterical. Mother and Papa came up and John ran up after them. And there I was in my petticoat.' She laughed. 'I think I was incoherent. I told them the pendant had been snatched off and I said it was jinxed and I refused to touch it again. It belonged to someone else. It wasn't mine. I had no right to be wearing it. John picked it up as though it were red hot and wrapped it in his hanky and tucked it into his breast pocket. He wasn't afraid.'

'Did you ever find out who it belonged to?' Vicky whispered.

Her grandmother shook her head. 'No. I was in such a state I refused to go out with John that night. It was stupid but I was afraid. I couldn't compete with it, you see. He refused to part with it. I knew we shouldn't have taken it. We had done something terribly wrong. I begged him to go back to Scotland and put it back where he had found it, but he wanted to find out about it. Where it was made. Who it belonged to. Things like that. It was so like him. He cared more for things than for people. I told him I would only go out with him again if we took it back. He refused. I met your grandfather shortly after that. I never saw John again.'

The story still fresh in her mind, Vicky turned to the old man. 'Do you still have the phoenix here?' she asked in a whisper.

He nodded. Leaning heavily on his walking stick he made his way to the far side of the room. There in a locked china cabinet were several pieces of old silver. Amongst them lay the phoenix. Some of the enamels were chipped, and one or two small stones were missing, but still it seemed to glow with inner fire. They stood staring down at it in awe. Then at last Vicky spoke.

'May I touch it?'

John gave a harsh, short laugh. 'Want to see if the same thing happens to you, eh?'

'No!' she cried. Then again, 'No. I just want to see it more closely.'

John reached into his pocket and produced a bunch of small keys. Unerringly he selected the right one and slipped it into the lock.

The phoenix was icy in her hands. It lay staring up at her unwinkingly from tiny red eyes. 'Did you ever find out who it belonged to?' she asked at last, awed.

'No. It was an impossible task. I assumed it belonged to one of the ladies of the castle. It was almost certainly made in Scotland, probably medieval.' He shrugged. 'I don't suppose we'll ever know more than that.'

'Was it lost in the siege, do you think?'

'Ah. So Julia remembered about the siege did she? She hated that castle. She said it was spooky.' He paused, his eyes going back to the jewel in Vicky's hand. 'The castle was rebuilt several times and it could have come from any period. The bird is a crude representation, which makes me think it is quite early, although the enamelling is very fine. What is unusual, is the subject. A phoenix. That is not something which features very much in medieval lore and it's not Celtic. It must have been made for a special reason.'

'And for a special person.' Vicky smiled. Her fingers closed over the pendant. The enamel still felt cold. It was unyielding; spiky. 'You should have taken it back.'

John shrugged. 'I suppose so. It's all so long ago now. I'd forgotten it, to be honest. And I don't think anyone ever missed it. The castle is one of those busy repointed, carefully preserved things now. Heritage.' He made the word sound like an expletive. 'How can people feel the atmosphere of these places when they are sterilised like that? No room is left for the imagination.'

Vicky smiled. 'Not everyone can arrange to go and excavate a romantic ruin, Mr Fraser. Not everyone can be there to see it in the moonlight.'

He sniffed. 'I suppose not. But the fact remains. I couldn't return it now, if I wanted to. There won't be a blade of grass long enough to cover it; nowhere to put it; nowhere to hide it.'

'It should go back to the castle. Your grandmother was right.' For a moment Giles couldn't believe the words had issued from his own mouth.

'It should?' Vicky stared at him. It was a romantic notion.

'Of course it should. We could take it.' The idea was growing on him as he thought about it. 'I'm sure we would find somewhere to put it. It would be right for you to do it, Vicky, if your grandmother was the one to find it.'

John was looking at him closely. 'Others have said the same, over the years. We shouldn't have taken it. It was wrong. Sometimes, when I've been in here I've thought there was someone watching – someone who resents me for touching it.' He laughed, embarrassed. 'I don't usually have much of an imagination when it comes to ghosts and things, but when I look at that phoenix . . .' He glanced at Vicky. 'Would you take it back? You're not afraid of it?'

'Afraid?' Vicky looked at him in astonishment. 'Why should I be afraid?' She glanced from one man to the other. They were both looking down at the pendant in Giles's hand.

They wrapped it in a handkerchief which Vicky put in her canvas shoulder bag. It seemed strange to none of them that John should trust two strangers with something so obviously valuable. Then they picnicked together on the terrace of John's house looking across the gardens.

'Have you met her grandmother?' John asked Giles at last, watching as Vicky took her sketchbook down to the lake. He began to light his pipe for the umpteenth time.

Giles shook his head.

'I wonder why she sent you.' John sucked the flame of his match hard into the bowl of the pipe and watched in satisfaction as the small nugget of tobacco glowed. 'I never married, you know. I wonder if she knew that.'

Giles shrugged.

'You really will put it back?'

'Scouts' honour!' Giles grinned. 'Of course,' he paused, leaning back in his chair, 'once it's gone back, there would be nothing to prevent you ringing Julia. After all, Vicky's grandfather died years ago.'

For a moment John stared at him, then his face broke into a smile. 'You know, I think I might do just that,' he said.

'You're going to put it on, aren't you,' Giles said that evening as they sat in the semi-darkness of the living room of her London flat. They still had not moved in together. He had a place near the Temple, she the first floor of a little Victorian house in Wandsworth. He worked at Lincoln's Inn, she in a solicitor's office in Fulham.

He leaned forward and topped up her glass with white wine, the phoenix between them on the coffee table. 'It seems a shame to take it back. It must be valuable – quite apart from its historical importance.'

Vicky looked up sharply. 'We must take it back. We promised.'

Giles put down the wine bottle and scooped the phoenix into his palm. 'What do you think it was? A ceremonial thing? It must be heraldic, I suppose?'

Vicky shook her head. 'It was a lover's gift.'

Smiling, Giles put it down again. 'You old romantic. Well, it's a lovely excuse for a weekend north of the border. Do you think you can get this Friday afternoon off?'

'I'll try.' Her eyes were shining. 'Giles, how will we hide it if the castle is all touristy? I'd hate it to be found by some uncaring person who would just steal it . . .'

'We'll think of something.' Giles tossed back his wine. 'Listen, I'm going back to my flat tonight. I've got some briefs to study and an early start. I'll call you tomorrow and we'll liaise about Scotland,' and he gathered her into his arms.

She watched him drive away from the window, then she went to the phone.

'Grandma, I've got something to tell you . . .'

The conversation took over an hour. It wasn't until much later, when she had bathed and put on her nightdress, that the temptation proved too strong.

Sitting on the edge of her bed, with the moonlight flooding through the undrawn curtains, she stared down at the pendant in her hands. She had taken a fine gold chain from a drawer and threaded it through the loop, feeling the gold links slide through her fingers. Gently she touched the bird's head with her little finger, then slowly she raised the chain and fastened it around her neck.

The pendant was heavy, just as her grandmother had said. It slid down between her breasts and nestled there, coldly. She held her breath, staring at the open window. Outside, the traffic noise was muted behind the high wall, and she could smell the honeysuckle which climbed the trellis at the back of the house.

Impulsively she stood up and walked over to the window, leaning with her elbows on the sill. Her hand went to the pendant and she stroked it. It was still cold against her skin. Heavy. Unresponsive. Alien. She shivered as a stray breeze from the garden whispered across her breasts.

The touch when it came was so gentle, so slight she didn't recognise it as a touch at all. A slight pressure on her shoulder beneath the lace, the barest caress along her collar bone, the tiptoeing of two fingers across her throat and down towards the mound of her breasts.

She closed her eyes. Her mouth had gone dry with fear; she couldn't move. Her breathing was jerky, her hands suddenly slippery with perspiration as they fell away from the pendant and hung limply at her sides. She could feel him now behind her, a presence so close she could have leaned back a little against him and drawn his arms around her. The fear was going; her body was responding. She wanted to turn; she wanted to raise her lips. . .

The blast of anger was so sudden she threw her arms across her face as if to shield herself from a physical blow. With a sob she staggered back from the window as the pendant was torn from her neck. The chain disintegrated as the phoenix flew into the corner of the room and skittered under the chest of drawers. With a whimper of fear Vicky ran to the door and dragged it open. She fled down the passage into the living room and, slamming the door behind her she locked it. She was shaking violently.

'I'm sorry,' she murmured out loud. 'I shouldn't have put it on.' Her cheeks were wet with tears. 'We'll take it back, I promise.'

She fell asleep at last on the sofa as dawn was breaking. In the garden a blackbird was singing, the notes clear and cold. Under the chest of drawers the phoenix lay on the dusty boards, a short length of golden chain beside it.

It was Saturday afternoon when the Porsche at last threaded its way the last few miles through the mountains. Giles glanced at Vicky. She was pale and tired and for the last hour she had been growing increasingly tense.

He reached across and put his hand over hers. 'What's wrong?'

'How do we know we're doing the right thing? How can we be sure that's what he . . . she . . . it . . . wants?'

Giles shrugged. He removed his hand from hers to change gear as the car purred up towards the top of the pass. 'You were the one who was so sure. If it isn't then he, she or it will have to tell us. Anyway, I thought you said it was a he. Definitely a he.' He smiled. 'It seems to me that he is well able to make his feelings clear.' She had told him what had happened. When he went back to the flat on Friday to collect her, the pendant was still lying on the floor; she hadn't dared to touch it. Picking it up he had glanced round, nervously, waiting for something to happen. Nothing had. Wrapping it in tissue paper he packed it into a small box and put it in his pocket.

They paid their entrance fee, bought a guide book and began the walk across the field towards the grey stone ruins of the castle. The pendant was in Giles's pocket.

'There are a lot of people about,' Vicky said nervously as she followed him through the gate.

He nodded. He had already spotted the triple windows high in the stone wall. 'Look, that must be where they found it. In what used to be the chapel.' He took her hand. Side by side they stood gazing up at the broken stone; at the remnants of once beautiful decoration. 'It must have been wonderful, excavating this. Can you imagine it? All wild and broken and covered with grass, and camping out here in the storm.' His hand had gone to his pocket. His fingers curled around the pendant.

'There's nowhere to put it, Giles.' She looked round desperately. The restoration was immaculate. Short grass, gravel, newly mortared stone.

Giles was staring up at the windows again. They affected him strangely. Such grace and beauty; such a striving towards the sublime in a castle built for war. And they had survived, where the great curtain walls had fallen. 'I wonder what really happened,' he said. He moved forward and rested his hand on the cold granite of a door jamb. 'Did she lose it? Was it stolen from her? Perhaps she was buried here in the chapel and the phoenix was buried with her.'

'It doesn't seem right to bury a phoenix,' Vicky said softly. 'A phoenix should die in the fire and then be reborn.'

'You're right.' Suddenly Giles was businesslike. 'We can't hide it here. Not with all these people. We'll come back tonight, when the castle is closed.'

'How?' Vicky's eyes were enormous with doubt and disbelief and excitement.

'We'll climb over the fence. I have a feeling that whoever he was, he will show us what to do.'

There was a full moon. The broad strath and the distant mountains were silvered and silent as they climbed the fence and dropped into the field. Grazing sheep looked up startled as, hand in hand, they crept towards the castle.

Vicky's shoes were soaked with dew as, half exhilarated, half terrified, she followed Giles towards the gate. Beyond it, within the ruined walls black pools of shadow contrasted sharply with the clear moonlight.

'I'll give you a leg up,' Giles whispered. He bent so she could stand on his knee and vault across the padlocked gate. Following her he caught her hand again and they stood still.

'Can't you see the headlines?' Vicky breathed in his ear. 'Barrister arrested for breaking into Highland ruin for rendezvous with ghost.'

Giles smiled. He gave a quick glance over his shoulder. 'No one is going to get arrested. We're not doing any harm. Come on.'

He led the way between what remained of the gatehouse towers, then, keeping to the grass they crept towards the site of the chapel.

Inside the walls the air was icy cold; the shadows were thick. Vicky clutched Giles's arm. 'I'm scared.'

He stopped, looking up at the windows. 'So am I.'

'Have you got it?'

'Of course.' He touched the pendant in his inner pocket, then he reached for his torch.

'Could we bury it under the grass?' she whispered.

'I was wondering that.' He had brought a penknife. He could cut a turf and replace it so no one could see.

Slowly he walked towards the wall and ran his hands across the stone. It was cold and unyielding.

Behind him Vicky stood in the moonlight, staring round.

Was he here, the jealous owner of the phoenix? Was she, the woman to whom he had given it?

'Where are you?' Her lips framed the words. 'What do you want us to do with it?' She shivered, remembering the touch of the unseen man's hands on her body.

'Can you smell burning?' Giles whispered suddenly.

She could smell it too now. Not the gentle, autumn smell of woodsmoke. This was acrid. Unpleasant. The smell of dead fire, dowsed by water, and it was inside the walls.

Giles was peering into the shadows, directing the torch towards the corner. 'Look. There's a stair in the thickness of the stone. How odd. I don't remember noticing that before.' He tiptoed towards it and stood, his hand on the newel post, staring up into the darkness. Then he began to climb.

Wordlessly Vicky followed him up the tight spiral. It was pitch dark. They had to feel their way upward, following the narrow torch beam.

Ahead of Vicky Giles climbed steadily. She could hear his heavy breathing. Abruptly he stopped. She heard a gasp.

'What is it?' Behind him on the narrow stairway she could see nothing. The skin was prickling on the back of her neck.

'Look.' He stepped through a doorway and suddenly the stair above her was empty.

'Giles. Wait!' She sped up the last few steps.

The staircase led into a dark upper chamber. The smell of burning was unpleasantly strong up here and the floor was thick with debris. The pale beam of light from Giles's torch showed fallen masonry and burned timbers, tumbled on stone. At the far end the three lancet windows rose up, close above them now, against the starlight. The torch beam picked out the details of the ravaged chapel – the breached, gaping walls, the collapsed roof open to the stars, the broken, exploded floor tiles, and beneath the windows a black gaping hole. Picking his way across the rubble Giles flashed the torch inside. 'There's something here.' He reached down.

'Be careful.' On her knees beside him, Vicky peered into the hole.

'There's a little box down here. It's half burned.' Lifting it out he put it on the floor. 'It must have been beautifully carved. You can just see the remnants of the decoration. What is it? Wood? Bone?'

'It's ivory.' Awed, Vicky picked up the box. The lid was warped and twisted but she managed to prise it off. It was empty.

Their eyes met. Around them the shadows shifted. Beyond the windows in the moonlight an owl hooted. Taking the phoenix from his pocket Giles handed it to her. It was the first time she had touched it since it had been snatched from around her neck. Reverently she laid the pendant in the box. 'It will be safe there,' she said quietly. She smiled. 'He must have loved her so much.'

Putting back the lid, she gave the box to Giles, and he reached down and wedged it into the hole. Then carefully he began to fill it with rubble. On the top he balanced some of the broken tiles.

They stood for a moment in silence. 'I hope you're together, wherever you are.' Giles's quiet words hung for a moment in the air before he turned towards the stairway.

The moon was setting and the shadows had moved and thickened. On the grass below the lancet windows they stopped and stared upwards, but deep in the blackness of the wall there was no sign of the place where they had been.

'Come on. I'm freezing.' Giles reached for her hand. In his inside pocket was a small velvet box. In it was a locket, but suddenly the moment did not seem right. The shadows were too sad. Tomorrow, in the sunshine, he would bring her back and tell her he loved her and give it to her. Tomorrow, when, he knew, there would be no sign of the burnt chapel; no staircase in the wall. When grass and ruins would be as stark and neat as when they had first seen them earlier that afternoon.

When the Chestnut Blossoms Fall

A Trilogy

THE MISTRESS

IT WAS WINTER OUTSIDE. The restaurant was dimly lighted and they saw each other's faces over the saucered candles as pale blurs, half dazzled against the flock wallpaper and the crowded, faded Victorian prints. A waiter hovered, a less substantial figure even than they, in the shadows with his coffee pot and the world-weary stoop to his shoulders.

'More coffee, Tina?' Derek smiled gently and she smiled back, hoping that he wasn't going to reach into his pocket for his glasses to read the bill, a gesture which made him prematurely old.

She shook her head. 'Let's have it at my place, shall we?'

The spell was broken completely when he glanced at his watch. At once she felt a surge of resentment; always the watch came between them; always the time limit; the barrier, the gate through which he passed out of her life and back into someone else's.

He had turned to the waiter. 'No more coffee, thank you. The bill.'

The man bowed – the bill was already made up – and Derek fumbled for his glasses.

'There's just time to come back, Tina, I'd like that.' He

turned to her with a quick smile which never failed to win her back from her agonised depressions. Then he took her coat from the waiter, and helped her on with it, so his hands were already round her shoulders as they went out through the door and into the wet road and it was natural to stay like that as they trod the shiny reflections of the pavement lamps into muddy opacity and lowered their faces before the cold of the slanting rain.

She had left the fire on in her flat. Either way it helped – if he felt he had to go back to his wife it made the loneliness more bearable for Tina; if he didn't, if he came back with her, it made the place inviting and homelike – his second home. She glanced up at him with a quick surge of warm happiness. This time he was there.

She threw off her coat and ran to the kitchen to find two cups, two saucers, two glasses for two people.

'What would you like with the coffee, Derek?' she called. He had lowered himself, by the fire, into the chair which she always thought of as his own.

'Scotch if there's any left. You know, Tina, we must do something about this room. Would you like me to buy you a new carpet? It might cheer it up a bit.'

She stopped, frozen in her tracks. He thought her room cheerless. He didn't like it. Her hand shook a little as she began pouring again and her voice was guarded as she answered. 'That would be nice. I should like that.'

At once he seemed aware of what was wrong, and he levered himself out of the chair and came to lean in the doorway of the kitchen, watching as she fixed the coffee. He took the Scotch from her hand. 'I love the room, Tina. As it is. It's comfortable. A haven, you know that. I just thought some more colour might cheer it up for you when I'm not here . . .'

So he did know how she felt. Of course; he was sensitive and that was why she loved him. One of the reasons. He was sensitive, warm, friendly, everything that that cow of a wife of his did not understand or appreciate.

Tina had never told him about the grey, aching evenings when he was not there. Or of the long empty nights; of the nervy solitary breakfast table when occasionally she would forget her promise to him to give up smoking and grab a cigarette with her black coffee instead of toast. She only told him about happy things, funny things, things which would bind him to her. She turned and smiled up at him. 'You are a darling, Derek.' She slipped her arms around his neck. A little of his Scotch spilled on her shoulder as she returned the hug and, smiling, he nuzzled it, pretending to lick where it had soaked darkly into the wool of her dress.

'God, I wish I could stay tonight!' Suddenly he was holding her in earnest. He felt blindly for the worktop behind her and, clumsily, set down the glass.

'Why don't you?' she whispered. She knew he would shake his head. He would probably glance at his wrist over her shoulder and hurriedly calculate the time it would take to drive home.

'Oh Derek!' She pushed him away exasperated. 'Ask her for a divorce. I can't go on like this. I want you so much and it's not as though she loves you – you've told me that.'

He had picked up his glass again, agitated as always when she touched on forbidden territory.

'No. I said she doesn't understand me, Tina, that's different. She does love me, my dear. That's the problem. That is why I can't hurt her. She loves me very much.'

'You can't hurt her and yet you hurt me every day!' She hated herself for saying it. She pushed past him and threw herself down on her knees before the fire in the dim light of the table lamp. 'And she hurts *you*,' she couldn't resist adding over her shoulder as he remained in the kitchen doorway. 'She knows how much you want a family, yet she refuses to give you any children. I should have thought that alone was grounds for divorce.'

'Perhaps.' He shook his head slowly as he came back to his chair. 'It's too soon, Tina. Perhaps eventually . . . I don't know.' He shrugged helplessly and sat there, gazing at the gently hissing flames in the elements.

'And I want children so much,' she went on piteously, half to herself. 'Life is so terribly unfair.'

He didn't answer. His eyes were still fixed on the fire. Perhaps he hadn't even heard her.

'Would you divorce her if I had a baby?' She looked up suddenly. 'You know, Derek, I think she would understand, if you told her that.' But he was still looking blankly at the columns of blue flame, his eyes vacant, not listening.

'Did you hear what I said?'

Visibly pulling himself together with an effort he focused on her again and smiled. 'I am sorry I was miles away. What did you say?' His face was haggard in the soft light.

She scrambled to her feet, her eyes shining from the idea which had at that moment been born, but her voice was gentle as she stood before him, gazing down into his eyes. 'You're tired.'

He nodded and slowly stood up. 'Perhaps I had better go. It's late and it's a long drive.'

For once she did not try to stop him. She clung to him for the last, treasured, kiss of the night and then stood watching as he walked down the echoing hall outside the flat door. At the corner by the lift he stopped and turned for a second as he always did, then he was gone.

She closed the door and leaned with her back against it. Shutting her eyes she could feel her heart hammering inside her rib cage as, taking a deep breath, she went into the bedroom. She kept her contraceptive pills in the top drawer of the chest of drawers under the window. There were three packets there. It took as many minutes to carry them out to the rubbish bin.

As she clanged the lid shut on them she could feel her hands trembling and she was wiping her palms nervously on her dress as she walked back into the flat. She had made her decision; there was no going back. She picked up Derek's bottle and poured herself a large drink. It was the first time she had ever done that alone.

Derek had promised to take her to the country at the weekend. It was bitterly cold and she sat beside him in the car hugging herself, smiling with excitement beneath her woollen hat.

'What's up? You look as though you've come into a fortune.'

She grinned happily at him. 'I'm just happy, that's all. Look at the frost on the trees, Derek. It's so beautiful after being in town; one forgets.' For once she did not even care that he lived in the country; that his house was probably decorated with hoarfrost even on weekdays and that his wife could see the snow on the boughs of their apple tree from her kitchen window.

They parked at the edge of the beechwoods and began slowly to walk through them, their shoes sinking into thawing leaf mould around ice-rimmed puddles, glancing up at the soaring silver trunks of the trees and the azure sky beyond. They held hands, his gloves leather, hers wool, and the smoke of their breath singled as they laughed. She wanted to run, but she was afraid to because he might remember he was so much older than she and pant and grow red in the face and say he was too old for that sort of thing and spoil it all.

They had tea in a little restaurant in front of a blazing log fire, asking for second helpings of scones and clotted cream and Derek looked at her and smiled. 'It wouldn't do you any harm to put on a little weight, sweetheart. You're as thin as a bean pole.'

And she smiled back, and almost told him what she had done, but didn't quite dare.

They seldom discussed Derek's wife after that. Janet receded in importance as Tina's happiness grew. She didn't care any more what Janet did or thought. She had stopped worrying about her and thought only of what would happen when at last she could tell Derek that she was going to have his baby. She had no doubts about what he would do. She was utterly happy.

He bought the new carpet for her flat. It was deep red and over it there was a soft shaggy hearth rug for her to sit on because it was her favourite place – on her knees before the fire, reading or talking, or listening to music.

Months passed. Spring slowly began to shade the trees and take the edge off the coldness of the mornings. Anxiously now, she counted off the weeks, waiting, hoping, each time again disappointed.

Derek seemed more relaxed and happy to see her happy, and he brought her more and more presents – but he came less often to see her.

There was always a busy time at his office in the spring, she remembered from last year, or thought she did. The excuses he gave his wife of working late, of seminars and conferences, were now true, as he assured her, for these few months. Tina missed him dreadfully, but still, there were the afternoons. One day a week he managed to slip away for a couple of hours. They would stay in her flat, turning their backs on the glory of the spring outside, lying close in her shady bedroom, both too conscious of the alarm they had to set to remind them when their time was up.

She had almost given up hope when at last it happened. A month stretched out to five weeks – six – seven. Breathless with excitement she waited, counting the days, wondering when she dared tell him.

At last she could wait no longer. He was surprised when she greeted him at the door of her flat, fully dressed; for the past weeks she had worn a kimono or a negligée, playing the part of his mistress to woo him. He smiled, pleased to see her excited, and he accepted the drink she had ready. The windows were wide open and they could hear the steady roar of traffic below, though all they could see was the foaming beauty of the horse chestnuts on the pavements.

'You look very smart today,' he said, glancing at her bright skirt and fashionable sandals. 'Do you want to go out somewhere?'

She shook her head. She had grown her hair long to please him and it swung heavily round her shoulders. He longed to take a handful and feel the weight of it in his palm. He turned away and took a sip of his drink.

'I've something to tell you, Derek. I hope you're going to be pleased.' She hesitated. Not until that moment had it crossed her mind that he might be anything but happy at what she had done. She swallowed and glanced down at the floor. The sun was shining in through the leaves outside, throwing a moving fretwork of patterns on the rich pile of the carpet. Derek's carpet.

'What is it, Tina?' He was watching her, amused at her sudden confusion. Not guessing.

She looked up and took a deep breath. 'I am going to have your baby.'

There was a long hush in the room. Even outside the road was empty for a moment as the traffic was halted by some distant red light. Then the deep throbbing roar of a bus passed, the high red roof brushing beneath the branches, shaking the tree so some of the blossom fell.

'Are you absolutely sure?' He sounded appalled.

Shaken, she looked away. 'Well, I'm nearly sure. I haven't had a test or anything, but . . .'

'Then you must.' All at once he was solicitous. Not for the first time he reminded her of her father. 'Once we know we'll be able to decide what to do.'

'But, Derek! Surely there's nothing to decide.' She could feel a strange coldness gripping her stomach as she looked at his face. 'Your wife will give you a divorce at once if she knows about the baby. You know she will. Then we can get married and –'

'*No!*'

He set down his glass and walked over to the window, looking down at the street below. 'I am sorry, Tina. Perhaps I haven't made myself clear. As you hadn't mentioned it for so long I thought you had decided to accept the situation. There can be no question of a divorce.'

'But you wanted a baby. You told me you wanted a baby.'

'I want my wife's baby, Tina.' His voice was gentle. 'I'm sorry, my dear, if you misunderstood the situation, but I really don't see how you could have. I've made no secret of the fact that I wanted a family.'

'That's why I wanted to get pregnant.' Her voice was small.

He swung round on her. 'You mean you did it deliberately?'

She nodded.

'Christ!' He hit his forehead with the flat of his hand. 'Oh, Tina, I am so sorry. But it cannot be. Not like that. You must get rid of it. I know it's hard, but . . . there's nothing else to do.'

'No, Derek.' She spoke quietly, suddenly calm. 'Your wife has everything. You; a proper home; your name. This baby is all I have of yours. I don't care how hard it is, but it's happened, and I shall keep it.'

'You can't, Tina!'

'Try and stop me!' She was angry now and very bitter. 'It's my decision, Derek.'

'Then it would be the end of us, Tina. I am not prepared to run a second family behind Janet's back.'

'Oh no,' she held back her tears with difficulty. 'Yet you were quite prepared to run a mistress for two years.'

She turned away from the sunny room and from him and ran into the bedroom, slamming the door behind her.

Left alone he groped for his cigarettes and shook one out of the packet, his hands trembling. Then he stood looking down out of the window, watching the cars go by. It was nearly four. In five minutes he would have to go back to the office.

He glanced towards the bedroom which was quite silent; he had dreaded the sound of sobbing. With a sigh he stubbed the scarcely smoked cigarette out in the ashtray and quietly he let himself out of the flat.

Tina heard the front door close as she lay on her bed. She wasn't crying. She felt too shocked and disappointed for that; too numb perhaps to register what had happened. It was a long time before she got up. She kicked off her sandals and wandered listlessly back into the sitting room. The sun had sunk behind the roofs opposite and the room was in shadow now. She could hear a blackbird whistling from the trees, its song clear over the roar of traffic.

She sat down at the table and drew a piece of paper towards her slowly. She had never written to Derek before; it had been part of their understanding.

'My Darling Derek,' she wrote, her hand shaking a little as she thought out what she was going to say to him. 'I am so sorry that I misunderstood what you wanted. I truly thought that it would make you happy. Please forgive me. We have had such a lovely two years together – and I love you so much. I could not bear it to end like this. I want very badly to keep the baby, but I promise I will make no claims on you now or in the future. Just love us a little, and keep in touch. You will have my love always, Tina.'

Slowly she read it through, then she folded it into the envelope and addressed it to his home. She thought for a moment and then wrote *Private*, on the top of the envelope.

She ran to the box with the letter before she could change her mind, and then slowly walked back to the flat.

It was very hard to sleep that night. She lay tossing and turning on the bed in a turmoil of indecision and misery. Each time she dozed off she thought she heard Derek's voice but then as her eyes flew open in the dark she knew she was alone and that he had left her. 'But I have the baby,' she thought, hugging herself. His baby. The pillow was hot. She turned it over and beat it desperately with her fists. Her eyes were sore. They wanted sleep as much as she. She got up and wandered into the kitchen where the tiles were cool beneath her feet and she poured herself a glass of milk.

She began to shiver as she sipped the cold milk. For the first time Derek had shown her, without a shadow of doubt, that if it came to choosing between Janet and herself, he would stay with Janet, whatever happened.

'He's a coward,' she whispered furiously at the half-lowered blind across the dark window. 'A coward and a liar.' She did not let herself think she might have been wrong.

Strangely, she fell asleep almost at once when she got back into bed, and slept for a few hours, dreamlessly. When she woke it was just beginning to get light. The street was quiet except for the tentative notes of one or two of the first birds in the dawn. She wondered for a moment what had awakened her. Then she knew. The familiar aching pain in the small of her back. The knotted cramp in her stomach. 'Oh no.' She leaped out of bed. 'Please God, no.' Trembling she switched on the bedside lamp and pulled back the blanket. There on the sheet was the small tell-tale patch of blood. There was no baby. There never had been.

THE MAN

It was winter. The garden lay beneath a crisp layer of frost, grey-green and unreal in the glittering sun as Derek made his way to the breakfast table. His wife, already seated, pouring out the coffee, glanced up with a smile. 'Hello you. You're going to be late again if you're not careful.'

'What about you, then?'

'Me, too.'

He went by car, she, hating the traffic, by train. They were both silent for a while, then she looked up. 'Is it tonight that you're working late again? I might stay up in town and do some shopping; perhaps even go to a show.'

He frowned, a little shamed by her tolerance. 'Janet, I hate leaving you on your own so often, I really do.' He meant it.

He reached for the toast rack. A piece of toast fell on the cloth in a shower of crumbs and he laughed a little uneasily. 'I'm lucky you understand. Not many men have high-powered business women for wives.' He intended it as a compliment, but at once she frowned.

'Don't let's go into that now, Derek, for goodness' sake. I'm fed up with hearing how high-powered I am. You know damn well it's just a job, same as thousands of other women do.'

'I know, I know.' Irritated, he dug the knife into the butter dish. 'It's just that thousands of other women manage to combine careers with families these days.' He pushed his chair back abruptly, so that it caught on the rush matting on the kitchen floor and nearly fell sideways.

'I don't happen to like children, Derek.' Her voice was energetically patient. 'For God's sake, do we have to discuss it every day? I love my job. I made it quite clear before we married how I felt; I didn't deceive you in any way; I've been telling you every day for the last eight bloody years! How many more times must I tell you?'

'You don't have to tell me at all. Please, let's not quarrel.' He went to put his arm round her, dropping a kiss on her head. 'I'm sorry. I never mean to bring the subject up.' He laughed uneasily. 'I must be feeling old again; seeking the immortality of sons, or something.'

Was it that? After all, Janet was only thirty-two and there was plenty of time for her, but he, well, he was nearly twice her age. He frowned as he opened the garage doors and slowly backed down the drive, watching the clouds of exhaust wreathing back over the car, enveloping him in a personal, isolating fog. He backed cautiously into the road and swung round towards London. Or was it that he was jealous of Janet's independence? It irked him a little, he had to admit, that she could afford to go off and buy things, big things, for the house for instance, without having to ask him for money. He had always liked the idea – it seemed romantic and cosy, of couples, young couples, putting their heads together to discuss things; working out budgets, agonising and saving and choosing, together. It must bring them close.

He swore as he reached the level crossing. The barrier was falling and that meant that he would have to wait for at least three commuter trains in quick succession. He drummed his fingers on the steering wheel impatiently. Then he thought of Tina.

With her he was the one who did the buying without consultation. He produced the goods for her flat with beneficence, feeling big because of it although he knew she would like to go out and choose with him sometimes; but he shied away from the idea. That would be too near the bone. Too much like setting up home together. It would admit to a permanence he denied.

He often cross-examined himself guiltily about Tina and he always came to the same conclusion. He was fond of her of course. He found her attractive and her home a refuge and a convenient pied-à-terre in London, but when he was not with her he liked to think that she probably ceased to exist; or rather that she became someone quite different; someone confident, poised, invulnerable and whole.

His conscience would never quite face the idea that she lived and loved for him alone. Once or twice he had taken the idea out, so to speak, examined it cursorily, and put it away again as being too uncomfortable to peruse further.

Two trains flashed by in opposite directions, their windows crossing like the flicks of a camera shutter, each hiding and revealing a microcosm of life behind the condensation, and then the barrier arm slowly began to rise. Derek checked his watch as he carefully pressed down the accelerator pedal. Late again.

* * *

He was due to meet Tina at six. It was a cold evening. Wet. The sleet, frosty and clean in the country, was unpleasant and depressing in London and he sighed a little, almost wishing he could go straight home to relax by the ash-whitened logs which Janet always kept burning in the evenings, regardless of the extra work it gave her.

Then he saw Tina, early as she always was, waiting in the foyer of his offices, sheltering from the cold, and his heart gave a little lift. Her dark hair was streaked blue-black by the rain, and swung loosely on her shoulders, still disarrayed by the scarf she had torn off as she came in.

'Hello Tina. Have I kept you waiting?' When her eyes met his he knew why he let it go on like this. He could never cease to be haunted by the clear grey honesty and the uncomplicated worship he saw there. And she made him feel young.

She put on the sodden scarf again, and turned up her coat collar, then he pushed the circular door for her, watching benevolently as like a child she half ran, her hand on the glass, until she was ejected breathless onto the front steps. She turned to him and laughed happily, watching as he followed.

Later, after the film, they both had *soupe du jour*. It was thick and hot and full of leeks. She always put salt in her soup regardless and it irritated him slightly that she didn't taste it first, but he said nothing. It was her evening. 'Did you enjoy the film?' he asked, watching as a strand of her hair strayed for a moment across her nose. She blew it off, suddenly gamine. 'I loved the bit where he chased after everyone in the car. That was really exciting!'

'Do you think I should drive like that?' He smiled tolerantly, reaching out to brush her hand quickly with his own.

She looked wistful. 'No one could drive like that in a staid saloon like yours, Derek! I wish you had a sports car!'

'Oh I'm too old for that! I had one when I was twenty.' He laughed a little wryly, not minding the joke against himself, but she, who was twenty, looked stricken. Once more he wished she would acknowledge the difference in their ages and laugh about it as Janet did, instead of constantly pretending it didn't exist.

'We must plan our day in the country, my dear,' he went on easily, reassuring her. 'I rather thought Burnham Beeches might be nice. What do you think?'

Janet had told him only a week ago about her conference and he had been hurt and angry. It was bad enough that her work encroached in the evenings sometimes, but to deprive him of a whole weekend! It had been to get his own back on Janet that he had rung Tina and the excitement and happiness in her voice when he suggested spending the two days together had soothed him a little, restoring his self-confidence.

The waiter had begun to hover again and he sighed. He wanted to linger. 'More coffee, Tina?' He smiled to hide his irritation.

She shook her head, and glancing at the waiter she leaned forward to whisper conspiratorially, 'Let's have it at my place.'

Surreptitiously he glanced at his watch. It wasn't all that late. Perhaps he could stay for half an hour before driving home through the rain. Hunting for his glasses he turned to the waiter and beckoned for the bill.

He loved the way she left the fire and the side-lamp switched on in her flat. Once or twice at the beginning he had reproached her for her extravagance but she had been so hurt that it had dawned on him she did it for him and he had been very touched. It didn't cross his mind it might cheer her too, should she have to return alone.

He sat down in the chair by the fire, relaxing, and glanced round the room while she was in the kitchen, making the coffee. It was comfortable and happy, if a little threadbare. He closed his eyes and gave a deep sigh of contentment. If only he could do something about it – buy her something new perhaps. He squinted down at the worn carpet and had an idea. For a moment she looked crestfallen when he suggested it and he was taken aback; he went into the kitchen and helped himself to the Scotch she had poured him. 'I love the room, Tina,' he murmured awkwardly. 'I thought it might cheer you up when I'm not there, that's all . . .'

She turned and flung herself into his arms, spilling his drink. Putting down his glass, he drew her close to him, feeling the accustomed longing as he smelled the fragrance of her hair. He glanced cautiously at his watch behind her head and swore soundlessly. There was no time.

At the surreptitious movement of his hand which freed the watch from his sleeve he felt her body tense. She knew what he was thinking and she resented it. She pushed him away. He could see the tears welling in her eyes. He knew what was coming and he braced himself, picking up his glass. It was weeks since she had mentioned Janet and divorce and all the unhappy, unmentionable things which would throw him into a panic and force him to realise how the situation could not be allowed to go on. Once, in a foolish unforgivable moment of self-pity he had mentioned the fact that Janet refused to give him any children and she had seized on the fact and nursed it and now, every so often, she would bring it up and throw it at him, imagining it to be a lever against her rival.

She pushed past him, still sobbing, and flung herself on her knees near the fire. He shook himself wearily. What was she saying? Something about Janet understanding. How naïve could she get?

Then she was getting to her feet again, her mood inexplicably gone as fast as it had come. She smiled gently, her face serene. 'You're tired.' She kissed him as he nodded.

'Perhaps I had better go, Tina. It is late and it's a long drive.'

They kissed goodbye and he left her, walking slowly down the long carpeted corridor towards the lifts.

Janet was asleep when he crept up to the darkened bedroom. He undressed quietly in the bathroom, and stood for a while looking at himself in the steamy mirror. His face was strained taut into lines which grooved his cheeks and furrowed his forehead with weariness and worry. He frowned and the lines deepened.

'You're working too hard, Derek.' Janet's voice from the darkened landing made him jump. She appeared in the doorway and smiled. 'Poor darling. I wish you would take a day or two off and let up for a bit. Shall I get you a hot drink?'

Still looking in the mirror he saw her, pretty and feminine, in the lacy negligée he had bought her, her immaculate hair tousełled and softened from the pillow, and his own face, in front of hers in the glass, visibly relaxing and lighting before his eyes at the sight of her. He turned.

'Darling.'

'What is it?'

'Do you have to go away this weekend?' He had forgotten Burnham woods.

'You know I must.'

He sat on the edge of the bath, his shoulders slumped, and she came to him, taking his head in her arms and cradling it on her breast.

'I am going to work less afterwards, though, Derek. I've been thinking about it for a while, and there is quite a bit I can delegate.' She smiled and dropped a kiss on his head. 'I've been ignoring my husband shamefully.'

He glanced up at her. Her eyes were bright and her face relaxed and pretty. He quite suddenly wanted her very badly. He stood up slowly and took her into his arms.

He would give Tina this one last treat. Then he must tell her that it had to end. Almost he dreaded picking her up on Saturday, but when it came the time passed in a haze of happiness. She did not once mention Janet, or the possibility of divorce; nor did she say anything which made him feel old. They laughed and joked together in the sun-bright frost and watched their breath mingle in clouds of whiteness and

Derek forgot that he had meant to end it. A few more meetings could do no harm and they gave her such pleasure. Each time as the weeks passed, when his conscience pained him, he would buy her a present; less often now something for the flat; things like flowers and chocolates which required less thought.

Slowly he began to realise that there was something about his wife which was different and it pleased him immensely. They no longer bickered and after a while he realised it was because she was not on the defensive any more. It was as though she had relaxed, accepted something, he was not quite sure what, which she had been fighting for a long time. Puzzled, but pleased, anxious not to endanger their new-found happiness together, he found it surprisingly easy to leave the office earlier now, and as the frosts relaxed their hold and the countryside began to stir he would look forward to the long slow drive through the rush-hour towards home.

He took to snatching a couple of hours in the afternoon every now and again to see Tina. She too had changed. She had grown more composed, more self-reliant; almost preoccupied now. And she radiated a new inner happiness which he hated to endanger, but he knew he had to tell her sometime. It was unfair to her to let her go on loving him. A little he hoped that she had found someone else and that that was the reason for her happiness. He hated the idea, but at the same time he wanted, in a cowardly way, for it to be true. Then he need never tell her.

It was a relief on this last day, when he had nerved himself for the final break, that she had opened the door to him fully dressed. He had not said as much to her, but it had shocked him slightly that over the past weeks of their afternoon meetings she had met him undressed at the door like a whore, too blatantly waiting for him to make love to her. He grinned at her now, relieved. Perhaps today she was going to give him his marching orders and save herself the hurt.

He went in and automatically she poured his drink. She had on a scarlet and orange skirt which swayed and flared as she walked. It was seductive. Now that he had made up his mind to leave her he felt a strange, urgent longing to make love to her again. He turned towards the window and looked out at the noisy street, sipping his drink. Her flat was on the first floor, level with the thickly flowering horse chestnuts which lined the street, and he could almost touch the blossoms through the open window.

'I've something to tell you, Derek; I hope you're going to be pleased.' Her voice was hesitant, almost lost beneath the roar of the bus which accelerated into the stream of traffic outside.

'What is it, Tina?' He turned and smiled to make it easier for her to tell him.

She hesitated for a brief moment, and then, 'I'm going to have your baby.'

The smile stuck on his face for a moment, wooden. Then slowly it faded as he felt the draught cold from the window behind him. Christ Almighty! How could he have been so stupid? But surely, surely, she had been on the pill? Taking a deep breath to steady himself he smiled again; he must reassure her.

'Are you absolutely sure?'

'Well, I'm nearly sure. I haven't had a test or anything, but . . .'

'Then you must. Once we know we'll be able to decide what to do.'

He was wondering how much it would cost; and then of course he would want to send her away for a really good holiday. But she was still talking, rushing on, not listening to him, her eyes panicking suddenly . . . divorce . . . marry her . . . keep the baby . . . divorce . . . divorce Janet

'*No*!' His voice came out much louder than he had intended. Oh Christ, why had he let it go on so long? Why had she not understood? Why had he ever mentioned children to her at all? He cursed himself silently as he turned back to the window, to give himself some time, not able to look at her frantic face. No. No. There was no way he was going to allow her to blackmail him like that, to force his hand, to betray Janet any more. He set his teeth grimly. He was fond of the girl; he even loved her still, in a way, but Janet had to come first.

Later she ran from the room crying, defiantly shouting that she wanted to keep the baby with or without him and she had slammed her bedroom door in his face. He reached for a cigarette, shaken, expecting to hear her sobs from behind the door. But the bedroom was silent. After a few moments he stubbed out the cigarette. Automatically he glanced at his watch. It was time to go back to the office.

Should he say anything before he went? Better not. In a day or so he would ring her; he would see she lacked for nothing whatever she decided but he would never see the baby. Whatever happened he would never do that to Janet.

With a shrug he gave a final glance round the room and slowly he walked out, carefully closing the front door behind him.

THE WIFE

Rows with Derek at breakfast always left me quivering with resentment and hurt. By and large they followed the same pattern each time, as though they had been scripted for us by a hack writer, and later I would try and shrug them off, pouring myself another coffee, my hand shaking a little. Glancing at my watch I could time him exactly. Two minutes to the door to collect his briefcase and coat, three minutes out to the garage. Another three to start the car and crunch slowly backwards up the drive – then silence.

I nearly always had twenty minutes or so to spare from that

moment before I left to catch the commuter train to my office. I could not bear the traffic and the crawl for hours through the suburbs as Derek could, I am too impatient, so I would never accept a lift with him.

This time the quarrel had ended on a conciliatory note. He had apologised, trying humorously to rationalise. 'I must be seeking the immortality of sons or something,' he had laughed as he refolded the paper to fit into his briefcase. I groped in my bag for my cigarettes, frowning. That throw-away comment had reached me where so many other arguments had failed. He was after all so much older than I and it meant so much to him, having children. But then, I reminded myself crossly, I had never had any desire for a family, and had made that clear before we married. He taunted me with the description 'high-powered business woman' and I knew from him it was no compliment, but that is what I was, and I revelled in it.

'Morning Mrs H.' Maggie's cheerful voice echoed through the hatch from the kitchen. I stood up slowly and taking my cup and my cigarette went thoughtfully out to her.

'It's cold this morning! You wrap up warm, dear, and watch out for the ice on the way to the station!' My cleaning lady was a cheerful, plump, motherly woman. I watched her take off her coat and hang it behind the door and suddenly I wanted to confide in her, ask her opinion. I took a sip from the cup. It would be foolish of course and all round the village in no time. 'Have some coffee, Maggie. It's still hot.'

'Thanks, dear. You know, I will this morning. It'll warm me nicely.'

'Maggie.' I was strangely embarrassed, not knowing how to put it. For so long I had been used to people – friends, above all relatives – saying, 'And when are you going to start a family?' to which I replied indignantly that it was none of their business. But we had been married, what, eight years now, and the questions had for the most part stopped. Except from Derek.

'Maggie, do *you* think I'm wrong not to want children?'

She gaped at me for a moment. Then she grinned comfortably. 'Well, each to his own way, that's what I say. We can't all want babies I suppose; and it would be wrong for you to have one after all this time if you didn't want it – not that you wouldn't love one if it came. I was only saying to my Harry last week, what this house needs is some little ones. Mr H, he'd be a lovely father.' She was pouring herself some coffee and she crossed to refill my cup at the same time. 'You enjoy your job too much though, don't you, dear?'

She began to stack the breakfast things. 'You'll miss your train if you don't hurry.'

'I suppose I could have a baby and go on working. People do. They get nannies or au pairs or something.'

She beamed going to the sink with the loaded tray. 'I'd give you all the help I could too. Love kiddies, I do.'

I set down the cup and reached for my coat. 'Don't say anything to anyone about this Maggie, will you? I am still thinking about it.' I pulled a wry face as I buttoned my coat and she smiled confidentially.

'Mum's the word, Mrs H. Now you run for your train, or you'll miss it. And mind the ice!'

It was a busy day and went reasonably well. At six I closed my desk diary and put it away with a sigh. Then I stood up and stretched. Outside, the evening was black, but the towering office blocks were bright with thousands of lights. London throbbed at this time of day and I loved it. I grabbed my handbag and made my way out to the Ladies to patch up my make-up. It was one of the days Derek was going to be late home; he was under a lot of pressure at the office and two or three nights a week he had been out till after midnight. In a way it was a relief. It meant I had no need to switch from thoughts of international currency exchange to worries about whether Maggie had done all the shopping and remembered to turn on the oven. I could go on being myself for the evening and not pretend to be more domesticated than I was.

The evening was mine. I slung my bag over my shoulder and ran down the steps to the entrance hall. Digby, the commissionaire, dapper as always, wished me a knowing good-night as he opened the door and I was outside. I took a deep breath of the cold damp air. It has a strange quality all of its own, London air. Not sharp like country air; not sweet like that of the hills. It has a bitter, sour smell that combines traffic fumes and hurrying people and wet scummy pavements and the excitement of the lights, the noise and the constant vibrant hurry. I adore it.

I thought of Derek stuck in that smoky boardroom in the City and I suddenly felt very benevolent towards him, poor darling. He always worked so hard.

Then I thought again of my plan. It was late-night shopping and I had decided to do a little research into my own psyche! The thought had come to me gradually as the day had progressed and I had faced it with equilibrium. It was, after all, the sensible way to analyse my own state of mind.

I pushed with the crowds into the store and allowed myself to be steered at random between counters stacked high and unattractively with Sale goods. Once or twice I stopped and allowed myself to be tempted but I was restless. I was suddenly eager to get on with what I had come for. I made my way to the escalators and let them carry me up out of the crowds. One, two, three, four floors. Why so high? It was much quieter up there. The crowds were thin. I stepped off the moving concourse and stood and looked around. Before me stretched lines of cots and prams, elegant, glittering and empty. I swallowed. I hadn't expected it to be quite so soulless. Slowly I began to walk.

For ten minutes I wandered around that department, out of the prams towards the soft toys, the tiny clothes, the powder and the rattles. There were no real babies there. I suppose it was too late for them to be out. I glanced at my watch. It was after seven. Once more round the display of baby buggies, each with a fluffy teddy bear as occupant, and I made thoughtfully for the *Down* sign.

I could feel myself frowning as I descended slowly into the crowds again. The visit had not been in any way decisive. I had not been repelled by what I saw and I must confess that I had been scared that I might be, but I hadn't been won over, either. I thought about all the babies I knew. The trouble was that I didn't actually *know* any. I always inspected from a safe distance, usually a little distastefully, shrinking from the sour milky smell so many of them seemed to have.

'For Christ's sake, Janet,' Derek had said in one of our earlier rows, when he still had the energy to go into the practicality of things. 'You needn't even look after it if you don't want to. Just give birth, that's all I ask. We'll get someone from the village to come in. I can afford it. Damn it, *you* can afford it, if you insist on going on working.'

'If you want to know, the idea of being pregnant repels me,' I had retorted, to hurt him. '*You* don't have to go around looking like the back of a bus, suffering from varicose veins and God knows what else for three-quarters of a bloody year!'

Poor Derek. It was to his credit that he had stuck so gently but so firmly to his guns for so long. Not that I had seen it like that. I had been on the point of leaving him over it, and yet. . .

The problem was a straight choice. I loved my husband and my home. Even more I loved my job and my independence. I loathed the idea of having to go to anyone and ask them for money and if I gave up work I would in a sense be giving up my right to be an individual – even if it was only for a few months or so.

That was the way I saw it.

I put my key in the lock and pushed open the front door.

The house was warm and welcoming. Nothing had changed of course. It was still home. With a grateful sigh I kicked off my boots and wandered into the living room to turn on the lamp. In the winter Maggie lights the fire before she leaves in the afternoon and she had done it today, not realising I would be late home. It had died to embers. I threw on a couple of logs and poured myself a drink.

In theory three months off work should be no problem. But there was always Ronnie Maxton. Ronnie, who had come in as my assistant, waiting, watching, full of drive and an ambition which I had straightaway pinpointed as ruthless. I am good at my job, but when it comes to it, if I took maternity leave Ronnie would still be there ready with his own schemes.

I lit a cigarette and began to pace up and down the hearth-rug. Would there be a place for me when I went back? The logs were blazing up now, on their bed of ash, shooting sparks up the chimney, scenting the room with the lovely fragrance of burning apple. I threw the half-smoked cigarette into the red heart of the fire.

I had a long leisurely bath and wandered into the bedroom. The rain had stopped earlier and when I drew back the curtains and glanced out I could see the black sky was pierced with a myriad shimmering stars and the garden was glittering with frost. I hoped the roads would not be too icy for Derek when he drove back from his meeting.

I kept my contraceptive pills in the bathroom cabinet. Last thing each night I would take one meticulously before I cleaned my teeth. Tonight I took them out and looked at them, turning the unopened new pink-and-white packet in my hand. It was the right moment, as far as I understood it, to stop – If I was going to stop. I took a deep breath.

I didn't have the courage to throw them away. I took the packet into the bedroom and tucked it into the back of the top drawer of my dressing table. It didn't seem somehow quite so irrevocable an act as putting them in the waste bin.

I was asleep when Derek came home at last. I woke when

he tiptoed into the bedroom and then out into the bathroom again and I lay there thinking sleepily, listening to the bath water flowing, watching the wisps of steam curling across the landing in the hall light and disappearing into the dark. Then at last I could lie still no longer. I got up and pulled on my dressing gown.

He looked so tired. I stood and watched him as he cleaned his teeth. Then he stood, stooping forward over the basin, gazing for a long time at his reflection. He looked haggard and my heart went out to him.

'You're working too hard, Derek,' I whispered, hardly realising that I was speaking out loud. 'Poor darling. I wish you would take a few days off and let up for a bit. Shall I get you a hot drink?'

He was still looking in the mirror. As if half asleep he raised his arm and rubbed the steamy reflection with the sleeve of his bathrobe. Our eyes met for a second in the glass. He turned.

'Janet.' He looked so anguished that for a moment I was afraid.

'What is it?'

'Do you have to go away this weekend?'

I jumped. This weekend. The two-day conference I had been looking forward to so much. It had slipped my mind altogether. For a moment I was tempted to let Ronnie go and keep the weekend free for Derek, but I knew that just this once more I had to be there.

'You know I must.'

His shoulders slumped a little and suddenly I desperately wanted to tell him what I had done; about the pills in the dressing-table drawer, but I knew I must keep it a secret. Supposing he had been right when once, not so long ago, he had said I would soon be too old to conceive. Suppose I had been too long on the pill? Supposing tomorrow I panicked and changed my mind?

He sat down suddenly on the edge of the bath looking pitifully defeated and I went to take him in my arms. I could at least promise him that I would allow no more weekends to come between us. Slowly his arms came up and round me, and at his touch I felt relaxed and happy – more so than I had felt for years.

We both began to be happy again after that. Derek seemed a different person and it was weeks and then months since we had had a row. He stopped coming home late, as well. I suppose the urgent order had been finished at last; and now that I no longer, guiltily, saw criticism and sarcasm in his every word we talked happily without the hurtful, loaded comments.

I was content – most of the time. Sometimes I would panic though, as I had known I would. I would sit in my office clutching the edge of my desk, feeling the sweat breaking through the careful make-up on my forehead, unable to bear the thought of giving it all up. Those days I would bring work home, clutching my briefcase like a talisman. Then after a few days the curse would come and I would relax again, perhaps even a little disappointed, knowing that it hadn't happened this time.

Slowly winter passed. I watched the birth of spring, a time I had always loved, with the swelling buds in the garden and the slow emergence of the bulbs and then the glory of the daffodils and narcissi in the orchard. It was a glorious season.

When at last it happened there was no panic and no doubt. I found that I knew quite calmly that this time it was for real. I waited for two months, hugging my secret, then I went to see Dr Forbes.

It was a sunny spring day, glorious with streaming clouds, the milky horse chestnut blossom outside the surgery showering a confetti of white petals on to the pavement as I walked home up the lane. It was hard not to tell Maggie, though I think with her unerring woman's instinct she guessed the second I had said I was taking a few days off work.

'It's a celebration, is it?' she enquired when I began to

prepare the supper that afternoon; all Derek's favourite things.

I nodded, trying to hide my excitement and she didn't ask any more.

He came home early, but the moment he entered the front door I realised that something was very wrong. He had the grey hunted look of the winter again and he went straight to the drinks tray and poured himself a large Scotch before he said hello.

Only then did he smile, acknowledging with a brief widening of the eyes that he liked my new dress.

'What is it, Derek?' I kept my voice carefully neutral as I poured myself a drink.

'Oh sorry, I should have got you one. It's nothing, Janet. A lousy day at the office, that's all.'

I didn't press him. He poured himself another drink and walked over to the fire, kicking the logs, so that the sparks shot up. It was still cold in the evenings and I had lit the fire to make the room more attractive, knowing how much he liked it.

He picked up the poker, the hand holding the glass resting on the mantelpiece and began to draw patterns in the dead white ash round the edge of the fire and I sat down pretending not to watch him, trying to ignore the selfish little lump of disappointment which had firmly lodged in my throat. I had for so many months been consciously and unconsciously preparing for this moment that I had forgotten that Derek knew nothing about it; had had nothing particular to look forward to this evening. It was obvious that he was in no mood for a celebration.

He did his best to hide his mood and his obvious worry. I wanted him to tell me what was wrong, so perhaps I could help him, but I knew better than to ask. I had kept my secret so long I could keep it another day or two.

We ate the celebration meal in a silence broken only by

the quiet record which I put on in an attempt to dispel the tension in the room. He did not seem to notice the choice of his favourite food, or the wine, which he drank fast and desperately. I had no inkling of what was really wrong. Until the next morning.

The post was early. He brought it as usual to the breakfast table, two for me, two for himself. I saw him turn one of the envelopes over and over, puzzled, as though not recognising the hand. I kept my eyes on my plate. He had slept badly, tossing and turning and getting up at least twice in the night and I had hoped that the coming of the morning might persuade him to confide in me. But no.

He picked up his knife and slid it into the envelope. He pulled out a sheet of pale blue paper and read it slowly. I sipped my coffee.

He put the letter back into the envelope without comment and tucked it into the newspaper beside his plate. Then he drank his own coffee and rose, glancing at his watch as usual. 'I must go Janet. Usual time tonight, darling.' He smiled, a strained, absent smile and picked up the newspaper to put it in his briefcase.

The letter fell out of it to the floor unnoticed and I said nothing. Had I, even then, instinctively guessed what was in it?

My Darling Derek, it said in a loopy, so very feminine hand. ***I am so sorry that I misunderstood what you wanted. I truly thought it would make you happy. Please forgive me. We have had such a lovely two years together*** – Two years! – ***and I love you so much. I could not bear it to end like this. I want very badly to keep the baby, but I promise I will make no claim on you now or in the future. Just love us a little, and keep in touch. You will have my love always, Tina.***

I put the letter carefully back into the envelope and only then did I notice that it said *Private* on the top left-hand corner.

It was my own ignorance which hurt most. The fact that I had trusted and believed and been proved naïve. I poured myself another cup of coffee, my hand shaking so much I slopped it on the table cloth. Then as I sipped it I felt a sudden constriction in my stomach. I set down the cup with a crash. I was shivering suddenly and there was no doubt at all, I was going to be sick. And I was already late for my train.

The Inheritance

LOOKING DOWN at her empty cup Jacqueline fixed her attention with determination on the muddy dregs in the bottom; she had made up her mind it would not be right to show any emotion at all when her turn came. Out of the corner of her eye she saw her mother's hand beginning to shake as she opened the letter and the sight unnerved her. The solicitor's letter held no surprises for Mrs Percival of course; she knew exactly what she had inherited. Her hand was probably shaking because the letter had reminded her of her own mother's death and Jacqueline could tell from the strained expression and the two white dimples beneath her cheekbones that her mother was determined not to cry.

'This letter concerns you three.' She looked up at her children and sniffed. Then she smiled wanly. 'I hope you'll be pleased. Great-Grandma has left you all something. Debbie, you and Greg, you each get five thousand pounds.' She glanced at each of the twins in turn. 'That's a lot of money,' she added unnecessarily. 'And you must be careful what you do with it.'

Debbie and Greg stared at her open-mouthed, then Greg let out a whoop of delight. 'I can get that new racing bike at last.' He launched himself from behind his plate of scrambled eggs and planted a kiss on his mother's head. Debbie seemed to have been struck dumb. She sat there with a glazed look on her face and then slowly began to crumble a piece of toast between her fingers onto the table cloth.

Once again Jacqueline began to gaze earnestly into the depths of her coffee cup. She swallowed. She was by a long way the eldest, and had been the acknowledged favourite.

She closed her eyes and breathed deeply as her mother chose that moment to set the letter down amongst the plates and empty cups and sticky knives and blow her nose. Then she glanced up. It came almost as an afterthought. 'Granny has left you her clock, Jackie, of course.'

Jacqueline waited expectantly.

Her father at last emerged from behind the paper. He refolded it noisily and glanced down at his watch. 'Come on, twins; I'll drop you off at school if you're quick. Jackie, you're going to be late for work again.' He stood up, obviously unmoved by the news; perhaps he hadn't heard it at all; dropped an absent-minded kiss on his wife's hair and strode from the room, followed by his two younger children, who were trying with scant success to keep the triumph out of their faces.

Jacqueline sat where she was, her eyes fixed on the letter. Her mother hadn't picked it up again. Her mother was standing up. She had begun to stack the plates.

'Come on, Jackie; get a move on. You heard your father.' She was bustling; efficient; trying to make up for the blown nose.

'Is that all?' Jacqueline's voice came out at last, strangled.

'Is what all, dear? Come on, come on.' Mrs Percival had swept the letter away and thrown it on the dresser.

'The clock. Don't *I* get any money?' She knew it was a dreadful thing to say. Swallowing guiltily she stood up.

As expected her mother turned on her. 'All? All! That clock was your great-grandmother's most treasured possession! She adored that clock!' She burst suddenly into a storm of noisy tears.

'I know.' Jacqueline was anguished. 'I'm sorry; I don't mean to be ungrateful; it's just that I hoped – well, I hoped for some money like the twins. Then I could pay for the modelling course and give up that job with Mr Grenside . . .' Her voice tailed away as she saw her mother's lips tighten into their accustomed thin line.

Mrs Percival groped for her handkerchief once more. 'Oh Jackie, can't you get that ridiculous idea out of your head. Your father and I must have told you a hundred times. You've got a good job with Grenside. It's solid and respectable and it's well-paid. Modelling is so insecure. It's not the glamorous life you think, really it isn't. I wish you wouldn't keep mentioning it.'

Jacqueline knew better than to argue. She turned and disconsolately began to shrug herself into her coat. It wasn't as if she had expected any money in the will at all; none of them had. But in the glorious few minutes between hearing of the twins' bequest and her own she had known real, ecstatic hope. For a moment she toyed with the idea of trying to borrow the money from the twins, then she shrugged it aside. There wouldn't be a chance.

When the clock was at last delivered Jacqueline retired with the brown paper parcel to the privacy of her bedroom and sat down with it on the bed. She remembered the clock clearly. It had always sat in its battered leather case on the chest of drawers in her great-grandmother's bedroom, surrounded by sewing boxes and bags of old stockings and patent medicine bottles. The white face, startlingly clear and precise in the surround of scratched red morocco through which it peered, had seemed to her to be insufferably pompous. 'That's my most treasured possession.' Great-Granny's voice echoed back to her as she began to fumble with the string. 'That clock is a little beauty. It belonged to my grandfather you know, and one day it will belong to you Jacqueline, as you're the eldest.'

Jacqueline patiently coaxed the string from the parcel into a neat coil and dropped it on her bedside table. Of course, ever since she could remember Granny had been saying that. Most of the family things would go to Mum and then probably to Greg, just because he was the boy, but the clock would come to her.

She removed the paper and threw it on the floor and there was the clock, its face as prim as ever, peering from the case. For once it was wrong. Its hands had stopped together at midday – or was it midnight? Gazing at it Jacqueline wondered suddenly if it had stopped the moment Great-Granny died, never-to-go-again.

'It keeps perfect time, that clock. Perfect time.' Her great-grandmother's voice sounded in her ears.

Taped inside the case was an envelope. Inside was a key.

So all it needed was winding.

She smiled at the clock and then child-like, stuck her tongue out at it. 'Supposing I never wind you up again. You wouldn't be so smug then.'

She put it on her own chest of drawers and instantly was reminded of the rather sour old-people smell of her great-grandmother's bedroom. Her own began to take on a different look. All it needed was the thick stockings and the bottles of linctus. Shuddering she picked it up. Immediately the room became itself again.

Eventually she wedged it into a gap between some books on one of her shelves. It held them upright nicely.

She never gave it another thought until she knocked her alarm clock off the bedside table. She shook it hopefully and was rewarded with an ominous rattle; no tick. She dropped it off at the jeweller on her way to work and that evening pulled Great-Granny's clock from its position between Dylan Thomas and Jilly Cooper. She blew off the dust. It wouldn't have an alarm of course, but with a noisy twin on either side of her she didn't really need one.

She pulled the envelope off and took out the key. Surprisingly it was exquisitely chased gilt. Tiny and delicate.

Gingerly she undid the leather case. Inside, the clock nestled down into a velvet lining, its gilt handle folded neatly down on a glass top. Gripping it, she lifted the clock out of its case and sat it on her bedside table beside her lamp.

She looked at it for a long time.

The gilt winked and glittered in the lamplight, untarnished and perfect. All round the sides and corners the clock was decorated with a tiny glittering inlay of coloured enamels, and around the face was a ring of minute diamonds. It was exquisite. Inside, through the glass panels at the top and round the sides, she could see the intricate details of the movement which gleamed like gold. Liberated from its case at long last the white ivory of the face no longer looked prim. It was beautiful.

With a shaking hand Jacqueline fitted the key into one of the two holes at the back and began to wind. The tick was surprisingly loud for such a small clock. She put the key into the other hole, expecting it to move the hands, and the clock chimed; a delicate silvery chime followed by twelve mellow velvet notes.

The clock was alive and she was enchanted.

She kept glancing at it as she changed from her office skirt into her jeans. Then she knelt down beside it and rested her finger lightly on the glass top. It vibrated with energy.

It was a long while before she called the rest of the family.

'In all the years I remember that clock I've never seen it without its case,' her mother exclaimed. 'No wonder your great-grandmother made such a fuss about it.'

'It's lovely, Jackie, you lucky thing.' For the first time Greg seemed to have a moment's regret about his share in the bequest, over which he had not stopped crowing unkindly.

'Are those real diamonds?' Debbie had fallen to her knees before it to get a better view as it stood on the low table. 'Oh Jackie, it's lovely. Why on earth have you left it so long to take it out of its case?'

'That clock must be worth a fortune, Jackie,' her father commented, frowning. 'I suppose we ought to see about getting it insured. Unless you want to sell it, of course?' He glanced at her and winked. 'I reckon that would pay a good bit towards that course you were hankering after.' He grinned.

'Roger!' Mrs Percival turned on him. 'How could you suggest such a thing. Sell grandmother's clock! Of course she wouldn't. I've never heard such nonsense. She must keep it forever.' She sat down heavily on the bed and groped for her handkerchief. 'It's the most beautiful thing I've ever seen.' She sniffed. 'And to think that none of us realised . . .'

The modelling course. Jacqueline looked at the clock and then at her father.

'How can we find out what it's worth?' Her heart was beating with excitement.

'I can take it up to town with me on Wednesday. I should think I could find someone to give me a rough idea.' He leaned forward and picked it up. 'Pretty thing. But better sold, I'd say, if it's worth anything.'

It was worth a great deal. The jeweller to whom he showed it respectfully mentioned Sotheby's or Christie's and padded the clock with several layers of corrugated cardboard before allowing Mr Percival to carry it home. Once there, through tact or natural caution, he said nothing to his wife, waiting for his daughter to come in.

Jacqueline went straight to her room, flinging the curtains shut and turning on the light and gas fire before beginning to unbutton her dress. She was in her dressing gown when her father knocked on the door.

'It's more money than one could ever hope to be handed, Jackie,' he said quietly, after he had told her. They sat side by side on the bed, gazing at the clock, as with a small important series of clicks and whirrs it prepared to strike the hour.

'It's the most beautiful and valuable thing I've ever owned.'

Wistfully Jackie pulled her dressing gown closer round her.

'It would buy you that course, Jackie, and leave you a nest egg to put in the bank.' Mr Percival put his arm round her. 'I know how much you've wanted to have a go at modelling, love. I think you deserve the chance. You've got a lovely figure and face. You've got what it takes, I'm sure of it.' He smiled at her fondly.

'Mummy doesn't think so; she's always been dead against it.' She frowned.

'Your mother's a sensible woman. She knows how much hard slog and possible heartache is involved.' He got up and, with his back to the fire, he stood looking down at her. 'She's wanted to save you from disappointment, Jackie, and I agree, up to a point. But,' he sighed. 'There's another way of looking at it. After all, faint heart never won fair lady, and all that.'

Jackie smiled at him fondly. 'You think I should have a go?'

'I think you'll wonder for the rest of your life if you could have been a cover girl if you don't. Better know, one way or the other.'

Jacqueline stared at the clock. There was a strange lump in her throat. 'The awful thing is,' she said suddenly, 'I can't bear the idea of selling it.'

'No. It's a beautiful thing, certainly.'

'I collected my alarm clock today.' She dived into her bag and brought out a box. She stood the clock up beside her bed. 'It works now; it's accurate. It only cost a couple of pounds to mend. It has an alarm. It's really much more useful in every way . . .'

Mr Percival smiled. 'But it doesn't have a pretty chime and glitter with diamonds, eh?'

'Oh Daddy, I don't know what to do. If I sell the clock I'll have the money, yes. But supposing I am a lousy model? It would be such a waste. I could never buy another clock like that.'

Mr Percival rubbed his chin thoughtfully.

'As I see it there's no easy way to decide, love. I know what I'd do. I'd sell. I know what your mother would do. She'd keep it for sentimental reasons. And she'd keep it even if she were half starving.' He shook his head slowly. 'But there's no real hurry, is there? If I were you I'd think about it for a while.'

Jacqueline sat on the bed gazing at the clock for a long time after he had gone downstairs.

For half an hour she thought, listening as twice the clock chimed the quarters; then slowly she reached under her pillow for the magazine. It was folded back as always at the modelling school's advertisement. *For further particulars, write to. . .*

There was no harm in writing. After all, it didn't commit her to anything, did it? Carefully she filled in her name and address. Then, hungry, she turned out the light and went downstairs.

Dance Little Lady

THE YACHT was in the bay again, anchored off the point, as I had hoped she might be. For a moment I forgot the need to hurry as I stood at the tall bay window of my bedroom and stared at it, hugging my dressing gown around me. The breeze off the sea touched my skin and I shivered. I was thinking about the evening to come.

'Only a few people this weekend, darling,' Sylvia had said anxiously as she met me off the train. 'It won't be too tiring.'

It is strange how solicitous some people are when they know you are recovering from a broken love affair; as if you had been ill. Except that I was the one who had broken it off, because for me it had never really existed. I was grateful, though, for her gentleness. I liked the woman my father lived with, even though I hated my father. It was because of her I still came home. Her, and the money my father paid for my London flat.

I turned reluctantly from the window. My hopes of a quiet weekend, swimming and sailing on my own while I thought things out, were gone. Instead the weekend had to be endured. But somehow the presence of the yacht, out there on the water, comforted me. I had seen her there several times that summer, always with the same man on board. I had surreptitiously studied him through binoculars. He was tall, fair and tanned. The opposite of Ben.

Dear Ben. I was still fond of him in spite of all the things he had called me. Perhaps he was right; perhaps I was immature and frigid; perhaps I did live in a dream world – my fantasy about the skipper of that white yacht rather proved that – but was it so very terrible to reject the cynicism and world weariness that people like Ben, and my father, wore round them like a cloak? I was sure the man out on that yacht was different; an independent spirit.

My father's guests were assembled in the drawing room when I went down. The only car I had recognised when Sylvia brought me home had been my brother David's Alfa and I saw him now with two other men by the open French windows. Sylvia was by the sideboard; with her was David's wife, Betinne. My heart sank. I loathed my sister-in-law.

She looked me up and down as I accepted a glass of champagne from Sylvia. 'I hear Ben ditched you, Anna,' she said. 'I can't say I'm surprised.' She sipped her own drink. 'Don must be relieved though, if it means you can dance attendance on his guests.' She managed to make her words sound suggestive.

I saw Sylvia frown, but I didn't want her to defend me. I hastily turned to look round the room. 'Where is Father? I haven't seen him yet.'

'Don is next door. With Parker Forbes,' Sylvia said quietly.

'*The* Parker Forbes,' Betinne emphasised. She was still watching me with a rather strange look in her eye.

Parker Forbes; the multi-millionaire; owner of half the West End of London. My father had been trying to pin him down to a deal for ages and his name had been the most frequent topic of conversation at weekends for months.

Sylvia was eyeing me anxiously. 'I think you'll like him, Anna. He's very attractive. And he likes music.'

Suddenly I understood. The urgent invitation home; the sudden concern over my welfare; the interest in my break-up with Ben. And I had thought Sylvia was on my side!

Once before my father had done this; he had invited a

colleague home and then proceeded to throw me at him for the entire weekend. I had been younger then, and more naïve. The man had taken pity on me; laughed at my gaucheness, and signed anyway. But I had a feeling Parker Forbes was different. His reputation had percolated through even to my particular corner of the College of Music.

I turned away without a word, conscious of their eyes following me as, sickened, I crossed the room towards David. I should have walked away then, but I knew my brother would cushion my shyness as he always did and sure enough he reached out and pulled me close for a hug. 'Anna, how's the college? I don't see enough of you these days,' and he introduced me to his two companions.

David was the only person in that house who knew me as I really was; who knew me in London, in my own world, away from father's wealth and the shallow pleasure-seeking life he led. In London I had my own career with music. Ben had almost bridged those two worlds but something had gone wrong. I eyed the two men standing with us. They were typical of father's colleagues; wealthy, brash, hard-drinking, laughing a little too much – and I sighed. The whole weekend to be got through.

I did not meet the other guests until dinner. Melanie Whittacker, the wife of one of David's companions, was a strangely mousey woman; quiet, cowed I suspected by her boorish husband. I was immediately sorry for her. With her were two other women: Naomi who I gathered was a model and Jane Peters. The final two guests were Robin Hamilton, the journalist – and Parker Forbes.

Robin sat opposite me. He was a tall, attractive man, tanned, fit, charming – the kind of man who makes every woman instantly aware of him, and knows it. Betinne was hanging on his every word as he regaled her and Melanie Whittacker with a stream of scandalous gossip, but I got the feeling that he did not reciprocate her enthusiasm. Once, looking up, he caught my eye over the glow of the candles and I was almost sure he winked. I felt a quick thrill of pleasure and was instantly furious with myself.

I had no chance to think about it, though, as my attention was once more drawn back to my father and Parker Forbes.

'You must get Anna to take you out onto the terrace later, Parker,' my father was saying for the second time. 'Let her show you our Sussex moon . . .'

I couldn't believe that he could be so blatant! I glanced desperately round for David, but he was talking at the other end of the table. There was nothing I could do except smile and nod and pretend that I agreed.

And I was still pretending half an hour later when Parker edged me towards the French windows and we stepped out with our coffee cups in our hands, into the velvet night. It was heavenly to get away from the hot cigar smoke and fumes of the wine. The sea air was balmy, softened with honeysuckle and the sweetness of new-mown hay.

He wasted no time. 'I had no idea that Don had such a beautiful home,' he murmured. We had paused at the edge of the terrace looking down across the lawn towards the sea which I could hear sighing gently against the rocks. 'And such charming ladies too. How long has he known Sylvia?'

'A couple of years,' I replied. Sylvia was the latest, and by far the nicest, of the succession of girlfriends my father had lived with since my mother had left him ten years before. Ma now lived with a horse breeder in Argentina. I never blamed her for going. My father had always been a ruthless, selfish bastard. I only wished I had had the strength of character and the courage to turn my back on him as well.

Parker and I began to walk again, slowly this time, towards the summer house which Sylvia had had perched on the top of the low cliff. I could feel the dew beginning to soak through my thin sandals and dragging at the hem of my skirt. Somewhere near a gull called in the night.

'Do you like her?' he asked curiously. He still hadn't looked at me.

'Very much,' I answered.

'I imagine she takes a lot of work off your hands. Don told me you used to act as his hostess.'

I laughed uneasily. 'I was never very good at it I'm afraid.'

'I can't believe that.' His voice was caressing. 'In fact, had I know what a welcome his house would have for me I would have been doing business with Don months ago.'

He turned to look at me, a long appraising glance which swept slowly up and down me leaving me feeling naked and self-conscious, then he took the cup out of my hand and put it down on the step of the summer house with his own. He was much taller than I, and powerfully built, and as his hands came down on my shoulders pulling me towards him I felt a surge of real fear.

'Mind if I join you?' As the cool, deep voice from the darkness interrupted us Parker released me abruptly and turned, his face set and angry. The journalist Robin Hamilton strolled towards us, the glowing butt of a cigar in his hand. He stopped, and stood looking at the view about three feet from me. 'You must not catch cold, Anna,' he said quietly. 'That dress is soaking, dragging in the dew.'

'You're right.' I could have kissed him from sheer relief. 'Excuse me, Parker, but I think I will go in.'

I didn't wait to see Parker's face. I flew towards the lights of the house.

My father cornered me ten minutes later. His handsome face was harsh.

'Anna? I thought you were looking after Parker?'

I liked the looking after bit! 'I was. I came in.' I faced him. 'I'm not going to let him make passes at me, Don, just to make him more amenable to your schemes. The man is detestable!'

My father's face darkened visibly. 'And you don't like it? What the hell are you, Anna, a twelve-year-old virgin? For God's sake grow up. Do you realise what Parker's signature on that agreement means to me?' We were standing in the corner of the dining room where I had been finding myself some more coffee and we were alone, but with a glance over his shoulder towards the open door into the hall, he dropped his voice to an ugly whisper.

'You be nice to Parker, Anna. You hear me? Everyone in this house pulls their weight and if they don't they're out, understand?' He stared at me for a full twenty seconds then he swung on his heel and left me alone in the room.

Mechanically I finished filling my cup and carried it over to the window seat. But the drink stayed untouched as I gazed at the coloured reflections in the glass.

The sound of the door closing behind me made me turn. It was Betinne. 'I saw Don leave you,' she said softly. 'He looked livid. What did he say?'

'Is that your business?' I snapped.

Her face was flushed and had a predatory excitement about it. 'It is if it involves Parker.' She stepped nearer. 'He wants to sleep with you doesn't he? He couldn't keep his eyes off you at dinner. I was watching. Doesn't Don like the idea?'

'You know very well what Don wants,' I retorted.

Betinne came and stood very close to me. 'And little miss pure pants doesn't like the idea?' she breathed scornfully.

'Would you?' I blazed at her and then suddenly I saw. The wide grey eyes, the large deep pupils gazing at me, the naked hunger in them. 'You would, wouldn't you?' I answered my own question quietly. 'You would sleep with him.'

'Sleep with him,' she echoed sarcastically. 'Of course I'd sleep with him; I'd do anything he wanted. Have you any idea how much money that man has? How much power?'

We stared at each other for a moment. I felt sick.

'Poor David,' I said at last.

'Leave David out of this!' she hissed viciously.

'Well you obviously have,' I retorted. 'Look Betinne. If you want Parker Forbes then you have him. Don will no doubt be delighted as long as some woman in this family nets him. But count me out. Please!'

I pushed past her, my cheeks flaming with heat, and let myself into the hall just as Robin Hamilton came back from the garden. I saw him look at me swiftly then glance over my shoulder into the dining room. Then he grinned. 'Hi. I hope you didn't mind me interrupting you out there.'

'You saved my life,' I said with rather more vehemence than I meant. 'That is –'

'I understand,' he said, laughing quietly. 'You needn't explain.' He hesitated. 'Your sister-in-law looked pretty heated in there.'

'She was.' I had no intention of telling Robin Hamilton, or anyone else for that matter, what I had quarrelled with Betinne about, but his presence soothed me as we went into the drawing room where the Whittackers were seated with my father and David. The four of them were laughing. My father looked up and I saw his glance harden as it swept over us. Then he stared out towards the terrace. Following his look I saw Sylvia out there with Parker. As I watched Betinne joined them.

The next day dawned hot and beautiful. After breakfast most of the house party collected towels and broad-brimmed hats and beach bags and headed for the rustic flight of steps which led down the cliff to our private beach. To my intense irritation Parker sat down beside me. He grinned.

'Pity we were interrupted last night, Anna. I was going to suggest a midnight bathe perhaps; an assignation under the stars? I tried your door later. Why do you lock it?' He was speaking in a low confidential voice but I could see Robin watching me, a quizzical expression on his face.

'Because I need my beauty sleep,' I managed to retort with a smile. I could feel my skin crawling as he leaned towards me and put his hand on my ankle, stroking it gently. His palm was damp.

I moved away a little and it was then that my father's shadow fell across us. 'I hope my daughter is entertaining you, Parker,' he said softly. 'We aim to keep our guests happy, don't we Anna?'

I looked up and at that moment I felt real loathing for my father but I was still so conditioned by my upbringing, by what we are taught are good manners, that I merely smiled stiffly. 'Of course,' I said. I wriggled out of Parker's reach and jumped to my feet. 'We aim to please always, don't we Don?' I ran towards the water. 'Come on Parker. Let's swim!'

The water was ice cold. Parker did not move. It was Robin who followed me, pacing me easily as I made for the raft which was anchored about fifty yards off the beach. He grabbed it as I pulled myself up onto it, and looked up at me.

'He can't get you here, eh?' He shook the water out of his eyes, laughing. We both glanced towards the beach where Betinne, oiled and sleek, had taken my place on the rug beside Parker.

'My father – ' I stopped abruptly, biting off the words. I had been about to confide in him; about to tell him what my father was doing, but something stopped me. Robin was a journalist after all. And who could resist the kind of headline my story could generate?

Robin grinned. 'Stand up for yourself, kiddo,' he said quietly. 'You're a free agent, remember?'

He gave me a long searching look, then he dived and was swimming back towards the beach. Robin Hamilton, I thought, knows exactly what is going on. And I had a feeling he was on my side. I watched him reach the shore and wade out of the water to grab a towel. He was extremely handsome as well as being nice and I found myself wishing suddenly that he was the one my father wanted me to seduce! The thought made me smile to myself. If Ben knew what had crossed my mind he would not have believed it. Physically Ben and I had not been a success; perhaps that was because any man to whom my father introduced me was suspect.

Beyond Robin, I saw Betinne roll over onto her stomach

and reach behind her to unhook her bikini top, cushioning her heavy breasts in the sand. It would only be a matter of minutes before Parker would be asked to oil her back. I almost envied her her casual sensuality. But Ben was right after all. I did not seem to know how to let myself go. Or was it that I had not yet met the right man? Almost unconsciously I found my eyes searching once more for Robin, then with a sigh I shifted round so that I could lie and watch the sea. The yacht was still there, her dinghy lying astern. I could see two brightly coloured towels fluttering from the rigging. If I was really a free agent, I thought ruefully, I would have been out there in my own little sailing dinghy thumbing a lift out of Don's world forever. But I didn't have the courage, then.

The heat was building. We ate a cold luncheon in the shade of the cedars on the lawn and then the guests drifted off towards their rooms for a siesta. I followed suit.

My bedroom was shaded by the soft pink curtains and I slipped out of my sundress to lie naked on the cool sheets thankful to be out of that blazing sun. Two seconds later I got up. I had forgotten to lock the door. I ran across the carpet and reached to turn the key, but it had gone. Puzzled I searched for it on the carpet, thinking it had fallen out, then I opened the door and groped for it on the outside. It wasn't there either.

As I stood there, not wanting to believe the suspicion which had flashed through my mind, I heard another door open in the corridor.

I grabbed my bathrobe off the chair and was knotting it around me as my door began to move.

Parker was wearing a navy and maroon striped silk dressing gown and a great deal of cologne, and, I was fairly sure, not much else. He came in and closed the door behind him, then triumphantly he felt in his pocket and produced the key. Locking the door he turned to me and grinned.

'Don said he hoped we'd get to know each other better

this afternoon,' he said softly. 'What do you say we give it a try?'

There was no fear or revulsion in me this time. As he walked towards me and put his hands on my shoulders as he had done before I felt nothing but white hot anger. His strength was enormous as he pushed me back against the wall but he wasn't expecting me to give more than a token resistance. As his mouth closed over mine I brought my knee up into his groin with all the force I could muster, my fingers clawing for his eyes. Then I dived for the door, fumbling desperately with the key.

Behind me he was doubled up, groaning. He made no attempt to follow me as I fled down the hall, but instinctively I made for the attics where I used to hide as a child, knowing that no one would find me in that network of old interconnecting lofts.

I stayed there a long time. It was hot under the roof and smelled of wood and dust and it was completely safe, but I knew I would have to come down eventually, if only to catch the last train back to London. There was no way I was going to spend another night in my father's house. Ever!

It was only the sound of the gong in the distance which made me realise how late it really was. Cautiously I went down at last. The house was deathly quiet; when I peered into my room it was deserted and the key was still in the door. Thankfully I went in and locked it, then I had a slower and lay down on my bed, trying to think.

It was Sylvia who came. 'Anna?' She knocked gently. 'Anna? Are you there?'

I got up and let her in. 'I'm not coming down,' I said defiantly. 'I have a terrible headache.'

I could see her eyes on me and there was real concern in her face. I wondered if Parker had said anything. On the whole I suspected not. It would not do his image much good if it became known that one of his victims had fought back. And won.

'Anna dear.' She sat down on the bed. 'I'm sorry. I know what you must be thinking; your father is a little insensitive at times.' She was looking lovely in a silvery evening dress which showed her tan. 'Please come down.'

'I really do have a headache,' I said. 'The weather is so thundery. I'll be all right in the morning.' I refused to meet her eye.

She sighed and stood up. 'I'll ask them to bring something up for you, shall I?'

When she had gone I relocked the door and went to stand by the window. There was no breath of air and, I realised suddenly, it was true: my head was splitting but I was still determined to go. I would drive myself to the station in my old Mini. I left it at the house during the week as it seemed pointless to keep it in London, but it would then get me to the train. And it would give me time to lie down for an hour, to let my head clear.

I was about to go back to bed when there was a furious knocking. It was my father. 'Anna, open this door at once!'

I obeyed him, waiting defiantly as he strode into the room. 'What the hell have you done?' he shouted. 'Parker is threatening to leave the house!'

'I warned you, Don.' For the first time in my life I wasn't afraid of him. I saw him for what he was, a ranting, bullying, weak man, terrified of failure. 'If Parker wanted your deal nothing would stop him signing,' I said, and I realised it was true. 'If he's looking for an excuse to back out it is because he has no faith in you, not because I refused to sleep with him.'

My father's face was puce.

'If you are determined that one of your family should prostitute herself for you then ask Betinne. She's more than willing,' I went on. 'I'm going back to London tonight.'

My father controlled himself with an effort. 'You are not. You are going to apologise to Parker. I don't know what happened between you but my God Anna you are going to apologise.'

His gaze swept across my dressing table where my handbag stood open. He dived for it, rifling through the contents. 'You needn't think you're going to creep out of this house. You're staying here until I tell you to go.'

Speechless, I watched him stride from the room and slam the door behind him. For one incredulous moment I thought he was going to lock me in, but I heard his steps move off down the hall. I ran to my bag and stared into it. He had taken my money, my return ticket and my car keys.

I sat down on the bed. My legs were shaking, and I was more angry, I think, than I have ever been in my life. I was more or less a prisoner.

I suppose I slept at last from sheer exhaustion, but when I next opened my eyes my headache had gone and the room was growing dark, and I could hear the sound of voices and laughter outside my window. I got up and went to look out. The dinner guests were all out on the terrace below me with their drinks. I counted them slowly. No one was missing; Betinne was talking to Parker in the corner by the wisteria. I saw the gleam of gold around her throat as she laughed up at him. Nearby I could see my father. He was watching them intently.

The yacht lay quite still on a sea which looked like oiled silk. The dinghy was gone. He must have come ashore, probably to the pub on the quay in the village a mile down the coast. I could see the reflection of the boat wavering gently below her. Beyond her, the arms of the bay had become indistinct in the darkening haze. Great black clouds were building in the distance and I heard a faint rumble of thunder as I turned from the window. I had awakened knowing exactly what I meant to do.

I slipped some jeans and a T-shirt on and pulled on some rope-soled espadrilles, then I let myself out into the empty corridor. If my father thought to keep me in his house till Parker came for me that night he was mistaken. I had other ideas. The kitchens were deserted; the staff had tidied up and retired as usual as soon as they had finished clearing away dinner so I was able to let myself out into the yard unnoticed. My old bicycle was still there – the tyres didn't even need pumping.

It took me ten minutes to reach the quay. I leaned the bike against the wall and peered down into the water. It was moving gently in a subdued swell as in the distance I heard another faint rumble of thunder.

I walked down to the end of the jetty where several small dinghies were tied, and carefully lowering myself into one of them, undid the painter and felt for the oars. I was awkward with them at first, out of practice and, I must confess, a little panicky when I saw the door of the pub open and the light flood out over the water as three figures walked down to the edge of the quay. I was expecting to hear angry shouts at any moment, but none came. I settled down to a steady pull, glancing over my shoulder to make sure I was heading in the right direction as I felt the drag of the tide. I think I was a little mad, that night; I would never dare to do such a thing again. But at that moment I felt no fear, only excitement and a sense of incredible freedom. The fear only came when it was too late to do anything about it.

My hands were blistered before I was half-way there, but I gritted my teeth against the pain and went on. I think if I had stopped for a rest my nerve would have failed, but always out of the corner of my eye I could see the blaze of lights on the cliff which was my father's home. The sight of it spurred me on.

There was a ladder over the side. I grabbed it, shaking with exhaustion, and pulled myself up onto the deck. Behind me, the dinghy tossed like a cork without my weight to steady it, bumped its way down the white side of the yacht, and then disappeared into the darkness. I watched it go with an almost detached relief. Now I could not go back if I wanted to; I was marooned.

I turned and made my way down into the cockpit. The main hatch had been left half open and I peered down into the darkened cabin, cursing myself for not thinking of bringing a torch. I knew he had light – I had seen it flooding from the portholes in the dark, but I didn't want to draw attention to myself too soon. I stepped down into the companionway and held my breath, listening, wondering for the first time what I would do if he had left someone on board, but the boat was silent. Uncannily silent save for the occasional gurgle and slap of water down her sides and once more an ominous growl of thunder in the west.

I reached out, feeling my way forward, and my hand found a rack just inside the hatchway; amongst the charts was a large rubber-cased torch. I switched it on and the beam of light flooded the cabin.

She was a beautiful yacht, fitted out to sleep five, with two main cabins, a shower cubicle, a galley and a forward sail locker which was large enough for the fifth bunk. The whole boat was immaculately tidy, everything stowed neatly into place, a chart already fixed to the chart table. Above me a halyard had begun to tap against the mast and I felt the floor beneath me move a little as a wave slide beneath the hull. The wind was rising.

I went out into the cockpit and, switching off the torch, looked around. The sky was black now – black with cloud that blotted out the moon and stars, leaving only the riding light at the masthead showing as the boat began to turn and tug at her anchor. I strained my eyes in the direction of the shore and then I saw it – the outline of his dinghy already half-way out towards the boat, the white dip of the oars showing against the black water.

My heart gave a sudden little kick of fright and I turned to go back into the cabin. My nerve had failed at last and I found myself desperately looking round for somewhere to hide. It wasn't a logical decision; the sensible thing would have been to show myself at once, and if he was angry ask him to put me ashore, but I was no longer thinking logically. The anger which had sent me flying from Don's house, the thundery air pressing down on the boat, my aching head and bleeding hands and the image of Parker, his aroused body naked beneath his dressing gown as he pushed me against the wall, all combined to reduce me to a frightened animal and like a frightened animal I looked for a dark corner to hide in. The quarter berth was the obvious place – the berth opposite the chart table which was half settee but which slotted down under the cockpit, so the sleeper could insert his legs to obtain a full-length bed. I wriggled down into that space now, relieved to find it quite roomy, and pulled the two berth cushions behind me, blocking me from sight. Unless he actually moved those cushions I could not be seen. It was an uncomfortable position. I could not sit up nor stretch out, I had to lie curled up in the darkness, listening to the beating of my heart above the slap of the water on the other side of the thin planking by my ear.

There was a slight lurch as the dinghy came alongside and I heard the thud of rubber soles almost immediately above my head. Minutes later the cabin was flooded with light; the cushions were not after all big enough to block me in entirely and I shrank back, praying he would not notice that they had been moved.

'Check everything's stowed and put out those lights as soon as you can. I want to save the battery.' His voice was so close I thought for a moment he must know I was there and be talking to me. I held my breath. He spoke with a distinct public school accent, but the voice was already moving as his footsteps ran over the deck. Someone else was in the cabin near me. I bit my lip, not daring to move, wondering who was with him. I had never seen anyone on the yacht besides him.

A female voice, husky, attractive and American, called out, 'Pete? Surely we can wait till morning. That guy in the pub said there was a gale warning, and I sure as hell don't like the sound of that thunder.'

The footsteps approached once more. 'Not afraid are you, Sam?' His tone, from the cockpit now, was mocking. 'I thought you told me you were prepared to risk everything to get your hands on that much dope. You shouldn't have got involved if you couldn't take the pace. The pick-up is arranged. And I'm going to make it. If you want out, you can swim for it.' His tone made the hairs stand up on the back of my neck.

The girl swore softly. 'Okay, okay. I guess you know what you're doing.'

Minutes later the lights went out and I heard the hatchway close. I was trapped and very afraid. Independent spirit this man might be; there was no doubt he was also potentially very dangerous and I cursed myself miserably. But there was no way of escape.

My hiding place was growing uncomfortably hot; I eased my position slightly and moved one of the cushions to give me some air; then I heard the roar and clap of loosened canvas overhead as the main sail was hauled up. Minutes later the thundering stopped as the sails filled, the yacht listed sideways and from my point of view downwards, and we were obviously on course out of the bay. She hit a heavy swell as soon as we were clear of the headland and the noise of the sea became deafening. In despair I cradled my head as best I could in the crook of my elbow and closed my eyes, trying hard to concentrate on anything other than what was happening to me. A long time later I heard the hatchway being slid back and the lights came on in the cabin. Above my head I could hear the drumming of rain on the decks.

'Coffee or soup?' I heard the woman's voice call. I did not catch the response, only the roar of the wind and waves, and suddenly very loud above them the crash of thunder.

The boat seemed to be slamming hard into wind and I could see the woman now as she made her way up the cabin towards the galley, clinging on to every handhold she could find. She was wearing dripping yellow oilskins, but her head was bare – her hair was long and blonde. She slid back the galley door and wedged herself in the corner whilst she fumbled with matches and locked a kettle into place on the gimballed cooker. The roar and smell of the bottled gas flame and the lights in the cabin were strangely comforting against that terrible background noise of the elements. I studied her face from my hiding place, trying to pluck up the courage to come out and throw myself on her mercy. She looked as though she was in her mid-twenties, although her face was strained and drawn and there were dark circles beneath her eyes. She did not look particularly sympathetic. On the whole I was not hopeful.

She stayed with the kettle until it boiled, then she made two mugs of coffee.

'Pete?' she yelled. 'Come and have it down here!'

There was no response. With a sigh she drank one of the mags, pulled up the hood of her oilskin and came back towards the hatchway. 'Come on Pete, I'll take a turn while you have a break,' she called, and she vanished out of my line of vision.

I held my breath as another figure appeared. He too was dressed in dripping oilskins, but he peeled his off, leaving them lying on the cabin floor. Dressed in a sweater and jeans he was, as I had seen through my binoculars, tall, rugged, fairly good-looking with, I now saw, sun-bleached hair and piercing blue eyes; his face like hers was hard and he had a deep frown on his brow. He pulled his way up to the galley just as the woman had done and collected his mug, then to my terror he came back and sat on the quarter berth only about eighteen inches from my head. He only had to glance my way – I froze, holding my breath as he sipped from the mug and then leaned forward gazing intently at something ahead of him. The chart table of course.

He worked for some time, making careful measurements and calculations, then at last he threw down his pencil, and leaned back. With a grunt of surprise he felt around behind him for the cushions which should have been there, then he turned and looked straight at me.

For a moment I don't think he believed what he saw; then I saw his face darken with anger.

'Who in the name of God's own Hell are you?' he whispered. He didn't give me a chance to extricate myself from my hiding place with any dignity. He lunged forward and grabbed my arm, pulling me headlong onto the floor of the cabin where I lay for a moment at his feet, too winded and too stiff to move.

'Well? I asked you a question!' he yelled at me again.

'I'm sorry,' I heard myself stammer. 'I'm so sorry. I did it for a joke.'

'A joke!' His voice rose in anger.

Shaking with fear and embarrassment I tried to pull myself up but the narrow space and the motion of the boat made it almost impossible, and I found myself kneeling at his feet clutching at the chart table to steady myself.

'I really am sorry,' I said again, trying to control my voice as I heard it waver like a child's. 'I thought I would stow away for fun; you have so often anchored off the beach near our house. I didn't mean any harm.' There was a brilliant flash of lightning from outside, filling the cabin, dimming the light for a moment, then a clap of thunder immediately overhead. I felt myself flinch but he did not move. There was no softening in his face, no sign of humour.

Behind him the hatch slid back and the girl's head appeared, dripping with rain. 'Did you say something, Pete? Christ this storm is bad! I wish you'd come up –' she broke off in astonishment as she suddenly noticed me.

'It seems we have a stowaway,' he said.

She went on staring for a moment, then she pushed the hatch right back and climbed in, to sit dripping on the companionway steps.

Pete too had not taken his eyes off me, but he swore at her sharply. 'You're supposed to be on watch, Sam,' he said.

'There's nothing on the radar,' she retorted. 'Nobody is such a bloody fool as to be out on a night like this; we're out of the shipping lanes and there's no point in having self-steering gear if you don't use it. Who is she?'

He raised an eyebrow. 'Who indeed.'

I swallowed, trying to regain a little of my composure, but it was difficult kneeling there between them on the hard lurching floor. 'My name is Anna Marshall,' I began. And I went on to try and explain.

They both listened frostily as I explained how I had taken the dinghy and hidden while they were in the pub. When I had finished there was a moment's silence broken only by another roar of thunder from above.

'What are you going to do with her?' Sam asked at last. She said it quietly but her tone sent a shiver up my spine.

Pete was watching me closely. 'I'm sure you are intelligent enough to realise, Miss Marshall,' he said, 'why stowaways are not welcomed on this boat.'

I had heard enough to know that. My eyes were fixed on his face, but I shrugged. Then I glanced at Sam, and I saw something – excitement – flickering behind her eyes. 'She's scared Pete. Scared as shit!'

'So she should be, we don't take passengers.' He moved forward slightly onto the edge of the bunk and I felt myself shrink back in terror, but he was craning to look out of the half open hatchway. Abruptly he reached down for the oil-skins. 'The wind's veered. I'll have to go up. Watch her, Sam.'

He stepped over me and vanished up the companionway, pulling the hatch closed after him.

The girl was watching me half fascinated, half, I was sure, afraid herself, now that Pete had gone. I took my chance and pulled myself up onto the bunk where he had been sitting. I felt less at a disadvantage off my knees. I gave a feeble smile. 'You couldn't spare some of that coffee you were making, could you?'

She stared at me a moment longer and I thought she was

going to refuse but she stood up and groped her way to the galley. A second later she was back with a mugful. She handed it to me without speaking and I drank it gratefully. It was only just warm and very bitter but it comforted me a little.

'Thanks,' I said.

She was still watching me in silence when Pete reappeared some minutes later.

Sam turned to him. 'You can't throw her overboard, Pete. That would be murder.'

'And aren't you prepared to murder, sweetheart, for a million pounds?' he asked her sarcastically.

I saw her lips tighten till the flesh round her mouth drained of colour but she shook her head. 'Not murder, Pete.'

He looked at me for a moment – he had not taken off his waterproofs this time – then he stooped and caught my elbow, pulling me to my feet. I cried out with fear, but instead of dragging me up on deck he pushed me in front of him towards the bows of the boat. 'You'll have to forgive us if we deprive ourselves of your company Miss Marshall,' he said with meticulous politeness. 'Until I decide what to do with you. It's a wild night as you cannot have failed to notice and I need Sam to help me sail this tub.'

He pushed me into the forward sail locker and pulled the door shut behind me, leaving me alone in the dark. I had already seen there was a padlock on the outside of the door; I did not need to hear the click to know he had locked me in.

The spare berth was furnished with a plastic-covered foam mattress; apart from the neatly stacked sailbags which more than half filled the small space, it was empty. There were no portholes.

I sat down hugging my arms around me to try and keep warm as the tears began to slip down my cheeks.

Later I wrapped myself in one of the sails; the cold crackly Terylene was little comfort but it was better than nothing and I must have dozed a little for I awoke to find the motion had lessened. I could hear feet above my head. I peered up half expecting the forehatch to open but it didn't. Instead I heard a deafening roar as the anchor chain began to run.

We had been rocking gently for some time when the sound of an outboard engine came to my ears. It drew close, hovered for a while then drew away again. Then at last the lock rattled and the door was pulled open. The light which streamed in was blinding after the darkness.

'Good morning Miss Marshall. I trust you slept well.' Pete reached in and took my arm.

This time we were going on deck. He propelled me up the companionway into the cockpit and, dazed, I glanced round. Sam was standing at the wheel. The oilskins were gone; she was dressed in shorts and a striped T-shirt, her blonde hair blowing in the sun. She grinned at me.

'I hope you can swim,' she said.

I tried to struggle but his arms were round me, lifting me over the rail, and there was nothing I could do to save myself. No time to think. I heard myself scream and then the icy water closed over my head.

I fought it madly, choking desperately until at last in a haze of bubbles I rose back into the air and only then did I realise that I was less than a hundred yards from the shore. As I began to swim I glanced over my shoulder at the yacht. Her sails set, she was already drawing away on a starboard tack. Only Sam turned to see if I had surfaced. The yacht, I noticed suddenly, had no name.

I lay on the beach until my clothes dried on me and I stopped shaking, then half faint with exhaustion and hunger I made my way up over the sand towards the dunes. My head throbbed but I was so grateful to be back on land and in one piece I could ignore it. I slipped and staggered as I walked but there at last was a road and in the distance I thought I could see a house.

I was still staring at the road sign incredulously when a lorry drew up beside me with a squeal and hiss of brakes. The driver leaned down from his cab and grinned. '*Salut!*' he said.

I stared at him. The first thing that came into my head was a sob of disbelief. 'This isn't France!' I said.

I saw the easy smile vanish off his face. He looked at me hard for a moment, taking in my crumpled, salt-stained clothes and tangled hair, then the huge panting engine was silenced and he opened his door, jumping down beside me. He was a tall man, in his forties, broadly built, with brawny arms and his face as he looked down into mine was gentle and concerned. 'You are English, yes? What do you mean this is not *La France*?' His accent was heavy.

I shook my head trying to blink back my tears; he would never believe me. No one would ever believe me.

But he did. Two minutes' gentle probing revealed to him that I had no money, no papers and had not eaten for nearly twenty-four hours. The last news seemed to cheer him slightly. It was something he could put right.

That French *routier* restored my faith in men. The vast lorry stowed safely off the road, he escorted me into a small restaurant in the next village and proceeded to order what seemed to me to be a feast.

'There. Better. Yes?' He said at last. We had not spoken while the soup was on the table. It was scalding, full of onions and cheese and quite beautiful.

'Much better.' I managed a quite presentable smile. I had borrowed his comb and washed the salt off my face. 'I don't know what I should have done if you hadn't arrived.'

He leaned forward and put his brawny arms on the table, pushing the plates aside. 'Now, when we are finished you will telephone home, yes?' He poured me some more of the *ordinaire* wine.

'But I was running away from home,' I protested. 'If I ring –'

He interrupted with a very Gallic shrug. '*Bien sûr*. But to run away without money; without passport; that was not well planned, eh?'

The *patron* took away our soup plates and replaced them with succulent helpings of fish dressed in a rich sauce.

I sighed. 'You are right. I will have to ring my father,' I said. It seemed a terrible thing, after my terrifying bid for freedom, to have to admit defeat.

'This father he is a tyrant, yes?' Jean-Pierre was watching me. I could see a flicker of amusement in his eyes. 'This I do not understand. I thought English girls were, how you say, liberate.'

'Liberated.' I smiled back. 'They are, most of them.'

'*Bon*. Then perhaps you can phone someone else. Your boyfriend?' He tore a piece of bread from the baguette which lay between us on the red and white chequered cloth and began to chew it thoughtfully.

Boyfriend. Ben? What would Ben say if I rang him and told him that I was marooned in France without money or passport, wining and dining with a lorry driver after being thrown overboard by drug smugglers? The only thing missing was the shark-infested sea!

I saw him grin. 'You have thought of something funny yes? That is good. You are not unhappy any more. Things are never so bad as they would seem, yes?'

'Yes,' I agreed. Suddenly I knew what I was going to do. 'I have thought of someone,' I said.

We had a *café filtré*, then at last we commandeered the *patron*'s telephone and made the call. I don't know who answered but when Jean-Pierre went back to our table he had summoned Robin Hamilton to the phone.

'Robin? It's Anna. Listen I'm in France.'

'I thought you were in bed with a headache!' I could hear the amusement in his voice over the phone. 'Did you do a bunk?'

'Sort of. I'll explain later. Robin, can you come and get me? Can you bring my passport and some money?'

'Where will I find them?'

'You mean you will?' I was incredulous for a moment.

'The party is appalling without you and I can be on the next hovercraft. Where do I find your things?' His voice was matter of fact as though he was asked things like this every day. Perhaps journalists are. Behind it I could hear the sound of music and laughter.

When I rejoined Jean-Pierre he had ordered another carafe of wine. '*Tout va bien?*' he asked.

I nodded. 'I told him where I'd be, just as you said. Are you sure you don't mind . . .' I was embarrassed suddenly. This complete stranger had become a friend in the space of less than two hours; a real friend. His lorry was empty and he was on his way home for twenty-four hours' rest before taking a load back to Paris, and he assured me he could think of no more delightful way of passing some of the time than with me!

We met Robin at seven that evening. He had taken the ferry to Boulogne and hired a car there. In the back was one of my own suitcases. He had gone to my room, rifled my drawers and cupboards and made his own selection of clothes. I saw Jean-Pierre eyeing him with obvious approval and I was pleased. I didn't think I was going to regret throwing myself on Robin's mercy. Nevertheless I was sad when Jean-Pierre had to go. One day, we promised, we would visit him, but before then I had a way of life to change.

When he had gone Robin produced my passport from his pocket and handed it to me. 'There you are,' he said. 'But you also need money. It was conspicuous by its absence in your handbag.'

He was looking at me closely. 'Do I get an explanation?'

I nodded. 'I rather think you do. Also, probably, a good story. I owe you a lot for coming like this.'

He grinned. 'You do indeed.' He opened the door of the red Renault for me. 'But first of all, I think, a change of clothes and dinner. I've checked us into a hotel.'

It was a double room.

'One of the things I owe you?' I asked, looking round. Strangely I did not feel angry.

He swung my case onto the bed and went to push back the shutters. Outside the street was noisy with traffic; two men were having an argument immediately beneath the wrought iron balcony; the air was full of the sound of their shouting and the smell of French cooking.

He turned and leaned with his shoulder against the wall, looking at me. 'Not unless you want,' he said. 'I could just about restrain myself to a chaste neighbourliness, provided I get my explanation; I am not quite such a lecher as Parker. Do I gather you told him where to go? The atmosphere at your idyllic home has not been all sweetness and light since you left.'

'Did Don lose his contract?' I had taken my silk négligé from the case.

Robin shrugged. 'Still not signed as far as *I* know. He'll get it though. Parker doesn't do business entirely with his balls. He'll make Don sweat but if he got as far as going down to Sussex, he'll sign.'

To my surprise I found I didn't really care. The house; Don; they were already in the past, as were, I suspected, my flat, my allowance and my car! I had a leisurely bath and then we went out to dinner.

By half-way through I was beginning to realise that I liked Robin Hamilton very much. He was unlike any other man I had known; relaxed, humorous, totally unconventional and, for the first time I found, as his fingers closed over mine on the table, a man whose touch did not leave me rigid with dislike. On the contrary I felt an unmistakable tingle of excitement.

There was a lot to talk about that evening and some of it involved the police. Robin was not prepared to ignore the method of my arrival in France. He took it very seriously indeed.

And he used the story. It made the headlines in most of the papers in England, but as far as I know they never caught Pete and Sam.

The other story, the one about a businessman who tried to sell his daughter for a contract, Robin kept to himself.

In our bedroom that first night together, as I waited for him to come upstairs from phoning his paper and Don, to tell him where I was, I went once more to the window and looked out. The sound of an accordion floated up from the café across the street and I could hear laughter and the sound of singing. I thought for one short moment about Ben. It was without regret.

When Robin returned at last he came over to the window and put his arms around me. 'I told Don, among other things,' he said softly, 'that you and I were driving on down to the Riviera for a few days.'

I turned to look up at him. His face was only inches from mine. 'I should like that,' I said.

He smiled. 'No strings attached. We'll see how it goes, shall we?'

I remembered Ben and all the strings that had surrounded that relationship and laughed. 'No strings,' I agreed, and I was surprised to realise that I really meant it. I was content to see what time, and the freedom to be myself at last, would bring.

'I told Don that his little Anna has grown up,' Robin added. 'She makes her own decisions from now on.'

'She does indeed,' I whispered. 'And one of my first is about you.'

While I was waiting for him to come upstairs from his phone calls I had changed into my négligé, and now, loosening the belt I let the pale blue silk slide gently from my shoulders to the floor. Robin had not packed any night-dresses, so of course I wasn't wearing one.

Rosemary and Thyme

THE SOUND OF THE FLUTE had taken her completely by surprise. It was as pure in its way as the sound of the robin's song which was cascading with icy beauty across the garden. This was not a small child painfully practising before school, this was adult music, expert, complex. Elizabethan. Shivering, as she listened, Lesley glanced down with distaste at her mud-caked gardening gloves. They were cold, clinging to her fingers, no longer comforting against the earth. Peeling them off she stooped and picked up her thermos. A secret indulgence this: steaming bitter coffee, redolent of past breakfasts, but here in the cleansing air of dawn safely apart from memories. Sipping, she could feel the darkness of her mood lifting and dispersing with the music.

Beyond the herb beds and the low box hedges she could see the sea. The sun, hard silver behind bars of dawn cloud, threw no heat yet across the glitter of the water. Behind her, in contrast, the churchyard wall was smothered in warm blossom. Espaliered pears clung unpruned the whole length of the soft old red brick and as she turned to watch a wren darted in and out of the white flowers.

From the yew tree behind the wall the robin was pouring out its heart to the dawn, the sweetness of the song a sharp counterpoint to the sudden harsh ringing cry of a gull overhead until, as though indignant at being outclassed by the music of the flute, it stopped singing and with a flirt of its tail vanished.

Unable to contain her curiosity, Lesley put down her mug and tiptoed across the beds, brushing aside the delicate fronds of rosemary with their veil of blue flowers. At the wall she reached up and cautiously she peered over. She could see nothing. The shadows in the depths of the churchyard were thick and dark. Suddenly the music stopped.

'Oh no!'

She had spoken involuntarily and half embarrassed she waited, expecting some response from the musician.

None came.

The silence unnerved her slightly. She had expected a voice, or a face amongst the holly branches, or even the sound of retreating footsteps. Uncomfortable with the intensity of the quiet she raised herself on her toes and peered further over the wall.

'Hello?' she called.

At the sound of her voice a blackbird hurtled out of the hollies near her, shrieking in alarm. Otherwise there was no sound.

Turning, she followed the wall to where an old wooden gate led from the garden into the churchyard itself. She pushed at it. It was swollen and stiff to open but with a protesting creak it allowed her to pass. Beyond the wall, where a few moments before she had stood and listened to the music, the sun was gaining strength. A small streak of gold touched the clouds.

The gravel path was thickly overgrown, but still it crunched beneath her feet as she moved cautiously forward. The church was locked. The old ivy-covered graves slept in silence.

The music when it came again was quieter, sadder. She listened, turning slowly round, trying to work out where it was coming from.

Beyond the church the path wound between the graves

towards the lych gate and the lane which led up from the village.

Slowly she walked on, following the music towards the avenue of majestic yews and a tangled thicket of old rose bushes. Leaving the path she walked on feeling the dew soaking, ice cold, over the top of her boots from the long, uncut grass.

The young man was standing looking down at a newly dug grave. Tall and slim he appeared to be dressed entirely in black. In his hand she could see the long outline of the instrument he had been playing. She stopped. He had his back to her, he hadn't seen her yet; she could still turn back. She hesitated, unwilling to leave, but not wanting to intrude on his obvious grief.

Seconds ticked by. Beside her the robin, reassured by her stillness, hopped out of the ivy which clung around the stone coping of a vault and came to rest only two feet from her. It bowed and half spread its wings and danced across the arm of a cross near by. Distracted, she watched it for a few seconds. When she glanced back at the young man, he had gone.

She shrugged. He must have looked round and caught sight of her. Slowly she made her way back towards the gate, conscious of the newly rising sun throwing warmth through the still-bare branches of the trees. She could understand grief too raw, too new to be shared, but at the same time she was overwhelmed with regret for the beauty and emotion of the music which had gone with him.

She did it automatically, as she would have done for a friend, conscious that she had scared the mourner away, putting together in recompense the nosegay of rosemary with its intense blue flowers, the gaudy bells of lungwort, cowslips and sweet violets, then retracing her steps, she followed the path towards the grave, her own offering to whoever lay beneath that soft black earth, a bright, fragrant bouquet in her hand.

The robin led the way, bobbing ahead with flirtatious friendliness, its beady eyes fixed on her face.

The church door was open. Someone must have been there to unlock it while she was preparing the flowers. Unable suddenly to face the thought of meeting anyone, of speaking, embarrassed by the presumptuousness of her little posy for the unknown grave, she tiptoed on the grass, following the path between the yew trees past the vault to the tangled rose bushes. Now the light was stronger, the shadows gone, she could see how old they were – great thick woody stems, most of them dead, or only sustained by suckers, threaded with thistle and goose grass, entwined with ivy. Beyond them there was an old grave, surrounded by railings, the stone moss-covered, cracked and crumbling. She glanced round, lost. Surely it was here she had been standing when she saw the young man. Feeling foolish suddenly she cast around, searching for the mound of newly turned dark earth.

'Can I help you? Are you looking for someone?'

She spun round with an involuntary cry of surprise at the diffident voice behind her. A man, painter's overalls over his thick green sweater, stood there on the path. He was about her own age she guessed, and about her height, but stocky, his thick curly hair awry, his face lit by a friendly smile. 'Sorry. I startled you.' His voice was low and musical.

'I didn't hear you coming.' Her uneasiness had been caused not so much by his sudden appearance as by the seeming disappearance of the grave. It had thrown her out of kilter. She had lost her bearings totally.

'I'm painting over some damp patches in the church.' He shrugged. 'Any job, you know, when one is temporarily unwaged.' His humorous scowl at the euphemism made her smile. 'You must be Mrs Davis?' His head to one side, he surveyed her with open curiosity. 'I saw you coming through the gate from Stables Cottage. You are very much a mystery lady. Everyone in the village is falling over themselves with curiosity about you.'

'Are they?' She stared at him, half her mind still on the grave behind her, half shocked by this revelation. It was threatening. Intrusive.

He read her mind with ease. 'I'm sorry. It's none of my business either. I'll leave you to it. Unless,' he hesitated, his eyes going to the flowers in her hand. 'Did you want help finding a grave? Whose is it?'

'I don't know.' She felt foolish as she had known she would. 'I was here earlier. I saw someone – '

It seemed easier suddenly to start from the beginning, and strangely, now that she had started talking she wanted to go on, wanted to end the self-imposed loneliness of the past weeks. She told him about the garden, the cold dawn, the hot coffee, the music drifting across the churchyard wall.

When she had finished he was looking puzzled. 'I don't quite understand. I'm not a great authority on local funerals, but I don't think there's been a burial here for months. So many people go to the crematorium these days. There are certainly no new graves.'

'Perhaps the grave was months old then.' She gave a wry smile. 'I'm not an expert on them either. Would they still look new?'

He grinned. 'All I know about graves is to be found in *Hamlet*, I'm afraid. "Water is a sore decayer of your whoreson dead body," and all that. The latest village graves are on the far side of the church, near the path. They certainly wouldn't be down here. These are all ages old.' He gestured towards the dead roses. 'I'll show you if you like – '

'No!'

He frowned, surprised at her vehemence.

'It was here. Near the yews; the roses. It was here.' She pointed to the railings.

'*Mary Elizabeth Weaver.*
Born 3rd May 1672. Died 5th August 1696'

he read, squinting at the inscription almost worn away and covered in lichen, and he shook his head. There was a long pause. 'I don't know of anyone in the village who plays the flute or the recorder. Not properly. Not if you don't count the school kids.' It was said absently as though he were mentally scanning a list of names. 'You are sure it wasn't a tape?'

'I saw him. He had the flute in his hand.'

'A visitor then. Come to see the grave of an ancestor?'

'It was a new grave.' She put her hand to her face wearily and he could see the earth encrusted round her nails. The sight made him feel strangely protective. She was very beautiful this stranger who had bought the cottage so close to the centre of the village but who remained so determinedly an enigma. Beautiful and sad.

The sadness vanished suddenly as she turned to him and her face lit with a smile. 'I must have been imagining it. Dreaming.' Crouching down she put her hand through the railings and laid the posy on the grave. 'There. She can have them with my love.' She stood up again and turned to him. 'Are you very busy? If the damp patches can wait come and have a cup of coffee. Then you can tell the villagers that you've met me and earn lots of Brownie points!'

He laughed. She had read his mind, but only to a certain extent. He would not tell them anything. He sensed a secret here to be guarded and cherished.

'I'd like some coffee. Thanks.'

Her cottage was comfortably furnished, the kitchen separated from the living room by only a few oak studs. Sitting down at the round pine table he was able to stare appreciatively around her whole domain, then watch as she put the kettle onto the stove. There were so many questions he wanted to ask but he knew he would ask none of them. He would wait for her to volunteer.

She took two heavy earthenware mugs down from the dresser and went to the fridge for a jug of milk. 'You are my first visitor from the village and I don't even know your name.' She had her back to him as she fished in a biscuit tin and brought out some flapjacks which she arranged on a plate.

'Philip. Phil.'

'And does Phil have a second name?'

He grinned. Enigma for enigma. 'He does.'

'But I'm not to know it?'

'My turn for a question perhaps?' He helped himself to a biscuit as she pushed the plate towards him.

'Fair enough.' She sat down too as they waited for the kettle to boil. 'Fire away. Just one.'

'Do you live here alone?'

She nodded. The barrier was closing around her again. The friendliness, the banter, they were good, but why had he homed in on the one thing she could not discuss? Because it was the most important thing in her life, of course. The gap at her side. The empty place in her bed. The missing laughter even in this house that had never known him, that she had thought would comfort her after the aching emptiness in the home they had shared.

Phil was watching her closely and she had a feeling he could read every thought passing through her mind. He turned to look out of the window. 'You're working on the old herb garden. I used to visit it when I was a boy. I loved the smells. It seemed so strange that you could stand in such a warm, safe, fragrant place and yet look out to the sea and watch the cold squalls of rain racing across the waves in the distance.' He paused. She didn't say anything so he went on. 'My parents lived on the other side of the church, in the old rectory. When my father died my mother bought a cottage up the other end of the village so when I was made redundant in the City I came back here for a bit to help her sort things out.'

'And you live alone with your mother?' Standing up she began to make the coffee.

He smiled and nodded. 'Three years of marriage and a fairly good-tempered divorce under my belt. Once bitten twice shy.'

There was silence. This was the moment to tell him. My

husband died. That was all she had to say. No need to talk about the hospice and the long weeks as she sat and watched the man who was her whole existence slip slowly beyond reach. Just the bare facts.

Outside the window the robin perched on the budding wisteria and burst into song. Phil smiled. 'He's followed us from the churchyard. Nosy fellow. Look at those bright eyes.' The moment had gone.

She nodded. 'I'll find him some crumbs.'

Pushing wide the casement she held her breath suddenly. 'Phil, listen!'

The beautiful haunting melody from the churchyard was drifting across the garden. In silence they listened for several minutes, then, his finger to his lips, Phil stood up and silently he opened the door. They crept down the path towards the gate and round the church, following the direction of the sound.

The young man was standing where she had seen him before, near the grave of Mary Elizabeth Weaver. But now the railings were missing, the headstone gone. The earth was newly turned. On it lay Lesley's posy of spring herbs. As the young man played they waited motionless, seeing the tall slim body, dressed all in black, sway gently in rhythm to the music, absorbed as they were by the beauty of the sound.

Lesley realised suddenly that she was clutching Phil's hand. They were both holding their breath. Behind them the robin bounced cheerfully into the hollies and, puffing up its scarlet breast feathers, it began to sing.

The young man lowered his instrument at last. He stood for a moment, looking down at the grave then he half glanced back over his shoulder as though he too could hear the cheerful song of the bird. For half a second more the vision remained, then a squirrel ran along the path in front of them and they realised he had gone.

Lesley slowly released her companion's hand. She took a deep breath. 'Tell me you saw him too.'

'I saw him too.'

She stared at him, her eyes wide, her face suddenly pale. 'He was a ghost.'

He nodded. 'I think he must have been.'

'But not frightening.'

'No. Just sad.' He smiled.

'That beautiful music!' She was strangely breathless. 'Trapped in time. Still existing.'

'We're privileged.' He looked at her. 'I hope it's comforting. To know people can come back. Can still love each other beyond whatever boundary it is we cross when we die.'

So he had guessed. Perhaps the villagers with their gossip and their grapevine already knew. She nodded. 'It is.' For a few seconds she thought about it, reassured as he had meant her to be, but then she frowned. 'But where is *she*? Where is Mary Elizabeth? Why haven't they met out there beyond the boundary?' She began slowly to walk forward towards the grave. Standing staring down through the railings she focused on the bunch of herbs. 'But perhaps he did find her.' She was talking to herself now. 'The music. The shadow of the man. They are just echoes. Images in the mirror. That's all.' She turned to face him and the sadness in her eyes had gone. 'We were idiots. We should have tried to tape the music. If there's a next time shall we have a go?'

He liked the 'we'. He could feel comfortable with that. And he could live with the shadows. 'What was your husband's name?' It was the right time to ask. He made no attempt to step closer to her.

'Jeff.'

He could see it was an effort even to say it.

He nodded. 'Lesley, I must get on with my painting. Would you come out to supper one evening? Perhaps go to a concert?' He gave wry grin. 'We both like music. It's a start.'

He could see her considering. She was staring at the robin, perched now on the railings round the grave. Suddenly she smiled. 'You're right,' she said slowly. 'It's a start.'

Flowers for the Teacher

I SHUT THE FRONT DOOR thankfully behind me and stood for a moment leaning against it, gazing round the cool living room of my tiny cottage. Almost at once I began to feel calm, it was so peaceful in there.

It had been the most terrible week since I had taken over as the teacher at the village school at Sherbridge. There had been times when I had thought I would never survive until Friday at all. And it was all due to one new boy who had arrived at half term.

His name was Paul Danefield and he was eight. He was a small sturdy child with freckles and his sole aim as far as I could see was to reduce the school to chaos and me to tears. He had very nearly succeeded in both.

With a sigh I dropped my books on a chair and went to plug in the kettle. I was worn out. Kicking off my shoes I ran my fingers through my hair and gazed out of the kitchen window at the lavender and sweet marigolds in the bed outside. Then someone knocked on the front door. I was tempted not to answer, but as I had soon discovered when I moved to Sherbridge, the teacher was considered public property rather as the district nurse was. If I was in I was available. And they would all know by now that I was in.

I opened the door to a tall young man in a smart grey suit. Puzzled, I tried to think who he was. I knew most of the villagers by now, and certainly all the parents, but I could not remember having seen him before.

'Miss Stanley?' His voice was low and even. 'I wonder if I might have a word with you. My name is James Danefield. It is about my son, Paul.'

My heart sank, but I smiled and beckoned him in, wishing I had thought to put my shoes on again before I opened the door. I felt ridiculously defenceless in bare feet.

'I expect you can guess why I'm here.' His grey eyes surveyed me rather grimly and I saw them taking in my dishevelled hair and my toes at a glance. He rather obviously disapproved of what he saw.

'I assume you want to discuss Paul's work,' I said rather weakly. I was about to add, 'And his rude uncouth behaviour,' but I bit back the words, not wanting to antagonise the man.

The kettle lid was beginning to jump up and down next door so I offered him a cup of tea. He accepted, rather curtly, I thought, and waited, his lips pursed, as I went through into the kitchen.

As I made the tea I found a comb in the drawer and my sandals under a chair so I was feeling slightly less untidy when I carried the tray into the living room.

'We haven't met before, Miss Stanley.' Mr Danefield refused to sit down and stood watching me pour out, his back to the fireplace. 'As you know it was my sister you saw at the time Paul joined your school. He has no mother.' He hesitated a moment as though wondering whether to tell me what had happened to her. Then obviously thinking better of it, he went on, 'And I have been away in London for the last few weeks.'

He took the cup I offered him and stirred it absently. 'Miss Stanley, I am extremely concerned about the way you have been treating my son.'

'I beg your pardon?' I looked at him blankly.

'He is a sensitive and unhappy child,' he went on as though I hadn't spoken, 'and he is still upset at having lost his mother.

I am most perturbed to find that you have been picking on him, making an example of him before the whole school and even using corporal punishment.'

'I've what?' My tea slopped into the saucer as I dropped my cup onto it. I was furious. 'Is that what he's told you? Well, I've news for you, Mr Danefield. Your son seems to me to be anything but sensitive. He has been going out of his way to wreck the school and everything I'm trying to do. He's unpleasant, rude, disobedient and spiteful. Ever since he came there's been nothing but trouble. And I have never, ever, used corporal punishment on him or any of the children!'

I was shaking with anger. I had managed to keep my temper all week in spite of Paul's single-minded attempts to make me lose it, but this was the last straw.

Mr Danefield put his cup down rather deliberately, his tea untouched. He looked at me for a long moment without speaking, his handsome face quite without expression, then he said, 'I am sorry, Miss Stanley, but this is obviously a matter for the school authorities.' Without another word he walked out and closed my front door behind him.

I stood gazing after him in disbelief for a moment and then I threw myself full length on the sofa and burst into tears.

How could I have been so stupid as to say all those things to him? Where was all my training, my tact, all that I had learned in psychology lectures, even my own natural politeness? How could I be such a fool? I loved this job and I loved Sherbridge and now I should probably be dismissed because I had lost my temper after the most awful week since I had finished my training; the sort of week every teacher dreads and prays will never happen. What I should have done was discuss things rationally with the child's father. Perhaps Paul *was* sensitive; perhaps his behaviour *was* solely due to his unhappiness. Why hadn't his aunt explained to me about his mother? I racked my brains trying to remember what she had said, but I am sure she had only told me that both his parents were away.

Worn out by tears and exhaustion I fell asleep eventually on the sofa and it was almost dark when I awoke at last and looked around me. The tea on the tray beside me was stone cold and a milky film had formed on the liquid in the cups. I shuddered at the sight, and picking up the tray went slowly into the kitchen. Through the open window came the smell of night-scented stock and the sound of the flitting bats as they squeaked in the dusk.

Instead of being the relaxed, happy weekend I had hoped for the next two days were a torment for me. I saw James Danefield in the village on Saturday afternoon, but either he didn't see me, or he pretended he didn't. He was dressed more casually this time, in a roll-neck sweater, and as he was chatting to Mrs Crowell outside the baker's I saw, with an unexpected little pang of misery, that he had a very attractive smile. But it was not directed at me.

Paul came to school as usual on Monday and I thought he seemed a little subdued. Certainly he was far better behaved and I had no need of my careful resolution to treat him with kid gloves.

Tuesday was the same and it really seemed as though the class was settling down again. But I couldn't relax. Every day now I was expecting a letter or a visit from the school authorities, for I had every reason to think that that cool grim-faced man meant every word he said about informing them. And who would take my word against his?

Then on the Thursday something very strange happened. Paul was very late. I had begun to think that he would not be coming when I saw him slinking into the back of the class. As he offered no apology or explanation I decided to ignore him until break and then ask him what had happened, but to my astonishment, as soon as the others had been dismissed I saw him making his way of his own accord towards my desk. His face was tear-stained and he was holding something behind his back.

'Good morning, Paul,' I said quietly. To my surprise I felt my heart going out to the child. He looked so crestfallen and unhappy.

'Please miss,' his voice was almost a whisper. 'I brought you these.' From behind his back he produced a bunch of wilted flowers. 'I'm sorry I've been naughty, miss.' So saying he turned and fled.

I was so touched and astonished I just sat there for a while, looking down at the bedraggled posy, gently separating out the bruised stems of pansies, primulas and buttercups from a few straggling pieces of grass. The little boy must have been clutching them tightly all morning. Eventually I fetched a jam jar for them from the cupboard and putting them carefully in water I set it on the front of my desk.

I noticed Paul's face light up a little at the sight when he returned to the classroom, but for the rest of the day he sat in silence and at the end of school he shot off on his own before any of the other children had left their desks.

I was still debating what had happened after I had had my supper that evening. I was sitting by the open window reading in the last of the daylight when there was a knock at the door.

It was James Danefield again. But this time he was wearing an open-necked shirt, and he carried a large bunch of red roses.

'Miss Stanley. I am sorry to call so late. I wonder if I could have a word with you?' I saw his eyes drop immediately to my feet which were yet again bare. 'I . . .' he hesitated. 'I want to apologise.' His face reddened slightly and I saw what a tremendous effort it was for him to say it.

Standing in front of the fireplace as he had before, still holding the roses, he smiled at me for the first time.

'I had a word with Mrs Greville who lives next door to me. Her son shares a desk with Paul, I believe. She seemed to agree with your view of Paul. So I tackled the wretched child about it and he admitted having lied to me, and having been badly behaved and rude to you. I hope you will forgive us both for our ill manners.'

He looked amazingly like Paul as he pushed the roses at me, half smiling, half embarrassed. I almost expected him to turn and run away as his son had done, but he didn't. He sat down on the sofa.

'I owe you an explanation,' he said, pulling a wry face. 'My wife and I have been separated for some time, and our divorce came through six months ago. She remarried recently and Paul feels it very badly. She doesn't really want anything to do with him, you see, although he does visit her once a fortnight.' He paused, as though looking for words. 'I think Paul was misbehaving because he wanted to attract your attention. He was seeking affection, although he was going the wrong way about getting it.' He glanced up at me under his long eyelashes. 'Besides telling me that you beat him . . .'

'I never did,' I interrupted indignantly.

'I realise that now. But besides that, you know, he told me you had hair the colour of polished conkers and that you were very beautiful. Quite discerning for a child of eight, I should say.' He grinned and I felt myself blushing scarlet.

'But of course,' he went on, 'he also said that "Miss" had this terrible temper, which goes with hair the colour of conkers.'

'And I obligingly proved it for him last time you came over.' I was contrite. 'It's I who should apologise, Mr Danefield. I should never have said those things to you, even if they were true. Poor little Paul. I should have realised there was something wrong.'

'Please, call me James.' He stood up and held out his hands to me. 'Will you have dinner with me on Saturday? We'll forget all our mutual apologies and start again from the beginning, and we can work out a plan for what to do with my errant son.' He smiled down at me and I could feel myself melting in the warmth of his charm.

Of course I should have said no. I should have insisted on a strictly parent-teacher relationship and politely sent him on his way. But I found myself smiling back at him. 'I'd love to,' I replied. 'Thank you for asking me.'

'Fine. I'm glad.' He beamed at me. 'But there is just one thing.' He hesitated and I saw a mischievous look come into his eyes. 'The restaurant where I plan to take you has some really rather nasty gravel in the front. It might be advisable, possibly, to wear some sort of shoes . . .'

He was already making for the front door, but the cushion I threw caught him on the shoulder. Laughing, he picked it up and tossed it back. Then he was gone.

I gathered up his beautiful roses and almost danced into the kitchen to find a vase for them. Perhaps my job at Sherbridge was not doomed to a premature end after all. And perhaps . . . But I was not going to build any dreams just yet. I would just wait and see what happened.

A Family Affair

PART ONE

THANKFULLY I CLOSED THE DOOR on the dusty New York street and ran up the steps to my cousin's apartment.

'Minna?' I called as I let myself in. 'Would you believe, Martin has let me come home early!'

I worked for Martin George, the world famous ecologist and TV personality, and I adored the job, but the hours were long and erratic: my work had to be my whole life, except for Chris of course. Chris and I were close, but not lovers. Maybe that would come later, but for the moment he was that rarest of animals, a male friend. And for once I could call him and tell him I could make it, shower and actually have time to relax for five minutes before he could get from his advertising offices on Madison Avenue to the brownstone where I was temporarily sharing my cousin's apartment.

'Minna, are you home?' Puzzled by the silence I checked my watch. My cousin's job was as regular as mine was variable and she should have been back an hour before.

Then I heard a sob.

I ran into the living room and found her, with her head in her arms, on the couch. She was crying.

'Uncle Julian phoned from England,' she sobbed.

'Pa?' I stared at her, feeling cold fingers run down my spine. 'What's happened?'

'It's Grandfather. He's dead!'

Stunned I sat down beside her, unable to say a word, and silently we held hands. Grandfather had meant so much to me. With my mother dead, and my father virtually an invalid from a bad heart, Grandfather had brought me up, his home at Kingley Manor my home, his world my world. Only in the last few years as I had grown up and he had become frail had he allowed Pa and me to move out of the manor house into one of the old farmhouses on the estate.

When I had recovered enough I rang my father back. 'He died in his sleep, Kate,' he assured me. 'It's the way he would have wanted to go. And he didn't want you to fly back for the funeral. "Tell the kids to hold a wake with the air fare money when I go," you know yourself that is what he said.'

Strange that home-loving Grandfather's three grandchildren should all be living in the States when he died. I, because I followed Martin and my job around the world, Minna because she had never lived in England – her mother had married an American, and she was as American as the Empire State Building, and Richard. Our cousin Richard Bradshaw, the only son of Grandfather's only son, an enigma, and if the gossip columnists were to be believed, a jet-setting millionaire, lived somewhere near Boston. Neither Minna nor I had ever met him, and neither of us thought of contacting him now. If he had wanted to keep in touch with his family, no doubt he would have done so, but like his father, who having met and married the Boston-born heiress to the Bay View millions had cut off all contact with Kingley, Richard had never as far as I knew made any attempt to see Grandfather, or visit the family home.

So the shock was doubly great when the will came through. Pa had phoned us again as soon as he knew what it said. 'Minna has been left Gatehouse Farm and the home Paddocks, and some money,' he shouted down the phone. Father always shouts on telephones. 'And you, sweetheart, get our beloved Kingley Farm and also the whole of Kingley Woods and the Marshes – and some money too.' He chuckled.

'And the main estate?' I asked. 'The manor house?'

There was a short silence. 'Richard gets all of that,' he said bleakly. 'Richard gets everything else!'

'It's so unfair!' Minna stamped her foot when I told her. 'What the hell has he done to deserve it! He never even visited grandfather! And he's as rich as Croesus already!'

Privately I agreed with her, but I was so overjoyed with my own bequest, our home and the woods and marshes I had adored since I was a child, that I didn't think too much about the main estate. Neither Minna nor I were business-minded, nor were we farmers, and I had always secretly thought the manor house too big and spooky ever to be really a home. If Richard were a businessman, he could run the estate and welcome.

Chris, when I mentioned my cousin to him, to my surprise knew all about him, and he whistled.

'He owns half of Boston, for Chrissake,' he said, when I told him over a hamburger lunch about the Bradshaw inheritance. 'Hey, Katie honey, you'll soon be out of my class!' We laughed together as we walked hand in hand down the street, and suddenly I began to feel better about grandfather's death. He would not have wanted me to grieve.

'So, you're a rich girl now,' Martin said jovially when I told him my news. 'You won't want to work for me any more!' He looked at me, his ruddy face twisted with mock sadness, his gold-rimmed spectacles twinkling, and I laughed.

'Of course I will, you know that. And I'm not rich. The money wasn't all that much, but I haven't told you the best bit.' I could hardly contain my excitement. 'I now own Kingley Marshes!'

He stared at me. 'Do you now,' was all he said. It was enough. In the world of conservation that name was famous – the last resort of several endangered species of flowers and butterflies. 'We'll do a TV special on it,' Martin said, and I was overjoyed.

Two days later Martin and I had to fly to Palm Beach and between spells in the conference centre and the sweltering TV studios I managed to find time to go shopping in anticipation of my money coming through, to buy what Martin laughingly called 'rich-lady' beach clothes, and to lie on the sand collecting what I hoped was a fairly respectable tan. By the time we were back in New York my hair had bleached out to honey highlights and I was quite proud of the way I looked. But my happiness was short-lived.

Minna had disappeared.

Frantically I called everyone I could think of, appalled at the smelling mouldy food I had found in the kitchen, and the unmade bed in her room, which was so unlike her, but no one knew where she was. She had not checked in at work for over a week. In the end, after tearfully consulting Martin and Chris I called the police department.

They were not interested. So many people disappear in New York, what was one more to them? They confirmed that her body had not been identified in any morgue, nor was she in any hospital as far as they knew, and presumably they slotted her name into a computer and forgot about her, leaving me shivering at all the unimaginable horrors which might have happened to her as I prowled the apartment and waited.

I had to wait two days before the phone rang.

'Hi! Is this Katherine Parrish?' a deep, unfamiliar voice drawled.

Listlessly I said that it was.

'My name is Dave Conway. I'm PA to your cousin Richard. Listen, Kate. Can you get up here to Salem? Minna is here, it's kind of a family reunion, and Richard would so like to meet you . . .'

I had already stopped listening. Minna was safe! And the enigmatic Richard Bradshaw had at last come out of hiding.

Martin agreed to give me a few days off – we had long ago

decided that he owed me months and months of overtime if truth were known – and Dave Conway arranged to pick me up by car. 'I'm in New York on business, and I have to make one short call on my way back, but I'd sure like to have your company,' he said. I needed no persuading.

Deliriously happy now, I whirled round the apartment, cleaning it like a new pin – I hadn't had the heart before – and then I set to, organising myself. I spent some more of that not-yet-arrived money on some new clothes and fashionable shoes, I had my hair done, and I was ready.

Dave was due to pick me up at Martin's downtown office and exactly on time a beige Cadillac slid to a halt outside the building.

Dave was tall, very thin, with grey hazel eyes, and utterly charming. I felt relaxed with him at once. He admired our chaotic office, shook hands with Martin, who responded with his usual warmth, and at last he bent to pick up my two new bags. I was following him out of the door when one of the telephones rang, and automatically I reached for it.

'Kate? Thank God I caught you!' It was Minna. Her voice sounded strangled and hysterical.

'Minna? What is it? Where are you?' Astonished I stared down at the receiver in my hand, then I put it back to my ear.

'Kate! For God's sake don't go. You mustn't – ' There was a gasp and the line went dead.

I replaced the receiver and stared up at Dave. 'That was Minna,' I said. I had gone cold all over.

He was watching my face closely and I had the sudden feeling that he knew exactly what Minna had been trying to tell me.

'Poor Minna,' he said, shaking his head. 'I'm afraid she has not been well. How did she sound?'

I saw Martin's worried frown in the distance, but my eyes were taken up with analysing Dave's expression. 'She sounded hysterical,' I said cautiously. Minna was one of the calmest people I knew.

Dave nodded. 'She has had some kind of a virus up at Bay View. She is on the mend though, you've no need to worry.' I wanted to believe him, but a strange foreboding was tugging somewhere at the back of my mind. It did not last however as Dave gave an apologetic grin. 'She was so sure she was infectious, poor thing, that is why we didn't call you up before, but the doc says she's not. I guess it'll do her more good than anything else to see you.' He stooped once again to pick up my bags.

I had no reason not to believe him. Reassured, I said goodbye to Martin and followed Dave down to the car.

As it slid silently and effortlessly through the heavy New York traffic and out onto the freeway I sat back in my seat and prepared to enjoy the journey. Dave was a good companion, handsome, amusing, strangely gentle in some ways for a high-powered businessman, and prepared to talk about his employer.

'He never saw his family in England,' I explained. 'I expect Minna told you. So he is a great mystery to us all. What's he like?'

He pondered a minute, swinging the car out to overtake a huge truck. 'He's quiet; strong; clever; a bit of a loner.'

'He's not married?' I asked innocently. I knew that much. Every gossip column invariably described him as 'eligible bachelor millionaire Richard Bradshaw' but I wanted Dave to confirm it.

'Nope; he's not married. And not likely to.' For a moment his good-natured grin vanished. Then it was back. 'He lives mainly at Bay View, but he has houses in France and Long Beach too.' He guided the car expertly round a long bend. 'You'll love Bay View. It's an old colonial place; our English guests always feel at home there.' He gave a throaty chuckle. I was liking Dave more and more. He made me feel relaxed and happy and I forgot my nervousness about meeting my millionaire cousin at last.

We stopped for lunch at Hertford, then Dave had a short meeting at one of the office blocks in the city centre. Afterwards we drove on through the hot afternoon towards Boston.

Bay View was every bit as breathtaking as Dave had promised. Entirely surrounded by a high wall, on the edge of the ocean, the estate was invisible from the road. We slowed before the enormous iron gates and miraculously they swung open before us, closing as soon as we were through. We drove up the long tree-lined drive and there was the house.

It was a large, square, white-painted building with three storeys topped by an elegant balustrade. Innumerable windows flanked by immaculately painted shutters, porticoes and pillars marked it out as a beautiful piece of early nineteenth century architecture. The velvet lawns, glorious grounds and clustered stables and outbuildings showed it was the home of a very rich man.

We swept up to the front door and drew to a halt. As Dave helped me out of the car the door was opened by the most beautiful woman I had ever seen. She was tall and painfully thin, with high, angled cheekbones and enormous dark eyes. She stared down at me from the top step. 'So, the country cousin is here,' she said softly.

I was stunned by the hostility which oozed from her as we stared at each other and I could sense that I was going scarlet, feeling already gauche in the pale linen dress of which I had been so proud.

'Let me introduce Jacqueline Overton,' Dave said quietly at my elbow.

Taking a deep breath I held out my hand as I mounted the steps. The woman's clasp was ice cold. 'I am Richard's fiancée,' she said.

I felt my mouth drop open. His fiancée? Why had Dave made no mention of a fiancée; surely he had said that Richard was unlikely to marry? I turned to him reproachfully but already he had moved to the back of the car to fetch my cases and I found myself entering the huge cool hall, carpeted with scattered Persian rugs. Jacqueline went without pause towards the sweeping staircase and mesmerised, I followed her.

'Richard is not back from Boston yet,' she said over her shoulder as she went up ahead of us. She had a way of talking in short, clipped sentences which required no reply. I was aware suddenly that Dave was no longer anywhere in sight.

I cleared my throat tentatively. 'How is Minna?' I enquired. 'I had half expected her to be on the doorstep waiting for me.'

Jacqueline stopped so suddenly that I almost bumped into her. 'Minna?' she said.

I was two steps below her on the stairs, and she looked down at me with withering scorn.

'She is here, isn't she?' I said. I could hear the uncertainty in my own voice.

'No,' she said. 'She's not here,' and she resumed her way upstairs.

I followed her, almost running. 'But she phoned me! David said –'

'What did Dave say?' She turned on me again. 'Minna Munro is no longer here. Richard didn't need her any more.' I thought she was going to say something else, but after a second she merely turned and continued up the stairs, leaving me to follow her, all my doubts and suspicions flooding back. If Minna wasn't there, where was she, and why had she tried so desperately to phone me?

Jacqueline stopped outside a door in the long, deeply carpeted corridor. 'Ring if you need anything,' she said haughtily. 'The housekeeper will help you,' and so saying she turned away, sweeping out of sight along the passage.

I opened the door and went in. The room was flooded with sunlight and I stared round, my delight for a moment obliterating my fears, quite dazzled by the white carpet and drapes and the lovely soft velvet of the chairs. A huge bowl of damask roses stood on the dressing table, filling the room with their heady scent.

Beyond the bedroom was a bathroom. Both bathroom and bedroom were equipped with enamelled bell-pulls. I hesitated, then defiantly pulled one.

Almost at once the door opened and a figure appeared, a tall dark-haired woman in her fifties, dressed in impeccable black. Her austere features did not betray the glimmer of a smile as she looked me up and down. I had the feeling she was judging me and was uncomfortably uncertain about the decision she had reached.

'Good afternoon Miss Parrish,' she said, in a strong Bostonian accent. 'I am Edith Marlesford, Mr Bradshaw's housekeeper. I trust you have everything you need?'

She sounded as if she were challenging me to find fault with something if I dare, and my question about Minna froze on my lips. I found myself giving her a tentative smile. 'The room is lovely, thank you. I was wondering if someone could bring up my cases.'

She bowed slightly. 'They are on their way.'

'When will my cousin return from Boston?' I asked.

'About eight, I believe,' she said. 'Dinner is at nine. There is one other guest here at present. Mr Calder, from England like yourself.' She paused, then almost unwillingly she went on, 'Perhaps you would like some refreshment brought up to your room now? Some iced tea?' It was obviously a great concession and gratefully I nodded assent.

An hour later, showered, changed and refreshed I leaned on the low window sill looking out into the deserted gardens, wondering what I was expected to do until Richard returned. I was not inclined to seek out the beautiful Jacqueline.

There was a phone beside the bed and on impulse I dialled Chris in New York. I had to talk to someone.

'How is it?' he asked. 'What's the tycoon like?'

I laughed nervously. 'He's not here yet, but his house is

fantastic.' It was reassuring to hear Chris's voice. I had begun to feel very lonely.

'Chris,' I went on. 'Minna isn't here.'

I could almost hear him shrug. 'She's probably had enough of the high life and come home. I shouldn't worry; I can't help thinking you'd have a lot more fun without her, Kate.' I might have known he would not take my worries seriously.

We talked for a few minutes more, then, my courage bolstered, I set off to explore the house. Slipping down the staircase I peered into first one cool high-ceilinged room, then another. All were spacious, all impeccably furnished with English antiques, and all deserted. Eventually I found some doors which led onto the lawns and I slipped outside with relief. I was tempted to take off my shoes and run barefoot on the velvet grass but somehow I resisted. I was still too awed by my surroundings.

I had been wondering where Dave Conway had got to all this time, and then in the distance I thought I caught sight of him, sitting on the edge of a stone fountain. I ran towards him with relief.

'Dave, thank goodness, I thought you'd abandoned me!'

The figure turned slightly and I recognised in embarrassment that it wasn't Dave at all, but a tall broad-shouldered dark-haired man with brilliant blue eyes; he was the most attractive man I had ever seen. He rose courteously and held out his hand. 'Katherine Parrish, I presume,' he said in an impeccable English accent. 'I'm sorry to disappoint you. Were you feeling very abandoned?' There was a hint of a smile in his eyes.

Flustered, I gave a little laugh. This was obviously the other guest, Mr Calder, and now I was close I saw no resemblance to Dave. Where Dave was charming and quiet with relaxed understated good looks, this man exuded a kind of vibrant magnetism which was almost palpable.

'Lost is a better word perhaps,' I said, confiding in him in spite of my shyness. 'I wasn't sure what I was expected to do until my cousin returns. I could find no one in the house.'

He nodded. 'How very remiss of everyone. I must apologise. Dave has his own quarters at the back. I expect he is there, and Jacqueline is probably resting.' He tightened his lips slightly and I received a strong impression that he did not like Jacqueline. 'So,' he went on with a smile, 'allow me to show you round the gardens. It will help to fill in the time before dinner.'

He slipped the note book he had been writing in into his hip pocket and gestured towards the vista of lakes and flower beds which led down towards the sunset.

I walked beside him, conscious every second of how attractive the man was as I wondered how he fitted into the household. He obviously knew who I was but had made no attempt to introduce himself. 'You must be Mr Calder?' I asked tentatively at last.

'Must I?' He turned his blue eyes on me and grinned. 'If you say so.'

That smile was irresistible. I found my own unease evaporating. 'Are you a colleague of my cousin's?' I asked as I followed him over the grass.

'Something like that,' he said unhelpfully.

'Have you known him long?' I persisted. My curiosity about Richard was at fever pitch now that I was actually in his house.

'All my life, I suppose.' He led me around the corner of a huge hedge and we stopped, looking down the broad grass terraces to a view of the distant sea.

'What is he like?' I asked.

He seemed to consider for a moment, his thumbs hitched into his belt. 'Hard,' he said. 'In fact, he's really rather a swine. You mustn't trust him.'

I swallowed. I had not expected such an outspoken assessment of our host, and it threw me; I was not sure how to take it.

'But you like him,' I stammered at last.

He considered for a moment. 'No,' he said. 'Sometimes I don't like him at all.'

I stared at him in complete silence. He was gazing into the distance, and for a second I received a sharp impression that he no longer knew I was there. I felt my skin suddenly grow cold as if a shadow had swept across the bright garden.

'There you are!' A woman's voice interrupted us and I swung round to see a tall red-haired figure appearing from the shelter of the hedge. She was dressed in a low-cut, green evening gown which revealed every detail of her fantastic figure. She eyed me with open antagonism.

'Is this the other cousin?' she asked, slipping her arm possessively through my companion's. Until that moment, I realised suddenly, he had not bothered to turn to face her.

'This is Katherine Parrish,' he agreed, his voice hard now. He swung round to me. 'Katherine, let me introduce Sara Dashwood.'

I held out my hand uncertainly. 'Please, call me Kate,' I said.

The woman ignored my gesture. 'Hi Kate,' she said dismissively, and one of her hands crept up to the front of his shirt and as I watched, fascinated, it slipped inside, caressing his chest possessively. 'What about coming in for a drink?' she whispered huskily. She could not have made it more clear that I was in the way.

I could feel my cheeks growing scarlet but Mr Calder gripped her wrist firmly and pushed her away. 'Good idea,' he said calmly. 'Katherine, you must forgive Sara. Her manners are not all they might be.' I caught my breath at his acid tone and was in time to see the vindictive look she flashed me, but he went on coolly. 'You don't mind if I call you Katherine, I hope. It suits you so much better than Kate.' His glance was warm and appraising, and I began to feel better but a moment later he had crushed me by his next remark. 'May I suggest that you should go and change now, Katherine. Dinner is in half an hour,' he consulted the wafer-thin gold watch on his wrist, 'and we like to keep it formal here.'

I fled.

Luckily I had brought a long dress with me and trembling with humiliation and rage I slipped into it, conscious that next to Sara and Jacqueline I would indeed look like some hick country cousin. I swept my long hair into what I hoped was a more sophisticated style and clipped my antique pearl studs into my ears. I was studying myself in the mirror when there was a knock at the door.

It was the housekeeper once more and I saw her eyeing me critically as she stood in the doorway. It was impossible to judge what she thought. Her face was as demonstrative as marble.

'If you are ready, Mr Richard would like to speak to you before dinner,' she said. So, he had returned at last.

I followed her down, my heart hammering with fear. I was no longer looking forward to our meeting.

The huge dim study was illuminated by a single alabaster table lamp which threw a pool of warm light on the leather-topped desk by the window. Two men were seated in the room and as I appeared they both rose to their feet.

To my relief my companion from the garden was there, dressed in a dinner jacket. With him was a much older man. I looked round, puzzled. I had imagined Richard to be in his thirties – certainly no more.

'Katherine, there you are. Allow me to present John Calder, my English lawyer,' my Mr Calder said. I had not missed the quick look of admiration which he flashed in my direction as he took in my dress and hair.

I stared at him. 'I . . . I don't understand. Mr Calder? But then who are you?' Then overcome with embarrassment I understood suddenly. 'You mean you are Richard? But why didn't you say?' I felt anger sweep over me as I saw the amusement in his eyes.

Impassively John Calder, the real John Calder, produced

a glass and put it into my hand. 'A drink, Miss Parrish,' he murmured. I took it, but my gaze had not left my cousin's face. 'I thought you were an American born and bred,' I went on. 'You don't sound American!'

'Indeed?' He replied at last, and his tone was suddenly icy. 'I can't think why I should.'

Once more he consulted his watch. 'Please, sit down Katherine. There is some business I wish to discuss with you before we dine.' He snapped his fingers. 'The papers, John.'

Obediently the other man reached for a leather document wallet as I seated myself in a chair near the desk and arranged my skirts around me as calmly as I could. The hands I clasped around my glass were trembling slightly as I surveyed my cousin's face in the lamplight. He was still the most handsome man I had ever seen, but the humour in his eyes had vanished. His face was hard and unemotional as he took the sheaf of papers from his colleague and came round the desk to sit on the edge of it, facing me.

'I have here deeds making over to me your share of the inheritance at Kingley,' he said. 'I have arranged that you have life tenancy of the farmhouse where your father lives at present – I am not interested in the building – but I want immediate possession of the land so that the woods can be cleared and the marshland drained. I am prepared to give you the current market value for the acreage in cash. You may of course have an independent valuation if you wish.'

I stared at him, unable to speak for a moment in my surprise. Then I felt the first white hot anger clamp down on my heart. His eyes had lost their charm; they were as hard as steel. Rising to my feet I put down my glass, shaking my head. 'I am sorry Richard. I am not selling.'

He did not seem surprised. 'I have paid Minna five hundred thousand pounds for her share,' he said softly.

I gasped. 'She agreed to sell?'

'She agreed.' He picked up his own glass and drained it.

I thought of Minna's phone call, her sobbing voice, her strangled warning and I felt suddenly very sick. 'Where is Minna?' I asked sharply. 'I want to see her. What have you done to her?'

'Done?' He raised an eyebrow coldly. 'I have done nothing other than make a rich woman of her. As to where she is, I assume she has gone back to New York.'

They were both looking at me and I could see nothing but menace in their faces. A picture of the lovely marshes at home, the sun reflecting on the golden reeded water flashed before my eyes and I shuddered violently. 'No,' I repeated again, looking wildly round. 'No, I will not sell.'

A gong sounded somewhere in the depths of the house. It seemed to dispel the sinister atmosphere which was building round us. Almost magically Richard's face cleared and he was once more all charm. 'Dinner,' he said quietly. 'You may of course have as much time as you need to consider your decision, but I should like your signature before you return to New York. Let us leave business now. My chef would be very upset to think that we even contemplated such a thing when one of his meals was in the offing. Allow me to show you the way . . .' His hand on my bare shoulder was warm and firm, his touch electric as he ushered me towards the door.

The others were already gathered in the dining room. To my relief Dave was there, handsome in a blue tuxedo, between Sara, her flaming hair glowing in the candlelight, and Jacqueline, thin and exquisite in silver lace.

We took our places and I found myself staring around the table, my hands still shaking, as the two uniformed maids served the soup course. What kind of man was my cousin? Handsome, charming, undeniably attractive to women as I myself had found, but it was he who had said he was hard and unlikeable, even to himself. I glanced from Sara, whose eyes were fixed possessively on him, to Jacqueline, who was toying listlessly with her food and I frowned. A fiancée and a mistress, if I read the signs aright, under the same roof, and at the same table. Was it possible?

I turned to Dave in some relief as he began to ask me about my job and somehow I managed to get through the meal, conscious the whole time of the silence of the other two women and my cousin as I chatted lightly with Dave and Calder, describing my work and the life I led with Martin. It was a very uncomfortable hour. Afterwards, coffee was served outside by the swimming pool and I found myself seated beside Richard. He was watching me carefully. 'You really care about your work?' he said.

I nodded. 'You must see why I cannot sell that land. It is a wildlife sanctuary of enormous importance,' I said earnestly.

He beckoned a servant over and asked for a cigar. I watched him flick his gold Dunhill into life. 'Unfortunate, but it can't be helped,' he said thoughtfully after a moment. 'Draining the marshes doubles the efficiency of the main estate.' He blew a column of fragrant smoke into the night sky.

'I'll never sell,' I said quietly.

I saw his eyes gleam. 'You will,' he said. 'I'm prepared to pay you half a million sterling for it. That is way over the market price for that acreage of uneconomic land.'

I stared at him, but he wasn't looking at me. I followed his gaze and saw that Sara was standing at the edge of the swimming pool, a brandy balloon in her hand, talking to Dave. Even in the twilight of the pool lights she looked voluptuous.

Abruptly I hauled myself to my feet from the low chair, overcome with a stifling sense of claustrophobia. I looked down at Richard, conscious that behind us everyone had turned to watch me. 'I told you, I am not going to part with that land,' I said softly. 'Grandfather intended me to have it; he knew what it meant to me, and I am going to hang on to it. Now, if you don't mind I should like to leave. Perhaps someone could drive me to the airport?'

Richard had not moved from his chair. He crossed his

ankles lazily, seemingly engrossed in the glowing point of his cigar. 'Tomorrow,' he said.

'I should like to go tonight,' I insisted, my voice rising slightly.

'You can't, Katherine, I'm sorry. The gates are locked on a time switch at dusk.' He smiled up at me, all charm once more. I licked my lips nervously trying to keep calm. 'But surely you can override it?'

'I can. But I don't choose to. Not tonight.' He stretched out comfortably and tapped a gobbet of glowing ash onto the paving stones. 'You must restrain your urge to leave until morning,' he said. 'If you are consumed with restlessness, why don't you have a swim?' He indicated the warm aquamarine water at our feet, and once again I saw the amusement in his eyes.

I was trapped. Trapped in an awful silken web of luxury.

Trying to hide my agitation I went over to the serving table and helped myself to more coffee, conscious that he was watching me, a slight smile on his lips. Then angrily I turned away and walked to the edge of the pool, whilst behind me Sara had slipped into my vacated chair at his side. I heard her soft laugh as she leaned towards him.

I made my way over to Dave and we wandered out of earshot on the far side of the pool.

'You've got to get me out of here,' I whispered urgently. 'Please, help me.'

He looked at me. 'I'm sorry, Kate, I can't do that.'

My heart sank, but I was determined not to show it. 'You said Minna was here, ill,' I whispered accusingly, 'but she's not, and now I find myself being kept here against my will! What the hell is going on?'

He had turned away to stare back across the pool, to where Richard and Sara were talking, their heads almost touching as they leaned towards one another in the low chairs. Calder and Jacqueline were strolling about on the terrace engaged in deep conversation, no longer interested in me.

'I understand Minna decided she was well enough to return home,' Dave replied guardedly.

'Now that Richard has got his way?'

My voice had risen slightly and I saw him frown. 'I don't know what you are suggesting, Kate –'

'Oh yes you do,' I interrupted. 'I am suggesting that she was kept here a prisoner until she signed over her farm. How he forced her I don't know, but she rang me to warn me and I took no notice, fool that I am.' I paused bitterly. 'And now I am a prisoner here in my turn!'

He looked at me in astonishment. 'A prisoner? Oh Kate, come on. You're imagining things.'

'Am I?' I caught at his arm. 'Then why aren't you prepared to help me leave?'

He sighed. 'Of course you can leave, Kate. In the morning. I'll drive you to the airport myself if it will make you feel happier, and you can take the first plane back home then. I promise.'

And with that I had to be content.

As soon as I decently could I excused myself and made my way to my bedroom, conscious of several pairs of eyes following me as I left the terrace and disappeared into the house. For a moment I wondered if anyone would follow me, but I was alone as I made my way through the darkened rooms to the stairs. Only then did I allow myself to run. I fled towards my room, finding to my relief that there was a key in the lock, and turning it, I slipped it under my pillow.

I kept telling myself that my suspicions were unfounded; that I was becoming paranoid if I thought Richard intended to find some way of forcing me to sign his wretched piece of paper, but I could not rid myself of my strange terror. Some instinct told me that I was in danger and nothing I could do would dispel it.

I had been in bed for less than twenty minutes trying to make myself relax between the cool peach-coloured silk sheets when I heard a knock at the door. I sat up, my heart thumping with terror, and clutched the sheet tightly to my throat. 'Who is it?' I whispered.

There was no answer, but as I watched, horrified, I saw the handle turn and heard a key in the lock on the outside. Whoever was there had a duplicate of my own and was using it to enter the room.

The door opened slowly and I saw the tall figure of the housekeeper silhouetted in the doorway.

'I'm sorry to disturb you,' she said, 'but Miss Sara would like to see you before you go to sleep.'

To my relief she had not made a move to enter the room.

'As you see I am already in bed,' I said, defiantly trying to keep my voice steady. 'Perhaps you would tell her I'll see her in the morning.'

'She would like to see you now,' the woman repeated mechanically, and there was something in her tone which defied argument. With a sigh I reached for my robe and pulled it on. I could not think what Sara Dashwood could possibly have to say to me.

I followed Edith Marlesford down several passages until we reached a door. She knocked on it once, then left me.

There was a murmur from behind the door and I pushed it open and went in.

Sara, dressed in a short nightdress which left nothing to the imagination, was lounging on a huge double bed, a glass in her hand which she waved at me languidly as she saw me.

'Come in and close the door,' she said.

I did so, staring round me in astonishment, half expecting to see Richard there, but she was alone. The walls of her room were hung with deep red silk and the bed itself repeated the colour in a darker shade. The only relief came from the windows which were wide open onto the garden so the moonlight flooded into the room.

She sat up and put down the glass. 'You'll have to sign, you know,' she said.

I was staring at her in horrified fascination. The long

elegant arms and legs curled languidly on the soft covers and her flaming hair hung provocatively over the low neckline of her nightdress.

'May I ask why it should interest you what I do?' I said, pulling myself together with an effort. I felt as little as a rabbit must feel confronted by a snake.

'Everything that interests Richard interests me,' she said softly. She smiled. 'If he wants your land, he'll get it one way or the other, believe me.'

I felt a return of my earlier fear, but I was determined not to show it. Tearing my eyes away from hers I walked across to the window and stared out.

'He's going to be unlucky this time,' I said firmly. 'That land means too much to me to sell it, and you can tell him as much.'

'Then you're a fool!' The scorn in her voice was like a whiplash. 'You're no match for him!'

Was it jealousy, I wondered, which made her so hostile? Well, however possessive she was, she had no need to fear me; there was no way I ever wanted to see my cousin Richard again.

I opened my mouth to say so, but she had risen from the bed in one sinuous movement and came to stand beside me. 'Do as he asks, Kate Parrish,' she hissed, her green eyes glinting in the moonlight. 'Otherwise something unpleasant could happen. You might have an accident and be found floating face down in the pool, or you might find yourself cornered in some lonely New York street and beaten up! It's happened before, you know.'

I gasped. 'You're not serious,' I said weakly. 'You're just trying to frighten me. He would never do such a thing!'

She gave me a withering look and then she smiled, a long beautiful smile which left me chilled to the marrow. 'Richard does anything he likes,' she said huskily. 'Do you want to know how you'd look when he'd finished with you?' Before I could speak she reached down and with one quick movement she had pulled her flimsy nightdress up and over her head. She flung it on the floor and stood before me naked, the moonlight shining coldly on her ivory skin. Her body was disfigured with bruises.

For one whole minute I could not drag my eyes away from the marks on her flesh, then I was running for the door. Appalled and terrified I was afraid I was going to be sick as I heard her laughter echoing up the passage behind me. I fled back to my room, slammed the door and locked it with shaking hands. Then, taking no chances, I wedged the back of a chair beneath the handle before I staggered trembling to the telephone.

I misdialled twice before I reached Chris.

'Kate? Do you know what time it is, for Chrissake?' he said as I sobbed his name into the receiver.

'Chris! Chris, you must come and fetch me, please,' I begged.

'Honey, it's three in the goddam morning!' he repeated patiently. 'Look, I couldn't even get to you for three or four hours. You've had a nightmare, Katie. Come on now, calm down!' He was beginning to sound irritated. 'If you hate it there so much leave, okay? Take the first shuttle out of Boston in the morning and I'll meet you at the airport. No sweat. Now go back to bed, Kate!'

There was no point in arguing. I knew he did not believe me. Trembling I climbed back into bed and pulled the bedclothes tightly round me. But I could not sleep a wink. Every time I closed my eyes, all I could see were those livid bruises on Sara's pale skin.

The first tentative rays of light were beginning to steal across the carpet when someone tried my door-handle once more. Somehow I stopped myself from screaming out loud as I crawled, aching, from the bed.

'Who is it?' I stammered.

There was a faint knock. Then I heard a whisper. 'Let me in, quickly. It is Jacqueline.'

'What do you want?' I answered suspiciously. I edged towards the door, my bare feet silent on the thick white carpet.

'I want to help you. I can get you away.'

Her voice, from the keyhole, sounded distant and very tired.

Cautiously I pulled away the chair and put the key in the lock. Jacqueline was dressed in jeans and a thick roll-neck sweater, her dark hair pulled back severely from her face. Her skin was paper white and her eyes had a drawn, haunted look which was inexpressibly painful to see. She slipped into my room and pushed the door silently shut behind her.

'Get dressed as quickly as you can,' she ordered quietly. 'My car is round the back.'

I did not bother to argue. I wanted more than anything on earth to be out of that house. Grabbing my clothes I ran to the bathroom and dressed, then flinging my things into the cases I put on my thin coat and I was ready. She had been watching me silently and now, with her finger to her lips, she tiptoed towards the door.

The corridor was deserted, and holding my breath I followed her through the sleeping house to the polished gleaming kitchens where the back door stood wide open. Outside stood a sleek red two-seater Mercedes. We climbed in without a word, pulling the doors closed silently, then she started the engine. I was sure the throaty roar would bring heads to every window in the house, but there was no sign of life as she swung away, the gravel spurting beneath the wheels, and headed up the drive, the headlights cutting swathes of brightness through the fresh silent dawn.

The gates opened at the touch of a button on her dashboard and then we were outside Bay View at last.

Only then did I feel I could breathe. I leaned back on the pale leather upholstery with a sigh.

'Why are you helping me?' I asked at last.

She did not take her eyes off the road, but I saw her

knuckles whiten on the wheel. 'Richard has ruined enough lives,' she said briefly.

'Won't he be angry with you?' I asked.

She gave a harsh humourless laugh. 'It doesn't matter if he is. There is nothing more he can do to me,' she said.

Already the car was slowing down and she drew into the side. I saw we were on a lonely road which overlooked a sea that was grey and endlessly empty. She opened the door and got out.

Then she bent and looked in at the window. 'Take the car, Katherine,' she said. 'I shall walk back along the beach.' She smiled for the first time. 'Don't let him catch up with you. He always ends up getting his way and it's time someone stood up to him. Good luck.'

Already she was threading her way down through the steeply growing undergrowth towards the shore. She did not look back, and I did not wait to watch her go. I had to put as many miles between myself and Richard Bradshaw as I could before he found out that I had gone.

PART TWO

Slipping across into the driver's seat I started the engine and gingerly began to ease off the handbrake. The Merc was the fastest car I had ever driven and for a moment I was tempted to take it all the way to New York, but the traffic was becoming heavier, and my nervousness was increasing as I craned in the mirror, wondering if I had been missed. I headed straight for Boston in the end and the airport, where I abandoned the Mercedes and caught the first available flight to New York after phoning Chris to come and meet me. He was there too; dear, dependable solid Chris, ready by now to listen to my story but still not prepared to believe more than half of it.

'Kate honey, Richard Bradshaw is as sound a businessman

as I ever heard of,' he said as he drove me into the city. 'There is no way he'd resort to the sort of things you are describing.' He laid a huge comforting hand on my knee. 'Come on. You need a good night's sleep, that's all. You'll see it differently when you've had a do'nut and some coffee.' Chris's universal panacea!

He dropped me off at the apartment, then he swung away from the kerb, already late for a business appointment, leaving me to let myself in. Pushing open the door I stared round cautiously. There were flowers in the room; things had been moved.

'Minna?' I called. 'Minna, are you there?'

She was lying face down on her bed, her hair tumbled over her shoulders, and for one awful moment I thought she was dead. Then I saw her drag herself almost unwillingly to wakefulness.

'Kate?' she murmured blearily. 'Are you all right?'

We hugged each other in silence for a long time. Then, over black coffee, she told me her story.

She too had been driven up to Bay View by Dave Conway in the beige Cadillac. She too had been ordered to sign over her inheritance. But she, eventually, had given in.

'Richard's a fiend, Kate,' she said weakly. 'He was so charming, so nice at first, then he changed completely. He became hard and cruel, and yet he was offering so much money.' She looked at me earnestly. 'More money than it was worth, Kate. And it's not as if Kingley means as much to me as it does to you.'

'I understand, Minna,' I said. She looked so miserable and guilty. 'I only wish we had never met him. Either of us!'

She nodded mournfully. 'If you really don't want to sell you'll have to get right away!'

I stared at her. 'I have got away,' I said warily. 'You don't think he'll try again?'

But of course I knew in my heart he would. Our fight was only just beginning.

She stood up pushing her hair off her face. 'Kate, I think he'll keep at you till he gets what he wants. He's that kind of man. And he knows where you live so you're not safe here any more.' I could hear the hysteria in her voice. It was very near the surface.

'What shall I do then?' I asked, feeling her panic beginning to creep through me. She was right of course. I was no safer in this apartment than I had been in my locked bedroom at his house.

It was my boss who solved the problem. Martin listened attentively to my story then he scratched his head.

'It seems to me, Kate, that it is time you took a vacation,' he said thoughtfully. 'Put yourself right out of his reach for a while. I can spare you a little now the series has finished. Why not take a month; that'll give him a chance to simmer down. And while you're there,' he grinned knowingly, 'you can do some preliminary research on our documentary.'

I stared. 'You mean I should go home? To Kingley?'

'Where else?' he said.

Chris agreed with him, though I could see he still thought I was over-reacting, and so without giving myself time to think I went to Pan Am and booked my flight to England. Only when the huge jet was safely in the air would I be safe again.

I settled back into my seat in relief the next day, looking out of the window at the beautiful misty morning and resolved, as the plane soared up over Long Island, that at last I could relax.

It was as the stewardess was serving coffee that I happened to turn to look back down the aisle and my heart stopped beating. On the opposite side, two rows back, sat David Conway.

He smiled at me apologetically. 'Hi,' he said. 'Richard's orders. He didn't want you getting lost or anything. Not before you've signed the documents, anyway . . .'

Far below, the mist and cloud had vanished and I could see the sparkling blue miles of the Atlantic Ocean. Why had

I ever thought Kingley would be safe? It was so obvious that I would go there and so obvious that he would follow.

Dave kept close to me through customs and out into the huge concourse at Arrivals and there for a moment I thought I had lost him; but I wasn't quick enough. As I scanned the ranks for an empty cab I felt a hand on my arm.

'If you're going to Kingley you might as well let me drive you,' he said. 'I've a hire car waiting for me, and it'll be much easier.'

Easier for whom, I wondered, but in the end I gave in. There was no point in pretending I wasn't going home, and I had no real fear of Dave. It was my cousin Richard I was afraid of.

With a sigh, I settled back on the smart leather upholstery and let him drive; he seemed to know his way round London and out into the dark countryside. Once I even felt myself doze off, worn out by the long journey, and was jerked into wakefulness only when we stopped at a service station for coffee. There, facing each other across a checked tablecloth, we talked about my cousin.

'Is he really so hard?' I asked, stirring my cup obsessively as I watched his face.

He scratched his ear. 'He's a very clever businessman,' he said.

'And he's ruthless?' I prompted.

He looked very serious. 'Yes,' he said slowly. 'He's probably the most ruthless man I've ever met. It doesn't do to cross him. Many a tough opponent has discovered that.'

Tougher than me, he was implying.

'You make him sound a very unpleasant person,' I said frankly. I could feel the almost familiar creep of fear playing over my skin once more, as it seemed to at every mention of Richard Bradshaw's name.

Dave shook his head. 'No. You've met him and you know better than that,' he replied. 'He's charming; he's a good friend. The best. But he makes a bad enemy and,' he looked up and held my gaze for a long moment, 'Kate, in case you should get any ideas about it, he dislikes women.'

I felt myself colour. I had found him attractive, I had to admit it. I swallowed nervously. 'What about Jacqueline and Sara? For a man who hates women he has more than average under his own roof!'

He gave a slow smile. 'Perhaps women like him,' he said cryptically.

A sudden suspicion crossed my mind. 'Are you telling me he's gay?' I asked.

He gave a harsh laugh. 'Oh no, Kate,' he said. 'He's not that.'

It was late when we reached Kingley and he dropped me off at the farm before driving on up to the old half-timbered manor house which now belonged to my cousin. One look at my father told me that I should never be able to confide my worries to him; he had grown so frail since I had seen him, his white hair a silver cloud around his head, his face paper white and thin as he greeted me. He drew me into the kitchen and made me a mug of hot milk and gradually the old house began to envelope me once more in its usual warm peace, so that for the remainder of that night I slept soundly for the first time since I had come across Richard Bradshaw.

Next day I went up to the manor, approaching it with some trepidation, afraid that seeing it with Grandfather gone would be more than I could bear, but it was just the same, a huge rambling Elizabethan building, the small leaded windows letting in little light, and it was still pervaded with the faint scent of burning apple boughs and, perhaps, a little of my grandfather's pipe.

I was greeted with open arms by Hill, the butler, and Mrs Dawson, Grandfather's cook-housekeeper, and was left in no doubt at once that they had no reservations about Grandfather's will. 'Of course we are all looking forward to meeting Mr Richard,' Hill said slowly. 'I hope that perhaps he will one day make his home here, but meanwhile he has appointed a first-class manager to take care of the estate.' Mrs Dawson nodded agreement. 'And that nice Mr Conway,' she said beaming. 'So American, Miss Kate, and so charming!'

I smiled to myself. They were right about Dave and what was the point of worrying them with my doubts about Richard?

I enjoyed the next few days enormously. The weather was heavenly and I took a horse each day from the Kingley stables and rode out across the land: my land, where the marshes stretched out towards the sea, ringed by woods hundreds of years old where the sunlight dappled through the young leaves onto carpets of bluebells. The air smelled of sweetness and salt and the warmth of the soft sunlight, and I blessed Minna for suggesting I came.

My happiness was reinforced by the visit I had made to the family lawyer.

Old Mr Kenton had stared at me in amazement when I had told him a carefully edited version of my story. 'Well, of course I knew your cousin Minna had made her share of the inheritance over to Mr Bradshaw,' he said. 'Frankly, it did not surprise me. I understand she has always lived in the States and she can have no emotional ties to the land, but there is no way the will can be broken, Katherine, other than by agreement. The bequest was quite unconditional.'

'So Richard cannot force me to part with Kingley Farm?'

He stared at me, his faded eyes concerned. 'There is no question of it. Kingley Farm and Marshes are yours and yours alone. That is definite.'

And without my consent Richard could not ever lay his hands on them.

Richard himself arrived at the Manor two weeks later. I had heard nothing of his arrival and was quite unprepared when the ringing of the phone brought me in from the garden where I had been weeding the rose beds whilst Father was resting.

'Oh Miss Kate!' It was Mrs Dawson on the line, and I

could hear she had been crying. 'Mr Richard is here and he has sacked us all!'

For a moment I could not believe my ears, then I knew what I had to do.

'I'm coming straight over,' I said.

It was beginning.

It was less than a mile up to the manor house and it looked the same as usual as I drove up, the mellow timbers and pink-washed walls dozing in the sunlight. Only the sapphire-blue Rolls Royce outside was different and I knew that already I had become a stranger there.

I went in without knocking, instinctively making for my grandfather's study.

Only when I was several feet into the room, propelled by my anger, did I see who the sole occupant of the study was. Sara Dashwood was poring over some papers on the desk. Her eyes widened as she recognised me and a slow smile spread across her features.

'Kate!' she said, her low voice purring. 'Welcome!'

I could feel my muscles tensing with dislike, but somehow I managed to smile. 'Is Dave Conway here?' I asked as pleasantly as I could. I was wondering if Jacqueline too had come to England, and if Richard had ever found out about her part in my escape.

She shook her head. 'Sorry Katie. Dave drove to London to collect some papers. He won't be back until tomorrow. Richard is here though. But I expect you know that. *Richard!*' She raised her voice only slightly to call him and I realised that the door into the library was open.

Seconds later Richard appeared. He was more handsome than ever, dressed in an open-necked blue shirt and slacks, his face deeply tanned, and I felt my heart give an illogical little jump at the sight of him.

'So, Katherine. How kind of you to call,' he said quietly. I had forgotten what a pleasant voice he had, but something in its tone frightened me.

I was not going to give my fear its head, however. This was, or had been, my territory, and I had a mission.

'I should like to speak to you alone, Richard,' I said looking pointedly at Sara. She had moved behind me to the door and as I watched she reached for the key and turned it. She smiled at me sweetly. 'Just in case you feel like leaving suddenly again,' she said. She tossed the key onto the desk and walked into the library.

I bit back my anger at her childishness. 'I came to speak to you about the staff,' I said stiffly, turning back to Richard.

He sat down on the edge of the desk watching me attentively, but as he said nothing, I went on: 'They have been with my grandfather for years. Kingley is their home. You cannot sack them.'

He raised an eyebrow. 'Grandfather is dead, Katherine. His ancient retainers are no use to me. But I assure you I am not as hard as you think. I am not completely insensitive. They are all being given pensions.'

'Money isn't everything!' I retorted hotly, wishing he wasn't so damned attractive. 'They are broken-hearted. They were looking forward to working for you.'

He gave a faint smile. 'Then I'm sorry to disappoint them, but I'm not a charitable institution.'

'Then you should be,' I said. 'It is part of the duty of a landowner to care for the people on his land.'

'I'll tell you what,' he said helpfully. 'Supposing I make cottages available for them on the estate and increase their pensions, would that appease you?'

I looked up suspiciously and met his glance. 'Is there a catch?' I asked.

He laughed softly. 'Of course,' he said. 'Your signature in exchange for their peace of mind.'

Somehow I controlled my anger. 'Just why do you want that land so badly?' I asked. 'It's right on the edge of the estate, and its clearance doesn't affect the efficiency of the rest of the place at all.' I held his gaze as calmly as

I could and was incensed to see the humour in his eyes.

'Maybe it does, maybe it doesn't,' he said. 'My reasons are not relevant.'

'They are to me,' I retorted. 'You can't ride roughshod over people like this!' I had begun to pace up and down the carpet. 'There is more to life than money! There is such a thing as beauty and kindness and loyalty and – love!' To my shame I could feel tears of anger pricking my eyelids.

He hadn't moved from the desk but I could see his eyes following me. He was grinning. 'You know, I can't help admiring you,' he said. 'You've got a lot more spirit than a great many of my business opponents. I like that in a woman.'

'That's not what I've heard!' I said sharply.

His eyes narrowed. 'Have you also heard that I am never defeated in a business battle?' he murmured. 'I think I shall enjoy defeating you, Katherine. It is a pity that Grandfather's old servants must suffer for your intransigence.'

'They won't suffer!' I had already thought what I was going to do. 'They can come to Kingley Farm.'

He laughed out loud. 'And how will you pay them?'

'From my inheritance. Grandfather left me some money too, you know.'

'I know exactly how much money Grandfather left you,' he said. 'If you spend it on a pack of idle servants you will be left penniless.' He stood up and walked over to the open window. The scent of the grass and fresh earth drifted in across the sill and I could see him breathing it in. Then he turned back to me.

'You really care about them, don't you,' he said.

'They are family to me,' I replied. 'I've known most of them since I was a baby.'

He was looking at me rather quizzically. 'Sentiment is not something I admire,' he went on. 'It leaves people vulnerable. But you have courage and as you said, loyalty, which I do admire. It makes you a worthy opponent. I suggest we take our battle of words further. But not here. Over dinner at the White Hart which I hear is not a bad hostelry.'

I was speechless for a moment at his change of tactics, but not so Sara, who had obviously been listening from the library the whole time. She erupted through the door, her green eyes blazing. 'You promised you would take me there tonight!' she accused.

Richard gave her a look of pure contempt. 'Another time,' he snapped. 'This is business.'

I should have turned him down there and then, but something made me agree to go out with him. Partly I think it was to get back at Sara, whom I had begun to dislike excessively, partly because now that my anger rather than my fear was uppermost, I had almost begun to enjoy sparring with him. But most of all, if I admitted the truth to myself, because I was finding him more and more attractive.

He drove me home first and waited in the Rolls whilst I changed. I did not ask him in to meet my father, who was in the event still asleep anyway, so I left him a note, then having donned a cream linen dress and my pearl earrings, I made my way out to the car once more.

Richard had obviously made up his mind not to mention our quarrel at all, nor did he mention Jacqueline. Not once did he antagonise me as we sat opposite each other in the candlelight and, baffled by his change of tactics, I found myself relaxing under his charm, almost enjoying myself as I sipped the wine.

In one corner of my mind I kept reminding myself that this man was dangerous and I must not trust him, but slowly my caution, and my antagonism, were slipping away. Without my noticing he ordered a second bottle of the Chateau Lafitte and, with my cheeks burning from the candles and the warmth of the room, I drank far more than I was used to. At last I saw the flames begin to blur and waver before my eyes and I caught myself nodding dangerously close to them. Finally Richard reached across the table and touched my hand and I jerked myself upright as if he had stung me.

'I'm sorry,' I said.

'You're tired.' He looked concerned. 'Perhaps it would be better if I took you home?'

I must have dozed again on the drive back for when I awoke we were drawing up outside the Manor.

'I thought you were taking me home!' I said, looking round in alarm.

'A coffee first, I think,' he replied firmly, and I had no alternative but to allow him to help me out of the car.

He was still holding my arm as we walked slowly up the moss-covered steps when the oak front door swung open and Sara stood there framed in the light of the hall.

I would have stopped, but Richard did not hesitate, urging me on until we passed through the wisteria-covered porch. Only then did I see the expression on Sara's face.

She was laughing. 'So, you got her drunk,' she said gleefully. 'How very clever. I might have known it wasn't the pleasure of her company you wanted!'

I drew back but Richard's arm was round me, propelling me forward into the study, and as I watched Sara slammed the door behind me. This time, when she had locked it, she dropped the key triumphantly into her cleavage.

Richard pushed me into one of the chairs then he turned to her. 'Go and make some coffee,' he said curtly, and I was aware that he had her by the elbow and was hustling her towards the door to the library beyond which lay the kitchens. Closing it behind her he strode back to me.

My head had begun to ache unbearably. 'You got me drunk deliberately,' I managed to say. 'I had begun to trust you.'

He laughed softly. 'That was a bad mistake, Katherine,' he said. 'No one should ever trust me. But I assure you, I did not get you drunk deliberately. I had imagined you would have a harder head than this. Why should I want to, anyway?' He sat down on the arm of my chair very close to me. 'Did you think I wanted to seduce you?' He was still laughing as his head dropped close to mine. 'I assure you, if I want a woman, I'll take her. I don't need to get her drunk!'

His lips were firm and warm, and I did not resist as his hands moved gently over my shoulders to slip inside my dress, caressing my breasts. All I knew was that I wanted him more than I had ever wanted any man in my life before.

'What the hell is going on?' Sara's sudden hiss of fury pierced my dazed thoughts and I shrank away from him, but he merely straightened up slowly and turned to her, mildly annoyed.

'I suggest you learn to knock on doors,' he said with awful quietness.

'And I suggest you stick to getting her signature!' she almost spat at him.

Shock cleared my head a little and I staggered to my feet, ducking under his arm. He did not appear to notice. They were regarding each other with too much anger and I was beginning to wonder if she would physically attack him when the silence between them was broken by the doorbell.

'See who that is!' he ordered abruptly.

She glared at him, then began to fumble in her blouse for the key. When she finally found it and opened the door I shot out of the room after her.

'Are you leaving so soon?' Richard had followed me into the hall, but he made no effort to restrain me.

'I am indeed,' I said as Sara pulled open the door and I saw the way of escape appear across the moonlit gravel before me. On the doorstep stood Dave Conway.

'I thought I'd come back tonight after all,' he said.

'Good.' Suavely Richard blocked his way. 'You are just in time to drive Katherine home.'

I saw the surprise on Dave's face, but already I was past him. 'There's no need,' I called over my shoulder. 'I'll drive myself.'

'You're had too much to drink,' Richard shouted sharply. 'Let Dave take you.'

I swung to face him. 'These are private roads. I'll be a

danger to no one but myself, and I seem to have sobered up astonishingly,' I replied.

He was still standing in the hall and the light showed he was smiling. 'You have indeed,' he said. 'Very well. We'll continue our little talk another time. And conclude our business transactions then as well.'

I held his gaze for a moment across that narrow stretch of gravel and I did not like what I saw there at all. All his charm had vanished. He was once more my antagonist and a dangerous man.

I accomplished the drive home without mishap and found my father waiting up for me.

'Katie! I was worried. Did Richard not drive you back?'

I shook my head. 'I had my car at the Manor so he dropped me there.' I didn't want him to see my face, but it was too late.

'Katie? Is something wrong? Have you and Richard quarrelled?'

There was no use denying it. I was too agitated. 'I suppose we have,' I admitted. 'Nothing serious, but I do think I should go away for a few days. Just to calm down a little.' I forced myself to laugh, as I knelt beside his chair. 'Will you promise me something so I can go? Will you have Mrs Dawson and Hill to work for you here?'

He smiled sadly. 'So it is true that Richard has sacked everyone up at the Manor?'

I nodded.

'Is that why you quarrelled?'

I nodded again and he reached for my hand. 'It's his decision to make Katie, but I should like people to help here. We'll afford it somehow.'

I only managed four hours' sleep. By eight next morning my case was in the car and I was driving through waist-high mist towards the main road, an enormous sense of relief bolstering me. Without my signature my woods were safe and as long as I was out of reach, Richard could not win.

* * *

I had not told my father where I was going. Sally and Duncan Graham were my best friends and the only people in England I could think of to whom I could tell my story. It was a good two-hour drive to their house and I found myself glancing constantly in the driving mirror for the sign that I was being followed, but as far as I could see there was no one behind me and with every mile I felt happier and more relaxed.

Coffee with a slug of Scotch was their first remedy. Then they listened intently to my story.

'My God, Kate! The man sounds a fiend,' Sally said with feeling. 'Yet if I read you right,' she looked at me sideways, 'you fancy him, don't you?'

I could feel my cheeks growing hot. 'Is it so obvious?' I said.

She laughed. 'Only to an expert like me.'

Duncan was frowning, however. 'I think you could be in real danger Kate,' he said. 'Not of your life or anything like that, but I suspect a man like that knows how to put the pressure on. He sounds most unsavoury to me.' Something Minna had echoed every time I had phoned her.

The Grahams' solution was immediate. They were leaving for a holiday at their Scottish cottage, and I should go with them. Duncan seemed to think that once I had dropped completely out of Richard's sight, I would be safe. 'He'll get tired of the new estate and get involved in some new deal, then you can slip home,' he said with a grin.

Twenty-four hours later I was ensconced with them in a stone-built cottage on the west coast of Scotland, a lifetime away from Kingley and Richard Bradshaw.

But my relief was all too short-lived. After dinner that first evening as we sat with our coffee around the crackling drift-wood fire I asked Duncan if I could ring my father. I let the dialling tone purr in my ear for a long time before I admitted no one was going to answer and hung up.

'Surely he could have gone out?' Sally said, shrewdly watching my face.

I shook my head slowly. 'He practically never does. And even if he had, someone should be there.'

I tried again an hour later and finally, just before we went to bed. Then I rang the Manor. An American voice answered.

'Who is that?' I asked cautiously. The receiver felt clammy in my hands.

'David Conway. May I help you?'

'Dave? Listen, do you know where my father is?'

'Kate? Where are you?'

'Never mind where I am. Where is my father?'

There was a short silence, then I heard him say cautiously, 'Kate, I think you had better come home.'

I felt panic beginning to mount in my throat, and I knew my face had gone white. Sally had risen to her feet and came to stand beside me, her hand on my arm. Somehow I managed to repeat my question.

'He's in Switzerland, Kate.'

'*Switzerland*?'

Duncan had stood up and came to stand beside Sally. They both had their eyes fixed on my face.

'He had a bad turn, Kate. Nothing too serious. Richard heard about it and naturally he wanted to help. He had a specialist come in and they arranged for Mr Parrish to be taken to a clinic in Switzerland.'

'Where is it? Give me the address.' My voice was shaking.

'I can't do that Kate,' he said softly. 'Richard has all the details. He's in New York just now, but he'll be back on Friday. You'll have to speak to him. In person, Kate.'

'You can't go!' Sally said later. 'It's a trap, you must see that.'

I knew she was right. And I also knew that I had no choice. Richard had found my weak point. Miserably I repacked my case and asked Duncan to drive me to catch the first train from Oban next morning.

Dave was waiting for me at King's Cross with the Rolls. 'I don't usually get involved in Richard's personal affairs, Kate,' he said as we threaded our way through the traffic. 'But in business I know him. He is completely ruthless honey, and without sentiment. He doesn't understand or care what you feel about that land. To him it's acreage on a piece of paper; more for his empire. You are a challenge and so, true to form, he's found your Achilles heel and gone straight for it.' He glanced across at me, his hazel eyes worried. 'Don't fight him, Kate. For God's sake. Do I have to spell out what I'm trying to say?'

'He'd actually hurt my father?' My fingers had twisted my skirt into a fan of tiny pleats.

For a moment he didn't answer. Then he nodded slowly. 'He stops at nothing to get what he wants honey, believe me.'

I believed him. I sat in a coma for the rest of that drive and, persuading Dave to drop me off at the farmhouse alone, I walked up the drive feeling as though the weight of the world were on my shoulders.

Mrs Dawson was in the kitchen and the place was full of sunlight and flowers with the kettle singing on the hob. But the house was empty without my father and I knew I was beaten.

Late that afternoon I went for a walk over my land and realised that I was saying goodbye. The bluebells still scented the shade of the oak woods and the marshland smelled of salt and sweet grasses and I stood for a long time watching the redshanks running about on the mud, their slender feet making light tracks which stayed a minute then vanished as if they had never been. 'Forgive me,' I whispered into the wind. 'Forgive me, for what I'm going to do.'

I walked back slowly, the setting sun in my face, and made my way back home exhausted and defeated. Mrs Dawson was waiting for me by the gate, her kind face wrinkled with worry. 'Miss Kate, you've been so long.'

'I'm sorry. I had to think by myself for a bit,' I said. Then I added hopefully, 'Has there been any word from my father?'

Any word which would bring reprieve.

She shook her head. 'Only Mr Richard phoned.' The tone of her voice told me what she thought of him. 'He said he was expecting you to dinner at the Manor.'

I dressed carefully in a long dress of palest eau de nil and piled my hair into a chignon. My car was still at Sally and Duncan's house, but Richard had said he would send the Rolls and I found myself smiling faintly at the chauffeur as I stepped in, feeling like Marie Antoinette as she mounted the tumbril for her last ride through Paris.

Richard seemed to be alone in the study – as far as I could see the only room in the house which he used – and I glanced round, expecting to see Sara somewhere in the background as usual, but no; there was no one else there. I was not sure whether or not I should be relieved.

I looked him straight in the eye as he rose to greet me. 'So, you've won. I suppose you think you're very clever.' I did not try to keep the bitterness out of my voice.

I was astonished at the way my heart had started to jerk uncomfortably somewhere under my breastbone at the sight of him. He was casually dressed in a cord jacket with a cravat at the open neck of his silk shirt and looked unbearably handsome. But I was determined not to be won over. 'It must be marvellous to be so rich you can ride roughshod over everyone and everything,' I went on relentlessly, 'manipulating lives, as if they were pawns on a chessboard.'

He had begun to smile slightly and I could feel my eyes blazing with anger.

'You are not a good loser I see, Katherine,' he said softly. 'Perhaps a drink would help a little?'

It was champagne.

I threw my purse down on a chair and took the tall tulip glass from him with as steady a hand as I could manage.

'I may not be a good loser, Richard,' I breathed, 'but I'm not a stupid one. I have to have proof my father is all right before I sign anything at all.'

He was watching me closely and now he sat down on the

corner of his desk. Putting his own glass down on the blotter, he folded his arms. 'And you also want to see the colour of my money, of course.'

'Of course.' It hadn't even crossed my mind, but I wasn't going to let him guess that. My eyes were fixed on the spray of tiny bubbles rising from his glass, too small to stain the royal blue blotting paper beneath them as they landed.

He laughed quietly. 'You know, Katherine, I'm almost disappointed in you. I had thought you would hold out to the death.'

I looked at him at that. 'My own perhaps,' I whispered. 'But not my father's.'

He picked up his glass. 'Then let us drink to his recovery,' he said smoothly. 'What proof do you want that he is safe and well? Will your own eyes convince you?'

I nodded.

Without a word he swivelled to pick up the phone on the desk. After a few murmured orders he turned back to me. 'We have time to eat a quick dinner, then the car will call at your place so that you can collect your passport,' he said, and he picked up his glass.

If only it could have been under different circumstances I would have enjoyed that flight in the executive jet across France. The sky was clear and starlit and the ground far beneath us bathed in silver moonlight as we cruised towards Switzerland and my father. It was too late to visit him when we arrived and a car whisked us into the centre of Geneva where hotel rooms were awaiting us, and I was shown with meticulous politeness to a private suite.

Exhausted, I fell asleep almost instantly and was only awakened by the chambermaid bringing a breakfast of coffee, croissants and black cherry jam.

Richard was waiting for me in the foyer. He greeted me with a brotherly kiss on the cheek. 'It's an hour's drive,' he said cheerfully. 'I've rung the clinic and your father is expecting us.'

I had never been to Switzerland before, and the beauty of those circling mountains took my breath away. In spite of my determination not to unbend towards Richard in any way, I could not prevent myself exclaiming in delight as the hired BMW drove us ever higher. The clinic was huge, white painted and obviously excessively expensive, and my father, greeting us in the muted, flower-filled reception room, looked better than I had seen him look for years.

'Richard, my boy,' he said after he had hugged us both. 'I don't know how to thank you. I've been given a new lease of life!' He turned to me and pulled my hair playfully. 'I had got the impression from you Katie, that this chap was some kind of Machiavellian monster. What were you thinking of you naughty child?'

'I can't imagine,' I said dryly.

We spent a couple of hours with father, wandering slowly in the gardens, and then we went back inside. As Richard said goodbye and went out to the car I lingered behind for a moment.

'You really are happy to be here, Pa? They are looking after you?' I asked.

He kissed me on the forehead. 'Reichman is the best there is in his field, Kate. I couldn't be in better hands. I don't know how I can ever thank Richard. This place costs a fortune you know.'

I smiled. 'He's glad to do it, Pa.'

'And you're in love with him, Kate, aren't you?' He was looking down into my face, his eyes reflecting all the pride and joy he had always shown me. I opened my mouth to deny it, but I knew suddenly that it would spoil everything for him if I did. Instead, I managed to smile. 'Perhaps a little,' I said. 'It's early days yet.'

'He's a good man, Katie, you could do no better,' he said hopefully. 'And he adores you, you know, I can see it in his eyes.'

* * *

By tea time we were once more circling the airport back home. The Rolls was waiting outside the terminal. At the wheel was Sara, her hair glowing above a black shirt and tight white jeans. She was laughing as she saw us emerge from the building. 'What, no cuckoo clocks and duty free brandy?' she said as she gunned the car viciously into life. 'I am surprised, Kate. And was the beloved parent alive and well?'

'That is enough Sara!' Richard's voice cut like a whiplash across her sarcasm and she fell silent, but my eyes met hers for an instant in the driving mirror and I saw the flash of triumph in them with a sinking heart.

I asked to be dropped off at the farm, but Richard refused. 'You have a small duty to perform before you go home, Katherine. A signature, remember?'

How could I forget?

At the Manor I headed for the study automatically, but Sara barred my way.

'There's a room for you upstairs,' she said. She eyed my suit as if it were something the cat had dragged in. 'I'm sure you would like to freshen up and change before dinner.'

I took a shower and slipped on the shantung dress which I had in my overnight bag. I brushed my hair down on my shoulders and carefully applied some make-up, then taking a deep breath I made my way back downstairs.

Richard was alone in the study. There was no sign of Sara, nor, I noted, Jacqueline. He too had changed and was now formally dressed in a dinner jacket. A new bottle of Krug stood already opened on the desk and when I appeared he poured out a second glass.

'To our business deal,' he said.

The windows were opened onto the twilit garden and I could hear a blackbird singing in the distance. The sound was somehow heart-breaking in its beauty.

'Well,' I said sharply, wishing I were not so conscious of how handsome he was looking. 'Let me sign and get it over.'

He glanced at his watch. 'Calder should be here soon. He's

on his way down from London. He has the papers with him.'

I put down my glass untouched. 'You should be feeling very pleased with yourself,' I said sadly. 'The fact that you are going to destroy so much that is beautiful and irreplaceable means nothing to you?'

'Should it?' He strode over to the window and glanced out.

'Haven't you enough money?'

Turning he looked at me. 'Does anyone ever have enough?'

I closed my eyes, hoping I wasn't going to cry. I had no arguments left.

John Calder arrived, dapper and cool in spite of his long drive, and produced a sheaf of legal documents from his briefcase. One by one they were put before me and one by one I signed, hardly seeing what I was doing through a haze of tears. Then all the papers were locked away in the safe behind Grandfather's portrait on the wall.

Richard pushed a scrap of paper towards me as I turned away. 'Don't forget your cheque, Katherine. Better put it somewhere safe.'

I picked it up without looking at it and slipped it into my pocket.

Calder and Richard drank more champagne, and then the former took his leave, shaking hands with us both in turn. 'I am so glad this has ended happily,' he said as he made his farewells and he slipped unobtrusively from the room. Outside the blackbird was still singing.

Richard was watching me closely. 'You look a little pale,' he said. 'Dinner won't be long.'

I shook my head. 'I don't want any dinner. I'm going home.'

He was at the door before me, his hands on my shoulders. 'I insist. You can't disappoint the chef. Then you can go home.'

I was too tired and too miserable to argue.

Only when we were seated once more in the huge, gloomy

dining room, lit by candles in the two silver candelabra, did I notice that Sara was still missing.

'Isn't your lady friend joining us?' I asked wanly as Richard poured white wine into two crystal glasses.

'She is not.' His voice was suddenly uncompromisingly hard.

'I can't believe she approves of you dining with me alone,' I said.

'She has no say in the matter,' he replied sitting down and picking up his napkin. 'She's locked in her room.'

I stared at him, shocked out of my apathy. 'You're joking!'

'Am I?' He met my gaze steadily for a moment. 'I wonder.'

The door opened and a maid appeared with the hors d'oeuvres. Only when she had gone did I look at Richard again. His eyes were gleaming maliciously in the candlelight. 'I hope you are going to eat this time. You've been picking at your food ever since I met you, and you are already too thin for my liking,' he said.

'Indeed,' I retorted. 'Well, if Sara is the shape you like, you can keep her. I'll never have a figure like that!'

He looked thoughtful. 'She is beautiful, that's true, but stupid. Very stupid.' He grinned. 'And a real bitch.'

'You haven't really locked her in?' I persisted uneasily in spite of myself. I wasn't at all sure that he was joking.

One of Grandfather's crested silver forks gleamed in his hand as he toyed with a minute curl of smoked salmon. He looked at me for a long moment, then he raised his glass. His face was alive with amusement.

'I did. She has a vicious temper. I gather she told you I beat her,' he went on conversationally.

I felt myself grow cold. 'Do you?' I asked.

He laughed and the sound made my skin crawl. 'I always beat my women,' he said softly.

There was a long silence in the room as, seemingly unconcerned, he continued eating.

'I don't believe a word you say!' I said at last.

He looked up. 'Don't you? You should see your face!'

Despite my feelings, I smiled. 'All I can say is thank God I am not one of your women, so I need never find out the truth.'

'Ah, but you are,' he said.

'I beg your pardon?' I stared at him.

'You are one of my women, Katherine,' he repeated softly.

'How do you make that out?'

'I've bought you, sweetheart. Body and soul.' He laughed again and I felt the hairs rise on the back of my neck.

'That cheque in your pocket,' he went on. 'Only half that money was for the land; the price I originally offered you. What do you think the rest is for?'

I stared at him for one full minute, then I reached into my pocket and unfolded the cheque, holding it to the candlelight so that I could read it.

It was made out for one million pounds sterling.

'Don't tear it up my dear, will you.' His voice came from miles away beyond the glow of the candlelight. 'You've signed now, and I shall not write you another one for less!'

For a moment I remained where I was, paralysed, then I pushed my chair back and stood up. 'You're crazy!' I cried. 'Quite, quite crazy!'

Again that low, pleasant laugh. 'Quite, quite possibly,' he echoed, 'but not too crazy to be able to collect what is mine.'

And with that he rose and began to walk towards me round the long table. . .

PART THREE

I found I could not move. Paralysed, I watched as Richard approached me round that long Georgian dining table, his face illumined by the flickering candles. My brain had ceased to function – then he touched me. His hands rested lightly on my elbows, and he drew me to him without a word. Obediently I lifted my lips to his and felt his kiss burning against my mouth. Slowly his arms slipped around me, holding me against him so tightly I could barely breathe, and I closed my eyes, feeling my whole body come unwillingly alive at his touch, powerless to resist him.

But somewhere, somehow, my mind was fighting back. This man was my enemy; however masterly a lover he was, however much I wanted him, nothing could change that. He was in search of conquest and only when I was completely his would his craving for power over me be satisfied. It was not me, Kate Parrish, whom he wanted. I had been a rival and I had to be completely defeated.

Besides, he was engaged. The thought broke the spell and at last I regained the power of movement. I began to struggle, pushing him away.

'How could you!' I managed to say. 'Doesn't it make you feel just the smallest bit guilty, making love to every woman who crosses your path, when you have a beautiful fiancée waiting for you in the States?'

He stiffened imperceptibly, then he let me go. 'I no longer have a fiancée,' he said, his voice cold. He walked across to the window and leaned out, his elbows on the sill.

'You mean you broke it off?' I asked incredulously.

There was a long silence. 'You could say that she broke it off,' he replied after a moment.

'All right then, what about Sara?' I flung at him. 'Your mistress is upstairs in this very house!'

He turned and gazed at me. Then he began to shake his head in mock despair.

'Mistress is such a quaint term; but are you going to make me get rid of all my women, Katherine?'

This time I could have moved, but I didn't try. I wanted him to kiss me again.

As his arms closed round me I heard the telephone ring in the distance. For a moment I thought he would ignore it, but reluctantly he pushed me away. 'I'll be back,' he whispered, touching the tip of my nose with his finger, and he was gone.

Seconds later he reappeared. He looked mildly amused rather than annoyed. 'It's for you,' he said.

The phone was in the study and, still dazed, I followed him and picked up the receiver.

'Kate? It's Chris. Can you get over here right away?'

'Chris?' For a moment I was non-plussed. Chris. My dependable, nice American Chris, ringing me at Kingley Manor? 'Where are you?' I stammered.

'I'm over at your place. Mrs Dawson here told me where you were. Look, Kate, you've got to get back here quickly.'

'Is something wrong? Is it Father?'

'I'll tell you when you get here.'

'Chris? Chris, *wait* . . .' I shouted, but he had hung up.

Richard was watching my face. 'What's wrong?'

Shaking my head, I was still staring at the phone. 'I don't know. I must go back . . .'

I expected him to argue, but to my surprise he offered to drive me home straightaway. Like me he obviously thought it must have something to do with my father.

At the farm he helped me out of the car. 'Do you want me to come in?' he said, his voice unexpectedly gentle.

I shook my head, and without a word he climbed back into the Rolls. 'You know where I am if you need me,' he said. 'Remember the plane is there if you want to go to him,' and he was gone.

I stood for a moment, watching the tail lights disappearing up the long tree-lined road back to the Manor, then I went into the farmhouse. Chris was sitting in the cosy living room, drinking coffee. There was no sign of Mrs Dawson. He rose as I went in, and I was enveloped in a huge bear hug. 'Kate honey, have I missed you!'

'Chris, what is it? Is it Pa?' Unable to think of anything else I stood, my hands clutching Chris's shirt-front, trying to read his face.

'Hey, relax honey. Why should it be to do with your Pa?' He guided me to the sofa and pulled me down beside him. 'I was sorry to hear from Minna that he'd been ill, but I understood from your nice Mrs Dawson that he was at some swanky clinic in Switzerland.'

'He is.' I was beginning to breathe evenly again. 'But what did you want to tell me so urgently then?'

'I'll tell you.' He reached for his coffee. 'Do you want some of this stuff? Okay, now, listen. Just before I was due to come over here, I had dinner with your boss, and he told me he'd been doing some research into your precious Kingley Woods.'

I felt my heart sink. What would Martin think of me when he heard I'd sold out?

'He's discovered the reason your millionaire cousin is so all-fired eager to get his paws on that land.'

'Don't tell me, Chris. It's too late,' I said desperately.

He stared at me. 'Too late?'

I nodded. 'I sold.'

For a moment I thought he was going to have a fit. His face went puce, then white. 'Why, for Chrissake?' he managed to say at last.

I got to my feet and feeling in my pocket I found the cheque and threw it down on the coffee table in front of him. 'There's the reason,' I said bitterly.

He reached for the piece of paper and opened it, and his mouth dropped open. 'One million. One lousy million! Kate, Martin has discovered that several years ago test borings were done on that land. There is oil under there.'

I gasped. 'And Richard knew that?'

'Sure he knew.'

For a moment I was too stunned to speak, then suddenly I began to laugh. Chris stared at me as if I had gone off my head as, too weak to explain, I threw myself back on the sofa, the cheque in my hand, and waved it at him.

'Only half this was for the land,' I spluttered hysterically. 'Half a million for the land. The other half was for me!'

It took him a minute to follow what I was saying, but eventually he understood. I have never seen Chris angry before, but this time I thought he'd hit the ceiling.

'The bastard!' he yelled, beside himself. 'The lousy, no-account bastard! Who the hell does he think he is anyway? My God! When I think . . .' He was beyond speech for a moment. Then he went on. 'When was this, anyway?'

'Just now,' I said with a harsh little laugh. 'You called up just as he was about to haul me off to bed.' I didn't add that, seduced by wine and candles and kisses, I would probably have gone without too much of a struggle. His next words however left me completely cold with horror, every ounce of bitter laughter drained from my body.

'I knew he was a shit,' he said slowly. 'But this takes some beating. Did he tell you his fiancée killed herself a couple of days back?'

Outside an owl had started hooting in the old walnut tree on the side lawn. It was the only sound in that room for a long time.

'Jacqueline?' I whispered at last.

'Jacqui Overton. That's right.'

'How?' Stiffly my lips framed the question.

He hesitated for a moment. 'She shot herself. Hey, Katie, I'm sorry honey. You look shattered. I didn't realise you knew her.'

I shook my head. 'I only met her once, but . . .' My eyes had filled with tears. 'She was kind to me, in her own way.'

Her last words to me had come flooding back. 'There is nothing more Richard can do to me,' she had said and I remembered suddenly the despair I had seen in her eyes.

I looked at Chris bleakly. 'You know, I would like that coffee after all,' I said huskily.

I did not sleep that night. I had shown Chris to the spare room and with one look at my face he had kissed me good-night and meekly closed the door behind him. I went to my own bed alone. My head was whirling with images: Jacqui, her face white, her eyes great aching pools of misery; Richard, his handsome profile stone-carved against the candlelit velvet curtains; my father, his eyes bright and happy above lips which still showed that tell-tale tinge of blue; and Sara, her mouth scarlet, laughing at me, laughing as she was dragged away by some of Richard's minions; and above all I kept seeing my woods and marshes, bright and sun-filled no longer, disfigured by a choking blanket of oil.

When I awoke it was raining. I lay for a long time listening to the regular splatter on the window then I dragged myself, my head splitting, out of bed.

Chris was sitting at the kitchen table demolishing a plate of bacon and eggs. I slid into the chair opposite him and tried to smile. 'How long can you stay?' I asked.

Mrs Dawson put a cup of coffee before me. 'Do you want bacon, Miss Kate?' she asked. I could see her eyeing my face doubtfully.

I shook my head. 'Just coffee thanks.' My hand was shaking as I picked up the cup.

'I'll stay as long as you like,' Chris said gently. 'And the first thing I'm doing is driving you to the bank to pay this in.' He reached into his pocket and produced the cheque. He laughed quietly. 'You know I found it on the floor this morning! You must get it cleared before our friend changes his mind and cancels it.'

I grimaced and reached for the wooden sugar bowl. 'I'm going to return it to him.'

'No, you're not.'

'Chris! I told you what the money was for!'

'Okay, so you pay the cheque in and write him another for half the sum.'

I had never thought of that.

My triumph was short-lived. Two days later I received my cheque to Richard through the post. It had been neatly torn in half and in spite of myself I was once more a millionairess and in his debt.

I told Chris, tears of frustration in my eyes, and he gave a dry laugh. 'Don't worry, honey,' he said. 'We'll win.'

Leaving Chris sitting in the garden I walked over to the stables and borrowed a horse, determined to gallop the misery out of my system, feeling the wind and rain and sun in my hair and on my face, but I was to wish bitterly that I hadn't. Automatically I took the bridle path which led round the acres Minna had sold to Richard, already shimmering green beneath their crop of winter wheat, and headed towards my woods. One more ride, surely, could do no harm, and Richard wasn't there to see me; I had heard that he had gone back to Boston.

But at the edge of Kingley Wood I had to pull the horse to a rearing halt. Instead of the broad soft leafy path I was used to I was confronted by a solid wire fence which led off in both directions as far as I could see into the distance. I stared at it. He must have had men working to fence off the wood at dawn the day after I had signed it over.

I walked the horse home, no longer interested in where I went. All I wanted was to go away and never see Kingley again.

Chris provided a temporary solution. 'We'll go and see your father,' he said. 'Spend a week or two in Switzerland. It's best like that, Katie, surely?'

Mutely I nodded. I had already heard the distant whine of a chainsaw echoing across the fields and I knew I could not hang around to watch those great oaks fall.

The flight to Switzerland was very different this time. I could not bring myself to touch the money in the bank, so we went economy, a pedal plane, as Chris laughingly called it, full of tourists and children and harassed stewardesses, and then hired a Hertz car to take us out to the clinic.

My father had a small private room on the second floor, a bright room full of flowers, and he seemed astonishingly well. At his recommendation Chris and I found ourselves rooms at the inn in the local village which we could use as a base for exploring the countryside.

'It looks to me as if you need this air as much as I do, Katie,' Pa said gently as I sat beside him on the window seat in his room. The doctor to whom I had spoken on our arrival had said he was so much better he would be able to go home within a few weeks. 'But I'm disappointed not to see Richard.' He looked at me searchingly. Chris had gone off to collect some newspapers.

I tried to keep my face impassive. 'He had to go to Boston on business,' I said, as calmly as I could.

'I see.' He was still watching me. 'I like Chris, of course, but I had hoped, Katie, that you and Richard –' he stopped as I jumped to my feet.

'No, I'm sorry, but there can never be anything between Richard and me!' As I said it I realised that I would have given my right arm to have been able to please him. But I never wanted to see Richard again.

Luckily Chris appeared at that moment, a pile of newspapers under his arm. 'Hi,' he said. 'I took the chance to ask them to bring up some coffee and pastries. I hope that's all right?' He looked from one to the other of us, obviously puzzled by our silence. 'Would you like me to go away again?' he asked humbly.

I grabbed his arm. 'Of course not. I was just telling Pa that Richard had gone to Boston.'

'Such a pleasant young man,' my father muttered defiantly.

Unfortunately Chris heard him. 'You're kidding,' he said. 'After the stunt he pulled over those woods!'

I aimed a kick at his ankle, but it was too late. My father rounded on him sharply.

'What are you talking about?'

Chris ignored my frenzied signals. 'He forced Kate to sell him her inheritance, that's all,' he said. 'The man is an unprincipled bastard.'

My father had gone white. 'You've sold the marsh, Katie?

It's not true? I can't believe it. Your grandfather wanted you to have it forever.'

'Pa,' I took his hands in mine. 'Don't be upset.'

'Upset!' He rounded on me. 'What made you do it? What in the world made you do it?'

I could not reply, but Chris stepped in. 'Why do you think Richard had you brought here?' he said quietly. 'The man has proved himself an unscrupulous blackmailer!'

For a moment there was complete silence in the room, then my father clutched at his chest. Through a haze of horror I saw his face go white and then blue as he began to stagger towards the bed, gasping for breath.

'*Chris!*' I screamed.

He had the presence of mind to press the bell and within seconds the room was full of doctors and nurses and Chris and I were hustled away.

'Oh Kate, I'm sorry.' Chris was holding his head. 'I never thought! I never realised . . .'

'It doesn't matter,' I heard myself say tonelessly. 'You weren't to know.'

Later the doctor came and spoke to us. He was very reassuring. 'He'll be fine after a good rest,' he said kindly. 'Come and see him tomorrow, for five minutes only.'

We walked slowly towards the inn with heavy hearts. I had not realised just how precarious my father's health was, but I could not be angry with Chris. He was on my side, after all.

We walked into the bar at the inn and ordered ourselves a drink. There seemed nothing else to do.

Seated in silence at the table for a while we watched the coming and going of the other guests, then Chris idly pulled one of the American newspapers out of the bag he was carrying, and opened it.

I heard his gasp and looked up. 'What is it?'

'Kate, you're not going to believe it!' he said, his voice

shaking. He folded the paper and pushed it towards me, his finger pointing at a double column article at the bottom of the page. The light was dim, but I could just make it out. The headline read: *Boston Murder Enquiry*. Below it there was an account of Jacqui's death and the police decision that it had not been suicide after all, but murder. There was a photo of Jacqui and another of Richard. I reread the last paragraph: *Police said last night that they were anxious to interview the deceased's fiancé, millionaire businessman Richard Bradshaw, at present believed to be visiting his family estates in England. They admitted that he could not be ruled out as a suspect. . .*

The room had started to spin and I closed my eyes, not realising that Chris had left the table until he returned with a brandy and pressed the glass into my hand.

'Drink it,' he ordered softly. Then he took the paper back and scrutinised it again, shaking his head.

I went to my room shortly afterwards, and spent the next hour sitting in a daze on the bed, staring at the wall. It was not possible. I did not believe it. Whatever I thought of Richard, whatever I had said, I did not, could not, believe he was capable of murder. Whatever Sara and David had said, and Jacqui herself, the man I knew, the man who had held me in his arms, could not be a killer.

I was only brought back to myself by a knock at the door. It was Chris.

'Kate, there's a David Conway in the bar asking for you. He went up to the clinic and they told him we were here.'

I heard myself gasp.

'If you don't want to see him, I'll tell him to get lost.' Chris was bristling with suspicion at once. But I shook my head. 'I'll come,' I said. 'Give me one minute and I'll come down.'

I washed my face and ran a comb through my hair. Then I went to join them.

Dave was looking tired, but reasonably cheerful, I thought. 'Seen the papers?' he said.

I nodded, sliding in close to Chris on the bench.

'Mrs Dawson said you'd flown out to see your father,' he went on. 'I thought I'd better come right out and reassure you. Needless to say Richard had nothing to do with this dreadful business. You do believe that, don't you?' He glanced first at me, then at Chris, his hazel eyes warm and sincere.

Obviously we both looked doubtful so he went on. 'You didn't know about Jacqui, Kate. There's no reason why you should as Richard protected her the whole time, even keeping up the pretence that they were engaged. She had a big drug problem, and she had tried to kill herself a couple of times before.'

I stared at him. 'But the paper said – '

'The papers say Richard is suspected of murdering her,' David said softly, 'because the police received information – anonymously of course – that he did.' He paused, his eyes steadily on mine. 'Hell has no fury, someone once said, and the woman Richard scorned was Sara Dashwood!'

'*She* told them he was a murderer?' I repeated, scandalised.

'She did. He had given her her marching orders, stupid bitch, and she got her own back very neatly.'

'Then he can prove he's innocent, surely?' I asked in a whisper.

He gave me a reassuring smile. 'He'll manage somehow.'

My head was reeling with the implications of what he had said.

'What made him decide to get rid of Sara at last?' I asked after a moment.

He looked at me, his head a little to one side.

'Can't you guess?'

Something in his expression made me blush. 'For Jacqui?' I murmured.

'No, for you.' For a moment we sat in silence looking at

each other. Then abruptly he stood up. 'Let me get us all another drink,' he said.

'What was that last bit about?' Chris said as Dave headed for the bar.

'You know as well as I do,' I said sharply. 'But I never thought he'd actually go as far as telling her to go!'

'You asked him to?' He raised an eyebrow.

'I asked him what the hell he meant by trying to seduce me with a fiancée – ' I stopped abruptly, then I went on, 'and at the same time another woman upstairs in the same house.'

'I see.' He didn't sound convinced.

David returned with three drinks. 'I've got to get going,' he said. 'I'm booked on a flight from Geneva this afternoon.'

'It was good of you to come here.' I could feel the strain showing on my face as I forced myself to smile.

He grinned. 'I just wanted to put your mind at rest. And the two most important things I haven't even mentioned yet. First, whatever happens Richard wants you to know that your father's bills at the clinic will be met. And second, the Kingley Wood trust is all but set up.'

'The Kingley Wood trust?' I echoed blankly.

He nodded. 'The land he bought from you.' He stopped and stared at me, his puzzlement showing clearly for a moment. 'He's put it in trust in perpetuity as a conservation area!'

I felt my mouth drop open. 'Are you *sure*?'

'I'm sure.'

'You mean he didn't know about the oil?'

'He knew.' He laughed at the look on my face. 'I don't know what you've done to him, Kate Parrish, but it's the first unbusinesslike move I have ever known him make! He could have made millions from that deal.'

I thought about that statement a great deal that night as I lay alone in bed, staring out of the open window at the moonlight reflecting on the soaring mountain peaks outside my window.

* * *

The next morning Richard's face was on all the front pages. *Millionaire Sought for Murder of Fiancée*, screamed the headlines. Chris looked at me across the breakfast table. 'You believe Conway? That he's innocent?'

I nodded. 'He's ruthless, Chris. But not a murderer!'

Chris looked sceptical. 'I'm sorry, Kate, but I'm not convinced. I'm just glad you're right out of it here. You may have lost your land, but at least *your* life is safe!'

'Chris. We've been unfair to him.' I could feel myself growing hot with indignation. 'He's saving the land. He's not going to let it go for oil.'

'So Conway says.' Chris raised an eyebrow. 'Sweet, innocent Kate. I don't know what the rules in Britain are, but sure as hell, if your government wants that oil, they'll get it, no matter what kind of rare bird has built its nest on top of it. They'll shift that bird's ass so fast – and who'll get the money, while he's bitterly regretting the betrayal of his attempt at conservation? Mr Richard Bradshaw!' He did not lighten the remark with a smile. Pushing his chair back he stalked out of the dining room, and left me with my thoughts.

I was completely torn. My head kept telling me that Chris was right. Richard was hard, ruthless, unsentimental at his own admission, and capable of violence. Hadn't I seen Sara's bruises with my own eyes? But my heart kept telling me that inside he was not like that at all, that perhaps he had become a little fond of me and that whatever or whoever he was, I had to admit at last that I had fallen in love with him.

And Chris knew it.

Two days later, after a spate of reporting in the press and on the TV news which I had watched at the inn, trying to hide the shaking of my hands as I saw the handsome face of my cousin on the screen, Chris insisted that we go for a walk.

'I'm going back home to New York, Kate,' he said.

'But Chris – ' I stared at him.

'No, Kate.' He took my hands in his and held my gaze steadily. 'Honey. You've got your father here, and no doubt

Conway will keep you in the picture about Bradshaw. I'm not going to stay and watch you destroying yourself over a man like that. If you need me, call me, but as long as you're in love with him, don't bother.'

Had I been as obvious as that? Overcome with remorse I threw my arms around his neck. 'Oh Chris,' I cried. 'I didn't mean to hurt you. But you and I –' I hesitated. 'It was never –'

'I know, Katie.' Gently he disengaged himself. 'And I hope it all works out the way you want.'

Two hours later I watched him climb into the local taxi and disappear out of sight.

I was very sad when I made my way up to the clinic that afternoon. Chris had been my prop and reassurance. I knew in my heart that I hadn't been fair to him, but already I missed him desperately.

In the corridor near my father's room I was waylaid by a doctor. 'Only ten minutes today, Miss Parrish,' he said. 'Your father is not feeling very strong.' He frowned. 'I gather he has learned more news which appears to have upset him considerably. I don't know if you can reassure him at all?' I had of course told him how much Chris regretted his indiscretion and about the Trust. It had cheered him and seemed to be helping him on the road to recovery. I had not mentioned a word about the murder.

Of course he had been bound to find out. In a way I was surprised he had not heard already.

Sure enough, as soon as I went in he groped under his pillow for a newspaper and showed it to me. 'You knew, Kate?'

I nodded. 'He's innocent of course. And he has a cast iron alibi. It will all be sorted out soon, you'll see.'

He seemed reassured, but I could see he was still unhappy. 'I don't understand it all, Kate. He seemed such a pleasant man and I had such hopes . . .' he went on after a moment.

He surveyed my face wistfully and I felt myself blush scarlet.

'It'll all work out in the end, Pa,' was all I could say and I patted his hand.

I didn't stay long, but as I left he brought me up in my tracks. 'Kate, I want you to go back to Kingley till this is all over,' he said.

I stared at him. 'But I want to be with you!'

He smiled rather wanly. 'I'm in good hands here; I couldn't be better off. But there is no one to take care of things at home. I'm sure Richard has an efficient manager but it's not the same as one of the family being there.'

In the end I had to agree with him. 'Okay. I'll fly straight home.' I kissed him fondly. 'If you promise to get completely well soon.'

'I promise,' he said.

The estate looked quite fabulous beneath the June sun. I stood and looked about me as I climbed out of the car, sniffing the sweetness of the honeysuckle and pinks and the soft air, so different from the biting purity of the mountains.

My father's worries, at first sight anyway, seemed groundless. The estate was working like clockwork under the direction of Richard's astute manager and the houses were being efficiently run. In fact Mrs Dawson had lavished so much love on Kingley Farm I wondered if she would polish away some of the furniture altogether. The woods and marshes had been completely fenced and as far as I could tell, allowed to go their own way, although the solicitor told me no further progress could be made on forming the trust without Richard's signature. Of Richard there was no word. He had vanished into thin air.

I had begun to relax, lying on a deckchair beneath the apple trees in the soft sunshine, feeling the warmth soaking into my skin, when Mrs Dawson brought me the news. Her normally gentle eyes were hard and excited.

'They've got him!' she announced. 'It was on the eleven o'clock news. He's been arrested in New York and taken to Boston where he's being charged.'

I looked up at her, thankful for my dark glasses which must have hidden some of my expression, conscious of the terrible despair welling up in me.

'You sound glad, Mrs Dawson.'

She nodded grimly. 'He's been nothing but trouble, that man. I'm glad he's going to get his come-uppance,' she said.

I had forgotten that he had sacked her from the manor.

I was glad that it was her evening off. The gleam in her eyes for the rest of that day had been more than I could bear as she stomped around with her dusters almost singing her triumph. My own heart was heavy. Several times I thought of picking up the phone and calling David at Bay View, but each time I stopped myself. If there were news, he would tell me soon enough, and anyway what was Richard Bradshaw to me?

I stayed out in the garden long after Mrs Dawson had gone, wandering around the lawns in the dusk. Then at last I went in. The house seemed very empty without her or my father there and restlessly I paced from room to room, touching the old oak furniture, running my finger lightly across the back of the books, blowing the powdering of pollen which had fallen from the bowl of flowers onto a polished table.

Slowly it began to grow dark. I turned on the small table light and tried to read, but my mind wasn't on my book.

When I heard the knock at the door I glanced at my watch. It was after eleven. I padded out to the hall and listened. There was no sound from outside, then the knocking came again, loud and insistent.

'Who is it?' I asked.

There was no reply. For a moment I didn't know what to do, but the wild hope had shot through me that it might be Richard; that the news had been wrong and that he had managed to reach home – and me.

With shaking hands I pulled back the bolt and eased the door open. For a moment I could see no one in the darkness, then a figure lurched out of the shadows. It was a woman.

With an exclamation of surprise I stepped back and tried to

push the door shut in her face, but she was too quick for me.

'I want to talk to you, honey,' Sara said thickly.

'I can't think why.' I looked at her in distaste. She was wearing a low-cut, tight-fitting green dress and she reeked of alcohol as she threw out her arm to steady herself against the wall.

'I thought you'd like to hear the news,' she said. 'Get me a drink.' She pushed past me into the living room and stood staring round. 'So this is where the little country cousin lives. I might have known it would be all chintz and schmaltz.' The look she threw round the quiet, much-loved room filled me with wild anger, but I managed to restrain myself.

'We don't all have the same tastes,' I said quietly.

'Except in men, it seems!' she flashed back at me. Her red hair was dishevelled and her skin had a damp white pallor which was most unattractive.

I took a step back. 'I'm not sure I know what you mean,' I said cautiously.

She laughed. 'Oh come, you're not as stupid as that. You were determined to get your hooks into Richard the moment you set eyes on him. Well, I've come to tell you, you're not going to get him.'

She threw herself down on the sofa, exposing a great deal of white thigh, and dropped her little clutch bag on the cushion beside her. 'Have you got any bourbon?'

I shook my head, feeling myself stiffly awkward in my dislike and disapproval. 'I can't see why you've come, and I think you should leave now,' I said. I moved hopefully towards the door, but she didn't attempt to rise. She eyed me insolently from beneath her eyelashes and smiled.

'You know who told them that Richard killed Jacqui?'

'I know,' I said quietly. 'And I also know it's a lie.'

'How can you be so sure?' Her eyes were gleaming in the lamplight. 'Richard is a schizo.'

'He's not a murderer,' I said as witheringly as I could. 'And you know it.'

'You know where Richard is?' she asked.

'I heard he's been arrested.'

She stretched her arms out along the back of the sofa and I heard the rasp of her nails in the heavy material.

'He was, but they released him on bail.' She narrowed her eyes. 'He's not supposed to leave town, but he's jumped it already.'

Again that chilling laugh.

'How do you know?' I was watching her in fascination, knowing that she was enjoying every moment of my discomfort but unable to stop myself asking.

'Because I called him up.' She moved her head to one side. 'He didn't want to speak to me, but I made him listen.'

There was something incredibly sinister about her, sitting there on the sofa, exuding malice, and I could feel the goose flesh creeping across my skin as I watched her.

'I suppose you're going to tell me what you said?' I went on unwillingly.

She was still enjoying herself. 'I sure am.' Stretching out her elegant legs she crossed them. 'Haven't you got anything at all to drink?' she repeated, and I suddenly realised that her hands were trembling.

'There's some Scotch in the sideboard,' I said guardedly.

'It'll do.'

I poured her some, and as an afterthought poured myself a small one as well. I thought I needed it.

She drank hers at one gulp and let the empty glass fall negligently onto the cushions. 'Richard is a fool,' she said, almost affectionately. 'A goddam, bastard fool.'

Her eyes were closing.

'Why don't you go home, Sara?' I said softly at last. I didn't want her falling asleep on my sofa.

'Home,' she said. 'Home? Do you know where home is? Richard thinks it's California.' She gave a strange, bitter giggle. 'But it isn't. It's Brooklyn.'

'What did you tell him on the phone, Sara?' I asked patiently, bringing her back to the subject.

She seemed to drag her eyes open with an effort. 'I told him I was going to kill you.'

For a moment I was speechless, conscious only of those brilliant, lazy green eyes watching me. 'It was a test,' she went on, enunciating each word carefully. 'To see if he loved you. If he dropped everything to come to you, I'd know.'

'And did he?' I whispered.

She smiled. 'When I rang that old fool Marlesford, he'd left for the airport.' She groped for the glass and lurching to her feet, moved towards the bottle. 'Bad luck for you,' she murmured, raising her glass in a toast.

'I'd have thought it was good,' I said with a spark of defiance. 'If it means he loves me.'

'What it means, honey, is that I really am going to have to kill you!' She said it so softly I hardly heard the words. 'And the beauty of it is,' she went on, filling her glass with elaborate care, 'that he will arrive here just in time to collect the rap.'

'You're mad,' I stammered, panic beginning to run up and down my spine.

'Very probably,' she said sweetly. She drained the glass and set it down on the table, staggering very slightly as she walked over to the sofa. Then she picked up her purse.

'Poor little Katherine,' she went on, half scornfully. 'His two million bucks didn't get Richard very far did it? Did he get any change out of it at all I wonder?' The laugh she gave was unmistakably crude.

I was eyeing the phone, wondering desperately if I could get to it; she was too drunk to reach me, I was sure of it, and if she did I could fight her off, but I had not anticipated the horror of the next two minutes.

Casually she pulled open the flap of her purse and reached inside.

Seconds later I was staring, mesmerised with terror, at the

barrel of a small revolver, and I heard the slight click as she eased off the safety catch.

PART FOUR

The gun was weaving in the air and Sara, with a laugh, brought up her other hand to steady it. My mouth was dry; I could not believe that this was happening to me.

I knew I had to talk, to distract her somehow, but terror had clamped down on my vocal cords and I could not utter a word. The smell of Scotch was overpowering in the room.

'If Richard comes, he won't come alone, you know,' I managed to gasp at last. 'And if you hurt me, he'll know it was you.'

'I intend him to know it was me,' she said with emphasis. 'If it weren't for the cops, I'd sign my name on your corpse.' Suddenly her eyes filled with tears. 'You lousy little bitch,' she shrieked. 'If you hadn't come along he would still have loved me!'

She was beyond reason. Taking two steps forward, clutching the gun in front of her she knocked against the table and let out a string of curses. Then she fired. Again and again she squeezed the trigger and, my ears ringing with shots, I waited to die. Only when four or five useless clicks showed that the gun was empty did I realise that she had missed me completely. Perhaps she had not really tried to hit me; a lifetime later we found five bullets embedded in various parts of that room.

Once the gun was empty she hurled it towards the chimney, where it knocked a pretty Staffordshire figurine off the mantelpiece and fell amid a shower of porcelain into the empty hearth. Then she threw herself face down on the sofa and began to cry.

I stared at her, too shaken for a moment to move. Then, dazed, I made my way towards the phone.

I called the Manor. It was by far the closest and the estate manager had seemed a solid, dependable man. All I wanted was someone to come. Anyone. Quickly.

A familiar voice answered the phone however and I felt a quick surge of relief.

'Dave? Is that really you?'

'Sure.' He sounded sleepy. 'Who's that?'

'It's Kate. Dave, can you come over to the farm? Sara's here. She tried to kill me!' And suddenly I started to cry.

'Where is she now?' He was fully awake at once, his voice clipped and urgent.

'Here. In the living room. She's drunk.'

I heard a low mutter at the other end of the line.

'Kate? Open the front door for me, then get the hell out of there. I'm on my way!' A second later I was listening to an empty line.

I met Dave at the gate. He drew up in one of the estate Range Rovers and leaped out. 'Are you okay?'

I nodded. 'Just a bit shaky. She missed me.'

'*Missed you*?' He stared. 'Are you telling me that she had a gun?'

'A revolver. In her purse.' I gave an unsteady laugh. 'I don't think she knew what she was doing.'

'Like hell she did. You wait out here.'

He strode past me and disappeared into the house. Moments later he was back. 'Okay. Come on. She's passed out for the moment.' His face was grim as he led me in and shut the front door. He took me into the kitchen. 'Now, tell me what happened exactly.'

Briefly I explained, and he gave a silent whistle. 'Of course we knew she had told the cops Richard killed Jacqui, but this is unbelievable! You say Richard has jumped bail?'

'So she said.'

'Christ!' He was gnawing the joint of his thumb. Then he reached for the wall phone.

He dialled Bay View and then Boston airport. At the latter they confirmed Richard's jet had filed a flight plan for London and taken off two hours before.

Dave put his head in his hands. 'What a mess,' he said. He looked up and gave a wan grin. 'Come on, Kate. Black coffee, then I'll take the lady home.'

'What'll you do?' Automatically I took down the jug and reached into the fridge for the coffee beans.

He shrugged. 'We'll keep her up at the Manor till Richard comes and then let him decide. I'm sure he's plenty of ideas about what to do with our Sara.'

I did not like the look of the grim expression which had clamped down on his features at all. 'Aren't you going to call the police?'

He shook his head. 'And have them waiting when Richard lands? No way, honey. This is a private matter.'

'You think *she* killed Jacqui, don't you?' I said after a moment. The idea had been hovering at the back of my mind since the first moment I had seen her gun.

Dave was plugging in the grinder for me and I couldn't see his face. 'It had occurred to me,' he said guardedly. 'She was over there when it happened.'

Almost unwillingly I found myself glancing over my shoulder towards the door as the roar of the grinder echoed through the house, terrified she would awake. But seconds later when Dave switched it off, I once more heard the rhythmical snores coming from the living room where Sara lay sprawled on the floor.

'She won't wake, Kate,' he said, catching my glance with a sympathetic grin. 'It'll take her hours to sleep off that lot. I've known lushes like her before. You've nothing more to fear, I promise.'

I turned back to him. 'It's almost as if she hates him now,' I said softly. 'Did he really beat her, Dave?'

He gave a harsh laugh. 'If he did, which I doubt, it's because she likes it. Oh come on, Kate! What kind of man do you think he is?' He reached out and put his hand under my chin. 'Richard's okay, honey. Business, he's ruthless in, even dangerous; but he's no Bluebeard.'

I wanted so much to believe him.

He carried Sara, who was still asleep, out to the Range Rover and put her in the back, then he turned to me.

'Get some sleep if you can, and I'll call you in the morning, okay?'

I lay a long time, tossing restlessly, listening to the ticking of my little clock in the dark, watching the sky slowly grow light behind the curtains. Then at last I must have fallen asleep for the room was brilliant with sunshine when I was awoken by the shrilling of the phone.

'Kate?' It was Dave. 'Richard has sent his plane for you. It arrived in the night and it's all right; he didn't come himself. I told his boys there is no panic and you're okay but they're anxious to get back. How soon can you be ready?'

I blinked up at the ceiling. 'You mean he wants me to fly back to the States?'

'Looks like it. I think you should go, Kate.' There was something in his voice which did not brook argument. And suddenly I didn't want to argue. I had been thinking about Richard almost without ceasing for weeks now, and all I wanted was to see him again, to find out if my love for him was real; if the love he felt for me existed at all.

Richard's plane was waiting at the local airport and it seemed hardly any time before I was ensconced alone in state in the cabin, being served breakfast and fragrant coffee as we winged our way out across the Atlantic. I was completely relaxed. The quiet tough men who had driven me to the airport looked competent to deal with any eventuality and I could understand Richard being content to send them to save me from Sara.

From Boston, after a minimum of formalities they drove me straight out to Bay View. I had hoped that Richard would be at the airport, but there was no sign of him, and by now the silence of my escorts was beginning to worry me. I had had time to think on the long flight; time to have second thoughts.

Why in heaven's name had I agreed to come? I had not been in danger any longer from Sara at home, but now, what was I heading for? My obscure longing to see a man who, even though he protested his innocence, had been charged with murder, had brought me, in the company of strangers, back to the States. And suddenly I was afraid again.

But it was too late to turn back; my escort would see to that.

Edith Marlesford greeted me at the door of the mansion and showed me to the room I had had before with the same gloomy silence, which she broke only when I asked her if Richard was in the house. Shaking her head she said reluctantly, 'I don't know where he is at present.' That was all, and turning she left me to myself.

I looked round the room with a shiver, remembering my last brief visit; that one night which I had spent sleepless with terror under Richard's roof. And I thought about Jacqui. I was in a bedroom only two doors away from the room in which she had died. I didn't want to stay. Miserable and afraid, I did not even unpack my case; I dragged a comb through my hair and sat on the bed thinking, then I reached for the phone and dialled Minna's number in New York. There was no reply, so I tried Chris's. It rang and rang in the silence, and then I heard a click. 'Chris Hannaway is out just now,' came the voice, mechanical and without animation. 'At the tone will you leave your name . . .' I hung up without a word, conscious suddenly that I was crying.

I would have sat there all day had not Mrs Marlesford knocked, and after a moment entered the room again. She looked to be in an even blacker humour than before.

'The police are here,' she said grimly. 'They want to speak to you.'

'To me?' I felt my stomach turn over apprehensively. 'Why?'

She shrugged austerely. 'They're downstairs.'

Literally shaking, I followed her.

Two men were standing in the dining room, gazing out of the windows across the garden towards the ice-blue pool. They turned as I came in. 'Miss Parrish?' one of them asked. I nodded. He had a note book in his hand and consulting it he went on, 'You are Richard Bradshaw's cousin from England, I understand? May I ask when and where you last saw him.'

I stumbled through his questions, doing my best to answer, not understanding where they were leading. The men were bland, seemingly only half interested. Then suddenly came one sneaky as a knife: 'I gather someone tried to kill you too, Miss Parrish?' The hard brown eyes were no longer evasive. They bored into my skull.

'How do you know that?' I said, shaken.

'We get to hear about most things, in the end,' he said laconically. 'Now, you recently sold some land in England to your cousin. Is that right?'

I nodded.

'As did a third cousin, Miss Minna Monro?' He was looking at his note book.

I nodded again.

'And neither of you wanted to part with your property?'

'Well, no, but –'

'Pressure was brought to bear on you, and in the end you agreed, Miss Parrish, isn't that right?' There was a moment's silence. He put his note book away and looked me straight in the eye. 'Did Bradshaw try to kill you?'

'No! No, you've got it all wrong!' Desperately I tried to explain. I told them about Sara and the gun, floundering as they asked question after question. How many shots had been fired? What time was it? Why hadn't I called the British police? Why had Sara hated me enough to want to kill me? And again, when had I last seen Richard?

At long last they went. I was left with two pieces of information, both of which frightened me. One, that by admitting my attraction to Richard, I had somehow perhaps implicated myself, and two, that Richard had not been seen since he was released on bail. He had completely disappeared.

As the front door closed on the two police officers I stood uncertainly in the hall and wondered what to do. The house seemed deserted. Then I heard a distant sound from somewhere at the back. Hesitantly I made my way towards it and found myself in the huge gleaming kitchens. Edith Marlesford was making coffee, her back to the door, and I stood for a moment watching her in her absorption with her task. Eventually I cleared my throat. 'I . . . I'm sorry.' I found I was stammering. 'I . . . I could smell the coffee . . .'

She turned quickly, a jug of cream in her hand. 'Did they give you a rough time?'

Collapsing into a chair at the kitchen table I nodded wordlessly. She eyed me, then she brought the percolator to the table and produced two shallow French coffee bowls. 'What did they say?' she asked sharply.

I was too tired and too upset to be on my guard. Sipping the coffee gratefully I poured out the whole story yet again, conscious that her black eyes never left my face. When I reached the bit about Sara I saw the malicious gleam increase.

'And you told them all that?' she asked.

'I had to.'

She laughed out loud. 'They'll call the English police and that will fix that lady for good. Save Mr Richard the trouble of doing it himself, and good riddance to her!'

Something in the way she said those words made me stare at her.

'You do know where he is?'

She looked away. 'I might. I might not.'

Cupping my hands round my bowl and sipping the coffee gratefully I watched as she stirred her own. She drank it black, without sugar or cream, and yet she stirred it endlessly, gazing down into the black eye of the whirlpool she was making with her spoon.

'Will you tell me something?' I asked after a long silence.

She put her head slightly on one side. 'What?'

'Did Jacqui kill herself or was she murdered?' I held my breath as I waited for her reply, knowing instinctively that she would have the answer.

There was a further long pause. Then: 'Richard wanted her dead, honey.'

I felt myself growing cold. 'You mean he did kill her; it wasn't Sara at all?' I breathed.

She laughed out loud. 'Oh it wasn't Sara!'

'Then it was Richard?' I persisted. I was sick with horror.

Shaking her head she smiled down at her coffee. 'Not with his own hands. Richard gives orders and they are obeyed.'

Somehow I stood up. 'What's the difference?' I cried in despair. 'He's the killer! Even if he got someone else to do it. He killed her!'

Blindly I turned for the door and ran out into the hot sunlight. I had to get away. I had to leave that evil, frightening house.

But I had forgotten the security which surrounded the estate. Pounding across the yard I dodged through the stables and ran as fast as I could across the grass towards the distant gates, only to find them locked fast. Sobbing, I beat feebly on the heavy painted iron with my fists, but I knew it was no good. I was trapped.

Edith Marlesford found me there and I felt her arm slip stiffly around my shoulders. 'Come back to the house, honey,' she said calmly.

Too exhausted to argue, I went with her, allowing her to lead me back to my chair at the kitchen table. I sat there, still crying silently as she busied herself once more with a new brew of coffee.

'I know it's a shock, honey.' She was talking softly, almost to herself. 'You're an English lady, not used to our way of doing things. Not like that trash, Sara. She was good for nothing, that one, and Jacqueline. Useless. Not the right ones for Mr Richard at all, either of them.' She put the freshly filled coffee bowl down before me. 'There, drink that.' Sitting down opposite me, she put her hand over mine. It was ice cold. 'You've nothing to fear, Katherine,' she said again. 'Nothing at all. He likes you.'

I drank the coffee slowly, half listening to her almost hypnotic voice droning on, reassuring, soothing, wondering sleepily why the events of the last two days and the long flight had left me more exhausted than I had thought possible. I no longer felt I could cope with what was happening to me as a warm drowsiness began to creep through my veins.

With an effort I pulled myself together and forced myself to listen to what she was saying, propping my head on my elbow as I tried to focus on her face.

'I've always taken care of Richard, since his momee died,' she was explaining. 'I've known what's best for him since he was five years old. Hundreds of women have chased him; but none of them were good enough. I've gotten rid of them all. Then Jacqueline came along. She was too dependent, too weak. She wouldn't let him go so easily, so I had to make her.'

I stared at her, trying to keep my eyes open with an effort, my brain struggling as I tried to understand. 'What are you saying?' I murmured.

She laughed, almost gaily. 'Don't you know?' she asked.

'You killed her?' I whispered. '*You* killed Jacqueline?'

'It was what he wanted,' she replied complacently. 'I've always been the instrument of his wishes. That's what I'm here for.'

Her face was swimming before me, in a haze, as I tried to stand, and I realised suddenly that I couldn't.

'What have you done to me?' I heard myself crying. 'You've poisoned me. In the coffee!' My mind had gone numb; I wasn't even afraid as, smiling, she rose slowly to her feet.

'No, no,' she said reassuringly. 'Not poison. I'm not going to hurt you, Katherine. You are the right one for him. I knew it the first time I saw you. You are what he needs; the others were wrong, but not you.' She was coming round the table towards me and I could do nothing but watch. I felt her arm go round my shoulders. 'Come, I'll help you to bed. This will help you sleep, honey, that's all. You're overwrought by everything that's happened.'

I seemed unable to argue. Her grip was surprisingly strong and I could feel her almost carrying me along the hall and up the stairs towards my bedroom. There she helped me to the bed and I fell on it heavily, my eyes closing. I heard the rattle of the curtains as she shut out the sunlight, then she came back to the bedside and I felt her removing my shoes. 'There, Katherine Parrish,' she said from a long way away. 'Relax and you'll soon be comfy.'

Dimly I realised that she was pulling off my dress, then the rest of my clothes, and I felt the satin sheets cold against my burning body. Her hand brushed my breast for a moment, caressing my skin, then gently she pulled the cover over me and tucked me in. I was unable to struggle, unable to move as I fought in vain against the terrible sleepiness which was overwhelming me.

'This'll keep you safe and quiet, honey,' she murmured, bending over me and touching my hair. 'Ready for him when he comes home . . .'

Through eyelids heavy as lead I saw her tiptoe across the shadowy carpet, remove the key from the lock and, taking it with her, slip out of the room. Seconds later I slid into unconsciousness.

When I awoke the room was almost dark. I lay there for a while conscious only of the painful throbbing behind my eyelids, feeling the numbness slowly ebbing from my limbs as gradually I remembered where I was.

'So, she's waking up.'

Only when I heard the voice did I realise at last that someone was sitting on the bed beside me and, as my eyes grew used to the gloom, I recognised Richard. His weight on the sheet was pinioning me to the bed, but I was suddenly painfully conscious that beneath the smooth satin I was naked.

He laughed softly and I felt the whisper of fear begin to play once more about me. This man was a murderer.

'I'm glad you decided to pay off your debt after all,' he said, still smiling as he reached out and touched my cheek with the back of his hand. 'You are beautiful, Katherine. I can see why Mrs M is so taken by you.'

I shrank away from his touch, but the sheet held me fast and I found I could not move as he leaned forward over me and began gently to kiss my lips.

So I did not resist or turn my head away. Perhaps I was still drugged; perhaps I had realised even then that I could not fight him, but slowly I felt a quick tingle of desire mingling with my fear. Even as I realised it Richard released me and straightened up with a grin. 'There is no time for this now,' he said standing up. 'Do you feel strong enough to get dressed? We must hurry.'

Hurry, before the police could find him. I stared at him, trying to see a murderer in the face of the man I had imagined myself in love with; a man who was prepared to let others kill for him; a man with the blood of a beautiful, helpless woman on his hands.

'The police know I'm here,' I stammered at last – the first words I had spoken to him since a lifetime ago he had driven me back to the farm with his cheque for a million pounds in my pocket.

'Ah yes. The police.' He picked up my clothes and tossed them to me.

'They are probably watching the house,' I stammered, sitting up, the sheet pulled up to my chin. 'They'll catch you, you know. You mustn't stay . . .' I realised for the first time that behind the curtains the sky was dark. I must have been asleep for hours.

He was watching me closely, his expression inscrutable, but for a moment I thought I saw a smile hovering behind his eyes. 'I don't intend to stay. And they're not going to bother me where I'm going.' He paused, then he corrected himself slowly. 'Where *we* are going, Katherine.' Gently but firmly he unfolded my fingers from my sheet and pulled it back. Then he smiled and reached to touch a strand of my hair which lay curling across my bare shoulder. 'Hurry up, my love. Put on that dress and come down. My car is at the door.'

I watched as he left the room, a tall, slim figure in immaculately cut jeans, and I shivered suddenly as I remembered the burning touch of his hands on my skin and realised that I did still love him. But how could I love a murderer? How could I have borne such a touch?

My fingers trembling, I reached for my clothes and began to put them on. I pushed my feet into my sandals and stood shakily up, grabbing my bag, then I ran for the stairs. The front door stood wide and outside, drawn up before the steps, I recognised the red Mercedes, the same car Jacqueline had driven when she rescued me before from Bay View. There was no sign of Richard.

I looked round cautiously, and then tiptoed out onto the steps. In the light from the porch I could see the keys in the ignition. Without another thought I ran down, pulled open the door and threw myself in. The car started at the first turn of the key. I slammed down the accelerator and hurtled down the drive as if all the hounds of hell were after me.

The tall iron-bound gates were still closed, but I remembered the button on the dashboard in time. At a touch the heavy green wings began to swing slowly open and I could see the black ribbon of the road stretching away into the darkness beyond.

I turned the car southbound with a squeal of tyres and drove with my foot flat on the boards. After the first hour I stopped glancing in the mirror to see if I was being followed; after two I dared to pull in for gasoline and picked up a sandwich and a paper cup of coffee to help keep me awake. It was the early hours when I reached New York and only as the traffic thickened and swirled around me, sucking me with it closer and closer to the heart of the city, did I feel safe at last.

Even so, I did not dare to go to Minna. It was the first place Richard would look. Instead I swung the car through the streets, threading my way towards Chris's apartment. It was three in the morning when I rang his bell.

For one awful moment I thought he wasn't there, then at last I saw a light come on in the hall and he swung the door open.

'Hi Chris,' I said.

'Kate!' He did not seem pleased to see me. 'What the hell are you doing here?'

'Oh Chris I'm sorry. You've got to help me!' I slipped past him. 'It's Richard!'

I heard a murmured curse behind me, but he closed the door to my relief and I watched as he put on the chain. 'What about Richard?' he said wearily. 'I thought it was all sorted out.'

'Sorted out?' I swung round on him. 'Chris! It's a mess!'

'It's that all right. I saw the old witch on the TV news last night.'

I was stunned for a moment. Then I heard myself repeat: 'On the news?'

'Sure. Edith Marlesford.' He must have noticed my blank face. 'Don't you know? She gave herself up to the cops last night. Confessed everything. Richard is in the clear.'

I sat down abruptly on the chest by the door. 'Richard is not under suspicion any more? Not even for wanting Jacqui dead, for incitement or whatever it's called?' I was dizzy with relief.

'Not for anything. Hell Kate, I thought you were the one who believed in him!'

Yes, I had believed in him. Hadn't I?

'Oh God!' I said. I grabbed the phone and with shaking hands I punched out the number to Bay View while Chris stared at me in astonishment.

A man's voice answered; not Richard.

'Who is that?' it asked suspiciously.

'It's Kate Parrish. I must speak to Richard.'

There was an infinitesimal pause. Then the voice asked: 'Where are you calling from, Miss Parrish?'

'Never mind where,' I said. 'Can I speak to him?'

'I must know where you are Miss Parrish,' the voice went on relentless.

'No chance. Look, just tell him I'm sorry. But if he'd explained what had happened perhaps it would have been better!' I said, my hurt and anger slowly building as I realised that he had deliberately let me go on thinking the worst. 'Tell him I'll mail the car keys!' I hung up.

My hands were still shaking as I pushed away the phone. Why had he not told me? Why had he let me go on thinking the police were after him?

Miserably I preceded Chris into the living room, then I stopped dead, jolted from my thoughts. A woman's clothes were scattered over the carpet.

'Oh hell, Chris! You've got someone here.'

'Top marks!' He reached into the pocket of his robe and brought out a pack of cigarettes.

Strangely I found I didn't mind. I smiled at him apologetically. 'Chris, I don't want to cause any hassle. I just had to have somewhere to go tonight, somewhere he couldn't find me. Tomorrow I'm flying back home.'

Behind me I heard the door open. A tall blonde girl appeared, swathed in a bed sheet. She gazed at me in silence.

I sighed. 'Sorry to intrude,' I saw awkwardly. 'Look, can I just fix myself some coffee, then I'll go.'

'Hell, no. You can stay,' Chris said at last. 'If you don't mind the couch.'

Maggie turned out to be very nice. She made me coffee and then made up a bed on the couch. I fell into it without bothering to undress and was asleep in seconds.

I slept, too, most of the way back to London and was still too desperately tired when I reached home to do any thinking.

My faith in Richard had not been strong enough. I had not believed in him at the end and he had seen the terror in my eyes. I did not even know if he had loved me, but if he did, it was my own fault that I had lost him. My own fault that I would never see him again without both of us realising that for a few short hours I had believed him a murderer. And this was something I could not bear to face, and something I could forget only in the oblivion of sleep.

When at last I let myself in at Kingley Farm I looked round in disbelief. Was it really only the day before yesterday I had scribbled that quick note to Mrs Dawson, packed my bag and left? I tried to count up the hours on my fingers and gave up.

'Is that you Miss Kate?' Mrs Dawson called from the kitchen, just like any other day when I came in from a ride or from the garden. 'I've just put the kettle on for tea, my dear.'

I went into the warm, sunny room and stared round. It was full of flowers and the smell of baking, and after the nightmare I had lived through in the last day or so the sheer relief of being home made me want to cry.

There was something I had to do, though, before I could rest. I waited until Mrs Dawson had gone outside to hang some sheets in the sun, then I grabbed the phone.

A secretary answered. Yes, she said. Mr Conway was still at the Manor.

'Kate?' He came on the line slightly breathless. 'Thank goodness. Are you home?'

'Never mind where I am,' I said, automatically cautious, though it could not matter any more now. 'What has happened to Sara?'

'She's in hospital. A complete nervous breakdown. Your police came and interviewed her, but they say it's up to you whether you want to press charges.'

'Oh no,' I said hastily. I hesitated. 'Dave? Have you heard from Richard?'

He laughed. 'I have indeed. I gather you kidnapped his Merc!'

I wondered what else Richard had told him.

'Kate,' he went on. 'Do tell me where you are. I want to see you.'

'You and who else,' I retorted. 'I'm in Scotland, Dave, so tell Richard to forget it for now, okay?'

Of course he would find out where I was within seconds if he wanted to, but I wanted a breather; the chance to compose myself, and put my thoughts in order.

Richard's face was still haunting me as I walked up to the marshes, climbing through the double threads of barbed wire which surrounded them and wandering in the gold and peace of the English summer, but I thought perhaps I was winning. I would be able to put the memory of what might have been behind me.

I was still thinking about him so much that when the phone rang that evening for a moment I was convinced it would be him. I almost did not answer it at all, then at last I picked it up and waited cautiously for someone to speak.

'Kate? Kate, are you there? Hello?' A familiar voice crackled over the wire and I found I was breathing again.

'Pa! Are you all right?' I had phoned him that morning as I phoned him every morning.

'I'm just fine, Katie. The doctors are very pleased with me.'

His voice sounded strong and confident. 'But I'd be better if you came over here again for a few days!'

It seemed a wonderful idea. Joyfully I put down the phone. I had lost Chris; I had no hope of Richard, but at least I still had my father.

He was propped up in bed when I reached the clinic at last, his colour better than I could remember seeing it for years, his eyes sparkling with pleasure.

I kissed his forehead. 'You look very pleased with yourself,' I said, laying the huge bunch of freesias which I had brought him on the bed cover. 'I expected to find you looking pale and interesting and you sit here looking as if you could beat me in straight sets at tennis!'

He laughed. 'I feel as if I could,' he said softly. 'I have a surprise for you, Katie, my love,' he went on.

'Oh?' I looked at him suspiciously, but he merely went on grinning at me. 'No,' he said, maddeningly. 'Not yet. Tonight.'

And with that I had to be content for the time being. I returned to the clinic at seven, having been lucky enough to secure a room at the inn after a cancellation, and went straight up to my father. He was sitting in a chair beside his bed, dressed in a new silk dressing gown and on his knee was a box wrapped in gold paper and tied with scarlet ribbon. I eyed it. 'No one told me it was Christmas,' I said with a smile.

He beamed at me. 'Well, it is,' he replied. He held out the box to me. 'Open it and see.'

I took it and shook it gently. It felt as if it were empty. With a suspicious look at my father I began to untie the ribbon and peeled off the paper. Beneath it was a plain white box which, when I took off the lid, was empty save for an envelope. Behind me the door opened and I heard someone enter, but my attention was on the envelope on my knee and I did not look up. As I tore it open I glanced up only once and caught sight of my father's face. He looked radiantly happy.

I could not make head or tail of the closely typed pages which I drew from the envelope. 'What is it?' I asked bewildered.

The voice which answered was not my father's.

'It is a deed making you co-trustee of the Kingley Marshes Sanctuary,' Richard said softly from the window seat behind me.

For a moment I did not move, then, slowly, I turned and look at him. 'How did you know I was here?' I asked when at last I had found my voice.

He smiled enigmatically. 'Shall we say I guessed,' he said.

My father chuckled. 'Rubbish. He came and told me to call you.'

'And you did?' I swung back to my father.

'Of course.' Pa was looking very pleased with himself.

'I told him the whole story Kate,' Richard said, standing up. 'Even the sorry tale of how I bullied and frightened you. I've apologised to him and now I want to do the same to you. I should have realised you would be terrified. It was unforgivable of me.'

I could feel my cheeks beginning to burn. 'I was not terrified!' I denied hotly.

Smiling unrepentantly he bowed slightly. 'You were apprehensive, should I say. But I still want to apologise.'

'So I should hope,' I said, beginning to recover from my shock. 'You are the most overbearing, tyrannical, unscrupulous man I have ever met.'

He laughed. 'To all that I plead guilty,' he said. 'And I promise, I will try to reform.'

'And you must let the man take you out to dinner, Kate,' came my father's voice from his corner. 'Alas, I cannot join you as yet, but I dare say you will find enough to talk about without me there!'

He was right of course. But there were still several things

that bothered me enough to make me pause, once we were outside on the beautifully raked gravel on the forecourt of the clinic.

'I know what you are going to ask, Kate,' Richard said, facing me and taking my hands. 'I never even hinted to Edith that she do that terrible thing. You must believe that. Jacqui had everything to live for at the end. She had agreed to go away for a cure, and she had met someone I believe she could have loved. I had nothing to gain by wanting the poor girl dead.'

I did believe him. But there was something else.

'And Sara,' I said softly. 'I saw her bruises.'

The sadness on his face vanished and I saw a malicious twinkle appear in his eyes. 'Still afraid I might beat you?' He tucked my hand comfortably beneath his arm and began to walk towards the car. 'Well, I must confess that, much though she deserved it, I didn't lay a finger on her. Those bruises, Kate, came from a fall she had when she was drunk.'

I should have guessed.

'Any other problems, ma'am?' He was opening the car door for me and helping me in. 'Because if there are I would rather sort them out now. This meal is going to be one which is not interrupted by telephone calls, or quarrels, or trans-Atlantic flights or you falling asleep and setting fire to yourself in the candles.' He leaned down to tuck my skirt out of reach of the door and I felt his lips brush my hair.

I pretended to think. 'Actually, there is one other thing that's been worrying me,' I murmured demurely, hoping he could not see how fast my heart was beating at his touch. 'I don't like the colour of your Rolls Royce.' I looked up at him, my eyes wide. 'I really don't.'

Taking several paces back he looked at me hard, then he shrugged. 'I can see you're going to be a tough lady to please,' he said cheerfully. 'Okay, we'll get a new one on our wedding day, and you can choose the colour. How does that appeal?' So saying, he climbed into the driving seat of the hired car and we set off down the road towards the mountains.

Networking

'THAT'S IT. That is absolutely it!' Denzil Johnson threw the front door of his flat shut behind him, sent his briefcase skidding up the polished pine floorboards and headed for the bottle of Scotch. He poured himself a hefty dose.

'Meg! Meg? I'm home.'

His wife put a cautious head round the door. She smiled nervously. 'I know, darling. I heard your key in the lock. Bad day?' Her face registered careful sympathy.

'Bad! Bad? It was bloody terrible!' He flung himself into a chair, swallowing the Scotch down with ostensible effort as if he disliked the taste.

Meg emerged further, ready to retreat if necessary. Her husband's adrenaline count had to be treated with caution these days. One approached him rather as one might the dial on a jammed steam engine.

'Was it Carter again, Den? The man's a swine. A perfect swine.' Coming from her, the epithet sounded genteelly judicious in the extreme.

Denzil was still fuming. 'Him and just about everyone else in that firm. They're unethical, Meg. They're immoral. If they don't want me on their staff why don't they say so? Why don't they transfer me, or make me redundant and pay me the whack they damn well owe me instead of this endless war of nerves. More Scotch.' He held out his glass.

Meg unscrewed the bottle slowly. 'Shall I put some water in this time, darling?' she asked hopefully.

He shook his head violently. 'No way. Milk and water – that's been my trouble all along and that's enough. Never again. I'm going to fight them. From tomorrow I'm going to fight. They can't do this to me Meg. Either they employ me or they transfer me to Bristol or they make me redundant. They are not going to chase me out. It's happening all the time, now, you know: putting pressure on people to make them resign. It's appalling! I'm going to fight, and fight all the way.'

His wife walked over to the window and drew the curtains against the glare of the recently lit street lamps outside. The table was already laid for supper but she ignored it with a sigh.

'TV darling, or are you going jogging this evening?' she asked in a conciliatory tone.

The tone did not this time have the desired effect.

'Neither. Hell, neither! I mean it this time, Meg. I'm going to fight. And before anything else I'm going to put the fear of God into those guys at work. What I need is a good QC.'

'Oh no, Denzil.' She was alarmed suddenly. 'We can't afford to take anyone to court, you know we can't.' She picked up the Scotch again. It was for herself this time.

He laughed wryly. 'Oh no, not to take them to court. Or a tribunal. I just want someone to talk to them. Someone who will shake them into taking me seriously. The very words "Queen's Counsel" will terrify them. *Terrify them.*' He repeated the words, almost lasciviously.

Meg took a sip of neat Scotch. He didn't usually go this far. His fury was usually dissipated after a drink and a day-dream, while she steamed the potatoes, about the lovely garden they could have if Carter would only recommend him for a transfer to the Bristol branch.

She swallowed. 'You'd have to pay him, darling.'

'So, I'll pay him if I must. But surely we ***know*** one, don't we? Doesn't your mother know a QC? She knows just about every bloody person in London!'

He put down his glass and set about loosening his tie, slipping it noose-like upwards over his head and leaning back at last in his chair, his eyes closed. A muscle twitched spasmodically in his cheek.

Meg looked at it, worried, unsure as to whether or not to take him seriously this time. She decided he probably did mean it, for he had thrown her a challenge and she knew it. And family solidarity demanded that her mother know a QC.

She glanced at the phone. No, she wouldn't do it now. Perhaps later, when he was in the bath. She didn't want him to overhear the conversation, larding it with provocative comments from the wings, antagonising her mother before she had consulted the inimitable address book which lodged somewhere in the deeply recessed memory banks of her brain.

He had opened his eyes and was watching her. For the first time he had noticed her wan, tense expression and he frowned as he leaned forward.

'Meggie, I'm sorry. I'm a boar. Go on, tell me. I'm so obsessed with the office I can't think about anything else. How was the dentist?'

She smiled radiantly. 'The dentist was last week, Den.'

For a moment his face fell. Then he laughed. 'Forgive me?'

'Of course I forgive you. Shall I go and put the food in the oven now darling?' She dropped a paper-light kiss onto the top of his head. In spite of everything, she noticed, his hair was as thick and boyishly ruffled as the day she had first met him.

It wasn't until he was safely in the bath that she rang her mother.

'Mummy? It's Meg. Do you happen to know any QCs?' She frowned as her straightforward query was greeted with an outburst of near hysteria.

'No dear, no one has murdered anyone. Yet. I just wanted to know. For Denzil.'

She turned, the receiver still pressed to her ear, and parting the curtains she gazed down at the dark street below. It had begun to rain.

'No Mummy. Uncle James was a solicitor. It's different. And anyway he's dead.'

Her mother was obviously scraping the bottom of the barrel. She decided to cut short the flow of reminiscence which had been let loose the other end of the line before it reached her mother's last parking fine outside Harrods – a case which had in any case been undefended, and undefensible.

'Look Mummy, I must ring off. There's someone at the door –' time-worn, time-honoured excuse, '– if you think of anyone let me know, there's a dear.'

She hung up and took a deep breath. It wasn't often her mother was stumped for someone who knew someone. . .

If only there was some other way she could help Denzil in his war with Carter. Moral support from behind the lines did not seem to be of much use at the moment.

She had a sudden brainwave and dialled before she could change her mind.

'Mary? It's Meg. Yes, I know, hasn't it been ages? You must come and have dinner with us soon.' She blanched visibly. 'All right, next week. Yes, that would be nice. Look Mary, didn't you go out with a barrister before you married David? Do you still know him by any chance?'

Her lips twitched imperceptibly at Mary's indignation.

'No, of course not. No, well, we wanted a QC and I remembered . . . what? Oh no, I don't think Denzil wants to use his solicitor. It's not that kind of *legal* thing. We want a QC who's a *friend*.'

She hung up wearily and reached for her diary, cursing her own weakness. She had let them in for a boring dinner party and achieved nothing into the bargain.

She jumped as the sitting room door opened. Denzil

appeared, wrapped in a bathrobe, glowing gently from the bath.

'Meg. I've had an idea. There's a chap I was at school with. I'm pretty sure he was a QC last time I heard. I think I'll give him a buzz.'

Meg lowered her eyes and shut her diary. 'That's a good idea, darling.' She hesitated. 'Den, why a QC? What's wrong with asking our own solicitor?'

He was rifling through the phone book. 'Doesn't pack enough wallop,' he commented absent-mindedly. 'Need the real thing for those bastards at the office.'

'But I gather you're only supposed to get an introduction through a solicitor, darling.' She did not dare tell him yet about the dinner party.

'Rubbish. Straight to the top, that's my motto.' He ran his finger down a page, squinting.

'Ellis. Let's see. Here we are. This must be him. I'll try.'

He punched out the number slowly and deliberately as he always did, with the action of a seasoned executive.

'Hello, is Fred Ellis there? What? Mr Justice Ellis? Oh no. I'm sorry, must be the wrong man.' He hung up swiftly and glanced at his wife rather sheepishly. 'Too much wallop,' he commented dryly.

It was as they were at last climbing into bed that the phone rang. Meg glanced at her watch. It was nearly midnight.

'You go.' Denzil pulled the sheet up to his chin. 'If it's for me I'm out.'

She gave him a withering look and padded barefoot into the sitting room, groping for the switch of the table lamp as she picked up the phone.

'Yes, who is it?' She tried to sound as though she'd just been woken up – an instinctive ploy to make the caller feel guilty. It didn't work. It was her sister. 'Jill! do you know what time it is? Yes I know I called Mummy. No, Denzil isn't in trouble. He just needs a . . . what?'

She gripped the receiver more tightly. 'You know one? Who?'

She listened intently as Jill explained a tenuous but definitely real line of contact and reached excitedly for her diary.

'But are you sure he knows he owes Don a favour?' she asked slowly as she wrote. Don was her brother-in-law.

She was reassured and a few minutes later was hurrying back to the bedroom.

She eyed her husband's recumbent and snoring form. 'Jill and Don have asked us to go for drinks on Thursday,' she announced triumphantly. 'They've got a QC lined up for you.'

She was answered by a snort.

At nine the next morning her mother was on the phone again. This time she was excited. She had obviously spent the night in deep communion with her address book.

'I've just remembered, darling,' she announced before Meg could draw breath. 'Your brother's godmother's husband was a QC. I think he's retired, but that won't matter will it? It's just as good, I'm sure. I've asked them over for tomorrow. Make sure you come early then Denzil will have plenty of time to talk to him . . .'

Mary called back at ten forty-five. 'Meg. You know, I thought about what you said yesterday and it did seem a super excuse to call Roland. He remembered me, and he sounds fabulous – a very *rich* sort of voice, I thought –' there was a short pause on the line while she licked her lips. 'And guess what? He's just been made a QC. So everything's perfect. He's agreed to come to have drinks with us Friday at six. All right? Of course I didn't tell him about Denzil wanting to speak to him, I mean how could I? I'm sure it's unethical or something, but you'll have to work that out . . .'

Meg put down the phone and stared at her diary. No one could say she hadn't tried. Three QCs, three days running!

She gave a little secret smile and picking up the phone

dialled Denzil's work number. It was a while before he came on the line, but when he did he sounded breathless.

'Meg? The most fantastic news!'

She stiffened suspiciously. 'Den, you haven't found a QC have you?'

'QC? What are you talking about? Good Lord, no, forget all that. Darling, I decided to take the bull by the horns and I went and saw the MD himself this morning and asked for a transfer. And guess what. He's agreed. No questions, no arguments. He said because of my seniority I can have the next posting there and one is coming up in about three months' time. It was as simple as that.'

As simple as that? She glanced down at her diary.

Wednesday:	Mummy's QC – 7.30
Thursday:	Jill's QC – 8.30
Friday:	Mary's QC – 6.00

She closed her eyes and taking a deep breath began to count slowly to ten.

When the phone rang again a little while later she automatically reached for her diary. There was only Saturday left. This week.

'Meg dear? It's Aunt Hattie. Your mother tells me you're anxious to find the name of a Queen's Counsel. Well, I happen to know one. He's a most delicious young man . . .'

I wonder how many QCs there are, Meg thought to herself idly as she listened, and reaching for her pen she began to doodle round the tiny picture of the moon which appeared on the page heralding the start of the following month.

Catherine's Cat

THEY WERE THERE AGAIN. The eyes. High up on top of the old-fashioned wardrobe in the corner of her room. Gleaming in the dark. Golden. Elliptical.

Of course, she knew they were really the locks on the suitcase, catching the reflection from the street lamp outside her window, but sometimes in the long sleepless nights as her aching lids refused to stay shut she would half focus on them and know that up there there lurked a big hungry cat.

With a shiver she pulled the duvet up over her mouth and nose leaving only her eyes exposed, eyes which refused to close. Soon she would hear her mother and father coming up to bed; the footsteps on the stairs, the quiet talking, sometimes laughter – always discreet, always thoughtful, not wanting to wake her up. It was reassuring, hearing them there, sensing them close, just across the landing. She didn't like it when she was upstairs by herself. It was frightening; lonely.

She heard their bedroom door close. In a few minutes it would open again and one of them would go into the bathroom. Sometimes they would run the bath before they shut the door, going backwards and forwards between the two rooms and sometimes, very faintly, she could smell the sweet lavender of her mother's bath oil. It comforted her to think that they were there so close. Within call if something awful should really happen. Her eyes went quickly from the thin bright line down the side of her bedroom door to the top of the wardrobe again.

It was still there, the sleepy cat; watching. Tonight it seemed more alert than usual; the eyes bigger. She glanced hastily out of the window, hardly daring to move her head lest she draw attention to herself, and saw the light outside in the street. It too seemed brighter. It was blue instead of a softer yellow. Perhaps they had changed the bulb. She looked back at the cat and heard a soft unmistakable growl.

Her heart thudding with fear she shrank back into the bed, trying to slip out of sight, trying to shrink herself to nothing. She didn't dare hide completely though. If she stopped watching it might move – leap down from its high perch and attack.

It had never done it yet but there was always a first time for everything – her father had told her that.

She could hear its tail swishing now – a rhythmic brushing against the wood of the wardrobe door and then in the silence she heard the slight rasping as it flexed its claws.

'Mummy –' Her call was so quiet it was no more than a whisper. She was too afraid it would hear her. 'Mummy, can you come here.'

If she called as her mother came out of the bathroom she might hear; might come straightaway, but then supposing the cat leapt and landed on her mother?

She ducked even further out of sight, not daring to call out again, her eyes red with staring.

'Frances? Come on. What are you doing in there? Did you fall asleep in the bath?' Her father's sudden call was shockingly loud. She tensed, waiting for the animal to jump, but it didn't move.

Couldn't move, she reminded herself sternly. It was after all a suitcase. Just a suitcase.

'Frances?' His voice was sharper, somehow more anxious. 'Are you all right?'

She held her breath.

Her father's footsteps padded across the landing and she heard the bathroom door open. 'Frances!' His call was peremptory and a little afraid. 'Frances!' It was louder again. He had come back out onto the landing. It sounded as if he were just outside her door. 'Frances!' The word was quieter yet louder as though he were speaking with his lips to her keyhole, yet not wanting to awaken her. Her eyes went up automatically to the cat. It watched sleepily, not moving.

'Frances!' It was a whisper this time but her door was opening – the crack of light widening cautiously as it pushed with a slight shushing sound across the pile of the carpet. The cat's eyes disappeared.

'Frances, are you in there?'

'Daddy?' Catherine sat up. 'Daddy, what's wrong?'

For a moment he hesitated then he groped for the light switch by the door. In the sudden brightness Catherine screwed up her eyes, blinking.

'I thought Mummy was in here,' he said slowly. 'I'm sorry, pudding. I didn't mean to wake you.'

'I wasn't asleep.' Catherine clutched her duvet more tightly.

'No.' He sounded suddenly bleak.

She stared at him. He was wrapped in his dark-blue dressing gown and his legs and feet were bare. She glanced at his legs and then averted her eyes. They were very white with black hairs growing on them. 'Where's Mummy gone?' she asked.

He gave a small tight smile, his hand going back to the light switch.

'Downstairs. I expect she's gone to make us some cocoa. Back to sleep now, pudding. God bless. I'll see you in the morning.'

The light clicked off and the door closed. The room was suddenly in total darkness. She froze, not daring to move.

The cat opened its eyes.

'Frances? Where are you, darling?' She heard her father's voice as he ran downstairs; the soft thump of his bare feet on each step. '*Frances!*' The anxiety was real now, sharp, although fainter. 'Oh God, please Frances, no. I can't live without you.'

Catherine's fists were knotted into the fabric of the duvet cover. She pressed her face into it, where it draped across her knees, to stop the scalding tears before they ran down her cheeks.

The house was silent. In the bed she began slowly to rock backwards and forwards in her misery, her loneliness and terror like an ice wall around her.

On the wardrobe the cat moved slightly. A paw flexed on the fretted wooden gallery above the doors and a deep groove appeared in the richness of the wood.

'Frances! Frances, my darling, I love you! Don't you see. I love you!'

Catherine stiffened. The voice was very loud once more, clear in the stillness of the night. It came not from the house but from outside her window. For a moment she couldn't move, then she pushed back the duvet and slid out of bed, running to stare out, shocked and terrified to see her father, still in his dressing gown and bare feet, standing in the middle of the road. Behind him the garden gate swung open, the path clear in the light of the street lamp. The road in both directions was completely empty. His hair was tousled and his face, clearly visible in the blue cold light, contorted with pain.

Her fingers clutched at the window sill so tightly her hands were white and bloodless; her attention was focused so hard on her father she did not hear the thud as the cat leapt down and stood for a moment on the carpet near her bed. It regarded the child's thin shoulders with an air of detached, almost academic interest and then it leapt onto the bed. Turning round once it settled down, the long tail brushing the floor on one side, a huge velvet paw casually draped over the other. It watched her sleepily, its eyes slowly closing, its nose resting comfortably on the soft black fur of a forepaw.

Catherine swallowed hard, trying not to cry, empathising with her father's pain and not able to articulate her own.

'Mummy?' The whisper was strangled.

After several minutes he turned and walked back towards the house. She could see his bare feet on the gritty tarmac of the road in the lamp light and she stared fascinated by this terrible abnormality in a life which had seemed so sane and ordered for every day of her existence.

He came through the gate and left it open as he walked slowly back towards the house. As he reached the front door, so like the others in the suburban avenue with its blue and green stained-glass flowers let into the panel above the letter box, he passed out of her sight.

Catherine didn't move. She heard him close the front door and knew with some part of herself that he was leaning against it, defeated, and sobbing silently.

She didn't dare move. Her world had crumbled. The love and security with which she had been surrounded all her life had gone. Reality was the loneliness of the darkened bedroom, the hungry angry cat lying on the wardrobe waiting to pounce.

She stared down the road with eyes blinded by tears. It was still empty.

'Daddy?' Her lips framed the word but she knew he couldn't come. She was no longer the centre of his world; she was no longer the centre of any world. He had forgotten her.

When she at last turned from the window, cold and stiff, trembling in every limb, she did not even look at the wardrobe; nor did she notice the shadow-like black shape taking up so much room on the end of her bed. Crawling under the pillows she burrowed out of sight and began to sob again. It was only as she was falling asleep that, stretching out a little, she felt the solid weight on the duvet near her feet and, taking comfort from the warmth, without further conscious thought, snuggled down against it.

She did not know how long she had been asleep when she was awakened by the sound of a door banging. She tensed, her eyes, swollen by crying, still tightly shut.

'Frances?' Her father's voice in the distance was croaky with exhaustion.

Catherine crept out of bed and went to the door. Pulling it open she peered out. The lights upstairs were all on. From where she stood she could see the top of the stairs and the banister around the head of the stairwell close to the bathroom door. In the bathroom the water for her mother's bath had long ago gone cold. Only a slow monotonous drip from one of the taps broke the silence.

'Frances? You came back?'

Behind her only a large oval indentation and a few black hairs on Catherine's bed cover showed where the cat had lain.

'I couldn't do it, Freddie.' Her mother's voice was barely audible.

Catherine crept across the landing and crouched down, peering through the banister rails. Her mother was standing just inside the front door, her hair wet with rain. When had it started raining? She was dressed in her old jeans with a heavy blue sweater and her red woollen jacket that Catherine liked to dress up in sometimes because on her it came down to the ground. Her mother's face was white and strained – it was to Catherine's shocked eyes no longer the face of the beautiful young princess-like figure who had figured in so many of the child's fantasy games, but that of an old ugly woman.

'I'm sorry for all the things I said.' Frances hadn't moved any further into the hall. Her hands were pushed down into the pockets of the jacket and her shoulders were hunched defensively. 'It was hateful of me.'

'They were true.' Freddie was sitting on the stairs with his back to Catherine and he had not stood up. He looked defeated. They were both, Catherine realised suddenly, frightened. She bit her lip. Her world had started to spin again; parents are never afraid.

'I am boring. I am stuck in a rut. You could have done much better than me. Everyone always thought that.'

'No!' Frances was shaking her head. 'No, Freddie –'

'Yes!' He buried his face in his hands. 'And I am too old for you. I always knew it. But I loved – love – you so much.' He looked up.

Catherine chewed her lip. She pressed her face closer to the bars. She could feel her father's pain; his absolute despair. Her eyes narrowed as her gaze went to her mother. For the first time in her life she was seeing her as a separate thing – a frightening, unpredictable stranger. She studied her mother's face with hostile intensity, noting the pale, unmade-up skin, the huge shadowed eyes with mud-coloured circles under the lower lids, the thin almost paper-coloured lips, usually so joyously scarlet and full, and she registered an infinitesimal shiver of dislike. Frances's hair was hanging round her shoulders in rats' tails, dripping down her neck and she pushed it away with cold near-lifeless fingers. 'I think I'll go upstairs and have a bath.' Her voice was lacklustre and defeated.

'Why did you come back?' Freddie was still sitting on the stairs. To go up to the bathroom she would have to climb over him.

She stood still, her hands spread in a gesture of helplessness.

'Wouldn't he have you?' Freddie's voice was suddenly harsh.

Her eyes went to his and Catherine noted dispassionately that they were now brimming with tears. 'I never reached his house.'

There was a long silence. Freddie didn't seem to know what to say. His shoulders had slumped as he sat there below her and Catherine saw the sharp angles of his bones beneath the blue towelling of his robe. Above the collar his neck rose, thin and defenceless, and above that his tousled hair. As if he could feel his daughter's gaze he ran distracted fingers through it and then sank his head once more into his hands. 'You could still go.'

She drew in her breath sharply. 'Do you want me to?'

'No.' He raised his head wearily. 'No of course I don't want you to, but I don't want you to stay if you're unhappy and it's all over between us.'

'It's not all over, Freddie. It was never there.' She turned back towards the front door and put her hand on the latch. For a moment it stayed there, then it slid away. Frances leaned forward, her forehead resting against the leaded panes of coloured glass, her hands hanging limply at her sides. 'I don't know what to do.' It was a child-like call for help.

'Stay. Please stay. Think of Catherine.'

Catherine's grip tightened on the banister rails until her hands hurt.

Frances turned wearily. 'Catherine wouldn't even miss me. She's always loved you best.'

Freddie didn't say anything for a moment, then he shrugged. 'That's silly. She loves both of us.'

'No.' Frances shook her head violently. 'No. She's never loved me. She's a cold uncaring child. I sometimes can't believe I even gave birth to her. She'd be much happier if I weren't here. Then she could have you all to herself.'

'Frances!' His voice was stronger suddenly. 'You don't know what you're saying.'

'No?' There was a strange half-sneer on Frances's lips. 'Do you want me to ask her?'

Catherine shrank back out of sight. She was very cold. Climbing unsteadily to her feet she crept back along the landing towards her bedroom door, her skin like ice beneath her thin cotton pyjamas.

The room was very dark; she was half-way across the carpet before she remembered the cat. She glanced up at the wardrobe. The animal had gone. She could see the wall clearly. No suitcase. She frowned, distracted. Had her father moved it? Then she heard the growl.

She found she couldn't breathe any more. Turning slowly back towards her bed she saw the huge black shape sitting there, saw the golden almond-shaped eyes with dark diamond slits, and heard the knife-like claws unsheathed, massaging the soft pink candy stripes of the duvet. She could smell the feral warmth of its fur.

Slowly it stood up. Arching its back with casual luxuriousness it jumped off the bed. Only a few feet from her now, it stood with its shoulder level with hers, its head raised almost at a height with her own.

She moistened her lips nervously with her tongue, her eyes on the cat's, and it echoed the movement revealing for a moment two hooked, white canine fangs.

Then it moved.

Anaesthetised by her fear Catherine stayed where she was. Only her eyes followed the cat as it padded once round the room before coming to a stop beside her and pressed its huge head against her, nuzzling her shoulder. Her small hand went cautiously to the ruff of stiff fur behind its ears and as she began to scratch it she was rewarded with a barely audible, deep vibrating purr.

'Catherine! Wake up. You'll be late for school.'

Her mother's voice cut through her dream like a serrated knife. For a moment Catherine lay quite still, then cautiously she opened her eyes.

Cold sunshine flooded into the bedroom; on the top of the wardrobe the old suitcase was stacked as usual beside her grown-up brother's empty rucksack and a broken kite.

She turned to look at her mother. Frances's face was pale beneath her make-up and she looked tired, but otherwise she was much as usual, bustling over to the stripped pine chest of drawers and pulling the top drawers open for clean blouse and knickers and socks. She tossed them onto the bed. 'Five minutes. Breakfast is almost ready,' she said and turning she went out of the room.

Catherine sat up in bed, hugging her knees, her eyes on the suitcase. It was a dream. It had to have been a dream. All of it.

She sat down in front of her bowl of cornflakes without enthusiasm, her eyes going to her father's place.

'Where's Daddy?'

'He caught the early train.' Her mother retrieved two pieces of toast from the toaster and juggled them into the rack. 'I'm driving you to school this morning.' She was the same as usual, apart from the funny blurred look on her face – efficient, slightly impatient, impersonal, trying to read the headlines of the paper as she drank her instant coffee and poured Catherine's hot milk from the saucepan.

'Mummy, can we have a kitten?' Catherine unscrewed the honey jar and stuck her knife into the grainy waxy sweetness, knowing it would call forth a cry of anger from her mother who had carefully put a long-handled spoon beside the jar.

'What, darling?' Seemingly engrossed in the paper Frances had not noticed the honey.

'A kitten. I would so love to have a kitten.'

'Mm.' The noise was too non-committal to be a yes; it was a reflex action, no more, and meant her mother hadn't heard.

'Daddy says I can.' That was chancing her arm and she knew it.

'What?' Frances looked up and threw the paper on the table. 'Come on. You're going to be late. Go and brush your teeth. Quickly.' She hadn't heard a word about the kitten. Not a word. 'Have you got your satchel? Don't forget your history book. It's in the dining room still, and your ballet things are in the airing cupboard.'

They were the things she always said. Normal, naggy, caring things. The kind of things mothers always said.

Catherine slid from her chair, still chewing on her toast. 'So, can I have a kitten?'

Her mother heard. She frowned. 'No, of course you can't have a kitten! What a ridiculous idea.'

'Daddy said –'

'I don't care what Daddy said. I say no. Now go and clean your teeth.'

Catherine walked sedately out of the room and up the stairs. Going into the bathroom she reached for her pink toothbrush and then the tube of paste. Carefully she cleaned her teeth and rinsed out her mouth, then she walked back across the landing and into her bedroom. She took her blazer out of the wardrobe and then she looked up.

'Mummy doesn't like kittens,' she said softly but clearly. 'I don't think Mummy likes cats either.'

The animal was lying, head on paws, surveying her through sleepy eyes. Its tail, hanging down the side of the cupboard, twitched slightly, softly stroking the polished walnut.

She could feel it now, the soft ruff of fur, the warmth, the coils of steel-strong muscle, relaxed and pliant beneath her fingers, the heavy head beside hers on the tear-hot pillow as she cried herself to sleep and she stared up at it unafraid. It was the first time she had seen it in daylight. It was huge; big enough to eat someone.

She smiled as she buttoned her blazer. 'Mummy doesn't like me either,' she said, her tone conversational. 'That's because Daddy likes me best.'

The cat blinked with lazy interest.

'Catherine!' Her mother's shout on the landing made her jump. 'For goodness' sake, hurry!'

'If you're hungry, you could probably eat her, you know.' She said it quickly under her breath, half afraid, half defiant, a last-minute instruction as she turned towards the door. Opening it she glanced back. In a patch of early morning sunlight the suitcase on the wardrobe had changed from shadowy black to the rich chestnut of old leather.

Sitting in her classroom Catherine glanced across her neighbour towards the window. The sun was shining brightly now and the heat was striking through the glass. The roar of traffic in the busy road outside was muted into a muffled continuous sound which with the heat of the sun falling across her desk made her feel very sleepy. It was Monday, the day her mother hung out the washing on the line in the narrow back garden, the day she would go into Catherine's room and change the bed linen so that tonight, Catherine's favourite night, the sheets and pillows would smell of flowers and grass and fresh country things.

Her mother would be going into the bedroom, alone, unsuspecting, her arms full of clean pillowcases and clothes and with her back to the wardrobe she would set them all down as she always did, on the small frilled stool which stood in front of Catherine's dressing table. She might glance up into the little mirror and catch a glance of the black face with the golden almond-shaped eyes as it sprang, she might not. She might never know what had attacked her at all.

'Catherine?'

All they would find would be a pile of clean laundry and perhaps her mother's silver bangles, lying on the carpet near the bed.

'Catherine, what is it? Are you ill?' Miss Pitman had heard the child's strangled gasp and seen her eyes fill with tears. She put her arm round Catherine's shoulders and squatted down beside her chair. 'What is it, sweetheart? What's wrong?'

Catherine's face was white and she was shaking. The other children in the class looked at her with interest. 'She's going to be sick,' a small voice announced from the end of the row with the certainty of long experience and with some satisfaction.

'No she's not, Edward.' Miss Pitman put her other hand gently over Catherine's. 'What's wrong, Cathie? Aren't you feeling well?'

Catherine shook her head. She was trembling too much to speak.

There was a procedure in place for occasions such as these

and it was set in motion without delay. While Catherine was led to the sick room the class was put on its honour to do some copying in silence and as on all occasions before she and Miss Pitman had reached the corner of the passage the noise behind them was crescendoing out of control; but for once Miss Pitman did not storm back to fling open the door and shout, without having to even look who it was, at young Edward and his two best cronies. The child beside her was worrying her too much.

She sat her on the bed and put a professionally cool hand on Catherine's forehead to feel skin burning like fire. 'What is it, Catherine? Where are you hurting?'

Catherine shook her head, incapable of speech. Before her eyes she could see clearly her mother's dismembered body, an arm lying near the dressing table, a foot on the bed where the cat had taken it to eat, holding it meticulously between two soft velvet paws, as it licked delicately at the toes, its eyes half shut in concentration.

Mrs Harriman, the principal, summoned from her mathematics class, frowned thoughtfully. 'Has something happened at home to upset you, Catherine?' She bent down a little in front of Catherine putting a hand on each shoulder, peering through circular spectacle lenses which enlarged her eyes into startling blue-irised globes.

Catherine nodded between hiccuping sobs.

'You must calm down and tell me so I can help. What's happened? What has upset you so much?'

'I've done something,' Catherine's words were all but inaudible, 'terrible.'

'You've done something terrible?'

She nodded miserably, hiccuping in earnest now, her eyes swollen and red.

'What have you done, Catherine?'

The quiet authority in the headmistress's voice was beginning to calm her. Catherine took a deep shuddering breath. Her hot hands kneaded the front of her pleated school skirt into a damp crushed rag. 'Mummy's dead.' The words were so quiet, so indistinct, at first, that neither woman thought she had heard aright.

Mrs Harriman collected herself visibly. 'Did you say there was something wrong with your Mummy, Catherine? But I saw her this morning when she brought you to school. She looked fine.'

'I've killed her.' The words were clearer this time, almost defiant. 'I killed her,' she repeated. 'Because she doesn't love me.'

Miss Pitman turned away from Catherine to the table near the window. Picking up a box of tissues, she pulled out a wad and put it into Catherine's hand. 'Blow your nose, sweetheart, and stop crying,' she said in her most bracing voice. 'Of course your mother loves you. How silly.' She raised an eyebrow in the direction of her superior. 'Do you think we'd better ring home?'

Mrs Harriman nodded. 'Give her a drink. I'll be back in a minute.'

It was a long minute. A mug of cocoa and two digestive biscuits later, with reinforcements sent to quell the two teacherless classrooms, Miss Pitman and Catherine were sitting side by side on the sick room bed and slowly the story was emerging.

Miss Pitman hid a smile. 'So, you told this panther or whatever it is, which lives on the wardrobe, that it could eat your mother, because your mother doesn't love you any more?'

Catherine nodded.

'And because you didn't love your mother any more either?'

Catherine nodded again.

'And you wanted to punish her?'

The nod was so small it was hardly visible.

'And now you're sorry you told the cat it could hurt her because you really love her very much.'

The nod this time, eyes huge, fixed desperately hopeful on Miss Pitman's face, was unmistakable.

Miss Pitman smiled. 'Catherine, the cat won't have attacked your mother! I'm sure you'll find she's safe and sound. It knows you really love her, just as it knows she really loves you. You know,' she stopped, wondering how far she dared go in reassuring the child on the subject of parental rows, 'grown ups do sometimes say things they don't mean at all when they are cross and it sounds to me as if your mummy and daddy were a bit cross with each other, doesn't it. I don't think they meant you to hear their quarrel. I think your mummy would be very upset indeed if she knew you heard her say something she didn't mean about you.'

'Does the cat know?'

Miss Pitman smiled again. 'Oh yes, the cat knows. The cat knows everything, because I think some of the time that silly old cat is just a story inside your head.'

Catherine surveyed her solemnly. Surely something inside her head could not scratch the wardrobe with its sharp claws; tear at her duvet cover the way it had.

'Anyway – ' Miss Pitman reached once more for the biscuit packet and passed it to her. 'You'll soon see your mummy is all right.'

She glanced up as the door opened. Sarah Harriman's face was white as she beckoned Miss Pitman out of the room. In the hall she pulled Miss Pitman away from the door and began to talk in an urgent whisper. 'There was no reply from the house so I rang the father at his office. They told me there he had been called to the hospital. His wife has had an accident.' She glanced over her colleague's shoulder towards the closed door of the sick room and lowered her voice even further. 'They think she was attacked by some kind of animal.'

The women stared at each other for a moment in silence as her words sank in and the shock registered on Miss Pitman's face. The word which she finally chose to relieve her feelings was not one usually heard even in the playground.

'Quite.' Sarah endorsed it without the flicker of an eyelash.

'So, what do we do?'

'Is she badly hurt, do they know?'

'All they know is that Freddie Carter dropped everything and raced off to be at her bedside.'

'You'd better ring the hospital.' Miss Pitman bit her lip. 'I'll go back to Catherine.' She hesitated. 'She says it was a cat; a cat to which she made the suggestion that it eat her mother.' There was another short pause. 'I suppose it could be a real cat – some moggy she's enticed into her bedroom?'

Her headmistress narrowed her eyes. 'What do you mean it *could* be a real cat? What else could it be?' They held each other's gaze for a moment and both looked away simultaneously. 'Look, go back to the child. Stuff her with biscuits. Take her back into class if she's calmed down enough. Tell her her mummy is out shopping and can't come and get her for a while – anything. Anything. I'll see what I can find out.'

Freddie came to collect his small daughter two hours later. Before he was allowed to see her, Sarah Harriman showed him into her study.

'How is your wife?' She studied his face, noting that though he was tired and obviously under some strain he was equally obviously not prostrate with grief. Inwardly she sighed with relief even before he spoke.

'She's okay. They're keeping her in over night. She's got one or two deep scratches but most are superficial. She's very shocked, though.'

'What was it, do you know?'

Sitting behind her desk, she was playing nervously with her pen.

'The police think a stray cat must have got into the house but there was no sign of it when we went back to look.'

'A stray cat.' Sarah nodded slowly.

She looked down at her blotter. 'I see.' She glanced up again and took a deep breath. 'I think it's possible Catherine may have enticed it in. She has been telling us a little about it this morning, but she's obviously been very upset.'

In the car going home Freddie glanced at his daughter's face. It was still a little puffy from her earlier storm of crying when he had told her what had happened to her mother, and he noticed not for the first time how heartbreakingly like Frances she was.

'We'll go home and have tea, then later we'll go to the hospital to see Mummy, okay?' He smiled at her, changing down as they reached the corner of their road, wondering yet again just how such a little girl was going to live with the trauma of her guilt and her pain, if as Mrs Harriman seemed to think, Catherine knew about the cat.

Catherine nodded. She had grown more and more quiet as they approached the house.

'What is it, sweetheart? There's nothing to be afraid of.' Drawing up outside he reached for her hands. 'The police have searched every corner of the house and the animal has gone.' So had the blood. He had cleaned it up himself before setting out to fetch Catherine. He looked at her hard for a minute and then he turned away to gaze out of the windscreen. He hadn't reached for the door-handle. 'It must have sneaked in when Mummy was hanging out the washing, or,' he hesitated, 'did you let it in, Cathie? Had you been giving it some milk or something?' The police had found the black hairs on his daughter's duvet and noted the deep jumping scratches on the top of the wardrobe from which the creature had leapt onto Frances's back. The lacerations across her shoulders had been ferociously deep.

The puzzle had been where the cat had gone. Frances had not seen it at all. Flinging the clinging creature from her back with a scream she had run from the room, half fallen down the stairs and locked herself, shaking and hysterical, in the kitchen. From there she had phoned a neighbour before she collapsed, and the neighbour taking one look at her unconscious friend and her blood-soaked sweater had called an ambulance and then the police. No door had been forced, no window was open more than a crack, yet the cat was undoubtedly gone.

'No one is cross, sweetheart. You couldn't have known it had a vicious streak. I'm just relieved it didn't hurt you as well.' He put his arm round her and she snuggled against him, comforted. 'That was it, wasn't it? You let it in.'

Catherine shook her head.

'You didn't?' He looked down at her with a frown.

She shook her head again. 'It's always lived here. In my room.' She waited for her father to say something and when he didn't she took a deep breath and she began to speak.

At the end of her story he was sitting staring sightlessly out of the windscreen. For a long time he said nothing and at last, timidly, she touched his hand.

'Daddy?' She was very afraid.

He turned to her and the sorrow on his face was so great she had to look away. 'I'm sorry,' she whispered. 'I'm sorry.'

'Darling, it's me who should be sorry. Mummy and me. We had no idea you were there listening. No idea at all.' He bit his lip, still making no move to get out of the car. It was as if he were afraid to go into the house.

He sighed. 'Listen. You have to believe me. You have to. Mummy loves you as much as I do and that is so much it would drown mountains.' He managed a smile. 'She only said she didn't love you so much and you didn't love her because she knew how cross it would make me! Grown ups do that every now and then, you know. Just to wind each other up. It's a sort of game they play. Then they make up and everything is all right. They know none of the things they said meant anything.' If only it were true. Please God, let it be true.

His hand on hers was ice cold and shaking slightly. She reversed the grip, taking his in her own two hot little palms and trying to give him comfort.

'I didn't mean her to get hurt. Truly.'

'I know you didn't. Cathie, it's not your fault. The cat didn't listen to what you were saying. It couldn't have!'

But even as he said the words he wondered.

Inside at last he gave her hot cheese on toast on her knee in front of the television, not arguing when she refused to go to her room, until she had been home for an hour and he couldn't stand it any longer. He reached down for her hand. 'Come on. We're going to check it out upstairs.'

She shook her head.

'Yes. We need to look at your room, find you a night light so you're never scared in the dark again, and look at this silly old suitcase.'

It was where it always was, on top of the cupboard. For a long time they both stared at it, then Freddie collected her dressing table stool and put it in front of the wardrobe. 'Hold it for me so I don't fall off.'

'Careful.' Her mouth was dry with terror.

'I will be.' He grinned at her.

Standing on tiptoe he reached for the worn leather handle and gave it a tug. It didn't move. He tugged again, realising he was going to have to lift it over the small ornate parapet which ran around the top of the wardrobe. For a moment it resisted then at last he dragged it free and swung it down, surprised at its weight. 'This old case belonged to my father,' he said to her as he laid it down on the floor and knelt before the huge brass locks. 'It went all over the world with him. Look at the labels.' He glanced up at her. 'There's nothing to be afraid of, Cathie. The case is empty.'

She had backed away, her hands tightly clasped together behind her back, her face like chalk.

He was struggling with the locks now, fighting them back, sure it wasn't locked, until at last one clicked back and then the other.

He stared down. The child's fear was infectious. Suddenly he didn't want to open it.

He had an irrational feeling that the cat was inside; but how could it be?

'When we've put this away up in the attic where it belongs, we'll go and see Mummy shall we?' He smiled up at her.

She nodded wearily.

'I don't think we'll tell her about all this, do you, Pudding?' he went on carefully. 'I think it's a special secret thing between you and me. Poor Mummy thinks it was just a silly old wild cat from the garden. I think it's better that way, don't you?' She also thought the cat was some kind of punishment for what she had done. His hand was on the lid of the case and Catherine was watching it, mesmerised.

'See this lovely old leather? That's why the case is so heavy; almost too heavy to lift even though it's empty. We should be glad modern suitcases are so light. In the old days they were all like this unless they were made of cardboard.' His fingers stroked the surface and rested one by one on the torn stickers. 'Look. India. Burma. China. What memories the case must have.' He bit his lip. All places where big cats roamed free.

Taking a deep breath he began to ease back the lid. Slowly it rose, revealing nothing but a rubbed faded lining and a few nondescript bits of rubbish. Tickets, a hairpin, an old envelope. The smell inside the suitcase was of old leather, dust and musty long-forgotten cologne.

For a long time Catherine and her father stared down into the case, then he let the lid fall shut. Neither of them had noticed the clump of black hairs caught in the inner buckled straps.

Pulling down the attic steps Freddie humped the case up out of sight and came back down again shutting the trap door behind him.

'Right?' He dusted his hands together. 'Now, we'll go and see Mummy. And I think you'll find she's got an idea for you.' He smiled. She had been devastated in the hospital about her harshness to Catherine that morning, remembering only her small daughter's crestfallen face and her tears, so resolutely held back as she walked into school. She would do everything in her power to make it up to the child, as she would to him. 'I think, as Mummy is a bit off cats at the moment, that it might involve a puppy.'

Catherine gave a gasp of delight but half-way down the stairs she stopped and glanced back. Obviously her father hadn't heard the click of claws on top of the trap door or the small querulous growl, but then perhaps she hadn't either.

Stranger's Choice

THE SUN WAS SLANTING through the feathery branches of the larch tree. Fiona stood for a while in the dappled shade, looking down at the broad sweep of the river at her feet. It was a still, gentle evening. Behind her she could see the stones of the old kirk nestling up in the wooded slopes of the hill.

Her heart beat fast and she checked her wristwatch. Half past, the minister had said. She clutched her music case a little more tightly and sat down on the river bank to wait, trying hard to think of anything but the coming test and the tunes she had so carefully practised.

Setting the case down on the grass as gently as she would had it contained some of the eggs from her mother's hens, she picked up a sprig of larch cones. Nervously she twisted them between her fingers, picking off the tiny scales. Then a bird caught her eye as it swept low over the water, just skimming the surface with its beak before it angled sharply up into the wood and disappeared. Fiona shivered. That was how she wanted to play the organ. The low easy skimming, the swift, controlled flights of ecstasy, the breathless, dizzy grace. She looked down at her hands. They were sturdy and red from the gardening, not the kind of hands to produce ethereal music.

From across the trees came the echoing single note of the clock striking the half hour. Fiona scrambled to her feet in horror. Her watch must have stopped. She began to run up through the dim woods, fighting her way between the closely planted firs, her sandals sinking into the soft carpet made by their needles.

The hillside was very steep, and when at last she arrived at the little grey-built kirk she was breathless and dishevelled. There was no sign of Mr Seton, the minister. Her heart sank. She knew he was a busy man. It had only been with reluctance that he had agreed to come and hear her play this evening at all. Indeed he had not even seemed to want to admit that the position of organist would be free when Sandy Gregor moved away. She knew he thought her too young for the post. To him, as to everyone else she was still Mrs Macrae's 'wee Fiona'.

Ducking into the low porch she listened for a moment to the noisily squabbling birds in the roof beams. They had an untidy nest up there, she saw, with two gaping beaks protruding from it. The sight made her smile as, cautiously, she pushed at the heavy door. To her surprise it was unlocked.

The kirk was very still. She thought for a moment it was empty, then she noticed a figure sitting on one of the benches to the side, near the organ. She approached on tiptoe and nervously cleared her throat.

He did not appear to hear her. He was dressed in his customary black suit, his head resting on his hand, his shoulders hunched. For a moment she stood beside him in awed silence, not knowing what to do. Then she spoke softly.

Slowly the man raised his head, and he gave her a grave smile. It was not Mr Seton.

'Oh, I'm sorry.' Fiona backed away in alarm, seeing the grey, tired face and red-rimmed eyes. 'I shouldn't have disturbed you. I thought you were the minister.'

Again the same smile. 'Think nothing of it, lassie. It was time I was leaving anyway.' He looked around the empty building, his eyes dwelling momentarily on the bowl of daffodils and narcissi before the lectern. The sun slanting through the tiny panes of glass in the west window was casting chequered patterns across the floor, lighting the blooms in a glorious radiance.

The man smiled. 'This is a beautiful place, young lady,' he said, his voice sad. Rising to his feet, he began to make his way towards the door. Then he paused and looked back.

Already Fiona, preoccupied with her own worries, had made her way to the organ and was running her fingers soundlessly over the keys. Her stomach was tied in a nervous knot, and she wondered suddenly if she would be able to remember a single note if Mr Seton came.

'Do you know how to play it?'

She jumped as the stranger's words carried back to her beneath the echoing roof vault.

'A little.' She smiled nervously. 'I've come to play for the minister, to see if I'm good enough for the services.'

'Indeed.' The man slowly retraced his steps. He stood behind her for a moment. 'Play something for me now.'

'Oh I couldn't.' Fiona was embarrassed. 'Besides, I must wait for Mr Seton.'

'He won't mind. Come on. I want to hear some music.'

Fiona slipped uncomfortably into the seat, then she let out a stifled cry.

'My music! Oh, I've left my music down by the river.' She looked round, anguished. 'Oh what am I to do?' The easy tears were already brimming in her eyes.

'Hush, hush.' The man put a gentle hand on her shoulder. 'Look there's plenty of music there, on the shelf.'

'But it's not mine,' wailed Fiona. 'I had it especially prepared. I had practised special things.' A tear fell on the keyboard and she hastily dabbed at it with her handkerchief.

The man chuckled. 'I'm thinking that these are the tunes you'll be asked to play: hymns and carols, not organ sonatas and party pieces.' He reached down a pile of tattered folios and began slowly to leaf through them.

Fiona watched him miserably. It had all gone wrong. She knew now that she would fail the test. She would never be able to play; her hands were shaking too much. Once again she was Mrs Macrae's wee Fiona and she wanted to run back to her mother's house.

The man looked over several pieces and then she saw him pause at one. He frowned and then gave a little laugh. Placing it before her, he smoothed back the page. 'Play me that,' he commanded.

Sniffing, she tentatively ran her fingers over the stops, and then slowly, softly, picked out the tune, touching in an occasional chord to give the music depth. It was something she had never heard before – sad, haunting and very beautiful.

Gradually she became absorbed in the music. She forgot herself and her mother, and the reason she was in the kirk. She did not even notice as the strange man, after listening for a few moments, his eyes distant with memory, slowly made his way back to the door and let himself out into the still evening.

Neither did she notice when a while later Mr Seton slipped into the kirk, still panting from his climb through the wood.

Not until the notes of the final chord had died away did she become conscious once more of her surroundings. Mr Seton rose from the seat he had taken at the back of the kirk and walked slowly up the aisle. 'That was very beautiful, Fiona,' he said. He reached over her shoulder and took the music. 'A strange choice though, I think, for the kirk. A lovely song, but more suited for a lover's wooing than one of my services.'

Fiona blushed. 'I'm sorry, Mr Seton. That gentleman chose it for me. And he took it from the music here by the organ, so I thought it was all right.'

'Indeed.' Mr Seton's eyebrows shot up, but he seemed amused. 'In that case I must have a wee word with Sandy Gregor before he leaves. I think it's time he had a sort through the music.' The minister himself picked up the pile of scores, and after a moment handed her another. 'What gentleman was that, Fiona?'

'He was in the kirk when I arrived. I disturbed him, thinking it was you, but he wasn't from these parts at all. I told him I'd left my music down by the river and he chose that song for me to play for him.'

'Indeed.' The minister smiled once more. 'I'm sorry I didn't see him. It seems he has a sense of humour, your strange friend. Enough. Play me the *Crimond* there, and we'll see how that sounds.'

Fiona sighed with relief. This was something she did know. She wished Mr Seton wouldn't stand quite so close behind her, checking every note she played, but on the whole she thought she got through it well enough. Her nervousness had not returned. He seemed pleased. She played two more hymns for him and that was all he wanted.

She sat quietly on the narrow seat, her sandals tucked well up on the crossbar, waiting for him to speak after she finished the last piece. He had retired during the last couple of verses to the end of the nave where he stood, his hands behind his back, seemingly lost in thought.

Then at last he spoke. 'Well, Fiona. I think you've got yourself a job, my dear, if you'd like it.' He smiled. 'I had no idea you had such a talent. My congratulations.'

Blushing, Fiona wriggled from her place and almost skipped down between the rows of empty seats to where he stood. Solemnly he shook hands with her.

She followed him out of the kirk, paused while he locked the door and went with him across the mown grass of the graveyard in the gradually dimming light.

'Will you go back by the river, Fiona, to collect your music?' The minister grinned at her mischievously. 'I know you won't make a habit of leaving it there before service.'

'Oh I won't,' Fiona agreed with him fervently. 'Indeed I won't.'

She stood and watched as he made his way out of the gate into the lane, then slowly she turned once more into the fragrant larches. Below her the evening sun, reflected in the river, turned the waters to a broad sweep of red gold.

Her music case was where she had left it on the river bank, the leather damp with dew. Clutching it to her she stood for a moment gazing out across the water.

She could hear someone singing. The voice, distant and melodious, seemed to be coming from further down the river. She strained her ears to make out the tune above the sound of the water: gradually she began to distinguish the notes. He was singing the love song she had played in the kirk.

She strained her eyes in the gloaming to see him. Was that a figure standing further down river near the rocks? She wasn't sure. Already the sound of the music was fading.

Raising her hand she waved in its direction, although she knew he couldn't see her.

'I'll never know who he was,' she reflected with a strange certainty, 'but maybe I'll play that tune for him again one day.' Whoever he was, his quiet smile and gentle choice of music had won her back her confidence and given her the job of her dreams.

She turned away from the water slowly and once more clutching her music case to her heart she began to make her way home in the dusk.

Aboard the Moonbeam

I STRETCHED LUXURIOUSLY and lay looking up at the dappled white reflection playing over the ceiling. It puzzled me for a moment. Then I remembered. I had arrived late the night before at the old house on the edge of Chichester Harbour. Outside my bedroom window stretched a vast expanse of ice-rimmed water.

Pulling my dressing gown around me with a shiver, half of excitement, half of cold as my feet met the floorboards beneath my bed, I got up and went over to the window to look out. It was early morning still and the harbour was deserted. Over towards the east the water was tinged with red from the morning sun. On either side cats' paws flecked the water into slate and silver shadow.

A solitary boat, large and black, was moored across the channel. I gazed at it fascinated for a while, lost in a dream, and then forgot it as I heard a call from downstairs.

My cousin, Jim, was in the kitchen.

'Granny stays in bed till lunch,' he explained, 'and I'm driving into town, so there's nothing for you to do but relax, and get well.' He smiled.

I was not really ill but long months of glandular fever had left me exhausted and depressed. My great aunt, Andrea, who had already offered Jim a home, now said she would be glad to have me for a few months as well. I think she guessed how lonely and unsettled I was and she knew how much I had loved my childhood holidays in her house.

After Jim had gone, I settled back to enjoy a second cup of coffee in the peaceful dining room, and inevitably my thoughts went back to Graham.

I looked ruefully at the engagement ring on my finger. It was a little loose still. We had never got round to having it altered to fit me properly. Dear Graham. He had said nothing; neither had I, but I had a feeling that when next we met it would be for me to return that ring. He had been too eager to go back to New Zealand without me, had too easily accepted my reason for postponing the wedding. Indeed he seemed almost relieved when I said I would not follow him until later.

This time I had not cried when we parted. There was a tight restriction in my throat, but also, unaccountably, a sense of sudden freedom.

I was so immersed in my thoughts that it was a moment before I realised that someone was knocking on the side door. A young man stood outside, a muffler pulled well up to his chin. I supposed him to be one of the local fishermen.

'Morning.' He stared at me, obviously wondering who I was. 'I just thought I'd let you know. ***Moonbeam***'s signalling.'

'***Moonbeam***?' I stared at him, bewildered.

He nodded. 'Is Jim here? 'E always goes over.'

'He's gone up to town.' That at least I could answer.

The man scratched his head. He looked worried. 'Might be urgent. 'E don't often signal.' He saw that I still didn't understand. 'Chap lives over there on the ***Moonbeam***.' He indicated the black hulk I had noticed earlier. 'Your Jim rows over most days and takes him food and papers and that. Edward Avon, that's 'is name, has an emergency signal if 'e needs help.'

'Why can't he come here?' I was indignant. It seemed a strange, one-sided arrangement to me.

'Broke 'is leg. Mrs Andrea, she offered to have 'im to stay, of course, with 'er heart of gold, but he wouldn't 'ear of it; didn't want to put 'er out, so 'e said. Never mind. I'll see if anyone from the village can go over.'

'I know how to row.' I don't know what made me say it. Perhaps I was curious. Perhaps it was the light way this young man assumed that I would be of no use. 'If you show me where the boat is I'll go over and see.'

'You sure you can manage?' He looked at me hard from piercing blue eyes.

I grinned. 'Give me one moment to fetch my jacket.'

I followed him out into the exhilarating autumn sunshine, down to the edge of the quay, and climbed into the rowing boat which was tethered there. He pushed me off and I managed quite well on the whole, as I pulled at the oars with unaccustomed muscles, a fixed grin on my face as he stood to watch me go. To my relief he only stayed a minute, I suppose to make sure this town woman really could row, and then he turned and hurried away towards the village.

It was much further than I thought across the harbour. I rowed slowly, losing my breath in the brisk salty wind, cursing the fact that I hadn't remembered to bring any gloves. My fingers turned red, blue and white in turns, and soon I felt my strokes beginning to fail. I had forgotten my own stupid weakness, and the fact that this harbour, unlike the lake at home where I had learned to row, had a tide.

As I felt myself weaken I kept glancing over my shoulder towards the singularly misnamed *Moonbeam*, where she lay black and forbidding against a bank of reeds. Uncomfortable waves of panic began to crawl up and down my spine as I wondered whether I could get there at all, and what would happen to me if I didn't. The tide had such effortless hidden strength as it swept up the broad channel, bringing with it great lumps of green spinach-like seaweed.

Eventually I did get there, even though for a while I had the strength only to hang gasping onto one of the heavy mooring ropes, slimy with weed. Then at last I began to swing my little dinghy round towards the ladder which hung over the side. I was beginning to call Edward Avon all kinds of rude names under my breath. Didn't the silly man have a mobile phone, or a radio or something sensible like that? Why didn't he appear and at least help me up his beastly ladder? I wasn't sure I had enough energy left to climb it on my own.

I squinted up at the flag hanging from the stumpy mast above me. On it there was a pretty yellow boat, and it was flying upside down. That was the signal, I supposed, as I scrabbled my way feebly around the side of the boat with frozen hands.

At last I reached the ladder and managed to pull myself up precariously onto the slippery deck. I looked around. The boat seemed deserted. Making my way to the cabin door, I tapped on it, shaking with cold. There was no reply so I pushed it open and peered in.

The cabin was neat and warm, an oil light burning above the table. In the corner I could see a bunk and on it the huddled form of a man, the plaster cast encasing his ankle dragging at an awkward angle on the floorboards beside the berth.

'Hello, can I come in?' I was surprised by the tremor in my voice. My teeth were chattering.

He did not stir. I supposed he was asleep and timidly stepped down into the cabin.

His pillow was soaked in blood.

For a moment I had to fight off a wave of terrified faintness and nausea and then miraculously I was clear-headed again. Very gently I touched his head, easing back the fair hair, which was matted black with blood. He groaned as I touched him, but he didn't open his eyes.

I sat down at the little table for a moment, trying to decide what to do. I hadn't enough strength to row back for help. Of that I was sure. Somehow I had to attract the attention of someone in the village.

He let out another groan and I pulled myself to my feet to go to his side. Somehow I had to help him myself. Eventually, very gently I managed to sponge away most of the blood. He seemed to have a deep cut on his temple and a massive, spreading bruise across his forehead. Cautiously I lifted his heavy cast up onto the bed and straightened his legs, throwing a rug over them. At least he looked more comfortable.

It was as I tried easing the blood-soaked pillow away and replacing it with a cushion that he suddenly opened his eyes. They were clear slits of silver in his weather-beaten face. He looked at me blankly for a moment and then he smiled.

'I'm sure you can't be an angel,' he said clearly. Then he mumbled something I couldn't make out and closed his eyes.

I looked down at him, amused. 'I'm afraid I'm not,' I was about to reply, but I could see he had slipped away into unconsciousness again.

He was, I guessed, about thirty, perhaps a little more, and his face had a pleasant, thoughtful expression as though he were puzzling out some strange but not too unpleasant problem. There were little laughter lines at the corners of his eyes.

I was worried. Obviously he needed a doctor, and obviously I shouldn't really have touched him at all. Supposing he had a fractured skull? I quickly tried to put the idea out of my head as I searched fruitlessly for the radio or phone which I had already guessed he didn't possess and then went back out onto the freezing deck and looked around for the way to make another signal. Aunt Andrea's house seemed so far away now, across the still water, and the village, the other side of the point, turned nothing but stone walls to the cold harbour view. I could see no signs of life.

Perhaps I should after all row back for help. I went to the ladder and peered down uncertainly.

The rowing boat had gone.

There were tears in my eyes as I made my way back into the cabin. How could I have been so foolish; so stupid? I wondered if I had even tried to tie it up. I suspect I had been so relieved to get to the ladder I had stepped out of the little boat and forgotten it.

'There she is again.' The voice was slightly muffled but more coherent this time. 'I dreamed I saw a lady, and she tried to walk away with my foot.'

I laughed. 'Well, I picked it up onto your bed. I'm sorry. I hope I didn't hurt it.'

'Bunk.' He smiled disarmingly.

'I beg your pardon?' I was indignant. Was he being deliberately rude?

'You don't have beds on boats, you have bunks.' He held out his hand. 'Come nearer, young lady; you have your back to the light and I can't see you. You're not the district nurse I suppose?'

I wasn't sure if he was being facetious. 'I am not. I am staying with Aunt Andrea and when we saw your signal I came to see what was wrong. Jim, who is my cousin, had already left for town.'

He looked a little puzzled.

'Signal? Andrea?' He put his hand to his head, and winced suddenly. 'I remember now. I tripped on deck with my stupid foot, and hit my face. There was blood everywhere. My foot hurt like hell, and I was scared. I put the signal up hoping to catch Jim before he left. Then I remember coming back down and the pain, and then . . .' he shook his head. 'I suppose I blacked out for a bit.'

Gingerly I reached out and touched his forehead. 'The bleeding has stopped. Have you a first aid box anywhere? I think I ought to put something on it until the doctor comes.'

I bit my lip suddenly as I remembered the dinghy, and my inability to call the doctor now.

'What's wrong?' His eyes were acute now that he was completely conscious.

'You'll think I'm such a fool. I've lost my boat. I didn't tie it up properly when I got here.'

To my surprise he let out a shout of laughter. 'Thank God!

You're not as efficient as you look. Don't worry, your boat will go for help without you. The tide will take it straight back to Andrea's. Then they will come and fetch you. I did that myself once just after I came here.'

'Haven't *you* got a dinghy? Then I could go back in that,' I said a little stiffly. 'Or a phone?' I didn't much like being laughed at. 'Or do you always rely on other people?'

'Now, now.' He tapped my hand reprovingly. 'I do have a dinghy, as it happens, but it is on deck, and I doubt if you could lower it on your own into the water, however strong and capable you are. Modern technology I eschew. It has its uses, I admit. But I did not envisage having any need of it.'

I withdrew my hand, where his own had casually come to rest, and backed away from his bunk.

'In that case shall I put on the kettle? I suppose you have one of them? Where did you say the first aid box is?'

His eyes twinkled. 'If you're thinking of making tea, I'd rather have medicinal brandy. And I prescribe it for you, too . . .' he paused, his head on one side. 'Does my angel of mercy have a name?'

'Christine,' I mumbled. 'Christine Harper.'

'Well, excellent Christine Harper; if you proceed through there,' he pointed vaguely to a door, 'to what would in your landlubber language be called the front end of the boat, you will find in a locker, or cupboard, which probably has the door open, a selection of bottles. Scrabble about a bit and see what you can find. And Christine –' he called after me as I made my way to the door, 'there's a box of plasters on the sink.'

Gingerly I let myself into the next cabin and gasped. It was flooded with light. Nearly half the roof had been replaced by an enormous skylight. There was an easel, a table, and everywhere paints, canvasses and jam jars of brushes and pencils and palette knives.

Shutting the door behind me I went over to the easel and examined the picture on it. It showed a flock of geese paddling about on the saltings. Eagerly I turned other paintings towards me. Most of them were of birds, although some showed boats and harbour scenes. It was the most fascinating room, and immediately explained a great deal about Edward's solitude. I found a small unopened bottle of brandy in the cupboard as he had predicted, behind a few empty beer cans and several bottles of turps and linseed oil. Collecting the elastoplast I returned to the main cabin.

'You're a painter!' I remarked rather foolishly, holding out the bottle to him. He was sitting up now, his head in his hands.

'Full marks for observation.' He grimaced slightly as he reached for the brandy. 'I'm more of an illustrator actually. The glasses are in the locker over there.'

I found them, and seeing how his hands were shaking, took the bottle back and poured out two small measures myself. Sitting down next to him I handed him a glass.

'I hope Aunt Andrea won't be terribly worried when the rowing boat drifts back without me. I didn't tell her I was coming here. She was still in bed when I left.'

'Your Aunt Andrea is not a worrier,' he smiled. 'At least not until you've spent the night here with me, then she might.' He chuckled.

I glanced at him sideways. 'Do I gather you have a reputation then?'

'I do.' He sounded quite pleased about it. 'The villagers think I live a life of utter debauchery over here, partly because people always think that about painters; partly because they saw my sister here in her bikini last summer. But, alas, I live like a hermit. Or did until now.' He looked at me speculatively. But I could see the twinkle was still there.

'I see I shall have to watch out.' I was beginning to enjoy his teasing manner. 'I can always swim for the shore if you get too persistent.'

We both looked down at his cast, and laughed.

'You'll outrun me for a while yet, Christine, so don't risk

hypothermia on my account. When are you getting married?'

I was astonished. His sharp eyes had missed nothing. Ruefully I twisted the ring on my finger. 'I don't think I am. My fiancé has gone back to New Zealand and I have a feeling I shan't be following him.'

'I'm sorry.' His voice was suddenly gentle. 'What went wrong?'

I shrugged. 'What does go wrong? We'd been apart for several months and when he came back we just didn't seem to be so right any more. We couldn't discuss things as we used to. The spark had gone, somehow.'

'And you came down here to make up your mind?'

I nodded. 'And to convalesce. I've been ill.'

'What a pair we are.' His voice was suddenly bright once more. 'More brandy?' He held out his glass.

We were on our third 'dose' and I was beginning to feel extremely light-headed when there was a loud knocking on the side of the boat. A moment later we heard heavy footsteps on deck.

'Anyone in?' a hearty voice called out. I looked at my companion wide-eyed.

'Come on down, Mac. It's Dr Macintosh,' he laughed at me, and then turning to the doorway, 'Are you psychic, or did you see me fall through your telescope?'

A large, jovial-faced man stepped cautiously down into the cabin. 'Neither. I gather you need me young man, but if you had any memory at all you would have remembered that I was coming over to see you this morning anyway.' He turned to me with a smile and stuck out a huge hand. 'Christine Harper, I presume. Your aunt asked me to look in this morning to give you a quick check-up, but you had gone out. I might have known Edward here would have enticed you over.'

I was indignant. 'Why did she want you to see me? She never mentioned it.'

'Oh just to catch up on your list of ailments.' He laughed

reassuringly. 'I gather you've been poorly for some time. But if you've the strength to row across here and indulge in a drunken orgy with this reprobate . . .' He grinned, leaving his sentence unfinished.

'Have one, doctor, while there's still some left.' Edward held out the battle.

The doctor poured himself a tiny measure, but his attention was already on Edward's head. He set down the glass untouched and made his patient lie down, thoroughly examining him as I watched. 'Did the lady hit you over the head?' he enquired thoughtfully as his fingers gently touched the wound.

'She did, doctor.' Edward's voice was mournful.

I could see the two of them were good friends, and very much on the same wavelength. And I was beginning to feel outnumbered.

'Does this convince you you're not fit to stay here alone?' the doctor said as he sat back at last, after putting on a dressing. He picked up his glass.

Edward shook his head. 'I'm unrepentant. Did you come to take off my cast?'

The doctor laughed. 'You've a while yet I'm afraid, before you can start thinking of that.'

When he stood up to go, I was making ready to follow when Edward took my hand.

'You will come again, Christine, please? I get so few visitors.'

'That's because you threaten to throw them off your boat,' Dr Macintosh commented over his shoulder as he climbed out of the door.

'Shut up, Mac.' Edward's voice was quite threatening. 'Please, Christine?'

'I'll think about it,' I said with a grin. I was beginning to like this Edward Avon – and his doctor – very much. 'But perhaps I'll get Jim to row me over next time. It might be wiser.' I ducked out under the low door before he had a chance to argue, and gingerly followed the doctor down the ladder into his motor launch.

Two days later I went into Chichester and posted my engagement ring to New Zealand. I was not going to follow it.

I visited the *Moonbeam* two or three times in the safely recovered dinghy, with Jim at the oars, and then as I regained my strength and nerve for rowing I began to do the trip on my own. The first time I did this Edward was awaiting me on deck, balancing with a walking stick near the rail. As I climbed the ladder he presented me with a little book on knots.

'Now,' he commented, 'you're not coming in until you've learned to tie a bowline and having done so have looped it over the appropriate bollard – or knob to you.' He grinned.

'And knobs to you too,' I retorted. But I obediently sat down in the freezing wind and twisted the dinghy's long painter into the correct knot.

Two weeks later when I arrived, still slightly breathless from the rowing, he greeted me on deck, jubilant. His cast had been removed.

'Now there's no escape,' he gloated with a grin. 'Even if I still have to hop I can go faster than you.'

But we both knew by now that he would not have to run. My initial attraction had swiftly developed into something much deeper, and although neither of us ever mentioned it I sensed that he felt the same way.

Autumn turned to winter and at last Christmas Eve arrived. I rowed over to the *Moonbeam* in the morning, a small Christmas tree propped up in the bow of the dinghy. He was coming to spend Christmas Day with us at Andrea's house, but I wanted the celebration to start early, with just us two there.

Carefully tying the dinghy to the ladder I climbed it and hauled the tree up after me.

'So now she wants a garden on board too!' He was looking

at me through the open cabin door, his eyes laughing as he watched my exertions.

'More like a forest,' I retorted. 'You might come and help.'

I had a box full of decorations and together we set up the tree in the main cabin. It took up an awful lot of space but it did look beautiful.

'Now,' he commanded. 'Make the coffee. I'm busy.' He retreated into his studio and closed the door.

'Make it yourself,' I answered back happily. There was something else in the dinghy which I wanted to fetch. His present.

The door reopened and he appeared, frowning. 'Did I hear you disobeying orders?'

'You sure did.' I stuck my tongue out at him.

'You realise that this is mutiny?' He strode towards me and grabbed my wrist. 'I don't hold with mutiny on my ship. I have ways of dealing with it.'

He had never kissed me before. As his arms went round me and he drew me to him, I felt myself starting to tremble. I did not believe it was possible to be so happy.

He broke away from me abruptly. 'As I was saying, I have ways of dealing with troublemakers.' He fished for a moment in his pocket and then he brought out a slim gold bangle. 'I clap them in irons. It generally keeps them in line.' He clipped it on my wrist, and gave me another quick kiss. '*Now*, will you make the coffee. Please?'

I put on the kettle.

The next morning he rowed across to us dressed, unbelievably, in a smart suit. Just before church he whisked Aunt Andrea away into the dining room. Moments later they reappeared together, smiling.

'This delightfully old-fashioned boy has asked me if he may propose to you, Chris,' said Aunt Andrea, her whole face alight with laughter. 'I said I thought probably that would be all right.' Picking up her prayer book with a little chuckle she went out into the hall, pointedly closing the door behind her.

I looked at Edward. He was grinning. 'As I told you, Christine, I don't hold with mutiny. You do as you're told.' He held out a little box. 'Try it for size, if you please.'

This engagement ring fitted me perfectly.

'Happy Christmas, darling,' he whispered, and he took me into his arms.

Choices

HE WAS TALL for an old man, perhaps over six foot in spite of his stoop, with a large ungainly frame to match his size, his skin dried up, leather-like, desiccated by eighty years of wind and weather and pain. Up and down he plodded, his feet leaving damp circles in the sand, rhythmically sweeping back and forth with the heavy disk on its long handle, slowly, methodically beating the tide back towards the setting sun.

Louise narrowed her eyes. She should have left for home by now. Hers was the last car in the car park on the cliff but still she lingered, watching. There was something so dogged, so determined, in his persistence. She had first seen him earlier in the café at the top of the cliff and had been struck then by his self-contained poise as he sat and drank his cup of tea and slowly reached into his pocket for the coins to pay. The tip he left the waitress was, she noticed, as much again as the price of the drink. He had reached down for the metal detector lying under the table, stooping painfully, and then straightened with a groan.

'Not found your treasure yet, Granddad?' The waitress grinned at him, pocketing her fifty pence.

He smiled. 'Not yet, sweetheart. You'll be the first to know.'

He walked slowly past Louise and out of the café and turned along the path out of sight.

'What's he hoping to find?' Louise had pulled out her

purse and was counting the money for her own bill.

'Gawd knows!' The girl tossed her head. 'Silly old goat.'

Louise frowned. The tone seemed so cruel. The girl was young, her flesh plump and pink and moist. She had her life before her. Surely she could spare a kind word about an old man. What, Louise wondered, would she say about her? A middle-aged woman, still slim, still, she liked to think, attractive, but probably, well, past it! Gathering up her things Louise made her way out and looked after him. Already he had plodded down the wooden steps against the cliff and was walking out across the sand.

She had come out to the beach to think. After all, it was a fair bet at this time of year that it would be empty. All the children were back at school and the guest houses and hotels were emptying fast now that the sun had grown hazy, allowing healing mists to drift up the beach and across the dried gold of the countryside. The shops on the small seafront further along the cliff were one by one being boarded up now, before the autumnal gales hurled the sand across the esplanade and piled rank weed, dredged by the storms from the depths of the sea, onto their doorsteps.

All day she had worried at her problem, tearing it to shreds, tossing the pieces back and forth, hand to hand, like a juggler, watching the alternate possibilities glitter in the sun and spin in and out of reach. Man or career; love or money; adventure or security. Only one. Not both. Not possibly both. If either one had come six months ago without the other there would have been no contest, no problem, but now. . .

The man had come first. Tall, tanned, his hair a short wild tangle of exuberance, his eyes a piercing blue. He was no Lothario. For a long time she had thought he had not even noticed her as he sat at his library desk, surrounded by heavy tomes, scribbling away at his notes. Twice she had found him books from the book stacks in the cellars and carried them to his desk, but the face he turned to hers for a second had been distracted, preoccupied, with – she had glanced at the titles again – the history of South America, the ancient peoples of Peru, the Nasca lines.

When he saw her in the restaurant behind the library however he had come over without hesitation, charming, diffident, apologetic. Magnetic. Within five minutes she was terrifyingly, totally in love.

Love – wild, abandoned, passionate love – always seemed to have bypassed Louise and she had thought she was probably temperamentally unsuited to the state. It was not that men did not find her attractive. They had always pursued her – if sometimes a little more respectfully than she might have wished. Even now she was tiptoeing around the idea of accepting that she was perhaps on the verge of middle age, they still came, still admired, still with the old-fashioned courtesy she seemed to inspire in them, taking her to concerts and theatres and art galleries. They were in fact so respectful that they did not even seem to resent each other. When, as must happen from time to time, one found out about another, there was no bristling of hackles, no flare of testosterone, no drawing of swords. Just a polite, perhaps reproachful, hurt.

Fraser was different. It did not occur to him that to love her would be disrespectful. He did not seem to see her grey hair as a warning or treat her intellect as a barrier or notice her sensible mien. What he had seen was the hidden passion, the longing, the warmth, the desire for romance even she had not known were there.

Galleries and museums, yes. Concerts and plays, no. No time. He took her instead to Avebury, to Stonehenge and to the Rollright Stones, to sites of geomantic significance and electro-magnetic force. He lectured her on ley lines and geophysics and geopathic stress and particles and he was completely honest: he had a wife; a wife he still quite liked. They were not divorced, but they no longer lived together. 'She wanted a home, I'm a wanderer.' He shrugged and smiled. 'I tried. I really tried. I'm still fond of her, but she's found herself another chap. He'll give her everything I can't. So I wish her well.' The way he shrugged had alerted her suspicions though. She would not be going into anything blind.

His other, greater love and one he admitted to freely, was for the planet, for Gaia, for his studies.

She was exhilarated, excited, horrified, dumbfounded by this other passion, by his eclectic intellectual curiosity and what she saw as his blinkered dismissal of recognised science. He was brilliant, shocking, everything she had ever wanted in a man – and he was going to South America in October.

He had told her about that too on the first day they had met; it wasn't until almost the last that he asked her to go with him. She was delirious with excitement, but something in her said, Stop. Consider. Two days later she was offered the post of senior archivist at the City Museum.

The sun was dropping towards the horizon fast; the shadow of the old man grew longer, an ectomorph etched in the sand by the last dying rays. Unconsciously she was following his path, her shadow parallel with his, turning when he turned, walking when he walked as she worried at her problem, tearing at it like some tangle of woven thread.

When he headed up towards her, his back to the sea, she did not at first notice. Her eyes were fixed on the scatter of shells lying in the rippled tide wrack. It was several seconds before she noticed that their shadows had merged and now were one. She looked up, startled. The metal detector was switched off now, at rest, hanging from its strap on his shoulder. The old man's eyes were on the heaped crimson clouds far to the west. 'Be dark soon.' His voice was rich and rumbling, projected from his chest. When she didn't respond he went on. 'I saw you up there in the café drinking Trish's best.' He gave a rueful chuckle. 'Little miss! Bad mouth me, did she, when I left?'

Louise smiled. 'Nothing too awful.'

The chuckle turned into a full blown belly laugh. 'Tactful lady, aren't you! Trish and I understand each other. I've got to know her quite well. She makes a wonderful cheese sandwich with home-made pickle.'

'Do you come here every day then?' Of one accord, companionably, they had begun walking again, slowly, heading away from the darkening sea towards the cliff.

He nodded. 'Most.'

'Have you ever found anything exciting?'

He nodded. 'One or two things. Jewellery mostly, that people have lost.'

'Was it worth much?'

He shook his head. 'I take it to the police. Sometimes I don't hear any more. People take it and that's it. No word of thanks. One or two things I was given when no one claimed them. I got a reward once.'

From the sigh in his voice she received the distinct impression that rewards were not the purpose of his search. She glanced at him sideways and found she was reluctant to probe further. A veil of sadness and of prohibition fluttered between them in the dusk.

'Would a sympathetic old ear help at all?' He glanced at her.

It was her turn to give a rueful smile. 'Is it that obvious?'

' 'Fraid so.'

'I have to make a decision.'

'Does it involve a man?'

She nodded.

'Heart versus head?'

She nodded again.

'If you say "no" will you regret it for the rest of your life?'

'Probably.'

'And all your friends are standing back and falling over themselves not to give advice?'

'I haven't discussed it with my friends.' It was true. In fact she had barely seen any of her friends for weeks.

The old man had glanced at her face and she had the feeling he could read her thoughts. 'Because your friends will back up your head and common sense and you, the you who is at the core of your being, want your heart to triumph.'

She laughed. 'I suppose so.'

'Am I allowed to know the choices?'

'The job of my dreams – one that won't come up again – versus –' she hesitated.

'The man of your dreams? There will be other jobs; you are clearly a talented and intelligent woman. Not the same job perhaps, but others. Will there be another . . .' he paused. 'What is his name?'

'Fraser.'

'Fraser, like you, is a unique human being. There will be other human beings; there will never be another Fraser.'

'You think I should go with him.' Her mouth had gone dry and she realised with surprise that it was with fear at the thought of reaching a decision.

They had reached the steps that led up the cliff and they stopped and faced each other. 'I asked a woman to marry me sixty years ago. She said yes, but then, for reasons unlike yours, but as troubling, she changed her mind. In my unhappiness I went abroad. To India.' He paused. 'I had no way of knowing that she would regret changing her mind and spend forty years looking for me.' Abruptly he turned and began climbing the steep stair, pulling himself up on the wooden handrail. She followed him and at the top he turned and swung round. 'It's her ring I'm looking for down there. The ring she gave back to me down on the beach. I was so upset I threw it into the sea. It was too late when I found out. She was dead.'

'I'm so sorry.' Louise put her warm hands over his cold ones. 'I'm so sorry.'

'Don't be. I'm a silly old goat. That's what Trish calls me. Sentimental. I tell her it helps to pass the time.' He was panting from the climb. 'Shall we go and plague Trish? She's usually open for another half-hour or so, till the market packs up. I'll get her to make us a sandwich.'

Louise stood still as he walked away. The letter she had

written to the museum accepting the job was in the pocket of her coat. She touched it with cautious fingers. Louise: the Louise who had run her life since she was a small child, sensibly, calmly, rationally – successfully – would post the letter now, in the box in the wall beside the café. That Louise always won in the end and she had never regretted it. But the other Louise, the passionate, impetuous, excited Louise; the Louise whose heart had finally rebelled; the Louise who longed to walk on desert sand and sail the turbid waters of the Amazon. What of her?

The old man had stopped. He looked back and saw her draw the envelope out of her pocket. Slowly she walked after him towards the café. In front of the red rectangular box in the old flint wall she raised her hand and held the letter for a moment before its gaping mouth.

He held his breath.

Her hand had begun to shake. She stepped back, staring down at the envelope, then abruptly she tore it in two.

Looking up she smiled at the old man and shrugged. 'Come on,' she said, 'let's have that cheese and pickle sandwich.'

Two's Company

MATTHEW GAZED into her eyes, made sapphire in the candlelight, and smiled as he reached for the bottle of wine. The evening had gone well. They had eaten gloriously and drunk elegantly and Petra had confided in him details of family and friends, of hopes and dreams, of fantasies and fears.

The fears intrigued him. There were so many. The huge eyes with their infinite depths of blue set off by the glossy chestnut curls and skin of creamiest porcelain grew larger and more eloquent with every terror she listed. Acrophobia, which meant abnormal fear of heights, she told him with a certain modest pride, spiders and lifts and thunder and wasps, and above all, ghosts.

'Ghosts?' He wondered, not for the first time, if she were winding him up. Increasingly he thought she was. 'To be afraid of ghosts, you have to see them.'

She smiled. 'I do.'

He risked a long, melting gaze into the fathomless blue and decided that, wound up or not, if he were not to risk drowning he must have her, and soon. The glimmer of a plan was emerging. 'Do you like ghost stories?'

She nodded. Her eyes held his. She did not appear to need ever to blink those sweeping lashes.

First a joke story. She was too serious. He needed to see her relax, to see for sure if she had a sense of humour. There could be no long-term relationship without a sense of humour.

'I could tell you the shortest ghost story in the world,' he said. He paused for a reaction – encouragement perhaps, or even a scowl. She continued to gaze, so, a little laboriously, he went on, ' "Do you believe in ghosts?" asks a man of his companion, on a train. "No," says the companion. "Oh, don't you," says the first man. And disappeared.'

He paused expectantly. It was usually good for a groan, at least.

She greeted the story with silence. Her eyes grew, if anything, larger. He suppressed a sigh.

'Do you have a ghost in your flat, then?'

He topped up her glass again, though she hadn't touched it since the waiter had brought their coffee and now the wine was held from spilling by only the meniscus.

When he had first met this girl at the office party he had assumed himself well in when she agreed to dinner. Now he was uneasy. She had talked too much, lightly, filling silences, but telling nothing. Nothing of her inner soul.

Perhaps she was a ghost herself. Amused at the thought he sat back and surveyed her through half closed eyes. Haloed by candlelight, shimmering in her blue shirt and dark silk jacket, she certainly looked ethereal. He reached out a cautious finger and touched her hand as it lay on the table. It was suspiciously cold and he withdrew with a shiver, almost convinced by his own fantasy.

'I'll introduce you to him, if you like.'

He realised suddenly that she was speaking again in that curiously husky drawl which he had found at first so attractive and now was in danger of finding monotonous.

'To him?' he echoed, puzzled. Some lover? Some husband? Some father then, heaven forbid, who would condemn utterly his politically incorrect motives for taking this beautiful creature to dinner and thence, hopefully, to bed.

'My ghost.' She smiled.

He sighed with relief. 'I'd like that.' He looked sincere. He was sincere. After all, was that not the point of the ploy? His ghost story – his next, real, more frightening and possibly true, ghost story about the fiend that lurked in the attics of the house in which he had been brought up as a child – was supposed to scare her, lead to his putting his arm around her shoulders, apologising for terrifying her, comforting her, reassuring her. Instead she had anticipated his next move for him and was, presumably, not afraid of this her own, private ghost.

'Is he your flatmate?' He asked with a smile. It sounded cool. Not witty perhaps, but at least humorous. And tolerant. No one could accuse him of being – not racist exactly. Corporealist perhaps?

She did not reply for a moment, then he saw the laughter, there at last behind the blue. 'You could say so. There's no one else.'

Now, that was bonus information. A double bonus. An empty flat waiting for them and, at last, signs of a sense of humour. He reached automatically for the bottle to top up her glass again but still she hadn't touched it. He refilled his own instead and glanced round for the waiter. The bill, a taxi back to her place and then with a bit of luck – heaven.

They had to wait for the taxi in the cold, but on the plus side she did not demur when he put his arm around her shoulders to counteract her shivering when at last they settled into its seat.

She lived in Notting Hill. A top-floor flat in a substantial house with pillared porch and white blistered paintwork. There was no lift and he was panting when they reached her door. The landing was dimly lit. He watched her pull her key out of her jacket pocket. 'Why aren't you afraid, living all alone with a ghost?'

He saw her smile, quickly hidden, as she turned to the door and inserted the key. 'We've grown used to each other.'

The flat was in darkness. She groped for a switch and a

shaded lamp came on at the far end of a pale-carpeted corridor.

'Throw your coat here.' She indicated a chair as she led the way into the living room and turned on more lights.

He looked round intrigued. The room was low-ceilinged, cosy, furnished simply with a generous scatter of cushions and throws. He rather liked it. Accepting another glass of wine – so, she did drink the stuff sometimes – and the promise of a coffee when the kettle had boiled, he threw himself down on the sofa and smiled. 'So, where is this flatmate?'

She was choosing a CD from the pile in the corner and he couldn't see her face.

'He'll be along, I expect.'

Soft music filled the room. Nothing he recognised. Strings. A harp. An occasional arpeggio on a pan flute. Taking off her jacket she threw it down and kicked off her shoes. Then she sat down, not next to him, but on a chair several feet away.

And for the first time that evening really looked at him hard.

Embarrassed by the scrutiny he dropped his gaze to the ruby depths in his glass. She smiled. Not bad looking. An eight out of ten, perhaps. Gold credit card – he had used it to pay for dinner, and in his name, not the business's, so money no obvious problem. Good job. He was after all her new boss. Sufficiently unattached or detached to take her out to dinner. His marital status did not bother her; a wife out of sight in the country was a wife out of mind; a ring and a marriage contract were not what she wanted. She wanted intellectual stimulation. Money, excitement, fun, companionship.

And sex of course.

She stretched languidly and saw his eyes flicker away from the wine towards the buttons on her blouse. Performance could only be judged by experience, but he had one or two other little tests to pass before she allowed him to seduce her. She smiled secretly. How strange that it never dawned on men even in this age of equal opportunity that they might be the prey.

'If we're lucky he might not come.' He would of course. He always did.

He looked up, surprised. 'Who?'

'My flatmate.' She did not want him to feel too secure, too comfortable. Not yet.

The trouble was she was fussy about her men. Her real men. She needed to know if he could handle irony. If he had wit and intellect. And courage. So far she was not convinced. His only attempt at a joke had been puerile.

'I'll make the coffee.' She gave him the half-lidded smile which men found enigmatic and headed, not for the kitchen, but towards the bedroom. It was here she kept her books, her flute, her tapes of poetry and drama. And her ghost.

Boris had been there since she had moved in. Companionable, gentle, not frightening at all once she had got used to him. Perhaps a little lonely. He was a friend, a confidant and, when she needed one, a chaperone who could chase away the most persistent of men.

Making sure the door was shut she slipped out of her shirt and trousers, stood for a moment naked in front of her mirror, and then pulled on the green silk wrap which turned her eyes to aquamarine and her hair to living fire.

Then she switched on the tape. Most of it – fifty-five minutes exactly – was silence.

In the shadows Boris watched it all and smiled. He had been lonely before she came, she was right. She had brought interest and sometimes excitement to the stasis of his existence. And she had given him a purpose. She thought she chose the men that stayed, but that was his self-appointed task. A task he performed with care and discrimination.

Matthew ignored the coffee, his eyes fixed, as she had known they would be, on the cleavage artfully revealed by the slippery silk. His physical reaction was, she noticed, a gratifying and unmissable ten out of ten.

He was not sure about the book she had produced though, puzzled by her timing, she thought, rather than appalled by the literary flavour the evening had suddenly acquired. But he acquitted himself well and cheerfully. Almost apologetically he revealed a more than passable knowledge of Chaucer, Jung, Plath and Okri, the cornerstones, in her view, of a broad intellect. Through them she could test briefly and without fuss his knowledge of history, psychology, philosophy, modern literature and politics and mark each out of ten (eight to nine in this case, she reckoned, pleased). That only left the ability to laugh at himself. So many men failed that most crucial test.

She rather hoped he wouldn't.

Intrigued and a little confused by the response his attempt at seduction had evoked, Matthew was nonetheless content. In the restaurant he had marked her down, in his turn, eventually, as scatty and not very bright. A quick lay if he were lucky. No more. Now, given courage by her own environment she had proved herself intelligent, well-read, thoughtful. He liked her for it more and more.

But it was a bit of a turn-off.

Her signals were in conflict: the deep green silk a come-on; the conversation a hold-back. Unmarried and so far uncommitted, he did not yet know that to fall in love with a woman you must first fall in love with her mind. He wanted to take her in his arms, but she was deeply into a new theme now. Universal consciousness.

Perhaps this was where the ghost came in?

Glancing into the shadows thrown by the carefully placed table lamps he smiled, suddenly uneasy.

Recognising the sign she glanced at her watch. It was happening too soon. There were three more minutes of the silent tape to go. There was only one way to fill them.

His lap was very comfortable. His lips tasted pleasantly of wine and coffee. Ten out of ten again, she thought, sleepy now. Slowly, with practised fingers she began to unbutton his shirt. She would be sad if he failed the test. The last three men had failed. But they were wimps and she had let Boris chase them away. Boris's trouble was that he never made a sound. The sound effects she had to provide for him. And they were very subtle. The slightest signs. Footsteps on uncarpeted floors and then in the distance a forlorn, breathy whistle, almost a monotone rather than a tune.

She felt Matthew tense, saw his eyes refocus away from her breast into the corner of the room, felt the gentlest touch of cold cross his skin under her fingers.

'Ignore him,' she whispered. He was there, but Matthew would never see him. She held her breath. The ghostly laugh, especially recorded by her brother with his head in a drainage pipe, had unmanned the others, the wimps. It was coming now.

She had to admit that it made even her blood curdle. For a moment he froze. She felt him grip her arms as though he would throw her across the room, then all at once light dawned. She felt him relax, saw his eyes close as laughter rocked him, felt his kisses on her throat and breasts.

'Thank God, she's got a sense of humour after all,' he thought as he pulled away the last of the clinging silk.

He did not see Boris, a shadow, no more, lurking ever watchful, nodding approval, in the corner of the room.